Laurell K. Hamilton is the bestselling author of the acclaimed Anita Blake, Vampire Hunter novels. She lives near St Louis with her husband, her daughter, two dogs and an ever-fluctuating number of fish. She invites you to visit her website at www.laurellkhamilton.org.

Reviews for the Anita Blake, Vampire Hunter, novels

'Anita Blake is one of the most fascinating fictional heroines since Scarlett O'Hara' *Publishers Weekly*

'What *The Da Vinci Code* did for the religious thriller, the Anita Blake series has done for the vampire novel' *USA Today*

'Hamilton's complex, enthralling world is utterly absorbing' *Booklist*

'A hardcore guilty pleasure' *The Times*

'Always very, very sexy and exciting' *Dreamwatch*

'This fast-paced, tough-edged supernatural thriller is mesmerizing reading indeed' *Locus*

'The action never stops' *The New York Review of Science Fiction*

'Supernatural bad guys beware, night-prowling Anita Blake is savvy, sassy and tough' P N Elrod

'I was enthralled by a departure from the usual type of vampire tale . . .' Andre Norton

'A real rush . . . a heady mix of romance and horror' Jayne Ann Krentz

LAURELL K. HAMILTON

THE KILLING DANCE

AN ANITA BLAKE, VAMPIRE HUNTER, NOVEL

headline

First published in the United States of America in 1997
Reprinted by Orbit, an imprint of Little, Brown Book Group, in Great Britain in 2000

First published in this edition in 2010 by
HEADLINE PUBLISHING GROUP

5

Cataloguing in Publication Data is available from the British Library

ISBN 978 0 7553 5534 1

Typeset in Monotype Fournier by Ellipsis Books Limited, Glasgow

Printed and bound in Great Britain by
Clays Ltd St Ives plc

Headline's policy is to use papers that are natural, renewable and
recyclable products and made from wood grown in sustainable forests.
The logging and manufacturing processes are expected to conform to
the environmental regulations of the country of origin.

HEADLINE PUBLISHING GROUP
An Hachette UK Company
338 Euston Road
London NW1 3BH

www.headline.co.uk
www.hachette.co.uk

To Paty Cockrum, fan, friend, fine artist.
You should see the pictures she sends me of Jean-Claude.
She really is the voice of temptation.

ACKNOWLEDGMENTS

Marion Stensgard who answered my questions.

The Wild Canid Survival and Research Center (Wolf Sanctuary) for letting me use their library.

Bonnee Pierson, who helped with a very different kind of research.

The Alternate Historians: Rett Macpherson who went above and beyond the call of duty for research, N. L. Drew who heard parts of this book over the phone, Tom Drennan, whose book is finally ready to make the rounds, Mark Sumner who says everything will be all right, even when he doesn't know, Marella Sands who reminded me we're supposed to be having fun, and Deborah Millitello who holds my hand.

Sarah Sumner for bitching sessions.

Joan-Marie Knappenberger who let me use her house.

The Saint Louis Bread Company for letting me take up a table for hours at a time.

Join the Official Laurell K. Hamilton Fan Club at www.laurellkhamilton.org or write to LKH Fan Club, MaPetite Enterprises, LLC, 483 S. Kirkwood Road, Suite 106, Kirkwood, MO 63122 and request a membership form.

I

The most beautiful corpse I'd ever seen was sitting behind my desk. Jean-Claude's white shirt gleamed in the light from the desk lamp. A froth of lace spilled down the front, peeking from inside his black velvet jacket. I stood behind him, my back to the wall, arms crossed over my stomach, which put my right hand comfortably close to the Browning Hi-Power in its shoulder holster. I wasn't about to draw on Jean-Claude. It was the other vampire I was worried about.

The desk lamp was the only light in the room. The vampire had requested the overheads be turned out. His name was Sabin, and he stood against the far wall, huddling in the dark. He was covered head to foot in a black, hooded cape. He looked like something out of an old Vincent Price movie. I'd never seen a real vampire dress like that.

The last member of our happy little group was Dominic Dumare. He sat in one of the client chairs. He was tall, thin, but not weak. His hands were large and strong, big enough to palm my face. He was dressed in a three-piece black suit, like a chauffeur except for the diamond stickpin in his tie. A beard and thin mustache lined the strong bones of his face.

When he'd entered my office, I'd felt him like a psychic wind tripping down my spine. I'd only encountered two other people who had that taste to them. One had been the most powerful voodoo priestess I'd ever met. The second had been the second most powerful voodoo priest I'd ever met. The woman was dead. The man worked for Animators, Inc., just like I did. But Dominic Dumare wasn't here to apply for a job.

'Ms Blake, please be seated,' Dumare said. 'Sabin finds it most offensive to sit when a lady is standing.'

I glanced behind him at Sabin. 'I'll sit down if he sits down,' I said.

Dumare looked at Jean-Claude. He gave a gentle, condescending smile. 'Do you have such poor control over your human servant?'

I didn't have to see Jean-Claude's smile to know it was there. 'Oh, you are on your own with *ma petite*. She is my human servant, so declared before the council, but she answers to no one.'

'You seem proud of that,' Sabin said. His voice was British and very upper crust.

'She is the Executioner and has more vampire kills than any other human. She is a necromancer of such power that you have traveled halfway around the world to consult her. She is my human servant without a mark to hold her to me. She dates me without the aid of vampire glamor. Why should I not be pleased?'

Listening to him talk you'd have thought it was all his own idea. Fact was, he'd tried his best to mark me, and I'd managed to escape. We were dating because he'd blackmailed me. Date him or he'd kill my other boyfriend. Jean-Claude had managed to make it all work to his advantage. Why was I not surprised?

'Until her death you cannot mark any other human,' Sabin said. 'You have cut yourself off from a great deal of power.'

'I am aware of what I have done,' Jean-Claude said.

Sabin laughed, and it was chokingly bitter. 'We all do strange things for love.'

I would have given a lot to see Jean-Claude's face at that moment. All I could see was his long black hair spilling over his jacket, black on black. His shoulders stiffened, hands sliding across the blotter on my desk. Then he went very still. That awful waiting stillness that only the old vampires have, as if, if they held still long enough, they would simply disappear.

'Is that what has brought you here, Sabin? Love?' Jean-Claude's voice was neutral, empty.

Sabin's laughter rode the air like broken glass. It felt like the very sound of it hurt something deep inside me. I didn't like it.

'Enough games,' I said, 'let's get it done.'

'Is she always this impatient?' Dumare asked.

'Yes,' Jean-Claude said.

Dumare smiled, bright and empty as a lightbulb. 'Did Jean-Claude tell you why we wished to see you?'

'He said Sabin caught some sort of disease from trying to go cold turkey.'

The vampire across the room laughed again, flinging it like a weapon across the room. 'Cold turkey, very good, Ms Blake, very good.'

The laughter ate over me like small cutting blades. I'd never experienced anything like that from just a voice. In a fight, it would have been distracting. Heck, it was distracting now. I felt liquid slide down my forehead. I raised my left hand to it. My fingers came away smeared with blood. I drew the Browning and stepped away from the wall. I aimed it at the black figure across the room. 'He does that again, and I'll shoot him.'

Jean-Claude rose slowly from the chair. His power flowed over me like a cool wind, raising goose bumps on my arms. He raised one pale hand, gone nearly translucent with power. Blood flowed down that gleaming skin.

Dumare stayed in his chair, but he, too, was bleeding from a cut nearly identical to mine. Dumare wiped the blood away, still smiling. 'The gun will not be necessary,' he said.

'You have abused my hospitality,' Jean-Claude said. His voice filled the room with hissing echoes.

'There is nothing I can say to apologize,' Sabin said. 'But I did not mean to do it. I am using so much of my power just to maintain myself that I do not have the control I once did.'

I moved slowly away from the wall, gun still pointed. I wanted to see Jean-Claude's face. I needed to see how badly he was hurt. I eased around the desk until I could see him from the corner of my eye. His face was untouched, flawless and gleaming like mother of pearl.

He raised his hand, one thin line of blood still trailing down. 'This is no accident.'

'Come into the light, my friend,' Dumare said. 'You must let them see, or they will not understand.'

'I do not want to be seen.'

'You are very close to using up all my good will,' Jean-Claude said.

'Mine, too,' I added. I was hoping I could either shoot Sabin or put the gun down soon. Even a two-handed shooting stance is not meant to be maintained indefinitely. Your hands start to waver just a bit.

Sabin glided towards the desk. The black cloak spilled around his feet like a pool of darkness. All vampires were graceful, but this was ridiculous. I realized he wasn't walking at all. He was levitating inside that dark cloak.

His power flowed over my skin like icy water. My hands were suddenly steady once more. Nothing like having several hundred years' worth of vampire coming at you to sharpen your nerves.

Sabin stopped on the far side of the desk. He was expending power just to move, just to be here, as if, like a shark, if he stopped moving he'd die.

Jean-Claude glided around me. His power danced over my body, raising the hair at the back of my neck, making my skin tight. He stopped almost within reach of the other vampire. 'What has happened to you, Sabin?'

Sabin stood on the edge of the light. The lamp should have cast some light into the hood of his cloak, but it didn't. The inside of the hood was as smooth and black and empty as a cave. His voice came out of that nothingness. It made me jump.

'Love, Jean-Claude, love happened to me. My beloved grew a conscience. She said it was wrong to feed upon people. We were once people, after all. For love of her, I tried to drink cold blood. I tried animal blood. But it was not enough to sustain me.'

I stared into that darkness. I kept pointing the gun, but I was beginning to feel silly. Sabin didn't seem at all afraid of it, which was unnerving. Maybe he didn't care. That was also unnerving. 'She talked you into going vegetarian. Great,' I said. 'You seem powerful enough.'

He laughed, and with the laughter, the shadows in his hood faded slowly, like a curtain lifting. He threw it back in one quick flourish.

I didn't scream, but I gasped and took a step back. I couldn't help myself. When I realized I'd done it, I stopped and made myself take back that step, meet his eyes. No flinching.

His hair was thick and straight and golden, falling like a shining curtain to his shoulders. But his skin . . . his skin had rotted away on half his face. It was like late-stage leprosy, but worse. The flesh was puss-filled, gangrenous, and should have stunk to high heaven. The other half of his face was still beautiful. The kind of face that medieval painters had borrowed for cherubim, a golden perfection. One crystalline blue eye rolled in its rotting socket as if in danger of spilling out onto his cheek. The other eye was secure and watched my face.

'You can put up the gun, *ma petite*. It was an accident, after all,' Jean-Claude said.

I lowered the Browning, but didn't put it up. It took more effort than was pretty to say calmly, 'This happened because you stopped feeding off of humans?'

'We believe so,' Dumare said.

I tore my gaze away from Sabin's ravaged face and looked back at Dominic. 'You think I can help cure him of this?' I couldn't keep the disbelief out of my voice.

'I heard of your reputation in Europe.'

I raised my eyebrows.

'No modesty, Ms Blake. Among those of us who notice such things, you are gaining a certain notoriety.'

Notoriety, not fame. Hmmm.

'Put the gun away, *ma petite*. Sabin has done all the – what is your word – grandstanding he will do tonight. Haven't you, Sabin?'

'I fear so, it all seems to go so badly now.'

I holstered the gun and shook my head. 'I honestly don't have the faintest idea how to help you.'

'If you knew how, would you help me?' Sabin asked.

I looked at him and nodded. 'Yes.'

'Even though I am a vampire and you are a vampire executioner.'

'Have you done anything in this country that you need killing for?'

Sabin laughed. The rotting skin stretched, and a ligament popped with a wet snap. I had to look away. 'Not yet, Ms Blake, not yet.' His face sobered quickly; the humor abruptly faded. 'You school your face to show nothing, Jean-Claude, but I read the horror in your eyes.'

Jean-Claude's skin had gone back to its usual milky perfection. His face was still lovely, perfect, but at least he'd stopped glowing. His midnight blue eyes were just eyes now. He was still beautiful, but it was a nearly human beauty. 'Is it not worth a little horror?' he asked.

Sabin smiled, and I wished he hadn't. The muscles on the rotted side didn't work, and his mouth hung crooked. I glanced away, then made myself look back. If he could be trapped inside that face, I could look at it.

'Then you will help me?'

'I would aid you if I could, but it is Anita you have come to ask. She must give her own answer.'

'Well, Ms Blake?'

'I don't know how to help you,' I repeated.

'Do you understand how dire my circumstances are, Ms Blake? The true horror of it, do you grasp it?'

'The rot probably won't kill you, but it's progressive, I take it?'

'Oh, yes, it's progressive, virulently so.'

'I would help you if I could, Sabin, but what can I do that Dumare can't? He's a necromancer, maybe as powerful as I am, maybe more. Why do you need me?'

'I realize, Ms Blake, that you don't have something specifically for Sabin's problem,' Dumare said. 'As far as I can discover, he is the only vampire to ever suffer such a fate, but I thought if we came to another necromancer as powerful as myself – ' he smiled modestly – 'or nearly as powerful as myself, perhaps together we could work up a spell to help him.'

'A spell?' I glanced at Jean-Claude.

He gave that wonderful Gallic shrug that meant everything and nothing. 'I know little of necromancy, *ma petite*. You would know if such a spell were possible more than I.'

'It is not only your ability as a necromancer that has brought us to you,' Dumare said. 'You have also acted as a focus for at least two different animators, I believe that is the American word for what you do.'

I nodded. 'The word's right, but where did you hear I could act as a focus?'

'Come, Ms Blake, the ability to combine another animator's powers with your own and thus magnify both powers is a rare talent.'

'Can you act as a focus?' I asked.

He tried to look humble but actually looked pleased with himself. 'I must confess, yes, I can act as a focus. Think of what the two of us could accomplish together.'

'We could raise a hell of a lot of zombies, but that won't cure Sabin.'

'True enough.' Dumare leaned forward in his chair. His lean, handsome face flushed, eager, a true convert looking for disciples.

I wasn't much of a follower.

'I would offer to teach you true necromancy, not this voodoo dabbling that you've been doing.'

Jean-Claude made a soft sound halfway between a laugh and a cough.

I glared at Jean-Claude's amused face but said, 'I'm doing just fine with this voodoo dabbling.'

'I meant no insult, Ms Blake. You will need a teacher of some sort soon. If not me, then you must find someone else.'

'I don't know what you're talking about.'

'Control, Ms Blake. Raw power, no matter how impressive, is not the same as power used with great care and great control.'

I shook my head. 'I'll help you if I can, Mr Dumare. I'll even participate in a spell if I check it out with a local witch I know first.'

'Afraid that I will try and steal your power?'

I smiled. 'No, short of killing me, the best you or anyone else can do is borrow.'

'You are wise beyond your years, Ms Blake.'

'You aren't that much older than I am,' I said. Something crossed over his face, the faintest flicker, and I knew.

'You're his human servant, aren't you?'

Dominic smiled, spreading his hands. '*Oui.*'

I sighed. 'I thought you said you weren't trying to hide anything from me.'

'A human servant's job is to be the daytime eyes and ears of his master. I am of no use to my master if vampire hunters can spot me for what I am.'

'I spotted you.'

'But in another situation, without Sabin at my side, would you have?'

I thought about that for a moment. 'Maybe.' I shook my head. 'I don't know.'

'Thank you for your honesty, Ms Blake.'

Sabin said, 'I am sure our time is up. Jean-Claude said you had a pressing engagement, Ms Blake. Much more important than my little problem.' There was a little bite to that last.

'*Ma petite* has a date with her other beau.'

Sabin stared at Jean-Claude. 'So you are truly allowing her to date another. I thought that at least must be rumor.'

'Very little of what you hear about *ma petite* is rumor. Believe all you hear.'

Sabin chuckled, coughing, as if struggling to keep the laughter from spilling out his ruined mouth. 'If I believed everything I heard, I would have come with an army.'

'You came with one servant because I allowed you only one servant,' Jean-Claude said.

Sabin smiled. 'Too true. Come Dominic, we must not take more of Ms Blake's so valuable time.'

Dominic stood obediently, towering over us both. Sabin was around my height. Of course, I wasn't sure if his legs were still there. He might have been taller once.

'I don't like you, Sabin, but I would never willingly leave another being in the shape you're in. My plans tonight are important, but if I thought we could cure you immediately, I'd change them.'

The vampire looked at me. His blue, blue eyes were like staring down into clear ocean water. There was no pull to them. Either he was behaving himself or, like most vampires, he couldn't roll me with his eyes anymore.

'Thank you, Ms Blake. I believe you are sincere.' He extended a gloved hand from the voluminous cloak.

I hesitated, then took it. His hand squished ever so slightly, and it took a lot not to jerk back. I forced myself to shake his hand, to smile, to let go, and not to rub my hand on my skirt.

Dominic shook my hand as well. His was cool and dry. 'Thank you for your time, Ms Blake. I will contact you tomorrow and we will discuss things.'

'I'll be expecting your call, Mr Dumare.'

'Call me Dominic, please.'

I nodded. 'Dominic. We can discuss it, but I hate to take your money when I'm not sure that I can help you.'

'May I call you Anita?' he asked.

I hesitated and shrugged. 'Why not.'

'Don't worry about money,' Sabin said, 'I have plenty of that for all the good it has done me.'

'How is the woman you love taking the change in your appearance?' Jean-Claude asked.

Sabin looked at him. It was not a friendly look. 'She finds it repulsive, as do I. She feels immense guilt. She has not left me, nor is she with me.'

'You'd lived for close to seven hundred years,' I said. 'Why screw things up for a woman?'

Sabin turned to me, a line of ooze creeping down his face like a black tear. 'Are you asking me if it was worth it, Ms Blake?'

I swallowed and shook my head. 'It's none of my business. I'm sorry I asked.'

He drew the hood over his face. He turned back to me, black, a cup of shadows where his face should have been. 'She was going to leave me, Ms Blake. I thought that I would sacrifice anything to keep her by my side, in my bed. I was wrong.' He turned that blackness to Jean-Claude. 'We will see you tomorrow night, Jean-Claude.'

'I look forward to it.'

Neither vampire offered to shake hands. Sabin glided for the door, the robe trailing behind him, empty. I wondered how much of his lower body was left and decided I didn't want to know.

Dominic shook my hand again. 'Thank you, Anita. You have

given us hope.' He held my hand and stared into my face as if he could read something there. 'And do think about my offer to teach you. There are very few of us who are true necromancers.'

I took back my hand. 'I'll think about it. Now I really do have to go.'

He smiled, held the door for Sabin, and out they went. Jean-Claude and I stood a moment in silence. I broke it first. 'Can you trust them?'

Jean-Claude sat on the edge of my desk, smiling. 'Of course not.'

'Then why did you agree to let them come?'

'The council has declared that no master vampires in the United States may quarrel until that nasty law that is floating around Washington is dead. One undead war, and the anti-vampire lobby would push through the law and make us illegal again.'

I shook my head. 'I don't think Brewster's Law has a snowball's chance. Vampires are legal in the United States. Whether I agree with it or not, I don't think that's going to change.'

'How can you be so sure?'

'It's sort of hard to say a group of beings is alive and has rights, then change your mind and say killing them on sight is okay again. The ACLU would have a field day.'

He smiled. 'Perhaps. Regardless, the council has forced a truce on all of us until the law is decided one way or another.'

'So you can let Sabin in your territory, because if he misbehaves, the council will hunt him down and kill him.'

Jean-Claude nodded.

'But you'd still be dead,' I said.

He spread his hands, graceful, empty. 'Nothing's perfect.'

I laughed. 'I guess not.'

'Now, aren't you going to be late for your date with Monsieur Zeeman?'

'You're being awfully civilized about this,' I said.

'Tomorrow night you will be with me, *ma petite*. I would be a poor . . . sport to begrudge Richard his night.'

'You're usually a poor sport.'

'Now, *ma petite*, that is hardly fair. Richard is not dead, is he?'

'Only because you know that if you kill him, I'll kill you.' I held a hand up before he could say it. 'I'd try to kill you, and you'd try to kill me, etc.' This was an old argument.

'So, Richard lives, you date us both, and I am being patient. More patient than I have ever been with anyone.'

I studied his face. He was one of those men who was beautiful rather than handsome, but the face was masculine; you wouldn't mistake him for female, even with the long hair. In fact, there was something terribly masculine about Jean-Claude, no matter how much lace he wore.

He could be mine: lock, stock, and fangs. I just wasn't sure I wanted him. 'I've got to go,' I said.

He pushed away from my desk. He was suddenly standing close enough to touch. 'Then go, *ma petite*.'

I could feel his body inches from mine like a shimmering energy. I had to swallow before I could speak. 'It's my office. You have to leave.'

He touched my arms lightly, a brush of fingertips. 'Enjoy your evening, *ma petite*.' His fingers wrapped around my arms, just below the shoulders. He didn't lean over me or draw me that last inch closer. He simply held my arms, and stared down at me.

I met his dark, dark blue eyes. There had been a time not so long ago that I couldn't have met his gaze without falling into it and being lost. Now I could meet his eyes, but in some ways, I was just as lost. I raised up on tiptoe, putting my face close to his.

'I should have killed you a long time ago.'

'You have had your chances, *ma petite*. You keep saving me.'

'My mistake,' I said.

He laughed, and the sound slid down my body like fur against naked skin. I shuddered in his arms.

'Stop that,' I said.

He kissed me lightly, a brush of lips, so I couldn't feel the fangs. 'You would miss me if I were gone, *ma petite*. Admit it.'

I drew away from him. His hands slid down my arms, over my hands, until I drew my fingertips across his hands. 'I've got to go.'

'So you said.'

'Just get out, Jean-Claude, no more games.'

His face sobered instantly as if a hand had wiped it clean. 'No more games, *ma petite*. Go to your other lover.' It was his turn to raise a hand and say, 'I know you are not truly lovers. I know you are resisting both of us. Brave, *ma petite*.' A flash of something, maybe anger, crossed his face and was gone like a ripple lost in dark water.

'Tomorrow night you will be with me and it will be Richard's turn to sit at home and wonder.' He shook his head. 'Even for you I would not have done what Sabin has done. Even for your love, there are things I would not do.' He stared at me suddenly fierce, anger flaring through his eyes, his face. 'But what I do is enough.'

'Don't go all self-righteous on me,' I said. 'If you hadn't interfered, Richard and I would be engaged, maybe more, by now.'

'And what? You would be living behind a white picket fence with two point whatever children. I think you lie to yourself more than to me, Anita.'

It was always a bad sign when he used my real name. 'What's that supposed to mean?'

'It means, *ma petite*, that you are as likely to thrive in domestic bliss as I am.' With that, he glided to the door and left. He closed the door quietly but firmly behind him.

Domestic bliss? Who, me? My life was a cross between a preternatural soap opera and an action adventure movie. Sort of *As the*

Casket Turns meets *Rambo*. White picket fences didn't fit. Jean-Claude was right about that.

I had the entire weekend off. It was the first time in months. I'd been looking forward to this evening all week. But truthfully, it wasn't Jean-Claude's nearly perfect face that was haunting me. I kept flashing on Sabin's face. Eternal life, eternal pain, eternal ugliness. Nice afterlife.

2

There were three kinds of people at Catherine's dinner party: the living, the dead, and the occasionally furry. Out of the eight of us, six were human, and I wasn't sure about two of those, myself included.

I wore black pants, a black velvet jacket with white satin lapels, and an oversized white vest that doubled for a shirt. The Browning 9mm actually matched the outfit, but I kept it hidden. This was the first party Catherine had thrown since her wedding. Flashing a gun might put a damper on things.

I'd had to take off the silver cross that I always wore and put it in my pocket because there was a vampire standing in front of me and the cross had started glowing when he entered the room. If I'd known there were going to be vamps at the party, I'd have worn a collar high enough to hide the cross. They only glow when they're out in the open, generally speaking.

Robert, the vampire in question, was tall, muscular, and handsome in a model-perfect sort of way. He had been a stripper at Guilty Pleasures. Now he managed the club. From worker to management: the American dream. His hair was blond, curly, and cut quite short. He was wearing a brown silk shirt that fit him perfectly and matched the dress that his date was wearing.

Monica Vespucci's health club tan had faded around the edges, but her makeup was still perfect, her short auburn hair styled into place. She was pregnant enough for me to have noticed and happy enough about it to be irritating.

She smiled brilliantly at me. 'Anita, it has been too long.'

What I wanted to say was, 'Not long enough.' The last time I'd seen her, she had betrayed me to the local master vampire. But Catherine thought she was her friend, and it was hard to disillusion her without telling the whole story. The whole story included some unsanctioned killing, some of it done by me. Catherine's a lawyer and a stickler for law and order. I didn't want to put her in a position where she had to compromise her morals to save my ass. So Monica was her friend, which meant I had been polite all through dinner, from appetizer all the way to dessert. I'd been polite mainly because Monica had been at the other end of the table. Now, unfortunately, we were mingling in the living room and I couldn't seem to shake her.

'It doesn't seem that long,' I said.

'It's been almost a year.' She smiled up at Robert. They were holding hands. 'We got married.' She touched her glass to the top of her belly. 'We got knocked up.' She giggled.

I stared at them both. 'You can't get knocked up by a hundred-year-old corpse.' Okay, I'd been polite long enough.

Monica grinned at me. 'You can if the body temperature is raised for long enough and you have sex often enough. My obstetrician thinks the hot tub did us in.'

This was more than I wanted to know. 'Have you had the amnio yet?'

The smile faded from her face, leaving her eyes haunted. I was sorry I'd asked. 'We've got another week to wait.'

'I'm sorry, Monica, Robert. I hope the test comes back clean.' I did not mention Vlad syndrome, but the words hung on the air. It was rare but not as rare as it used to be. Three years of legalized vampirism and Vlad syndrome was the highest rising birth defect in the country. It could result in some really horrible disabilities, not to mention death for the baby. With that much at stake, you'd think people would be more cautious.

Robert cradled her against him, and all the light had faded from her face. She looked pale. I felt like a heel.

'The latest news was that a vampire over a hundred was sterile,' I said. 'They should update their information, I guess.' I meant for it to be comforting, like they hadn't been careless.

Monica looked at me, and there was no gentleness in her eyes when she said, 'Worried?'

I stared at her all pale and pregnant and wanted to slap her anyway. I was not sleeping with Jean-Claude. But I was not going to stand there and justify myself to Monica Vespucci – or anyone else, for that matter.

Richard Zeeman entered the room. I didn't actually see him enter. I felt it. I turned and watched him walk towards us. He was six foot one, nearly a foot taller than me. Another inch and we couldn't have kissed without a chair. But it would have been worth the effort. He wove between the other guests, saying a word here and there. His smile flashed white and perfect in his permanently tanned skin as he talked to these new friends that he'd managed to charm at dinner. Not with sex appeal or power but with sheer good will. He was the world's biggest boy scout, the original hail fellow, well met. He liked people and was a wonderful listener, two qualities that are highly underrated.

His suit was dark brown, his shirt a deep orangey gold. The tie was a brighter orange with a line of small figures down the middle of it. You had to be standing right next to him to realize the figures were Warner Brothers cartoons.

He'd tied his shoulder-length hair back from his face in a version of a french braid, so the illusion was that his brown hair was very short. It left his face clean and very visible. His cheekbones were perfect, sculpted high and graceful. His face was masculine, handsome, with a dimple to soften it. It was the kind of face that would have made me shy in high school.

He noticed me watching him and smiled. His brown eyes sparkled with the smile, filling with heat that had nothing to do with room temperature. I watched him walk the last few feet, and felt heat rise up my neck into my face. I wanted to undress him, to touch his bare skin, to see what was under that suit. I wanted that very badly. I wouldn't, because I wasn't sleeping with Richard, either. I wasn't sleeping with the vampire or the werewolf. Richard was the werewolf. It was his only fault. Okay, maybe one other: he'd never killed anybody. That last fault might get him killed someday.

I slid my left arm around his waist, under the unbuttoned jacket. The solid warmth of him beat like a pulse against my body. If we didn't have sex soon, I was simply going to explode. What price morals?

Monica stared at me very steadily, studying my face. 'That's a lovely necklace. Who got it for you?'

I smiled and shook my head. I was wearing a black velvet choker with a cameo, edged by silver filigree. Hey, it matched the outfit. Monica was pretty sure Richard hadn't given it to me, which meant, to Monica, that Jean-Claude had. Good old Monica. She never changed.

'I bought it to match the outfit,' I said.

She widened her eyes in surprise. 'Oh, really?' like she didn't believe me.

'Really. I'm not much into gifts, especially jewelry.'

Richard hugged me. 'That's the truth. She's a very hard woman to spoil.'

Catherine joined us. Her copper-colored hair flowed around her face in a wavy mass. She was the only one I knew with curlier hair than mine, but its color was more spectacular. If asked, most people described her from the hair outward. Delicate makeup hid the freckles and drew attention to her pale, grey green eyes. Her dress was the color of new leaves. I'd never seen her look better.

'Marriage seems to agree with you,' I said, smiling.

She smiled back. 'You should try it sometime.'

I shook my head. 'Thanks a lot.'

'I have to steal Anita away for just a moment.' At least she didn't say she needed help in the kitchen. Richard would have known that was a lie. He was a much better cook than I was.

Catherine led me back to the spare bedroom where the coats were piled in a heap. There was one real fur coat draped over the pile. I was betting I knew who owned it. Monica liked being close to dead things.

As soon as the door was shut, Catherine grabbed my hands and giggled, I swear. 'Richard is wonderful. My junior high science teachers never looked like that.'

I smiled, and it was one of those big, dopey smiles. The silly kind that say you're in horrible lust if not love, maybe both, and it feels good even if it is stupid.

We sat down on the bed, pushing the coats to one side. 'He is handsome,' I said, my voice as neutral as I could make it.

'Anita, don't give me that. I've never seen you glow around anyone.'

'I don't glow.'

She grinned at me and nodded. 'Yes, you do.'

'Do not,' I said, but it was hard to be sullen when I wanted to smile. 'All right, I like him, a lot. Happy?'

'You've been dating him for nearly seven months. Where's the engagement ring?'

I did frown at her then. 'Catherine, just because you're deliriously happily married doesn't mean everyone else has to be married, too.'

She shrugged and laughed.

I stared into her shining face and shook my head. There had to be more to Bob than met the eye. He was about thirty pounds heavier than he should have been, balding, with small round glasses on a rather nondescript face. He did not have a sparkling personality, either. I'd been ready to give her the thumbs down until I saw the way he looked at Catherine. He looked at her like she was the whole world, and it was a nice, safe, wonderful world. A lot of people are pretty, and clever repartee is on every television set, but dependability, that's rare.

'I didn't bring Richard here to get your stamp of approval; I knew you'd like him.'

'Then why did you keep him such a secret? I've tried to meet him a dozen times.'

I shrugged. The truth was because I knew she'd get that light in her eyes. That maniacal gleam that your married friends get when you're not married and you're dating anyone. Or worse yet, not dating, and they're trying to fix you up. Catherine had the look now.

'Don't tell me you planned this entire party just so you could meet Richard?'

'Partly. How else was I ever going to?'

There was a knock on the door.

'Come in,' Catherine said.

Bob opened the door. He still looked ordinary to me, but from the light in Catherine's face, she saw something else. He smiled at her. The smile made his whole face glow and I could see something shining and fine. Love makes us all beautiful. 'Sorry to interrupt the girl talk, but there's a phone call for Anita.'

'Did they say who it is?'

'Ted Forrester; says it's business.'

My eyes widened. Ted Forrester was an alias for a man I knew as Edward. He was a hit man who specialized in vampires, lycanthropes, or anything else that wasn't quite human. I was a licensed vampire hunter. Occasionally, our paths crossed. We might even on some level be friends, maybe.

'Who's Ted Forrester?' Catherine asked.

'Bounty hunter,' I said. Ted, Edward's alias, was a bounty hunter with papers to prove it, all nice and legal. I stood and went for the door.

'Is something wrong?' Catherine asked. Not much got past

her, which was one of the reasons I avoided her when I was ass deep in alligators. She was smart enough to figure out when things were off-center but she didn't carry a gun. If you can't defend yourself, you are cannon fodder. The only thing that kept Richard from being cannon fodder was that he was a werewolf. Although refusing to kill people made him almost cannon fodder, shapeshifter or not.

'I was just hoping not to have to do any work tonight,' I said.

'I thought you had the entire weekend off,' she said.

'So did I.'

I took the phone in the home office they'd set up. They'd divided the room down the middle. One half was decorated in country with teddy bears and miniature gingham rockers, the other half was masculine with hunting prints and a ship in a bottle on the desk. Compromise at its best.

I picked up the phone and said. 'Hello?'

'It's Edward.'

'How did you get this number?'

He was quiet for a second. 'Child's play.'

'Why did you hunt me down, Edward? What's up?'

'Interesting choice of words,' he said.

'What are you talking about?'

'I was just offered a contract on your life, for enough money to make it worth my while.'

It was my turn to be quiet. 'Did you take it?'

'Would I be calling you if I had?'

'Maybe,' I said.

He laughed. 'True, but I'm not going to take it.'

'Why not?'

'Friendship.'

'Try again,' I said.

'I figure I'll get to kill more people guarding you. If I take the contract, I only get to kill you.'

'Comforting. Did you say guard?'

'I'll be in town tomorrow.'

'You're that sure someone else will take the contract?'

'I don't even open my door for less than a hundred grand, Anita. Someone will take the hit, and it'll be someone good. Not as good as me, but good.'

'Any advice until you get into town?'

'I haven't given them my answer yet. That'll delay them. Once I say no, it'll take a little time to contact another hitter. You should be safe tonight. Enjoy your weekend off.'

'How did you know I had the weekend off?'

'Craig is a very talkative secretary. Very helpful.'

'I'll have to speak to him about that,' I said.

'You do that.'

'You're sure that there won't be a hitter in town tonight?'

'Nothing in life is sure, Anita, but I wouldn't like it if a client tried to hire me and then gave the job to someone else.'

'You lose many clients at your own hands?' I asked.

'No comment,' he said.

'So one last night of safety,' I said.

'Probably, but be careful anyway.'

'Who put the hit out on me?'

'I don't know,' Edward said.

'What do you mean, you don't know? You have to know so you can get paid.'

'I go through intermediaries most of the time. Keeps down the chance that the next client is a cop.'

'How do you find wayward clients if they piss you off?'

'I can find them, but it takes time. Anita, if you've got a really good hitter on your tail, time is something you won't have.'

'Oh, that was comforting.'

'It wasn't supposed to be comforting,' he said, 'Can you think of anyone who hates you so badly and has this kind of money?'

I thought about that for a minute. 'No. Most of the people that would fit the bill are dead.'

'The only good enemy is a dead enemy,' Edward said.

'Yeah.'

'I heard a rumor that you're dating the master of the city. Is that true?'

I hesitated. I realized I was embarrassed to admit the truth to Edward. 'Yeah, it's true.'

'I had to hear you say it.' I could almost hear him shake his head over the phone. 'Damn, Anita, you know better than that.'

'I know,' I said.

'Did you dump Richard?'

'No.'

'Which monster are you with tonight, bloodsucker or flesh-eater?'

'None of your damn business,' I said.

'Fine. Pick the monster of your choice tonight, Anita, have a good time. Tomorrow we start trying to keep you alive.' He hung up. If it had been anybody else, I'd have said he was angry about me dating a vampire. Or maybe *disappointed* would be a better word.

I hung up the phone and sat there for a few minutes, letting it all sink in. Someone was trying to kill me. Nothing new there, but this someone was hiring expert help. That was new. I'd never had an assassin after my butt before. I waited to feel fear wash over me, but it didn't. Oh, in a vague sort of way, I was afraid, but not like I should have been. It wasn't that I didn't believe it could happen. I did believe. It was more that so much else had happened in the last year that I couldn't get too excited yet. If the assassin jumped out and started shooting, I'd deal with it. Maybe later I'd even have an attack of nerves. But I didn't get many attacks of nerves anymore. Part of me was numbing out like a combat veteran. There was just too much to take in, so you stop taking it in. I almost wished I had been scared. Fear will keep you alive; indifference won't.

Somewhere out there, by tomorrow, someone would have my name on a to-do list. Pick up dry cleaning, buy groceries, kill Anita Blake.

3

I stepped back into the living room and caught Richard's eye. I was sort of ready to go home. Somehow, knowing an assassin was out there, or would be soon, had put a damper on the evening.

'What's wrong?' Richard asked.

'Nothing,' I said. I know, I know, I had to tell him, but how do you tell your sweetie that people are trying to kill you? Not in a room full of people. Maybe in the car.

'Yes, there is. You've got that tension between your eyebrows that means you're trying not to frown.'

'No, I'm not.'

He smoothed his finger between my eyes. 'Yes, you are.'

I glared at him. 'Am not.'

He smiled. 'Now you are frowning.' His face sobered. 'What's wrong?'

I sighed. I stepped closer to him, not for romance but for privacy. Vampires had incredibly good hearing, and I didn't want Robert to know. He'd tattle to Jean-Claude. If I wanted Jean-Claude to know, I'd tell him myself.

'It was Edward on the phone.'

'What does he want?' Richard was frowning now, too.

'Someone tried to hire him to kill me.'

A look of total astonishment blossomed on his face, and I was glad his back was to the room. He closed his mouth, opened it, and finally said, 'I would say you're kidding, but I know you're not. Why would anyone want to kill you?'

'There are plenty of people who would like to see me dead,

Richard. But none of them have the kind of money that's being put out for the hit.'

'How can you be so calm about this?'

'Would it solve anything if I had hysterics?'

He shook his head. 'It's not that.' He seemed to think for a second. 'It's that you're not outraged that someone's trying to kill you. You just accept it, almost like it's normal. It isn't normal.'

'Assassins aren't normal, even for me, Richard,' I said.

'Just vampires, zombies, and werewolves,' he said.

I smiled. 'Yeah.'

He hugged me tightly and whispered, 'Loving you can be very scary sometimes.'

I wrapped my arms around his waist, leaning my face against his chest. I closed my eyes, and for just a moment I breathed in the smell of him. It was more than his aftershave; it was the smell of his skin, his warmth. Him. For just a moment, I sank against him and let it all go. I let his arms be my shelter. I knew that a well-placed bullet would destroy it all, but for a few seconds, I felt safe. Illusion is sometimes all that keeps us sane.

I pushed away from him with a sigh. 'Let's give our regrets to Catherine and get out of here.'

He touched my cheek gently, looking into my eyes. 'We can stay if you want.'

I nestled my cheek against his hand and shook my head. 'If the shit hits the fan tomorrow, I don't want to spend tonight at a party. I'd rather go back to my apartment and cuddle.'

He flashed me that smile that warmed me down to my toes. 'Sounds like a plan to me.'

I smiled back because I couldn't not smile back. 'I'll go tell Catherine.'

'I'll get the coats,' he said.

We did our various tasks and left early. Catherine gave me a very knowing smile. I wished she was right. Leaving early to jump

Richard's bones beat the heck out of the truth. Monica watched us leave. I knew that she and Robert would report back to Jean-Claude. Fine. He knew I was dating Richard. I hadn't lied to anybody. Monica was a lawyer at Catherine's firm – frightening thought all on its own – so she had a legitimate reason to be invited. Jean-Claude hadn't arranged it, but I didn't like being spied on, no matter how it came about.

The walk to the car was nerve-racking. Every shadow was suddenly a potential hiding place. Every noise a footstep. I didn't draw my gun, but my hand ached to do it. 'Dammit,' I said, softly. The numbness was wearing off. I wasn't sure it was an improvement.

'What is it?' Richard asked. He was suddenly scanning the darkness, not looking at me while he talked. His nostrils flared just a little, and I realized he was scenting the wind.

'Just jumpy. I don't see anyone out here, but I'm suddenly looking too damn hard.'

'I don't smell anyone close to us, but they could be downwind. The only gun I smell is yours.'

'You can smell my gun?'

He nodded. 'You've cleaned it recently. I can smell the oil.'

I smiled and shook my head. 'You are so blasted normal, sometimes I forget you turn furry once a month.'

'Knowing how good you are at spotting lycanthropes, that's quite a compliment.' He smiled. 'Do you think assassins would fall from the trees if I held your hand right now?'

I smiled. 'I think we're safe for the moment.'

He curved his fingers around my hand, and a tingle went up my arm like he'd touched a nerve. He rubbed his thumb in small circles on the back of my hand and took a deep breath. 'It's almost nice to know that this assassin business has unnerved you, too. I don't want you afraid, but sometimes it's hard to be your guy when I think you may be braver than I am. That sounds like macho crap, doesn't it?'

I stared up at him. 'There's a lot of macho crap out there, Richard. At least you know it's crap.'

'Can this male chauvinist wolf kiss you?'

'Always.'

He leaned his face downward, and I rose on tiptoe to meet his mouth with mine, my free hand against his chest for balance. We could kiss without me going on tiptoe, but Richard tended to get a crick in his neck.

It was a quicker kiss than normal because I had this itching in the middle of my back, right between the shoulder blades. I knew it was my imagination, but I felt too exposed out in the open.

Richard sensed it and pulled away. He went around to the driver's side of his car and opened his door, leaning across to unlock mine. He didn't open the door for me. He knew better than that. I could open my own bloody door.

Richard's car was an old Mustang, sixty something, a Mach One. I knew all this because he had told me. It was orange with a black racing stripe. The bucket seats were black leather, but the front seat was small enough that we could hold hands when he wasn't using the gear shift.

Richard pulled out onto 270 South. Friday night traffic spilled around us in a bright sparkle of lights. Everybody out trying to enjoy the weekend. I wondered how many of them had assassins after them. I was betting I was one of the few.

'You're quiet,' Richard said.

'Yeah.'

'I won't ask what you're thinking about. I can guess.'

I looked at him. The darkness of the car wrapped around us. Cars at night are like your own private world, hushed and dark, intimate. The lights of oncoming traffic swept over his face, highlighting it, then leaving us in darkness.

'How do you know I'm not thinking about what you'd look like without your clothes on?'

He flashed me a grin. 'Tease.'

I smiled. 'Sorry. No sexual innuendo unless I'm willing to jump your bones.'

'That's your rule, not mine,' Richard said. 'I'm a big boy. Give me all the sexual innuendo you want, I can take it.'

'If I'm not going to sleep with you, it doesn't seem fair.'

'Let me worry about that,' he said.

'Why, Mr Zeeman, are you inviting me to make sexual overtures to you?'

His smile widened, a whiteness in the dark. 'Oh, please.'

I leaned toward him as far as the seat belt would allow, putting a hand on the back of his seat, putting my face inches from the smooth expanse of his neck. I took a deep breath in and let it out, slowly, so close to his skin that my own breath came back to me like a warm cloud. I kissed the bend of his neck, running my lips lightly up and down the skin.

Richard made a small, contented sound.

I curled my knees into my seat, straining against the seat belt so I could kiss the big pulse in his neck, the curve of his jaw. He turned his face into me. We kissed, but my nerves weren't that good. I turned his face away. 'You watch the road.'

He shifted gears, his upper arm brushing against my breasts. I sighed against him, putting my hand over his, holding it on the gear shift, keeping his arm pressed against me.

We stayed frozen for a second, then he moved against me, rubbing. I scooted out from under his arm, settling back into my seat. I couldn't breathe past the pulse in my throat. I shivered, hugging myself. The feel of his body against mine made places all over my body tighten.

'What's wrong?' he said, his voice low and soft.

I shook my head. 'We can't keep doing this.'

'If you stopped because of me, I was enjoying myself.'

'So was I. That's the problem,' I said.

Richard took in a deep breath and let it out, sighing. 'It's only a problem because you make it one, Anita.'

'Yeah, right.'

'Marry me, Anita, and all this can be yours.'

'I don't want to marry you just so I can sleep with you.'

'If it was only sex, I wouldn't want you to marry me,' Richard said. 'But it's cuddling on the couch, watching *Singing in the Rain*. It's eating Chinese and knowing to get that extra order of crab Rangoon. I can order for both of us at most of the restaurants in town.'

'Are you saying I'm predictable?'

'Don't do that. Don't belittle it,' he said.

I sighed. 'I'm sorry, Richard. I didn't mean to. I just . . .'

I didn't know what to say because he was right. My day was more complete for having been shared with Richard. I bought him a mug that I just happened to see in a store. It had wolves on it, and said, 'In God's wildness lies the hope of the world – the great fresh, unblighted, unredeemed wilderness.' It was a quote from John Muir. No special occasion, just saw it, knew Richard would like it, bought it. A dozen times a day I'd hear something on the radio or in conversation, and I'd think, I must remember and tell Richard. It was Richard who took me on my first bird-watching trip since college.

I had a degree in biology, preternatural biology. Once I'd thought I'd spend my life as a field biologist like a preternatural version of Jane Goodall. I'd enjoyed the bird-watching, partly because he was with me, partly because I'd enjoyed it years ago. It was like I'd forgotten that there was life outside of a gun barrel or a grave side. I'd been neck deep in blood and death so long; then Richard came along. Richard who was also neck deep in strange stuff, but who managed to have a life.

I couldn't think of anything better than waking up beside him, reaching for his body first thing in the morning, knowing I'd be coming home to him. Listening to his collection of Rodgers and Hammerstein, watching his face while he watched Gene Kelly musicals.

I almost opened my mouth and said, let's do it, let's get married, but I didn't. I loved Richard; I could admit that to myself, but it wasn't enough. There was an assassin after me. How could I involve a mild-mannered junior high teacher in that kind of life? He was one of the monsters, but he didn't accept it. He was in a battle for leadership of the local werewolf pack. He'd beaten the current pack leader, Marcus, twice, and twice refused the kill. If you didn't kill, you didn't get to be leader. Richard clung to his morals. Clung to values that only worked when people weren't trying to kill you. If I married him, his chance at any kind of normal life was gone. I lived in a sort of free-fire zone. Richard deserved better.

Jean-Claude lived in the same world that I did. He had no illusions about the kindness of strangers, or anyone else for that matter. The vampire wouldn't be shocked at the news of an assassin. He'd simply help me plan what to do about it. It wouldn't throw him, or not much. There were nights when I thought that Jean-Claude and I deserved each other.

Richard turned off onto Olive. We were soon going to be at my apartment, and the silence was getting a little thick. Silences don't usually bother me, but this one did. 'I'm sorry, Richard. I am truly sorry.'

'If I didn't know you loved me, this would be easier,' he said. 'If it wasn't for that damned vampire, you'd marry me.'

'That damn vampire introduced us,' I said.

'And he's regretting it, don't think he isn't,' Richard said.

I looked at him. 'How do you know that?'

He shook his head. 'All you have to do is see his face when we're together. I may not like Jean-Claude, and I hate the thought of you with him, but we aren't the only two hurting here. It's a threesome, don't think it's not.'

I huddled in my seat, suddenly miserable. I'd have almost welcomed a hit man appearing out of the darkness. Killing I understood. Relationships confused me. Admittedly, this relationship was more confusing than most.

Richard turned into the parking lot of my apartment building. He parked the car and turned off the engine. We sat there in the dark, the only illumination the distant glow of a street light.

'I don't know what to say, Richard.' I stared out through the windshield, concentrating on the side of the building, too cowardly to look at him while I talked. 'I wouldn't blame you for just saying to hell with it. I wouldn't put up with this kind of indecision from you, and I wouldn't share you with another woman.' I finally looked at him. He was staring straight ahead, not looking at me.

My heart sped up. If I was truly as brave as I thought I was, I'd have let him go. But I loved him, and I wasn't that brave. The best I could do was not sleep with him. Not take the relationship that next step forward. That was hard enough. Even my self-control wasn't limitless. If we'd been planning a wedding, I could have waited. With an end in sight, my self-control would have appeared endless, but there was no end in sight. Chastity works better if you don't keep testing it quite so often.

I unbuckled the seat belt, unlocked and opened the door. Richard touched my shoulder before I could get out. 'Aren't you going to invite me up?'

I let out a breath I hadn't realized I was holding and turned back to him. 'Do you want to be invited up?'

He nodded.

'I don't know why you put up with me,' I said.

He smiled. He leaned into me, a light brush of lips. 'Sometimes I'm not sure, myself.'

We got out. Richard held his hand out to me, and I took it.

A car pulled in behind us, beside my own Jeep. It was my

neighbor, Mrs Pringle. She had a huge television box tied into her trunk.

We walked to the sidewalk and waited for her to get out. She was a tall woman, stretched almost painfully thin with age. Her snow white hair was done in a bun at the back of her head. Custard, her Pomeranian, jumped out of the car and stood yapping at us. He looked like a golden powder puff with little cat feet. He bounced forward on stiff legs. He sniffed Richard's foot and looked up at him with a small growl.

Mrs Pringle tugged on his leash. 'Custard, behave yourself.'

The dog quieted, but I think it was more Richard's steady glare than Mrs Pringle's admonishments. She smiled at us. She had the same light in her eyes that Catherine had had. She liked Richard and made no bones about it.

'Well, now, this is advantageous. I need some strong young arms to carry that monstrous television up the stairs for me.'

Richard smiled at her. 'Happy to oblige.' He walked around to the trunk and started trying to undo the knots.

'What'd you do with Custard while you shopped?' I asked.

'I carried him with me. I've spent a great deal of money at that store before. The salesmen fairly salivate when I come through the doors, so they indulge me.'

I had to smile. There was a sharp twang as the ropes broke. 'I'll help Richard.' I walked back to the trunk. The rope was an inch thick and flopped, broken, onto the pavement. I raised eyebrows at him and whispered, 'My, my, Grandma, what strong hands you have.'

'I could carry the television up alone, but it might arouse suspicions.'

It was a thirty-inch wide screen. 'You could really carry it up the stairs by yourself?'

'Easily,' he said.

I shook my head. 'But you're not going to because you are a mild-mannered science teacher, not an alpha werewolf.'

'Which is why you get to help me,' he said.

'Are you having trouble undoing the rope?' Mrs Pringle asked. She'd walked back to us with Custard in tow.

'No,' I said, giving Richard a look. 'We've got the rope.' If people found out Richard was a lycanthrope, he'd lose his job. It was illegal to discriminate, but it happened all the time. Richard taught children. He'd be branded a monster, and most people didn't let monsters near their children.

Mrs Pringle and Custard led the way. I went up backwards, sort of steadying the box, but Richard took all the weight. He walked up the stairs like the box weighed nothing, pushing with his legs, waiting for me to go up another step. He made a face at me, soundlessly humming under his breath as if he was bored. Lycanthropes are stronger than your run-of-the-mill human being. I knew that, but it was still a little unsettling to be reminded.

We made it to the hallway, and he let me have some of the weight. The thing was heavy, but I held on, and we kept moving towards Mrs Pringle's apartment, which was right across the hall from mine.

'I've got the door opened,' she called.

We were at the door, starting to maneuver through, when Custard darted between us, underneath the box, trailing his leash. Mrs Pringle was trapped behind the television. 'Custard, come back here.'

Richard lifted with his forearms, taking the weight. 'Get him. I can get inside.'

I let him pretend to struggle inside the apartment and went for the dog. I expected to have to chase him down the hall, but he was sniffing at my door, whining. I knelt and grabbed the end of his leash, pulling him back towards me.

Mrs Pringle was at her door, smiling. 'I see you caught the little rascal.'

I handed her the leash. 'I've got to get something out of my apartment. I'm sure Richard can help you set up the TV.'

'Thanks a lot,' he called from inside the apartment.

Mrs Pringle laughed. 'I'll give you both some iced tea, unless you have better things to do.' There was a knowing look in her blue eyes that made me blush. She winked at me, I kid you not. When the door was safely closed with her and Richard on the other side, I walked toward my apartment. Three doors down, I crossed the hallway. I took the Browning out and clicked the safety off. I eased back towards my door. Maybe I was being paranoid. Maybe Custard hadn't smelled anybody in my apartment. But he'd never whined at my door like that before. Maybe Edward's phone call was making me jumpy. But better jumpy than dead. Paranoid it was.

I knelt by the door and took a breath, letting it out slowly. I took my keys out of my jacket pocket left-handed. I scrunched down as low as I could get and still have a decent shooting stance. If there was a bad guy in there, he'd probably shoot at chest level. On my knees I was a lot shorter than chest level. I pushed the key in the lock. Nothing happened. The apartment was probably empty, except for my fish wondering what the hell I was doing. I turned the knob, pushed the door inward, and a hole exploded out through the door, thundering over my head like a cannon shot. There was no sound for a second. The door swung closed with the force of the shot, and through the hole in the door I saw a man with a shotgun raised to his shoulder. I fired once through the hole. The door bounced open, still reverberating from the shotgun blast. I threw myself onto one side, gun pointed through the open door.

The shotgun fired again, showering the hallway with bits of wood. I fired twice more, hitting the man in the chest both times. He staggered, blood blossoming on his coat, and fell straight back. The shotgun fell to the carpet near his feet.

I got to my knees, back pressed to the wall near my kitchenette. All I could hear was a roaring in my ears, then dimly my own blood rushing through my head.

Richard was suddenly there in the doorway, like a target. 'Get down! He may not be alone!' I wasn't sure how loud I was yelling. My ears were still ringing.

Richard crouched beside me. I think he said my name, but I didn't have time for it. I pushed upward, my back to the wall, gun in a two-handed grip. He started to stand. I said, 'Stay down.' He did. Point for him.

I could see that there was no one in front of my apartment. Unless there was somebody hiding in the bedroom, the hit man had been alone. I approached him, slowly, gun pointed at him. If he'd twitched, I'd have shot again, but he didn't move. The shotgun was by his feet. I'd never seen anybody use a gun with their feet, so I left it where it was.

He lay on his back, one arm thrown up over his head, one down at his side. His face was slack with death, his eyes wide and unseeing. I didn't really need to check for a pulse, but I did it anyway. Nothing. There were three holes in his chest. I'd hit him with the first shot, but it hadn't been a killing blow. That had nearly cost me my life.

Richard came up behind me. 'There's no one else in the apartment, Anita.'

I didn't argue with him. I didn't ask if he knew this by smell or by hearing. I didn't bloody care. I checked the bedroom and bathroom just to be thorough and came back out to find Richard staring down at the dead man.

'Who is he?' Richard asked.

It occurred to me that I could hear again. Bully for me. I still had a faint ringing in my ears, but it would pass. 'I don't know.'

Richard looked at me. 'Was he the . . . hitter?'

'I think so.' There was a hole in the door big enough to crawl through. It was still open. Mrs Pringle's door was closed, but the doorjamb was splintered like something had taken a big bite out of it. If she'd been standing there, she'd have been dead.

I heard the distant wail of police sirens. Couldn't blame the neighbors for calling them. 'I'm going to make some phone calls before the cops get here.'

'Then what?' he asked.

I looked at him. He was pale, the whites of his eyes showing just a little too much. 'Then we go with the nice police officers down to the station to answer questions.'

'It was self-defense.'

'Yeah, but he's still dead on my carpet.' I walked into the bedroom, searching for the phone. I was having a little trouble remembering where I'd left it, as if it ever moved from the nightstand. Shock is always fun.

Richard leaned in the doorway. 'Who are you going to call?'

'Dolph, and maybe Catherine.'

'A friendly policeman I understand, but why Catherine?'

'She's a lawyer.'

'Oh,' he said. He glanced back at the dead man, who was bleeding all over my white carpet. 'Dating you is never boring, I'll give you that.'

'And it's dangerous,' I said, 'Don't forget dangerous.' I dialed Dolph's number from memory.

'I never forget you're dangerous, Anita,' Richard said. He stared at me and his eyes were amber, the color of a wolf's eyes. His beast slid behind those eyes, peering out. Probably the smell of fresh blood. I stared into those alien eyes and knew I wasn't the only dangerous thing in the room. Of course, I was armed. The dead man could vouch for that. Laughter tickled the back of my throat. I tried to swallow it, but it spilled out, and I was giggling when Dolph answered the phone. Laughing was better than crying, I guess. Though I'm not sure Dolph thought so.

4

I sat in a straight-backed chair at a small, scarred table in an interrogation room. Oh, sorry, interview room. That's what they were calling it now. Call it what you will, it still smelled like stale sweat and old cigarettes with an overlay of disinfectant. I was sipping my third cup of coffee, and my hands were still cold.

Detective Sergeant Rudolph Storr leaned against the far wall. His arms were crossed over his chest, and he was trying to be unobtrusive, but when you're six foot eight and built like a pro wrestler, that's hard. He hadn't said a word during the interview. (Just here to observe.)

Catherine sat beside me. She'd thrown a black blazer over the green dress, brought her briefcase, and sat wearing her lawyer face.

Detective Branswell sat across from us. He was in his midthirties, black hair, dark complected, with eyes as black as his hair. His name was English, but he looked Mediterranean, like he'd just stepped off the olive boat. His accent was pure middle Missouri.

'Now, Ms Blake, go over it just one more time for me. Please.' He poised his pen over his notebook as if he'd write it all down again.

'We'd helped my neighbor carry up her new television.'

'Mrs Edith Pringle, yeah, she confirms all that. But why did you go to your apartment?'

'I was going to get a screwdriver to help install the television.'

'You keep a lot of tools, Ms Blake?' He wrote something on his notepad. I was betting it was a doodle.

'No, detective, but I've got a screwdriver.'

'Did Mrs Pringle ask you to go get this screwdriver?'

'No, but she'd used it when she bought her stereo system.' Which was true. I was trying to keep the lies to an absolute minimum.

'So you assumed she'd need it.'

'Yes.'

'Then what?' He asked like he'd never heard the answer before. His black eyes were intense and empty, unreadable and eager at the same time. We were coming to the part that he didn't quite buy.

'I unlocked my door and dropped my keys. I squatted down to pick them up and the first shotgun blast roared over my head. I returned fire.'

'How? The door was closed.'

'I shot through the hole in the door that the shotgun had made.'

'You shot a man through a hole in your door and hit him.'

'It was a big hole, detective, and I wasn't sure I hit him.'

'Why didn't the second shotgun blast take you out, Ms Blake? There wasn't enough left of the door to hide behind. Where were you, Ms Blake?'

'I told you, the blast rocked the door inward. I hit the floor, on my side. The second blast went over me.'

'And you shot the man twice more in the chest,' Detective Branswell said.

'Yes.'

He looked at me for a long moment, studying my face. I met his eyes without flinching. It wasn't that hard. I was numb, empty, and distant. There was still a fine ringing in my ears from being so damn close to two shotgun blasts. The ringing would fade. It usually did.

'You know the man you killed?'

Catherine touched my arm. 'Detective Branswell, my client has been more than helpful. She's told you several times that she did not recognize the deceased.'

He flipped back through his notebook. 'You're right, counselor. Ms Blake has been helpful. The dead man was James Dugan, Jimmy the Shotgun. He's got a record longer than you are tall, Ms Blake. He's local muscle. Someone you call when you want it cheap and quick and don't care how messy it is.' He stared at me while he talked, studying my eyes.

I blinked at him.

'Do you know anyone who would want you dead, Ms Blake?'

'Not right offhand,' I said.

He closed his notebook and stood. 'I'm going to recommend justifiable homicide to the DA. I doubt you'll see the inside of a courtroom.'

'When do I get my gun back?' I asked.

Branswell stared at me. 'When ballistics is done with it, Ms Blake. And I'd be damn grateful that you're getting it back at all.' He shook his head. 'I've heard stories about you from some of the cops who answered the last call from your apartment. The one with the two killer zombies.' He shook his head again. 'Don't take this wrong, Ms Blake, but have you considered moving to a new jurisdiction?'

'My landlord is probably going to suggest the same thing,' I said.

'I'll just bet he is,' Branswell said. 'Counselor, Sergeant Storr.'

'Thanks for letting me sit in on this, Branswell,' Dolph said.

'You said she was one of yours. Besides, I know Gross and Brady. They were the first officers on scene for the zombies. They say good things about her. I've talked to half a dozen officers that say Ms Blake saved their butt or stood shoulder to shoulder with them under fire and didn't blink. It cuts you a hell of a lot of slack, Blake, but that slack isn't unlimited. Watch your back, and try not to shoot up any innocent bystanders.' With that, he left.

Dolph stared down at me. 'I'll drive you back to your place.'

'Richard's waiting for me,' I said.

'What's going on, Anita?'

'I told Branswell everything I know.'

Catherine stood up. 'Anita has answered all the questions she's going to answer tonight.'

'He's a friend,' I said.

'He's also a cop,' Catherine said. She smiled. 'Isn't that right, Sergeant Storr?'

Dolph stared at her for a minute. 'That is certainly true, Ms Maison-Gillette.' He pushed away from the wall. He looked at me. 'I'll talk to you later, Anita.'

'I know,' I said.

'Come on,' Catherine said. 'Let's get out of here before they change their minds.'

'Don't you believe me?' I asked.

'I'm your lawyer. Of course I believe you.'

I looked at her. She looked at me. I got up. We left. I wondered if Richard would believe me. Probably not.

5

Richard and I walked toward his car, through the police station parking lot. He hadn't said a word to me. He'd shaken hands with Catherine and headed for the car. He got into his side. I slid into the passenger side. Richard started the engine and backed out of the parking slot.

'You're mad about something,' I said.

He eased out onto the street. He always drove carefully when he was angry. 'What could I possibly be mad about?' The sarcasm was thick enough to eat with a spoon.

'You think I knew there was a hit man in my apartment?'

He flashed me a look that was pure rage. 'You knew, and you let me go inside and set that damned TV up. You got me out of harm's way.'

'I wasn't sure, Richard.'

'I bet you had your gun drawn before he fired.'

I shrugged.

'Dammit, Anita, you could have been killed.'

'But I wasn't.'

'That's your answer to everything. If you survive, it's all right.'

'It beats the alternative,' I said.

'Don't make jokes,' Richard said.

'Look, Richard, I didn't go out hunting this guy. He came to me.'

'Why didn't you tell me?'

'And you would have done what? Go through the door first? You'd have taken a chest full of buckshot and survived. How would you have explained that? You'd have been outed as a lycanthrope. You'd have lost your job, at the very least.'

'We could have called the police.'

'And told them what? That Custard sniffed at the door? If they had investigated, they'd have gotten shot. The guy was jumpy as hell. He shot through the door, remember? He didn't know who he was firing at.'

He turned onto Olive, shaking his head. 'You should have told me.'

'What would it have changed, Richard? Except maybe you'd have tried to play hero, and if you survived, you'd have lost your career.'

'Dammit, dammit.' He smashed his hands into the steering wheel over and over. When he looked at me, his eyes had gone amber and alien. 'I don't need you to protect me, Anita.'

'Ditto,' I said.

Silence filled the car like ice water. Nobody but the bad guy had died. I'd done the right thing. But it was hard to explain.

'It wasn't that you risked your life,' Richard said, 'it was that you got rid of me before you did it. You didn't even give me a chance. I have never interfered with you doing your job.'

'Would you have considered this part of my job?'

'Closer to your job description than mine,' he said.

I thought about that for a minute. 'You're right. One of the reasons we're still dating is you don't pull macho crap on me. I apologize. I should have warned you.'

He glanced at me with eyes that were still pale and wolfish. 'Did I just win an argument?'

I smiled. 'I admitted I was wrong. Is that the same thing?'

'Exactly the same thing.'

'Then give yourself a point.'

He grinned at me. 'Why can't I stay mad at you, Anita?'

'You're a very forgiving person, Richard. One of us has to be.'

He pulled into my parking lot for the third time that night. 'You can't stay at your place tonight. The door is in pieces.'

'I know.' If I'd been kicked out of my apartment because it was being painted, I had friends I could stay with, or a hotel, but the bad guys had proven they didn't care who got hurt. I couldn't risk anybody, not even strangers in the next room at a hotel.

'Come home with me,' he said. He parked in an empty space closest to the stairs.

'I don't think that's a good idea, Richard.'

'The shotgun blast wouldn't have killed me. I'd have healed, because it wasn't silver shot. How many of your other friends can say that?'

'Not many,' I said quietly.

'I've got a house set back in a yard. You won't be risking innocent bystanders.'

'I know you have a yard, Richard. I've spent enough Sunday afternoons there.'

'Then you know I'm right.' He leaned towards me and his eyes had bled back to their normal brown. 'I have a guest room, Anita. It doesn't have to be more than that.'

I stared at him from inches away. I could feel his body like a force just out of reach. It wasn't his otherworldly wolf powers. It was simply sheer physical attraction. It was dangerous agreeing to go to Richard's house. Maybe not to my life, but to other things.

If Jimmy the Shotgun had had a partner inside the apartment tonight, I'd be dead now. I'd been so busy concentrating on killing him that a second perp could have blown me away. Edward had told his contact no by now, and it takes a little while to find another hitter of Edward's caliber. So, instead of waiting, they hired cheap and local, taking the chance that cheap might take me out and they'd be saved several hundred grand. Or maybe they wanted me dead really quickly for some reason that I didn't understand. Either way, they wanted me dead pretty damn badly. Usually, when someone wants you dead that badly, they succeed. Not tonight or tomorrow, but unless Edward and I could find out who had put the contract out on me, the line of talent would just keep coming.

I stared into Richard's face, almost close enough to kiss. I thought about never seeing him again. About never touching him again. About never satisfying that growing hunger that perfumed the air whenever I was with him. I touched his face, lightly running my fingertips down his cheek. 'Okay.'

'You look so serious. What are you thinking, Anita?'

I leaned in and kissed him. 'Blood, death, and sex. What else is there?'

We got out of the car. I filled my automatic fish feeder full of enough food for a week. In a week's time, if the assassin was still after me, and if I was still alive, I'd have to come back. All the bad guys had to do was stake out my fish tank, and they had me if they were patient enough. Somehow I didn't think they would be.

I packed a few things, including my stuffed toy penguin, Sigmund, every weapon I owned, a few clothes, an outfit for tomorrow's date with Jean-Claude. Yeah, probably I wouldn't be going, but I didn't want to come back to the apartment, not for anything. I left a message on Ronnie's machine. We usually worked out together on Saturday morning, but I didn't want Ronnie in the line of fire. She was a private detective, but Ronnie wasn't a shooter, not like I was. She had a certain respect for life that could get you killed.

Richard waited while I changed. Black jeans, a royal blue polo shirt, white jogging socks with a blue stripe, black Nikes, and I felt more myself. I laid the Browning's shoulder holster in my suitcase. The Browning was my main gun, and I missed it. I'd have missed it under normal circumstances, but now my hand ached for the gun.

I guess that's what backup guns are for. The Firestar 9mm is a good gun and fits my hand well. My hands are small enough that a lot of 9mms are just too big. The Browning was about the limit of a comfortable grip. I wore the Firestar in an interpants holster, set for a forward cross draw, which meant you could see the gun. I wasn't sure I cared tonight.

I put on wrist sheaths and both knives. These were the last two of a foursome that I'd had custom made for my hands, with the highest silver content possible in the steel. I'd had to have two of them replaced; monsters ate them. I put the two new knives in the suitcase still in their felt-lined box. They were pretty and sharp enough to cut your skin if you ran a thumb along the edge.

While I was having the lost knives replaced, I'd ordered a new one. It was nearly a foot long, more a sword than a knife. I'd had a leather harness made that let me carry it down my spine, with the hilt under my hair. I hadn't used it before, but I'd seen it in a catalog and couldn't resist.

I had a Derringer, a sawed-off shotgun, two full-sized, pump-action shotguns, a twelve gauge, and a mini-Uzi. The Derringer, the Uzi, and the sawed-off shotgun were all gifts from Edward. Not Christmas or birthday gifts. No, we'd be out hunting vampires together, and he'd give me a new toy. I'd asked for the shotgun.

The full-sized shotguns wouldn't pack in either the suitcases or the gym bags. I put them in their individual carrying cases, with straps. The gym bags held my vampire hunting kit and my zombie paraphernalia. I put extra ammo in both bags for temporary keeping. Heck, I shoved extra ammo in the suitcase, too. You could never have too much.

I caught a glimpse of myself in the mirror. The gun was pretty obvious against the bright blue of the shirt. I finally put a black jacket over it, what they call a boyfriend's jacket, because it's sort of big through the shoulders and body. The sleeves rolled back to expose the silky lining. I liked the jacket, and with one button fastened, it hid the Firestar, though not completely. You'd still catch glimpses of it when I moved, but maybe people wouldn't run screaming.

I felt naked without the Browning, which was kind of funny, considering I had an Uzi in my suitcase. But hey, I slept with the Browning.

Richard never said a word about the two shotguns. Maybe he would have complained about the rest if he'd seen them, but he picked up one suitcase, put one gym bag over his shoulder, one shotgun carrying case on the same shoulder, and let me pick up my share.

'Can you carry both suitcases?' I asked.

'Yeah, but I'm shocked you asked. The last time I tried to carry something unasked, you nearly handed me my head in a basket.'

'I want one hand free for my gun.'

'Ah,' he said, 'of course.' He took the other suitcase without another word. He really is a very wise man.

Mrs Pringle stepped out of her door as we were leaving. She had Custard in her arms. He growled briefly at Richard, and she hushed him. 'I thought I heard you out here. Are you all right, Anita?'

I glanced at the hole by her door. 'I'm fine. How 'bout you?'

She hugged Custard, raising his tiny furry body near her face. 'I'll be all right. Are you going to be charged?'

'It doesn't look like it.'

'Good.' She glanced at the suitcases. One for clothes, one for weapons. 'Where are you going?'

'I think I'm a little too dangerous to be around right now.'

She searched my face like she was trying to read my mind. 'How bad is this mess, Anita?'

'Bad enough,' I said.

She gently touched my hair, 'You be very careful out there.'

I smiled. 'Always. You take care of yourself, too.'

'Custard and I will take care of each other.'

I petted Custard, rubbing his little fox ears. 'I owe you a box of doggie treats, furball.' He licked my hand with a tiny, pink tongue.

'When you can, give me your new phone number,' she said.

'When I can, I'll come back.'

She smiled, but her pale eyes stayed worried.

We left because we had to. My imagination has always been too good for my own peace of mind. I had a very clear image of Mrs Pringle splattered against the wall, that lovely, aging face blown away. If she had opened the door at the wrong moment, I wouldn't be imagining it. Too close, too damn close.

6

Richard's house was a one-story, half-brick ranch. It looked like a house for children, and Mommy baking cookies in the kitchen. It wasn't even set that far back off the road, but it had plenty of yard on either side and the backyard was an acre of woods. You could look out both the sides and the back and not see a neighbor, except in winter when the bare trees revealed distant glimpses across the valley. From the front picture window, you could see the corner of the next house half obscured by overgrown shrubs. No one had lived in it the entire time I'd been visiting. The place was a little isolated. Richard liked that, and whether I did or not, I needed it now.

The place looked like an invitation for an ambush, but neighbors would have been cannon fodder. Most bad guys try not to take out innocent bystanders. It's not moral outrage, just bad for business. The cops tend to put the heat on if you waste a lot of bystanders.

Richard hit the garage door opener and eased the Mustang into the garage. His four by four was already inside. I followed him in my Jeep. I idled out on the street, waiting for him to move the four by four out so I could put the Jeep in. Parking my Jeep out in front of his house seemed like making the bad guys' job a little too easy. He pulled out. I pulled in. He parked behind me in the driveway and walked into the garage. I unloaded the suitcases, and he hit the button by the interior door.

The door opened into the kitchen. The walls were lined with Hogarth prints of dogs and more modern hunting scenes. A Warner

Brothers canister set; Bugs to Tweety Bird sat on the off-white cabinets. The countertops were off white. The cabinets light honey colored oak. There were dishes draining on a towel by the sink, even though Richard had a dishwasher. A glass, a bowl, a spoon; he'd washed his breakfast dishes before he left for work this morning. I'd have poured water in them and left them in the sink. Of course, I never ate breakfast.

Richard walked through into the living room, carrying one suitcase. I followed, carrying the suitcase with the weapons in it. I also had the two gym bags.

The living room had deep forest green carpet and pale yellow walls. Cartoon lithographs took up the far wall. The near wall was taken up with a wooden entertainment center that Richard had built himself. There was a large-screen TV, a miniature stereo system that made mine sound like humming through a comb, shelves of books, and closed doors that hid part of his extensive video collection and a portion of his CDs. The rest of his books were in the basement, set in shelves along every wall. There were still boxes he hadn't unpacked because he ran out of shelf space.

There was a large couch and a heavy wood coffee table. The couch was green and brown, patterned with a yellow afghan thrown across it that his grandmother had made. A small antique armoire sat against the far wall. There was no other furniture in the room.

He'd set the suitcase in the smaller bedroom. It had a twin bed, a nightstand, and a lamp. The walls, the drapes, and the coverlet were all white, like he hadn't really decided what to do with the room yet.

I laid the gym bags on the bed, put the suitcase on the floor, and stared at it all. My life sitting in little bags on the carpet. Seemed like there should have been more.

Richard came up and hugged me from behind, arms wrapping

around my shoulders. 'I think this is where I'm supposed to ask what's wrong, but I know the answer already. I'm sorry the bad guys invaded your house.'

That was it exactly. The bad guys were not supposed to come home with you. It should have been against the rules. I knew it wasn't, it had happened before, but not like this. Not where I knew I couldn't go back. Even when this was over, I couldn't risk Mrs Pringle and my other neighbors again.

I turned in his arms, and he loosened them so I could do it. I hugged him around the waist. 'How did you know that was exactly what was bothering me?'

He smiled. 'I love you, Anita.'

'That's not an answer.'

He kissed me on the forehead. 'Yes, it is.' He kissed me gently on the lips and stepped back. 'I'm going to get out of this tie. Change into your jammies if you want to.' He left, closing the door behind him.

I opened the door and called after him. 'Can I use the phone?'

He answered from his bedroom. 'Make yourself at home.'

I took that for a yes, and went into the kitchen. The phone was on the wall. I got a card out of my fanny pack, which I'd been forced to carry like a purse. You couldn't fasten the jacket over the fanny pack, and the open jacket would have shown off the gun.

The card was white with a number printed in black script, nothing but the number. I dialed and got Edward's twenty-four-hour answering service. I left a message, saying to call me ASAP, and Richard's number.

Richard's answering machine sat on the counter, connected by wires to the wall-mounted phone. The message light was blinking, but it wasn't my machine, so I didn't check it.

Richard came into the kitchen. His hair fell around his shoulders in tight, foaming waves, curlier from the French braid. His hair was brown, but light of almost any kind brought out golden highlights, hints of bronze. He was wearing a flannel shirt, forest green, with the sleeves rolled above his elbows, showing the fine muscles in his forearms. I'd seen the shirt before. It was high-quality flannel, soft as a blanket to touch. He had on jeans and no socks. He padded barefoot towards me.

The phone rang. It was nearly one o'clock in the morning. Who else could it be but Edward? 'I'm expecting a call,' I said.

'Help yourself.'

I picked it up, and it was Edward. 'What happened?' he asked.

I told him.

'Somebody wants you dead quick.'

'Yeah. When you said no, they went out and bought some cheap local talent.'

'You get what you pay for,' Edward said.

'If there'd been two of them, Edward, I wouldn't be here.'

'You aren't going to like my news.'

'How much worse could it get?' I asked.

'I answered a message just before yours. They upped the offer to five hundred thousand dollars, if you were dead within twenty-four hours.'

'Sweet Jesus, Edward, I'm not worth that kind of money.'

'They knew you blew away their hitter, Anita. They knew the hit had failed.'

'How?' I asked.

'I don't know yet. I'm trying to find out who's putting up the money, but it'll take a little time. The safeguards that keep me out of it protect the client, too.'

I was shaking my head back and forth. 'Why twenty-four hours for the hit?'

'Something's happening that they want you out of the way for, something big.'

'But what?'

'You know what it is, Anita. You may not be aware that you know, but you do. Something worth this kind of money that you could put a stop to. There can't be that many choices.'

'I can't think of a single thing, Edward.'

'Think harder,' he said. 'I'll be there as early as I can tomorrow. Watch your back. Don't drive your car.'

'Why not?'

'Bombs,' he said.

'Bombs,' I repeated.

'For half a million dollars, Anita, they'll get someone good. A lot of professionals will do you from a nice, safe distance. A bomb, a high-powered rifle.'

'You're scaring me,' I said.

'Good, maybe you'll be careful.'

'I'm always careful, Edward.'

'I apologize. You're right, but be more careful. I didn't expect them to try a local hit.'

'You're worried,' I said.

He was quiet for a second. 'We can keep taking out the hitters, but eventually we've got to get to the man with the money. As long as the contract's out there, somebody'll keep taking it.'

'It's just too much damn money to pass up,' I said.

'A lot of professionals won't take a hit with a time limit on it,' he said. 'Some of the best are out of the running because of the deadline. I won't take a hit with special circumstances.'

'I hear a "but" coming up,' I said.

He laughed, quietly. 'For half a million dollars, people will break their rules.'

'Not comforting,' I said.

'Not meant to be,' he said. 'I'll be at Richard's tomorrow early.'

'Do you know where it is?'

'I could find it, but let's not play games. Give me directions.'

I did. 'I would tell you to stay indoors, but you've been dating

Richard for months. A good hitter will be able to find you. I don't know if you're safer inside or on the move.'

'I'll pack extra firepower and be more paranoid than usual.'

'Good. See you tomorrow.' He hung up, and I was left holding the buzzing phone.

Richard was staring at me. 'Did I hear you say twenty-four hours for the hit?'

I hung up the phone. 'I'm afraid so.' I hit the message button on his machine out of habit. It whirred as it rewound.

'Why, for God's sake?' Richard asked.

'I wish I knew.'

'You mentioned money twice. How much?'

I told him.

He sat down in one of the kitchen chairs, looking shocked. Couldn't blame him. 'Anita, don't take this wrong. To me you're worth any amount of money, but why would somebody pay half a million dollars to kill you?'

For someone who knew nothing about assassins, he'd grasped the big question quite nicely. I walked over to him. I ran my fingertips through his hair. 'Edward says I must already know what the big event is, that I wouldn't be worth this kind of money, with this kind of deadline, unless I was already intimate with the situation.'

He looked up at me. 'But you don't know, do you?'

'Not a clue.'

He laid his hands on either side of my waist, pulling me against him, wrapping his arms completely around my waist.

The message machine clicked to life and made us both jump. We laughed nervously, not just from fear. There was a heat to his eyes as he stared up at me that made me want to blush or kiss him. I hadn't decided which.

Two hang-ups, his younger brother Daniel, sorry Richard had canceled their rock climbing tomorrow.

I leaned towards Richard. His lips were the softest I'd ever kissed. The taste of him was intoxicating. How could I be thinking of giving him up?

The last message began playing: 'Richard, this is Stephen. Oh, God, pick up. Please pick up. Please be there.'

We froze, listening.

'They're trying to get me to do one of those movies. Raina won't let me leave. Richard, where are you? They're coming. I've got to go. Oh, God, Richard.' The phone clicked dead. A mechanical voice said, 'End of messages.'

Richard stood up, and I let him. 'I thought Raina had stopped making pornographic movies,' I said.

'She promised not to make snuff films, that was all.' He replayed the message. The time on it was 12:03.

'That's less than an hour ago,' I said.

'I can't leave you alone here tonight. What if another killer comes?' He paced in a tight circle. 'But I can't abandon Stephen.'

'I'll go with you,' I said.

He shook his head, walking for the bedroom. 'I can survive the games that the pack plays, Anita. You're human, they'll tear you up.'

'They'll tear you up, too, Richard.'

He just kept walking. 'I can handle myself.'

'Are you at least going to call some of the pack that's on your side? Get some backup?'

He sat down on his bed, pulling on socks. He glanced up at me, then shook his head. 'If I take my army, this'll turn into a war. People will get killed.'

'But if you go in alone, you only endanger yourself, is that it?'

He glanced up at me. 'Exactly.'

I shook my head. 'And what happens to Stephen if you go out there and get killed? Who rescues him?'

That stopped him for a second. He frowned, fishing his shoes out from under the bed. 'They won't kill me.'

'Why not?' I asked.

'Because if Marcus kills me outside the challenge circle, he doesn't retain leadership of the pack. It's like cheating. The pack would turn on him.'

'What if you accidentally died in a fight with someone else?'

He was suddenly very interested in tying his shoes. 'I can handle myself.'

'Meaning if someone else kills you in a legitimate fight, Marcus is off the hook, right?'

He stood up. 'I guess.'

'Raina is Marcus's mate, Richard. She's afraid you're going to kill him. This is a trap.'

He shook his head stubbornly. 'If I call in the wolves on my side and we go over there in a mass, they'll be slaughtered. If I go over there alone, I may be able to talk my way through it.'

I leaned against the doorjamb and wanted to yell at him, but bit it back. 'I'm going with you, Richard.'

'You have enough problems of your own.'

'Stephen risked his life to save mine once. I owe him. If you want to play politician, fine, but I want Stephen safe.'

'Going out where the assassin can find you isn't a smart idea, Anita.'

'We've been dating for months, Richard. If a professional assassin hits town, it won't take him long to find me here.'

He glared at me, jaw tight enough that I could see the small muscle on the side. 'You'll kill someone if I take you.'

'Only if they need killing.'

He shook his head. 'No killing.'

'Even to save my own life? Even to save Stephen's?'

He looked away from me, then back, anger turning his dark eyes almost black. 'Of course you can defend yourself.'

'Then I'm coming.'

'All right, for Stephen's sake.' He didn't like saying it.

'I'll get my jacket.' I got the mini-Uzi out of the suitcase. It was amazingly small. I could have shot it with one hand, but for accuracy, I needed two. Though accuracy and machine guns were sort of mutually exclusive. You pointed it a little lower than you meant to hit and held on. Silver ammo, of course. I slid the strap over my right shoulder. It had a little clip that attached to my belt at the small of my back. The clip kept the Uzi from sliding all over the place, but left enough play for me to slide the gun out and fire it. The gun rode at the small of my back, which was irritating, but no matter what I told Richard, I was scared, and I wanted at least two guns with me. The police had the Browning. I didn't have a holster big enough for the sawed-off, not to mention it was illegal. Come to think of it, wasn't the machine gun? I had a permit to own it, but they didn't hand out carry permits for fully automatic weapons, not to civilians, anyway. If I got caught with it, I might be going to court after all.

I put the jacket on and whirled around. The jacket was bulky enough that it didn't show. Amazing. The Firestar was more noticeable in its front-draw holster.

My pulse was beating hard enough that I could feel it thrumming against my skin. I was scared. Richard was going to play politics with a bunch of werewolves. Shapeshifters didn't play politics much, they just killed you. But I owed Stephen, and I didn't trust Richard to save him. I'd do whatever it took to see him safe; Richard wouldn't. Richard would hesitate. It would almost surely get him killed one day. Tonight, for the first time, I realized it might get me killed.

No way should we walk into one of Raina's little shows without more people. No way. Jean-Claude would never have tolerated Raina and Marcus's games. They'd be dead by now, and we'd all be safe. I would have trusted Jean-Claude at my back tonight. He wouldn't flinch. Of course, he'd have brought his own little army of vampires and made it a true battle. The shit could hit the fan tonight and be over before morning. Richard's way, we'd rescue Stephen, survive, escape, and Raina would still be alive. Nothing would be settled. It may have been civilized, but it was a bad way to stay alive.

Richard was waiting by the front door, keys in hand, impatient. Couldn't blame him.

'Stephen didn't say where he was. Do you know where they make the films?'

'Yeah.'

I looked a question at him. 'Raina took me to watch the filming a few times. She thought I'd overcome my shyness and join in.'

'You didn't.' It wasn't a question.

'Of course not. Let's go get Stephen.' He held the door for me, and just this once I didn't tell him not to.

7

I expected Richard to drive into the city, to some disreputable warehouse in a seedy section of town. Instead, he drove further into Jefferson County. We drove down Old Highway 21 between soft, rolling hills, silvered in the moonlight. It was early May, and the trees were already thick with leaves.

Woods hugged the sides of the road. An occasional house would break out of the trees, but for the most part, we were alone in the dark, as if the road stretched out forever and no other human had ever set foot on it.

'What's the plan?' I asked.

Richard glanced at me, then back to the road. 'Plan?'

'Yeah, a plan. If Raina's there, she won't be alone, and she won't like you taking Stephen.'

'Raina's the alpha female, the lupa. I'm not allowed to fight her.'

'Why not?'

'An alpha male becomes Ulfric, wolf king, by killing the old leader, but the winner chooses the lupa.'

'So Raina didn't have to fight for her place?'

'She didn't have to fight to be lupa, but she did have to fight to be the most dominant female in the pack.'

'You once told me that the pack considers me a dominant. What's the difference between being a dominant and being an alpha female? I mean, can I be an alpha?'

'Alpha is the equivalent to being a master vampire, sort of,' he said.

'So what is a dominant?'

'Anyone not pack, not lukoi, that's earned our respect. Jean-Claude is a dominant. He can't be more unless he becomes pack.'

'So you're alpha, but you're not pack leader.'

'We have about half a dozen alphas, male and female. I was Marcus's second in command, his Freki.'

'Freki is the name of one of Odin's wolves. Why would second wolf be named after something out of mythology?'

'The pack is very old, Anita. Among ourselves, we are the lukoi. There can be two seconds, Freki and Geri.'

'Why the history lesson and the new vocabulary?'

'To outsiders, we keep it simple. But I want you to know who and what we are.'

'Lukoi is Greek, right?'

He smiled. 'But do you know where it's from?'

'No.'

'King Lykaon of Arcadia was a werewolf. He didn't try and hide it. We call ourselves the lukoi in his memory.'

'If you're not Freki anymore, what are you?'

'Fenrir, challenger.'

'The giant wolf that kills Odin at Ragnarok.'

'I'm impressed, not many people would know that.'

'Two semesters of comparative religion,' I said. 'Can a woman be Ulfric?'

'Yes, but it's rare.'

'Why?'

'They'd have to win a knock-down drag-out physical battle. All the power in the world won't stop someone from pounding your face into the ground.'

I would have liked to argue, but I didn't. He was right. Not because I was female. Small men get their asses kicked, too. Size matters if both people are equally well trained.

'Why don't the female alphas have to duke it out to win the top spot?'

'Because the Ulfric and his lupa are a mating pair, Anita. He doesn't want to get stuck with a woman he can't stand.'

I looked at him. 'Wait a minute. You're next in line to lead the pack. If you succeed Marcus, do you have to sleep with your lupa?'

'Technically, yes.'

'Technically?' I said.

'I won't choose one. I won't sleep with someone just so the pack can feel secure.'

'Glad to hear it,' I said, 'but does that jeopardize your standing in the pack?'

He took a deep breath, and I heard it sigh outward. 'I have a lot of support among the pack, but some of them are bothered by my morals. They think I should pick a mate.'

'And you won't, because . . . of me?'

He glanced at me. 'That's a big part of it. It wouldn't be only one time, Anita. An alpha couple binds for life. It's like a marriage. They usually marry each other in real life, not just in the pack.'

'I can see why the pack leader gets to pick his mate.'

'I've picked my mate,' Richard said.

'But I'm not a werewolf.'

'No, but the pack considers you a dominant.'

'Only because I killed a few of them,' I said.

'Well, that does tend to impress them.' He slowed down. There was a line of pine trees along the left-hand side of the road, too regular and too thick to be natural. He turned down a gravel driveway in the middle of them.

The driveway curved downhill, and at the bottom of a shallow valley was a farmhouse. Hills thick with trees poured out around the house. If there had ever been fields, the forest had reclaimed them.

The driveway opened into a small gravel lot that was crowded with cars, at least a dozen of them. Richard jerked the car into park and was out the door before I could unbuckle my seat belt. I had to run to catch up and was at his back just as he flung open the barn door. There was a thick wall of cloth hanging inside the door, not a curtain but more a barrier. Richard pulled it aside, and light flooded out around us. He stalked into that light, and I trailed after him.

There were lights everywhere, hanging from the rafters like large, ugly fruit. About twenty people stood around the open interior of the barn. Two cameras were trained on a set, made up of two walls and a king-size bed. Two cameramen were sort of draped on the cameras, waiting. A long table thick with take-out bags and cold pizza was set near the entrance. Over a dozen people were clustered around the food. They glanced at us as we entered. A handful of humans looked hurriedly away and began inching back. The lycanthropes stared, their eyes almost motionless, intent. I suddenly knew what it must feel like to be a gazelle near a lion pack.

At least two-thirds of the people in the barn were shape-shifters. Probably, they weren't all werewolves. I couldn't tell what animal they might be by looking, but I knew they were all shapeshifters. Their energy burned through the air like a hint of lightning. Even with the Uzi, if things went wrong, I was in trouble. I was suddenly angry with Richard. We shouldn't have come alone like this. It was too careless for words.

A woman stepped out of the group. She had what looked like an industrial-strength makeup kit on her shoulder. Her dark hair was shaved close to her head, leaving a very pretty face open and clean, without a drop of makeup on it.

She moved uncertainly towards us as if afraid she'd get bitten. The air vibrated around her, a tiny shimmer, as though reality was just a little less firm than it should be around her. Lycanthrope. I wasn't sure what flavor, but that really didn't matter. Whatever the flavor, they were dangerous.

'Richard,' she said. She stepped away from the watching crowd, small hands running up and down the strap of her bag. 'What are you doing here?'

'You know why I'm here, Heidi,' he said. 'Where's Stephen?'

'They aren't going to hurt him,' she said. 'I mean, his brother's here. His own brother wouldn't let him get hurt, would he?'

'Sounds like you're trying to convince yourself, not us,' I said.

Her eyes flicked to me. 'You must be Anita Blake.' She glanced behind at the watchers at her back. 'Please, Richard, just go.' The aura of energy around her was vibrating harder, almost a visible shimmer in the air. It prickled along my skin like ants.

Richard reached out towards her.

Heidi flinched but stood her ground.

Richard smoothed his hand just above her face, not quite touching her skin. As he moved his hand, the energy around her quieted, like water calming. 'It's all right, Heidi. I know the situation Marcus has put you in. You want to join another pack, but he has to give permission. To get his permission, you do what he says, or you're trapped. Whatever happens, I won't hold it against you.'

The anxiety seeped away. Her otherworldly energy quieted until it was barely there at all. She might have passed for human.

'Very impressive.' A man stepped forward. He was at least six foot four, maybe an inch taller, his head bald as an egg, only his eyebrows showing dark above pale eyes. His black T-shirt strained over the muscles in his arms and chest, as if the shirt was the skin of an insect about to split and let loose the monster. Energy boiled off him like summer heat. He moved with the confident strut of a bully, and the power crawling over my skin said he might be able to back it up.

'He's new,' I said.

'This is Sebastian,' Richard said. 'He joined us after Alfred died.'

'He's Marcus's new enforcer,' Heidi whispered. She stepped

back, halfway between the two men, her back to the curtain we'd entered through.

'I challenge you, Richard. I want to be Freki.'

Just like that, the trap was sprung.

'We are both alpha, Sebastian. We don't have to do anything to prove that.'

'I want to be Freki, and I need to beat you to do it.'

'I'm Fenrir now, Sebastian. You can be Marcus's Freki without fighting me.'

'Marcus says no, says I have to go through you.'

Richard took a step forward.

'Don't fight him,' I said.

'I have to answer challenge.'

I stared at Sebastian. Richard is not a small man, but he looked small beside Sebastian. Richard wouldn't back down to save himself. But for someone else . . . 'And if you get killed, where does that leave me?' I asked.

He looked at me then, really looked at me. He turned back to Sebastian. 'I want safe passage for Anita.'

Sebastian grinned and shook his head. 'She's dominant. No safe passage. She takes her chances like the rest of us.'

'She can't accept challenge, she's human.'

'When you're dead, we'll make her one of us,' Sebastian said.

'Raina has forbidden us to make Anita lukoi,' Heidi said.

The glare that Sebastian gave her made her cringe against the curtain door. Her eyes were round with fear.

'Is that true?' Richard asked.

'It's true,' Sebastian growled. 'We can kill her, but we can't make her pack.' He grinned, a brief flash of teeth. 'So we'll just kill her.'

I drew the Firestar, using Richard's body to shield the movement from the lycanthropes. We were in trouble. Even with the Uzi, I couldn't kill them all. If Richard would kill Sebastian, we might salvage the situation, but he'd try not to kill him. The other shapeshifters watched us with patient, eager eyes. This had been the plan all along. There had to be a way out.

I had an idea. 'Are all Marcus's enforcers assholes?'

Sebastian turned to me. 'Was that an insult?'

'If you have to ask, then indeedy-do, it was.'

'Anita,' Richard said, low and careful, 'what are you doing?'

'Defending myself,' I said.

His eyes widened, but he didn't take his glance from the big werewolf. Richard understood. There was no time to argue about it. Sebastian took a step forward, big hands balled into fists. He tried to step around Richard to get to me. Richard moved in front of him. He put out his hand, palm outward like he had with Heidi, and that roiling energy damped down, spilling out like water from a broken cup. I'd never seen anything like it. Calming Heidi was one thing. Forcing a lycanthrope to swallow such power was something else.

Sebastian took a step back, almost a stagger. 'You bastard.'

'You are not strong enough to challenge me, Sebastian. Don't ever forget that,' Richard said. His voice was still calm, with the barest hint of anger underneath. It was a reasonable voice, a voice for negotiating.

I stood behind Richard with the Firestar held at my side, as unobtrusive as I could make it. The fight was off, and my little show of bravado hadn't been needed. I'd underestimated Richard's power. I'd apologize later.

'Now, where is Stephen?' Richard asked.

A slender black man stalked towards us, moving like a dancer in a shimmering wash of his own energy. His hair was braided in shoulder-length cornrows with colored beads worked into them. His features were small and neat, his skin a rich solid brown. 'You may be able to control us one at a time, Richard, but not all at once.'

'You were kicked out of your last pack for being a troublemaker, Jamil,' Richard said. 'Don't make the same mistake twice.'

'I won't. Marcus will win this fight because you are a fucking bleeding heart. You still don't get it, Richard. We aren't the Young Republicans.' Jamil stopped about eight feet back. 'We are a pack of werewolves, and we aren't human. Unless you accept that, you are going to die.'

Sebastian stepped back to stand beside Jamil. The rest of the lycanthropes moved up behind the two men. Their combined energy flowed outward, filling the room like warm water with piranha in it. The power bit along my skin like tiny electric shocks. It rose in my throat until it was hard to breathe, and the hair on my head stood at attention.

'Will you be pissed if I kill some of them?' I asked. My voice sounded squeezed and harsh. I moved closer to Richard, but had to step back. His power poured over me like something alive. It was impressive, but there were twenty lycanthropes on the other side, and it wasn't *that* impressive.

A scream shattered the silence, and I jumped.

'Anita,' Richard said.

'Yeah.'

'Go get Stephen.'

'That was him screaming?' I asked.

'Go get him.'

I looked at the mass of lycanthropes and said, 'You can handle this?'

'I can hold them.'

'You can't hold us all,' Jamil said.

'Yes,' Richard said, 'I can.'

The scream sounded again, higher, more urgent. The sound came from deeper in the barn where it had been divided into rooms. There was a makeshift hallway. I started towards it, then hesitated. 'Will you be pissed if I kill people?'

'Do what you have to do,' he said. His voice had grown low, with an edge of growl to it.

'If she kills Raina with a gun, she still won't be your lupa,' Jamil said.

I glanced at Richard's back. I hadn't known I was being considered for the job.

'Go, Anita; now.' His voice was dying down to a growl. He didn't have to add, hurry. I knew that part. He might be able to stall, but he couldn't fight them all.

Heidi walked towards me, behind Richard's back. He didn't turn any attention to her, as if he didn't consider her a danger at all. She wasn't powerful, but you didn't have to be powerful or even strong to stab someone in the back, claw or knife, what did it matter? I pointed the gun at her. She passed within inches of Richard and he did nothing. My gun was the only thing guarding his back. Even now, he trusted Heidi. Right this minute, he shouldn't have trusted anyone but me. 'Gabriel's with Raina,' she said. She said his name like she was afraid of him.

Gabriel wasn't even a member of the pack. He was a were-leopard. He was one of Raina's favorite actors, though. He'd appeared in her porno flicks and even one snuff film. I almost asked her who she feared most, Raina or Gabriel. But it didn't matter. I was about to confront them both.

'Thanks,' I said to Heidi.

She nodded.

I went for the hallway and the sound of screams.

8

I entered the hallway and followed the sounds of voices to the second door on the left. I heard at least two different male voices, soft, murmuring. I couldn't make out the words. The screams changed to yelling. 'Stop, please, stop. No!' It was a man, too. Unless they were torturing more than one person tonight, it had to be Stephen.

I took a deep breath, let it out, and reached for the door with my left hand, gun in my right. I wished I knew the layout of the room. Stephen yelled, 'Please, don't!'

Enough. I opened the door, shoving it against the wall so I'd know there was no one behind it. I meant to sweep the room, but what I saw on the floor stopped me cold, like some kind of flash-frozen nightmare. Stephen lay on his back, a white robe open, revealing his nude body. Blood trailed down his chest in thin scarlet ribbons, though there were no apparent wounds. Gabriel held Stephen's arms, pinned underneath his body, behind his back as if they might already be tied. Stephen's waist-length yellow hair spilled over Gabriel's leather-clad lap. Gabriel was naked from the waist up, a silver ring through his right nipple. His curly black hair had spilled over his eyes, and when he looked up at me, he looked blind.

A second man knelt on the far side of Stephen. Curling blond hair fell to his waist. He wore an identical white robe, fastened. When he looked at the door, his slender, nearly pretty face was a mirror of Stephen's. Had to be his brother. He was holding a steel knife. He was in midslice when I came through the door. Fresh blood welled from Stephen's skin.

Stephen screamed.

There was a naked woman curled over Stephen's body. She straddled his lower body, pinning his legs. Her long auburn hair fell like a curtain, hiding the last indignity from sight. Raina raised her head from Stephen's groin. Her full lips parted in a smile. She'd worked him to erection. Even with his protests, his body had gone on without him.

It took a heartbeat to see it all, a sort of slow-motion shorthand. I sensed movement to my right and tried to turn, but it was too late. Something furred and only half-human slammed into me. I hit the far wall hard enough to make it shudder. The Firestar went spinning, and I fell, stunned, to the floor. A wolf the size of a pony loomed over me. It opened jaws big enough to crush my face, and growled, a sound low and deep enough to stop my heart.

I could move again, but that face was an inch from my cheek; I could feel its breath on my face. A line of saliva fell from its mouth to glide down the edge of my mouth. It lowered its muzzle that last inch, lips drawn back like it was going to take a nibble. The Uzi was pinned between my back and the wall. I went for one of the knives, and knew I'd never make it.

Human arms curved around the wolf, tore it back, away from me. Raina stood holding the struggling wolf like it was no effort. Her beautiful naked body rippled with muscles that didn't show until they were used. 'Draw no blood from her, I told you that.' She tossed the wolf into the other wall. The wall cracked and buckled. The wolf lay still, eyes rolled back into its skull.

It gave me the time I needed. I pulled the Uzi around on its strap. When Raina turned back to me, I was pointing it at her.

She stood over me, naked, perfect, slender where she was supposed to be slender, curved where she was supposed to be curved. But since I'd seen her sculpt her body at will, I wasn't that impressed. When you could manipulate your body like she could, who needed plastic surgery?

'I could have let her kill you, Anita. You don't seem very grateful.'

I sat on the floor, propped against the wall, not completely trusting that I could stand yet. But the Uzi was pointed nice and steady. 'Thanks a lot,' I said, 'Now, back up, slowly, or I will cut you in half.'

Raina laughed, a low, joyous sound. 'You are so dangerous. So exciting. Don't you think so, Gabriel?'

Gabriel came to stand beside her. Both of them looking down at me was too much, so I used the wall to brace myself and stood. I could stand. Great. I was beginning to think I could even walk. Better.

'Back up,' I said.

Gabriel stepped around her, bringing him almost close enough to have reached out and touched me. 'She's perfect for anyone who's into pain and has a death wish.' He reached out, as if to run his fingers down my cheek. I pointed the machine gun at his waist, because it would kick upward. Aim too high and you can actually miss.

'The last time you pushed me, Gabriel, all I had on me was a knife. You survived having me gut you, but even you can't heal from a submachine gun burst. At this range, I'll cut you in half.'

'Would you really kill me just for trying to touch you?' He seemed amused, his strange grey eyes almost fever bright as they peered out of the tangle of his hair.

'After what I just saw, you bet.' I stood away from the wall. 'Back up or we'll find out how much damage you can take.'

They backed up. I was almost disappointed. The Uzi with silver ammo would do exactly what I'd said it would do. I could cut them down, kill them, no muss, no fuss, just a hell of a mess. I wanted them dead. I looked at them for a heartbeat and thought about it, thought about pulling the trigger and saving us all a lot of trouble.

Raina backed up, pulling Gabriel with her. She stared at me as she moved, back towards the wall where the ponysized wolf was staggering to its feet. Raina looked at me and I saw the knowledge on her face of how close she'd come. I think until that moment she hadn't realized I could kill her and not lose sleep. Hell, leaving her alive would cost me more sleep.

A roaring scream came from the other room. Howling vibrated through the barn. There was a moment of breathless silence, then growls, shrieks. The floor shuddered with the impact of distant bodies. Richard was fighting without me.

Raina smiled at me. 'Richard needs you, Anita. Go to him. We'll take care of Stephen.'

'No thanks.'

'Richard could be dying while you waste time.'

Fear flowed over me in a cool wash. She was right. They'd lured him here to die. I shook my head. 'Richard told me to get Stephen, and that's what I'm going to do.'

'I didn't think you took orders that well,' she said.

'I take the ones I like.'

Stephen had curled onto his side, pulling the robe over his body. His brother sat beside him, smoothing his hair and murmuring, 'It's all right, Stephen. You're not hurt.'

'You sliced him up, you son of a bitch.'

He spread Stephen's robe, exposing his chest. Stephen tried weakly to close his robe. His brother slapped his hands lightly. He wiped his hands across the bloody chest. The skin was perfect. The cut had healed already, which meant that all the blood was Stephen's.

'Get off of him, right now, or I will blow you away.'

He eased back from him, eyes wide. He believed me. That was good, because it was true.

'Come on, Stephen. We've got to go.'

He raised his head and looked at me, tears sliding down his cheeks. 'I can't stand.' He tried to crawl to me, but collapsed on the floor.

'What did you give him?' I asked.

'Something to relax him,' Raina said.

'You bitch.'

She smiled. 'Exactly.'

'Go over and stand by them,' I said to the brother.

The man turned a face to me so like Stephen's it was startling. 'I wouldn't let them hurt him. He'd enjoy it if he'd just let himself go.'

'He is hurt, you son of a bitch! Now get over there, right now, or I'll kill you. Do you understand me? I will kill you and be happy about it.'

He got to his feet and went to stand beside Gabriel. 'I made sure no one hurt him,' he said softly.

The walls shuddered. There was a sound of splintering wood. Someone had been thrown through the wall of the room next to us. I had to get us out of there. I had to get to Richard. But if I was careless, I'd never make it. Richard wasn't the only one in danger of getting his throat ripped out.

With this many lycanthropes in a room so small, they were too close. They could jump me if I went to help Stephen stand, but with a machine gun in my hand, I was betting most of them would be dead before they reached me. It was a comforting thought.

I spotted the Firestar in the far corner. I picked it up and holstered it without having to look. Practice, practice, practice. I kept the machine gun out. It just made me feel better.

I knelt by Stephen without taking my eyes off the others. It was hard not to at least glance down, but I was too damn close to them. The wolf had been unbelievably fast, and I didn't think Raina would save me a second time. I was lucky she didn't want me wounded. I got my arm around Stephen's waist, and he managed to throw his arms around my neck. I stood, and he was almost dead weight, but we both managed to stand, and with my help, Stephen kept his feet. I was glad he was about my size. Bigger would have been harder. His robe flapped open, and he took one arm from around my shoulders and tried to tie it closed, but he couldn't do it. He started to take his other arm off my shoulders.

'Leave it, Stephen, please. We've got to go now.'

'I don't want people to see me.' He stared at me from inches away, his face vague and unfocused from the drugs, but a single tear trailed from the corner of one cornflower blue eye. 'Please,' he said.

Shit. I braced him around the waist, and said, 'Go ahead.' I stared at Raina while he tied his robe, clumsy and slow from the drug she'd slipped him. He was making a low whimpering sound deep in his chest by the time he got it closed.

'In some ways you are as sentimental as Richard,' she said. 'But you could kill us, all of us, even Stephen's brother, and feel nothing.'

I met her honey brown eyes and said, 'I'd feel something.'

'What?' she asked.

'Safer,' I said.

I backed us towards the open door and had to glance behind to make sure nothing was coming up at me. When I looked back at them, Gabriel had moved forward, but Raina had a hand on his arm, stopping him. She was looking at me like she'd never really seen me before. Like I'd surprised her. I guess it was mutual. I'd known she was twisted, but not in my wildest dreams would I have accused her of raping one of her own people.

Stephen and I stepped out into the hall, and I took a deep breath, feeling something in my chest loosen. The sounds of fighting crashed over us. I wanted to run towards the fight. Richard was alive, or they wouldn't have still been fighting. There was time. There had to be.

I called to Raina, 'Don't show your face out here until after we're gone, Raina, or I'll shoot it off.' There was no answer from the room. I had to get to Richard.

Stephen stumbled and nearly took us both down. He hung from

my shoulders, his arms pressing into my neck, then he got his feet under him. 'You with me, Stephen?'

'I'm all right. Just get me out of here.' His voice sounded weak, thready, like he was losing consciousness. I could not carry him and shoot, or at least I didn't want to try. I got a firmer grip on his waist and said, 'Stay with me, Stephen, and I'll get you out.'

He nodded, long hair spilling around his face. 'Okay.' The one word was almost too soft to hear above the fighting.

I stepped out into the main room, and it was chaos. I couldn't see Richard. There was just a mass of bodies, arms, legs, a clawed form rose above the rest, a man-wolf close to seven feet tall. He reached down and drew Richard out of the mess, claws digging into his body. Richard shoved a hand that was too long to be human, and not furry enough to be wolf, under the werewolf's throat. The creature gagged, spitting blood.

A wolf almost as long as Richard was tall leapt upon his back. Richard staggered, but didn't fall. The mouth sank teeth into his shoulder. Furred claws and human hands grabbed at him from every side. Fuck it. I fired the machine gun into the wooden floor. It would have looked more impressive if I'd fired into the over-head lights, but bullets come down at the same speed they go up, and I didn't want to catch my own ricochet. Holding the machine gun one-handed was a trip. I held on and sprayed a line from me to the bed. I ended with the gun pointing at the fight. Everyone had frozen, shocked. Richard crawled out of the mess, bleeding. He got to his feet, swaying a bit, but moving on his own power. I could never have carried both him and Stephen, let alone the machine gun.

He stopped in front of the curtain, waiting for me to come to him. Stephen sagged against me, arms limp. I think he'd passed out. It was an agonizingly slow walk to Richard. If I tripped and went down, they'd be on me. They watched me move with eyes, human and wolf, but nothing I could have talked to. They watched me like they wondered what I'd taste like and would enjoy finding out.

The giant man-wolf spoke, its furry jaws thick and strange around human words. 'You can't kill us all, human.'

He was right. I raised the machine gun a little. 'True, but who's going to be first in line?'

No one else moved as I walked. When I reached Richard, he took Stephen from me, cradling him in his arms like he was a child. Blood seeped down his face from a cut on his forehead. It covered half his face like a mask. 'Stephen is never to come back here, not ever,' Richard said.

The man-wolf spoke again, 'You are not a killer, Richard. That is your weakness. Even if we bring Stephen back here, you will not kill us for it. You will hurt us, but not kill us.'

Richard didn't say anything. It was probably true. Damn.

'I'll kill you,' I said.

'Anita, you don't understand what you're saying,' Richard said.

I glanced at him, then back to the waiting masses. 'Killing is all they understand, Richard. If you aren't willing to kill them, Stephen isn't safe. I want him safe.'

'Enough to kill for it?' Richard asked.

'Yeah,' I said, 'enough to kill for it.'

The wolfman stared at me. 'You are not one of us.'

'It doesn't matter. Stephen is off limits. Tell Raina if he gets dragged back here, I'll hold her personally responsible.'

'Tell me yourself.' Raina stood in the hallway, naked, and totally comfortable as if she'd been wearing the finest silk. Gabriel was at her back.

'If anyone brings Stephen back here, tries to force him into the movies, I'll kill you.'

'Even if I have nothing to do with it.'

I smiled, like I would believe that. 'Even if, no matter who does it, or why, it'll be your ass on the line.'

She nodded her head, almost a bow. 'So be it, Anita Blake. But know this, you have challenged me in front of my pack. I cannot let that stand unanswered. If you were another shapeshifter, we would duel, but your being human poses a problem.'

'You know this, bitch. I am human, so if you expect me to drop my gun and fight you one on one, you're crazy.'

'That would hardly be fair, would it?'

'I didn't think you worried much about being fair, after what I saw in the back room.'

'Oh, that,' she said, 'Stephen will never rise in the pack. There is no more challenge to him. He is anyone's meat that is higher in the pack.'

'Not anymore,' I said.

'You offer him your protection?' she asked.

I'd been asked this question once before and knew it meant more than it sounded like it did, but I didn't care. I wanted Stephen safe, and I'd do what it took, killing or making myself a target. Hell, the assassin would probably finish me soon, anyway. 'Yeah, he's under my protection.'

'He's already under *my* protection, Anita,' Richard said.

'Until you're willing to kill to back it up, it doesn't mean a whole lot to these people.'

'You will kill to support Richard's claims of protection?' Raina asked.

'She doesn't understand what you're asking,' Richard said. 'It isn't a fair question unless she understands it.'

'Then explain it to her, Richard, but not tonight. It grows late, and if we are to get any filming done, we must hurry. Take your little human and explain the rules to her. Explain how deep a hole she's dug herself tonight. When she understands the rules, call me. And I will think of a way to make a duel between us as fair as possible. Perhaps I could blindfold myself or tie one arm behind my back.'

I started to say something, but Richard said, 'Come on, Anita.

We have to go now.' He was right. I could kill a lot of them, but not all. I hadn't brought a spare clip for the machine gun. I hadn't thought I'd need it. Silly me.

We got out the door with me walking backwards, ready to shoot anyone who stuck a head out. No one followed us. Richard carried Stephen through the late spring night and didn't look back, as if he knew they wouldn't follow.

I opened the door, and he laid Stephen in the backseat. 'Can you drive home?' he asked.

'Yeah, how bad are you hurt?'

'Not bad, but I'd like to ride back here with Stephen in case he wakes up.'

I couldn't argue with that. I drove. We were safe. We were all actually still alive. But if they'd rushed us, we wouldn't be. Now that we were safe, I could be mad. 'Well, we survived. No thanks to your little plan,' I said.

'And no one died, thanks to my little plan,' Richard said.

'Only because I was better armed than usual.'

'You were right,' he said, 'it was a trap. Happy?'

'Yeah, I'm happy,' I said.

'Glad to hear it.' Underneath the sarcasm he was tired. I could hear it in his voice.

'What are you supposed to explain to me, Richard?' I glanced in the rearview mirror but couldn't see his face in the dark.

'Raina backs up Marcus's orders. She's his lupa. He uses her to do things he doesn't approve of, like torture.'

'So I set myself up as your lupa.'

'Yes, I'm the Fenrir. Normally, I'd already have a lupa picked out. The pack is divided, Anita. I've given my protection to my followers so that if Marcus tries to hurt them, I come after him, or my followers will act to protect each other with my blessing. Without a Fenrir or a pack leader to back you up, it's a sort of mutiny to go against the pack leader's orders.'

'What's the penalty for mutiny?'

'Death or mutilation.'

'I thought you guys could heal anything short of a death wound.'

'Not if you shove burning metal into it. Fire purifies and stops the healing process, unless you reopen the wound.'

'It works that way with vampires, too,' I said.

'I didn't know that,' he said, but not like he really cared.

'How have you risen to next in line to lead and not killed anyone? You had to fight a lot of duels to get to the top of the heap.'

'Only the fight for Ulfric has to be to the death. All I had to do was beat them all.'

'Which is why you take karate and lift weights, so you'll be good enough to beat them.' We'd had this discussion before when I asked if lifting weights when you could bench press a small car was redundant. He'd replied, not if everyone you're fighting can lift a car, too. He had a point.

'Yes.'

'But if you won't kill, then your threat doesn't have much bite, no pun intended.'

'We're not animals, Anita. Just because this is the way it's always been in the pack doesn't mean things can't change. We are still people, and that means we can control ourselves. Dammit, there has to be a better way than slaughtering each other.'

I shook my head. 'Don't blame it on the animals. Real wolves don't kill each other for dominance.'

'Only werewolves,' he said. He sounded tired.

'I admire your goals, Richard.'

'But you don't agree.'

'No, I don't agree.'

His voice came from the darkness out of the backseat. 'Stephen doesn't have any wounds. Why was he screaming?'

My shoulders hunched, and I made myself sit up straight. I turned onto Old Highway 21, and tried to think of a delicate way to tell him, but there was nothing delicate about rape. I told him what I'd seen.

The silence from the backseat lasted a very long time. I was almost to the turnoff for his house when he said, 'And you think if I'd killed a few people along the way, this wouldn't have happened?'

'I think they're more afraid of Raina and Marcus than they are of you, so yeah.'

'If you back my threat with killing, it undermines everything I've tried to do.'

'I love you, Richard, and I admire what you're trying to do. I don't want to undermine you, but if they touch Stephen again, I'll do what I said I'd do. I'll kill them.'

'They're my people, Anita. I don't want them dead.'

'They're not your people, Richard. They're just a bunch of strangers that happen to share your disease. Stephen is your people. Every shapeshifter who threw their support to you and risked Marcus's anger, they're your people. They've risked everything for you, Richard.'

'When Stephen joined the pack, I was the one who told Raina she couldn't have him. I've always stood by him.'

'Your intentions are good, Richard, but they didn't keep him safe tonight.'

'If I let you kill for me, Anita, it's the same as doing it myself.'

'I didn't ask your permission, Richard.'

He leaned on the back of the seat, and I realized he wasn't wearing his seat belt. I started to tell him to put it on, but didn't. It was his car, and he could survive a trip through the windshield. 'You mean if they take Stephen again, you'll kill them because you said you'd kill them, not for me.'

'A threat's not worth anything if you aren't willing to back it up,' I said.

'You'd kill for Stephen. Why? Because he saved your life?'

I shook my head. It was hard to explain. 'Not just that. When I saw him tonight, what they were doing to him . . . He was crying, Richard. He was . . . Oh, hell, Richard, he's mine now. There are a handful of people that I'd kill for, kill to keep safe, kill to revenge. Stephen's name got added to the list tonight.'

'Is my name on the list?' he asked. He rested his chin on my shoulder over the seat. He rubbed his cheek on my face and I could feel a faint beard stubble, scratchy and real.

'You know it is.'

'I don't understand how you can talk about killing so casually.'

'I know.'

'My bid for Ulfric would be stronger if I were willing to kill, but I'm not sure it would be worth it.'

'If you want to martyr yourself for high ideals, fine. I don't like it, but fine. But don't martyr the people who trust you. They're worth more than any set of ideals. You nearly got yourself killed tonight.'

'You don't just believe in something when it's easy, Anita. Killing is wrong.'

'Fine,' I said, 'but you also nearly got *me* killed tonight. Do you understand that? If they had rushed us, I wouldn't have made it out. I will not go down in flames because you want to play Gandhi.'

'You can stay home next time.'

'Dammit, that isn't what I'm saying, and you know it. You're trying to live in some Ozzie and Harriet world, Richard. Maybe life used to work like that, but it doesn't anymore. If you don't give up on this, you're going to get killed.'

'If I really thought I had to become a murderer to survive, I think I'd rather not survive.'

I glanced at him. His expression was peaceful, like a saint. But you only got to be a saint if you died. I looked back at the road. I could give Richard up, but if I left him, he was going to end up dead. He'd have gone in there tonight without anyone, and he wouldn't have made it out.

Tears burned at the back of my eyes. 'I don't know if I'd survive it if you died on me, Richard. Doesn't that mean anything to you?'

He kissed my cheek, and something warm and liquid seeped down my neck. 'I love you, too.'

They were only words. He was going to get killed on me. He was going to do everything short of suicide. 'You're bleeding on me,' I said.

He sighed and leaned back into the darkness. 'I'm bleeding a lot. Too bad Jean-Claude isn't here to lick it up.' He made a bitter sound low in his throat.

'Do you need a doctor?'

'Get me home, Anita. If I need a doctor, I know a wererat that makes house calls.' He sounded tired, weary, as if he didn't want to talk anymore. Not about the wounds, or the pack, or his high ideals. I let the silence grow and didn't know how to break it. A soft sound filled the quiet dark, and I realized that Richard was crying. He whispered, 'I'm sorry, Stephen. I am so sorry.'

I didn't say anything because I didn't have anything good to say. Just lately I had noticed that I could kill people and not blink. No attack of conscience, no nightmares, nothing. It was like some part of me had turned off. It didn't bother me that I was able to kill so easily. It did bother me that it didn't bother me. But it had its uses, like tonight. I think every last furry one of them had believed I'd do it. Sometimes, it was good to be scary.

9

It was 4:40 in the morning when Richard carried the still uncon-
scious Stephen into his bedroom. Blood had dried the back of
Richard's shirt to his skin. 'Go to bed, Anita. I'll take care of
Stephen.'

'I need to look at your wounds,' I said.

'I'm all right.'

'Richard . . .'

He looked at me, half of his face covered in dried blood, his eyes
almost wild. 'No, Anita, I don't want your help. I don't need it.'

I took in a deep breath through my nose and let it out. 'Okay,
have it your way.'

I expected him to apologize for snapping at me, but he didn't.
He just walked into the other room and closed the door. I stood
there in the living room for a minute, not sure what to do. I'd hurt
his feelings, maybe even offended his sense of male honor. Fuck
it. If he couldn't take the truth, fuck him. People's lives were at
stake. I couldn't give Richard comforting lies when it could get
people killed.

I went into the guest room, locked the door, and went to bed.
I put on an oversized T-shirt with a caricature of Arthur Conan
Doyle on it. I'd packed something a little sexier. Yes, I admit it. I
could have saved myself the trouble. The Firestar was lumpy under
the pillow. The machine gun went under the bed within reach. I
laid an extra clip beside it. Never thought I'd need that much firepower, but between assassination attempts and packs of werewolves,
I was beginning to feel a little insecure.

When I shoved the silver knives half under the mattress so I could get to them if I had to, I realized just *how* insecure I was feeling. But I left the knives out. Better insecure and paranoid than dead.

I got my stuffed toy penguin, Sigmund, out of the suitcase and cuddled under the covers. I'd had some vague idea that spending the night at Richard's house might be romantic. Shows how much I knew. We'd had three fights in one night, a record even for me. It probably wasn't a good sign for the longevity of the relationship. That last thought made my chest tight, but what was I supposed to do? Go into the other room and apologize? Tell him he was right when he wasn't? Tell him it was okay to get himself killed and take the rest of us down with him? It wasn't okay. It wasn't even close to okay. I hugged Sigmund until he was nearly squeezed in two. I refused to cry. Question: Why was I more worried about losing Richard than about the assassins? Answer: Killing didn't bother me; losing Richard did. I fell asleep holding my penguin and wondering if Richard and I were still dating. Who would keep him alive if I wasn't around?

Something woke me. I blinked up into the dark and reached under my pillow for the Firestar. When it was secure in my hand, I listened. A knock, someone was knocking at the locked bedroom door. Soft, hesitant. Was it Richard come to apologize? That would be too convenient.

I threw back the covers, spilling Sigmund to the floor. I put him back in the suitcase, lowering the lid without closing it, and padded barefoot to the door. I stood to one side of it, and said, 'Who is it?'

'It's Stephen.'

I let out a breath I hadn't known I was holding. I crossed to the other side of the door, gun still ready, and unlocked the door. I opened it slowly, looking, listening, trying to make sure it was just Stephen.

He stood outside the door wearing a pair of Richard's cutoff sweat pants. The shorts hung nearly to his ankles. A borrowed T-shirt covered his knees. His long yellow hair was tousled, like he'd been asleep.

'What's wrong?' I lowered the gun to my side, and he watched me do it.

'Richard went out, and I'm afraid to be alone.' His eyes wouldn't quite meet mine when he said the last, flinching like he was afraid of what he'd see on my face.

'What do you mean he went out? Where to?'

'The woods. He said he'd keep watch for assassins. Does he mean Raina?' He did look up then, amazing blue eyes wide, the beginnings of panic sliding across his face.

I touched his arm, not sure it was the right thing to do. Some people don't want to be touched after a sexual molestation. It seemed to comfort Stephen. But he glanced behind him at the empty living room, rubbing his hands along his bare arms.

'Richard told me to stay in the house. He said I needed to rest.' He wouldn't meet my eyes again. 'I'm afraid to be alone, Anita. I . . . ' He hung his head, long yellow hair spilling like a curtain to hide his face. 'I can't get to sleep. I keep hearing noises.'

I put a finger under his chin and lifted his face gently. 'Are you asking to sleep in here with me?'

His eyes stared at me, wide and pain-filled. 'Richard said I could.'

'Run that by me again,' I said.

'I told him I couldn't stand to be alone. He said, Anita's here, she'll protect you. Go sleep with her.' He looked at me, his face awkward. Something must have shown on my face. 'You're mad now. I don't blame you. I'm sorry . . . I'll . . . ' He started to turn away, and I caught his arm.

'It's okay, Stephen. I'm not mad at you. Richard and I had a . . . disagreement, that's all.' I didn't want him to sleep in here with me. The bed was too small for two people, and if I was going to share it with anyone, I'd have preferred Richard, but that wasn't going to happen. Maybe not ever at the rate we were going.

'You can stay in here.' I didn't add, keep your hands to yourself. His face was raw with a need that had nothing to do with sex. He needed to be held, to be told the monster under the bed wasn't really there. I couldn't help him on the last. The monsters were real. But the first, I might manage that. Cold-blooded killer that I am, maybe I could share my toy penguin with him.

'Could you get an extra pillow from Richard's room?' I asked.

He nodded and fetched it. He clutched it to his chest like he'd have rather slept with it than on it. Maybe the penguin wasn't such a bad idea.

I locked the door behind us. I could have moved into Richard's room. It was a bigger bed, but it also had a picture window with a deck and bird feeders. The guest room only had one small window. Easier to defend. Unless I wanted to go out a window, they were both traps, so we stayed in the more secure room. Besides, I'd have had to move all the weapons and it would have been dawn before I finished.

I pulled the covers back and said, 'You first.' If something came through the door, I wanted to be the first to greet it, but I didn't say that out loud. Stephen was jumpy enough.

He climbed into bed with his pillow, pressing it against the wall, because there really wasn't room for two full-sized pillows. He lay on his back, staring up at me, his curling yellow hair falling around his face and bare shoulders like Sleeping Beauty. You didn't see many men with hair longer than mine. He was one of those men who was pretty rather than handsome, lovely as a doll. Staring up at me with his blue eyes, he looked about twelve. The look on his face was what did it, like he was expecting me to kick him, and he'd let me because he couldn't stop me. I understood in that moment what Raina had meant about him being anyone's meat. There was nothing dominant about Stephen, and it made me wonder about his background. Abused children will sometimes have that raw look to their eyes. And they'll take abuse, because it's normal.

'What's wrong?' Stephen said.

I'd been staring. 'Nothing, just thinking.' Tonight was not the night to ask if his father had beat him. I thought about throwing on a pair of jeans, but it would have been uncomfortable, not to mention hot. It was late spring, the heat hadn't set in. It was only seventy degrees, but it wasn't cool enough to wear jeans, especially if you had someone else in bed with you. Besides, I wasn't sure how Stephen would take me getting dressed to lie down beside him. Maybe he'd be insulted. It was too complicated for me. I turned off the light and climbed into bed beside him. If either of us had been much bigger, we'd have never fit. Stephen had to roll onto his side as it was.

He curled against my back, spooning his body against mine, one arm flung across my waist, like I was the stuffed toy. I stiffened, but Stephen didn't seem to notice. He buried his face into my back, and let his breath out in a sigh. I lay there in the dark and couldn't sleep. Two months ago after I'd nearly ended up a vampire, I'd had trouble sleeping. Close brushes with death, I could handle. Close brushes with becoming the undead, that scared me. But I got over it. I was sleeping just fine, thank you very much, until now. I pushed the button on my watch that made it glow. It was only 5:30. I'd had about an hour's sleep. Great.

Stephen's breathing deepened, and his body relaxed against me a muscle at a time. He whimpered softly in his sleep, arm convulsing around me, then the dream passed and he lay still and warm.

I drifted off to sleep, cuddling Stephen's arm around my body, He was almost as good as a stuffed toy, though he did have a tendency to move at the odd moment.

Daylight spilled through the thin white drapes, and at first I thought the light had awakened me. I woke stiff, in the same position that I'd fallen asleep in, as if I hadn't moved at all during the night. Stephen was still curled around me, a leg over my legs along with one arm like he was trying to get as close to me as he could, even in his sleep.

I lay there for a moment with his body wrapped around me and realized I'd never awakened with a man before. I'd had a fiancé in college and I'd had sex with him, but I'd never spent the night. I'd never actually slept in the same bed with a man. It was kind of odd. I lay in the circle of warmth of Stephen's body and wished it was Richard.

I had a vague feeling that something had awakened me, but what? I eased out from the covers and Stephen's clinging body. He rolled over on his other side, sighing, making small protesting noises. I tucked the covers around him and took the Firestar out from under my pillow.

According to my watch, it was nearly 10:30. I'd had about five hours of sleep. I slipped on a pair of jeans, got my toothbrush and some clean undies and socks out of the suitcase. I folded everything in a clean polo shirt and unlocked the door. I kept the Firestar in my hand. I'd put it on the top of the toilet while I cleaned up. I'd have done the same thing at home.

Someone passed in front of the door, talking. Two voices, one of them female. I laid the clothes on the floor, unclicked the safety on the gun, and put my left hand on the doorknob.

'Was that the safety on a gun I heard?' a man's voice said from the other side of the door. I recognized the voice.

I clicked the safety back in place, put the gun down the front of my pants, and slipped the T-shirt over it. Armed, but not visibly, I opened the door. Jason stood there, grinning at me. He was about my height. His blond hair was straight and baby fine, and cut just above his shoulders. His eyes were the innocent blue of spring skies, but the look in them wasn't innocent. He peered around me at Stephen still curled up in the bed.

'Is it my turn next?' he asked.

I sighed, picked up my clothes, tucked them under my arm, and closed the door behind me. 'What are you doing here, Jason?'

'You don't sound happy to see me.' He was wearing a fishnet T-shirt. His jeans were faded and soft with one knee completely out. He was twenty and had been a college student before he'd joined the pack. Now he was Jean-Claude's wolf, and playing body-guard and breakfast entrée to the Master Vampire of the City seemed to be his only job.

'Isn't it a little early in the morning for fishnet?'

'Wait until you see what I'm wearing to tonight's gala opening of Jean-Claude's dance club.'

'I may not be able to make it,' I said.

He raised his eyebrows. 'You spend one night under Richard's roof, and you break a date with Jean-Claude.' He shook his head. 'I don't think that's a good idea.'

'Look, neither of them own me, okay?'

Jason backed up, hands held up in mock surrender. 'Hey, don't shoot the messenger. You know it will piss Jean-Claude off, and you know he'll think you slept with Richard.'

'I didn't.'

He glanced at the closed door. 'I know that, and I am shocked, Anita, at your choice of bed partners.'

'When you tell Jean-Claude that I slept with Stephen, you make absolutely sure he knows we just shared the bed and nothing else. If Jean-Claude gives Stephen a hard time because of your word games, I'll be angry. You don't want me angry, Jason.'

He looked at me for a heartbeat or two. Something slid behind his eyes, his beast stirring to life, just a touch. Jason had a small streak of what Gabriel had a big streak of. A fascination with danger, pain, and simply being an all round pain in the ass. Jason was tolerable, not a bad guy, all in all; Gabriel was perverted; but it was still the same personality flaw done small. After what I'd seen last night, I wondered what Jason would have thought of the entertainment. I was almost sure he'd have disapproved, but not a hundred percent sure, which told you something about Jason.

'Did you really draw a machine gun on Raina and Gabriel last night?'

'Yeah, I did.'

A woman stepped out of Richard's bedroom with an armful of towels. She was about five foot six, with short brown hair so curly it had to be natural. She wore navy slacks and a short-sleeved sweater. Open-toed sandals completed the outfit. She looked me up and down, sort of disapproving or maybe disappointed. 'You must be Anita Blake.'

'And you are?'

'Sylvie Barker.' She offered a hand and I took it. The moment I touched her skin, I knew what she was. 'Are you with the pack?' I asked.

She took her hand back and blinked at me. 'How could you tell?'

'If you're trying to pass for human, don't touch someone who knows what they're looking for. Your power prickles down my skin.'

'I won't waste time trying to pass then.' Her power flooded over me, pouring like a blast of heat when you open an oven door.

'Impressive,' I said, glad my voice was steady.

She gave a small smile. 'That's quite a compliment, coming from you. Now, I've got to get these towels to the kitchen.'

'What's happening?' I asked.

Sylvie and Jason exchanged glances. She shook her head. 'You knew Richard was hurt?' She made it a question.

My stomach clenched tight. 'He said he'd be all right.'

'He will be,' she said.

I felt my skin go pale. 'Where is he?'

'Kitchen,' Jason said.

I didn't run, it wasn't that far, but I wanted to. Richard sat at the kitchen table, shirtless, his back to me. His back was a mass of fresh claw marks. There was a bite mark in his left shoulder where a piece of flesh was missing.

Dr Lillian was blotting blood off his back with a kitchen towel. She was a small woman in her mid-fifties with salt-and-pepper hair cut in a short, no-nonsense style. She'd treated my own wounds twice before, once when she was furry and looked like a giant man-rat.

'If you had called for medical attention last night, I wouldn't be having to do this, Richard. I do not enjoy causing my patients pain.'

'Marcus was on call last night,' Richard said. 'Under the circumstances, I thought it best to go without.'

'You could have let someone clean and bandage the wounds.'

'Yes, Richard, you could have let me help you,' I said.

He glanced back over his shoulder, his hair spilling around his face. There was a bandage on his forehead. 'I'd had enough help for one night.'

'Why? Because I'm a woman, or because you know I'm right?'

Lillian took a small silver knife to the lower half of a claw mark. She sliced the blade down the wound, reopening it. Richard took in a deep breath and let it out.

'What are you doing?' I asked.

'Lycanthropes heal, but sometimes without medical attention, we can scar. Most of the wounds will heal, but a few of them are deep enough that he really needs some stitching before the skin starts to close, so I'm having to reopen some of the wounds and add a few stitches.'

Sylvie handed Dr Lillian the towels.

'Thank you, Sylvie.'

'What are you two lovebirds fighting about?' Sylvie asked.

'Let Richard tell you, if he wants to.'

'Anita agrees with you,' Richard said. 'She thinks I should start killing people.'

I walked over to where he could see me without straining. I leaned against the cabinet island and tried to watch his face rather than Lillian's slicing knife. 'I don't want you to start killing people indiscriminately, Richard. Just back your threat up. Kill one person and the rest will back down.'

He glared up at me, outraged. 'You mean make an example of one of them?'

Put that way, it sounded sort of cold-blooded, but truth was truth. 'Yeah, that's what I mean.'

'Oh, I like her,' Sylvie said.

'I knew you would,' Jason said. They exchanged a glance that I didn't quite get, but it seemed to amuse the hell out of them.

'Am I missing a joke here?'

They both shook their heads.

I let it go. Richard and I were still fighting, and I was beginning to think this fight had no end. He winced as the doctor sliced open another wound. She was only adding a stitch here and there, but it was still more than I'd have wanted in my flesh. I didn't like stitches.

'No painkillers?' I asked.

'Anesthesia doesn't work well on us. We metabolize it too quickly,' Lillian said. She wiped the silver knife on one of the clean towels and said, 'One of the claw marks drops below your jeans. Take them off so I can see.'

I glanced at Sylvie. She smiled at me. 'Don't mind me. I like girls.'

'That's what you two were laughing about,' I said to Jason. He nodded, smiling happily.

I shook my head.

'The others will be here soon for the meeting. I don't want my ass hanging out as everyone comes in the door.' Richard stood up.

'Let's finish up in the bedroom.' There were a ring of puncture wounds just below his collarbone. I remembered the man-wolf lifting with its claws last night.

'You could have been killed,' I said.

He glanced at me. 'But I wasn't. Isn't that what you always say?'

I hated having my own words fed back to me. 'You could have killed Sebastian or Jamil and the rest wouldn't have jumped you.'

'You've already decided who I should kill.' His voice was thick with anger.

'Yeah,' I said.

'She's actually making pretty good choices,' Sylvie said.

Richard turned his dark, dark eyes to her. 'You stay out of this.'

'If it was just a lovers' quarrel, Richard, I would,' she said. She went to stand in front of him. 'But Anita's not saying anything that I haven't said. That most of us haven't begged you to do. For a few months, I was willing to try it your way. I hoped you were right, but it isn't working, Richard. Either you're alpha male or you're not.'

'Is that a challenge?' he asked. His voice had grown very quiet. Power flowed through the room like a warm wind.

Sylvie backed up a step. 'You know it's not.'

'Do I?' he said. The power in the room built, growing like a flash of electricity. The hairs on my arms stood to attention.

Sylvie stopped backing up, hands in fists at her sides. 'If I thought I could defeat Marcus, I'd do it. If I could protect us all, I would. But I can't do it, Richard. You're our only chance.'

Richard loomed over her. It wasn't just physical size. His power flowed over her, filled the room, until it was almost chokingly close.

'I won't kill just because you think I should, Sylvie. No one is going to force me into it. No one.'

He turned his gaze on me, and it took a lot to meet his eyes. There was a force to them, a burning weight. It wasn't a vampire's drowning power, but it was something. My skin shivered with his power, his energy, and I didn't turn away. I stared at the wounds just below his neck and knew I'd come close to losing him. That was unacceptable.

I walked closer until I could have reached out and touched him. His otherworldly energy whirled over me until it was hard to draw a good breath. 'We need to talk, Richard.'

'I don't have time for this right now, Anita.'

'Make time,' I said.

He glared down at me. 'Talk to me while Lillian finishes up. I've got people coming over for a meeting in about fifteen minutes.'

'What meeting?' I asked.

'To discuss the Marcus situation,' Sylvie said. 'He scheduled the meeting before last night's adventure.'

Richard stared at her, and it wasn't a friendly look. 'If I'd wanted her to know about the meeting, I'd have told her.'

'What else haven't you told me Richard?'

He turned those angry eyes to me. 'What haven't you told me?'

I blinked at him, genuinely puzzled. 'I don't know what you're talking about.'

'A shotgun fires over your head twice and you don't know what I'm talking about.'

Oh that. 'I did the right thing, Richard.'

'You're always right, aren't you?'

I looked at the floor and shook my head. When I looked back at him, he was still angry, but I was losing my anger. A first. This was going to be *the* fight. The one that ended it. I wasn't wrong. No amount of talking would change that. But if we were going to break up, we'd go down in flames. 'Let's finish this, Richard. You wanted to go into the bedroom.'

He stood up, body stiff with an anger that was deeper than I could comprehend. It was controlled rage, and I didn't understand where it was coming from. It was a bad sign. 'You sure you can stand to see me naked?' His voice was utterly bitter, and I didn't know why.

'What's wrong, Richard? What did I do?'

He shook his head too vigorously, making him wince as his shoulder caught the movement. 'Nothing, nothing.' He walked out of the room. Lillian looked at me, but followed him. I sighed and joined them. I wasn't looking forward to the next few minutes, but I wasn't going to chicken out. We'd say all the ugly things and make it as nasty as possible. Trouble was, I didn't have any nasty things to say. It made the fight a lot less fun for me.

Jason whispered as I walked by, very softly, 'Go, Anita, go, Anita.'

It made me smile.

Sylvie watched me with cool eyes. 'Good luck.' It didn't sound completely sincere.

'Do you have a problem?' I'd have much rather fought with her than Richard.

'If he wasn't dating you, then he might choose a mate. It would help things.'

'You want the job?' I asked.

'Yes,' she said, 'I do, but sex is integral and I'm not up for it.'

'Then I'm not standing in your way,' I said.

'Not in mine, no,' she said.

Which implied there were others, but I didn't give a shit, not today. I said, 'It is too damn early in the morning for furball politics. If someone wants a piece of me, tell them to go to the back of the line.'

She cocked her head to one side, like a curious dog. 'Is it a long line?'

'Lately, yeah.'

'I thought all your enemies were dead,' Jason said.

'I keep making new ones,' I said.

He smiled. 'Fancy that.'

I shook my head and walked towards the bedroom. I'd have rather faced Raina again than Richard. I almost hoped the assassin would jump out of the woodwork and give me something to shoot at. It would hurt less than breaking up with Richard.

Richard's bedroom was painted pale green, a vibrant rug thrown in front of the bed like a piece of stained glass. The bed was a heavy four-poster, and even hurt, he'd made the bed, pulling the solid red spread up over it. He had three solid spreads that he rotated on the bed; green, blue, and red. Each color picked up a different color in the rug and the painting over the bed. The painting was of wolves in a winter scene. The wolves were looking directly out of the picture as if you'd just come around a tree and surprised them. There was a deer bleeding on the snow, its throat torn out. It was an odd choice for a bedroom, but it fit somehow. Besides, I liked it. It had that quality that all fine paintings do, as if when you leave the room the painting will move, life suspended and captured on canvas. The green spread emphasized the evergreens, the blue spread caught the washed blue of the sky and the bluish shadows, the red caught the stain of blood on the snow.

Richard lay on his stomach across the crimson cloth. He was totally nude, his jeans thrown on the corner of the bed. His tanned skin looked dark and smooth and incredibly touchable against the red cloth. I felt heat rise up my face as my eyes followed the curve of his body, over the smooth expanse of his buttocks. Lillian had just finished sewing up a curve of claw that had spilled down from his buttocks. I looked away.

I'd seen Richard nude once when I first met him, but never since. We hadn't even been thinking about dating then. I had to look away, mainly because I wanted to look. I wanted to see him like that, and it was too embarrassing for words. I studied the contents of the built-in shelves on his bedroom wall like I'd memorize them. Bits of quartz, a small bird's nest. There was a lump of fossilized coral as big as my hand, a dark rich gold in color with streaks of white quartz. I'd found it on a camping trip and given it to him because he collected bits and pieces, and I didn't. I touched the bit of coral, and didn't want to turn around.

'You said you wanted to talk, then talk,' Richard said.

I glanced back. Lillian snipped the black thread she was using to close his skin. 'There,' she said. 'You shouldn't even have a scar.'

Richard folded his arms on the bed, resting his chin on his forearms. His hair spread around his face, foaming and touchable. I knew it was as soft as it looked.

Lillian glanced from one to the other of us. 'I believe I'll leave you two alone.' She began putting things into her bag, which was brown leather and looked more like a fishing tackle box than anything else. She looked at Richard and back to me. 'Take a piece of advice from an old lady. Don't screw up.'

She left with Richard and me both staring after her.

'You can get dressed now,' I said.

He glanced at his crumpled jeans, moving only his dark eyes. His eyes came back to me, and they were as angry as I'd ever seen them. 'Why?'

I concentrated on meeting those angry eyes and tried not to stare at his body. It was harder than I would have admitted out loud. 'Because it's hard to fight with you when you're naked.'

He raised up on his elbows, hair falling down into his eyes, until he stared at me through a curtain of brown gold hair. It reminded me of Gabriel, and that was unnerving as hell.

'I know you want me, Anita. I can smell it.'

Oh, that made me feel better. I blushed for the second time in five minutes. 'So, you're gorgeous. So what? What the hell does that have to do with anything?'

He raised up on all fours, knees, and hands. I looked away so fast it made me dizzy. 'Please put on your jeans.'

I heard him slide off the bed. 'You can't even look at me, can you?'

There was something about the way he said it that made me want to see his face, but I couldn't turn around. I just couldn't. If this was the last fight we ever had, I didn't want the memory of his body imprinted on my mind. It would be too cruel.

I felt him standing behind me. 'What do you want from me, Richard?'

'Look at me.'

I shook my head.

He touched my shoulder, and I jerked away.

'You can't even stand for me to touch you, can you?' For the first time, I heard pain in his voice, raw and hurting.

I turned then. I had to see his face. His eyes glittered with unshed tears, eyes wide so they wouldn't fall. He'd pushed his hair back from his face, but it was already spilling forward. My eyes traveled down his muscular chest, and I wanted to run my hands over his nipples, down his slender waist, and lower. I drew my eyes back up to his face with force of will alone, my face pale now, rather than blushing. I was having trouble breathing. My heart was beating so hard, it was hard to hear.

'I love it when you touch me,' I said.

He stared down at me, his eyes filled with pain. I think I preferred the anger. 'I used to admire you for saying no to Jean-Claude. I know you want him, and you keep refusing. I thought it was very moral of you.' He shook his head, one tear slid from the corner of his eye, trailing in slow motion down his cheek.

I brushed the tear from his face with my fingertip. He caught my hand in his, holding it a little too hard, but not hurting, only surprising. It was also my right hand, and drawing the gun left-handed was going to be a bitch. Not that I really thought I'd need the gun, but he was acting so strangely.

Richard spoke, staring down at me. 'But Jean-Claude's a monster and you don't sleep with monsters. You just kill them.' Tears slid from both of his eyes and I let them fall. 'You don't sleep with me, either, because I'm a monster, too. But you can kill us, can't you, Anita? You just can't fuck us.'

I jerked away from him, and he let me. He could have bench pressed the heavy cherry wood bed, so he let me go. I didn't like that much. 'That was an ugly thing to say.'

'But it's true,' he said.

'I want you, Richard, you know that.'

'You want Jean-Claude, too, so that's not very flattering. You tell me to kill Marcus, like it would be easy. Do you think it wouldn't bother me to kill him because he's a monster, or because I am?'

'Richard,' I said. This was an argument I hadn't seen coming. I didn't know what to say, but I had to say something. He was standing there with tears drying on his face. Even nude and gorgeous, he looked lost.

'I know it would bother you to kill Marcus. I never said it wouldn't,' I said.

'Then how can you urge me to do it?'

'I think it's necessary,' I said.

'Could you do it? Could you just kill him?'

I thought about that for a moment, then nodded. 'Yeah, I could.'

'And that wouldn't bother you?' he asked.

I stared straight at him, looked him right in his pain-filled eyes, and said, 'No.'

'If you really mean that, it makes you a bigger monster than I am.'

'Yeah, I guess it does.'

He shook his head. 'It doesn't bother you, does it, knowing that you could take a human life?' He laughed, and it was bitter. 'Or don't you consider Marcus human?'

'The man I killed last night was human,' I said.

Richard stared at me, fresh horror growing in his eyes. 'And you slept jut fine didn't you?'

I nodded. 'Pretty good, considering you sent Stephen to my bed.'

A strange look passed through his eyes, and for a split second, I saw him wonder.

'Sweet Jesus, you know me better than that.'

He looked down. 'I know. It's just that I want you so badly, and you keep saying, no. It makes me doubt everything.'

'Shit. I am not going to stroke your ego in the middle of a fight. You sent Stephen to me because you were mad. Said I could protect him. Had it occurred to you that I'd never slept – just slept – in the same bed with a man before?'

'What about your fiancé in college?'

'I had sex with him, but I didn't sleep over,' I said. 'The first time I woke up in the morning with a man curled around me, I wanted it to be you.'

'I'm sorry, Anita. I didn't know. I . . .'

'You didn't think. Great. Now, what's with the no clothes? What's going on, Richard?'

'You saw the fight last night. You saw what I did, what I can do.'

'Some of it, yeah.'

He shook his head. 'You want to know why I don't kill? Why I always stop just short of it?' The look in his eyes was almost desperate, wild.

'Tell me,' I said, softly.

'I enjoy it, Anita. I love the feel of my hands, my claws ripping into flesh.' He hugged himself. 'The taste of fresh, warm blood in my mouth is exciting.' He shook his head harder, as if he could erase the sensation. 'I wanted to rip Sebastian apart last night. I could feel it, like an ache in my shoulders, in my arms. My body wanted to kill him, the way I want you.' He stared at me, still hugging himself, but his body was speaking for him. The thought of killing Sebastian did excite him, really excite him.

I swallowed hard. 'You're afraid that if you let go and killed, that you'd like that, too?'

He stared at me, and that was the horror in his eyes: the fear that he was a monster, the fear that I was right not to touch him, not to let him touch me. You don't fuck the monsters, you just kill them.

'Do you enjoy killing?' he asked.

I had to think about that for a second or two. Finally, I shook my head. 'No, I don't enjoy it.'

'What does it feel like?' he asked.

'Like nothing. I don't feel anything.'

'You have to feel something.'

I shrugged. 'Relief that it wasn't me. Triumph that I was faster, meaner.' I shrugged again. 'It doesn't bother me to kill people, Richard. It just doesn't.'

'Did it once?'

'Yes, it used to bother me.'

'When did it stop bothering you?'

'I don't know. Not the first death, or the second, but when it gets to the point that you can't keep track of them all . . . It either stops bothering you or you find another line of work.'

'I want it to bother me, Anita. Killing should mean something other than blood, and excitement, or even survival. If it doesn't, then I'm wrong, and we are just animals.' His body reacted to the thought, too. And he did not find it exciting. He looked vulnerable and afraid. I wanted to tell him to get dressed, but I didn't.

He'd chosen to be naked very deliberately, as if to prove once and for all that I didn't want him, or that I did.

I didn't much like tests, but it was hard to bitch with the fear in his eyes. He'd walked away to stand in front of the bed. He rubbed one hand up and down the opposite arm as if he were cold. It was May in Saint Louis. He wasn't cold, at least not that kind of cold.

'You aren't animals, Richard.'

'How do you know what I am?' And I knew that he was asking the question more of himself than of me.

I walked over to him. I took the Firestar out of the front of my pants and laid it on the night stand beside his cut glass lamp. He watched me do it, eyes wary. Almost like he expected me to hurt him. I was going to try very hard not to do that.

I touched his arm, gently, where he was rubbing it. He froze under my touch. 'You are one of the most moral people I have ever met. You can kill Marcus and not become a ravening beast. I know that, because I know you.'

'Gabriel and Raina kill and look what they are.'

'You aren't like them, Richard. Trust me on that.'

'What if I kill Sebastian or Marcus, and I enjoy it.' His handsome face was raw with terror at the thought.

'Maybe it will feel good.' I gripped his arm tighter. 'But if it does, there's no shame in that. You are what you are. You didn't choose it. It chose you.'

'How can you say there's no shame in enjoying killing something. I've hunted deer and I love it. I love the chase, and the kill, and eating the warm meat.' As before, the thought excited him. I kept my eyes on his face as much as possible, but it was distracting.

'Everyone has different things that flip their switch, Richard. I've heard worse. Hell, I've seen worse.'

He stared down at me like he wanted to believe me and was afraid to. 'Worse than this.' He lifted his right hand from its grip on his arm, he held his hand in front of my face. His power prickled over my hand, down my arm, until I gasped. It was force of will alone that kept my hand on his arm.

His fingers elongated, stretching impossibly long and thin. The nails grew into heavy claws. It wasn't a wolf hand, rather his own grown into a claw. Nothing else had changed that I could see. Only that one hand.

I was having trouble breathing, for different reasons than before. I stared at the clawed hand and realized for the first time that he was right. Watching the bones in his hand stretch and pop sickened me, scared me.

I kept my hand on his arm, but I was shaking. I found my voice, and it shook, too. 'I saw Raina do that once. I thought it wasn't a common ability.'

'Only Raina, Marcus, and I can do it within our pack. We can partially change at will.'

'That's how you stabbed Sebastian last night.'

He nodded, eyes searching my face. I was fighting to keep it blank, but what he saw there wasn't reassuring enough. He turned away from me, and I didn't have to see his eyes to feel the pain.

I grabbed his hand and wrapped my fingers around those long, thin bones. I felt muscles under my hands that had never been in Richard's hand before. It took everything I had to hold that hand. To touch him like that. Everything. The effort left me shaking and unable to meet his eyes. I didn't trust what he'd see in them.

He touched my chin with his other hand and turned me slowly to face him. He stared down at me. 'I can taste your fear, and I like it. Do you understand? I like it.'

I had to clear my throat to talk. 'I noticed,' I said.

He had the grace to blush. He bent slowly to kiss me. I didn't try to stop him, but I didn't help, either. I usually rose on tiptoe to meet him halfway. I stood there, too scared to move, forcing his tall body to bend at the shoulders, to fold down towards me. The long, thin-fingered hand that I was holding convulsed around me, the claws playing lightly on my bare forearm.

I tensed, and his power poured over me. I held onto his hand while the muscles and bones slid back into place. I held on with both hands while his hand re-formed under mine. My skin shuddered with the spill of power.

His lips brushed mine, and I kissed him back, almost swaying. I let go of his hand, my fingers brushed his bare chest, playing over his hardened nipples. His hands slid around my waist, fingers kneading upward, over my ribs, along my spine. He whispered into my mouth, 'You're not wearing anything under this T-shirt.'

'I know,' I said.

His hands slid under the shirt, caressing my back, pressing our bodies together. His naked body touched me, and even through my jeans, it made me shudder. I wanted to feel his naked flesh against mine so badly, I could feel it like a hunger in my skin. I slipped the T-shirt off, and he made a sound of surprise.

He stared down at my bare breasts, and he wasn't the only one excited. He ran his hands over my breasts, and when I didn't stop him, he dropped to his knees in front of me. He looked up at me, his brown eyes filled with a dark light.

I kissed him while he knelt in front of me, as if I'd eat him from the mouth down. The feel of him against my naked flesh was almost too much.

He broke from the kiss and ran his mouth over my breasts. It brought a surprised moan from my throat.

There was a knock at the door. We froze. A woman's voice that I didn't recognize said, 'I didn't come all this way to listen to you make out, Richard. I'd like to remind you that all of us have incredibly good hearing.'

'Not to mention sense of smell.' That was Jason.

'Damn,' he said softly, head buried against me.

I leaned my head over him, burying my face in his hair. 'I think I'll just climb out the window.'

He hugged me around the waist and stood, passing his hands over my breasts one last time. 'I can't tell you how long I've wanted to do that.'

He reached for his jeans and underpants still lying on the bed. I touched his arm, bringing his attention back to me.

'I want you, Richard. I love you. I want you to believe that.'

He stared at me, his face grew strange and solemn. 'You haven't seen me change into a wolf yet. You need to see that before we go any further.'

The thought did not excite me, and I was glad I was the girl, so it didn't show. 'You're right, though if you'd played your cards right, we might have had sex first.'

'It wouldn't be fair to you.'

'So you're saying even if we'd been alone you'd have stopped and shapeshifted.'

He nodded.

'Because it wouldn't be fair to sleep with me until I'd seen the whole package?'

'Exactly.'

'You are such a boy scout, Richard.'

'I think I just lost one of my merit badges,' he said. The look on his face brought a rush of heat up my neck.

He grinned and slipped on his pants. He wore briefs. He pulled on his jeans and was careful zipping them up. I watched him get dressed with a proprietary air. An air of anticipation.

I picked the T-shirt up from the floor and pulled it back on. Richard came up behind me, sliding his hands under the shirt, cupping a hand around each breast, kneading them. I leaned back against him. He was the one who stopped, hugging me around the waist, picking me an inch off the floor. He turned me around and gave me a quick kiss. 'When you make up your mind to do something, you really make up your mind, don't you?'

'Always,' I said.

He took in a deep breath through his nose and out through his mouth. 'I'd try to make it a quick meeting, but . . . '

'Edward should be here soon, so it doesn't matter.'

He nodded, his face falling. 'I almost forgot that someone was trying to kill you.' He cupped my face in his hands and kissed me, eyes searching my face. 'Be careful.'

I touched the bandage on his shoulder. 'You, too.'

He pulled a black T-shirt from a drawer and slipped it on. He tucked it into his jeans, and I made myself stay away from him while he fumbled with his zipper. 'Join us after you get dressed.'

I nodded. 'Sure.' He left, closing the door behind him. I sighed and sat down on the edge of the bed. Damn. I didn't want to lose Richard. I really didn't. I wanted to sleep with him. I wasn't sure how I felt about seeing him change into full animal form. The hand thing had bothered me enough. What if I couldn't take it? What if it was too gross? Dear God, I hoped not. I hoped I was a better person than that. A stronger person than that.

Richard was afraid that if he started to kill, he'd just keep killing. It wasn't a completely unreasonable fear. I hugged myself tight. The feel of his body against mine clung to my skin. The feel of his mouth on me . . . I shivered, and it wasn't fear. It was stupid to love Richard. Having sex with him would make it worse. He was going to be dead soon if he didn't kill Marcus. Simple as that. Jean-Claude would never have endangered himself like that. Never. You could always trust Jean-Claude to survive. It was one of his talents. I was almost sure it wasn't one of Richard's. Last night should have proved to me beyond any doubt that I should dump him. Or that he should dump me. You could agree to disagree on politics, or even religion sometimes, but you either killed people or you didn't. Homicide was not something you could be neutral on.

Jean-Claude didn't mind killing people. Once upon a time, I'd thought that made him monstrous. Now I agreed with him. Will the real monster please stand up?

11

I'd finally gotten dressed, red polo shirt, black jeans, black Nikes, the Firestar 9mm in its inner-pants holster. The gun was very visible against the red shirt, but hey, why try to hide it? Besides, I could feel the roil of power just outside the door. Shapeshifters, not all of them happy. Strong emotions make it harder to hide their power. Richard was one of the best at hiding it that I'd ever met. He'd fooled me for awhile, made me think he was human. No one else had ever been able to do that.

I looked at myself in the mirror and realized that it wasn't facing a room full of lycanthropes that bothered me, it was facing a room full of people who knew that Richard and I had been making out. I preferred danger to embarrassment any day. I was used to danger.

The bathroom was just off the living room, so when I opened the door, they were all there, clustered on or around the couch. They glanced at me as I stepped out, and I nodded. 'Hello.'

Rafael said, 'Hello, Anita.' He was the Rat King, the wererats equivalent of pack leader. He was tall, dark, and handsome with strong Mexican features that made his face seem stern. Only his lips hinted that perhaps there were more smiles than frowns in him. He was wearing a short-sleeved dress shirt that left the brand on his arm bare. The brand was in the shape of a crown, and was the mark of kingship. There was no equivalent mark among the wolves. Being a lycanthrope meant different things, depending on the animal; different cultures as well as forms.

'I didn't know the wererats would be interested in the packs' internal squabbles,' I said.

'Marcus is trying to unify all shapeshifters under one leader.'

'Let me guess,' I said, 'he gets to be leader.'

Rafael gave a small smile. 'Yes.'

'So you've thrown in with Richard as the lesser evil?' I made it a question.

'I've thrown in with Richard because he is a man of his word. Marcus has no honor. His bitch Raina has seen to that.'

'I still think if we killed Raina, Marcus might be willing to talk with us.' This from a woman who I thought I'd seen before but couldn't place. She sat on the floor sipping coffee from a mug. She had short blond hair, and was wearing a pink nylon jogging suit, jacket open over a pink T-shirt. It was a jogging suit made for looking at, not working out in, and I remembered her. I'd seen her at the Lunatic Cafe, Raina's restaurant. Her name was Christine. She wasn't a wolf, she was a weretiger. She was here to speak on behalf of the independent shapeshifters. Those who didn't have enough people to have a leader. Not every kind of lycanthropy was equally contagious. You could get cut to pieces by a weretiger and not get it. A werewolf could barely cut you and you got furry. Almost none of the cat-based lycanthropy was as contagious as wolf and rat. No one knew why. It was just the way it worked.

Richard introduced me to about fifteen others, first names only.

I said hi and leaned against the wall by the door. The couch was full, and so was the floor. Besides, I liked being out of reach of any shapeshifter I didn't know. Just a precaution.

'Actually, I've met Christine before,' I said.

'Yes,' Christine said, 'the night you killed Alfred.'

I shrugged. 'Yeah.'

'Why didn't you kill Raina last night when you had the chance?' she said.

Before I could answer, Richard interrupted. 'If we kill Raina,' he said, 'Marcus will hunt us all down.'

'I don't think he's up to the job,' Sylvie said.

Richard shook his head. 'No, I still won't give up on Marcus.'

No one said anything, but the looks on their faces were enough. They agreed with me. Richard was going to get himself killed and hang his followers out to dry.

Louie came out of the kitchen carrying two mugs of coffee. He smiled at me. Louie was Richard's best friend, and he'd gone on a lot of hiking dates with us. He was five foot six, with eyes darker than my own, true black, not just darkest brown. His baby-fine black hair had been cut recently. He'd worn it long for all the time I'd known him, not a fashion statement like Richard; he just never got around to getting it cut. Now it was short enough that his ears showed, and he looked older, more like a professor with a doctorate in biology. He was a wererat, and one of Rafael's lieutenants. He handed me one of the mugs.

'These meetings have been so much more pleasant since Richard bought that coffeemaker. Thanks to you.'

I took a big breath of coffee, and felt better instantly. Coffee might not be a cure-all, but it was close. 'I'm not sure everyone is happy to see me.'

'They're scared. It makes them a little hostile.'

Stephen came out of the guest room dressed in clothes that fit too well to be Richard's. A blue dress shirt, tucked into faded blue jeans. The only man in the room that was close to Richard's size was Jason. Jason never minded sharing his clothes.

'Why does everyone look so grim?' I asked.

Louie leaned against the wall, sipping coffee. 'Jean-Claude withdrew his support of Marcus and threw in with Richard. I can't believe neither of them mentioned that.'

'They said something about having formed a bargain, but they didn't explain.' I thought about what he'd just told me. 'Marcus must be pissed.'

The smile faded from his face. 'That is an understatement.' He looked at me. 'You don't understand, do you?'

'Understand what?' I asked.

'Without Jean-Claude's backing, Marcus doesn't stand a chance of forcing the rest of the shapeshifters under his control. His dreams of empire building are finished.'

'If he doesn't stand a chance, why is everyone so worried?'

Louie gave a sad smile. 'What Marcus can't control, he has a tendency to kill.'

'You mean he'd start a war?'

'Yes.'

'Not just with Richard and the pack, you mean, but an all-out war with all the other shapeshifters in town?'

Louie nodded. 'Except the wereleopards. Gabriel is their leader and he sides with Raina.'

I thought about it for a second or two. 'Sweet Jesus, it would be a bloodbath.'

'And there'd be no way of containing it, Anita. Some of it would spill over onto the normal world. There are still three states in this country that will pay hundreds of dollars in bounty for a dead shapeshifter, no questions asked. A war like this could make the practice look practical.'

'Do you two have something better to do?' Christine asked. I was beginning not to like her. It was she that knocked on the door and interrupted Richard and me. Frankly, for that I was sort of grateful. The thought of everyone hearing us go further would have been too embarrassing for words.

Louie moved back to sit on the floor with the others. I stayed leaning against the wall, sipping my coffee.

'Are you going to join us?' she asked.

'I'm fine where I am,' I said.

'Too good to sit with us?' a man in his late thirties with dark blue eyes asked. He was about five foot eight; it was hard to tell with him sitting on the floor. He was dressed in a suit, complete with tie, as if he was on his way to work. His name was Neal.

'Not good enough,' I said, 'not good enough by half.'

'What the hell's that supposed to mean?' he asked. 'I don't like having a normal here.'

'Leave it alone, Neal,' Richard said.

'Why? She's laughing at us.'

Richard glanced back at me from his corner of the couch. 'Come join us, Anita?'

Sylvie was sitting beside Richard, not too close, but still, there was not enough room for me. Rafael sat on the end of the couch, spine straight, ankle propped on one knee.

'Couch looks full,' I said.

Richard held out his hand to me. 'We'll make room.'

'She isn't even pack,' Sylvie said. 'I won't give up my seat to her. No offense to you, Anita, you don't know any better.' Her voice was matter-of-fact, not hostile, but the look she gave Richard wasn't exactly friendly.

'No offense taken,' I said. I wasn't sure I wanted to sit on the couch surrounded by lycanthropes anyway. Even supposedly friendly ones. Everyone in the room was stronger and faster than I was, just a fact. The only leg up I had was the gun. If I sat right beside them, I'd never get it out in time.

'I want my girlfriend to sit with me, Sylvie, that's all,' Richard said. 'It isn't meant as a challenge to your position in the lukoi.' His voice sounded patient like he was talking to a child.

'What did you say?' Sylvie asked. She looked shocked.

'We are the lukoi. Anita knows that.'

'You shared our words with her?' Neal said, outrage thick in his voice.

I wanted to say that it was just words, but I didn't. Who says I'm not getting smarter?

'There was a time when sharing our secrets with normals could get you a death sentence,' Sylvie said.

'Even Marcus doesn't allow that anymore.'

'How much of our secrets do you know, human?'

I shrugged. 'A few words, that's all.'

Sylvie stared at me. 'You want your human girlfriend to cuddle up next to you, is that it, Richard?'

'Yes,' he said. There was no trace of anger in his voice. Personally, I didn't like the way she'd said 'human.'

Sylvie knelt on the couch, staring at me. 'Come human, sit with us.'

I stared at her. 'Why the change of heart?'

'Not everything has to do with the pack hierarchy. That's what Richard is always telling us. Sit by your lover. I'll scoot over.' She did, curling up on the couch, near Rafael.

The Rat King glanced at me. He raised an eyebrow, almost a shrug. I didn't trust Sylvie, but I trusted Rafael, and I trusted Richard, at least here, today. I realized that I would have trusted Rafael last night. He wouldn't have the moral qualms that Richard had. Poor Richard was like a lone voice crying in the wilderness. God help me, I agreed with the pagans.

Louie and Stephen were curled on the floor, close by. I was among friends. Even Jason, grinning up at me, wouldn't let me get hurt. Jason was Jean-Claude's wolf to call, as was Stephen. I think if they let me get killed, they might not survive much longer than I did.

'Anita?' Richard made it a question.

I sighed and pushed away from the wall. I was among friends, so why were the muscles in my back so tight it hurt to move? Paranoid? Who me?

I walked around the couch, coffee mug in my left hand. Sylvie patted the couch, smiling, but not like she meant it.

I sat beside Richard. His arm slid over my shoulders. My right arm was pressed against his side, not too tightly. He knew how much I hated having my gun hand impeded.

Leaning into the warmth of his body, I relaxed. The tightness in my shoulders eased. I took a sip of coffee. We were all being terribly civilized.

Richard put his lips against my face, and whispered, 'Thank you.'

Those two words earned him a lot of brownie points. He knew what it had cost me to sit down among the wolves, rats, and cats. Not sitting with him would have undermined him in front of the pack and the other leaders. I wasn't here to make the situation worse.

'Who saved you last night, Stephen?' Sylvie asked. Her voice was sweet, face pleasant. I didn't trust her at all.

Every eye turned to Stephen. He tried to huddle into the floor, as if he could go invisible, but it didn't work. He stared at Richard, eyes wide.

'Go ahead, Stephen, tell the truth. I won't be mad.'

Stephen swallowed. 'Anita saved me.'

'Richard was fighting about twenty lycanthropes at the time,' I said. 'He told me to get Stephen, so I did.'

Neal sniffed Stephen, running his nose just above the other man's face and neck, down his shoulder. It wasn't a human gesture, and it was unnerving in the well-dressed man. 'He has her scent on his skin.'

Neal glared at me. 'He's been with her.'

I expected an outcry, but instead, the others crowded around Stephen, sniffing his skin, touching him, and bringing their fingers close to their own faces. Only Sylvie, Jason, Rafael, and Louie stayed sitting. One by one, the rest turned to Richard and me.

'He's right,' Christine said. 'Her scent clings to his skin. You don't get that much scent just by carrying someone.'

Richard's hand tightened on my shoulder. I glanced at his face. It was calm, only a slight tightness around the eyes betrayed tension. 'I was patrolling the woods for assassins,' Richard said. 'Stephen didn't want to be alone. I sent him to Anita.'

'We know about the assassination attempts,' Sylvie said. I widened my eyes. 'You do, do you?'

'Richard wants us to help protect you. If we're going to take a bullet for you, we need to know why.'

I met her eyes. Her pretty face was harsh, the bones in her cheeks standing out.

'I'm not asking anyone to take my bullet,' I said. I scooted out from under Richard's arm, which put me closer to Sylvie, not an improvement.

Richard didn't fight it. He drew his arm back. 'I should have talked to you before I told them.'

'Damn straight,' I said.

Sylvie leaned her arms on the back of the couch, bringing her face inches from mine. 'Are you going to chastise our would-be pack leader, human?'

'You say *human* like it's a bad thing, Sylvie. Jealous?'

She drew back like I'd hit her. A look that was part pain, part rage passed across her face. 'Most of us here survived an attack, human. We did not choose this.' Her voice was chokingly harsh.

I'd expected a lot of things from her, but not the pain of a survivor. I was sorry I'd made the crack. 'I'm sorry. I didn't mean anything personal by it.'

'You have no idea how personal it is.'

'That's enough, Sylvie,' Richard said.

She rose on her knees to meet Richard's face over my head. 'Don't you even have the balls to be angry that she slept with a subordinate male?'

'Wait a minute,' I said. 'Stephen and I did not have sex. We literally slept together, nothing else.'

Neal plunged his face into Stephen's crotch and sniffed. It wasn't a human gesture. Stephen let him do it, and that wasn't very human, either.

Jason leaned in, sniffing my leg.

I put my coffee cup on my knee, in front of his face. 'Don't even think it,' I said.

Jason grinned up at me. 'Can't blame a guy for trying.'

'I can,' Richard said softly.

Jason smiled at him and scooted back.

Neal raised his face and shook his head. 'They didn't have sex.'

'He said she'd protect me,' Stephen said. The silence grew so thick you could have walked on it.

'Is that what you said?' Sylvie asked. She was staring at Richard like he'd done something very bad.

Richard took a deep enough breath that his shoulders shuddered. 'Yes, that's what I said.'

'Stephen,' Sylvie said, 'Did you believe she'd protect you? If Raina had come through the door, would you have trusted Anita to save you?'

Stephen looked at the floor, then up, his eyes darted to Richard, then to me. His eyes finally stopped, staring at me. 'She had me sleep near the wall so she'd be in front in case anything came through the door.'

And I'd thought I'd been subtle.

'What would you have done if Raina *had* come?' Sylvie asked.

Everyone was watching me, except Richard. Their eyes were very intent, and I knew the question meant more than it should have. 'I'd have killed her.'

'Not just shot her or wounded her?' Christine asked.

I shook my head. 'She got her free pass last night. If she comes after Stephen again, I'll kill her.'

'You mean that, don't you?' Sylvie said.

'Every word,' I said.

There was a hum of energy in the room, almost as if they were all sharing some telepathic message. I don't think they were, but something was happening. The energy level in the room was rising, and I didn't like it. I sat the coffee mug on the floor. I wanted both my hands free.

Sylvie grabbed me around the waist and rolled us off the couch. We were on the floor with her riding my back before I could react. I went for the gun, and her hand was there first. She jerked the gun out of its holster and tossed it away. She wasn't fast, she was miraculous, and I was in deeper shit than I could get out of.

The bend of her arm was tucked under my chin like in a strangle hold, positioned just right so she could black me out without killing me. Her legs locked around my waist, as close as she could get and not climb down my shirt.

A half dozen werewolves flowed between her and Richard. He was standing, hands in fists at his side. His power poured through the room, deeper and higher, until it was like being buried alive in some kind of static charge.

'Don't,' I whispered. I wasn't talking to Richard.

I felt something open inside Sylvie, a trembling, vibrating energy flowed from her skin across my body. It was almost hot, like opening the door to an oven. Where her skin touched me, I shivered. It was painful, like small electric shocks.

'What are you doing, Sylvie?' Richard asked. His voice had gone low and growling deep; it didn't sound human. I expected his eyes to be amber, but they were the same solid brown as always. Human eyes, but the look in them was not. The beast stared out of Richard's eyes. I knew in that moment that he was truly dangerous. I also knew that all that impressive power wouldn't save me if Sylvie wanted to rip my head off.

My pulse thudded against her arm like a trapped butterfly. I forced my voice calm. 'What's going on?'

'I'm going to make you his mate.'

'You're not contagious in human form,' I said.

'Really?' she said. The arm around my throat grew warm, pulsing like a beating heart. I felt the muscles slide under her skin.

'Richard.' My voice sounded high and wispy. Fear will do that to you.

Rafael and Louie were on their feet now. The werewolves that had joined Sylvie in this little protest fanned out to cover the rats, too.

I couldn't see Stephen. He was somewhere behind us, crouched on the floor, last I saw.

Jason crouched at Richard's feet, facing the other were-wolves. But at least ten of them just sat there, watching, not taking sides. 'You've been holding out on us,' Jason said.

Sylvie flexed the arm around my neck. I had a glimpse of a long-clawed hand. 'Only Raina is higher in the pack than I am, Jason.'

Richard faced the werewolves. He brought his hands upward, making a soothing gesture like he'd done at the movie set. The prickling energy in the room went down a notch. He was forcing their power back.

'All it takes is a scratch, Richard,' Sylvie said. 'You'll never reach us in time.'

'I forbid this,' Richard growled. 'No one is to be infected against their will. Especially Anita.'

'Why?' Sylvie said. 'Because if she wasn't human, you wouldn't want her? Not taking the pack to your bed is just another way of denying what you are, Richard.'

Something passed over his face behind the anger and the power: uncertainty.

I knew in that moment she was right.

Sylvie whispered in my ear, her breath warm on my face. 'See his face.'

'Yeah,' I said.

'He accuses you of not being able to sleep with him because you think he's a monster, but if I make you one of us, he won't want you. He thinks of all of us as monsters, but not good old Richard. He's better than the rest of us.'

'I will hurt you, Sylvie. I'll bleed you, do you understand,' Richard said.

'But you won't kill me, will you?' she said. Her arm flexed, long claws tickled down my face.

I put my hands on her arm, trying to hold it away from me, and not succeeding. '*I'll* kill you,' I said.

She went very still against my body. 'For changing you into one of us? For losing you Richard's love when he sees you monstrous and furry?'

I spoke very low, very carefully. 'You hate what you are, Sylvie.'

Her arm convulsed tight enough that I couldn't breathe for a second. 'I don't hate what I am. I accept what I am.' Her arm loosened.

I took a shaky breath and tried again. 'I saw the look on your face when I accused you of being jealous. You are jealous of me being human, Sylvie. You know you are.'

She held her other hand up in front of my face, letting me get a good look at the long, thin claws. The hand at my throat combed claws through my hair.

'You know that Raina has forbidden us to make you lukoi. She's afraid if you joined us, you'd be a better bitch than she is.'

'How flattering,' I whispered. I looked at Richard through the backs of the werewolves. His eyes had gone amber and alien. Even now, I knew, he wouldn't kill Sylvie. Even if she bled me, infected me, he wouldn't kill her. It was there in the pain on his face. The confusion replacing the fear.

Maybe Sylvie saw it. Maybe she'd made her point. Whatever, she uncurled herself from my body and stood carefully on the other side of me.

I scuttled away on all fours as fast as I could go. It wasn't pretty, it wasn't slick, but it was effective.

I crawled until I came to the far wall. I stayed sitting against it, as far away from everything in the room as I could get.

The other werewolves had faded away. Sylvie and Richard stood facing each other. Sylvie's eyes had gone a strange liquid grey, wolf eyes.

Richard flung his power outward. It ate along my skin, tore a gasp from my throat.

Sylvie stood in that flood of power and didn't flinch. 'The power is impressive, Richard, but it means nothing as long as Marcus lives.'

He backhanded her, in a blur of motion that was too fast to follow: Sylvie careened into the wall and slid to the floor, stunned.

'I am pack leader,' Richard's voice roared, and he raised clawed hands to the sky. He fell to his knees, and I didn't go to help. I stayed huddled against the wall, wishing I'd packed an extra gun.

Richard crouched on the floor, rocking gently. He curled on his knees into a ball, and I felt him swallow the power back. I felt it drain away. He stayed crouched on the floor, hugging himself for a long time after the power vanished from the room, head down, his hair hiding his face.

Sylvie got to her knees and crawled towards him. She crouched beside him, smoothing his hair back on one side. 'We would follow you anywhere if you would kill for us. She will kill for us. If your mate, your lupa, will kill for us, it might be enough.'

Richard raised his head up with a shudder. 'No one is to be infected against their will, that is my word, and my order.' He raised back on his knees.

Sylvie stayed crouched down, face near the floor, a sign of abasement. 'But you will not kill to enforce it.'

'I will kill to protect Anita,' Rafael said.

Everyone looked at him.

He met their eyes and didn't back down. 'If anyone touches her against her will, I and mine will hunt them down.'

'Rafael,' Richard said, 'don't do this.'

He stared at Richard. 'You bring a human among us, but you do not protect her. Someone has to.'

I wanted to say I could protect myself, but it wasn't true. I was good, but I was just human. It wasn't enough.

'I can't let you do my dirty work for me,' he said.

'I am your friend, Richard,' Rafael said. 'I do not mind.'

Sylvie hugged the ground at Richard's feet. 'Will you let the Rat King kill your pack? Is he our leader now?'

He stared down at her, and something happened to his face, not otherworldly, or wolf, but a hardness, almost a sadness passed over him. I watched it, and I didn't like it. If I'd had my gun, I might have shot Sylvie for making that look pass over his face. 'I will kill anyone who breaks my word. I have spoken, and it is law.'

Sylvie abased herself even lower, and the other wolves came crowding around, crawling on the floor, abasing themselves in front of him. Some of them licked his hands, touched his body. They moved around him until he was nearly hidden from sight.

Richard stood up, walking through them, their hands clinging to his legs. He bent down and picked up the Firestar from the floor and walked over to me. He looked normal enough, all the wolfish changes hidden away. He handed me the gun, butt first. 'Are you all right?'

I cradled the gun in both hands. 'Sure.'

'I value your humanity, Anita. Sylvie's right. How can I ask you to embrace my beast, when I can't do it myself?' The pain on his face was heartrending. 'I will kill to keep you safe. Does that make you happy?'

I stared up at him. 'No,' I said. 'I thought it would, but no.' I felt like Rafael, I'd kill for him. I'd kill to keep the pain out of his eyes.

I holstered the gun and raised my right hand to him. His eyes widened. He understood the gesture. He took my hand and raised me to my feet. He drew me with him towards the waiting wolves.

I hung back, pulling on his hand.

'I said I'd kill for you, Anita.' His voice was soft and harsh at the same time. 'Don't you believe I'd do it?'

His eyes were utterly sad. It was like something inside of him that he'd kept alive all these years was dead now. I believed the look in his eyes. He would kill to protect me, and the decision had cost him dearly.

The werewolves closed around us. I would have said they crawled around us, but that didn't cover what they were doing. Crawling wasn't graceful, or sensuous, but this was. They moved like they had muscles in places that people didn't. They circled us and rolled their eyes up at us. When I met those eyes, they looked away, all except Sylvie. She met my gaze and held it. It was a challenge, but I wasn't sure what I was supposed to do about it.

A hand touched me, and I jerked away from it. Only Richard's hand on mine kept me from going for my gun. He held both my hands in his and drew me to him, our bodies not quite touching. He met my eyes and held them. He wasn't afraid. I tried to relax, but it wasn't working.

'This is my lupa. Know her scent, know her skin. She has shed our blood, and shed her blood for us. She stands as protector for those weaker than herself. She will kill for us, if we ask. She is your alpha.'

Sylvie and Neal stood up. They both moved out of the circle. They stood, staring at me, at Richard. The others crouched on the floor, watching.

'She is not dominant to me,' Sylvie said.

'She is not even one of us,' Neal said, 'I won't bow to her. I could break her in half with one hand.' He shook his head. 'She isn't my alpha.'

'What's happening, Richard?' I asked.

'I tried to bring you into the pack, make you one of us without contaminating you.'

'Why?' I asked.

'If you're going to protect Stephen, then you deserve the protection of the pack. If you're going to take risks for us, then you deserve to have the benefits of our protection.'

'No offense,' I said, 'but I haven't been too impressed with your protection so far.' The minute I said it, I wished I hadn't. His face fell.

'You made it personal last night with Raina, Anita. You have no idea how dangerous she is. I wanted you to have everyone's protection in case something happened to me.'

I looked up at him. 'You will kill Marcus if he jumps you, right? No more being squeamish.' I touched his arm. I studied his face. 'Answer me, Richard.'

He nodded, finally. 'I won't let him kill me.'

'You will kill him; promise me.'

His jaw tightened, the muscle thrumming. 'I promise.'

'Well, hallelujah,' Sylvie said. She stared at me. 'I withdraw my challenge. You aren't dominant to me, but you can be his alpha female. You're a good influence on him.' She stepped back into the circle, but didn't kneel. 'Come on Neal,' she said, 'let it go.'

He shook his head. 'No, she isn't one of us. She can't be. I won't acknowledge her as alpha.'

'All you have to do is prove to Neal that you're serious,' Sylvie said. 'You just have to make him hurt a little.'

'Since he could probably survive a direct hit with a mack truck, how am I supposed to hurt him?'

She shrugged.

'I didn't think anyone would challenge you. I'm sorry,' Richard said.

'You expect people to be nice, Richard. It's one of your best qualities and greatest weaknesses,' I said.

'Refuse the challenge, Anita.'

'If I refuse, then what?'

'It's over. You won't be a member of the pack, but I can order them to protect you from Raina. It's almost as good.'

'I told you, I don't want anyone being ordered to take a bullet for me. Besides, no way am I volunteering to go one on one with a lycanthrope. I'll keep my gun, thanks anyway.'

The doorbell rang. It was probably Edward. Damn. I looked at the little group, and even though they were in human form, he'd know what they were. He was better at smelling monsters than I was, at least live ones. 'If you guys can tone it down a bit, I'll get the door.'

'Edward?' Richard made it a question.

'Probably,' I said.

He stared around at the group. 'Everybody up off the floor. He's another normal.'

They got to their feet, slowly, almost reluctantly. They seemed almost intoxicated, as if the power in the room had done more for them than for me.

I went for the door. I was halfway to it when Richard yelled, 'No!'

I dropped to the ground, rolling, and felt the air whistling over me where Neal had swung. If he'd been any good at fighting, he'd have nailed me. The missed swing put him off balance, and I foot-swept him to the floor, but he got to his feet again before I could stand, like there were springs in his spine. It was impressive as hell.

'Stop it, Neal,' Sylvie said.

'She didn't refuse the challenge. It's my right.'

I scuttled backwards, still on the ground, not sure what to do. The closed drapes of the picture window were at my back if I stood up. I wasn't sure standing up was my best bet. 'Give me the rules, quick,' I said.

'First blood,' Sylvie said. 'Human form only.'

'If he shapeshifts, you can shoot him,' Richard said.

'Agreed,' Sylvie said, others murmured their agreement.

Peachy. Neal leaped for me, leaving the ground completely, hands outstretched. I came up on one knee, grabbed his jacket, and rolled on my back, letting his amazing momentum carry us both. I shoved both feet into his stomach and pushed with everything I had. He flew over me in a near perfect arc. He'd set himself up for a textbook tomoe-nage throw.

He smashed through the window, taking the curtain with him. I rolled to my feet and stared at the gaping window. Broken shards of glass sprinkled onto the carpet and the yard beyond. Neal struggled out of the curtain, blood running down his face where the glass had cut him.

Edward was on the ground in a combat stance, gun out. He pointed it at Neal, as he struggled free of the curtain.

'Don't shoot him,' I said. 'I think the fight's over.'

Neal stood, kicking free of the clinging curtain. 'I'll kill you.'

I drew the Firestar and pointed it at him. 'I don't think so.'

Richard stepped up beside me. 'She drew first blood, Neal. The fight is over, unless you want to fight me, too.'

'And me,' Sylvie said. She stepped up on the other side of Richard. The rest of the pack stepped up behind us. Stephen crouched at my feet.

'She is pack now,' Sylvie said. 'You fight one of us, and you fight all of us.'

Edward raised his eyebrows at me. 'What is going on, Anita?'

'I think I've been adopted,' I said.

Neal glared at me.

'Do it, Neal,' Sylvie said.

Neal knelt in the glass and the curtain. The cuts were already beginning to heal on his face. Glass wasn't silver or the claws of another monster, so he healed almost magically.

'You are dominant. You are alpha.' The words were dragged from his throat. 'If this window hadn't been here, you couldn't have bloodied me.'

'Why do you think I moved in front of it, Neal?' I asked.

His eyes squinted. 'You planned this?'

I nodded and raised my gun skyward. 'I'm not just another pretty face.'

Richard took my left hand, squeezing it gently. 'That's the God's honest truth.'

I put up the Firestar.

Edward shook his head, smiling, but didn't put his gun up. He did stop pointing it at anyone. 'You are the only person I know who leads a more interesting life than I do.'

Jason patted me on the back. 'Tomorrow night we'll take you out chasing deer.'

'I thought you'd chase cars,' I said.

He grinned. 'What fun is that? Cars don't bleed.'

I smiled, and then stopped. His eyes were as innocent as spring skies, as joyous, and staring into them, I wasn't sure if he was kidding me or not. I almost asked, but didn't. I wasn't sure I wanted to know.

12

Edward was five foot eight, with blond hair cut very short and close to his head. He was blue-eyed and the epitome of WASP breeding. He was also the most dangerous man I'd ever met, living or dead.

He was amused as hell by the gathering of lycanthropes. The group broke up soon after his arrival, mainly because all the business had been taken care of. The meeting had mainly been a last-ditch effort to convince Richard to compromise his morals and kill someone. Barring that, for him to pick a lupa who would kill for him. We'd sort of killed two birds with one stone, pun intended. But I was very aware that I'd gotten lucky with Neal. If he'd had a background in any martial art, if he'd known anything about fighting, I'd have been toast.

Richard had boarded up the broken window and had a call in to a glass repair shop that was willing, for an exorbitant fee, to come out and repair the damage immediately. I'd offered to pay for the damages since I made them.

Edward, Richard, and I sat around the kitchen table. Edward and I sipped coffee. Richard drank tea. One of his few serious faults was a total dislike of coffee. Hard to trust a man who won't drink coffee.

'What have you found out?' I asked.

Edward sipped his coffee and shook his head. 'Not much. The contract has been picked up.'

'Even with the time limit?' I asked.

He nodded.

'When is the twenty-four hours up?' I asked.

'Let's say two o'clock. I got the offer about one o'clock last night, but we'll add an hour to be safe.'

'To be safe,' Richard said. I think it was sarcasm.

'What's wrong with you?' I asked.

'Am I the only one in this room who's worried?'

'Panicking won't help, Richard.'

He stood up, emptying his mug in the sink and rinsing it automatically. He turned, leaning his butt against the cabinets, arms crossed over his chest. 'You need a clear head to plan?'

I nodded. 'Yeah.'

He stared at us. I watched him thinking about something serious. He finally said, 'I don't understand how the two of you can be calm. I'm shocked that someone has put a contract out on Anita. Neither of you is shocked.'

I looked at Edward, and he looked back at me. We had one of those moments of perfect understanding, and I knew I couldn't explain it to Richard. I wasn't even sure I could explain it to myself. 'I've stayed alive this long because I don't react the way most people react.'

'You've stayed alive because you're willing to do things other people aren't.'

I nodded. 'That, too.'

His face was very serious, like a little boy asking about the facts of life. 'Let me ask one stupid question; then I'll shut up.'

I shrugged. 'Ask away.'

'Anita says she doesn't enjoy killing. That she feels nothing when she kills.'

I realized then that the question was going to be for Edward. I wasn't sure how that would go over.

'Do you enjoy killing?'

Edward sat very still in his chair, drinking his coffee quietly. His blue eyes were as neutral and unreadable as any vampire's, and in some ways just as dead. I wondered for the first time if my eyes ever looked like that. 'Why do you want to know?'

'I agreed to kill Marcus,' Richard said. 'I've never killed anyone.'

Edward stared up at him. He set his coffee down carefully and met Richard's eyes. 'Yes.'

'Yes, you enjoy killing?' Richard asked.

Edward nodded.

Richard was waiting for him to explain. You could see it in his face.

'He's answered your question, Richard.'

'But does he enjoy the sensation of killing? Is it physical? Or is it the planning that he enjoys?'

Edward picked up his coffee.

'The question and answer session is over, Richard,' I said.

A look halfway between stubbornness and frustration crossed Richard's face. 'But "yes," doesn't tell me anything.'

'After you kill Marcus,' Edward said, 'you can ask the question again.'

'And you'll answer it?' Richard asked.

Edward gave the barest of nods.

For the first time, I realized that Edward liked Richard. Not as a friend, maybe, but he didn't think Richard was a complete waste of time.

Richard stared into Edward's face for a long time, then shook his head. 'Okay.' He sat back down. 'No more questions. What's the plan?'

I smiled at him. 'To keep the hitter from killing me.'

'That's your entire plan?' Richard asked.

'And to take out the man with the money,' Edward said. 'As long as the money is out there, Anita won't be safe.'

'Any ideas how to accomplish this?' Richard asked.

Edward nodded and up-ended his coffee mug, finishing the last of it. He went to the counter and refilled it, like he was at home.

He sat back down. Good ol' Edward, comfortable wherever he was.

I sat waiting, watching him quietly. He'd tell us when he was ready and not before. Richard was practically dancing in place. 'What?' he finally asked.

Edward smiled, I think at Richard, or maybe at that eternal music that only he could hear. The rhythm that kept him self-contained and alive.

'The assassin might come here today, and we'll take precautions for that. A herd of shapeshifters was perfect. I'd have passed on the hit myself until they cleared out.'

I glanced around the quiet kitchen. The spot between my shoulder blades was itching. 'You think we're in danger now?'

'Maybe.' He didn't seem too worried. 'But I think they'll hit you tonight on your date with the Master of the City.'

'How did you know I had a date tonight?'

Edward just smiled. 'I know that the Master of the City is taking the Executioner to the opening of his dance club, Danse Macabre. I know that you'll be arriving in a limo.'

'I didn't even know that,' I said.

He shrugged. 'It wasn't hard to find out, Anita.'

'I was going to cancel my date tonight and hide out.'

'If you stay here, the assassin will almost certainly come here.'

I glanced at Richard. 'Oh,' I said.

'I can take care of myself,' Richard said.

'Could you kill a human being?' I asked.

He blinked at me. 'What do you mean?'

'I mean if someone came at you with a gun, could you kill them?'

'I said I'd kill to protect you.'

'That's not what I asked, Richard, and you know it.'

He stood up and paced a small circle in the kitchen. 'If it was standard ammunition, it couldn't kill me.'

'You wouldn't know whether it was silver ammo until it was too late,' I said.

He hugged his arms, ran his hands through his long hair, and turned to me. 'Once you decide to start killing, it never stops, does it?'

'No,' I said.

'I don't know if I could kill a human being.'

'Thanks for the honesty,' I said.

'But that means you'll take an assassin into a club crowded with people? You'll endanger all of them to keep me safe?'

'I would endanger almost anyone to keep you safe.'

Edward made a small sound, almost a laugh. His face was pleasant and empty. He sipped coffee. 'Which is why I don't want Richard in the line of fire. You'll be so busy worrying about him, it might make you careless.'

'But all those people, you can't put them in danger,' Richard said.

Edward looked at me and didn't say what he was thinking. I was grateful for that. 'I think Edward has a plan for that, too, Richard.'

'I think they'll hit you on the way home from the club. Why work in the middle of a crowd if they don't have to? Plant a bomb on the limo, or wait until you're alone on the drive back.'

'Is that what you would do?' Richard asked.

Edward looked at him for a moment, then nodded. 'Probably. Not the bomb, but I'd hit the limo.'

'Why not the bomb?' Richard asked.

I didn't ask, because I knew the answer. Edward's eyes flicked to me. I shrugged.

'Because I like to kill up close and personal. With a bomb there's no personal risk.'

Richard stared at him, studying his face. He finally said, 'Thank you for answering the question.'

Edward acknowledged him with a nod. Richard was gaining brownie points from both of us. But I knew that Richard had illusions. If Edward seemed to like him, Richard would assume Edward wouldn't kill him. I knew better. If the situation called for it, Edward could pull the trigger on anyone.

'Let's say you're right,' I said. 'I go on the date and let the hitter make his move. Then what?'

'We take him out.'

'Wait a minute,' Richard said. 'You're betting that the two of you are better than a professional assassin. That you'll get to him before he gets to Anita.'

We both nodded.

'What if you're not better?'

Edward looked at him like he'd said the sun wouldn't rise tomorrow.

'Edward will be better,' I said.

'You'd bet your life on that?' Richard asked.

'I am betting my life on that,' I said.

Richard looked a touch pale. He nodded. 'I guess you are. What can I do to help?'

'You heard Edward,' I said. 'You stay here.'

Richard shook his head. 'I heard, but surely in a crowd of people even Superman will need a few more eyes and ears. The pack can help watch your back.'

'It doesn't bother you to endanger them?'

'You said you'd risk almost anyone to keep me safe,' Richard said. 'I feel the same way.'

'If they want to volunteer, that's one thing, but I don't want them ordered into it. People aren't good bodyguards if they resent doing it.'

Richard laughed. 'Very practical. For a second there, I thought you were really worried about my wolves.'

'Practical will keep me alive, Richard, sentimentality won't.'

'If we had some extra watchers, it'd free me up a little,' Edward said.

I looked at him. 'You'd trust monsters to watch my back?'

He smiled, and it wasn't pleasant. 'Monsters make excellent cannon fodder.'

'They aren't cannon fodder,' Richard said.

'Everyone's cannon fodder,' Edward said, 'eventually.'

'If I really thought we were endangering innocent by-standers, I wouldn't go to the club. You know that, Richard.'

He stared at me for a second, then nodded. 'I know that.'

Edward made a small sound low in his throat. 'Innocent by-standers.' He shook his head, smiling. 'Let's get dressed,' Edward said. 'I bought some new toys for you to use tonight.'

I looked at him. 'Dangerous toys?' I asked.

'Is there any other kind?' We grinned at each other.

'You two are enjoying this,' Richard said. It was almost accusatory.

'If we didn't enjoy it, we'd both do something else,' Edward said.

'Anita doesn't kill people for money, and you do.'

I watched the humor drain from Edward's eyes like the sun sinking behind clouds, leaving them pitiless and empty. 'Think what you like, loverboy, but Anita could have chosen another line of work, one that wouldn't put her in harm's way. But she didn't. There's a reason for that.'

'She's not like you.'

Edward looked at me with empty eyes. 'Closer than she used to be.' His voice was soft, almost neutral, but it made me shiver.

I met his eyes, and for the first time in a long time, wondered what I'd given up to be able to pull the trigger. The same thing Edward had given up inside himself to be able to kill so easily? I looked up at Richard and wondered if he could do it. If, when the fur flew, he could really kill anyone. Some people couldn't. No shame in that. But if Richard backed out, he was dead. Not tonight or tomorrow, but eventually, because Marcus would see to it. Richard had beaten Marcus twice and refused the kill. I doubted Marcus would let him have another shot at it. They'd taken Stephen last night, knowing what Richard would do. If I hadn't been with him, he might he dead now. Shit.

All I had to do was kill the assassin before he or she killed me. Trust Richard not to let Marcus kill him. Keep Raina from killing me. And let's see, I was sure there was something else. Oh, yeah, decide whether I'm going to sleep with Richard, and if I did, what that would mean for Jean-Claude and myself. There were days when my life was too complicated even for me.

13

Finding dress-up clothes that you can hide a gun in is a bitch. I actually hadn't planned to carry a gun on my date with Jean-Claude. Of course, that was before the assassin. Now I wasn't going out without one. If I'd known I'd be needing a gun tonight, I'd have worn the little black dress yesterday and saved the pants suit. But who knew, and now all I'd packed besides jeans was the dress. It was a little black dress with just enough strap to allow a bra, if you were careful. I'd bought a black bra to be safe. Flashing a white bra strap in a black dress always looked so tacky. The jacket was a deep black velvet, a bolero cut that hit me at the waist. Black beading edged the collar and hem.

The jacket was hanging on the doorknob of Richard's closet. He was sitting forlornly on the bed, watching me put the last touches on my lipstick. I was leaning forward, peering at myself in the mirror on his dresser. The skirt was short enough that I decided to wear a black teddy under it, not for underwear but to go over my panty hose, so everything matched. Ronnie hadn't trusted me not to end over at least once tonight. She was right. So even if I forgot, the teddy covered more than most bathing suits. I'd have never picked out something so short on my own. Ronnie was a bad influence on me. If she'd known I was planning to wear it for Jean-Claude, she'd have probably chosen something else. She called him fangface. Or worse. She liked Richard.

'Nice dress,' Richard said.

'Thanks.' I turned in front of the mirror to check the way the skirt hung. It was just full enough to swing when I moved. The black knife sheaths on my forearms actually matched the dress. The knives made a nice touch of silver. The wrist sheaths almost covered the scars on my arms. Only the mound of scar tissue at my left elbow was visible. A vampire had torn up my arm once upon a time. The same vamp had bitten through my collarbone. The scars were normal for me, but every once in a while I'd be out enjoying myself and catch someone looking, staring. They'd look hurriedly away, or meet my eyes. It wasn't that the scars were awful to look at. They weren't that bad – really. But they told a story of pain and something out of the ordinary. They said I'd been places that most people hadn't, and I'd survived. Worth a stare or two, I guess.

The black straps that held the new knife down along my spine showed a little at the shoulders, but more across the back. The hilt was hidden under my hair, but I wouldn't be taking the jacket off.

'Why didn't you wear this last night?' Richard asked.

'The pants suit seemed more appropriate.'

He stared at me, eyes roving over my body more than my face. He shook his head. 'For seeing someone you're not going to sleep with, that is a very sexy outfit.'

I had never planned on Richard seeing the dress, at least not on the night I wore it for Jean-Claude. I wasn't sure what to say, but I'd try. 'I trust myself with Jean-Claude more than I trust myself with you, so he gets the short skirt and you don't.' That was the truth.

'You're saying I don't get the sexy outfit because I'm so irre-sistible?'

'Something like that.'

'If I ran my hands up your legs, would I find panty hose or garters?' He looked so solemn, hurt. With everything else going down, I shouldn't have had to worry about my boyfriend's hurt feelings, but there it was. Life goes on, even if you're ass deep in alligators.

'Panty hose,' I said.

'Will Jean-Claude find out what kind of hose you're wearing?'

'He could ask, like you did,' I said.

'You know that's not what I meant,' he said.

I sighed. 'I don't know how to make this easier on you, Richard. If there's anything that would make you feel more secure about this, ask.'

To his credit, he didn't ask me not to go. I think he knew he wouldn't like the answer. 'Come here,' he said and held out his hand to me.

I walked over to him and took his outstretched hand. He sat me on his lap, legs sideways like you'd sit on Santa. He encircled me with one arm, then laid his other hand on my thigh. 'Promise me you won't sleep with him tonight.'

'With assassins ready to jump out of the woodwork, I think that's a safe bet,' I said.

'Don't joke, Anita, please.'

I smoothed my hand through his hair. He looked so serious, so hurt. 'I've said no for a very long time, Richard. Why should you be worried about tonight?'

'The dress,' he said.

'I admit it's short, but . . . '

He smoothed his hand up my thigh until it vanished under the skirt. He rested his hand just below the lace of the teddy. 'You're wearing lingerie, for God's sake; you never wear lingerie.'

I would have explained about everything matching, but somehow I didn't think that would be comforting. 'Okay, I won't sleep with him tonight. I hadn't planned on it to begin with.'

'Promise me you'll come back and sleep with me.' He smiled when he said it.

I smiled back and slid off his lap. 'You'd have to shift first. I'd have to see your beast. Or so you keep telling me.'

'I could shift when you get back.'

'Could you take human form again quickly enough to do us any good tonight?'

He smiled. 'I'm strong enough to be Ulfric, Anita. One of the things I can do is change form almost at will. I don't pass out when I change back to human form like most shapeshifters.'

'Handy,' I said.

He smiled. 'Come back tonight, and I'll change for you. Sylvie's right. I have to accept what I am.'

'Part of that is trying it out on me, huh?'

He nodded. 'I think so.'

Staring into his solemn eyes, I knew that if he changed for me tonight and I couldn't deal with it, it would destroy something inside of him. I hoped I was up to it. 'When I come back tonight, I'll watch you shift.'

He looked grim as if he expected that I'd run screaming. 'Kiss me, and get out of here,' he said.

I kissed him, and he licked his lips. 'Lipstick.' He kissed me again. 'But underneath I can still taste you.'

'Hmmm,' I said. I stared down at him and almost didn't want to go. Almost. The doorbell rang, and I jumped. Richard didn't, as if he'd heard it before I had.

'Be careful. I wish I could be with you.'

'There'll be media all over the place,' I said. 'Wouldn't do to get your picture taken with a bunch of monsters. It might blow your cover.'

'I'd blow my cover if it would keep you safe.'

He loved teaching, yet I believed him. He'd come out of the closet for me. 'Thanks, but Edward's right. I'd be so worried about keeping you alive, I wouldn't be taking good care of myself.'

'You don't worry about Jean-Claude?'

I shrugged. 'He can take care of himself. Besides, he's already dead.'

Richard shook his head. 'You don't really believe that anymore.'

'No, he's dead, Richard. That I know. Whatever keeps him alive is a form of necromancy, different than my own powers, but still magic.'

'You can say it, but in your heart you don't believe it.'

I shrugged again. 'Maybe not, but it's still the truth.'

There was a knock on the door. Edward said, 'Your date's here.'

'I'm coming. Now I have to fix my lipstick all over again.'

He wiped fingers across his mouth, coming away with crimson stains. 'At least I'll be able to tell if you've been kissing him. This stuff will show up like blood on his white shirt.'

I didn't argue. Jean-Claude always wore black and white. I'd only seen him in one shirt that wasn't white. It had been black. I reapplied the lipstick and put it in the beaded black purse on the dresser. The purse was too small even for the Firestar. I did have a Derringer, but except at close quarters, it was pretty worthless. With an assassin I might not want to get that close. Edward had a solution. He'd loaned me his See-camps .32 autoloader. It was about the same size as a small .25, only a little wider than my own hand, and I had a small hand. It was a very nice gun, and for the caliber and the size, I'd never seen better. I wanted one. Edward informed me that he'd had to wait nearly a year for the gun to come in. It was pretty much a custom order. Otherwise, he'd have made it a gift. Fine, I'd order my own – if I survived the night. If I didn't, well, I wouldn't be ordering anything.

I'd managed not to think too much about that. I'd concentrated on dressing, putting the weapons in place, Richard, anything but that I was putting myself out as bait for someone good enough to earn 500,000 dollars a pop. I was having to trust that Edward would keep me alive. Because though Edward would have stopped the limo and fired only when he could see my face, most hit men wouldn't. Most professionals prefer to take you out from a nice, safe distance. A high-powered rifle could be yards or even miles away. Not much I, or even Edward, could do about that. I knew nothing about explosives. I was going to have to depend on Edward to take care of any bombs. I was putting myself in Edward's hands tonight, trusting him like I'd never trusted anyone before. Scary thought, that.

I checked the purse again; ID, lipstick, money, gun. I'd have normally carried a small travel hairbrush, but there wasn't room. I could live with messy hair for one night.

The thought made me check my hair in the mirror and run a brush through it one last time. I had to admit that it looked great. It was one of my best features. Even Ronnie couldn't improve on it. It was all natural curl. Even tonight I'd shoved hair goop in it after my shower and let it dry naturally. I'd had a woman get angry with me once in California because I wouldn't tell her where I'd gotten my hair permed. She wouldn't believe it was natural.

I slipped the purse over my shoulders so the thin strap went across my chest. It blended with the dress well enough that it looked almost as good with it as without. But the purse rode at my ribs, just a little lower than my shoulder holster. I tried drawing the gun a couple of times, and it wasn't too bad. Not as good as a holster, but what was? I slipped the jacket on and checked myself in the mirror for the umpteenth time. Neither the knives nor the gun showed. Great. I slipped my cross on last. I made sure the cross was inside the dress, then put a small piece of masking tape over it. This way I kept my cross, but it didn't spill out of my clothes and glow at Jean-Claude. I picked up the brush again and put it down without using it.

I was stalling. It wasn't just the assassin I was afraid of. I was dreading the moment Richard and Jean-Claude met tonight. I wasn't sure how they were going to react, and I wasn't up to an emotional confrontation. I rarely was.

I took a deep breath and went for the door. Richard followed me. It was his house. I couldn't ask him to hide in the bedroom.

Jean-Claude stood by the television, peering at the shelves of videos, as if studying the titles. He was tall and slender, though not as tall as Richard. He wore black pants and a short black jacket, cut just at the waist like my own. He had on high, leather boots that covered nearly his entire leg, the soft leather tops were held in place by black straps with small silver buckles. His black hair spilled over his shoulders, inches longer than when I first met him.

He turned at last, as if he hadn't known we were standing there. I made a small involuntary gasp as he faced me. His shirt was red, a pure, clear crimson that blazed inside his open jacket. The collar was high, held in place by three antique jet beads. The shirt gaped open below the collar, showing a large oval of his chest. The cross-shaped burn scar on his chest showed in the circle of red cloth as if it were framed for viewing. The circle of bare skin ended just above the black pants, where the shirt was safely tucked away.

The shirt looked splendiferous against his pale skin, the black wavy hair, his midnight blue eyes. I closed my gaping mouth, and said, 'Spiffy, very spiffy.'

He smiled. 'Ah, *ma petite*, always the perfect thing to say.' He glided across the carpet in his nifty boots, and I found myself wanting him to take the jacket off. I wanted to see his hair spill over that shirt, black over red. I knew it would look wonderful.

Richard came up behind me. He didn't touch me, but I could feel him standing there. A warm, unhappy presence at my back. I couldn't blame him. Jean-Claude looked like an advertisement for Wet Dreams 'R' Us. I couldn't blame anyone for being jealous.

Jean-Claude stood in front of me, close enough that I could have reached out and touched him. I stood between the two of them, and the symbolism wasn't lost on any of us.

'Where's Edward?' I managed to ask. My voice sounded almost normal. Good for me.

'He is checking the car. I believe for incendiary devices,' Jean-Claude said with a small smile.

My stomach clenched tight. Someone really wanted me dead by midnight tonight. Edward was sweeping the car for bombs. Even for me, it didn't seem quite real.

'*Ma petite*, are you well?' Jean-Claude took my hand in his. 'Your hand is cold.'

'Nice complaint, coming from you,' Richard said.

Jean-Claude looked over my shoulder at Richard. 'It was not a complaint but an observation.'

His hand was warm, and I knew that he had stolen that warmth from someone. Oh, they'd been willing enough. There were always people willing to donate to the Master of the City. But still, he was a blood sucking corpse, no matter what he looked like. Staring up at him, I realized part of me didn't buy that anymore. Or maybe I just didn't care anymore. Damn.

He raised my hand slowly to his lips, eyes watching not me but Richard. I drew my hand out of his. He looked at me. 'If you want to kiss my hand, fine, but don't do it just to get on Richard's nerves.'

'My apologies, *ma petite*. You are quite right.' He looked past me to Richard. 'My apologies to you as well, Monsieur Zeeman. We are in a . . . ticklish position. It would be childish to make it worse with game playing.'

I didn't have to see Richard's face to know he was frowning.

Edward came in and saved us. We could all shut up and leave. Hopefully.

'The car's clean,' he said.

'Glad to hear it,' I said.

Edward was dressed for the evening. A brown leather coat hung to his ankles and moved like something alive as he came into the room. The coat hung strangely heavy in places. He'd shown me some of his toys that were positioned here and there. I knew there was a garotte hidden in the stiff white collar of his shirt. A garotte was a little too up-and-close even for me.

His eyes flicked to the two men in my life, but all he said was, 'I'll follow the limo. Don't look around for me tonight, Anita. I'll be there, but we don't want the hitter alerted to the fact that you've got a bodyguard.'

'A second bodyguard,' Jean-Claude said. 'Your, how do you say, hitter will know I will be by her side.'

Edward nodded. 'Yeah, if they hit the limo, you'll be there. They'll have to plan on taking you out, too, which means it's got to be serious firepower.'

'I am both a deterrent and an invitation to up the stakes, is that it?' Jean-Claude asked.

Edward looked at him like the vampire had finally done something interesting. Edward didn't meet his eyes though. I was the only human I knew that could meet the Master's eyes and not be bespelled. Being a necromancer had its uses. 'Exactly.' He said it like he hadn't expected the vampire to grasp the situation. But if there was one thing Jean-Claude was good at, it was surviving.

'Shall we go then, *ma petite*? The party awaits us.' He made a sweeping motion with his arms, directing me towards the door but not taking my hand. He glanced at Richard, then at me. He was behaving himself terribly well. Jean-Claude was a world-class pain in the ass. It wasn't like him to be a good boy.

I glanced at Richard. 'Go on. If we kiss goodbye, it'll smear your lipstick again.'

'You are wearing quite enough of her lipstick already, Richard,' Jean-Claude said. For the first time tonight, I heard that warm edge of jealousy.

Richard took two steps forward, and the tension level in the room soared. 'I could kiss her good night again, if that would make you happy.'

'Stop it, both of you,' I said.

'By all means,' Jean-Claude said. 'She is mine for the rest of the evening. I can afford to be generous.'

Richard's hands balled into fists. The first trickle of power oozed through the room.

'I'm leaving now.' I made for the door and didn't look back. Jean-Claude caught up with me before I reached the door. He reached for the doorknob first, and then released it, letting me get it.

'I do forget your penchant for doors,' he said.

'I don't,' Richard said softly.

I turned and looked at him standing there in his jeans, his T-shirt molded to the muscles of his arms and chest. He was still barefoot, his hair a wavy mass around his face. If I'd been staying here, we could have cuddled on the couch in front of one of his favorite movies. We were beginning to have our favorite movies, songs, sayings that were ours. Maybe a moonlight walk. His night vision was almost as good as my own. Maybe later we could finish what we'd started before the meeting.

Jean-Claude slid his fingers through mine, drawing my attention to him. I stared up into those blue, blue eyes like a sky before a storm, or seawater where the rocks lie deep and cold. I could touch those three black buttons and see if they were really antique beads. My gaze traveled downward to the pale glimpse of his chest. I knew that the cross-shaped burn scar was a rough slickness to the touch. Looking at him made my chest tight. He was so beautiful. Would my body always feel the pull of him, like a sunflower turning towards the light? Maybe. But standing there holding his hand, I realized it wasn't enough.

Jean-Claude and I could have had a glorious affair, but I could see spending my life with Richard. Was love enough? Even if Richard killed for self-preservation, could he really accept my body count? Could I accept his beast, or would I be as horrified by it as he was himself? Jean-Claude accepted me lock, stock, and gun. But I didn't accept him. Just because we both looked at the world through dark glasses, didn't mean I liked it.

I sighed, and it wasn't a happy sound. If this was the last time I ever saw Richard, I should have jumped his body and given him a kiss he would never forget, but I couldn't do it. Holding Jean-Claude's hand, I couldn't do it. It would have been cruel to all of us.

'Bye, Richard,' I said.

'Be careful,' he said. He sounded so alone.

'Louie and you are going to the movies tonight, right?' I asked. He nodded. 'He should be here soon.'

'Good.' I opened my mouth to say more, but didn't. There was nothing to say. I was going with Jean-Claude. Nothing I said would change that.

'I'll wait up for you,' Richard said.

'I wish you wouldn't.'

'I know.'

I left, walking a little too fast out to the waiting limo. It was white. 'Well, isn't this shiny and bright,' I said.

'I thought black looked too much like a hearse,' Jean-Claude said.

Edward had come out also. He closed the door behind us. 'I'll be there when you need me, Anita.'

I met his eyes. 'I know you will.'

He gave the briefest of smiles. 'But just in case, watch your back like a son of a bitch.'

I smiled. 'Don't I always?'

He glanced at the vampire standing by the open limo door. 'Not as well as I thought you did.' Edward walked into the darkness towards his waiting car before I could think of a reply. It was just as well. He was right. The monsters had finally gotten me. Seducing me was almost as good as killing me, and nearly as crippling.

14

The name of the club, Danse Macabre, blazed in red neon letters nearly eight feet high. The letters were curved and flowed at an angle like some giant hand had just finished writing them. The club was housed in an old brewery warehouse. The place had stood on the Riverfront, boarded up and abandoned for years. It had been the only eyesore in a line of chic restaurants, dance clubs, and bars. Most of them were owned by vampires. The Riverfront was also known as The District, or Blood Square, though not in polite vampire company. For some reason, the nickname bugged them. Who knew why?

The crowd had spilled out from the sidewalk into the street, until the limo was stopped by the sheer weight of people. It was so bad that I spotted a uniformed cop trying to ease the people back enough for the cars to get through. I looked through the dark tinted windows at the press of people. Was the assassin out there? Was one of those well-dressed, smiling people waiting to kill me? I opened my purse and slipped the Seecamp out.

Jean-Claude eyed the little gun. 'Nervous, *ma petite?*'

'Yes,' I said.

He looked at me, head to one side. 'Yes, you are nervous. Why does one human assassin unnerve you so much more than all the preternatural creatures you have faced?'

'Everyone else who's wanted to kill me, it was personal. I understand personal. Whoever this is wants to kill me because it's business. Just business.'

'But why is that more frightening to you? You will be just as dead, regardless of your assailant's motives.'

'Thanks a lot,' I said.

He touched my hand, as it gripped the gun. 'I am trying to understand, *ma petite*, that is all.'

'I don't know exactly why it bothers me. It just does,' I said. 'I like to put a face on my enemies. If someone kills you, it shouldn't be only for money.'

'So killing for hire offends your moral sensibilities?' he asked. His voice was very bland, too bland, as if he were laughing silently to himself.

'Yes, dammit, it does.'

'Yet you are friends with Edward.'

'I never said I was consistent, Jean-Claude.'

'You are one of the most consistent people I have ever known, *ma petite*.'

'How consistent can I be if I'm dating two men?'

'Do you think being unable to choose between us makes you frivolous?' He leaned towards me as he said it, hand smoothing up the sleeve of my jacket.

The trouble was I had almost chosen. I almost told him, but I didn't. First, I wasn't a hundred percent sure. Second, Jean-Claude had blackmailed me into dating him. Date him or he'd kill Richard. He wanted a chance to woo me away from Richard. Which meant really dating him. As he put it, 'If you allow Richard to kiss you, but not me, it is not fair.' Supposedly, if I chose Richard, Jean-Claude would merely step aside. I think he was egotist enough to mean it. The Master of the City couldn't imagine anyone not being won over, eventually. Not if you had access to his lovely body. He kept offering it. I kept refusing. If I chose Richard over him, would he really bow out gracefully, or would he take us all down in a bloodbath?

I stared into his deep blue eyes and didn't know. I'd known him for years. Dated him for months. But he was still a mystery to me. I just didn't know what he would do. I wasn't willing to push that button, not yet.

'What are you thinking about so seriously, *ma petite*? Do not say it is the assassin. I would not believe you.'

I didn't know what to say, so I just shook my head.

His hand slid over my shoulders until I was resting in the curve of his arm. The feel of his body that close to mine made my stomach flutter. He bent forward as if to kiss me, and I stopped him, the back of my left hand against his chest. Since I was now touching bare skin, I wasn't sure this helped.

'You behaved yourself the entire drive up here. What gives now?' I asked.

'I am trying to comfort you, *ma petite*.'

'Yeah, right,' I said.

He wrapped his other arm around my waist, turning my upper body against him. The gun was still in my hand, but it began to seem awkward. I wasn't going to use it on Jean-Claude, and the assassin wasn't coming through the locked doors. That much violence in a crowd this large with cops directing traffic seemed a little bold even for a professional.

I slid my arm across his back, the gun still in my hand. 'If you kiss me, I'll have to redo my lipstick.'

He leaned his face close enough to kiss, lips so close to mine he could have breathed me in. He whispered just above my mouth. 'We mustn't have that.' He kissed my cheek, running his lips down the edge of my jaw.

I touched his face with the edge of the gun, moving his face where I could see it. His eyes had gone drowning blue. 'No necking,' I said. I meant that. I'd only volunteered once for blood donation and that was when he was dying. I did not share bodily fluids with the Master of the City.

He rubbed his cheek against the gun. 'I had something a bit

lower in mind.' He ducked his head to my collarbone, licking down my skin. For a second I wondered how low he was planning on going, then I pushed him off of me.

'I don't think so,' I said, half-laughing.

'Do you feel better now, *ma petite*?'

I stared at him for a heartbeat, then laughed. I did. 'You are a devious son of a bitch, did you know that?'

'I've been told that before,' he said, smiling.

The police had pushed the crowd back, and the limo moved forward. 'You did that just to cheer me up.' I sounded almost accusatory.

He widened his eyes. 'Would I do such a thing?'

I stared at him and felt the smile slide from my face. I really looked at him for a moment, not just as the world's greatest lust object, but as him, Jean-Claude. The Master of the City was worried about my feelings. I shook my head. Was he becoming nicer, or was I just fooling myself?

'Why so solemn, *ma petite*?'

I shook my head. 'The usual, trying to figure out how sincere you are.'

His smile widened. 'I am always sincere, *ma petite*, even when I lie.'

'Which is what makes you so good at it,' I said.

He nodded his head once, almost a bow. 'Exactly.'

He glanced ahead of us. 'We are about to embark on a sea of media, *ma petite*. If you could put the gun up? I think the press would find it a bit much.'

'Press?' I said. 'You mean local media?'

'Local, yes.'

'What aren't you telling me?'

'When the door opens, take my arm and smile, please, *ma petite*.'

I frowned at him. 'What is about to happen?'

'You are about to be introduced to the world.'

'Jean-Claude, what are you up to?'

'This is not my doing, *ma petite*. I do not like the limelight quite this much. The vampire council has chosen me to be their representative to the media.'

'I know you had to come out of the casket to the local vampires after you won your last challenge, but isn't it dangerous? I mean you've been pretending to be some mysterious master's number-one flunkie. It's kept you safe from outside challengers.'

'Most masters use a stalking horse, *ma petite*. It cuts down on challenges and human assassins.'

'I know all that, so why are you going public?'

'The council believes that skulking in the shadows gives ammunition to our detractors. Those of us who would make good media fodder have been ordered into the light, as it were.'

I stared at him. 'How into the light?'

'Put the gun away, *ma petite*. The doorman will open the door and there will be cameras.' I glared at him, but I slid the Seecamp into my purse.

'What have you gotten me into, Jean-Claude?'

'Smile, *ma petite*, or at least do not frown.' The door opened before I could say anything else. A man in a tux held the door. The flash of lightbulbs was blinding, and I knew it had to bother his eyes more than mine. He was smiling as he held a hand back for me. If he could stare that much light in the face without blinking, I could be gracious. We could always fight later.

I stepped out of the limo and was glad I was holding his hand. Flashbulbs were everywhere like tiny suns blasting off. The crowd surged forward, microphones shoved at us like knives. If he hadn't been holding my hand tight, I'd have crawled back into the limo. I moved closer to him, just to be able to keep my feet. Where the hell was crowd control?

A microphone nearly touched my face. A woman's voice yelled from far too close, 'Is he good in bed? Or would that be coffin?'

'What?' I said.

'Is he good in bed?' There was a moment of near silence, while everyone waited for my answer. Before I could open my mouth and say something scathing, Jean-Claude moved in, graceful as always.

'We do not kiss and tell, do we, *ma petite*?' His French accent was the thickest I'd ever heard it.

'*Ma petite* – is that your pet name for her?' a man's voice.

'Oui,' he said.

I looked up at him, and he leaned down as if to kiss my cheek. He whispered, 'Glare at me later, *ma petite*. There are cameras everywhere.'

I wanted to say that I didn't give a damn, but I did. I mean, I think I did. I felt like a rabbit caught in headlights. If the assassin had jumped out with a gun at that moment, I'd have stood there and let him shoot me. That thought, more than anything else, brought me back to myself, helped me to think again. I started trying to see past the lights, the microphones, a few tape recorders, and video cameras. I caught at least two major network emblems on the cameras. Shit.

Jean-Claude was fielding questions like a pro, smiling, gracious, the perfect vampire cover boy. I smiled and leaned into him, standing on tiptoe, putting my lips so close to his ear that I could have licked it, but I was hoping the microphones wouldn't pick up what I was saying. I was sure it looked coy and girlish as hell, but hey, nothing was perfect. I whispered, 'Get me out of here now, or I pull the gun and clear a path for myself.'

He laughed, and it flowed down my skin like fur, warm, and ticklish, and vaguely obscene. The reporters ooohed and aahed. I wondered if Jean-Claude's laugh worked off a recorder, or on video. That was a frightening thought.

'Oh, *ma petite*, you naughty girl.'

I whispered, 'Don't ever call me that again.'

'My apologies.' He smiled, waved, and began escorting me

through the press of reporters. Two vampire doormen had come out to help clear our path. They were both large and muscular, and neither of them had been dead long. They looked rosy-cheeked and almost alive. They'd fed on someone tonight. But then, so had Jean-Claude. It was getting harder and harder for me to throw stones at the monsters.

The door opened, and we slipped inside. The silence was wonderful. I turned on him. 'How dare you drag me into that kind of media coverage.'

'It does not endanger you, *ma petite*.'

'Had it occurred to you that if I chose Richard over you, that I might not want everybody in the world to know I was dating a vampire?'

He gave a slight smile. 'Good enough to date, but not good enough to go public with?'

'We've gone to everything from the symphony to the ballet together. I'm not ashamed of you.'

'Really?' The smile was gone, replaced by something else, not anger exactly, but close. 'Then why are you angry, *ma petite*?'

I opened my mouth, then closed it. Truth was that I would rather not have gone quite this public, because I guess I didn't really believe I could choose Jean-Claude. He was a vampire, a dead man. In that one moment I realized how prejudiced I still was. He was good enough to date. Good enough to hold hands with, and maybe a bit more. But there was a limit. Always a point where I knew I'd say stop because he was a corpse. A beautiful corpse, but a vampire is a vampire. You couldn't really fall in love with one. You couldn't have sex with one. No way. I'd broken Jean-Claude's one rule for dating both of the boys. I'd never really given Jean-Claude the same chance that I'd given Richard. And now, with national television coverage, the bat was out of the bag. It embarrassed me that anyone would think I might actually date him. That I might actually care for a walking dead man.

The anger washed away in the knowledge that I was a hypocrite. I don't know how much of it showed on my face, but Jean-Claude cocked his head to one side. 'Thoughts are flying across your face, *ma petite*, but what thoughts?'

I stared up at him. 'I think I owe you an apology.'

His eyes widened. 'Then this is a truly historic occasion. What are you apologizing for?'

I wasn't sure how to put it into words. 'You're right; I'm wrong.'

He put his fingers to his chest, face wide with mock surprise. 'You admit that you have treated me like some guilty secret, hidden away. Exiled from your true feelings while you cuddle with Richard and his living flesh.'

I frowned at him. 'Enough already. See if I ever give you another apology for anything.'

'A dance would suffice,' he said.

'I don't dance. You know that.'

'This is the grand opening of my dance club, *ma petite*. You are my date. Are you truly going to deny me even one dance?'

Put that way it sounded petty. 'One dance.'

He smiled, wicked, enticing. The smile that the serpent must have given Eve. 'I think we will dance well together, *ma petite*.'

'I doubt it.'

'I think we would do many things well together.'

'Give you one dance and you want the whole package. Pushy bastard.'

He gave a small bow, smiling, eyes shining.

A female vamp strode towards us. She was inches taller than Jean-Claude, which made her at least six feet tall. She was blond and blue-eyed, and if she'd looked any more Nordic, she'd have been a poster girl for the master race. She was wearing a violet blue body suit with strategic holes cut out. The body that showed through was broad-shouldered, muscular, and still managed to be full-breasted. Leather boots in the exact same color rode her long, muscular legs all the way up to her thighs.

'Anita Blake, this is Liv.'

'Let me guess,' I said. 'Jean-Claude chose the outfit.'

Liv looked at me from her considerable height as if simply being tall made her intimidating. When I didn't flinch, she smiled. 'He is the boss.'

I stared up at her. I almost asked why. I could feel her age pressing down on me like a weight. She was six hundred years old. Twice Jean-Claude's age or more. So why wasn't she the boss? I could feel the answer along my skin like a cool wind. Not enough power. She wasn't a master vampire, and no amount of age would change that.

'What are you staring at?' she asked. She looked me right in the eyes and shook her head. 'She really is immune to our gaze.'

'To your gaze,' I said.

She put her hands on her hips. 'What's that supposed to mean?'

'It means you don't have enough juice to do me,' I said.

She took a step forward. 'How about I just pick you up and squeeze some juice out of you?'

Here was where not having a gun in a holster was going to get me killed. I could get one of the knives out, but unless I was willing for her to come very close, it wouldn't help. I could slip my hand in the purse; most people didn't expect a gun to come out of a purse so small. Of course, if Liv caught me going for the gun, she could get to me before I could draw it. With a holster I'd have tried it. From a purse hanging from a strap, I didn't think so. Vampires are just that fast.

'How many vampire kills do you have now, Anita?' Jean-Claude asked.

The question surprised me, and my answer surprised me more. 'Over twenty legal kills.'

'How many kills altogether, *ma petite*?'

'I don't know,' I said. It had to be over thirty now, but truthfully,

I didn't remember anymore. I didn't know how many lives I'd taken. A bad sign, that.

'Liv is mine, ma petite. You may speak freely in front of her.'

I shook my head. 'Never admit to murder in front of strangers, Jean-Claude. Just a rule.'

Liv looked at me. She didn't seem to like what she saw. 'So this is the Executioner.' She shook her head. 'She's a little on the small side, isn't she?' She stalked around me like I was a horse for sale. When she was at my back, I opened the purse.

By the time she came around again, I had the gun out, behind the purse, unobtrusive, though in a pinch I guess I could have shot through the purse. But why, if I didn't have to?

Liv shook her head. 'She's pretty, but she's not very impressive.' She stood behind Jean-Claude, running her strong hands over his shoulders, his arms. She ended with her hands around his waist, fingers kneading his body.

I was getting very tired of Liv.

'I can do things that no human can do for you, Jean-Claude.'

'You are being rude to Anita. I will not remind you of it again.' There was a cold, even threat in his voice.

Liv unwrapped herself from him and stood between us, hands on hips. 'The great Jean-Claude driven to celibacy by a human. People are laughing behind your back.'

'Celibacy?' I asked.

Jean-Claude glanced at me, then sighed. 'Until you give up your nunnish ways, *ma petite*, I am playing monk.'

My eyes widened. I couldn't help it. I knew that Richard and I had each had one lover and chosen celibacy afterwards. But I'd never thought about Jean-Claude and what he might be doing to satisfy his needs. Abstinence would not have been one of my choices for him.

'You seem surprised, *ma petite*.'

'I guess anyone who exudes sex the way you do . . . I just never thought about it.'

'Yet if you discovered that I had been sleeping with another female, alive or dead, while we were dating, what would you do?'

'Drop you in a hot minute.'

'Exactly.'

Liv laughed, a loud, unattractive bray of sound. 'Even your human doesn't believe you.'

Jean-Claude turned to her, his eyes a blaze of sapphire flame. 'You say they laugh behind my back.'

She nodded, still laughing.

'But only you are laughing to my face.'

Her laughter died abruptly like a turned switch. She stared at him.

'A little more submissiveness, Liv, or is this a challenge to my authority?'

She looked startled. 'No, I mean . . . I never meant . . . '

He just looked at her. 'Then you had best ask my forgiveness, had you not?'

She dropped to one knee. She didn't look afraid, more as if she'd done some huge social gaffe and now had to make amends. 'I beg your forgiveness, Master. I forgot myself.'

'Yes, you did, Liv. Do not make it a habit.'

Liv got to her feet, all smiles, all forgiven. Just like that. The political maneuvering was thick in the air. 'It's only that she doesn't look nearly as dangerous as you painted her.'

'Anita,' Jean-Claude said, 'show her what you have in your hand.'

I moved the purse to one side, flashing the gun.

'I could have your throat in my hands before you could point that toy,' Liv said.

'No,' I said, 'you couldn't.'

'Is that a challenge?' she asked.

'Six hundred years of life, plus or minus a decade,' I said. 'Don't throw it away for a little grandstanding.'

'How did you know my age?'

I smiled. 'I am really not in the mood to bluff tonight, Liv. Don't try me.'

She stared at me, her extraordinary eyes narrowing. 'You are a necromancer, not just a corpse-raiser. I can feel you inside my head, almost like another vampire.' She looked at Jean-Claude. 'Why couldn't I feel her before?'

'Her power flares when she feels threatened,' he said.

This was news to me. To my knowledge, I wasn't using any power right now. But I didn't say it out loud. Now was not the time to ask stupid questions or even smart ones.

Liv stepped to one side, almost as if she was afraid. 'We're opening in an hour. I've got work to do.' She moved towards the door, never taking her eyes from me.

I watched her move, happy with her reaction but not understanding it.

'Come, Anita,' Jean-Claude said, 'I want to show you my club.'

I let him lead me into the main area of the club. They had gutted the warehouse until it rose three stories straight up with railings around each floor. The main dance floor was huge, shining and slick, gleaming in the subdued light. Track lighting was hidden away so it was hard to tell where the light was coming from.

Things hung from the ceiling. At first glance I thought they were bodies, but they were mannequins, life-size rubber dolls, crash-test dummies. Some were naked, one wrapped in cellophane, some in black leather or vinyl. One rubber doll wore a metal bikini. They were hung from chains at different levels. It was a mobile.

'That's different,' I said.

'A promising new artist did it especially for the club.'

I shook my head. 'It does make a statement.' I slipped the gun back into my purse but kept the purse open. That way I was able to get to the gun surprisingly quickly. Besides, I couldn't walk around all night with a loaded gun in my hand. Eventually, your hand starts cramping, no matter how small the gun is.

Jean-Claude glided across the dance floor, and I followed. 'Liv was afraid of me. Why?'

He turned gracefully, smiling. 'You are the Executioner.'

I shook my head. 'She said she could feel me in her head like another vamp. What did she mean?'

He sighed. 'You are a necromancer, *ma petite*, and your power grows with use.'

'Why would that scare a six-hundred-year-old vampire?'

'You are relentless, *ma petite*.'

'It's one of my best things.'

'If I answer your question, will you enjoy my club with me, be my date until the assassin shows up?'

'Thanks for reminding me.'

'You had not forgotten.'

'No, I hadn't. So, yeah, answer my question and I'll play date.'

'Play?'

'Stop stalling and answer the question.' I thought of one other question I wanted answered. 'Two questions.'

He raised his eyebrows, but nodded. 'Vampires are given powers in folklore and popular myth that we do not possess: controlling weather, shapeshifting into animals. Necromancers are supposedly able to control all types of undead.'

'Control? You don't mean just zombies, do you?'

'No, *ma petite*.'

'So Liv's afraid I'll take her over?'

'Something like that.'

'But that's crazy. I can't order vampires around.' The moment I said it, I wished I hadn't. It wasn't true. I had raised a vampire once. Once. Once had been enough.

Something must have shown on my face, because Jean-Claude touched my cheek.

'What is it, *ma petite*? What fills your eyes with such . . . horror?'

I opened my mouth and lied. 'If I could order vampires around,

Serephina wouldn't have cleaned my clock two months ago.'

His face softened. 'She is dead, *ma petite*. Well and truly dead. You saw to that.' He leaned forward and kissed my forehead. His lips were silken soft. He brushed his lips across my forehead, moving his body in closer, comforting me.

It made me feel guilty as hell. I did still have nightmares about Serephina, that much was true. Just saying her name out loud made my stomach clench. Of all the vampires I'd faced, she'd come the closest to getting me. Not killing me, that would happen sooner or later. No, she had nearly made me one of them. Nearly made me want to be one of them. She had offered me something more precious than sex or power. She'd offered me peace. It had been a lie, but as lies go, it had been a good one.

Why not tell Jean-Claude the truth? Well, it was none of his damn business. Frankly, what I'd done frightened me. I didn't want to deal with it. Didn't want to think about it. Didn't want to know what the philosophical ramifications of raising a vampire during daylight hours might be. I was very good at ignoring things I didn't want to deal with.

'*Ma petite*, you are trembling.' He pushed me back from him to search my face.

I shook my head. 'There's an assassin out to kill me, and you ask why I'm trembling.'

'I know you too well, *ma petite*. That is not why you tremble.'

'I don't like you using me like some kind of bogeyman for vampires. I'm not that scary.'

'No, but I have encouraged the illusion.'

I pushed away from him. 'You mean, you've been telling other vamps that I could control vampires?'

'A hint or two.' He smiled, and in that one simple expression, you just knew he was thinking wicked thoughts.

'Why, for heaven's sake?'

'I have taken a lesson from our diplomatic Richard. He has won over many wolves by simply promising to treat them well, not to force them to do things they do not want to do.'

'So?' I said.

'I have invited vampires to join my flock with the promise not of fear and intimidation but of safety.'

'Like Liv?'

He nodded.

'How do you make sure they don't stage a palace revolt?' I asked.

'There are ways.'

'Like threatening them with a necromancer,' I said.

He smiled. 'Indeed.'

'Not everyone will believe it.'

'I know I don't,' a voice said.

15

I turned to find another new vampire. He was tall and slender with skin the color of clean white sheets, but sheets didn't have muscle moving underneath, sheets didn't glide down the steps and pad godlike across a room. His hair fell past his shoulders, a red so pure it was nearly the color of blood. The color screamed against his paleness. He was wearing a black frock coat like something out of the 1700s, but his chest gleamed lean and naked inside it. The heavy cloth was nearly covered in thick embroidery, a green so vivid it gleamed. The embroidery matched his eyes. Green as a cat's eyes, green as an emerald. From the waist down, he was wearing green Lycra exercise pants that left little to the imagination. A sash was tied at his waist like a pirate belt, black with green fringe. Knee-high black boots completed the outfit.

I thought I knew all the bloodsuckers in town, but here were two new ones in less than two minutes. 'How many new vampires are in the city?' I asked.

'A few,' Jean-Claude said. 'This is Damian. Damian, this is Anita.'

'I feel silly in this outfit,' he said.

'But you look splendid, doesn't he, *ma petite*?'

I nodded. 'Splendid is one way of putting it.'

Jean-Claude walked around the new vampire, flicking imaginary specks of lint from the coat. 'Don't you approve, Anita?'

I sighed. 'It's just . . . ' I shrugged. 'Why do you make everyone around you dress like they stepped out of a sexual fantasy with a high costume budget?'

He laughed, and the sound wrapped around me, tugged at things lower than he'd ever gotten to touch. 'Stop that,' I said.

'You enjoy it, *ma petite*.'

'Maybe, but stop it anyway.'

'Jean-Claude has always had a killer fashion sense,' Damian said, 'and sex was always one of his favorite pastimes, wasn't it?' There was something about the way he said that last that made it not a compliment.

Jean-Claude faced him. 'And yet, for all my foppish ways, here you are, in my lands, seeking my protection.'

The pupils in Damian's eyes were swallowed by a rush of green fire. 'Thank you so much for reminding me.'

'Remember who is master here, Damian, or you will be banished. The council themselves interceded with your old master, rescued you from her. She did not want to give you up. I spoke for you. I ransomed you because I remember what it was like to be trapped. To be forced to do things you didn't want to do. To be used and tormented.'

Damian stood a little straighter but didn't look away. 'You've made your point. I am . . . grateful to be here.' He looked away, then to the floor, and a shudder ran through him. 'I am glad to be free of her.' When he looked back up, his eyes had returned to normal. He managed a smile that didn't quite reach his eyes. 'Wearing a few costumes is not the worst thing I've ever done.'

There was a sorrow to his voice that made me want to ask Jean-Claude to let him change into a pair of pants, but I didn't. Jean-Claude was walking a very fine line here. Damian was over five hundred years old. He wasn't a master, but that was still a hell of a lot of power. Jean-Claude might be able to handle Liv and Damian, but if there were more, Master of the City or not, he wasn't up to the job. Which meant these little dominance games were necessary. The others couldn't be allowed to forget who was Master, because once they did, he was done for. If he'd asked for my vote before he put out the invitations, I'd have said no.

A door at the far side of the room opened. It was a black door in the black walls, and it seemed almost magical as a woman stepped out. She was about my own height, with wavy, waist-length brown hair that foamed over the shoulders of her ankle-length black coat. She was wearing a pair of hot turquoise exercise pants with a matching sports bra. Crisscrossing straps went from pants to the bra, emphasizing her small waist. Black vinyl boots reached to her knees, with a small projection that covered the knees. She walked down the steps and strode across the floor with a free-swinging walk that was almost a run. She entered the room like it was her room, or maybe she was her own room, comfortable wherever she went.

She stopped by us, smiling, pleasant, hazel eyes greener because of the strip of turquoise around her neck. 'What do you think?'

'You look lovely, Cassandra,' Jean-Claude said.

'You look better in yours than I do in mine,' Damian said.

'That's a matter of opinion,' I said.

The woman looked at me. Her eyes flicked down the length of Damian's body. She met my eyes, and we both laughed.

Damian looked puzzled. Jean-Claude looked at me. 'Share your humor with us, *ma petite*, please.'

I met Cassandra's eyes again, swallowed another laugh, and shook my head. I took a few deep breaths. When I was pretty sure I could speak without laughing, I said, 'Girl humor, you wouldn't understand.'

'Very diplomatic,' Cassandra said. 'I'm impressed.'

'If you knew how hard diplomacy comes to *ma petite*, you would be even more impressed,' Jean-Claude said. He had gotten the joke, as if there'd been any doubt.

Damian was frowning at us, still puzzled. It was just as well.

Jean-Claude looked from Cassandra to me and back again. 'Do you two know each other?'

We shook our heads in unison.

'Cassandra, Anita. My newest wolf, meet the light of my life. Cassandra is one of your guards for the night.'

'You're very good. I wouldn't have picked up on it.'

Her smile widened. 'Richard said you didn't know he was a werewolf at first, either.'

Instantly, a little spark of jealousy flared. Of course, if she were a werewolf and with Jean-Claude, then she was one of Richard's followers. 'You weren't at the meeting.'

'Jean-Claude needed me here. He couldn't do without both Jason and me.'

I looked at Jean-Claude. I knew what Jason did for him. He bled Jason when he woke, and sucking blood was damn close to sex for a vampire. 'Really,' I said.

'Don't worry, *ma petite*. Cassandra won't share blood with me, either. She and Richard have many similarities. I believe that Richard chose her for me because she bears a certain resemblance to you, not just physically, but a certain *je ne sais quoi*.'

'*Je ne sais quoi* is French for nothing,' I said.

'It means an indefinable something that is difficult to put into words, *ma petite*. A quality that transcends vocabulary.'

'He does talk pretty, doesn't he?' Cassandra said.

'He has his moments,' I said. 'You can't be draining Jason every morning. Even a werewolf needs a little recoup time.'

'Stephen is a willing donor.'

'Why wasn't Stephen with you last night?' I asked.

'Is that an accusation?' Jean-Claude asked.

'Just answer the question.'

'He had requested an evening off to spend time with his brother. Who am I to stand in the way of familial obligations?' He stared at me while he answered like he wasn't completely happy with the conversation. Tough. Neither was I.

Stephen's own brother had betrayed him, acted as bait for the trap. Damn. 'Where is Stephen?'

'He's in the back room,' Cassandra said. 'He helped me get into this thing. I couldn't reach all the straps.' She dropped the coat off her shoulders and turned so I could see her back. The straps formed a tight web, most of them in places you couldn't have fastened without help. She slipped the coat back on and turned, looking at me. 'You're taking this alpha female thing seriously, aren't you?'

I shrugged. 'I'm serious about Stephen's safety.'

Cassandra nodded, face solemn, thoughtful. 'I like that. Sometimes alpha female is just a token position. Just a word for the pack leader's lover. Most of them aren't as active as Raina.' She made a face when she said the name, like she'd tasted something bitter.

Jean-Claude interrupted. 'I will leave you two girls to your conversation. I have things to attend to before the club opens.' He kissed the back of my hand and was gone, leaving us standing in the middle of the club, alone. Damian had gone at his heels as if he'd been asked.

For a moment, I was nervous. Cassandra and I were very much in the open. 'Let's go over there.' I motioned to the steps that led to the next level. We sat down on them, me having to smooth my skirts down. Even that didn't help. I had to keep my feet and knees together or I would have flashed the room. Sigh.

'Let me guess,' I said. 'Raina wanted you for her movies.'

'She wants everyone that is remotely attractive for her movies. Though sometimes sharing her bed for a tryout can get you out of it. She offered me to Gabriel for my tryout. That damn leopard is not even a pack member.'

'If he were, she'd make him pack leader,' I said.

Cassandra shook her head. 'Gabriel couldn't defeat Marcus, let alone Richard. He's the leader of the wereleopards only because there's no one stronger. He's an alpha, but he's flawed. It makes him weak.'

'Sexual perversion doesn't always mean you'll lose a fight,' I said.

'It's not that,' Cassandra said. 'He's into dangerous sex. Lycanthropes can take a lot of damage.' She shivered. 'The things he wanted to do to me.' She looked at me, and the fear showed in her eyes. 'He says you nearly gutted him once while he had you pinned to the ground.'

I looked away. 'Yeah.'

Cassandra touched my arm, and there was no sense of power. She was every bit as good as Richard at hiding what she was. She made Sylvie look like an amateur. The touch made me turn back to her. 'He's hot for you, Anita. I didn't tell Richard because, well, I'm new in the pack. Got into town about two weeks ago. I was afraid that if I told him what Gabriel had said about you, he might do something stupid. But meeting you, maybe telling you is enough. You can decide whether Richard needs to know.'

She looked so serious. It scared me. 'What did Gabriel say?'

Cassandra took a deep breath. 'He has a fantasy about you. He wants to arm you with knives and let you try to kill him, on film, while he rapes you.'

I stared at her. I wanted to say, you're kidding, but I knew she wasn't. Gabriel was just that twisted. 'How does the movie end in his version?'

'With you dead,' she said.

'While he rapes me?' I said.

She nodded.

I hugged myself, running my hands down my arms, tensing my back, feeling the weapons I was carrying. I was armed. I was safe, but shit.

She touched my shoulder. 'You all right?'

'Well, isn't this touching,' a man's voice on the stairs behind us. Cassandra was on her feet, facing it in an instant. I slid my hand into the open purse and drew the Seecamp out. The gun caught a bit on the cloth lining and cost me a couple of seconds, but it was out and ready. I felt better. I'd twisted on the steps, coming up on one knee, not bothering to stand. Sometimes, standing made you a better target.

Sabin stood about five steps above us. Frightfully close for neither of us to have sensed him. He was dressed as I'd seen him in the office; hooded cloak covering him from head to toe. I could see under the cloak now. There were no feet. He was floating above the step. 'I wish you could see the look on your face, Ms Blake.'

I swallowed my pulse back into my mouth and said, 'I didn't know you'd be here tonight, Sabin.'

Cassandra took a step towards him, a soft growl oozing from her throat. 'I don't know you,' she said.

'Calm yourself, wolf. I am Jean-Claude's guest, aren't I, Ms Blake?'

'Yeah,' I said. 'He's a guest.' I stopped pointing the gun at him, but I didn't put it up. He was awfully damn good to have snuck up on me and a werewolf.

'You know him?' Cassandra asked. She was still standing above me, blocking the vampire's path. She was taking this bodyguard thing very seriously.

'I've met him.'

'He safe?'

'No,' I said, 'but he's not here to hurt me.'

'Who is he here to hurt?' Cassandra asked. She still hadn't given any ground.

Sabin eased down the steps, cloak billowing around him in an odd motion, like the sleeve of an amputee. 'I have come to watch the night's entertainment, nothing more.'

Cassandra backed up to stand a step ahead of me. I stood but still kept the gun out. I was jumpier than normal. I was also remembering how Sabin had bled me from a distance with his laughter. Keeping a gun handy seemed like a good idea.

'Where's Dominic?'

'He's here somewhere.' His hood was a cup of darkness, smooth and empty, but I knew he was watching me. I felt his gaze like a weight.

He stayed on the step just above Cassandra, two steps above me. 'Who is your lovely companion?'

'Sabin, this is Cassandra; Cassandra, Sabin.'

A black-gloved hand slid out of the cloak. He reached towards Cassandra as if he'd caress her face.

She jerked back. 'Don't touch me.'

His hand froze in midmotion. A stillness washed over him. I'd seen other vampires fill with that utter quietness, but I'd thought it was made up of visual clues. There was no visual from Sabin, but that same emptiness flowed outward. The illusion was almost better this way as if it was just an empty cloak somehow hovering on the stairs.

His voice came out of that stillness. It was startling. 'Is my touch so repulsive?'

'You smell of sickness and death.'

Sabin drew his hand back inside his cloak. 'I am a visiting master. It is within my rights to ask for a bit of . . . companionship. I could ask for you, wolf.'

Cassandra growled at him.

'No one's forcing anyone into anyone's bed,' I said.

'Are you so sure of that, Ms Blake?' Sabin asked. He floated around Cassandra. The cloak brushed her, and she shuddered.

I couldn't smell him; I didn't have a werewolf's sense of smell. But I'd seen some of what was under that cloak. It was worth a shudder or two.

'Cassandra is only on loan to Jean-Claude. She belongs to the pack, so yeah, I'm sure.'

Cassandra glanced back at me. 'You'd protect me?'

'It's part of my job description now, isn't it?'

She studied my face. 'Yes, I suppose it is.' Her voice was soft, the growling like a distant dream. She looked terribly normal except for the outfit.

'You've seen what I am, Ms Blake. Do you shudder at my touch?'

I moved down a step until I was on the floor. Better footing than the stairs. 'I shook your hand earlier.'

Sabin floated to the floor. The darkness faded from inside the hood. He pushed it back to reveal that golden hair and that ravaged face.

Cassandra let out a hiss. She backed up until she hit the banister. I think Sabin could have pulled a gun and shot her right that second, and she wouldn't have reacted in time.

He smiled at her. His beautiful mouth pulling the rotted flesh loose. 'Have you never seen anything like this?'

She swallowed hard enough for me to hear, like she was trying not to throw up. 'I've never seen anything so horrible.'

Sabin turned back to me. His one eye was still a clear, pure blue, but the other had burst in the socket in a welter of pus and thinner liquid.

I did my own swallowing. 'Your eye was fine yesterday.'

'I told you it was virulent, Ms Blake. Did you think I was exaggerating?'

I shook my head. 'No.'

His gloved hand came out of hiding once more. I remembered the way his hand had squished when I shook it yesterday. I did not want him to touch me, but there was a look in his beautiful eye, some pain on what was left of his face, that made me hold still. I wouldn't flinch. I felt sorry for him, pretty stupid, but true.

That black glove hovered beside my face, not quite touching me. The Seecamp was forgotten in my hand. Sabin's fingertips brushed my face. The glove was liquid-filled, like some kind of obscene balloon.

He stared at me. I stared back. He spread his hand over my

lower jaw and pressed. There were solid things inside the glove, thicker pieces, and bone, but it wasn't a hand anymore. Only the glove gave it shape.

A small sound crawled out of my throat. I couldn't stop it.

'Perhaps I should ask for you?' he said.

I eased back out of his grip. I was afraid to move too quickly. Afraid that sudden movement might tear off the glove. I did not want to see him spill out in a flood of foul-smelling liquid. He was a horror show enough without that.

Sabin didn't try to hold me; maybe he was afraid of the same thing.

'Are you abusing my hospitality again?' Jean-Claude said. He stood on the dance floor, looking at Sabin. His eyes were pure blue light. His skin had gone pale and smooth like carved marble.

'You have not yet shown me true hospitality, Jean-Claude. It is customary to offer me companionship.'

'I didn't think there was enough of you left to have such needs,' Jean-Claude said.

Sabin grimaced. 'It is a cruel illness. Not all of my body has rotted away. The need remains, though the vessel is so grotesque that no one will touch me, not by choice.' He shook his head, and the skin split on one side. Something black and thicker than blood oozed down the side of his face.

Cassandra made a small sound. My bodyguard was about to be sick. Maybe it smelled bad to her.

'If one of my people angers me enough while you are in my territory, you may have them. But I cannot give someone to you just because you wish it. Not everyone's sanity would survive it.'

'There are days, Jean-Claude, when my own sanity is in doubt.' Sabin looked from Cassandra to me. 'It would break your wolf, I think. But your servant, I think she would survive.'

'She is off limits to you, Sabin. If you abuse my hospitality with such an insult, council edict or no council edict, I will destroy you.'

Sabin turned to him. The two vampires stared at each other. 'There was a time, Jean-Claude, when no one spoke to me like that, no one short of the council.'

'That was before,' Jean-Claude said.

Sabin sighed. 'Yes, before.'

'You are free to enjoy the show, but do not tempt me again, Sabin. I have no sense of humor where *ma petite* is concerned.'

'You share her with a werewolf but not with me.'

'That is our business,' Jean-Claude said, 'and we will never speak of this again. If we do, it will be a challenge between us, and you are not up to it.'

Sabin gave a half bow, hard to get the leverage for it without legs. 'You are Master of the City. Your word is law.' The words were correct. The tone was mocking.

Liv came up to stand behind and to one side of Jean-Claude. 'It is time to open the doors, Master.' I think that last was deliberate. Jean-Claude usually chastised his flock for calling him master.

Jean-Claude said, 'Everyone to their places then.' His voice sounded strangled.

'I will find a table,' Sabin said.

'Do so,' Jean-Claude said.

Sabin raised the hood back into place. He glided back up the stairs, headed for the tables on the upper level. Or maybe he'd just float in the rafters.

'My apologies, *ma petite*. I believe the sickness has progressed to his mind. Be wary of him. Cassandra is needed for the show. Liv will remain with you.'

I looked at the tall vampire. 'She won't take a bullet for me.'

'If she fails me, I will give her to Sabin.'

Liv paled, which is a neat trick for a vampire, even one that's fed. 'Master, please.'

'Now I believe she'll take a bullet for me,' I said. If the choices were sleeping with Sabin or getting shot, I'd take the bullet. From the look on Liv's face, she agreed.

Jean-Claude left to make his entrance.

Cassandra met my eyes. She wasn't just pale, she was green. She jerked her gaze from mine as if afraid of what I'd see. 'I am sorry, Anita.' She went for the door she'd first entered through. She seemed embarrassed. Guess I couldn't blame her.

Cassandra had failed the bodyguard test. She was a powerful lycanthrope, but Sabin had totally unnerved her. She'd have probably been just fine if the vampire had tried violence, but he'd just stood there and rotted at her. What do you do when the monsters start being piteous?

The doors opened, and the crowd flowed in like a tidal wave, spilling in a wash of thunderous noise. I slipped the gun back into the purse but didn't shut it.

Liv was at my elbow. 'Your table is over here.' I went with her because I didn't want to be alone in the jostling crowd. Besides, she was suddenly taking my safety very seriously. Couldn't blame her. Sabin's diseased body was a wonderful threat.

I'd have felt better if I hadn't believed Jean-Claude would do it. But I knew better. He'd give Liv to Sabin. He really would. There was a look in the vampire's eyes that said she knew it, too.

16

The table was the largest of a string of small, black lacquer tables. It blended nearly perfectly with the black walls. My dress matched the decor. I was really going to have to look into something in a different color scheme. The table was set away from the wall, near the railing so that the growing crowd couldn't block my view of the dance floor. It also meant that my back was exposed. I had scooted my chair so that the wall was at my back, but I was very aware that the edge of the railing curved around on my right side, so that someone could walk up and shoot me, relatively hidden from anyone else.

Of course, Liv was with me. She stood at my back, arms crossed over her stomach. All she needed was a sign over her head that flashed bodyguard.

Admittedly, my purse was open. The gun was within reach, and it was tempting to put it in my lap. I was spooked, but that wasn't the point. We had a plan. The plan did not include the assassin being scared away.

I touched Liv's arm.

She bent down.

'You're supposed to be unobtrusive.'

She looked puzzled. 'I'm supposed to keep you safe.'

'Then sit down and pretend to be my friend. The trap won't work if I look like I'm being guarded.'

She knelt by me; too far to bend down, I suppose. 'I will not risk being given to Sabin. I don't care if your assassin knows I'm here or not.'

It was hard to blame her, but I was willing to make the effort. I leaned into her. 'Look, either work with the program, or get away from me.'

'I obey Jean-Claude, not his strumpet.'

As far as I could remember, I'd never done anything in my life to deserve being called a strumpet. 'Jean-Claude said if you failed him, he'd give you to the rotting corpse, right?'

Liv nodded. Her eyes searched the crowd behind me. She really was trying to do the job, and the effort showed.

'He didn't say you'd be punished if I got hurt, did he?'

Liv's eyes flicked to me. 'What are you saying?'

'If you scare away the hitter and spoil the plan, that's failure.'

She shook her head. 'No, that's not what he meant.'

'He said never to fail him again.'

I watched her try to work out the logic. I was betting that logic wasn't one of her strong points.

'Clever, Anita, but if you get killed, Jean-Claude will punish me. You know he will.'

I was wrong. She was a lot smarter than she looked. 'But if you spoil our plan, he'll punish you anyway.'

Fear flashed through her eyes. 'I'm trapped.'

I felt sorry for her. Pity for two monsters – no three – in one night. I was losing my edge. 'If I don't get killed, I'll make sure you don't get punished.'

'You swear it?' She said the phrase like it meant more. Giving your oath was not a casual thing to her. A lot of vampires came from times when a man's or a woman's word was their bond.

'I give you my word.'

She stayed kneeling for a moment longer, then stood. 'Try not to get killed.' She moved into the crowd, leaving me on my own, like I'd asked.

The rest of the tables filled up quickly. The crowd spilled around the edges of the room on the raised area around the dance floor.

So many people stood at the fenced edges that if the table had been by the wall, I'd have lost my view of the dance floor. Under other circumstances, I'd have appreciated the thoughtfulness. Another bodyguard could come along at any time. I was ready for some company.

The crowd filled the two levels above, standing room only. I looked for Sabin's dark cloak, but didn't see him. The main dance floor was untouched. The way to the floor was barred by half a dozen vampires. They had quietly but firmly motioned everybody back to the sides of the room. Both male and female were dressed nearly identically, black lycra pants, boots, and black fishnet shirts. The women wore black bras under their shirts, but that was the only difference. I approved. Short little skirts or hot pants for the women would have pissed me off. The thought occurred that maybe Jean-Claude had dressed them with me in mind. He knew me too well in some ways and didn't have a clue in others.

I scanned the crowd for Edward and for anything suspicious, but it was hard to pick out any one person in the jostling, laughing crowd. I couldn't spot Edward. I had to just trust that he was there somewhere. And although I did trust him to be there, the tightness in my chest didn't ease.

Edward had cautioned me to be casual, not to look suspicious. Outwardly, I was trying. Inwardly, I was almost dizzy searching the crowd and that painful empty spot to the right and almost behind me where the railing went. I put my hands in my lap and forced myself to look down. If the assassin came now, I wouldn't be looking, but I had to get hold of myself. If I didn't, I was going to be so busy jumping at shadows, I wouldn't be ready when the real thing came. I was beginning to wish I'd let Liv stay.

I took deep, even breaths, in and out, concentrating on the rhythm of my own body. When I could hear the blood flowing inside my head, I raised my face slowly. I stared calmly out at the crowd and the dance floor. I felt empty, distant, calm. Much better.

A vampire came up to the railing in front of my table. Willie McCoy was dressed in a suit so horribly green it could only be called chartreuse. Green shirt, and a wide tie with Godzilla crushing Tokyo on it. No one would ever accuse Willie of matching any decor.

I smiled. I couldn't help it. Willie had been one of the first vampires to ever cross that line from monster to friend. He scooted one of the chairs around so his back was to the open space. He sat down like he hadn't done it on purpose. I didn't have to pretend to be happy to see him.

He had to lean a bit into me to be heard over the crowd's rising murmur. I could smell the sweet scent of the goop he used to slick back his short hair. Him being this close didn't even make me tense. I trusted Willie more than I trusted Jean-Claude.

'How ya doing, Anita?' He grinned enough to show fang. Willie hadn't been dead three years yet. He was one of the few vamps I'd known before and after death.

'I've been better,' I said.

'Jean-Claude said we were to bodyguard you, but to keep it casual. We'll drift in and out. But you looked spooked.'

I shook my head, smiling. 'That obvious?'

'To someone who knows ya, yeah.'

We smiled at each other. Looking into Willie's face from inches away, I realized that he was on my list. The list that Stephen was on. If someone killed Willie, I'd hunt them down. It surprised me to realize that any vamp had made the list. But Willie had, and come to think of it, I guess, so had one other vampire.

Jean-Claude appeared on the far side of the club. Speak of the devil. A spotlight hit him from somewhere. It had to be coming from a fly loft, but it was hidden away so that it was hard to tell.

A perfect place for a high-powered rifle. *Stop it, Anita. Stop tormenting yourself.*

I hadn't truly realized how crowded the opening would be. Edward by himself searching for one lone assassin in this mass of people would have been poor odds. Maybe the vamps and werewolves were amateurs, but their extra eyes couldn't hurt.

The lights began dimming until the only illumination was the spotlight on Jean-Claude. He seemed to glow. I wasn't sure if it was a trick or if he was making his own light from the skin outward. Hard to tell. Whichever, I was in the dark with an assassin, maybe, and I was not a happy camper.

Hell with it. I put the Seecamp in my lap. Better. Not perfect, but better. The fact that just the touch of a gun in my hand made me feel better was probably a bad sign. The fact that I missed my own guns was a worse one.

Willie touched my shoulder and made me jump enough that people near us glanced back. Shit.

He whispered, 'I got your back covered. Easy.'

Willie would make great cannon fodder, but he wasn't up to protecting me. He'd been a bit player before he died, and dying hadn't changed that. I realized if the shooting started and the bad guys were using silver bullets, I was worried about Willie. Worrying about your bodyguard is not good.

Jean-Claude's voice rose through the darkness, filling it with a sound that caressed my skin. A woman standing near the table shivered as if she'd been touched. Her date put his arm around her shoulders, and they huddled in the dark, surrounded by Jean-Claude's voice.

'Welcome to Danse Macabre. The night will be filled with surprises. Some wondrous.' Two smaller spotlights hit the crowd. Cassandra appeared balanced on the railing on the second floor. She swept the coat back, revealing her body, stalking along the inches-wide iron bar like it was the floor, nearly dancing. Wild applause broke out. The second spot hit Damian on the first floor. He glided out of the crowd, swishing the embroidered coat around him like a small cape. If he felt silly in the outfit, it didn't show.

He moved through the crowd with the spotlight following him. He touched a shoulder here, ran his hands through waist-length hair, put his arm around one woman's waist. Each one, man or woman, didn't seem to mind. They leaned into him or whispered in his ear. He came to a woman with long brown hair parted in the middle. She was dressed rather modestly for the crowd. Navy blue business skirt and jacket. Her white blouse had one of those big bows that are supposed to look like a tie but never do. Of the women around Damian, she looked the most normal. He circled her so closely that his body brushed her. She jerked away from every touch, eyes wide with fear I could see, even from across the room.

I wanted to say, 'Leave her alone,' but I didn't want to yell. Jean-Claude wouldn't allow anything illegal, at least not in front of this many witnesses. Bespelling a group of people wasn't illegal. Mass hypnosis wasn't permanent. But one on one, it was permanent. Which meant that Damian could stand under the woman's window and call her out some dark night, no time limitation.

Willie was leaning forward in his chair, his dark eyes on the woman and Damian. He didn't seem to be looking for assassins right that second.

I watched the woman's face go blank of all expression, until she was like one asleep. Her empty eyes stared at Damian. He took her hand and leaned against the railing. He rolled both legs over, ending on his feet, still holding her hand. She took two hesitant steps to the railing edge. He put his hands on her waist, under her jacket, and lifted her high in the air, effortlessly, setting her down on the dance floor in her sensible black pumps.

The spotlights on Jean-Claude and Cassandra died until the only light was that on Damian and the woman. He led her to the center of the dance floor. She walked, looking only at him as if the rest of the world no longer existed.

Dammit. What Damian was doing was illegal. Most of the crowd wouldn't pick it up. Vampires were allowed to use their powers for entertainment purposes so even the media, if they were inside, would be okay with it. But I knew the difference; I knew the law. Jean-Claude had to know I'd recognize what was happening for what it was. Was she an actress? A plant for the show?

I leaned into Willie, close enough to brush the shoulder of his suit. 'Is she an actress?'

He turned startled eyes to me, and I could see that the pupils had been swallowed by the brown of his eyes. Down a long dark tunnel there was a hint of fire.

I swallowed hard and eased back from him, glad of the gun in my lap. 'It's real, isn't it?'

Willie licked his lips nervously. 'If I say it is, you're going to do something to mess up the show. Jean-Claude will get mad at me. I don't want him mad at me, Anita.'

I shook my head but didn't argue with him. I'd seen what Jean-Claude did to vamps that angered him. Torture was putting it mildly. I had to find out what was going on but without disrupting things and drawing more attention to myself than I wanted tonight.

Damian stood the woman in the center of the light. He focused her face on something we could not see. She stood there, empty and waiting for his commands. He stood behind her, folding his arms around her waist, rubbing his cheek against her hair. He undid the bow at her throat, and the first three buttons of her blouse. He rubbed his lips along her exposed neck, and I couldn't take any more. If she was an actress, fine; but if she was an unwilling victim, this had to stop.

'Willie?'

He turned to me slowly, reluctantly. His hunger made him want to watch. His fear of what I was about to ask made him slower.

'What's up?'

'Go tell Jean-Claude that the show is over.'

Willie shook his head. 'If I leave your side and you get wasted, Jean-Claude will kill me. Slow and painful. I'm not leaving your side until I'm supposed to.'

I sighed. Fine. I leaned over the railing and motioned one of the vampire waiters over to me. He glanced off in the dark as if he could see Jean-Claude, even though I couldn't, then he walked over to me.

'What is it?' he whispered. He leaned in close enough that I could smell the mints on his breath. Nearly ever vampire I knew used breath mints.

I still had the Seecamp naked in my hand. I figured I could afford to get up close and personal with the new dead, so I leaned in and whispered back, 'Is she an actress?'

He glanced back at the little tableau. 'Just a volunteer from the audience.'

'She wasn't a volunteer,' I said. There had been a half dozen people that would have volunteered, but the vampire had chosen the one who was afraid. That extra little bit of sadism – they just couldn't resist it.

'Tell Jean-Claude that if he doesn't stop this, I will.'

He blinked at me.

'Just do it,' I said.

He walked around the edge of the dance floor, vanishing into the darkness. I could sort of follow him, more an impression of movement than anything else. I couldn't see Jean-Claude at all.

Damian passed his hand above the woman's face, and when his hand came away, she blinked, awake at last. Her hands flew to her blouse, eyes frantic. 'What's happening?' Her voice carried, thin with fear.

Damian tried to take her in his arms, but she drew away, and all he caught was a wrist. She strained against him, and he held her easily. 'Let me go, let me go, please!' She reached out to someone in the crowd. 'Help me!'

The crowd had gone very quiet, quiet enough that I could hear the voice of her supposed friend, 'Enjoy it. It's just part of the show.'

Damian jerked her around to face him, hard enough that there would be bruises. As soon as her eyes met his, her face went blank. She sagged to her knees, still held by one wrist.

He raised her to her feet, gently now. He clasped her against him and drew her hair to one side, exposing a long line of neck. He turned in a slow circle as if they were dancing, showing her bare flesh to all.

Willie leaned forward, tongue dancing over his lower lip as if he could taste her skin already. Willie was my friend, but it was good to remember that he was also a monster.

The vampire waiter was coming back. I could see him moving towards me.

Damian curled his lips, exposing fangs. He thrust his neck back giving everyone a view. I saw his neck muscles tense and we were out of time.

Willie looked up as if realizing the shit was hitting a different fan, but there was no time.

I shouted, 'Don't do it, Damian.' I pointed the gun at his back, about where the heart would be. When a vamp gets around five hundred, one shot to the chest, silver bullets or not, doesn't always guarantee a kill. But we would by God find out if he bit her.

Willie raised his hand toward me.

'Don't, Willie.' I meant it. Just because nobody else was allowed to kill him, didn't mean I couldn't.

Willie sank back into his chair.

Damian relaxed enough to turn his head and look at me. He turned so that the girl was in front of him like a shield. Her hair was still back on one side, her neck still exposed. He stared at me, running one finger down her naked flesh. Daring me.

A dim spotlight shone on me, and the illumination built as I walked very carefully to the two steps that led down to the dance floor. Vaulting the railing might have looked better, but it made it damn hard to hold a target. I could probably have made the head shot from the railing, but with an unfamiliar gun, it was too risky. I didn't want to accidentally shoot the woman in the head. Killing the hostage is always frowned upon.

The vampire waiters and waitresses didn't know what to do. If I'd been some schmuck off the street, they might have tried to jump me, but I was their master's beloved, which made things a little sticky. I kept a sort of peripheral eye on them. 'You guys back up and give me some room – right now.'

They all glanced at each other.

'You don't want to crowd me, boys and girls, so move it!' They moved.

When I was close enough to feel confident that I could make the shot, I stopped. 'Let her go, Damian.'

'She will not be harmed, Anita. Just a little fun.'

'She's unwilling. That's against the law, even for entertainment purposes, so let her go, or I'll blow your fucking head off.'

'Would you really shoot me in front of all these witnesses?'

'You bet,' I said. 'Besides, you're over five hundred years old. I don't think one shot to the head will kill you, not permanently at least. But it'll hurt like hell and may leave scars. You wouldn't want to spoil that beautiful face, now would you?' I was getting tired of holding one arm out. It wasn't that the gun was heavy, but it was hard to hold a one-handed pose for long without starting to waver. I didn't want to waver.

He stared at me for a space of heartbeats. He very carefully, very slowly licked the side of the woman's neck, strange green eyes staring at me the whole time. It was a dare. If he thought I was bluffing, he'd picked the wrong girl.

I let my breath out until my body was quiet, and I could hear my pulse in my ears. I sighted down my arm, down the gun, and . . . he was gone. He'd moved so suddenly it startled me. I moved my finger off the trigger and pointed the gun skyward, waiting for my heart to stop pounding.

He was standing just at the edge of the light, leaving the woman empty-faced, waiting. Damian stared at me.

'Are you going to interrupt our entertainment every night?' he asked.

'I don't like it,' I said, 'but pick a volunteer, and I have no quarrel with you.'

'A volunteer,' he said, turning in a circle to view the audience. They all stared at him. He licked his lips, and hands went up.

I shook my head and put the gun up. I took the woman's hand. 'Release her, Damian,' I said.

He glanced back at her and did it. Her eyes flew open wide, searching frantically like someone awakened from a nightmare to find it real. I patted her hand.

'It's all right. You're safe now.'

'What's happening? What's happening?' She caught sight of Damian and started sobbing hysterically.

Jean-Claude appeared on the edge of the light. 'You have nothing to fear from us, fair lady.' He glided towards us.

She started screaming.

'He won't hurt you,' I said. 'I promise. What's your name?'

She kept screaming. She was taller than me, but I touched her face, putting a hand on either side, forcing her to look at me. 'What's your name?'

'Karen,' she whispered, 'my name's Karen.'

'We're going to walk off this dance floor, Karen, and no one will hurt you. You have my word.'

She nodded over and over, breath coming so fast I was afraid she was going to pass out.

Cassandra walked into the light, but stayed back. 'Can I help?'

Jean-Claude had not moved since Karen started screaming. He just looked at me, and I still couldn't read his expression.

'Yeah,' I said, 'I could use some help.'

Karen shied away from her. 'She's not a vampire,' I said.

She let Cassandra take her other arm, and we led her off the dance floor away from the light. Jean-Claude stepped onto center stage, and his voice followed us into the darkness. 'Did you enjoy our little melodrama?' There was a puzzled silence. His voice was like fur wrapping the crowd in the dark, breathing in their fear, giving them back desire. 'We do not tease here at Danse Macabre. Who would like to experience the reality of Damian's kiss?' Someone would take him up on it. Someone always did. If anyone could salvage the show after the woman's hysterics, Jean-Claude could.

Liv came to help, I think. Karen took one look at the muscle-bound vamp and fainted dead away. She was not a small woman, and it surprised both Cassandra and myself. She sagged to the floor. Liv started to come closer, but I waved her off.

A woman from the crowd came towards us, hesitantly. 'Can I help?' she asked. She was about the same size as Cassandra and me, small, with long reddish hair that swung to her waist, straight and fine. She was dressed in a pair of dark brown dress slacks, the kind that run large and have cuffs and are usually linen. For a shirt she wore only a vest with a silk camisole under it.

I glanced at Cassandra. She shrugged. 'Thanks, if you could take her feet.' Cassandra could have flung the woman across her shoulders in a fireman's carry, but most lycanthropes didn't like to show off their strength. I could have carried her, too, even if she was so bloody tall. I could still have carried her for a short distance, but not fast, and not too far.

The woman shoved her clutch purse under one arm and took the unconscious woman's feet. We got moving a little awkwardly, but we managed to get a rhythm and Cassandra took us to the women's rest room. Or I should say, lounge. The front part had a couch and a lighted vanity. It was white and black, with a mural on the wall that was from a woodcut that I knew, entitled 'Demon-Lover.' The demon in this version looked suspiciously like Jean-Claude, and I doubted it was accidental.

We laid Karen on the black couch. The woman who was helping dampened some paper towels without being asked and brought them back. I laid them against Karen's forehead and neck. 'Thanks.'

'Is she going to be all right?' the woman asked.

I didn't answer, because that all depended on Damian. 'What's your name?'

The woman smiled almost shyly. 'Anabelle, Anabelle Smith.'

I smiled up at her. 'Anita Blake. This is Cassandra.' I realized I didn't know her last name. Jean-Claude always called his wolves by only their first names, like a pet. 'I'm sorry. I don't know your last name.'

'Cassandra is fine.' She shook Anabelle's hand. They smiled at each other.

'Should we report what happened to the police?' Anabelle asked. 'I mean that vampire was going to force himself on her. That's illegal, right?'

Karen stirred on the couch, moaning.

'Yeah, it's illegal,' I said.

Anabelle raised an interesting point. I could report it to the cops. If a vampire acquired three complaints against him or her, you could get a death warrant issued, if you got the right judge. I would talk to Jean-Claude and Damian first, but if they didn't give me the answers I wanted, maybe I should go to the cops. I shook my head.

'What are you thinking?' she asked.

'Nothing worth sharing,' I said.

The bathroom door opened. Raina walked in wearing a cream-colored dress as short as my own. The dark hose and stiletto high heels made her legs go on forever. She wore a fur jacket in a dusty red, probably fox. She was the only shape-shifter I'd met who wore real fur that wasn't her own.

She'd pulled her auburn hair on top of her head in a soft bun with loose strands of hair curled artfully around her face and neck.

Karen chose that minute to regain consciousness. I wasn't sure she was going to like her wake-up call. I knew I didn't.

I stood. Cassandra moved in front of me and a little to one side, not blocking me, but closer to the danger than I was. I wasn't used to anyone guarding me. It felt odd. I could take care of myself. That was the point, wasn't it?

'What's happening?' Anabelle asked.

Karen was looking around, eyes going wide again. 'Where am I?'

'Anabelle, can you sit with Karen, please?' I smiled when I asked, but I didn't take my eyes from Raina. The door had closed behind her, and there wasn't enough room to maneuver, not really. If Cassandra could hold her for a even a few seconds, I could get the gun out, but somehow I didn't think Raina had come to fight. I think she'd have worn different shoes.

Anabelle sat on the couch and literally held Karen's hand. But she was watching the rest of us. Hell, it might be a better show than what was outside.

'What do you want, Raina?' I asked.

She gave a wide smile with her lipsticked mouth, baring small, even white teeth. 'It's the ladies' room, isn't it? I came to powder my nose. And to see how our frightened guest is doing.' She took two steps into the room, and Cassandra moved in front of her, blocking her way.

Raina stared down at her. 'You forget yourself, wolf.' Her voice held a low edge of growl.

'I forget nothing,' Cassandra said.

'Then stand aside,' she said.

'What did you mean by *our guest*?' I asked.

She smiled at me. 'I am Jean-Claude's partner in this little enterprise. Didn't he tell you?' From the look on her face, she knew the answer and was enjoying it.

'I guess it slipped his mind,' I said. 'Why aren't you part of the show then?'

'I'm a silent partner,' she said. She pushed past Cassandra, body brushing the smaller woman. She knelt by the couch. 'How are you feeling, my dear?'

Karen stammered, 'I just want to go home.'

'Of course you do.' She glanced up and smiled. 'If one of you would help me get her to her feet, there's a cab waiting to take her anywhere she wants to go at the club's expense. Or did you want to ride home with your friends?'

Karen shook her head. 'They aren't my friends.'

'So wise of you to realize that,' Raina said. 'So many people put their trust in the wrong people.' She stared at me while she said the last. 'And they get hurt, or worse.'

Anabelle had moved away from Raina. She was staring at all of us, clutching her purse. I don't think she understood everything we were saying, but she obviously was not having a good time. One good deed and she was already being punished.

'Can you stand? Why don't you help me?' Raina asked Anabelle.

'No, let Cassandra help you,' I said.

'Afraid I might eat your newfound friend?'

I smiled. 'You'll eat anything that can't get away. We all know that.'

Her face tightened, anger flashing through her amber brown eyes. 'In the end, Anita, we will see who eats what.' She helped the woman to stand.

Cassandra whispered, 'Jean-Claude told me to guard you.'

'Make sure she gets into a cab that really is going to take her home. Then you can follow me around for the rest of the evening, okay?'

Cassandra nodded. 'Jean-Claude won't like it.'

'I'm not too happy with him right now, either,' I said.

'A little help here,' Raina said.

Cassandra sighed, but she took Karen's other arm, and they helped her through the door. When the door closed behind them, Anabelle let out a long sigh. 'What is going on?'

I turned to the lighted mirror, leaning my hands on the vanity top. I shook my head. 'It's too long a story, and the less you know, the safer you'll be.'

'I have to confess I have an ulterior motive.' I watched her through the mirror, and she looked embarrassed. 'I didn't just help out of the goodness of my heart. I'm a reporter, freelance. A quote from the Executioner would really put me on the map. I mean I could name my price, especially if you explained what just happened here.'

I bowed my head. 'A reporter. Not exactly what I needed tonight.'

Anabelle came up behind me. 'It was real on the dance floor, wasn't it? That vampire – Damian, right? He was really going to do her, right there, as part of the show.'

I watched her face in the mirror. She was vibrating with eagerness. She wanted to touch me. You could see her hands fluttering, nervous. It was a big story if I corroborated it. It would serve Jean-Claude right if I did.

Something went through Anabelle's eyes. Some of the brightness leaked away.

Several things happened almost simultaneously. Anabelle jerked my purse, the strap broke, she took a step back, and drew a gun from an inner-pants holster under her vest. The door opened, and three laughing women entered. The women screamed.

Anabelle looked at the door for just a heartbeat. I drew a knife and turned. I didn't try and walk those two steps to her. I dropped to one knee and lunged my body like a line with the knife as the point. The knife entered her upper stomach. The gun moved towards me. I used my left hand to sweep the arm away. The shot went wild, cracking the mirror. I shoved the knife upward, under her sternum, shoved it until the hilt met flesh and bone, and jerked the blade up and sideways. Her hand convulsed on the gun and another shot hit the carpeted floor. The silencer made each shot seem muffled, almost anti-climactic.

She sank to her knees, eyes wide, mouth opening and closing. I ran my hand down her arm and took the gun from her. She blinked at me, eyes unbelieving, then she fell abruptly as if her strings had been cut. She twitched twice and died.

Edward was at the door, gun out, pointed. He stared from me to the fresh corpse. He took in the knife still protruding from her chest, the gun with silencer in my hand. He relaxed, pointing the gun at the floor. 'Some bodyguard I turned out to be, letting you get dusted in the ladies' room.'

I stared up at him. I felt numb, distant with shock. 'She almost got me,' I said.

'But she didn't,' he said.

I heard men's voices shouting, 'Police! Everybody stay where they are. We'll check it out.'

'Shit,' I said softly and with feeling. I laid Anabelle's gun by her body and sat back on the carpet. I wasn't sure I could stand right then.

Edward holstered his gun and moved back from the door to join the crowd that was pushing forward to see the show. Just another part of the anonymous throng. Yeah, right.

I sat there beside the corpse and tried to think of something to tell the cops. I wasn't sure the truth was an option I could afford right now. I began to wonder if I was going to see the inside of a jail tonight. Watching the blood soak the front of Anabelle's vest, it seemed likely.

17

I was sitting in a straight-backed chair in Jean-Claude's office at Danse Macabre. My hands were cuffed behind me. They hadn't let me wash the blood off my right hand, and it had dried to a nice tacky substance. I was used to having dried blood on me, but it was still uncomfortable. The uniformed officers had taken the other knife and found the Seecamp in my purse. They had not found the big knife in the spine sheath. It had been a sloppy search to have missed a knife longer than my forearm, but the uniform that did it had at first assumed that I was another victim. It had shaken him to find out that the pretty little woman was a murderer. Oh, excuse me, alleged murderer.

The office had white walls, black carpet, a desk that looked like carved ebony. There was a red lacquer screen with a black castle done high on top of a black mountain. There was a framed kimono on the far wall, scarlet with black and royal blue designs. Two smaller frames held fans: one white and black with what looked like a tea ceremony painted on it, the other blue and white with a flock of cranes. I liked the cranes best, and I'd had plenty of time to make a choice.

One of the uniforms had remained in the room with me the entire time. They'd drunk coffee and not offered me any. The younger uniform would have uncuffed me, but his partner had pretty much threatened to beat the shit out of him if he did it. The partner was grey-haired with eyes as cold and empty as Edward's. His name was Rizzo. Looking at him, I was glad I'd put the gun on the floor before he came into the room.

Why, you may ask, wasn't I at the police station being questioned? Answer: The media had bayed us. Four uniforms had been enough to control traffic and keep the media from mobbing anyone – until they smelled a breaking story. Suddenly, there were cameras and microphones everywhere, like mushrooms after a rain. The uniforms had called for backup and barricaded the murder scene and the office. Everything else had fallen to the cameras and microphones.

There was a homicide detective standing over me – looming, actually. Detective Greeley was just under six feet tall, so broad-shouldered he looked like a big square. Most black people aren't truly black, but Greeley was close. His face was so dark it had purple highlights. His close-cropped greying hair looked like wool. But black, white, or brown, his dark eyes were neutral, secret, cop eyes. His gaze said he'd seen it all and hadn't been impressed by any of it. He certainly wasn't impressed by me. If anything, he looked bored, but I knew better. I'd seen Dolph get the same look right before he pounced on someone and tore their alibi apart.

Since I didn't have an alibi, I wasn't worried about that. I'd told my story before they read me my rights. After Greeley mirandized me, all I'd said was that I wanted a lawyer. I was beginning to sound like a broken record, even to me.

The detective pulled a chair around so he was sitting facing me. He even hunkered down trying not to be so intimidating. 'Once we get a lawyer in here,' Greeley said, 'we can't help you anymore, Anita.'

He didn't know me well enough to call me by my first name, but I let it go. He was pretending to be my friend. I knew better. Cops are never your friends if they suspect you of murder. Conflict of interest.

'It sounds like a clear-cut case of self-defense. Tell me what happened, and I'll bet we can do a deal.'

'I want my lawyer,' I said.

'Once we involve a lawyer, the deal goes out the window,' he said.

'You don't have the authority to make a deal,' I said. 'I want my lawyer.'

The skin around his eyes tightened; otherwise he looked the same, unmoved. But I was pissing him off. Couldn't blame him.

The door to the office opened. Greeley looked up, ready to be angry at the interruption. Dolph walked inside, flashing his badge. His eyes gave the briefest of flicks to me, then settled solidly on Greeley.

Greeley stood up. 'Excuse me, Anita. I'll be right back.' He even managed a friendly smile. He was putting so much effort into the act, it was almost a shame I wasn't buying it. Besides, if he was really being friendly, he'd have taken the cuffs off.

Greeley tried to get Dolph to step outside, but Dolph shook his head. 'The office is secure. The rest of the club isn't.'

'What's that supposed to mean?' Greeley said.

'It means your murder scene, complete with victim, is being flashed on national television. You ordered that no one was to talk to the press, so they've been speculating. Vampires run amok is the choice rumor.'

'You want me to tell the media that a woman attached to a police squad is being charged with murder?'

'You have three witnesses that all say Ms Smith pulled her gun first. That it was self-defense.'

'That's something for the assistant district attorney to decide,' Greeley said.

Funny how when he was talking to me he could make a deal. Now that he was talking to another cop, suddenly the ADA was the only one who could make a deal.

'Call them,' Dolph said.

'Just like that,' Greeley said. 'You want to cut her loose?'

'She'll make a statement after we get her and her lawyer down to the station.'

Greeley made a rude sound in his throat. 'Yeah, she's real hot for her lawyer.'

'Go talk to the press, Greeley.'

'And tell them what?'

'That vampires aren't involved. That it was just bad timing that the murder happened at Danse Macabre.'

Greeley glanced back at me. 'I want her here when I get back, Storr. No disappearing act.'

'We'll both be here.'

Greeley glared at me, all his anger and frustration filling his eyes for a second. The friendly mask was gone. 'Make sure you are. The brass may want you in on this, but this is a homicide case, *my* case.' He shoved a finger at Dolph, not quite touching him. 'Don't fuck with it.'

Greeley pushed past him and shut the door firmly. Silence thick enough to walk on filled the room.

Dolph pulled a chair up in front of the desk, next to me, and sat facing me. He clasped his big hands together and stared. I stared back.

'The three women say Ms Smith pulled her gun first. She ripped your purse off, so she knew where your gun was,' he said.

'I flashed it a little too much tonight. My fault.'

'I heard about you joining the show out there. What happened?'

'I had to police the show a little. The woman didn't want to play. It's illegal to use preternatural powers to coerce anyone into doing something they don't want to do.'

'You aren't a policeman, Anita.'

It was the first time he'd ever reminded me of that. Usually, Dolph treated me like one of his people. He'd even encouraged me to simply say I was with his squad so people would assume I was a detective.

'You kicking me off the squad, Dolph?' My stomach was tight as I asked. I valued working with the police. I valued Dolph and Zerbrowski and the rest of the guys. It would hurt more than I wanted to admit to lose all that.

'Two bodies in two days, Anita, both of them normal humans. That's a lot of explaining at headquarters.'

'If they'd been vamps or some other creepie-crawlie, everyone would look the other way, is that it?'

'Picking a fight with me isn't your best bet right now, Anita.'

We stared at each other for a second or two. I looked away first, and nodded. 'Why are you here, Dolph?'

'I handle the media a lot.'

'But you're letting Greeley talk to the press.'

'You've got to tell me what's going on, Anita.' His voice was quiet, but I knew by the tightness around his eyes, the way he held his shoulders, that he was angry. I guess I couldn't blame him.

'What do you want to hear, Dolph?' I asked.

'The truth would be nice,' he said.

'I think I need a lawyer first.' I wasn't going to spill my guts just because Dolph was my friend. He was still a cop, and I had killed someone.

Dolph's eyes narrowed. He turned to the uniform still leaning against the wall. 'Rizzo, go get some coffee, black, for me. What do you want in yours?'

Coffee was coming. Things were looking up. 'Two sugars, one cream.'

'Get some for yourself, Rizzo, and take your time.'

Officer Rizzo pushed away from the wall where he'd been leaning. 'You sure about this, Sergeant Storr?'

Dolph looked at him, just looked at him.

Rizzo held his hands out in a sort of push away gesture. 'I don't want Greeley riding my ass about leaving you two alone.'

'Get the coffee, Officer Rizzo. I'll take any heat that comes down.'

Rizzo left, shaking his head, probably at the stupidity of plain-clothes detectives. When we were alone, Dolph said, 'Turn around.'

I stood up and offered him my hands. He uncuffed me, but didn't pat me down again. He probably assumed Rizzo had done it. I didn't tell him about the knife they missed, which would piss him off if he found it later, but hey, I couldn't let the cops confiscate all my weapons. Besides, I didn't want to be unarmed tonight.

I sat back down, resisting the urge to rub my wrists. I was heap-big-vampire-slayer. Nothing could hurt me. Yeah, right.

'Talk to me, Anita.'

'Off the record?' I asked.

He stared at me, eyes flat and unreadable, good cop eyes. 'I should say no.'

'But,' I said.

'Off the record, tell me.'

I told him. I changed only one thing: that an anonymous call had alerted me to the contract on me. Other than that, it was the absolute truth. I thought Dolph would be happy, but he wasn't.

'And you don't know why someone would put a contract out on you?'

'For that kind of money, with a time limit on it, no.'

He stared at me, as if trying to decide how much truth I was telling him. 'Why didn't you tell us about the anonymous phone call earlier?' He put a lot of stress on the word *anonymous*.

I shrugged. 'Habit, I guess.'

'No, you wanted to hotdog it. Instead of hiding out, you came here and played bait. If the hitter had used a bomb, you could have gotten a lot of people hurt.'

'But she didn't use a bomb, did she.'

He took a deep breath and let it out slowly. If I hadn't known better, I'd have said he was counting to ten.

'You got lucky,' he said.

'I know.'

Dolph stared at me. 'She nearly did you.'

'If those women hadn't come in when they did, I wouldn't be talking to you now.'

'You don't seem worried.'

'She's dead. I'm not. What's to worry about?'

'For that kind of money, Anita, there'll be someone else tomorrow.'

'It's after midnight, and I'm still alive. Maybe the contract will be canceled.'

'Why the time limit?'

I shook my head. 'If I knew that, I might know who put the hit out on me.'

'And if you find out who put the money up, what will you do?' he asked.

I stared at him. Off the record or not, Dolph was still the ultimate cop. He took his job very seriously. 'I'll turn the name over to you.'

'I wish I believed that, Anita, I really do.'

I gave him my best wide-eyed, innocent look. 'What do you mean?'

'Can the little girl routine, Anita. I know you too well.'

'Fine, but you and I both know that as long as the money is out there, hitters will keep coming. I'm good, Dolph, but no one's that good. Eventually, I'll lose. Unless the money goes away. No contract, no more hitters.'

We stared at each other. 'We can put you in protective custody,' Dolph said.

'For how long? Forever?' I shook my head. 'Besides, the next hitter might use a bomb. You want to risk your people? I don't.'

'So you'll hunt the money man down and kill him.'

'I didn't say that, Dolph.'

'But that's what you're planning,' he said.

'Don't keep asking the question, Dolph. The answer won't change.'

He stood, hands gripping the back of the chair. 'Don't cross the line with me, Anita. We're friends, but I'm a cop first.'

'I value our friendship, Dolph, but I value my life and yours more.'

'You think I can't handle myself?'

'I think you're a cop, and that means you have to play by the rules. Dealing with professional hitters, that can get you killed.'

There was a knock on the door. 'Enter,' Dolph said.

Rizzo came in with a round tray and three slender black china mugs. There were little red coffee stirrers in each one. Rizzo glanced from Dolph to me. He stared at my uncuffed hands but didn't say anything. He sat the tray on the desk far enough from me that I couldn't have grabbed him. Officer Rizzo looked like a twenty-year man, and he was still treating me like a very dangerous person. I doubted that he'd have turned his back on Anabelle. If she hadn't grabbed my purse, she could have shot me in the back. Oh, I'd have seen it in the mirror, but I'd have never gotten my gun out in time. I'd never have let a man, no matter how friendly or how helpful, come up behind me like that. I'd made the same mistake with Anabelle that people made with me. I'd seen a small, pretty woman and underestimated her. I was a female chauvinist piglet. It had nearly been a fatal flaw.

Dolph handed me the mug that held the lightest-colored coffee. It was too much to hope that the cream would be real, but either way it looked wonderful. I'd never met coffee that wasn't wonderful. It was just a matter of how wonderful it was. I took a hesitant sip of the steaming liquid and made appreciative 'mmm' sounds. It was real coffee and real cream.

'Glad you like it,' Rizzo said.

I looked up at him. 'Thank you, Officer.'

He grunted and moved away from us to lean against the other wall.

'I talked to Ted Forrester, your pet bounty hunter. The gun in your purse is registered to him.' Dolph sat back down, blowing on his coffee.

Ted Forrester was one of Edward's aliases. It had stood up to police scrutiny once before when we ended up with bodies on the ground. He was, as far as the police knew, a bounty hunter specializing in preternatural creatures. Most bounty hunters stayed in the Western states where there were still substantial bounties on shapeshifters. Not all of them were particularly careful that the shapeshifter they killed was really a danger to anyone. The only criteria some states had was that after death, the body was medically certified as a lycanthrope. A blood test was sufficient in most cases. Wyoming was thinking of changing its laws because of three wrongful death suits that had made it all the way to their state supreme court.

'I needed a gun small enough to fit in the purse but with stopping power,' I said.

'I don't like bounty hunters, Anita. They abuse the law.'

I sipped coffee and stayed quiet. If he knew just how much Edward abused the law, he'd have locked him up for a very long time.

'If he's a good enough friend to bail your ass out of this kind of trouble, why haven't you mentioned him before? I didn't know he existed until that last trouble you had with those shapeshifter poachers.'

'Poachers,' I said and shook my head.

'What's wrong?' Dolph asked.

'Shapeshifters get killed, and it's poaching. Normal people get killed, and it's murder.'

'You sympathizing with the monsters now, Anita?' he asked. His voice was even quieter, so still you might have mistaken it for calm, but it wasn't. He was pissed.

'You're mad about something other than the body count,' I said.

'You're involved with the Master of the City. Is that how you keep getting all that inside info on the monsters?'

I took a deep breath and let it out. 'Sometimes.'

'You should have told me, Anita.'

'Since when is my personal life police business?'

He just looked at me.

I looked down into my coffee mug, staring at my hands. I finally looked back up. It was hard meeting his eyes, harder than I wanted it to be. 'What do you want me to say, Dolph? That I find it embarrassing that one of the monsters is my boyfriend? I do.'

'Then drop him.'

'If it were that easy, trust me, I'd do it.'

'How can I trust you to do your job, Anita? You're sleeping with the enemy.'

'Why does everyone assume I'm sleeping with him? Doesn't anybody but me date people and not have sex?'

'I apologize for the assumption, but you got to admit a lot of people are going to assume the same thing.'

'I know.'

The door opened, and Greeley came back inside. His eyes took in the handcuffs being gone, the coffee. 'You have a nice chat?'

'How'd your statement to the press go?' Dolph asked.

He shrugged. 'I told them Ms Blake was being questioned in connection with a death on the premises. Told 'em that no vamps were involved. Not sure they believed me. They kept wanting to speak to the Executioner. Though most of them were calling her the Master's girlfriend.'

That made me flinch. Even with a career of my own, I was going to end up being Mrs Jean-Claude in the press. He was more photogenic than I was.

Dolph stood. 'I want to take Anita out of here.'

Greeley stared at him. 'I don't think so.'

Dolph set his coffee on the desk and went to stand next to the other detective. He lowered his voice, and there was a lot of harsh whispering. Greeley shook his head. 'No.'

More whispering. Greeley glared at me. 'All right, but she comes down to the station before the night is over or it's your ass, Sergeant.'

'She'll be there,' Dolph said.

Rizzo was staring at all of us. 'You're taking her out of here, but not to the station house?' It sounded accusatory even to me.

'That's my decision, Rizzo,' Greeley said. 'You got that?' His voice growled the words. Somehow Dolph had pulled rank, and Greeley didn't like it. If Rizzo wanted to make himself a convenient target for that anger, fine.

Rizzo faded back against the wall, but he wasn't happy about it. 'I got that.'

'Get her out of here,' Greeley said. 'Try the back. But I don't know how you'll get past the cameras.'

'We'll walk through,' Dolph said. 'Let's go, Anita.'

I set my mug on the desk. 'What's up, Dolph?'

'I got a body for you to look at.'

'A murder suspect helping with another case. Won't the brass get mad?'

'I cleared it,' Dolph said.

I looked at him, eyes wide. 'How?' I asked.

'You don't want to know,' he said.

I looked at him. He stared back. I finally looked away first. Most of the time, when people said I didn't want to know, it meant just the opposite. It meant I probably needed to know. But from a handful of people, I'd take their word for it. Dolph was one of those people. 'Okay,' I said. 'Let's go.'

Dolph let me wash the dried blood off my hands, and we went.

18

I'm not a big one for idle chatter, but Dolph makes me seem loquacious. We drove down 270 in silence, the hiss of the wheels on the road and the thrum of the engine the only sounds. Either he'd turned off his radio or nobody was committing crimes in Saint Louis tonight. I was betting the radio was off. One of the good things about being a detective on a task force is you don't have to listen to the radio all the time, because most of the calls aren't your problem. If Dolph was needed somewhere, they could always beep him.

I tried to hold out. I tried to make Dolph talk first, but after nearly fifteen minutes, I broke. 'Where are we going?'

'Creve Coeur.'

My eyebrows raised. 'That's a little upscale for a monster kill.'

'Yeah,' he said.

I waited for more; there wasn't any more. 'Well, thanks for enlightening me, Dolph.'

He glanced at me, then back to the road. 'We'll be there in a few minutes, Anita.'

'Patience has never been my strong suit, Dolph.'

His lips twitched, then he smiled. Finally, he laughed, a short, abrupt sound. 'I guess not.'

'Glad I could lighten the mood,' I said.

'You're always good for a laugh when you're not killing people, Anita.'

I didn't know what to say to that. Too close to the truth, maybe. Silence settled over the car, and I left it alone. It was an easy, friendly quiet this time, tinged with laughter. Dolph wasn't mad at me anymore. I could stand a little silence.

Creve Coeur was an older neighborhood, but it didn't look it. The age showed in the large houses set in long, sloping yards. Some of the houses had circular drives and servants' quarters. The few housing developments that had crept in here and there didn't always have big yards, but the houses had variety, pools, rock gardens. No cookie cutter houses, nothing déclassé.

Olive is one of my favorite streets. I like the mix of gas stations, Dunkin' Donuts, custom order jewelry stores, Mercedes-Benz dealerships, and Blockbuster Music and Video. Creve Coeur isn't like most ritzy areas, at war with the peons. This part of the city has embraced both its money and its commerce, as comfortable buying fine antiques as taking the kiddies through the drive-up line at Mickey-D's.

Dolph turned on a road sandwiched between two gas stations. It sloped sharply, making me want to use the brake. Dolph didn't share this desire, and the car coasted down the hill at a nice clip. Well, he was the police. No speeding ticket, I guess. We sped past housing developments that branched off the road like true suburbia. The houses were still more distinct, but the yards had shrunk, and you knew that most of what you were driving past had never had servants' quarters. The road climbed just a touch, then evened out. Dolph hit his turn signal while we were still in the shallow valley. A tasteful sign said Countryside Hills.

Police cars clogged the narrow streets of the subdivision, lights strobing the darkness. There was a huddle of people being held back by uniformed police, people clutching light coats over their jammies or standing with robes tied tight. The crowd was small. As we got out of the car, I saw a drape twitch in a house across the street. Why come outside when you can peek from the comfort of your own home?

Dolph led me through the uniforms and the twist of yellow Do-

Not-Cross tape. The house that was the center of attention was one story with a brick wall as tall as the walls of the house forming an enclosed courtyard. There was even a wrought iron gate to the curved entrance, very Mediterranean. Except for the courtyard, the house looked like a typical suburban ranch. There was a stone path and square, rock-edged beds full of rosebushes. Floodlights filled the walled garden, lending every petal and leaf its own shadow. Someone had gone way overboard on the in-ground lighting.

'You don't even need a flashlight in here,' I said.

Dolph glanced at me. 'You've never been here then?'

I met his eyes and couldn't read them. He was giving me cop eyes. 'No, I've never been here. Should I have been?'

Dolph opened the screened door without answering. He led the way in, and I followed. Dolph prides himself on not influencing his people, letting them come in cold and make their own conclusions. But even for him, he was being mysterious. I didn't like it.

The living room was narrow but long with a TV and video center at the end of it. The room was so thick with cops there was barely room to stand. Every murder scene gets more attention than it needs. Frankly, I wonder if more evidence is lost with all the traffic than is found with all the busy hands. A murder can make a cop's career, especially that jump from uniform to plainclothes. Find *the* clue or *the* evidence, shine at the critical time, and people notice. But it's more than that. Murder is the ultimate insult, the last worst thing you can do to another human being. Cops feel that, maybe more than the rest of us.

The cops parted before Dolph, eyes shifting to me. Most of the eyes were male, and after the first glance, almost all of them did the full body look. You know the look. The one that if the face and top match, they just have to see if the legs are as good as the rest. It works in reverse, too. But any man that starts at my feet and ends with my face has lost every brownie point he ever had.

Two short hallways led straight off the living room at right angles, a dining room directly off of the first room. An open door revealed carpeted stairs leading to a finished basement. Cops were traveling up and down the stairs like ants, with bits of evidence in plastic baggies.

Dolph led me down one of the hallways, and there was a second living room with a fireplace. It was smaller and more boxlike, but the far wall was entirely brick, which made it seem warmer, cozier. The kitchen showed to the left through an open doorway. The top half of the wall was a pass-through, open like a window so you could work in the kitchen and still talk to people in the living room. My father's house had a pass-through.

The next room was obviously new. The walls still had that raw paint look of fresh construction. Sliding glass doors made up the left-hand wall. A hot tub took up most of the floor space. Water still clung in beads to its slick surface. They'd finished the hot tub before they'd painted the room. Priorities.

A hallway so roughed out it still had that heavy plastic they put down for workers to walk on led away from the tub. There was another larger bathroom, not quite finished, and a closed door at the end of the hall. The door was carved, new wood, light-colored oak. It was the first closed door I'd seen inside the house. That was kind of ominous.

Except for the cops, I hadn't seen a damn thing out of place. It looked like a nice upper-middle-class house. A family kind of house. If I'd walked straight into carnage, I'd have been all right, but this long buildup had tightened my stomach, filled me with dread. What had happened in this nice house with its new hot tub and brick fireplace? What had happened that needed my kind of expertise? I didn't want to know. I wanted to leave before I saw some new horror. I'd seen enough bodies already this year to last a lifetime.

Dolph put his hand on the doorknob. I touched his arm. 'It's not kids, is it?' I asked.

He glanced over his shoulder at me. Normally, he wouldn't have answered. He'd have said something cryptic like, 'You'll see in a minute.' Tonight, he said, 'No, it's not kids.'

I took a deep breath through my nose and let it out slowly through my lips. 'Good.' I smelled damp plaster, fresh cement, and underneath that, blood. The scent of freshly spilled blood, faint, just behind the door. What does blood smell like? Metallic, almost artificial. It isn't really much of a smell all by itself. The smell won't make you sick, it's what goes with it. We all know in some ancient part of ourselves that blood is the thing. Without it, we die. If we can steal enough of it from our enemies, we steal their lives. There's a reason that blood has been associated with almost every religion on the planet. It's primal stuff, and no matter how sanitized we make our world, part of us still recognizes that.

Dolph hesitated, hand still on the doorknob. He didn't look at me while he spoke. 'Tell me what you think of the scene, then I have to take you back for a statement. You understand that.'

'I understand,' I said.

'If you're lying to me, Anita, about any of this, tell me tonight. Two bodies in two days takes a lot of explaining.'

'I haven't lied to you, Dolph.' *At least not much*, I added in my head.

He nodded without turning around and opened the door. He went in first and turned so he could watch my face as I entered the room.

'What's wrong, Dolph?' I asked.

'See for yourself,' he said.

All I could see at first was pale grey carpet and a bureau with a large mirror against the right-hand wall. A cluster of cops blocked my view of the rest of the room. The cops stepped aside at a nod from Dolph. Dolph never took his eyes from me, my face. I'd never seen him so intent on my reaction before. It made me nervous.

There was a body on the floor. A man, spread-eagled, pinned

at wrists and ankles with knives. The knives had black hilts. He lay in the middle of a large red circle. The circle had had to be large so the blood didn't leak out and spoil it. Blood had soaked into the pale carpet, spread across it like a red ruin. The man's face was turned away from me. All I could see was short blond hair. His chest was bare, so slick with blood it looked like a red shirt. The knives held him in place. They hadn't been what killed him. No, what had killed him was a gaping hole in his lower chest just below the ribs. It was like a red-lined cave big enough to plunge both hands into.

'They took his heart,' I said.

Dolph looked at me. 'You know that from the doorway?'

'I'm right, aren't I?'

'If you were going to take his heart out, why not go straight down?'

'If you wanted him to survive, like heart surgery, you'd have to break the ribs and go down the hard way. But they wanted him dead. If all you want is the heart, going under the ribs is easier.'

I walked towards the body.

Dolph moved ahead of me, watching my face. 'What?' I said.

He shook his head. 'Just tell me about the body, Anita.'

I stared at him. 'What is your problem tonight?'

'No problem.'

It was a lie. Something was up, but I didn't press it. It wouldn't have done me any good. When Dolph decides not to share information, he doesn't share, period.

There was a king-size bed with purple satin sheets and more pillows than you knew what to do with. The bed was rumpled as if it had been used for something other than sleeping. There were dark stains on the sheets, nearly black.

'Is that blood?'

'We think so,' Dolph said.

I glanced at the body. 'From the murder?'

'When you're finished looking at the body, we'll bag the sheets and get them down to the lab.'

A subtle hint to get on with the job. I walked towards the body and tried to ignore Dolph. That was easier than it sounded. The body sort of stole the show. The closer I got, the more details I could see, and the more I didn't want to see. Under all that blood was a nice chest, muscular but not too much of a good thing. The hair was cut very short, curly and blond. There was something naggingly familiar about that head. The black daggers had silver wire curled around them. They'd been shoved to their hilts in the flesh, bones had broken when they'd been driven in. The red circle was definitely blood. Cabalistic symbols ran round the inside of the circle, traced in blood. I recognized some of them, enough to know that we were dealing with some form of necromancy. I knew the symbols that stood for death and the symbols that watched against it.

For some reason, I didn't want to enter the circle. I walked carefully around the edge of it until I could see the face. With my back leaning against the wall I stared into the wide eyes of Robert the vampire. Monica's husband. The soon-to-be daddy.

'Shit,' I said softly.

'You know him?' Dolph asked.

I nodded. 'Robert. His name's Robert.' The death symbols made sense if you were going to sacrifice a vampire. But why? Why like this?

I took a step forward and hit the circle. I stopped dead. It was like a million insects crawled and swarmed over my body.

I couldn't breathe. I stepped back off the blood line. The sensation stopped. I could still feel it like a memory on my skin, in my head, but I was okay now. I took a deep breath, let it out slowly, and stepped forward again. It wasn't like hitting a wall. It was more like hitting a blanket, a drowning, suffocating, maggot-crawling blanket. I tried to walk forward, tried to move past the circle, and couldn't. I staggered back from it. If the wall hadn't been there, I'd have fallen.

I let myself slide down until I was sitting with my knees tucked up. My toes were inches from the circle. I did not want to touch it again.

Dolph walked through the circle like it wasn't there and knelt beside me, part of him still in the circle. 'Anita, what's wrong?'

I shook my head. 'I'm not sure.' I stared up at him. 'It's a circle of power, and I can't cross it.'

He glanced back at his own body partially inside the circle. 'I can.'

'You're not an animator. I'm not a witch, and I don't know a lot of official magic, but some of the symbols are either death symbols or maybe symbols of protection from the dead.' I stared up at him, my skin still shivering from trying to cross the line. A new horror spread through my mind. 'It's a spell to both contain and keep out the dead, and I can't cross it.'

He stared down at me. 'What exactly does that mean, Anita?'

'It means,' said a female voice, 'that she didn't create the circle.'

19

A woman stood just inside the door. She was tall, slender, dressed in a purple skirt suit with a white man-tailored shirt. She walked into the room with an eagerness that made me knock about ten years off her age. She looked thirty, but she wasn't. Twenty-something and full of herself. Probably around my own age, but there was a shiny newness to her that I'd lost years ago.

Dolph stood, offering me a hand up. I shook my head. 'Unless you want to carry me, I can't stand yet.'

'Anita, this is Detective Reynolds,' he said. He didn't sound entirely happy about it.

Reynolds walked around the edge of the circle as I had, but she was coming for a better view of me. She ended up on the opposite side from Dolph. She stared down at me, smiling, eager. I stared up at her, skin still jumping from trying to force my way past the circle.

She leaned down and whispered, 'You're flashing the room, dear.'

'That's why the underwear matches,' I said.

She looked surprised.

There was no way for me to stretch my legs out without touching the circle again, so if I wanted to quit flashing the room, I had to stand up. I held my hand up to Dolph. 'Help me up, but whatever you do, don't let me fall into that thing.'

Detective Reynolds took my other arm without being invited, but frankly, I needed the help. My legs felt like spaghetti. The moment she touched me, the hair on my body stood at attention. I jerked away from her and would have fallen into the circle if Dolph hadn't caught me.

'What's wrong, Anita?' Dolph asked.

I leaned into him and tried to breathe slowly and evenly. 'I can't take anymore magic right this moment.'

'Get her a chair from the dining room,' Dolph said. He didn't speak to anyone in particular, but a uniform left the room, probably to get the chair.

Dolph picked me up while we waited. Since I couldn't stand, it was hard to protest, but I felt like a damn fool.

'What's on your back, Anita?' Dolph asked.

I'd forgotten about the knife in the spine sheath. I was saved from having to answer by the uniform bringing one of the straight-backed chairs into the room.

Dolph eased me into the chair. 'Did Detective Reynolds try a spell on you?'

I shook my head.

'Someone explain what just happened.'

An unhealthy flush crept up Reynold's pale neck. 'I tried to read her aura, sort of.'

'Why?' Dolph asked.

'Just curious. I've read about necromancers but never met one before.'

I looked up at her. 'If you want to do any more experiments, Detective, ask first.'

She nodded, looking younger, more unsure of herself. 'I am sorry.'

'Reynolds,' Dolph said.

She looked at him. 'Yes, sir.'

'Go stand over there.'

She glanced at both of us and nodded. 'Yes, sir.' She walked over to stand by the other cops. She tried to be nonchalant about it, but she kept looking over at us.

'Since when do you have a witch on the payroll?' I asked.

'Reynolds is the first detective ever with preternatural

abilities. She got her pick of assignments. She wanted to join our squad.'

I was happy to hear him call it 'our' squad. 'She said I didn't draw the circle. Did you really think I'd done that?' I pointed at the body.

He stared down at me. 'You didn't like Robert.'

'If I killed everyone I didn't like, Saint Louis would be littered with bodies,' I said. 'Why else did you drag me down here? She's a witch. She probably knows more about the spell than I do.'

Dolph stared down at me. 'Explain.'

'I raise the dead, but I'm not a trained witch. Most of what I do is just,' I shrugged, 'sort of natural ability. I studied basic magic theory in college, but for only a couple of classes, so if you want feedback on a detailed spell like this one, I can't help you.'

'If Reynolds hadn't been here, what would you have suggested we do?'

'Find a witch to undo the spell for you.'

He nodded. 'Any thoughts on who or why?' He jabbed his thumb behind his back at the body.

'Jean-Claude made Robert a vampire. That's a strong bond. I think the spell was to prevent him from knowing what was happening.'

'Could Robert have alerted his master from this far away?'

I thought about that. I wasn't sure. 'I don't know. Maybe. Some master vampires are better at telepathy than others. I'm not sure how good Jean-Claude is with other vampires.'

'This setup took a while,' Dolph said. 'Why kill him like this?'

'Good question,' I said. I had a nasty idea. 'It's a weird way to do it, but this might be a challenge to Jean-Claude's control over his territory.'

'How so?' Dolph had his little notebook out now, pen poised. It was almost like old times.

'Robert belonged to him, and now somebody's killed him. Could be a message.'

He glanced back at the body. 'But who is the message meant for? Maybe Robert pissed someone off, and it was personal. If it was a message for your boyfriend, why not kill him at Jean-Claude's club? That's where he worked, right?'

I nodded. 'Whoever did this couldn't have pulled off something so elaborate at the club, with other vampires around. No way. They needed privacy. They might have needed the spell just to keep Jean-Claude or some other vamp from riding to the rescue.' I thought about it. What did I really know about Robert? Not much. I knew him as Jean-Claude's flunkie. Monica's boyfriend, now husband. A soon-to-be daddy. Everything I knew about him was through other people's perceptions of him. He'd been killed in his own bedroom, and all I could think of was that it was a message for Jean-Claude. I was thinking of him like a flunkie because Jean-Claude treated him that way. Because he wasn't a master vampire, no one would want to kill him for his own sake. Geez, I was actually thinking of a Robert like disposable commodity. We could always make more.

'You've thought of something,' Dolph said.

'Not really. Maybe I've been hanging around vampires too long. I'm beginning to think like one of them.'

'Explain,' Dolph said.

'I assumed that Robert's death was connected to his master. My first thought was that no one would kill Robert for his own sake, because he wasn't important enough to kill. I mean, killing Robert won't make you Master of the City, so why do it?'

Dolph looked at me. 'You're beginning to worry me, Anita.'

'Worry, hell,' I said, 'I'm beginning to *scare* me.' I tried to look at the murder scene fresh, not like a vampire. Who would go to this much trouble to kill Robert? I didn't have the faintest idea. 'Except for this being a challenge to Jean-Claude's authority, I have no idea why anyone would kill Robert. I guess I don't really know that much about him. It could be one of the hate groups, Humans First or Humans Against Vampires. But they'd have to have some heavy magical know-how, and either group would stone a witch as fast as stake a vampire. They consider them both devil spawn.'

'Why would the hate groups single out this vampire?'

'His wife's pregnant,' I said.

'Another vampire?' Dolph asked.

I shook my head. 'Human.'

Dolph's eyes widened just a fraction. It was the most surprise I'd ever seen from him. Dolph, like most cops, doesn't ruffle easily.

'Pregnant? And the vampire is the father?'

'Yes,' I said.

He shook his head. 'Yeah, that might earn him a starring roll on the hate group hit parade. Tell me about vampire reproduction, Anita.'

'First, I need to call Jean-Claude.'

'Why?'

'Warn him,' I said. 'I agree this probably is something personal to Robert. You're right. Humans First especially would kill him in a heartbeat, but just in case, I want to warn Jean-Claude.' I had another thought. 'Maybe that's why someone wanted me dead.'

'What do you mean?'

'If they want to harm Jean-Claude, killing me would be a good way to do it.'

'I think half a million dollars is a little steep for bumping off someone's girlfriend.' He shook his head. 'That kind of money is personal, Anita. Someone's afraid of you, not your toothy boyfriend.'

'Two hired killers in two days, Dolph, and I still don't know why.' I stared up at him. 'If I don't figure this thing out, I'll be dead.'

He touched my shoulder. 'We'll help you. Cops are good for some things, even if the monsters won't talk to us.'

'Thanks, Dolph.' I patted his hand. 'Did you really believe Reynolds when she said I could have done this?'

He straightened, then met my eyes. 'For a second, yes. After that, it was a matter of listening to my detective. We hired her so she could help out on the preternatural stuff. It would be stupid to ignore her on her first case.'

Not to mention demoralizing, I thought. 'Okay, but did you really think I was capable of doing that?' I motioned towards the body.

'I've seen you stake vamps, Anita. I've seen you decapitate them. Why not this?'

'Because Robert was alive while they carved open his chest. Until they removed his heart, he was alive. Hell, when they took his heart, I'm not sure how long he might have lived. Vampires are strange when it comes to death wounds. Sometimes they linger.'

'Is that why they didn't take his head? So he'd suffer more?'

'Maybe,' I said. 'Jean-Claude needs to be told, in case it is a threat,' I repeated.

'I'll have someone call.'

'You don't trust me to tell him?'

'Leave it alone, Anita.'

For once I did what he asked. Even a year ago I wouldn't have trusted anyone dating a vampire. I'd have assumed they were corrupt. Sometimes, I still assumed that. 'Fine, just call him now. Be bad if Jean-Claude got wasted while we were debating who should warn him.'

Dolph motioned one of the uniforms over. He scribbled something in his notebook, tore the page out, folded it, and handed it to the uniform. 'Take this to Detective Perry.'

The uniform left, note in hand.

Dolph glanced back at his notes. 'Now, tell me about vampire reproduction.' He stared at what he'd written in his notebook. 'Even saying that sounds wrong.'

'Newly dead males often have leftover sperm from before death. That's the most common. Doctors recommend you wait six weeks before sex after you've become a vampire, sort of like after a vasectomy. Those babies are usually healthy. Being fertile is a lot rarer in older vamps. Frankly, until I saw Robert and his wife at a party, I didn't know vamps as old as he is could make babies.'

'How old was Robert?'

'A century and some change.'

'Can female vamps get pregnant?' he asked.

'Sometimes with the newly dead it happens, but the body spontaneously aborts or reabsorbs the baby. A dead body can't give life.' I hesitated.

'What?' Dolph asked.

'There have been two reported cases of an older female vampire giving birth.' I shook my head. 'It wasn't pretty, and it certainly wasn't human.'

'Did the babies survive?'

'For awhile,' I said. 'The case that's the best documented was from the early 1900s. Back when Dr Henry Mulligan was trying to find a cure for vampirism in the basement of Old Saint Louis City Hospital. One of his patients had given birth. Mulligan thought it was a sign that life was returning to her body. The baby had been born with a full set of pointed teeth and been more cannibal than vampire. Doctor Mulligan carried a scar on his wrist from the delivery until the day he died, which was about three years later when one of his patients crushed his face.'

Dolph stared down at his notebook. 'I write it all down. But frankly, this is one bit of information I hope I never have to use. They killed the baby, didn't they?'

'Yes,' I said. 'Before you ask, the father was not mentioned. The implication is that the father was human and may even have been Dr Mulligan himself. Vampires can't make babies without a human partner, as far as we know.'

'Nice to know humans are good for something besides blood,' he said.

I shrugged. 'I guess.' Truthfully the thought of giving birth to a child with severe Vlad syndrome scared the hell out of me. I never planned on having sex with Jean-Claude, but if it ever came up, we were definitely taking precautions. No spontaneous sex, unless it included a condom.

Something must have shown on my face, because he asked, 'Penny for your thoughts.'

'Just glad I have high moral standards, I guess. Like I said, until I saw Robert and his wife, I thought a vampire over a century was sterile. And considering the length of time you'd have to keep the vamp's body temperature up –' I shook my head – 'I don't see how it could be accidental. But they both claimed it was. She hasn't even gotten their amnio results back yet.'

'Amnio test for what?' he asked.

'Vlad syndrome,' I said.

'Is she healthy enough to stand up under this kind of news?' he asked.

I shrugged. 'She looked fine, but I'm no expert. I'd say she shouldn't be told over the phone, and she probably shouldn't be alone. I just don't know.'

'Are you friends with the wife?'

I shook my head. 'No, and don't even ask. I am not going to hold Monica's hand while she cries over her dead husband.'

'All right, all right, it's outside your job description. Maybe I'll let Reynolds do it.'

I glanced at the young woman. She and Monica probably deserved each other, but . . . 'Jean-Claude might know who Monica's friends are. If he doesn't, I know of one. Catherine Maison-Gillete and Monica work together.'

'Monica is a lawyer?' Dolph said.

I nodded.

'Great,' he said.

'How much are you telling Jean-Claude about this?' I asked.

'Why?' Dolph asked.

'Because I want to know how much I can tell him.'

'You don't discuss ongoing homicide cases with the monsters,' he said.'

'The victim was his companion for over a century. He's going to want to talk about it. I need to know what you're telling him so I won't let something slip by accident.'

'You don't have a problem withholding information from your boyfriend?'

'Not on a homicide. Whoever did this is at the very least a witch, and maybe something scarier. It's probably one of the monsters, one way or another. So we can't tell the monsters all the details.'

Dolph looked at me long and steady, then nodded. 'Keep back the heart and the symbols used in the spell.'

'He'll have to know about the heart, Dolph, or he'll guess. Head or heart, there isn't a lot else that'll kill a century-old vamp.'

'You said you'd withhold information, Anita.'

'I'm telling you what will wash and what won't, Dolph. Keeping back the heart from the vamps won't work because they'll guess. The symbols, fine, but even there, Jean-Claude's going to have to have to wonder why he didn't feel Robert die.'

'So what *can* we withhold from your boyfriend?'

'The exact symbols used in the spell. The knives.' I thought about it for a moment. 'How they got the heart out: Most people will still go through the ribs to tear out a heart. They see all the hospital shows on TV and they don't think about doing it differently.'

'So if we get a suspect, we ask how'd you get the heart out?'

I nodded. 'The crazies will start talking about stakes. Or be vague.'

'Okay,' he said. Dolph looked at me. 'If anyone hated the

monsters, I thought it was you. How can you date one of them?'

I met his eyes this time, not flinching. 'I don't know.'

He closed his notebook. 'Greeley's probably wondering where I took you.'

'What did you whisper to him? I would have bet money that he'd have held on to me.'

'Told him you were a suspect in another murder. Said I wanted to watch your reaction.'

'And he bought that?'

Dolph glanced back at the body. 'Close to the truth, Anita.'

He had me there. 'Greeley didn't seem to like me very much,' I said.

'You'd just killed a woman, Anita. Tends to give a bad first impression.'

He had a point. 'Do I need to have Catherine meet us down at the station?' I asked.

'You're not under arrest,' Dolph said.

'I'd still like Catherine to meet us at the station.'

'Call her.'

I stood.

Dolph touched my arm. 'Wait.' He turned to the other cops. 'Everybody wait outside for a minute.' There were some glances, but no one argued, they just went. They'd all worked with Dolph before, and no one present outranked him.

When we were alone behind closed doors, he said, 'Give it up.'

'What?'

'You've got some kind of freaking blade down your back. Let's see it.'

I sighed and reached under my hair to the hilt. I drew the knife out. It took a while. It was a long knife.

Dolph held out his hand. I handed it to him.

He balanced it on his open hands and gave a low whistle. 'Jesus, what were you planning to do with this?'

I just looked at him.

'Who frisked you at the club?'

'Rizzo's partner,' I said.

'Have to have a talk with him.' Dolph looked up at me. 'Be a bad thing to miss on someone who might use it. Is it the only weapon he missed?'

'Yep.'

He stared at me. 'Lean on the bureau, Anita.'

My eyebrows raised. 'You're going to pat me down?'

'Yeah.'

I thought about arguing but decided not to. There were no more weapons to find. I leaned on the bureau. Dolph laid the knife on the chair and searched me. If there'd been anything to fide, he'd have found it. Dolph was thorough in everything he did, methodical. It was one of the things that made him a great cop.

I looked at him in the mirror without turning around. 'Satisfied?'

'Yeah.' He handed the knife back to me, hilt first.

I must have looked as surprised as I felt. 'You're giving it back to me?'

'If you'd lied to me about it being your last weapon, I'd have kept it and everything I found.' He took a deep breath and let it out. 'But I won't take your last weapon, not with a contract out on you.'

I took the knife and resheathed it. It was a lot harder putting it back than getting it out. I finally had to use the mirror to sort of direct me.

'I take it it's a new weapon?' Dolph asked.

'Yeah.' I flipped my hair out over the sheath and presto, you couldn't see it. I was really going to have practice with it more. It was too good a hiding place not to use more often.

'Any other impressions of the scene before I take you back?'

'Was there forced entry?'

'No.'

'Someone he knew then,' I said.

'Maybe.'

I glanced at Robert's still form. 'Could we finish this discussion in another room?'

'This one bother you?'

'I knew him, Dolph. I might not have liked him, but I knew him.'

Dolph nodded. 'You can finish telling me all about it in the nursery.'

I looked at him. I could feel myself going pale. I was not up to seeing what Monica would have done with a nursery. 'You're developing a mean streak, Dolph.'

'Can't seem to get past the fact you're dating the Master of the City, Anita. Just can't shake it.'

'You want to punish me because I'm dating a vampire?'

He looked at me, a long searching look. I didn't look away. 'I want you to not date him.'

'You're not my dad.'

'Does your family know?'

I did look away then. 'No.'

'They're Catholic, aren't they?'

'I am not going to have this discussion with you, Dolph.'

'You need to have it with someone,' he said.

'Maybe, but not with you.'

'Look at him, Anita. Look at him, and tell me you could sleep with that.'

'Drop it,' I said.

'I can't.'

We stared at each other. I was not going to stand here and explain my relationship with Jean-Claude to Dolph. It wasn't any of his business. 'Then we have a problem.'

There was a knock on the door. 'Not now,' Dolph said.

'Come in,' I said.

The door opened. Goody. Zerbrowski walked in. Even better. I knew I was grinning like an idiot, but I couldn't seem to stop. The last time I'd seen him had been the day he got out of the hospital. He'd been nearly gutted by a shapeshifter, a wereleopard the size of a pony. His attacker had been not a lycanthrope but a shapeshifting witch. That was why Zerbrowski wasn't turning furry once a month. The witch had clawed him up horribly. I'd killed it. I'd held my hands over his stomach and pressed his intestines back into his body. I still had the scars from the same monster.

Zerbrowski's hair is normally curly and a mess, black going grey. He'd cut it short enough that it stayed in place. Made him look more serious, more grown-up, less like Zerbrowski. His suit was brown and looked like he'd slept in it. His tie was medium blue and matched nothing that he was wearing.

'Blake, long time no see.'

I couldn't help myself; I walked over and hugged him. There are benefits to being a girl. Though, before Richard came into my life, I might have resisted the urge. Richard was bringing out my feminine side.

Zerbrowski hugged me awkwardly, laughing. 'I always knew you wanted my body, Blake.'

I pushed away from him. 'You wish.'

He eyed me up and down, eyes glittering with laughter. 'If you dress up like that every night, I might leave Katie for you. If that skirt was any shorter, it'd be a lamp shade.'

Even with the teasing, I was glad to see him. 'How long have you been back on full duty?'

'Not long. I saw you on the news with your boyfriend.'

'News?' I said. I'd forgotten about the media blitz Jean-Claude and I had walked through.

'He sure was pretty for a dead guy.'

'Shit.'

'What?' Dolph asked.

'It was national media, not just local.'

'So?'

'My father doesn't know.'

Zerbrowski laughed. 'He does now.'

'Shit.'

'I guess you'll have that talk with your father after all,' Dolph said.

There must have been something in Dolph's voice or my face, because the humor faded from Zerbrowski's face. 'What's up, you two? You look like someone stepped on your puppy.'

Dolph looked at me. I looked at him. 'Philosophical differences,' I said finally. Dolph didn't add anything. I hadn't really expected him to.

'Okay,' Zerbrowski said. He knew Dolph well enough not to pry. Me alone, he'd have bugged the hell out of me, but not Dolph.

'One of the nearest neighbors is a serious right-wing vampire hater,' he said. That got our attention.

'Explain,' Dolph said.

'Delbert Spalding and his wife Dora sat on the couch, holding hands. She offered me iced tea. He objected to me saying that Robert had been murdered. Said you couldn't kill the dead.' Zerbrowski dug a wrinkled notebook out of his suit pocket. He flipped some pages, tried to smooth the page down, gave up, and quoted. 'Now that someone has destroyed that thing, the woman should abort that monster she's carrying. I don't believe in abortion normally, but this is abomination, pure abomination.'

'Humans Against Vampires, at the very least,' I said, 'Maybe even Humans First.'

'Maybe he just doesn't like living next door to a vampire,' Dolph said.

Zerbrowski and I looked at him.

'Did you ask Mr Spalding if he belonged to either of the hate groups?' Dolph asked.

'He had HAV's newsletters scattered on his coffee table, gave me one.'

'Great,' I said, 'evangelizing hatemongers.'

'HAV doesn't advocate this kind of violence,' Dolph said.

The way he said it made me wonder what mailing list Dolph was on. I shook my head. I wouldn't believe the worst of him just because he didn't like me dating the walking dead. A few months back, I'd have felt the same way. 'Humans First does,' I said.

'We'll find out if Mr Spalding is a member of Humans First,' Dolph said.

'You also need to find out if the Spaldings have any magical talent,' I said.

'How?' Dolph said.

'I could meet them, be in the same room with them. To be sure, I might have to touch them, shake hands.'

'I shook Mr Spalding's hand,' Zerbrowski said. 'It was like shaking anybody else's hand.'

'You're a great cop, Zerbrowski, but you're almost a null. You could shake the grand high pooh-bah's hand and not get more than a twinge. Dolph's a complete null.'

'What's a null?' Dolph asked.

'A magical null. Someone who has no magical or psychic ability. It's what let you cross the blood circle and kept me out.'

'So you're saying *I* have some magical ability?' Zerbrowski asked.

I shook my head. 'You're a tiny bit sensitive. Probably one of those people who get hunches that turn out to be right.'

'I get hunches,' Dolph said.

'I'll bet your hunches are based on experience, years of police work. Zerbrowski will make a leap of logic that makes no sense, but proves to be true. Am I wrong?'

They looked at each other, then at me, then both nodded. 'Zerbrowski has his moments,' Dolph said.

'You want to come shake the Spaldings' hands?' Zerbrowski asked.

'Detective Reynolds can do it. It's one of the reasons you brought her on board, right?'

They looked at each other again. Zerbrowski grinned. 'I'll get Reynolds and go back over.' He stopped at the door. 'Katie's been after me to invite you over for dinner, meet the kids, a real domestic affair.' He stared at me with his brown eyes guileless behind dark-rimmed glasses. 'I was going to tell you to bring Richard, but if you're dating Count Dracula now, guess that'd be awkward.' He stared at me, asking without asking.

'I'm still seeing Richard, you pushy son of a bitch.'

He smiled. 'Good. Bring him over a week from Saturday. Katie'll fix her famous mushroom chicken.'

'If I was only dating Jean-Claude, would the invitation still include my boyfriend?'

'No,' he said. 'Katie's a little nervous. I don't think she'd be up to meeting Count Dracula.'

'His name's Jean-Claude.'

'I know.' He shut the door behind him, and Dolph and I were alone with the body once more. The night was not looking up.

'What are we hunting for, Anita?' I was actually relieved that Dolph was talking business. I'd had enough personal chitchat to last the night.

'More than one murderer.'

'Why?'

I looked up at him. 'I don't know if there's enough humans in the world to pin a vampire to the floor like that. Even if it was other vampires or shapeshifters, it'd take more than one. I'd say two beings with abnormal strength to hold, and a third to put in the knives. Maybe more to hold, maybe more to do the spell. I don't know, but at least three.'

'Even if they were vampires?' Dolph asked.

I nodded. 'Unless one vamp was strong enough to have mind control over Robert.' I looked down at the body, careful not to touch the circle. I forced myself to stare at what had been done to him. 'No, once they started putting knives in him, I don't think any mind control would work. A human, yeah, they could have done this to a human and made him smile while they did it, but not another vamp. Did any of the neighbors see or hear anything? I mean the Spaldings may be involved, so they'd lie, but someone had to see or hear something. He didn't go quietly.'

'They say no,' Dolph said. He said it like he knew some or all of them had lied. One of the things cops learn first is that everyone lies. Some people to hide things, some people just for the hell of it, but everyone lies. Assume that everyone is hiding something, it saves time.

I stared at Robert's face, his mouth half-open, slack. There were rubbed marks at each corner of his mouth, a slight reddening. 'Did you notice the marks by his mouth?'

'Yes,' Dolph said.

'And you weren't going to mention them to me?'

'You were a suspect.'

I shook my head. 'You didn't really believe that. You're just playing all the details close to your chest, like always. I get tired of putting the pieces together when you've already done it.'

'So, what do you make of the marks?' he asked, his voice neutral.

'You know damn well what I make of them. He may have been gagged while they did this to him. The neighbors really might not have heard anything. But that still doesn't say how the killers got into the house. If vampires were involved, they couldn't cross the threshold without an invitation. Robert wouldn't have invited strange vamps into his house, so someone with them had to be known, or human, or at least not vampire.'

'Could a human cross the threshold and invite vampires inside?'

'Yes,' I said.

Dolph was making notes, not looking at me. 'So we're looking for a mixed group, at least one vamp, at least one not vamp, at least one witch or necromancer.'

'You got that last from Reynolds,' I said.

'You disagree?'

'No, but since I'm the only necromancer in town, it has to be outside talent.' The moment I said it, I realized that outside talent was in town now. Dominic Dumare.

'John Burke couldn't do it?'

I thought about that. 'John's a vaudun priest, but this isn't voodoo. I don't know if his knowledge of the arcane stretches this far. I also don't know if he's powerful enough to have done this, even with the knowledge.'

'Are you powerful enough?'

I sighed. 'I don't know, Dolph. I'm sort of new at necromancy. I mean, I've raised the dead for years, but not this formally.' I motioned at the body. 'I've never seen a spell like this.'

He nodded. 'Anything else?'

I hated dragging Dominic into it, but it was too bloody big a coincidence that a powerful necromancer hits town and a vamp gets taken out with necromancy. If he was innocent, I'd apologize. If he wasn't innocent, it was a death penalty case.

'Dominic Dumare is a necromancer. He just got into town.'

'Could he have done this?' Dolph asked.

'I only met the man once, Dolph.'

'Give me an opinion, Anita.'

I thought about the feel of Dominic in my head. His offer to teach me necromancy. The big thing was that killing Robert and leaving the body for us to find was stupid. Dominic Dumare didn't strike me as a stupid man.

'He could have. He's a vampire's human servant, so it gives you two of your mixed group.'

'Did the vampire know Robert?'

I shook my head. 'Not to my knowledge.'

'You got a number where we can reach Mr Dumare?'

'I can call our night secretary and get it for you.'

'Great.' Dolph stared down at his notes. 'Is Dumare your best suspect?'

I thought about that. 'Yeah, I guess he is.'

'You got any proof?'

'He's a necromancer, and this was done by someone with knowledge of necromancy.' I shrugged.

'The same reason we suspected you,' Dolph said. He almost smiled when he said it.

'Point taken,' I said. 'Prejudiced little me.'

Dolph closed his notebook. 'I'll take you down for your statement then.'

'Fine. Now can I call Catherine?'

'There's a phone in the kitchen.'

Zerbrowski opened the door. 'The wife's here, and she's pretty hysterical.'

'Who's with her?' Dolph asked.

'Reynolds.'

Through the open door, I heard a woman talking, just below the level of screaming. 'Robert, my husband, dead? He can't be dead. He can't be dead. I have to see him. You don't understand what he is. He isn't dead.' The voice was coming closer.

'She's doesn't need to see this, Anita.'

I nodded. I walked out the door and closed it tightly behind me. I couldn't see Monica yet, but I could hear her. Her voice rising, growing thinner with panic. 'You don't understand. He isn't really dead.'

I was betting that Monica wouldn't take my word for Robert being well and truly dead. I guess if it was Jean-Claude lying in there, I wouldn't, either. I'd have to see for myself. I took a deep breath and walked forward to meet the grieving widow. Damn. This night just kept getting better and better.

20

The hospital room was soft mauve with paintings of flowers on the wall. The bed had a mauve bedspread and pink sheets. Monica lay in the bed hooked up to an IV and two different kinds of monitors. A strap across her belly monitored the contractions. Gratefully, the lines had gone flat. The other monitor was the baby's heartbeat. The sound had scared me at first; too fast, like the heart of a small bird. When the nurses assured me the heartbeat was normal, I relaxed. After nearly two hours, the frantic beat had become a comforting sound like white noise.

Monica's auburn hair was plastered in wet tendrils to her forehead. Her careful makeup was smeared across her face. They had been forced to give her a sedative, though it wasn't great for the baby. She had fallen into a light, almost feverish sleep. Her head turned, eyes flicking behind her lids, mouth working, caught in some dream, a very bad dream probably, after the night she'd had. It was almost two o'clock, and I still had to go to the station and make my statement to Detective Greeley. Catherine was on her way to take my place at Monica's bedside. I'd be glad to see her.

I had little crescent nail marks on my right hand. Monica had clung to it like it was all that was holding her together. At the worst of the contractions, when it looked like Monica would lose her baby as well as her husband, her long, painted nails had bitten into me, and only when blood trickled down my hand in fine crimson lines did a nurse say something. When Monica calmed down, they had insisted on messing with the wounds. They'd used the cartoon bandages they kept for the babies, so that my hand was covered in Mickey Mouse and Goofy.

There was a television on a shelf on the wall, but I hadn't turned it on. The only sounds were the whirr of air circulating through the vents and the baby's heartbeat.

A uniformed cop stood outside the door. If Robert had been killed by a hate group, then Monica and the baby were possible targets. If he'd been killed for personal reasons, Monica might know something. Either way, she was in danger. So they'd put a guard on her. Fine with me, since all I had left was a knife. I was really missing my guns.

The phone on the bedside table rang, and I flung myself out of the chair, scrambling for it, terrified that it would wake Monica. I cupped the receiver against my mouth and spoke quietly while my pulse pounded. 'Yes?'

'Anita?' It was Edward.

'How did you know where I was?'

'All that matters is that if I can find you, so can someone else.'

'Is the contract still on?'

'Yes.'

'Damn. What about the time deadline?'

'Expanded to forty-eight hours.'

'Well, shit. Aren't *they* determined.'

'I think you should go underground for awhile, Anita.'

'You mean hide?'

'Yeah.'

'I thought you wanted me to be bait.'

'If you stay out as bait, we need more bodyguards. The were-wolves and vamps are monsters, but they're still amateurs. We're professionals, it's what gives us our edge. I'm good, but I can't be everywhere.'

'Like following me into the women's john,' I said.

I heard him sigh. 'I let you down.'

'I was careless, too, Edward.'

'So you agree?'

'To hiding? Yeah. You got some place in mind?'

'As a matter of fact, I do.'

'I don't like the tone in your voice, Edward.'

'It's the most secure place in town and has built-in bodyguards.'

'Where?' That one word sounded suspicious even to me.

'Circus of the Damned,' he said.

'You have got to be out of your freaking mind.'

'It's the Master's daytime retreat, Anita. It's a fortress. Jean-Claude's sealed up the tunnel we came through to get Nikolaos. It's secure.'

'You want me to spend the day bedded down with vampires. I don't think so.'

'You going back to Richard's house?' Edward asked. 'How safe are you going to be there? How safe will you be anywhere above ground?'

'Dammit, Edward.'

'I'm right, and you know it.'

I wanted to argue, but he *was* right. The Circus was the most secure place I knew. Hell, the place had dungeons. But the idea of voluntarily sleeping there made my skin crawl.

'How can I rest surrounded by vampires, even friendly ones?'

'Jean-Claude s offered you his bed. Before you get mad, he'll sleep in his coffin.'

'That's what he says now,' I said.

'I'm not worried about your virtue, Anita. I'm worried about keeping you alive. And I'm admitting that I can't keep you safe. I'm good. I'm the best money can buy, but I'm only one person. One person, no matter how good, isn't enough.'

That was scary. Edward admitting that he was in over his head. I never thought I'd live to see it. Come to think of it, I almost hadn't.

'Okay, I'll do it, but for how long?'

'You hide out, and I'll check some things. If I don't have to guard you, I can do more.'

'How long?'

'A day, maybe two.'

'What if whoever it is finds out I'm at the Circus?'

'They might try for you,' Edward said. His voice was very matter-of-fact when he said it.

'And if they do?'

'If you, a half dozen vampires, and almost that many were-wolves can't handle the action, then I don't think it matters.'

'You're just comforting as hell.'

'I know you, Anita. If I was any more comforting, you might refuse to hide.'

'Twenty-four hours, Edward, then I want another plan. I am not going to hide at the bottom of a hole and wait for people to kill me.'

'Agreed. I'll pick you up after you make your statement to the cops.'

'Where do you get your information?'

He laughed, but it was harsh. 'If I know where you'll be, so does someone else. Might ask your cop friends if they have a spare vest.'

'You mean a bulletproof vest?'

'Couldn't hurt.'

'Are you trying to scare me?'

'Yes.'

'You're doing a good job.'

'Thanks. Don't come out of the police station until I come in and get you. Avoid being in the open if you can.'

'You really think someone else will try to hit me tonight?'

'We're planning for worst-case scenarios from now on, Anita. No more chances. I'll see you then.' He hung up before I could say anything else.

I stood there holding the phone, scared. In all the panic with Monica and her baby, I'd almost forgotten that someone was trying to kill me. Probably not a good thing to forget.

I started to hang the phone up, but dialed Richard's number instead. He answered on the second ring, which meant he'd been waiting up. Damn.

'Richard, it's me.'

'Anita, where are you?' His voice sounded relieved, then cautious. 'I mean, are you coming back here tonight?'

The answer was no, but not for the reasons he feared. I told him what had happened, the shortest possible version.

'Whose idea was it that you stay with Jean-Claude?' There was a hint of anger in his voice.

'I am not staying with Jean-Claude. I am staying at the Circus.'

'And the difference is what?'

'Look, Richard, I am too tired to argue with you about this. Edward suggested it, and you know he likes Jean-Claude even less than you do.'

'I doubt that,' he said.

'Richard, I did not call you to fight. I called to tell you what's happening.'

'I appreciate the call.' I'd never heard him sound so sarcastic. 'Do you want your clothes?'

'Damn, I hadn't even thought about that.'

'I'll bring them to the Circus.'

'You don't have to do that, Richard.'

'You don't want me to?'

'No, I'd love to have my stuff, and not just the clothes if you get my drift?'

'I'll bring it all.'

'Thanks.'

'I'll pack a bag for myself.'

'Do you think that's a good idea?'

'I've stayed at the Circus before. Remember, I used to be one of Jean-Claude's wolves.'

'I remember. Should you ask Jean-Claude's permission before you invite yourself over?'

'I'll phone first. Unless you don't want me there tonight.' His voice was very quiet.

'If it's okay with Jean-Claude, it's fine with me. I could use the moral support.'

He let out a breath like he'd been holding it. 'Great. Great, I'll see you there.'

'I have to give a statement to the cops about the incident at Danse Macabre. It could take a couple of hours, so don't rush.'

'Afraid Jean-Claude will hurt me?' He was quiet for a moment. 'Or are you afraid I'll hurt him?'

I thought about that. 'Worried about you.'

'Glad to hear it,' he said, and I could hear him smile.

The reason I wasn't worried about Richard is he wasn't a killer. Jean-Claude was. Richard might start a fight, but Jean-Claude would finish it. I didn't say any of this out loud. Richard wouldn't have appreciated it.

'I'm looking forward to seeing you tonight,' he said.

'Even at the Circus?'

'Anywhere. Love you.'

'Love you, too.'

We hung up. Neither of us had said goodbye, a Freudian slip, perhaps.

I was betting that Richard and Jean-Claude would find something to fight about, and I was really too tired to mess with it. But if I'd told Richard to stay away, he would have assumed I wanted to be alone with Jean-Claude, which was certainly not true. So they'd have their little fight. Frankly, I had my own fight all picked out, one involving me, Jean-Claude, and Damian. They'd broken the law at Danse Macabre, broken it enough that with the right judge, I might have gotten a warrant of execution on Damian. We could have one great big glorious knock-down, drag-out fight.

I wondered where everybody would sleep, and with who.

21

Circus of the Damned is a combination of traveling carnival, circus, and one of the lower rungs of hell. Out front, fanged clowns dance above the lights that spell the name. Posters stretch the sides of the building, proclaiming, 'Watch zombies rise from the grave. See the Lamia — half-snake, half-woman.' There is no trickery at the Circus, everything advertised is absolutely real. It is one of the few vampire tourist attractions that welcome children. If I'd had a kid, I wouldn't have brought the little tyke near the place. Even I didn't feel safe.

Edward had picked me up outside the police station, just like he said he would. My statement had taken three hours, not two. The only reason I got out that soon was Bob, Catherine's husband and fellow lawyer, had finally told them to charge me or let me go. Truthfully, I thought they might charge me. But I had three witnesses saying the killing was self-defense, witnesses that I'd never met before tonight. That helped. The DA usually didn't charge on self-defense cases. Usually.

Edward took me into the Circus through a side door. There were no lights to mark it as special, but there was also no door-knob on the outside of the steel reinforced door. Edward knocked. The door opened, and in we went.

Jason closed the door behind us. I had missed him earlier at Danse Macabre. I certainly would have remembered the outfit. He was wearing a sleeveless plastic shirt, molded to his body. The pants were half crinkly blue cloth that looked like colored foil, with oval plastic windows, exposing his thigh, calf, and as he turned, one buttock.

I shook my head, smiling. 'Please tell me Jean-Claude didn't make you wear that out where people could see you.'

Jason grinned at me and turned so he flashed his butt at me. 'Don't you like it?'

'I'm not sure,' I said.

'Discuss fashion later, in a more secure place,' Edward said. He glanced at the door to our right that led into the main part of the Circus. It was never locked, though it had a sign above the door about authorized personnel only. We were standing in a stone room with an electric light dangling from the ceiling. It was a storage area. A third door was set in the far wall. Behind it was a stairway and the nether regions where the vampires stayed during the day.

'I'll be underground, literally, soon enough, Edward.'

Edward looked at me for a long moment. 'You promised to hide out for twenty-four hours. No going outside for any reason. Don't even go into the main part of the Circus when it's open to the public. Just stay downstairs.'

'Aye, aye, Captain.'

'This isn't a joke, Anita.'

I tugged at the bulletproof vest I'd put over my dress. It was too large for me, hot, and uncomfortable. 'If I thought it was funny, I wouldn't have worn this.'

'I'll bring you some armor that fits when I come back.'

I met his pale blue eyes and saw something I'd never seen before. He was worried.

'You think they're going to kill me, don't you?'

He didn't look away. He didn't flinch. But what I saw in his face made me wish he had. 'When I come back tomorrow, I'll have help with me.'

'What kind of help?'

'My kind.'

'What does that mean?'

He shook his head. 'Twenty-four hours means that you hide until dawn tomorrow, Anita. With luck, I'll have a name for us, and we can kill him. Don't be careless while I'm gone.'

I wanted to say something casual, joking, like 'I didn't know you cared,' but I couldn't. I couldn't joke staring into his serious eyes.

'I'll be careful.'

He nodded. 'Lock the door behind me.' He went outside and Jason locked the door.

Jason leaned against the door for a second. 'Why does he scare me?'

'Because you're not stupid,' I said.

He smiled. 'Thanks.'

'Let's get downstairs,' I said.

'Nervous?'

'It's been a long night, Jason. No games.'

He pushed away from the door and said, 'Lead the way.'

I opened the door to the stone stairway, which led downward. It was wide enough for us to walk abreast. In fact, there was almost room for a third, as if the stairway had been built for wider things than human bodies.

Jason closed the door with a resounding thunk. It made me jump. He started to say something, but the look on my face stopped him. Edward's parting comments had unnerved me. If I didn't know better, I'd have said I was scared. Naw.

Jason walked down the steps ahead of me, exaggerating his walk just a touch to show off his derriere.

'You can cut the peep show,' I said.

'You don't like the view?' He leaned against the wall, hands pressed behind him, showing off his chest.

I laughed and walked past him, clicking my nails down his shirt. It was solid and hard as a beetle's carapace. 'Is that as uncomfortable as it looks?'

He fell into step beside me. 'It's not uncomfortable. The ladies at Danse Macabre liked it a lot.'

I glanced at him. 'I bet they did.'

'I like flirting.'

'No joke.'

He laughed. 'For someone who doesn't flirt, you have a lot of guys after you.'

'Maybe because I don't flirt,' I said.

Jason was quiet as we walked to the bend in the stairs. 'You mean because you're a challenge, they keep coming around?'

'Something like that.'

I couldn't see around the bend of the stairs. I hated not being able to see around corners. But this time I was invited; I hadn't come to kill anybody. The vamps tended to be a lot friendlier when you weren't trying to kill them.

'Is Richard here yet?'

'Not yet.' He glanced back at me. 'Do you think it's a good idea to have them both here at the same time?'

'No,' I said, 'absolutely not.'

'Well, at least we all agree it's a bad idea,' he said.

The door at the bottom of the stairs was iron bound, made of a heavy, dark wood. It looked like a portal to another time – a time when dungeons were in vogue, and knights rescued ladies fair or slaughtered a few peasants and no one minded, except maybe the peasants.

Jason drew a key out of his pants pocket. He unlocked the door and pushed. It opened on well-oiled hinges.

'Since when did you get a key?' I asked.

'I live here now.'

'What about college?'

He shrugged. 'It doesn't seem very important anymore.'

'You plan on being Jean-Claude's lap-wolf forever?'

'I'm having a good time,' he said.

I shook my head. 'I fight like hell to stay free of him, and you just give in. I don't understand that at all.'

'You have a college degree, right?' he asked.

'Yeah.'

'I don't. But here we both are, ending up in the same place.'

He had me there.

Jason motioned me through the door with a low flourish that had imitation Jean-Claude written all over it. Jean-Claude made it seem courtly and real. Jason meant it for a joke.

The door led into Jean-Claude's living room. The ceiling stretched up into darkness, but silken drapes hung in black and white folds that formed cloth walls on three sides. The fourth side was bare stone, painted white. A white stone fireplace looked original, which I knew it wasn't. The mantlepiece was black-veined white marble. A silver fireplace screen hid the hearth. There were four chairs in black and silver grouped around a wood and glass coffee table. A black vase sat on the table filled with white tulips. My high heels sank into the thick, black carpet.

There was one other addition to the room that stopped me in my tracks. A painting hung above the fireplace. Three people dressed in the style of the 1600s. The woman wore white and silver with a square bodice showing quite a bit of décolletage, her brown hair styled in careful ringlets. She held a red rose loosely in one hand. A man stood behind her, tall and slender, with dark gold hair in ringlets over his shoulders. He had a mustache and a Vandyke beard, so dark gold they were almost brown. He wore one of those floppy hats with feathers and was dressed in white and gold. But it was the other man who made me walk towards the painting.

He was seated just behind the woman. He was dressed in black with silver embroidery and a wide lace collar and lace cuffs. He held a floppy black hat with a single white feather and a silver buckle across his lap. Black hair fell in ringlets over his shoulders. He was clean shaven, and the artist had managed to capture the sinking blue of his eyes. I stared at Jean-Claude's face painted hundreds of years before I was born. The other two were smiling. Only he was solemn and perfect, dark to their lightness. He was like the shadow of death come to the ball.

I knew Jean-Claude was centuries old, but I'd never had such obvious proof, never had it shoved in my face. The portrait bothered me for another reason. It made me wonder if Jean-Claude had lied about his age.

A sound made me turn. Jason had slumped into one of the chairs. Jean-Claude stood behind me. He'd taken off his jacket and his curling black hair spilled across the shoulders of his crimson shirt. The shirt cuffs were long and tight at the wrist, held by three antique jet beads just like the high neck of the shirt. Without the jacket to distract the eye, the pale oval of skin framed by the red cloth gleamed. The cloth covered his nipples but left his belly button bare and drew the eye to the top of his black pants. Or maybe it just drew me. It was a bad idea to be here. He was just as dangerous as the assassin, maybe more. Dangerous in ways I had no words for.

He glided towards me in his black boots. I watched him walk closer like a deer caught in headlights. I expected him to flirt or ask how I liked the painting. Instead, he said, 'Tell me of Robert. The police said he was dead, but they know nothing. You have seen the body. Is he truly dead?'

His voice was thick with concern, worry. It caught me completely off guard. 'They took his heart.'

'If it is only a stake through the heart, he might survive if it was removed.'

I shook my head. 'The heart was taken out completely. We couldn't find it in the house or the yard.'

Jean-Claude stopped. He slumped suddenly into one of the chairs, staring at nothing, or nothing I could see. 'Then he is truly gone.' His voice held sorrow the way it sometimes held laughter, so that I felt his words like a cold, grey rain.

'You treated Robert like dirt. Why all this weeping and wailing?'

He looked at me. 'I am not weeping.'

'But you treated him badly.'

'I was his master. If I had treated him kindly, he would have seen it as a sign of weakness. He would have challenged me and I would have killed him. Do not criticize things that you do not understand.' There was anger in that last sentence, enough to brush heat along my skin.

Normally, it would have pissed me off, but tonight . . . 'I apologize. You're right. I don't understand. I didn't think you gave a damn about Robert unless he could further your power.'

'Then you do not understand me at all, *ma petite*. He was my companion for over a century. After a century, I would mourn even an enemy's passing. Robert was not my friend, but he was mine. Mine to punish, mine to reward, mine to protect. I have failed him.'

He stared up at me, eyes gone blue and alien. 'I am grateful to you for seeing to Monica. The last thing I can do for Robert is to tend his wife and child. They will want for nothing.'

He stood suddenly in one smooth motion. 'Come, *ma petite*. I will show you to our room.' I didn't like the *our*, but I didn't argue. This new, improved, emotional Jean-Claude had me confused.

'Who are the other two in the painting?'

He glanced at it. 'Julianna and Asher. She was his human servant. The three of us traveled together for nearly twenty years.'

Good. He couldn't give me some bullshit about the clothing being costumes now. 'You're too young to have been a Musketeer.'

He stared at me, face carefully blank, giving nothing away. 'Whatever do you mean, *ma petite*?'

'Don't even try. The clothing is from the 1600s, around the time of Dumas's *The Three Musketeers*. When we first met, you told me you were two hundred and ten. Eventually, I figured out you were lying, that you were closer to three hundred.'

'If Nikolaos had known my true age, she might have killed me, *ma petite*.'

'Yeah, the old Master of the City was a real bitch. But she's dead. Why still lie?'

'You mean why am I lying to you?' he said.

I nodded. 'Yeah, that's what I mean.'

He smiled. 'You are a necromancer, *ma petite*. I would have thought you could judge my age without my help.'

I tried to read his face and couldn't. 'You've always been hard to read; you know that.'

'So glad I can be a challenge in some area.'

I let that go. He knew exactly how much of a challenge he was, but for the first time in a long time, I was bothered. Telling a vamp's age was one of my talents, not an exact science to be sure, but one I was good at. I'd never been off by this much. 'A century older, my, my.'

'Are you so sure that it is only a century?'

I stared at him. I let his power beat across my skin, rolled the feel of it around in my head. 'Pretty sure.'

He smiled. 'Do not frown so, *ma petite*. Being able to hide my age is one of my talents. I pretended to be a hundred years older when Asher was my companion. It allowed us freedom to wander through the lands of other masters.'

'What made you stop trying to pass for older?'

'Asher needed help, and I was not master enough to help him.' He looked up at the portrait. 'I . . . humbled myself to gain him aid.'

'Why?'

'The Church had a theory that vampires could be cured by holy items. They bound Asher with holy items and silver chains. They used holy water on him, drop by drop, trying to save his soul.'

I stared up at that handsome, smiling face. I'd been bitten by a master vampire once upon a time and had the wound cleansed with holy water. It had felt like a red-hot brand was being shoved into my skin, like all the blood in my body had turned to boiling oil. I had vomited and screamed and thought myself very brave for not passing out altogether. That had been one bite mark, one day. Having what amounted to acid dripped on you until you died was in the top five ways not to go out.

'What happened to the girl, Julianna?'

'She was burned as a witch.'

'Where were you?'

'I had taken a ship to see my mother. She was dying. I was on my way back when I heard Asher's call. I could not get there in time. I swear by all that is holy or unholy that I tried. I rescued Asher, but he never forgave me.'

'He's not dead?' I asked.

'No.'

'How hurt was he?'

'Until I met Sabin I thought Asher's scars the worst injury I'd ever known a vampire to survive.'

'Why did you hang the painting if it bothers you this much?'

He sighed and looked at me. 'Asher sent it as a present, to congratulate me for becoming Master of the City. The three of us were companions, almost family. Asher and I were true friends, both masters, both of near equal power, both in love with Julianna. She was devoted to him, but I had her favor as well.'

'You mean a ménage à trois?'

He nodded.

'Asher doesn't hold a grudge?'

'Oh, no, he holds a grudge. If the council would allow it, he would have come with the picture and had his revenge.'

'To kill you?'

Jean-Claude smiled. 'Asher always had a strong sense of irony, *ma petite*. He petitioned the council for your life, not mine.'

My eyes widened. 'What did I ever do to him?'

'I killed his human servant; he kills mine. Justice.'

I stared back up at the handsome face. 'The council said no?'

'Indeed.'

'You have any other old enemies running around?'

Jean-Claude gave a weak smile. 'Many, *ma petite*, but none in town at the moment.'

I looked up at those smiling faces. I didn't know quite how to phrase it, but said it anyway. 'You all look so young.'

'I am physically the same, *ma petite*.'

I shook my head. 'Maybe young isn't the word I want. Maybe naive.'

He smiled. 'By the time this painting was made, *ma petite*, naive was not a word that described me, either.'

'Fine, have it your way.' I looked at him, studying his face. He was beautiful, but there was something in his eyes that wasn't in the painting, some level of sorrow or terror. Something I had no word for, but it was there just the same. A vampire may not wrinkle up, but living a couple of centuries leaves its mark. Even if it's only a shadow in the eyes, a tightness around the mouth.

I turned to Jason, who was still slumped in the chair. 'Does he give these little history lessons often?'

'Only to you,' Jason said.

'You never ask questions?' I asked.

'I'm just his pet. You don't answer questions for your pet.'

'And that doesn't bother you?'

Jason smiled. 'Why should I care about the painting? The woman's dead, so I can't have sex with her. Why should I care?'

I felt Jean-Claude move past me, but couldn't follow with my eyes. His hand was a blur. The chair clattered to the floor, spilling Jason with it. Blood showed at his mouth.

'Never speak of her again in such a manner.'

Jason touched the back of his hand to his mouth and came away with blood. 'Whatever you say.' He licked the blood off his hand with long slow movements of his tongue.

I stared from one to the other of them. 'You are both crazy.'

'Not crazy, *ma petite*, merely not human.'

'Being a vampire doesn't give you the right to treat people like that. Richard doesn't beat people up.'

'Which is why he will never hold the pack.'

'What's that supposed to mean?'

'Even if he swallows his high morals and kills Marcus, he will not be cruel enough to frighten the rest. He will be challenged again and again. Unless he begins slaughtering people, he will eventually die.'

'Slapping people around won't keep him alive,' I said.

'It would help. Torture works well, but I doubt that Richard would have the stomach for it.'

'I couldn't stomach it.'

'But you litter the ground with bodies, *ma petite*. Killing is the best deterrent of all.'

I was too tired to be having this conversation. 'It's 4:30 in the morning. I want to go to bed.'

Jean-Claude smiled. 'Why, *ma petite*, you are not usually so eager.'

'You know what I mean,' I said.

Jean-Claude took a gliding step towards me. He didn't touch me, but he stood very close and looked at me. 'I know exactly what you mean, *ma petite*.'

That brought heat in a rush up my neck. The words were innocent. He made them sound intimate, obscene.

Jason righted the chair and stood, licking the blood off the corner of his mouth. He said nothing, merely watched us like a well-trained dog, seen and not heard.

Jean-Claude took a step back. I felt him move, but couldn't follow it with my eyes. There had been a time only months ago that it would have looked like magic, like he'd just appeared a few feet away.

He held his hand out towards me. 'Come, *ma petite*. Let us retire for the day.'

I'd held his hand before, so why was I left standing, staring, like he was offering me the forbidden fruit that once tasted would change everything? He was nearly four hundred years old. Jean-Claude's face from all those long years ago was smiling down at me, and there he stood with almost the same smile. If I'd ever needed proof, I had it. He'd struck Jason down like a dog he didn't much like. And still he was so beautiful, it made my chest ache.

I wanted to take his hand. I wanted to run my hands over the red shirt, explore that open oval of flesh. I folded my hands over my stomach and shook my head.

His smile widened until a hint of fang showed. 'You have held my hand before, *ma petite*. Why is tonight any different?' His voice held an edge of mockery.

'Just show me the room, Jean-Claude.'

He let his hand drop to his side, but he didn't seem offended. If anything, he seemed pleased, which irritated me.

'Bring Richard through when he arrives, Jason, but announce him before he comes. I don't want to be interrupted.'

'Anything you say,' Jason said. He smirked at us, at me, a knowing look on his face. Did everyone and their wolf believe I was sleeping with Jean-Claude? Of course, maybe it was a case of the lady protesting too much. Maybe.

'Just bring Richard to the room when he comes,' I said. 'You won't be interrupting anything.' I glanced at Jean-Claude while I said the last.

He laughed, that warm touchable sound of his that wove over my skin like silk. 'Even your resistance to temptation grows thin, *ma petite*.'

I shrugged. I would have liked to argue, but he'd smell a lie.

Even a run-of-the-mill werewolf can smell desire. Jason wasn't run-of-the-mill. So everyone in the room knew I was hot for Jean-Claude. So what?

'*No* is one of my favorite words, Jean-Claude. You should know that by now.'

The laughter faded from his face, leaving his blue, blue eyes gleaming, but not with humor. Something darker and more sure of itself looked out his eyes. 'I survive on hope alone, *ma petite*.'

Jean-Claude parted the black and white drapes to reveal the bare, grey stones that the room was made of. A large hallway stretched deeper into the labyrinth. Torchlight gleamed beyond the electricity of the living room. He stood there, backlit against the flame and the soft modern lights. Some trick of light and shadow plunged half his face into darkness and brought a pinprick glow to his eyes. Or maybe it wasn't a trick of the light. Maybe it was just him.

'Shall we go, *ma petite*?'

I walked into that outer darkness. He didn't try to touch me as I moved past him. I'd have given him a brownie point for resisting the urge, except I knew him too well. He was just biding his time. Touching me now might piss me off. Later, it might not. Even I couldn't guarantee when the mood would be right.

Jean-Claude moved ahead of me. He glanced back over his shoulder. 'After all, *ma petite*, you do not know the way to my bedroom.'

'I've been there once,' I said.

'Carried unconscious and dying. It hardly counts.' He glided down the hall. He put a little extra sway to his walk, somewhat like Jason had done on the stairs, but where it had been funny with the werewolf, Jean-Claude made it utterly seductive.

'You just wanted to walk in front so I'd have to stare at your butt.'

He spoke without turning around. 'No one makes you stare at me, *ma petite*, not even me.'

And that was the truth. The horrible truth. If in some dark part of my heart I hadn't been attracted to him from the beginning, I'd have killed him long ago. Or tried to. I had more legal vampire kills than any other vampire hunter in the country. They didn't call me the Executioner for nothing. So how did I end up being safer in the depths of the Circus of the Damned with the monsters than above ground with the humans? Because somewhere along the line, I didn't kill the monster I should have.

That particular monster was gliding up the hallway ahead of me. And he still had the cutest butt I'd ever seen on a dead man.

22

Jean-Claude leaned one shoulder against the wall. He'd already opened the door. He motioned me inside with a graceful sweep of his hand.

My high heels sank into the deep, white carpet. White wallpaper with tiny silver designs graced the walls. There was a white door in the left-hand wall near the bed. The bed had white satin sheets. A dozen black and white pillows were grouped at the head of the bed. A fan of black and white drapes fell from the ceiling, forming a partial canopy over the bed. The black lacquer vanity and chest of drawers still sat in opposite corners. The wallpaper and the door were new. Guess which bothered me more.

'Where does the door go?'

'The bathroom.' He closed the outer door and walked past me to sit on the edge of the bed. There were no chairs.

'A bathroom. That wasn't here last time,' I said.

'Not in its present form, but it was here just the same.'

He leaned back on his elbows. The movement strained the cloth of his shirt, exposing as much skin as the shirt would allow. The line of dark hair that started low on his belly peeked just above the cloth.

The room was getting warmer. I undid the Velcro fastenings on the bulletproof vest and slid it over my head. 'Where do you want me to put this?'

'Anywhere you like,' he said. His voice was soft and more intimate than the words themselves.

I walked around to the far side of the bed, away from him, and laid the vest across the satin sheets.

He laid back against the sheets, his black hair framing his pale face to perfection. Warmer, it was definitely getting warmer in here.

'Mind if I freshen up?'

'Whatever I have is yours, *ma petite*. You should know that by now.'

I backed into the door and opened it with a feeling of relief. I closed the door without really looking at the bathroom. When I looked up, I let out a silent *wow*.

The room was long and narrow. It had a double sink and mirrors with round white lightbulbs edging it. The sinks were black marble with white veins running through. Every faucet, every metal edge, gleamed silver. The floor was black carpeting. A half wall of silver and mirrored panels hid the black stool against a black wall. Another half wall graced the other side. Then there was the bathtub. Three marble steps led up to a black bathtub, big enough for four people. The faucet was a silver swan with outspread wings. There was no way to take a shower, which was my preferred method, and the swan was a bit much, but other than that, it was lovely.

I sat down on the cool marble edging. It was nearly five in the morning. My eyes burned from lack of sleep. The adrenaline rush of nearly getting killed had long since faded. What I wanted was to be comforted, held, yes, sex was in there somewhere, but that wasn't my highest priority tonight. I think both Richard and Jean-Claude would say it was never my highest priority, but that was their problem. Okay, it was our problem.

If it had been Richard stretched out on the bed in the next room, I would have jumped him tonight. But it wasn't Richard, and once Richard got here, we'd be sleeping in Jean-Claude's bed. Seemed pretty tacky to have sex for the first time in your other boyfriend's bed. But it wasn't just the boys suffering from sexual tension, I was drowning, too.

Was Richard right? Was the fact that Jean-Claude wasn't human the only thing keeping me out of his bed? No. Or at least I didn't think so. Out of Richard's bed? The answer, sadly, was yes, maybe.

I freshened up and couldn't help checking myself in the mirror. The makeup had faded a little, but the liner still made my large, dark eyes stand out in dramatic contrast. The blush was almost gone, and the lipstick had long ago vanished. I had lipstick in my purse. I could freshen that at least. But freshening my lipstick was like admitting I cared what Jean-Claude thought of me. I did care. That was the truly scary part. I did not put on more lipstick. I walked back into the bedroom as is, let him make of it what he would.

He was leaning on one elbow, watching me as I came through the door. '*Ma petite*, you are beautiful.'

I shook my head. 'Pretty, I'll give you, but not beautiful.'

He cocked his head to one side, sending a wave of hair over one shoulder. 'Who told you you were not beautiful?'

I leaned against the door. 'When I was a little girl, my father would come up behind my mother. He would wrap his arms around her waist, bury his face in her hair, and say, "How is the most beautiful woman in the world today?" He said it at least once a day. She would laugh and tell him not to be silly, but I agreed with him. To me, she was the most beautiful woman in the world.'

'She was your mother. All little girls think that of their mother.'

'Maybe, but two years after she died, Dad remarried. He married Judith, who was tall and blond and blue-eyed, and nothing like my mother. If he had really believed my mother was the most beautiful woman in the world, why did he marry some Nordic ice princess? Why didn't he marry someone small and dark like my mother?'

'I don't know, *ma petite*,' he said quietly.

'Judith had a daughter only a couple of years younger than me. Then they had Josh together and he was as blond and blue-eyed as the rest of them. I looked like a small dark mistake in the family photos.'

'Your skin is almost as pale as mine, *ma petite*.'

'But I have my mother's eyes and hair. My hair isn't brunette, it's black. A woman asked Judith once in front of me if I was adopted. Judith said, no, I was from her husband's first marriage.'

Jean-Claude slid off the bed. He moved towards me, and I had to look at the floor. I wanted badly to be held, to be comforted. If it had been Richard, I'd have gone to him. But it wasn't Richard.

Jean-Claude touched my cheek and raised my face until I had to look at him. 'I have lived for over three hundred years. In that time, the ideal of beauty has changed many times. Large breasts, small, thin, curved, tall, short, they have all been the height of beauty at one time or another. But in all that time, *ma petite*, I have never desired anyone the way I desire you.' He leaned towards me, and I didn't move away. His lips brushed mine in a gentle kiss.

He took that one last step to press our bodies together, and I stopped him, one hand on his chest, but all I met was bare skin. The slickness of his cross-shaped burn scar met my fingertips. I moved my hand and found his heart beating against my palm. Not an improvement.

He drew back, a breath, and whispered into my mouth, 'Tell me no, *ma petite*, and I will stop.'

I had to swallow twice before I could speak. 'No.'

Jean-Claude stepped away from me. He lay back on the bed as he had earlier, propped on his elbows, his legs from the knees hung off the bed. He stared at me, daring me to come join him, I think.

I wasn't that stupid. There was some dark part of me that was tempted. Lust has less logic than love, sometimes, but it's easier to fight.

'I have played the mortal for you these many months. I thought in March when you held my naked body, when you shared blood with me, that it would be a changing point for us. That you would give in to your desire and admit your feelings for me.'

A burning wash of color crept up my face. I had no good excuse for the foreplay that got out of hand. I was weak, so sue me. 'I gave you blood because you were dying. I'd have never done it otherwise. You know that.'

He stared at me. It wasn't vampire tricks that made me want to look away. It was a raw honesty that I'd never seen in his face before. 'I know that now, *ma petite*. When we returned from Branson, you threw yourself into Richard's arms as though he were a life-line. We continued to date, but you drew away. I felt it and did not know how to stop it.'

He sat up on the bed, hands clasped in his lap. A look of frustration and confusion passed over his face. 'I have never had another woman deny me, *ma petite*.'

I laughed. 'Oh, your ego isn't big.'

'It is not ego, *ma petite*, it is the truth.'

I leaned against the bathroom door and thought about that one. 'No one in almost three hundred years has ever said no to you?'

'You find that so hard to believe?'

'If I can do it, so can they.'

He shook his head. 'You do not appreciate how very harsh your strength of will is, *ma petite*. It is impressive. You have no idea how impressive.'

'If I'd fallen into your arms the first time we met, or even the dozenth time we met, you'd have bedded me, bled me, and dumped me.'

I watched the truth of my words fill his face. I hadn't realized until this moment how much control he kept over his facial expressions, how it was the lack of reaction that made him seem more otherworldly than he was.

'You are right,' he said. 'If you had giggled and fawned over me, I would not have given you a second glance. Your partial immunity to my powers was the first attraction. But it was your stubbornness that intrigued me. Your flat refusal of me.'

'I was a challenge.'

'Yes.'

I stared into his suddenly open face. For the first time, I thought I might see the truth in his eyes. 'Good thing I resisted. I don't like being used and tossed aside.'

'Once you were only a challenge, something to be conquered. Then I became intrigued by your growing powers. I saw possibilities that I could use you to strengthen my position if only you would join with me.'

Something like pain passed over his face, and I wanted to ask if it was real. If any of this was real, or if it was only another act. I trusted Jean-Claude to do whatever it took to stay alive. I didn't trust him to tell the truth sitting on a stack of Bibles.

'I saved your ass enough times. I'm your declared human servant. What more do you want?'

'You, *ma petite*.' He stood, but didn't come closer. 'It is no longer challenge or the promise of power that makes me look to you.'

My pulse was suddenly thudding in my throat, and he hadn't done a damn thing.

'I love you, Anita.'

I stared at him, my eyes growing wide. I opened my mouth, closed it. I didn't believe him. He lied so easily, so well. He was the master of manipulation. How could I believe him now? 'What do you want me to say?'

He shook his head, and his face fell back into its normal lines. That beautiful perfection that was what passed for ordinary. But I knew now that even this was a mask, hiding his deeper emotions.

'How did you do that?'

'After several centuries of being forced to school your face into pleasant, unreadable lines, you lose the knack of anything else. My survival has depended on my expression more than once. I wish you understood the effort that little display of humanity cost me.'

'What do you want me to say, Jean-Claude?'

'You love me a little, that I am sure of.'

I shrugged. 'Maybe, but a little isn't enough.'

'You love Richard a lot, don't you?'

I met his eyes and wanted to lie, to save his feelings, but those kinds of lies hurt more than the truth. 'Yeah.'

'Yet, you have not made your choice. You have not told me to leave the two of you to matrimonial bliss. Why is that?'

'Last time we had this talk, you said you'd kill Richard.'

'If that is all that is stopping you, *ma petite*, have no fear. I will not kill Richard merely because you go to his bed and not mine.'

'Since when?' I asked.

'When I threw my support to Richard, Marcus became my enemy. That cannot be changed.' He leaned his shoulder against the dark wooden bedpost closest to me. 'I had thought to petition another pack. There is always an ambitious alpha male out there somewhere. Someone who would like his own pack but either through sentimentality or lack of strength is doomed to play second forever. I could kill Richard and bring someone else in to kill Marcus.'

I listened to his plan told so matter-of-factly. 'What changed your mind?'

'You.'

'Come again?'

'You love him, *ma petite*. You truly love him. His death would destroy something inside of you. When Julianna died, I thought I would never feel for anyone again. And I didn't, until I met you.'

'You won't kill Richard because it would hurt me?'

'*Oui.*'

'So I could tell Richard when he gets here that I've chosen him, and you would let us go off, get married, whatever?'

'Isn't there one hurdle to your marriage besides myself?' he asked.

'What?'

'You must see him change into wolf form.' Jean-Claude smiled and shook his head. 'If Richard was human, you would meet at the door with a smile and a yes. But you fear what he is. He is not human enough for you, *ma petite*.'

'He isn't human enough for himself,' I said.

Jean-Claude raised his eyebrows. 'Yes, Richard runs from his beast, as you have run from me. But Richard shares a body with his beast. He cannot outrun it.'

'I know that.'

'Richard is still running, *ma petite*. And you run with him. If you were secure that you could accept him, all of him, you would have done it by now.'

'He keeps finding excuses not to change for me.'

'He fears your reaction,' Jean-Claude said.

'It's more than that,' I said. 'If I can embrace his beast, I'm not sure he'll be able to accept me.'

Jean-Claude cocked his head to one side. 'I do not understand.'

'He hates what he is so badly. I think if I can accept his beast, he won't . . . he won't love me anymore.'

'Being able to embrace his beast would make you what . . . perverse?'

I nodded. 'I think so.'

'You are trapped on the horns of a nasty dilemma, *ma petite*. He will not make love to you or marry you until you have seen and accepted his beast. Yet if you accept it, you fear he will turn from you.'

'Yeah.'

He shook his head. 'Only you could choose two men in one human lifetime that are this confusing.'

'I didn't do it on purpose.'

He pushed away from the bed. He stopped two small steps from me, staring down. 'I tried to play the mortal for you, *ma petite*. But Richard is much better at being human than I am. I have not been truly human for so very long. If I cannot be the better man, let me be the better monster.'

My eyes narrowed. 'What's that supposed to mean?'

'It means, *ma petite*, that Jason told me of what happened this afternoon. I know how close you and Richard came.'

How much had the lycanthropes been able to hear? More than I was comfortable with, that was for sure. 'I just love being spied on.'

'Do not be flippant, *ma petite*, please.'

It was the please that got me. 'I'm listening.'

'I told you once that if Richard could touch you and I could not, it would not be fair. That is still true.'

I pushed away from the door. He'd stepped over the line. 'Are you asking me to let you touch me where Richard touched me?'

He smiled. 'Such righteous indignation, *ma petite*. But have no fear. Forcing myself upon you in such a way would smack of rape. I have never been interested in such things.'

I took a step back, putting a little space between us. Unless I was really angry, it was never good to get that close. 'So, what are you saying?'

'You have always forbidden me to use vampire tricks, as you call them, with you.' He held a hand up before I could say it. 'I do not mean bespelling you with my eyes. I am not even sure that is possible anymore. I cannot be human, *ma petite*. I am a vampire. Let me show you that has pleasures beyond humanity.'

I shook my head. 'No way.'

'A kiss, *ma petite*, that is all I ask. A chaste kiss.'

'And the catch is?' I asked.

His eyes were solid, sparkling blue. His skin glowed like alabaster under lights.

'I don't think so,' I said.

'If you were truly sure of Richard, I would leave you to him. But does the fact that I love you not earn me so much as a kiss?'

He glided towards me. I backed up, but the door was right there, and there was nowhere to go.

He was like a living sculpture, all ivory and sapphire, too beautiful for words. Too beautiful to touch. His hands smoothed over my forearms, along my hands. I gasped. Power rushed along my skin in a smooth wash, like air dancing over my body.

I must have tensed up because Jean-Claude said, 'It will not hurt, that I promise.'

'Just a kiss,' I whispered.

'Just a kiss,' he whispered. His face lowered towards mine. His lips brushed mine, gently, slowly. The power flowed across his lips into my mouth. I think I stopped breathing for a second. My skin felt like it was melting away and I would sink into his body, into that shining power.

'Looks like I got here just in time.' It was Richard in the doorway.

I shoved my hand into Jean-Claude's chest and pushed him away hard enough for him to stumble. I was gasping for air like I'd been drowning. My skin pulsed and beat with the power that still crawled over me, into me.

'Richard,' I whispered. I wanted to say that it wasn't what it looked like, but I couldn't get enough air.

Jean-Claude turned, smiling. He knew exactly what to say. 'Richard, how good of you to join us. How did you get past my wolf?'

'It wasn't that hard.'

I stared at both of them. I was still having trouble breathing. It felt like every nerve in my body had been touched all at once. The line between pleasure and pain was damn narrow, and I wasn't sure which side this went on.

The light was seeping away from Jean-Claude, leaving him pale, lovely, almost human.

Richard stood directly inside the door. His eyes glowed not with inner light but with anger, an anger that made his eyes dance, tightened the muscles across his shoulders and down his arms so that the effort showed from across the room. I'd never been so aware of how physically large he was. He seemed to fill more space than he should have. The first skin-prickling rush of his power swirled over me.

I took a deep, shaking breath and started walking towards him. The closer I got, the thicker the power, until about six feet from him, it was like stepping into a nearly solid mass of pulsing, vibrating energy.

I stood there, trying to swallow my heart back into my throat. He was dressed in jeans and a green flannel work shirt with sleeves rolled over his forearms. His hair fell loose round his shoulders in a wavy mass. I'd seen him like this a hundred times, but suddenly it was all different. I had never been afraid of Richard, not really. Now, for the first time, I saw that there was something to fear. Something swam behind his eyes, his beast, he called it. It was there now just behind those true, brown eyes. A monster waiting to be set loose.

'Richard,' I said and had to cough to clear my throat, 'what's wrong with you?'

'Tomorrow is the full moon, Anita. Strong emotions aren't good right now.' Rage thinned his face, made those lovely cheekbones high and tight. 'If I hadn't interrupted, would you have broken your promise to me?'

'He still doesn't know what kind of hose I'm wearing,' I said.

Richard smiled, some of the tension easing away.

'Too smooth for garters,' Jean-Claude said. 'Panty hose, though they could be crotchless, of that I am not sure.'

Richard snarled.

I glanced back at Jean-Claude. 'Don't help me.'

He smiled and nodded. He'd leaned his back on one of the bedposts, fingers playing over the bare skin of his chest. It was suggestive, and he meant it to be. Damn him.

A low, bass growl brought my attention back to Richard. He stalked towards the bed as if each movement hurt. The tension sang through the building power. Was I going to get to see him change here and now? If he changed, there'd be a fight, and for the very first time, I was worried for Jean-Claude's safety, as well as Richard's.

'Don't do this, Richard, please.'

He was staring past me at Jean-Claude. I didn't dare look behind to see what mischief the vampire was doing; I had my hands full with the werewolf in front of me.

Something flickered across his face. I was sure Jean-Claude had done something behind my back. Richard made a sound more animal than human and rushed for the bed. I didn't move out of the way. I stood my ground, and when he was even with me, moving past me, I threw my body into him and threw him in a nearly perfect shoulder roll. His momentum did the rest. Maybe if I'd let go of his arm, we could have avoided the rest, but I made the classic mistake. I didn't think Richard would really hurt me.

He grabbed the arm that was holding him and flung me across the room. He was flat on his back and didn't have much leverage, and that was all that saved me. I was airborne for just a second and rolled along the carpet when I hit. The world was still spinning when my hand went for the knife. I couldn't hear anything but the blood rushing in my own head, but I knew, I knew he was coming.

He touched my arm, rolled me over, and I laid the silver blade against his neck. He froze, bent over, trying, I think, to help me stand. Richard and I stared at each other from inches away. The anger was gone from his face. His eyes were normal, as lovely as ever, but I kept the knife against the smooth skin of his neck, dimpling it so he knew I meant business.

He swallowed carefully. 'I didn't mean to hurt you, Anita. I am so sorry.'

'Back off,' I said.

'Are you hurt?'

'Back off, Richard. Now!'

'Let me help you.' He bent closer, and I pressed the blade in hard enough to draw a trickle of blood.

'Let go of me, Richard.'

He let go and moved slowly away. He looked puzzled and hurt. He touched the blood at his neck as if he didn't know what it was.

When he was out of reach, I let myself sag against the carpet. Nothing was broken, of that I was sure, and I wasn't bleeding. If he'd thrown me into a wall with that much force, it would have been a different story. I'd been dating him for seven months, nearly slept with him more than once, and in all that time, I hadn't fully appreciated what I was playing with.

'*Ma petite*, are you all right?' Jean-Claude was standing at the foot of the bed. He was watching Richard closely as he moved towards me.

'I'm all right, I'm all right.' I glared up at him. 'What did you do behind my back to piss him off?'

Jean-Claude looked embarrassed. 'I did tease Monsieur Zeeman. Perhaps I even wanted a fight. Jealousy is a foolish emotion. How was I to know you would not move out of the way of a charging werewolf?'

'I don't back up, not for anyone.' I almost laughed. 'Though next time, maybe I'll make an exception.'

'I didn't mean to hurt you,' Richard said. 'But seeing you together like that . . . Knowing you're with him isn't the same thing as having it rubbed in my face.' His anger had vanished the moment he'd hurt me. Horror at what he'd done, fear for my safety, sanity returning in a rush.

'We were only kissing, Richard, nothing else, no matter what he wants you to believe.'

'I was suddenly so jealous. I'm sorry.'

'I know it was an accident, Richard. I'm just glad there wasn't a wall closer.'

'I could have hurt you badly.' He took a step towards me, hands reaching, and stopped himself. 'And you want me to let the beast loose enough to kill. Don't you understand how hard I fight to control it?'

'I understand better than I did a few minutes ago,' I said.

'Your bags are in the hallway. I'll bring them in, then I'll go.' This was the look I'd been dreading. This crushed, puppy dog look. The anger had been easier to deal with, if more dangerous.

'Don't go.'

They both looked at me.

'Jean-Claude staged this.' I held a hand up before he could protest. 'Oh, I know you enjoyed yourself, but you still wanted Richard to see us together. You wanted to pick a fight. You wanted to show me he was as much a monster as you are. You succeeded on all counts beautifully. Now, get out.'

'You are throwing me out of my own bedroom?' He looked amused.

'Yeah.' I stood up and was only a little wobbly on the high heels.

Jean-Claude sighed. 'I am to be relegated forever to my coffin then, to never know the joy of your company for my slumber.'

'You don't go to sleep, Jean-Claude. You die. Maybe I lust after your warm, breathing body, but I'm not up to the full package yet.'

He smiled. 'Very well, *ma petite*. I will leave you and Monsieur Zeeman to discuss the last few minutes. I would ask one thing.'

'And that is?' I asked.

'That you not make love in my bed when I cannot join you.'

I sighed. 'It would be pretty tacky to make love with Richard in your bed. I think you're safe on that one.'

Jean-Claude glanced at Richard. His eyes seemed to take in every inch of him, lingering on the open wound at his neck, though maybe that was just my imagination. 'If anyone could withstand the temptation, it is you, *ma petite*.' Jean-Claude looked at me, his face unreadable. 'I am sorry you were nearly hurt. I did not mean for that to happen.'

'You always have good intentions,' I said.

He sighed, then smiled. He glanced at Richard. 'Perhaps I am not the better monster, after all.'

'Get out,' I said.

He left, still smiling. He closed the door behind him, and I was left with his power dancing over my skin, the feel of his lips and hands on my body. It was only a kiss. Foreplay. But even the rush of adrenaline, of nearly being thrown into a wall, couldn't chase away the aftereffects.

Richard stood staring at me, as if he could sense the power somehow. 'I'll go get the bags,' he said. He could have said so many things, but that was safest.

He went to get the bags, and I sat down on the bed. Richard could have killed me. Jean-Claude would never have lost control like that. I wanted Richard to embrace his beast, but maybe, just maybe, I didn't understand what that meant.

23

I sat on the edge of the bed, waiting for Richard to come back into the room. My skin was jumping from Jean-Claude's parting gift. Only a kiss, and Richard had nearly torn into Jean-Claude and me. What would Richard have done if he'd caught us doing something truly lascivious? It was better not to find out.

Richard set my suitcase and both bags inside the door. He went out and came back with his small overnight bag.

He stood there, just inside the door, staring at me. I stared back. Blood still trickled down his throat from where I'd cut him. Neither of us seemed to know what to say. The silence grew until it was so thick it began to have weight.

'I'm sorry I hurt you,' he said. 'I've never lost control like that before.' He took a step into the room. 'But seeing you with him . . .' He held out his hands, then let them fall to his sides, helplessly.

'It was only a kiss, Richard. That's all.'

'It's never only a kiss with Jean-Claude.'

I couldn't argue that.

'I wanted to kill him,' Richard said.

'I noticed.'

'You're sure you're all right?'

'How's your neck?' I asked.

He touched the wound and came away with fresh blood. 'Silver blade, it won't heal immediately.' He came to stand in front of me, looking down, so close that the legs of his jeans nearly brushed my knees. It was almost too close. The lingering brush of Jean-Claude's power made my skin ache. Richard's nearness made it worse.

If I stood up, our bodies would touch, he was that close. I stayed sitting, trying to swallow the last bits of Jean-Claude's kiss. I wasn't sure what would happen if I touched Richard now. It felt almost like whatever Jean-Claude had done reacted to Richard's body. Or maybe it was me. Maybe I was becoming that needy. Maybe my body was tired of saying no.

'Would you really have killed me?' Richard asked. 'Could you have plunged that blade home?'

I stared up at him and wanted to lie to the sincerity in his eyes, but I didn't. Whatever we were doing with each other, whatever we meant to each other, it couldn't be based on lies. 'Yes.'

'Just like that,' he said.

I nodded. 'Just like that.'

'I saw it in your eyes. Cold, dispassionate, like someone else was looking out. If I was sure I could kill coldly, it wouldn't scare me so much.'

'I wish I could promise you that you wouldn't enjoy it, but I can't.'

'I know that.' He stared at me. 'I couldn't kill you. Not for any reason.'

'It would destroy something in me to lose you, Richard, but my first reaction is to protect myself at all costs. So, if we ever have another misunderstanding like we did tonight, don't help me up, don't come close to me, until I'm sure you're not going to eat me. Okay?'

He nodded. 'Okay.'

The energy rush that Jean-Claude had given me was fading, calming. I stood up, and Richard's body touched mine. I felt an instant rush of warm energy that had nothing to do with the vampire. Richard's aura enveloped me like a breath of warm air. His arms slid behind my back. I slid my hands around his waist and laid my cheek against his chest. I listened to the deep throbbing of his heart, running my hands over the softness of the flannel shirt. There was a measure of comfort in Richard's arms that simply wasn't there when Jean-Claude held me.

He ran his hands through my hair, putting one on either side of my face. He pulled me back until he could see my face. He bent towards me, lips parted. I stretched on tiptoe to meet him.

A voice said, 'Master.'

Richard turned with me still in his arms, so we could see the door. Jason crawled across the white carpet, dripping crimson drops as he moved.

'My God, what happened to you?' I asked.

'I happened to him,' Richard said. He walked over to the crawling man.

'What do you mean, you happened to him?'

Jason abased himself at Richard's feet, face pressed to the carpet. 'I'm sorry.'

Richard knelt and raised Jason to a sitting position. Blood ran down his face from a cut above his eyes. It was deep and would need stitches.

'You threw him into a wall?' I asked.

'He tried to stop me from reaching you.'

'I can't believe you did this.'

Richard looked up at me. 'You want me to be pack leader. You want me to be alpha. Well, this is what it takes.' He shook his head. 'You should see your face. You look so damned outraged. How can you want me to kill another human being and be upset by a little rough and tumble?'

I didn't know what to say. 'Jean-Claude said that killing Marcus wouldn't be enough. That you'd have to be willing to terrorize the pack to rule it.'

'He's right.' Richard wiped the blood off Jason's face. The cut was already beginning to close. He put his bloody fingers into his mouth and licked them clean.

I stood there, frozen, staring, like an unwilling witness to a car crash.

Richard bent close to Jason's face. I thought I knew what he was going to do, but I had to see it to believe it. He licked the wound. He ran his tongue over the open wound like a dog will do.

I turned away. This couldn't be my Richard, my safe, comforting Richard.

'You can't stand to watch, can you?' he asked. 'Did you think that killing was the only thing I had refused to do?'

His voice made me turn back.

There was a smudge of blood on his chin. 'Watch it all, Anita. I want you to see what it takes to be alphic. Then you tell me if it's all worth it. If you can't stomach it, don't ever ask me to do it again.' The look in his eyes made it a challenge.

I understood challenges. I sat on the edge of the bed. 'Go to it. I'm all yours.'

Richard brushed the hair on one side, exposing the wound on his neck. 'I am alpha and I feed the pack. I spilled your blood, and now I give it back to you.' The warm rush of his power spilled through the room.

Jason stared up at him, his eyes rolled almost to white. 'Marcus doesn't do this.'

'Because he can't,' Richard said. 'I can. Feed on my blood, on my apology, my power, and never stand against me again.' The air was so thick with power it was hard to breathe.

Jason rose on his knees and put his mouth over the wound, tentatively at first, as if afraid he'd be turned away or hurt. When Richard didn't say anything, Jason pressed his mouth to the open wound and drank. His jaw muscles worked, his throat swallowed. One hand slipped behind Richard's back, one hand on his shoulder.

I walked around them until I could see Richard's face. His eyes were closed, his face peaceful. He must have felt me watching him, because he opened his eyes. There was anger there, anger at me, partly. It wasn't only about killing Marcus, it was about giving up pieces of his humanity. I hadn't understood that, not until now.

He touched Jason's shoulders. 'Enough.' Jason pressed himself harder against the wound, like a nursing puppy. Richard pulled him forcibly off of his neck. A hicky had already spread around the wound.

Jason lay back, half-cradled in Richard's arms. He licked the edges of his mouth, getting the last drops of blood. He giggled and rolled away from Richard, to kneel on the floor. He rubbed his face along Richard's leg. 'I've never felt anything like that. Marcus can't share power like that. Does anybody else in the pack know you can share blood?'

'Tell them,' Richard said. 'Tell them all.'

'You really are going to kill Marcus, aren't you?' Jason asked.

'If he gives me no other choice, yes. Now, go, Jason, your other master is waiting.'

Jason stood, and almost fell. He righted himself, rubbing his hands down his legs and arms as if he was bathing in something I couldn't see. Maybe it was the warm, ruffling power that he tried to tie around himself. He laughed again. 'If you'll feed me, you can hit me into a wall anytime.'

'Get out,' Richard said.

Jason got out.

Richard was still kneeling on the floor. He looked up at me. 'Do you understand now why I didn't want to do this?'

'Yes,' I said.

'Maybe if Marcus knows I can share blood, my power, he'll back down.'

'You're still hoping not to kill him,' I said.

'It's not only the killing, Anita. It's everything that goes with it. It's what I just did with Jason. A hundred things, none of them very human.' He looked at me, and there was a sorrow in his brown eyes that I had never seen before.

I understood suddenly. 'It isn't the killing exactly, is it? Once you take over the pack by blood and brute force, you have to keep the pack with blood and brute force.'

'Exactly. If I could force Marcus out somehow, if I could make him back down, then I'd have room to do things differently.' He came to stand in front of me, his face eager. 'I've brought nearly half the pack either to my side or at least to be neutral. They aren't backing Marcus anymore. No one's ever divided a pack like this without deaths.'

'Why can't you split into two packs?'

He shook his head. 'Marcus would never allow it. The pack leader gets a tithe from every member. It would cut not just his power but his money.'

'You getting money now?' I asked.

'Everyone's still tithing to Marcus. I don't want the money, and it's just one more fight. I think tithing should be abolished.'

I watched the light in his face, the plans, the dreams. He was building a power base of fairness and boy scout virtues with creatures that could rip out your throat and eat you afterwards. He believed he could do it. Watching his handsome, eager face, I almost believed it, too.

'I thought you could kill Marcus and that would be it. But it won't be, will it?'

'Raina will see to it that I'm challenged. Unless I put the fear of *me* into them.'

'As long as Raina is alive, she'll be trouble.'

'I don't know what to do about Raina.'

'I could kill her,' I said.

The look on his face was enough.

'Just kidding,' I said. Sort of. Richard wouldn't agree with the ultimate practicality, but if he was going to be safe, Raina had to die. Cold-blooded, but true.

'What are you thinking, Anita?'

'That maybe you're right and the rest of us are wrong.'

'About what?'

'Maybe you shouldn't kill Marcus.'

Richard's eyes widened. 'I thought you were angry with me for *not* killing Marcus.'

'It's not killing Marcus. It's endangering everybody by not killing Marcus.'

He shook his head. 'I don't see the difference.'

'The difference is that killing is a means to an end, not an end in itself. I want you alive. Marcus gone. The pack members that follow you safe. I don't want you to have to torture the pack to keep your place. If we can accomplish all that without you having to kill anyone, I'm okay with that. I don't think there's an option that doesn't involve killing. But if you can come up with one, I'll support you.'

He studied my face. 'Are you telling me that you think I shouldn't kill now?'

'Yeah.'

He laughed, but it was with more irony than humor. 'I don't know whether to yell at you or hug you.'

'I affect a lot of people that way,' I said. 'Look, when we went to rescue Stephen, you should have called a few people. Gone into the situation from a position of strength, with three or four lieutenants at your back. There is a compromise between playing Sir Lancelot and being Vlad the Impaler.'

He sat down on the edge of the bed. 'Being able to feed power through my blood is a rare talent. It's impressive, but it won't be enough. I'd have to have some major scary stuff to get Marcus and Raina to back down. I'm powerful, Anita, really powerful.' He said it like it was simply the truth, no ego, no pride. 'But it's not that kind of powerful.'

I sat down beside him. 'I'll do anything I can, Richard. Just promise me you won't be careless.'

He smiled, but it didn't reach his eyes. 'I won't be careless if you'll kiss me.'

We kissed. The taste of him was warm and sure, but underneath it was the sweet salt of blood, and Jason's aftershave. I drew away from him.

'What's wrong?'

I shook my head. Telling him I could taste other people's blood in his mouth was not going to be helpful. We were going to work so he didn't have to do things like that. It wasn't his beast that would steal his humanity, it was a thousand smaller things.

'Change for me,' I said.

'What?'

'Change for me, here, now.'

He stared at me, as if trying to read something in my face. 'Why now?'

'Let me see all of you, Richard, the whole package.'

'If you don't want Jean-Claude sharing the bed, you don't want a wolf in bed with you, either.'

'You wouldn't be trapped in wolf form until morning, you said so earlier.'

'No, I wouldn't,' he said softly.

'If you change tonight, and I can accept it, we can make love. We can start planning the wedding.'

He laughed. 'Can I kill Marcus before I have to kill Jean-Claude?'

'Jean-Claude promised not to hurt you,' I said.

Richard went very still. 'You've already talked to him about this?'

I nodded.

'Why wasn't he angry with me?'

'He said he'd step aside if he couldn't win me, so he's stepping aside.' I didn't add the part about Jean-Claude loving me. Save it for later.

'Call your beast, Richard.'

He shook his head. 'It isn't just my beast, Anita. It's the lukoi, the pack. You have to see them, too.'

'I've seen them.'

He shook his head. 'You haven't seen us at the lupanar. Our place of power. We're real there, no pretense, not even to ourselves.'

'I've just told you that I want to marry you. Did you pick up on that?' I asked.

Richard stood. 'I want to marry you, Anita, more than almost anything in the world. I want you so badly my body aches with it. I don't trust myself to be here tonight.'

'We've managed to stay chaste so far,' I said.

'By the skin of our teeth.' He picked up his overnight case. 'The lukoi call sex the killing dance.'

'So?'

'We use the same phrase for battles of succession.'

'I still don't understand the problem.'

He stared at me. 'You will. God help us both. You will.'

There was something so sad, so wistful about him suddenly, that I didn't want to let him go. Tomorrow he'd face Marcus, and just because he'd agreed to kill didn't mean he could. When the moment came, I didn't trust him not to flinch. I didn't want to lose him.

'Stay with me, Richard. Please.'

'It wouldn't be fair to you.'

'Don't be such a frigging boy scout.'

He smiled and gave a very bad Popeye imitation, 'I am what I am.' He closed the door behind him. I didn't even get to kiss him goodbye.

24

I woke to darkness and someone bending over me. I couldn't really see, but I felt something in the air above me like a weight. My hand slid under the pillow and came out with the Firestar. I shoved the gun into whoever it was, and they were gone like a dream. I slid off the bed, pressing my back against the wall, making myself as small a target as possible.

A voice came out of the darkness. I aimed for it, straining my ears for sounds of more intruders.

'It's Cassandra. The light switch is above you. I'll stay right here while you turn on the lights.' Her voice was low, even, the sort of voice you used for crazy people, or people who had guns pointed at you.

I swallowed past my pulse and scooted my back up the wall. I swiped my left hand up the wall until it hit the switch plate, then I knelt back down, fingers touching the switch. When I was as far down as I could get and still turn on the light, I hit it. Light flared. There was a moment of dazzling blindness while I hunkered on the floor, gun pointed blindly. When I could see, Cassandra stood near the foot of the bed, hands out to either side, staring at me. Her eyes were a little too wide. The lace on her Victorian nightgown fluttered with her breath.

Yes, Victorian nightgown. She looked delicate, doll-like. I'd asked her last night if Jean-Claude picked out the gown. No, she'd picked it out. Each to their own.

She stood on the carpet, frozen, staring. 'Anita, are you all right?' Her tone said she didn't think so.

I took a deep breath and pointed the gun at the ceiling. 'Yeah, I'm all right.'

'Can I move?'

I stood, holding the gun at my side. 'Don't try to touch me when I'm in a sound sleep. Say something first.'

'I'll remember that,' she said. 'May I move?'

'Sure. What's up?' I asked.

'Richard and Jean-Claude are outside.'

I checked my watch. It was one o'clock in the afternoon. I'd had nearly six hours of sleep. Or would have had if Cassandra and I hadn't talked for an hour. I hadn't had a sleep-over in years, and frankly, girl or no, she was still a lycanthrope that I'd met only that night. It felt strange to trust her at my back as my bodyguard. I've never been too fond of sleeping with strangers. It's not sexual. It's plain suspicion. Being deeply asleep is as helpless as most of us get.

'What do they want?'

'Richard said he has a plan.'

I didn't need to ask what plan. There was only one thing on his mind the day of the full moon: Marcus.

'Tell them I'm getting dressed first.' I went for my suitcase. Cassandra padded to the door. She opened it only a crack, speaking softly. She closed it firmly behind her and came back to me. She looked puzzled. In the nightgown with a puzzled frown on her face, she looked about twelve.

I knelt by the suitcase, clothes in my hands, looking up at her. 'What now?'

'Jean-Claude said not to bother getting dressed.'

I stared at her for a heartbeat. 'Yeah, right. I'm getting dressed. They can just bloody well wait that long.'

She nodded and went back to the door.

I went for the bathroom. I stared at myself in the mirror. I looked as tired as I felt. I brushed teeth, took care of necessities, and wished for a shower. It would have helped wake me up. I could have run a bath, but I wasn't sure the boys would last that long. Besides, a bath was something I did to get ready for bed, not for waking up. I needed something stimulating, not something soothing.

Richard had a plan, but Jean-Claude was with him. That meant that the vampire had helped come up with the plan. It was a scary thought.

Tonight Richard would fight Marcus. He could be dead by tomorrow. The thought made my chest tight. There was a pressure behind my eyes that had more to do with tears than anything else. I could live with Richard off somewhere. It would hurt if he wasn't with me, but I'd survive. I might not survive his death. I loved Richard. I really loved him. I didn't want to give him up. Not for anything.

Jean-Claude was being a perfect gentleman, but I didn't trust it. How could I? He always had a dozen different reasons for everything he did. What was the plan? The quicker I dressed, the quicker I'd find out.

I'd pretty much just grabbed stuff out of the suitcase. You can mix and match almost all the clothing I own. Dark blue jeans, navy blue polo shirt, white jogging socks. I hadn't dressed to impress anyone. Now that I was a little more awake, I wished I'd chosen something a little less practical. Love makes you worry about stuff like that.

I opened the door. Richard stood by the bed. The sight of him stopped me in my tracks. His hair was brushed until it fell like a frothy mass around his shoulders. He was wearing nothing but a pair of silky undershorts, royal purple. They were slit high on each side, giving glimpses of his thighs as he turned towards me.

When I could close my mouth and talk, I said, 'Why are you dressed like that?'

Jean-Claude leaned one shoulder against the wall. He was wearing a black ankle-length robe edged with black fur. His hair mingled with the fur collar until it was hard to tell where one blackness ended and the other began. His pale neck and a triangle of his chest showed almost perfectly white against the fur.

'You look like you've just stepped out of two different porno movies. Cassandra said something about a plan. What's the plan?'

Richard glanced at Jean-Claude. They exchanged a look between them that said better than words that they'd been plotting behind my back.

Richard sat on the edge of the bed. The shorts clung a little too close for comfort and I had to look away, so I looked at Jean-Claude. Not comforting, but at least most of him was covered.

'Do you remember some months ago, before Christmas, when we accidently set off some sort of magical energy in your apartment?' Jean-Claude asked.

'I remember,' I said.

'Monsieur Zeeman and I believe that the three of us could share power, become a triumvirate.'

I looked from one to the other. 'Explain.'

'There is a link between myself and wolves. There is a link between you, my little necromancer, and the dead. Lust and love have always held a magical energy. I can show you individual spells that can use the link between vampire and their animal, between necromancer and vampire. We should not be surprised that there is power between us.'

'Make your point,' I said.

Jean-Claude smiled. 'I believe we could call up enough power to back down a certain Ulfric. I know Marcus. He will not fight if he believes he has no hope of winning.'

'Jean-Claude's right,' Richard said. 'If I can shine with enough power, Marcus will back down.'

'How do you know we can even call this whatever-it-is up again?' I asked.

'I have done some research,' Jean-Claude said. 'There are two cases of master vampires who could call animals, who then made one of those animals in were-form a sort of human servant.'

'So?'

'It means that there is a chance of my being able to bind you both.'

I shook my head. 'No way, no vampire marks. Been there, done that, didn't like it.'

'There were no marks on either of you in December,' Jean-Claude said. 'I think it will work without any now.'

'Why are the two of you dressed like that?'

Richard looked embarrassed. 'It was all I brought. I thought we were going to be sharing the bed last night.'

I motioned at the shorts. 'Those would not have helped us stay chaste, Richard.'

Heat crept up his face. 'I know; sorry.'

'Tell me there is no lingerie in your suitcase, *ma petite*.'

'I never said there wasn't.' Ronnie had talked me into an outfit just in case I gave in to Richard. She was willing for me to bed him before the wedding if it would knock Jean-Claude out of the running.

'Who'd you buy it for?' Richard asked quietly.

'You, but don't distract me. Why the nice jammies?'

'Richard and I have made an attempt or two on our own to call the power. It does not work with only the two of us. His dislike of me has rendered it useless.'

'Is this true, Richard?'

He nodded. 'Jean-Claude says we need our third; we need you.'

'What's with the clothes?'

'Lust and anger were what drew the power the first time, *ma petite*. We have our anger. We are missing our lust.'

'Wait just a damn minute.' I stared from one to the other of them. 'Are you saying we become a ménage à trois?'

'No,' Richard said. He stood up. He walked towards me in his little shorts, flashing the room. 'No sex, I promise you that. Even for this, I wouldn't have agreed to sharing you with him.'

I ran my fingertips down the silk of his shorts, lightly, almost like I was afraid. 'Then why the costumes?'

'We're running out of time, Anita. If this is going to work, it's got to work fast.' He gripped my arms, his hands warm on my skin. 'You said you'd help me with a plan. This is the plan.'

I drew away from him slowly and turned to Jean-Claude. 'And what do you get out of it?'

'Your happiness. No wolf will challenge Richard if we are a true triumvirate.'

'My happiness, right.' I studied his calm, lovely face, and had an idea. 'You tasted Jason, didn't you? You tasted the power that he sucked off of Richard, didn't you? Didn't you, you son of a bitch?' I walked towards him as I talked, fighting an urge to hit him when I got there.

'What of it, *ma petite*?'

I stood right in front of him, throwing the words into his face. 'What do you gain from all this? And don't give me crap about my happiness. I've known you too long.'

His face was at its mildest, its most disarming. 'I would gain enough power that no master vampire, short of the council itself, would dare challenge me.'

'I knew it. I knew it. You don't do anything without a dozen ulterior motives.'

'I benefit in exactly the same way Monsier Zeeman benefits. We would both secure our power bases.'

'Fine, what do I get out of it?'

'Why, Monsieur Zeeman's safety.'

'Anita,' Richard said softly. He touched my shoulder.

I whirled to face him. My angry words died at the look on his face. So serious, so solemn.

He gripped my shoulders, one hand cupping the side of my face. 'You don't have to do this if you don't want to.'

'Do you understand what he's suggesting, Richard? We would never be free of him.' I touched his hand where he held my face. 'Don't tie us to him like this, Richard. Once he gets a piece of you, he never lets go.'

'If you really believed he was evil, you would have killed him a long time ago and been free of him.'

If I didn't do this, and Richard died tonight, would I be able to live with it? I leaned into him, pressing my face against his chest, breathing in his scent. No. If he died and I could have saved him, I'd never be rid of the guilt.

Jean-Claude came to stand near us. 'It may have been one of those freakish accidents that cannot be duplicated under controlled conditions, *ma petite*. Magic is often like that.'

I turned my face and looked at him, cheek still pressed to Richard's bare chest, his arms wrapped around my back. 'No vampire marks on either of us, right?'

'I promise. The only thing I would ask is that none of us back away. We need a true idea of how much power we can call. If it is not much, then it is moot, but if it is as I believe, then it will solve a great many problems.'

'You manipulative bastard.'

'Is that a yes?' he asked.

'Yes,' I said.

Richard hugged me. I let his arms hold me, comfort me, but it was Jean-Claude's eyes I met. There was a look on his face that was hard to describe. The devil must look like that after you've signed on the dotted line and given away your soul. Pleased, eager, and a little hungry.

25

'You and Monsieur Zeeman have a nice visit. I will take my turn in the bathroom, then join you.'

Just hearing him say it out loud made me want to refuse. But I didn't. 'Are you sure this isn't just your elaborate way of forming us into a ménage à trois?'

'Would I be so devious?'

'Yeah.'

He laughed, and the sound shivered over my skin like an ice cube dropped down my spine.

'I will leave you two alone.' He brushed past us into the bathroom.

I stalked after him and caught the door before it could close. He looked at me through the opening. 'Yes, *ma petite*?'

'There better be something under that robe besides skin.'

He smiled wide enough to show just a hint of fang. 'Would I be so crude, *ma petite*?'

'I don't know.'

He nodded and closed the door.

I took a deep breath and turned to face the other man in my life. Richard's clothes lay folded on my suitcase. He moved towards me. The shorts were slit high enough that I could see almost a clear line from foot to waist.

If we were truly alone, I would have gone to him. What should have been romantic was suddenly chokingly awkward. I was very aware of the sounds of running water from the bathroom. Jean-Claude planned to join us. Sweet Jesus.

Richard still looked scrumptious with his hair falling across one eye. He had stopped moving closer. He finally shook his head. 'Why is this suddenly so awkward?'

'I think the biggest reason is in the bathroom getting ready to join us.'

He laughed and shook his head again. 'It doesn't usually take us this long to be in each other's arms.'

'No,' I said. At this rate, we were going to be staring at each other like high school kids at a dance when Jean-Claude came back out.

'Meet me halfway,' I said.

Richard smiled. 'Always.' He walked to meet me. The muscles in his stomach rippled as he moved.

I was suddenly sorry that I was wearing jeans and a polo shirt. I wanted him to see me in the lingerie I'd bought. I wanted his hands to run over the silk and my body underneath.

Richard and I stopped inches away from each other, neither one touching. I could smell his aftershave faintly. I was close enough to feel the warmth of his body. I wanted to run my hands over his bare chest. I wanted to run my hands down the front of those silk shorts. The thought was so real I crossed my arms to keep my hands busy.

Richard leaned over me. He ran his lips over my eyebrows, kissed my eyelids ever so gently. He reached my mouth, and I rose on tiptoe to meet him. He slid his arms around me.

I fell against him, my hands searching his body, my mouth pressing against his. He bent and slid his arms under my butt, lifting me until our faces were even. I broke the kiss and started to say, 'Put me down,' but staring at his face from an inch away, I couldn't say it. I wrapped my legs around his waist. He braced his legs to catch his balance. I kissed him, and the first brush of power broke over me in a line of skin-prickling, belly-tickling warmth.

Richard made a small sound in his throat that was more growl than moan. He knelt on the floor with me still riding him, and when he took me to the floor, I didn't stop him. He raised his upper body over me, bracing with his arms, his lower body pressed against me. When he stared down at me, his eyes had gone wolfish. Something must have shown on my face because he turned his head so I wouldn't see.

I raised up underneath him, grabbed a handful of his thick hair, and turned his head back to me none too gently. Whether it was the pain or something else, he turned back with a snarl. I didn't flinch. I didn't look away.

Richard lowered his face towards mine, and I lay back on the floor. His mouth hovered over mine. There was a brush of warmth as our mouths met, as if I was tasting his energy, his essence.

The bathroom door opened. The sound froze me, making my eyes slide towards the open door. Richard hesitated for a second, mouth uncertain above mine, then he kissed the edge of my chin, running his lips down my neck.

Jean-Claude stood in the doorway, dressed in black silk pajamas. The long-sleeved top was unbuttoned so that it fanned around his naked upper body as he moved. The look on his face, in his eyes, panicked me.

I patted Richard's shoulder. He'd worked his way to the base of my neck and was nuzzling the collar of my polo shirt, as if he'd put his face inside the shirt. He raised those startling amber wolf eyes to me, and the only thing I could read on his face was desire, almost a hunger. His power breathed along my skin like a line of hot wind.

My pulse thudded against the skin of my throat until I thought it would burst the skin. 'What's wrong with you, Richard?'

'Tonight is the full moon, *ma petite*. His beast calls to him.' Jean-Claude padded across the carpet towards us.

'Let me up, Richard.'

Richard went to his hands and knees, leaving me to squirm out from under him. I stood, and he knelt in front of me, wrapping his arms around my waist. 'Don't be afraid.'

'I'm not afraid of you, Richard.' I stared at Jean-Claude.

Richard ran his hands down my ribs, fingers digging into the flesh as if he were massaging my back. It brought my attention back to him. 'I would never hurt you willingly. You know that.'

I did know that. I nodded.

'Trust me now.' His voice was soft and deep, with a roll of bass to it that wasn't normal. He started pulling my shirt out of my pants. 'I want to touch you, smell you, taste you.'

Jean-Claude padded around us, not coming any closer. He circled us like a shark. His midnight-blue eyes were still human, more human looking than Richard's.

Richard raised my shirt free of my pants, pushing it back until he exposed my stomach. He ran his hands over my bare skin and I shuddered, but it wasn't sex, or not only sex. That warm, electric power of his flowed from his hands across my skin. It was like having a low-level current tracing over me. It didn't quite hurt, but it might if it didn't stop. Or it might feel very good, better than anything else. I wasn't sure which thought scared me more.

Jean-Claude stood just out of reach, watching. That thought scared me, too.

Richard put his hands on either side of my exposed waist, holding the shirt up, draped over his wrists.

Jean-Claude took that last step, pale hand outstretched. I tightened up, fear overriding the remains of desire. He let his hand fall back without touching us.

Richard licked my stomach, a quick, wet motion. I stared down at him, and he stared back with brown eyes. Human eyes. 'I won't let anything happen to you, Anita.'

I didn't know what it had cost him to swallow his beast back down inside, but I knew it hadn't been easy. There were many lesser lycanthropes who could not go back once they started to change. It would have been more reassuring if his true brown eyes hadn't held a darkness all their own. But it wasn't his beast, it was something more basic, more human: sex. Even lust doesn't cover that look in a man's eyes.

Jean-Claude was standing behind me. I could feel him. Without touching me at all, I could feel his power, like a cool, seeking wind. He brushed his face against my hair. My heart was beating so loudly I couldn't hear anything but the thundering of my own blood in my head.

Jean-Claude brushed my hair to one side. His lips touched my cheek and his power burst over me in a quiet rush, cool as a wind from the grave. It flowed through me, seeking Richard's warmth. The two energies hit, mingled inside me. I couldn't breathe. I felt that thing inside me that could call the dead from the grave — magic, for lack of a better word — I felt it coil and flare against them both.

I tried to pull away from Richard, but his fingers dug into my ribs. Jean-Claude's arms tightened around my shoulders. 'Build the power, do not fight it, *ma petite.*'

I fought the panic, my breath coming in quick gasps. I was going to hyperventilate and pass out if I couldn't get a handle on it. I rode the power and my own fear, and I was losing.

Richard's mouth bit gently at my stomach. His mouth sucking my skin. Jean-Claude's lips touched my neck, nibbling gently. His arms cradled me against his chest. Richard was a growing warmth at my waist. Jean-Claude like some cool fire at my back. I was being eaten from both ends like a piece of wood going up in flames. The power was too much. It had to go somewhere. I had to do something with it or it was going to burn me alive.

My legs buckled, and only Richard's and Jean-Claude's hands on me kept me from falling. They lowered me to the floor, still cradled in their arms. My shoulder touched the ground, then my hand, and I knew what I could do with the power. I felt it surge through the ground, seeking, seeking the dead. I rolled onto my stomach. Jean-Claude's hands were on my shoulders, his face brushing mine. Richard's hands were under my shirt touching my back, roaming higher, but it was all secondary. I had to do something with the power.

I found the dead I needed, and it didn't work. The power continued to build until I would have screamed if I could have gotten enough air. A step, an ingredient, something was missing.

I rolled onto my back, staring up at both of them. They stared down at me. Jean-Claude's eyes had gone solid, midnight blue. They both leaned towards me at once. Richard went for my mouth, Jean-Claude went for my neck. Richard's kiss was almost a burning. I could feel the brush of fangs as Jean-Claude fought not to bite me. Temptation was everywhere. Someone's hand was under my shirt, and I wasn't sure whose it was anymore. Then I realized it was both of them.

What was one thing I needed for raising the dead? Blood. I must have said it out loud: 'Blood.'

Jean-Claude raised up, staring at me from inches away. His hand was just below my breast. I'd grabbed his wrist without thinking about it. 'What, *ma petite*?'

'Blood to finish it. We need blood.'

Richard raised his face up like a drowning man. 'What?'

'I can give you blood, *ma petite*.' Jean-Claude leaned into me. I stopped him with a hand on his chest, at the same time that Richard put a hand on his shoulder. The power poured over us in a searing wash, and I was seeing white spots.

'You won't use me to sink fangs into her for the first time,' Richard growled it at him. His anger fed the magic and I screamed.

'Give me blood, or get off me.' I held up my own wrist between them. 'I don't have a knife, someone do it.'

Richard leaned over me. He swept his hair back from one side of his neck. 'Here's your blood.'

Jean-Claude didn't argue. He leaned into him, lips drawn back. I watched in a sort of slow motion as he bit the side of Richard's neck. Richard tensed, a hiss of breath as the fangs sank home. Jean-Claude's mouth sealed over his skin, sucking, throat working.

The power roared through me, raising every hair on my body, creeping through my skin until I thought I'd come apart. I sent it all outward to the dead that I'd found. I filled them up and still there was too much power. I reached outward, outward, and found what I was looking for. The power left us in a cool, burning, rush.

I lay gasping on the floor. Jean-Claude lay on my left, propped on one elbow. Blood stained his lips, trickling down his chin. Richard lay on his stomach to my right, pinning my arm underneath his cheek. His chest rose and fell in great gasps, sweat glistening along his spine.

The world was gold-edged, almost floating. Sound returned slowly, and it was like I was listening down a long tube.

Jean-Claude licked the blood from his lips, wiping a shaking hand across his chin, licking the hand clean. He lay down beside me, one hand across my stomach, his head cradled on my shoulder. His bare chest and stomach lay across my arm. His skin was almost hot, feverish. He'd never felt like that before. His heart pounded against my skin like a captive bird.

His hair fell against my face. It smelled of some exotic shampoo and of him. He gave a shaky laugh and said, 'It was glorious for me, was it good for you, *ma petite*?'

I swallowed, and was too tired to even laugh. 'Trust you to know just what to say.'

Richard raised himself up on his elbows. Blood trickled down his neck where two neat fang marks showed. I touched the bite mark, and my fingers came away stained crimson.

'Does it hurt?' I asked.

'Not really.' He grabbed my wrist, gently, licking the blood off my fingers, sucking them clean.

Jean-Claude's strangely warm hand caressed my stomach under my shirt. He undid the button of my pants.

'Don't even think it,' I said.

'Too late, *ma petite*.' He bent and kissed me. I could taste the metallic sweetness of Richard's blood on his tongue. I rose up to meet him, pushing at his mouth. I'd asked for the blood, not either of them. The truth was, we weren't done with the bloodletting today. Whatever I'd called from the grave had to be put back. That would take blood, fresh blood. The only question was who would donate it and how would it be gathered. Oh, one more question, how much blood would we need?

26

Jean-Claude's fingertips slid along the edge of my pants. Richard grabbed his wrist. Anger flared from both of them, and that shared power flickered to life.

'You won't use this as an excuse to get into her pants, either,' Richard said. His voice was thick and dark with more than anger. His hand tightened on Jean-Claude's wrist.

Jean-Claude balled his hand into a fist and bent his arm at the elbow. Concentration and anger touched both their faces. I could feel the trembling effort through their chests. Their anger prickled along my skin. It was too soon to do all this shit over again. 'You can arm-wrestle later, boys, we've got to go see what I raised from the dead.'

There was a fraction of hesitation, then they both looked down at me. Their arms were still straining against each other. Richard's face showed the effort. Jean-Claude's face had gone blank and curious, as if it was no effort to hold off a werewolf. But I could feel the fine trembling through his body. Illusion was all with Jean-Claude. With Richard it was all nerve endings and reality.

'What did you say, *ma petite*?'

'She said she raised the dead,' Richard said.

'Yep, so get off me. You can fight later, but right now, we need to check on what I did.'

'*We* did,' Jean-Claude said. He eased away from Richard, and after a second, Richard released his hand.

'What we did,' I said.

Richard stood, the muscles in his bare legs moving under the skin, and it was hard not to touch them, feel the movement of him. He offered me a hand up.

'Give me a minute,' I said.

Jean-Claude stood as if drawn to his feet by strings. He offered me a hand, too.

They stood glaring at each other. Their anger played through the air like invisible sparks. I shook my head. I seemed to be more worse for wear than either of them, poor human that I was. I'd have actually taken a hand up, which was rare for me. I sighed, got my feet under me, and stood without help from either of them.

'Behave yourselves,' I said. 'Can't you feel what's in the air? Anger works just fine to call whatever it is, so stop it. We may have to do it again to lay to rest what we've already called from the grave.'

Jean-Claude looked instantly relaxed, at ease. He gave a low bow. 'As you like, *ma petite*.'

Richard rotated his neck, trying to loosen his shoulders. His hands were still balled into fists, but he nodded. 'I don't understand how what we did called zombies.'

'I can act as a focus for other animators. It's a way to combine powers and raise an older zombie or more than one or two zombies. I don't know how to do anything else but raise the dead, so when you shoved that much power in my face . . . ' I shrugged. 'I did what I know how to do.'

'Did you raise all of Nikoloas's old cemetery?' Jean-Claude asked.

'If we're lucky,' I said.

He put his head to one side, puzzled.

Richard looked down at himself. 'Can I get some pants on?'

I smiled. 'Seems a shame,' I said, 'but yeah.'

'I will fetch my robe from the bathroom,' Jean-Claude said.

'Help yourself,' I said.

'No comment about how it is a shame that I am getting dressed?'

I shook my head.

'Cruel, *ma petite*, very cruel.'

I smiled and gave him a little bow.

He returned the smile, but there was a challenge to his eyes as he walked towards the bathroom.

Richard was sliding into his jeans. I watched him zip them up and button them into place. It was fun just to watch him dress. Love makes the smallest movements fascinating.

I walked past him, towards the door, leaving him to put a shirt on if he was going to. The only way to ignore him was to just not look. The same theory worked with Jean-Claude most of the time.

I walked to the door. My hand was reaching for the knob when Richard grabbed me from behind, lifting me off my feet, carrying me back from the door.

My feet were literally dangling off the ground. 'What the hell are you doing? Put me down.'

'My wolves are coming,' he said, as if that explained everything.

'Put me down.'

He lowered me enough for my feet to touch the floor, but his arms stayed wrapped around me, as if he was afraid I'd go for the door. His face was distant, listening. I heard nothing.

A howl echoed up the corridor and raised the hairs on my arms. 'What's going on, Richard?'

'Danger,' he almost whispered it.

'Is it Raina and Marcus?'

He was still listening to things I could not hear. He pushed me behind him and went to the door, still shirtless, wearing nothing but his jeans.

I ran for the bed and the weapons. I got the Firestar out from under the pillow. 'Don't go out there empty-handed, dammit.' I dragged the Uzi out from under the bed.

A chorus of howls went up. Richard flung the door open and raced down the hallway. I called his name, but he was gone.

Jean-Claude came out of the bathroom in his black, furlined robe. 'What is it, *ma petite*?'

'Company.' I slipped the Uzi's strap across my chest.

The sounds of snarling wolves came distant. Jean-Claude ran past me, the long robe flying out behind him. He ran like a dark wind. When I got out to the corridor, he was nowhere in sight.

I was going to be the last one there. Dammit.

27

Running full tilt towards a fight was not the best way to stay alive. Caution was better. I knew that, and it didn't matter. Nothing mattered but getting there in time. In time to save them. *Them*. I didn't dwell on that; I ran, the Firestar gripped tightly in my right hand, the Uzi in my left. I was running like an idiot, but at least I was armed.

A roaring shout thundered off the walls ahead. Don't ask me how, but I knew it was Richard. I didn't think I could run any faster. I was wrong. I spilled into the open, breath coming in throat-closing gasps, not looking left or right. If someone had had a gun, they could have blown me away.

Richard stood in the middle of the room, a zombie held at arm's length above his head. A wolf the size of a pony had pinned another zombie to the floor, savaging it. Stephen stood at Richard's back in human form, but crouched and ready to fight. Cassandra stood back from them. She turned to me as I skidded into the room. There was a look on her face that I couldn't quite read, and didn't have time to puzzle over.

Jean-Claude was at the far left, away from the werewolves. He was staring at me, too. I couldn't read his face, but he was in no danger. He hadn't waded into the zombies. He knew better. Richard didn't.

The room had been a narrow rectangle, but the far wall had blasted outward, scattering rubble across the floor. It looked like the zombies had crawled out from behind the wall. A graveyard that I, at least, hadn't known was there.

The dead stood in front of the ruins. Their eyes shifted to me as I saw them, and I felt the weight of their gaze like a blow to my heart.

The fear for everyone's safety was gone, washed away in a rush of anger. 'Richard, put it down, please, it won't hurt you. Call Jason off the other one.' It had to be Jason unless there was another werewolf down here. And if it was someone else, where was Jason?

Richard turned his head to look at me, the zombie, once a human male, still held effortlessly above his head. 'They attacked Jason.'

'They wouldn't have done anything without orders. Jason jumped the gun.'

'They didn't attack us,' Cassandra said. 'They started pouring out of the wall. Jason changed and attacked them.'

The giant wolf had opened the zombie's stomach and was tearing at intestines. I'd had enough. 'Grab the wolf,' I said. The zombie under him locked its arms around the wolf's fore-quarters. The wolf sank teeth into the corpse's throat and tore it out in a spurt of dark fluid and flesh.

The rest of the zombies, somewhere between sixty and eighty, surged toward the wolf. 'Let him up, Jason, or I'll show you what it's like to be attacked by zombies.'

Richard bent his elbow and tossed the zombie away from him. The body tumbled through the air and landed in the mass of waiting zombies. They fell like bowling pins, except that these bowling pins got to their feet, though one lost an arm in the process.

Richard crouched by his wolves. 'You're attacking us?' He sounded outraged.

'Pull your wolf off my zombie and it stops here.'

'You think you can take us?' Cassandra said.

'With this many dead, I know I can,' I said.

Stephen's face crumpled, almost like he'd cry. 'You'd hurt us.'

Shit, I'd forgotten. I was their lupa now. I'd threatened to kill

Raina if she hurt Stephen again, and here I was about to feed him to zombies. There was a logic gap somewhere.

'If I'm supposed to protect you all, then you have to obey me, right? So Jason gets the fuck off my zombie or I beat the hell out of him. Isn't that pack protocol?'

Richard turned to me. There was a look on his face I'd never seen before: anger and arrogance, or something close to it. 'I don't think Jason really expected you to demand his obedience. I don't think any of us did.'

'Then you don't know me very well,' I said.

'*Mes amies*, if we kill each other, won't Marcus be pleased.'

We all turned to Jean-Claude. I said, 'Stop.' All the zombies stopped at once like a freeze frame. One tumbled to the floor, caught in midshuffle, rather than take that last partial step. Zombies were terribly literal.

The giant wolf tore another piece out of the zombie. The dead man made a small involuntary cry. 'Drag Jason off of it now, or we are going to do this dance. Fuck Marcus. I'll worry about it later.'

'Off of him, Jason, now,' Richard said.

The wolf reared back, tearing at the zombie's arm. Bone cracked. The wolf worried the arm like a terrier with a bone. Blood and thicker fluids flew in a spray.

Richard grabbed the wolf by the scruff of the neck, jerking it off its feet. He grabbed the front of its furry throat and turned it to face him. The muscles in his arms corded with the effort. The wolf's claws scrambled in the air while it strangled. The massive claws raked Richard's bare skin. Blood flowed in thin crimson lines.

He threw the wolf across the room into the waiting dead. 'Never disobey me again, Jason, never!' His voice was lost in a growling that turned into a howl. He threw back his head and bayed. The sound rose from his human throat. Cassandra and

Stephen echoed him. Their howls filled the room with a strange, ringing song.

I realized then that Richard might avoid killing Marcus, but he'd never control the lukoi without brutality. He was already casual about it. Almost as casual as Jean-Claude. Bad sign or good sign? I wasn't sure.

Jason scrambled out of the dead. He turned pale green wolf eyes to me, as if waiting for something. 'Don't look at me,' I said, 'I'm pissed with you, too.'

Jason stalked towards me on paws bigger across than my hands. The fur at his neck rose in a prickling brush. His lips curled back from his teeth in a silent growl.

I pointed the Firestar at him. 'Don't do it, Jason.'

He kept coming, each step so stiff and full of tension that it looked robotic. He gathered his body, legs squirming into position for a leap. I wasn't going to let him finish the movement. If he'd been in human form, I'd have aimed to wound, but in wolf form, I wasn't taking any chances. One scratch and I'd be alpha female for real.

I sighted down the barrel and felt that quietness fill me. I felt nothing while I stared down the gun at him. Nothing but a cool, white emptiness.

'Stop it, both of you!' Richard growled. He walked towards us. I kept my eyes on the wolf but had a peripheral sense of Richard moving closer.

He kept coming, easing himself between Jason and me. I had to aim the gun skyward to keep from pointing it at his chest. He stared at me, his face thoughtful. 'You won't need the gun.' He knocked the great wolf to the floor with his fist. The wolf lay stunned. Only the rise and fall of its chest showed it was still alive.

When he turned back to me, his eyes were amber, and no longer human. 'You are my lupa, Anita, but I am still Ulfric. I won't let you do to me what Raina has done to Marcus. I lead this pack.'

There was a hardness to his voice that was new. I'd discovered his male ego at last.

Jean-Claude laughed, a high, delighted sound that made me shiver. Richard hugged his bare arms as if he felt it, too.

'Don't you realize by now, Richard, that *ma petite* is either your equal or your master? She knows no other way to be.' He came to stand by us. He looked amused as hell.

'I want her to be my equal,' Richard said.

'But not within the pack,' Jean-Claude said.

Richard shook his head. 'No, I mean . . . No, Anita is my equal.'

'Then what are you bitching about?' I said.

He glared at me with his alien eyes. 'I am Ulfric, not you.'

'Lead, and I'll follow, Richard.' I stepped close to him, almost touching. 'But lead, Richard, really lead, or get out of the way.'

28

'As amusing as this is,' Jean-Claude said, 'and believe me, *ma petite*, Richard, it is amusing. We do not have time for this particular argument, not if Richard stands any hope of not being forced to kill tonight.'

We both glared at him, and he gave that graceful shrug that meant everything and nothing. 'We must call the magic again, but this time, Richard needs to try and pull some of it into himself. He needs to do something that would impress his pack. This,' he motioned to the zombies, 'though impressive, looks too much like Anita's work.'

'You've got a suggestion, I take it.'

'Perhaps,' he said. His eyes turned very serious then, the humor dying away until his face was lovely and blank. 'But first, I think I have a question or two for you, myself, *ma petite*. I think it is not only Richard that you are emasculating today.'

'What are you talking about?' I asked.

He cocked his head to one side. 'Perhaps you honestly do not know?' He sounded surprised. 'There is a small hallway to the right. Look inside it.'

I could see the archway at the top of the hall, but the zombies filled the space, hiding the rest from view. 'Move forward,' I said. The zombies moved like a single organism, their dead eyes watching my face as if I were all that mattered. To them, I was.

The zombies moved like a shambling curtain. I could see the smaller hallway now, and the figures waiting inside. 'Stop,' I said. The zombies stopped as if I'd hit a switch.

Liv, the blond bouncer from Danse Macabre, stood just inside the smaller hallway. She was still dressed in her violet body suit. Her extraordinary violet eyes stared at me, empty, waiting. My pulse thudded in my throat. There were other figures behind her.

Richard said softly, 'This isn't possible.'

I didn't argue with him. It would have been too hard.

'Bring them out, *ma petite*, let us see who you have called from their coffins.' His voice was warm with the beginnings of anger.

'What's eating you?'

He laughed, but it was bitter. 'I threatened my people with this, but you said nothing. You did not tell me you could truly raise vampires like any other zombie.'

'I've only done it once before.'

'Indeed,' he said.

'Don't get all pissy on me.'

'I shall get pissy if I want to,' he said. 'These are my people, my companions, and you have them walking around like puppets. I find that most disquieting.'

'So do I,' I said. I looked back at the vampires. Liv, who had been so animated last night, stood there like a well-preserved zombie. No. No, I'd never have mistaken her for a zombie. I could feel a difference. But there she stood, that muscular body waiting for my next order. There were others behind her. I couldn't see how many. Too many.

'Can you put my vampires back, *ma petite*?'

I continued to look at Liv, avoiding Jean-Claude's eyes. 'I don't know.'

He touched my chin, turning me to face him. He studied my face, eyes searching, as if some hint of truth might show through. I let anger fill my face, anger was always a great thing to hide behind.

'What did you do with the last vampire you raised, *ma petite*?'

I pulled away from him. He grabbed my arm unbelievably fast. Too fast to see. What happened next was simply automatic. He held my right upper arm, but I could still bend at the elbow and point the Firestar at him. The Uzi in my left hand pointed at him, too. He could have crushed my arm before I fired one gun, but not both. But for the first time, staring down the barrel of a gun at him was problematic. The sash of his robe had come loose and I could see a triangle of pale flesh. I could see where his heart would be. I could blow his heart out his back and sever his spine. And I didn't want to do it. I didn't want to splatter that beautiful body all over the wall. Damn.

Richard came closer. He didn't touch either of us. He just stared from one to the other. 'Is he hurting you, Anita?'

'No,' I said.

'Then should you be pointing a gun at him?'

'He shouldn't be touching me,' I said.

Richard's voice was very mild. 'He just finished touching you a lot more than this, Anita.'

'Why are you helping him?'

'He helped me. Besides, if you kill him over something small and stupid, you'll never forgive yourself.'

I took a deep breath and let it out. Some of the tension eased with the breath. I lowered the Uzi.

Jean-Claude released my arm.

I pointed the Firestar at the floor and looked at Richard. There was something in his eyes, even the wolf's amber eyes, that was all too human. Pain. He knew how much Jean-Claude meant to me. It was there in his eyes. That one comment said that he understood my relationship with the vampire, maybe better than I did.

I wanted to apologize to him, but I wasn't sure he'd understand what it was for. I wasn't even sure I could explain it. If you love someone, truly love them, you should never cause them pain. Never fill their eyes with something so close to grief.

'I'm sorry I got mad at you earlier. You want what's best for the pack, I know that.'

'You still think I'm a fool to want a bloodless coup,' he said.

I stood on tiptoe and kissed him gently. 'Not a fool, just naive, terribly naive.'

'Very touching, *ma petite*. And I do appreciate your interference on my behalf, Richard, but these are my people. I promised them certain freedoms when they joined me. I ask again. Can you put them back as they were?'

I turned to Jean-Claude, one hand still balancing against Richard's chest. 'I don't know.'

'Then you had better find out, *ma petite*.'

It sounded too much like a threat for my taste, but . . . there was a figure behind Liv the bouncer that I couldn't take my eyes off of. I walked towards the waiting vampires. I opened my mouth, but no sound came out. My stomach clenched into a hard lump, my chest was tight. I finally said it: 'Willie McCoy, come to me.'

Willie walked out from behind the tall blond vampire. He was wearing the same chartreuse suit he'd had on at Danse Macabre. His brown eyes seemed to see me, but they were empty of that spark that was Willie. He wasn't home. It was like watching a puppet moving, and I was the puppet master. I tasted something bitter at the back of my throat. My eyes were hot and tight. I wasn't sure if I was going to throw up or cry first.

I stopped him about two feet from me. Close enough that I couldn't pretend or wish it away. I swallowed hard, and tears hot enough to scald ran down my face. 'I didn't want to know this,' I whispered.

Jean-Claude came to stand beside me. 'Willie,' he said, his voice vibrated through the room. Willie's body thrummed to the sound like a tuning fork struck. 'Willie, look at me.'

The blank, familiar face turned slowly towards his master.

Something flickered through the eyes for a moment; something moved that I had no name for.

'This has possibilities,' Jean-Claude said.

'Willie,' I said, 'look at me.' My voice wasn't nearly as impressive as the vampire's, but Willie turned to me.

'No,' Jean-Claude said, 'look at me, Willie.'

Willie hesitated.

'Willie,' I said, 'come to me.' I held out a hand and he took a step towards me.

Jean-Claude said, 'Stop, Willie, do not go to her.'

Willie hesitated, almost turning to Jean-Claude.

I concentrated on that curl of power inside of me, that thing that allowed me to raise the dead and let it wash over me, flow out of me. I called Willie's body to me and nothing Jean-Claude could do would get him to turn away from me.

Richard said, 'Stop it, both of you. He isn't a doll.'

'He isn't alive, either,' I said.

'He deserves better than this,' Richard said.

I agreed. I turned to Jean-Claude. 'He's mine, Jean-Claude. They're all mine. When night falls, they will be yours again, but their empty shells are mine.' I stepped close to him, and that swirl of power lashed out.

He took a hissing breath and backed up. Holding his hand as if I'd struck him.

'Never forget what I am and what I can do. No more threats between us, ever, or it will be the last threat.'

He stared at me, and for just a second, there was a flash of something I hadn't seen before: fear. Fear of me for the first time. Good.

Willie stared at me with empty, waiting eyes. He was dead, well and truly dead. Tears flowed down my face, tight and hard. Poor Willie, poor me. He wasn't human. All these months of being his friend and he was dead. Just dead. Damn.

'What happened to the first vampire you raised, *ma petite*? Why didn't you put it back into its coffin?' A thought slid behind his eyes. I watched the idea form, and fall from his lips. 'How did Monsieur Bouvier get the lower half of his body melted away?'

Magnus Bouvier had been Serephina's mortal servant. It had been his job to keep me near Serephina's coffin until she rose to finish me off. I scrubbed at my face, trying to get rid of the tears. Always ruins the effect when you cry. 'You know the answer,' I said. My voice sounded strained and small.

'Say it aloud, *ma petite*, let me hear it from your own lips.'

'I feel like I'm missing part of this conversation,' Richard said, 'What are you two talking about?'

'Tell him, *ma petite*.'

'The vampire grabbed Magnus around the waist and held on. I'd planned on it slowing him down, nothing else. I got to the door and ran outside. The sunlight hit the vampire and it burst into flames. I expected Magnus to go back inside, but he didn't. He kept coming, dragging her into the light.' Saying it fast didn't make it any better.

I stood in the middle of the dead I had called, hugging myself. I still had dreams about Serephina. Still saw Magnus reaching out to me, begging me to save him. I could have shot him and never lost a moment's sleep, but burning him alive was torture. I didn't do torture. Not to mention that Ellie Quinlan had already risen as a vampire, which made her legally alive. I'd killed them both, and it hadn't been pretty.

Richard was looking at me, a look of something close to horror on his face. 'You burned the man and the vampire alive?' I watched the brown in his eyes swim back to the surface. The entire shape of the eye changed while I watched. It looked almost like it should hurt. If it did hurt, he never showed it.

'I didn't plan it, Richard. I didn't want it to happen, but I would have done anything to escape Serephina. Anything.'

'I don't understand that.'

'I know,' I said.

'There is no shame in surviving, *ma petite*.' I turned to Jean-Claude. There was no shock on his face. It was lovely and unreadable as a doll's.

'Then why can't I read your face right now?'

Life flowed back into his face, filled his eyes, moved behind his skin until he was there, staring at me. The look in his eyes wasn't what I expected. Fear was still there and surprise, but underneath was worry.

'Better?' he asked.

'Yes.' I frowned. 'What's worrying you?'

He sighed. 'All honesty is eventually punished, but not usually this quickly.'

'Answer me, Jean-Claude.'

His eyes went past me to the werewolves waiting at Richard's back. 'No one must speak of what has happened here, not to anyone.'

'Why not?' Richard asked.

'It would embarrass *ma petite*.'

'That's true,' I said, 'but that's not what you mean. You don't mind embarrassing me. Hell, this story would make a great threat for all your vampires. It'd scare the hell out of them.'

'That, *ma petite*, is the point.'

I sighed. 'Stop being obtuse and just tell us.'

'I do not want this,' he waved at the vampires, 'coming to the attention of the vampire council.'

'Why not?' Richard and I asked together.

'Put simply, *ma petite*, they will kill you.'

'I'm your registered human servant,' I said, 'you said you did that to keep me safe.'

'For this they will come and see for themselves, *ma petite*. Whoever they send will know instantly that you do not bear my marks. You are my servant in name only. That will not be enough for them. Without any binding between us, they will not trust you.'

'So they'll kill her, just like that?' Richard asked. He moved closer to me as if he'd touch me, but his hands hesitated above my shoulders.

Without looking at him, I said, 'One story about burning people alive and you don't want to touch me. You prejudiced little were-wolf, you.' I tried to keep my voice light but a harsh edge crept in.

His hands gripped my shoulders tightly. 'It really bothers you, what you did, doesn't it?'

I turned to see his face, his hands still on my shoulders. 'Of course it bothers me. I didn't just kill Magnus, I tortured him to death. Ellie Quinlan didn't deserve to be burned alive.' I shook my head and tried to step away from him. He slid his arms across my back, holding me gently against him.

'I'm sorry you had to do it.' He touched my hair with one hand, the other still against my back. 'Your eyes are haunted by it, by what you did. Don't take this wrong, but it makes me feel better to see that pain in your eyes.'

I pushed away from him. 'Did you think I could kill someone by torture and feel nothing?'

He met my eyes but it seemed like it was an effort. 'I wasn't sure.'

I shook my head.

Jean-Claude took my left hand; the other was still holding the Firestar. He turned me to face him. He raised my hand towards his lips as he bowed slowly towards me. He spoke as he moved, 'There is nothing that you could ever do that would make me not desire the touch of your body.' He kissed my hand. His lips lingered a little longer than was polite. His tongue licked across my skin, and I pulled away.

'It scares you that I can raise vampires like this.'

'Perhaps, *ma petite*, but I have frightened you for years and yet you are still here.'

He had a point. I stared at Willie. 'Let's see if we can put everyone back where they belong.' I hoped I could do it. I wanted Willie back, even if it was only a lie. He walked, he talked, it was still Willie. Or maybe, I just wanted it to be Willie. Maybe I needed it to be Willie.

29

'Take me to the coffin room,' I said.

'Why?' Jean-Claude asked. There was something in the way he said that one word that made me stare at him.

'Because I asked.'

'How would my flock feel if I allowed the Executioner to enter their private chamber while they slept helpless?'

'I'm not going to kill anybody today, not on purpose.'

'I do not like the way you said that, *ma petite*.'

'Uncontrolled power is unpredictable, Jean-Claude. All sorts of unpleasant things can happen. I need to see where the vampires will be resting. I want to try and put them back in a controlled manner.'

'What sorts of unpleasant things?' Richard asked.

It was a good question. Since I was pretty much flying blind, I didn't have a good answer. 'It takes less power to put back than it does to raise. If we just call it up wild and try to will them back . . . ' I shook my head.

'You could extinguish their life force,' Cassandra said.

I looked at her. 'What did you say?'

'You're going to put them back in their coffins as you would a zombie, but with a zombie you will it to be dead again, correct?'

I hadn't really thought of it that way, but she was right.

'If you will the vampires back in their coffins, you're in effect willing them dead again like a zombie, right?'

'Yeah.'

'But you don't want them permanently dead.'

My head was beginning to hurt. 'No, I don't want them permanently dead.'

'How do you know so very much about necromancy, Cassandra?' Jean-Claude asked.

'I have a master's degree in magical theory.'

'That must be useful on a résumé,' I said.

'Not in the least,' she said, 'but it might be useful now.'

'Did you know your newest pack member was so well-educated, Richard?' Jean-Claude asked.

'Yes,' he said, 'it's one of the reasons I gave her permission to move here.'

'Permission to move here?' I said, 'Why did she need your permission?'

'A werewolf has to get the permission of the local pack leader before they can enter a new territory. If they don't, it's considered a challenge to his authority.'

'Did she have to ask your permission or Marcus's?'

'Both,' Cassandra said. 'Most werewolves won't come near Saint Louis while this power struggle is going on.'

'Why did you come, then, my wolf?' Jean-Claude asked.

'I liked what I heard about Richard. He's trying to bring the pack into the twentieth century.'

'Did you come planning to be his lupa?' I asked. Yes, a little twinge of jealousy had reared its ugly head.

Cassandra smiled. 'Maybe, but the job's filled. I came here to avoid fighting, not to start it.'

'You have come to the wrong place, I fear,' Jean-Claude said.

She shrugged. 'If I waited until the battle was over and it was safe, I wouldn't be worth much, would I?'

'You came to fight at Monsieur Zeeman's side?'

'I came because I agree with what he's trying to do.'

'You don't approve of killing?' I asked.

'Not really.'

'Why, Richard, you have found a kindred spirit,' Jean-Claude said, smiling, and far too pleased.

'Cassandra believes in the sanctity of life; a lot of people do,' Richard said. He wouldn't look at me.

'If she's a better match for you than I am, I won't stand in your way.'

He turned to me, a look of astonishment on his face. 'Anita . . .' He shook his head. 'I'm in love with you.'

'You'd get over it,' I said. My chest was tight with the offer, but I meant it. Richard and I had a basic fundamental difference of opinion. It wasn't going away. One of us was going to have to compromise, and it wasn't going to be me. I couldn't quite meet Richard's eyes, but I didn't take it back.

He stepped in front of me, and all I could see was his bare chest. There was a scratch just below his left nipple, blood drying on his skin in darkening strings. He touched my chin, raising my face until I met his eyes. He studied my face like he'd never seen it before.

'I would never get over losing you, Anita. Never.'

'Never's a long time to tie yourself to a killer.'

'You don't have to be a killer,' he said.

I stepped away from him. 'If you're hanging around me waiting for me to soften up and become this good little girl, you might as well leave now.'

He grabbed my arms, pulling me against his body. 'I want you, Anita, all of you.' He kissed me, arms locked behind my back, raising me up against him.

I slid my hands behind his back, Firestar still in one hand. I pressed my body against his hard enough to know he was happy to see me.

We came up for air, and I pulled back, but not out of his arms, half laughing. I caught a glimpse of Jean-Claude standing to one side. The look on his face wiped the smile from my lips. It wasn't jealousy. It was hunger. Desire. Watching us together had excited him.

I drew back from Richard and found blood on my hands. It was hard to tell on the navy blue shirt but there were wet spots where I'd pressed myself against the bloody scratches. Some of the wounds were deep enough that they were still seeping blood.

Richard was looking at Jean-Claude, too, now. I stepped away from Richard, holding up the bloody hand. I walked towards the vampire, and his eyes stayed on the fresh blood, not on me. I stopped less than a foot from him, my hand held out in front of his face.

'Which would you rather have right now, sex or blood?'

His eyes flicked to my face, back to my hand, then to my face. I watched the effort it took for him to keep eye contact. 'Ask Richard which he would rather have just after he changes into a wolf, sex or fresh meat?'

I glanced back at Richard. 'What's your choice?'

'Just after the change, meat.' He said it like I should have known the answer.

I turned back to the vampire. I slid the Firestar into the front of my pants, and moved the bloody hand towards his lips.

Jean-Claude grabbed my wrist. 'Do not tease me, *ma petite*. My control is not boundless.' A tremor ran through his arm and down his hand. He looked away, eyes closed.

I touched his face with my right hand, turning him back to face me. 'Who says I'm teasing?' I said softly. 'Take us to the coffin room.'

Jean-Claude searched my face. 'What do you offer me, *ma petite*?'

'Blood,' I said.

'And sex?' he asked.

'Which would you rather have, right this minute?' I stared at him, willing the truth in his face.

He gave a shaky laugh. 'Blood.'

I smiled, and pulled my wrist away. 'Remember, it was your choice.'

A look passed over his face that was a mixture of surprise and irony. 'Touché, *ma petite*, but I am beginning to have hopes that this will not be the last time I am given the choice.' There was a heat to his voice, his eyes, just standing this close to his body, that made me shiver.

I glanced back at Richard. He was watching us. I expected to see jealousy or anger, but all I could read in his eyes was need. Lust. I was pretty sure that Richard's choice right this minute would be sex, but the thought of a little blood thrown in didn't seem to worry him. In fact, it seemed to excite him. I was beginning to wonder if the werewolf and vampire shared similar tastes in foreplay. The thought should have scared me, but it didn't. That was a very, very bad sign.

30

The last time I'd been in the coffin room under Circus of the Damned, I'd come to slay the current Master of the City. I'd come to slay every vampire in the place. My, how things had changed.

Track lighting in solid white fixtures clung to the walls, casting soft halos of light on each of seven coffins. Three of the coffins were empty, their lids propped open. All of the coffins were modern, new, roomy. They were all a rich varnished oak, stained nearly black. Silver handles graced the wood. The satin linings of the open coffins were different colors; white, blue, red. The coffin with the red interior held a sword in a specially made side sheath: a freaking two-handed sword as long as I was tall. A pair of the ugliest fuzzy dice I'd ever seen were suspended from the white satin coffin. It had to be Willie's. The blue satin held a small extra pillow. Standing over the coffin, the smell of herbs rose musty, vaguely sweet. I touched the small pillow and found it filled with dried herbs. 'Herbs for sweet dreams,' I said to no one in particular.

'Is there some purpose to you handling their personal belongings, *ma petite?*'

I looked at him. 'What keepsakes do you have in your coffin?'

He just smiled.

'Why all the same coffins?'

'If you came in here to kill us, where would you start?'

I looked around at the identical coffins. 'I don't know. If someone comes in, they can't tell who's the oldest or who's the Master of the City. It covers your ass but endangers the rest.'

'If someone comes to kill us, *ma petite*, it is to everyone's benefit if the oldest are not killed first. There is always a chance that one of the older ones could awaken in time to save the rest.'

I nodded. 'Why the extra-wide, extra-high interiors?'

'Would you want to spend eternity on your back, *ma petite*?' He smiled and came to stand beside me, leaning his butt against the open coffin, arms crossed over his chest. 'There are so many other more comfortable positions.'

I felt heat rise up my face.

Richard joined us. 'Are you two going to exchange witty repartee or are we going to do this?' He leaned on the closed end of the coffin, forearms resting on it. There was a bloody scratch on his right upper arm. He seemed at home. Jason, still furry and big enough to ride, padded over the stone floor, nails clicking. The wolf's head was high enough that it licked Richard's bloody arm while still on all fours. There were moments when I felt Richard was too normal to fit into my life. This wasn't one of them.

'Yeah, we're going to do it,' I said.

Richard stood, running his fingers through his thick hair, getting it out of his face, and showing his chest off to good advantage. For the first time, I wondered if he'd done it on purpose. I searched his face for that edge of teasing that Jean-Claude had, that knowledge that even that simple movement touched me. There was nothing. Richard's face was guileless, handsome, empty of ulterior motives.

I exchanged glances with Jean-Claude. He shrugged. 'If you do not understand him, do not look to me. I am not in love with him.'

Richard looked puzzled. 'Did I miss something?' He stroked under the wolf's throat, pressing the head against his chest. The wolf made a high whimpering sound of pleasure. Glad to be back in the pack leader's good graces, I guess.

I shook my head. 'Not really.'

'Why are we here?' Stephen asked. He was as close to the door as he could get and not be outside the room. His shoulders were hunched. He was scared, but of what?

Cassandra stood near Stephen, inside the room, closer to us. Her face was bland, unreadable except for a certain wariness around the eyes. They both wore jeans with oversized shirts.

Stephen's was a man's pale blue dress shirt. Cassandra had an oversized T-shirt a dull pine green with a wolf's head done large with huge, yellow eyes.

'What's wrong, Stephen?' Richard asked.

Stephen blinked and shook his head.

'We all heard Anita tell Jean-Claude she'd need more blood, fresh blood,' Cassandra said. She looked at me while she finished the thought. 'I think Stephen's worried where the fresh blood's coming from.'

'I'm not into human sacrifice,' I said.

'Some people don't consider a lycanthrope human,' Cassandra said.

'I do,' I said.

She looked at me, judging my words. Some lycanthropes could tell if you were lying. I was betting she was one of them. 'Then where are you going to get the blood?'

It was a good question. I wasn't sure I had a good answer. 'I don't know, but it won't take a death.'

'Are you sure?' she asked.

I shrugged. 'If it takes a death to put them back, they're dead. I'm not going to kill anybody else to bring them back.' I looked at the three waiting vampires after I said it. Liv, Willie, and surprisingly, Damian. Raising the vampires was impressive enough, raising one as powerful as Damian was downright scary. He wasn't a master vampire, never would be, but he'd have frightened me in a fair fight. Now he stood dressed only in the green Lycra pants and the pirate sash. His upper body gleamed like muscled marble under the glow of the lights. His green eyes stared at me with a patient waiting that only the truly dead can manage.

'You are shivering, *ma petite*.'

'We raise the power again, then we need blood.' I looked at Jean-Claude and Richard. 'If Richard has to fight Marcus tonight, I'm not sure he should be the one who supplies this round of blood.'

Jean-Claude cocked his head to one side. I expected him to say something irritating, but he didn't. Maybe even a very old dog could learn new tricks.

'He is not sinking fangs into you,' Richard said. Anger made his brown eyes dark and sparkling, he was lovely when he was angry. That aura of energy flared around him, close enough to creep down my bare skin.

'You can't donate twice this close together, with Marcus waiting for you,' I said.

Richard grabbed me by the upper arms. 'You don't understand, Anita. Feeding is like sex to him.'

Again, I half-expected Jean-Claude to chime in, but he didn't. I had to say it. Damn. 'It won't be the first time he's done it, Richard.'

Richard's fingers dug into my arms. 'I know that. I saw the fang marks on your wrist. But remember, you weren't under any mind control that time.'

'I remember,' I said. 'It hurt like hell.'

Richard drew me to him with his hands still holding only my upper arms, drew me to tiptoe as if he'd drag me to his face. 'Without mind control, it's like rape, not the real thing. It'll be real this time.'

'You're hurting me, Richard.' My voice was calm, steady, but the look on his face scared me. The intensity in his hands, his face, his body, was unnerving.

He eased down, but didn't take his hands away. 'Take blood from Jason or Cassandra.'

I shook my head. 'That might work or it might not. If the blood comes from one of us, I know it'll work. Besides, should you be offering up other people's blood without asking them first?'

Doubt slid behind his eyes, and he let me go. His long hair fell forward, hiding his face. 'You say you've chosen me. That you're in love with me. That you don't want to have sex with him. Now, you tell me you want him to feed off of you. That's as bad as sex.' He stalked the room, pacing around the waiting vampires, swinging back in an agitated stride that filled the room with a warm, creeping power.

'I didn't say I wanted to feed him,' I said.

He stopped in the middle of the room, staring at me. 'But you do, don't you?'

'No,' I said, and it was true. 'I've never been interested in that.'

'She speaks the truth,' Jean-Claude said at last.

'You stay out of this,' Richard said, pointing a finger at him.

Jean-Claude gave a small bow and fell silent. He was behaving himself far too well. Made me nervous. Of course, Richard was having enough of a fit for both of them.

'Then let me feed him again.'

'Isn't it sexual for you, too?' I asked.

Richard shook his head. 'It was you I was looking at, Anita, not him. A little pain is fine.'

It was my turn to shake my head. 'Are you truly saying that letting him sink fangs into my body would bother you as much as sinking . . . ' I let the thought die unspoken. 'I see donating blood as the lesser evil, Richard. Don't you?'

'Yes,' he hissed. His power was filling the room like warm, electric water. I could almost reach out and grab it.

'Then what are you bitching about?' I said. 'We wouldn't have done it the first time, but you wanted me to do it. You wanted us to do it.' I stalked towards him, finally angry myself. 'You don't want to kill Marcus, fine, but this is the price. You want enough power to cow the rest of the pack without losing your humanity, great, but that kind of power isn't free.' I stood in front of him, so close that his power danced over my skin like fine needles, like sex that rode that edge between pleasure and pain.

'It's too late to back out now. We are not going to strand Willie and the others because you're getting cold feet.' I took that last step, putting our bodies so close together that a deep breath would have made them touch. I lowered my voice to a whisper, though I knew everything in the room would still hear me. 'It isn't the blood that bothers you. What bothers you is that you enjoyed it.' I lowered my voice until it was almost a movement of lips with only a breath of sound. 'Jean-Claude isn't just seducing me, he's seducing us.'

Richard stared down at me, and the look in his true brown eyes was lost, hopeless. A little boy who's discovered the monster under the bed is actually real, and it's screwing Mommy.

Jean-Claude's power eased through the room, mingling with Richard's electric warmth like a cool wind from the grave. We both turned and looked at the vampire. He was smiling ever so slightly. He undid his robe and let it fall to the floor. He glided towards us, wearing nothing but his silk pajamas and a knowing smile. His own power making his long hair flare round his face like a small wind.

Richard touched my shoulders and even that chaste touch sent a line of warm, shivering energy along my skin. The power was there for the calling, just below the surface. We didn't need all the sexual charades.

Jean-Claude reached a pale hand out towards me. I met his hand with mine, and that one touch was enough. That cool, burning power flowed over me, through me, into Richard. I heard Richard gasp. Jean-Claude started to move forward, like he'd press his body against mine. I held him away from me with the hand that was entwined in his, straight-arming him. 'It's here, Jean-Claude, can't you feel it?'

He nodded. 'Your power calls to me, *ma petite*.'

Richard's hands slid over my shoulders, his face brushing my hair. 'Now what?'

'We ride the power this time, it doesn't ride us.'

'How?' Richard whispered.

Jean-Claude looked at me with eyes that were deep as any ocean and as full of secrets. 'I believe *ma petite* has a plan.'

'Yeah,' I said, 'I have a plan.' I looked from one to the other of them. 'I'm going to call Dominic Dumare and see if he knows how to put vampires back in their coffins.' Dominic had been cleared of Robert's murder. He had an airtight alibi. He'd been with a woman. Even if he hadn't been, I might have asked for his help. I wanted to save Willie more than I wanted to revenge Robert.

A strange expression crossed Jean-Claude's face. 'You, asking for help, *ma petite*? That is unusual.'

I drew away from both of them. We could get the power back, I was pretty certain of that. I looked at Willie's empty face and the fuzzy dice hanging from his coffin. 'If I make a mistake, Willie's gone. I want him back.'

There were times when I thought that it wasn't Jean-Claude who had convinced me that vampires weren't always monsters. It was Willie and Dead Dave, ex-cop and bar owner. It was a host of lesser vampires that seemed, occasionally, like nice guys. Jean-Claude was a lot of things; nice was not one of them.

31

Dominic Dumare showed up wearing a pair of black dress slacks and a black leather jacket unzipped over a grey silk T-shirt. He looked more relaxed without Sabin looking on, like an employee on his day off. Even the neatly trimmed Vandyke beard and mustache seemed less formal.

Dominic walked around the three vampires I'd raised. We'd moved back out into the rubble-strewn main area, so he could see the zombies and the vampires all at once. He paced around the vampires, touching them here and there. He grinned at me, teeth flashing in his dark beard. 'This is marvelous, truly marvelous.'

I fought the urge to frown at him. 'Forgive me if I don't share your enthusiasm. Can you help me put them back the way they were?'

'Theoretically, yes.'

'When people start using the word *theoretically*, it means they don't know how to do something. You can't help me, can you?'

'Now, now,' Dominic said. He knelt by Willie, staring up at him, studying him like a bug under a bioscope. 'I didn't say I couldn't help. It's true that I've never seen this done. And you say you've done this before.' He stood up, brushing off the knees of his pants.

'Once.'

'That time was without the triumvirate?' Dominic asked.

I'd had to tell him. I understood enough about ritual magic to know that if we withheld how we'd gotten this much power, anything Dominic helped us come up with wouldn't work. It would be like telling the police it was a burglary when it was really a murder. They'd be trying to solve the wrong crime.

'Yeah, the first time was just me.'

'But both times in daylight hours?' he asked.

I nodded.

'That makes sense. We can only raise zombies after the souls have flown. It would make sense that vampires can only be raised during the day. When darkness falls, their souls return.'

I wasn't even going to try and argue about whether or not vampires had souls. I wasn't as sure of the answer as I used to be.

'I can't raise zombies during daylight hours. Let alone vampires,' I said.

Dominic motioned at all the waiting dead of both kinds. 'But you did it.'

I shook my head. 'That's not the point. I'm not supposed to be able to do it.'

'Have you ever tried to raise normal zombies during daylight hours?'

'Well, no. The man who trained me said it wasn't possible.'

'So you never tried,' Dominic said.

I hesitated before answering.

'You have tried,' he said.

'I can't do it. I can't even call the power under the light of the sun.'

'Only because you believe you can't,' Dominic said.

'Run that by me again.'

'Belief is one of the most important aspects of magic.'

'You mean, if I don't believe I can raise zombies during the day, I can't.'

'Exactly.'

'That doesn't make sense,' Richard said. He leaned against

one of the intact walls. He'd been very quiet while I talked magic with Dominic. Jason, still in wolf form, lay at his feet. Stephen had cleared some of the broken stones and sat beside the wolf.

'Actually,' I said, 'it does. I've seen people with a lot of raw talent that couldn't raise anything. One guy was convinced it was a mortal sin so he just blocked it out. But he shone with power whether he wanted to accept it or not.'

'A shapeshifter can deny his power all he wants, but that doesn't keep him from changing,' Richard said.

'I believe that is why lycanthropy is referred to as a curse,' Dominic said.

Richard looked at me. The expression on his face was eloquent. 'A curse.'

'You'll have to forgive Dominic,' Jean-Claude said. 'A hundred years ago, it never occurred to anyone that lycanthropy could be a disease.'

'Concern for Richard's feelings?' I asked.

'His happiness is your happiness, *ma petite*.'

Jean-Claude's new gentlemanly behavior was beginning to bug me. I didn't trust his change of heart.

Cassandra said, 'If Anita didn't believe she could raise the dead during daylight hours, then how did she do it?' She had joined in the metaphysical discussion like it was a graduate class in magical theory. I'd met people like her in college. Theorists who had no real magic of their own. But they could sit around for hours debating whether a theoretical spell would work. They treated magic like higher physics, a pure science without any true way of testing. Heaven forbid the ivory tower magicians should actually try out their theories in a real spell. Dominic would have fit in well with them, except he had his own magic.

'Both occasions were extreme situations,' Dominic said. 'It works on the same principle that allows a grandmother to lift a truck off her grandchild. In times of great need, we often touch abilities beyond the everyday.'

'But the grandmother can't lift a car at will, just because she did it once,' I said.

'Hmm,' Dominic said, 'perhaps the analogy is not perfect, but you understand what I am saying. If you say you do not, you are merely being difficult.'

That almost made me smile. 'So you're saying that I could raise the dead in daylight if I believed I could.'

'I believe so.'

I shook my head. 'I've never heard of any animator being able to do that.'

'But you are not merely an animator, Anita,' Dominic said. 'You are a necromancer.'

'*I* have never heard of a necromancer that could raise the dead in broad daylight,' Jean-Claude said.

Dominic shrugged gracefully. It reminded me of Jean-Claude. It takes a couple hundred years to make a shrug pretty. 'I don't know about broad daylight, but just as some vampires can walk around during the day, as long as they are sufficiently sheltered, I believe the same principle would apply to necromancers.'

'So you don't believe Anita could raise the dead at high noon out of doors, either?' Cassandra said.

Dominic shrugged again. Then he laughed. 'You have caught me, my studious beauty. It may well be possible for Anita to do exactly that, but even I have never heard of such a thing.'

I shook my head. 'Look, we can explore the magical implications later. Right now, can you help me figure a way to put the vampires back without screwing them up?'

'Define screwing them up,' Dominic said.

'Do not joke, Dominic,' Jean-Claude said. 'You know precisely what she means.'

'I want to hear it from her lips.'

Jean-Claude looked at me and gave a barely perceptible shrug.

'When darkness falls, I want them to rise as vampires. I'm afraid if I do this wrong, they'll just be dead, permanently.'

'You surprise me, Anita. Perhaps your reputation as the scourge of the local vampire populace is exaggerated.'

I stared at him. Before I could say something that sounded like bragging, Jean-Claude spoke. 'I would think what she has done today is proof enough of how very much she deserves her reputation.'

Dominic and the vampire stared at each other. Something seemed to pass between them. A challenge, a knowledge, something. 'She would make an amazing human servant if only some vampire could tame her,' Dominic said.

Jean-Claude laughed. The sound filled the room with echoes that shivered and danced across the skin. The laughter swept through my body, and for the briefest moment, I could feel something touch me deep inside where no hand belonged.

In another context Jean-Claude might have made it sexual; now it was simply disturbing.

'Don't ever do that again,' Richard said. He rubbed his bare arms as if he were cold or trying to erase the memory of that invasive laughter.

Jason trotted over to Jean-Claude, to butt his head against the vampire's hand. He'd liked it.

Dominic gave a little bow. 'My apologies, Jean-Claude, you have made your point. If you wished to, you could cause the damage that my master caused by accident at your office.'

'My office,' I said. Personally, I didn't think that Jean-Claude could cause damage with just his voice. I'd been in situations where if he could have done it, he would have. No sense telling Dominic that, though.

Dominic gave an even lower bow in my direction. 'Your office, of course.'

'Can we cut the grandstanding?' I said. 'Can you help us?'

'I am more than willing to try.'

I walked up to him, picking my way over the broken stones. When I was standing as close as was polite and maybe an inch or so more, I said, 'These three vampires are not an experiment. This is not some graduate study in magical metaphysics. You offered to teach me necromancy, Dominic. I think you're not up to the job. How can you teach me when I can do things you can't? Unless, of course, you can raise vampires from their coffins?'

I stared into his dark eyes the entire time I spoke, watching the anger narrow his eyes, tighten his lips. His ego was as big as I'd hoped. I knew he wouldn't disappoint me. Dominic would do his best for us now. His pride was at stake.

'Tell me exactly how you called the power, Anita, and I will build you a spell that should work – if you have the control to make it work.'

I smiled at him, and I made sure it was just this side of condescending. 'You come up with it, I can pull it off.'

He smiled. 'Arrogance is not a becoming trait in a woman.'

'I find it a very becoming trait,' Jean-Claude said. 'If it's deserved. If you had just raised three vampires from their daytime rest, wouldn't you be arrogant, Dominic?'

His smile widened. 'Yes, I would be.'

Truth was, I didn't feel arrogant. I was scared. Scared that I'd screwed Willie up and he would never rise again. I felt bad too, about Liv and Damian. It wasn't a matter of liking them or not; I didn't mean to do it. You shouldn't extinguish someone's life force by accident. If I felt half as secure as my words to Dominic, why did my stomach hurt?

32

Dominic, Cassandra, and I came up with a spell. The part of the plan that was my idea was very simple. I had put zombies back in their graves for years. I was good at it. As far as I was able, I was going to treat this like just another job: laying the dead to rest, nothing special. Lay the zombies first, worry about the vamps later.

I had Cassandra fetch one of my knives and a wrist sheath from the bedroom. If I'd been acting as a focus for another animator, I wouldn't have let him sink teeth into me, so why did the blood have to come from Jean-Claude drinking it? It didn't, or I didn't think it did. Dominic agreed with me, but he wasn't a hundred percent sure. So zombies first. They'd be the practice. If the knife didn't work, we'd go to fangs, but what little normalcy was left to me, I was going to cling to.

I'd sent Stephen for a bowl to hold the blood. He'd returned with a small, golden bowl. I wondered if the size was deliberate, to encourage me not to spill too much blood. For a werewolf, Stephen didn't seem to like blood very much. The bowl was polished to a shine so bright it almost glowed. The inside showed the dimpled blows of hammer work. Beaten gold, and I knew as soon as I touched it, it was old. Why does everyone think you have to have something special to hold the blood? Tupperware would have worked.

We stood in the rubble-strewn room where the zombies waited, patient as only the dead can be. Some of the eyes that watched me were sunken like the blind eyes of dead fish, a few skulls were empty, and even without eyes, they all seemed to be looking at me.

I stood, knife strapped to my left wrist, facing them.

Richard stood to my left, Jean-Claude to my right. They weren't touching me, by my request.

Dominic had asked for enough details of the first triumvirate that I'd been embarrassed. He agreed with me that the power was probably there without us having to crawl all over each other. Agreeing to that alone earned him brownie points. After all, the plan was to raise the magic tonight in front of the whole pack. I didn't really want to be having sex in front of that many strangers. All right, it wasn't exactly sex, but it was close enough that I didn't want an audience.

The glow was fading. Staring at the partially rotting zombies, it was hard to regain the mood. 'My zombies usually hold together better than this,' I said.

'If you had pulled this much power from two other necromancers, the zombies would be better,' Dominic said.

'Perhaps it was the lack of control,' Jean-Claude said.

I turned and looked at him. 'I think Dominic means that some of the power that raised them was taken from a dead man.'

'Do you believe I am a dead man, *ma petite*?'

I stared into that lovely face and nodded. 'The vampires I raised are just corpses. Whatever you are, it's a form of necromancy. Necromancy only works when you start with a dead body.'

He cocked his head to one side. 'I hear your words, *ma petite*, but I do not think you believe them, not completely.'

I shook my head. 'I don't know what I believe anymore.'

'Actually,' Dominic said, 'I don't believe it matters that Jean-Claude is a vampire. I think it is more that neither he nor Richard know anything of raising the dead. That is your talent alone. I think with practice, you could channel the power into perfect zombies, but in a way, Jean-Claude is right. The wildness of it, the lack of control, made the zombies less perfect.'

Something must have shown on my face, because he said, 'You

had too many things to control to pay attention to all the details. I think you instinctively let the zombies go, because it was the part you were most sure of. You have excellent instincts.'

'Thanks, I guess,' I said.

He smiled. 'I know time is growing short. As we can see from Jean-Claude's presence, not all vampires sleep until full dark. I fear that if one of the vampires passes its waking hour, that he or she will be lost. But I would ask Anita to do one thing for me that has nothing to do with her problem, but everything to do with mine.'

'What problem?' I asked.

'Sabin,' Jean-Claude said.

Dominic nodded. 'Sabin's time is running short.'

'Sabin, the vampire at the club?' Cassandra asked.

'Yeah,' I said. 'What do you need, Dominic? Make it quick, and I'm your girl.'

Dominic smiled. 'Thank you, Anita. Concentrate on one of your zombies. Try to bring it closer to perfection.'

I frowned at him.

'Heal one of your zombies, *ma petite*.'

'You can't heal the dead,' I said, 'but I can make them more life-like.'

Dominic nodded. 'That would do very nicely.'

'I usually do that during the initial rush of power. I've never tried to fiddle with my dead once they were raised.'

'Please try,' Dominic said.

'We could raise the power between the three of us, then try it,' I said.

Dominic shook his head. 'I am not sure what that would do to the spell. I think it would be taking a great risk with your companions.'

I stared at him for a heartbeat or two. 'You'd risk leaving Sabin to rot to save our friends?'

'You asked for my help, Anita. I think you are not a woman who asks for help often. It would be poor payment of such a compliment if I let you risk your friends for mine. If you can heal your dead cold, as it were, so be it. If you cannot, we will proceed to save these three vampires.'

'A very honorable sentiment,' Jean-Claude said.

'There are moments when honor is all that is left,' Dominic said.

The vampire and the man seemed to have a moment of near perfect understanding. A wealth of history, if not shared, then similar, passed between them. I was odd woman out.

I looked to Richard and we had our own moment of perfect understanding. We valued our mortal life span. The fatalism in Dominic's voice had been frightening. How old was he? I could usually tell with a vampire, but never with a human servant. I didn't ask. There was a weight of years in Dominic's brown eyes that made me afraid to ask.

I looked at Jean-Claude's lovely face and wondered if I would be as honorable, or would I have risked anyone, everyone, to heal him? To see Jean-Claude dead would be one thing, but rotted away like Sabin . . . It would be worse than death in many ways. Of course, Sabin was dying. Powerful as he was, he couldn't hold himself together forever. Or maybe he could. Maybe Dominic could sew him up in a big sack, like the gloves the vampire wore on his hands. Maybe Sabin could go on living even after he'd been reduced to so much liquid. Now that was a hideous thought.

I stared at the standing dead. They looked back. One of the zombies was almost intact. Grey skin clung to the bones, more like clay than flesh. One blue eye stared at me. The other eye had shriveled like a raisin. It reminded me of what had happened to Sabin's eye.

It would make more sense to say I touched the eye and healed it. Or that I thought at it and smoothed the flesh like clay. It wasn't like that. I stared at the zombie. I touched that spark inside me that allowed me to raise the dead. I drew that part of me outward, coaxed it like feeding a small flame, and threw it outward into that one zombie. I whispered, 'Live, live.'

I'd watched it before, but it never ceased to amaze me. The flesh filled out, plumping, smoothing. A warm flesh tone spread like heat across the grey skin. The dry, strawlike hair grew and curled, brown and soft. The dead eye blew up like a small balloon, filling the socket. Two good eyes looked back at me. Even the tattered clothing mended itself. He wore a vest with a gold watch chain. His clothes were a hundred years or more out of date.

'I am most impressed,' Dominic said. 'If you changed his clothes, he could pass for human.'

I nodded. 'I make great zombies, but that won't help your master.'

'Call one of the vampires from the coffin room.'

'Why?' I asked.

Dominic drew a small silver knife from a sheath at his back. I hadn't known he had a weapon. Careless of me.

'What are you going to do with that?' Jean-Claude asked.

'With your permission, I will cut one of the vampires and ask Anita to heal the wound.'

Jean-Claude considered the request, then nodded. 'A small cut.'

Dominic bowed. 'Of course.'

The vamps could heal a small cut on their own eventually. If I couldn't heal it, no harm done. Though I wasn't sure the vampires would agree with me.

'Anita,' Dominic said.

I called, 'Damian, come to me.'

Jean-Claude raised his eyebrows at my choice, I think. If he expected me to call Willie, he didn't understand. Willie was my friend. Even dead, I didn't want to see him cut up.

Damian had tried to mind-rape a woman tonight at the club. Let him get cut up just a little.

Damian walked in, staring until he found me. His face was still blank and empty. Emptier than sleep, empty as only death can make it.

'Damian, stop.'

The vampire stopped. His eyes were the greenest I'd ever seen. Greener than Catherine's, more cat than human.

Dominic stopped in front of Damian. He stared at the vampire. He laid the silver blade against the pale cheek and pulled the point downward, sharply.

Blood flowed down that perfect paleness in a thin crimson wash. The vampire never reacted, not even to blink.

'Anita,' Dominic said.

I stared at Damian, no, Damian's shell. I flung power at him, into him. I willed him to live. That was the word I whispered to him.

The blood slowed, then stopped. The cut knit together seamlessly. It was . . . easy.

Dominic wiped the blood away with a handkerchief he'd drawn from his jacket pocket. Damian's pale cheek was flawless once more.

It was Cassandra who said it first, 'She could heal Sabin.'

Dominic nodded. 'She just might.' He turned to me with a look of triumph, elation. 'You would need the power of your triumvirate to raise Sabin during his daylight slumber, but once raised, I think you could heal him.'

'A shallow cut is one thing,' I said. 'Sabin is a . . . mess.'

'Will you try?'

'If we can put these three vamps back unharmed, yeah, I'll try.'

'Tomorrow.'

I nodded. 'Why not?'

'I cannot wait to tell Sabin what I have seen here today. He has been without hope for so long. But first, we must put your friends back. I will help you all I can.'

I smiled. 'I know enough of magic, Dominic, to know that all you can do is advise from the sidelines.'

'But it will be very good advice,' he said with a smile.

I believed him. For Sabin's sake, he wanted us to succeed. 'Okay, let's do it.' I held my hands out to Richard and Jean-Claude. They took my hands dutifully enough, and it was pleasant holding their hands. Both of them were warm and lovely, but there was no instant magic. No spark. I realized that in some strange way, the sexual interplay took the place of the ritual. Rituals aren't absolutely necessary to most magic, but they serve as a way to focus, to prepare yourself for the act of casting a spell. I had no blood circle to walk. I had no sacrifice to kill. I had no paraphernalia to use. All I had was the two men standing in front of me, my own body, and the knife at my wrist. I turned away from both of them.

'Nothing's happening,' I said.

'What do you expect to happen?' Dominic asked.

I shrugged. 'Something. I don't know.'

'You are trying too hard, Anita. Relax, let the power come to you.'

I rotated my shoulders, trying to ease the tension. It didn't work. 'I really wish you hadn't reminded me that some of the vamps could rise before dark. It's late afternoon, and we're underground. It could already be too late.'

'Thinking like that is not helpful,' Dominic said.

Jean-Claude walked up to me, and even before he touched me, there was a rush of power like a spill of warmth over my skin. 'Don't touch me,' I said.

I felt him hesitate behind me. 'What is wrong, *ma petite*?'

'Nothing.' I turned to face him. I held my hand just above his bare chest and that line of warmth traveled from his skin to mine. It was as if his body breathed against me. 'Do you feel that?'

He cocked his head to one side. 'Magic.'

'Aura,' I said. I had to fight an urge to glance at Dominic, like looking to a coach to see if this was the play he wanted. I was afraid to look away, to lose that thread. I held my hand out to Richard. 'Walk towards me, but don't touch me.'

He looked puzzled but did what I asked. When my hand was just above his skin, that same line of warmth came up, like a small, captive wind. I could feel their energy breathing against my skin, one to each hand. I closed my eyes and concentrated on the sensation. There. I could feel a difference, slight, almost indiscernible, but there. There was a prickling, almost electric tremble to Richard. Jean-Claude was cool and smooth. All right, we could touch auras, so what? Where did that get us?

I pressed my hands suddenly forward, through the energy, against their bodies. I forced that energy back into them, and got a gasp from both of them. The shock of it ran up my arms and I bowed my head, breathing through the rush of power. I raised my face up to meet their eyes. I don't know what showed on my face, but whatever it was, Richard didn't like it. He started to take a step back. I dug fingernails into his stomach just enough to get his attention.

'Don't break the connection.'

He swallowed. His eyes were wide and there was something close to fear in them, but he stayed put. I turned to Jean-Claude. He didn't look scared. He looked as calm and controlled as I felt.

'Very good, Anita.' Dominic's voice came soft, low. 'Combine their power as if they were simply two other animators. You are acting as focus. You've done that before. You've laid the dead to rest a thousand times. This is only one more time.'

'Okay, coach,' I whispered.

'What?' Richard said.

I shook my head. 'Nothing.'

I stepped back from them slowly, hands extended towards them. The power trailed between us like two ropes. There was nothing to see, but from the look on Richard's face, we all felt it. I unsheathed the knife and picked up the golden bowl without looking down, my gaze on the two of them. There was a difference between this and combining with other animators, there was lust. Love. Something. Whatever it was, it acted like fuel, or glue. I had no words for what it was, but it was there when I looked at them.

I held the gold bowl in my left hand, knife in the right. I walked back to them. 'Hold the bowl for me, one hand apiece.'

'Why?' Richard asked.

'Because I said so.'

He looked like he wanted to argue. I laid the flat of the blade against his lips. 'If you question everything I say, it spoils my concentration.' I took the knife away from his mouth.

'Don't do that again,' he said, voice soft, almost harsh.

I nodded. 'Fine.' I held my wrist over the empty bowl and drew the knife down the skin in one sharp movement. Blood welled out of the cut, falling in thick drops, splashing down the sides and bottom of the gleaming gold bowl. Yes, it did hurt.

'Your turn, Richard.' I kept my wrist over the bowl; no need to waste the blood.

'What do I do?'

'Put your wrist over the bowl.'

He hesitated, then did what I asked. He put his arm over the bowl, hand balled into a fist. I turned his hand over to expose the underside of his arm. I steadied his hand with my still bleeding hand. The bowl wavered where his free hand was still holding it with Jean-Claude.

I looked up at his face. 'Why does this bother you more than Jean-Claude tasting you?'

He swallowed. 'A lot of things don't bother me when I'm thinking about sex.'

'Spoken like someone with only one X chromosome,' I said. I drew the knife down his skin in one firm bite, while he was still looking at my face. The only thing that kept him from pulling away was my hold on him.

He didn't struggle after that initial surprise. He watched his blood splash into the bowl, mingling with mine. The bottom of the bowl was hidden from sight, covered in warm blood. I released his hand and he held his bleeding wrist over the bowl.

'Jean-Claude?' I said.

He held his own slender wrist out to me without being asked. I steadied his wrist as I had Richard's. I met his dark blue eyes but there was no fear there, nothing but perhaps a mild curiosity. I cut his wrist and the blood welled crimson against his white skin.

His blood splashed into the bowl. It was all red. Human, lycanthrope, and vampire. You couldn't tell who was who by just looking. We all bleed red.

There still wasn't enough blood to walk a circle of power around the sixty or so zombies. There was no way short of a true sacrifice to get that much blood. But what I had in my hands was a very potent magic cocktail. Dominic thought it would be enough. I hoped so.

A sound brought my attention away from the blood, and the growing warmth of power.

Stephen and Jason were crouched near us, one in human form, one wolf, with nearly identical looks in their eyes: hunger.

I looked past them to Cassandra. She was standing her ground, but her hands were balled into fists, and a sheen of sweat gleamed on her upper lip. The look on her face was near panic.

Dominic stood smiling and unaffected. He was the only other human in the room.

Jason growled at us, but it wasn't a real growl. There was a rhythm to the noise. He was trying to talk.

Stephen moistened his lips. 'Jason wants to know if we can lick the bowl?'

I looked at Jean-Claude and Richard. The looks on their faces were enough. 'Am I the only one in this room not lusting after the blood?'

'Except for Dominic, I fear so, *ma petite*.'

'Do what you have to do, Anita, but do it quick. It's full moon, and fresh blood is fresh blood,' Richard said.

The two other vamps I'd raised shuffled towards me. Their eyes still empty of personality, like well-made dolls.

'Did you call them?' Richard asked.

'No,' I said.

'The blood called them,' Dominic said.

The vampires came into the room. They didn't look at me this time. They looked at the blood, and the moment they saw it, something flared in them. I felt it. Hunger. No one was home, but the need was still there.

Damian's green eyes stared at the bowl with the same hunger. His handsome face thinned down to something bestial and primitive.

I licked my lips and said, 'Stop.' They did, but they stared at the freshly spilled blood, never raising their eyes to me. If I hadn't been here to stop them, they might have fed. Fed like revenants, animalistic vampires that know nothing but the hunger and never regain their humanity or their minds.

My heart thudded into my throat at the thought of what I'd almost loosed upon some unsuspecting person. The hunger wouldn't have differentiated between human and lycanthrope. Wouldn't that have been a fine fight?

I took the bloody bowl, cradling it against my stomach, the knife still in my right hand.

'Do not be afraid,' Dominic said. 'Lay the zombies to rest as you have a thousand times over the years. Do that and that alone.'

'One step at a time, right?' I said.

'Indeed,' he said.

I nodded. 'Okay.'

Everyone but the three vampires looked at me as if they believed I knew what I was doing. I wished I did. Even Dominic looked confident. But he didn't have to put sixty zombies back in the ground without a circle of power. I did.

I had to watch my step on the rubble-strewn floor. It wouldn't do to fall and spill all this blood, all this power. Because that's what it was. I could feel Jean-Claude and Richard at my back like two braids of a rope twisting inside me as I moved. Dominic had said that I would be able to feel both of the men. When I'd asked for specifics about how I would be able to feel them, he had gone vague. Magic was too individualistic for exactness. If he told me one way and it felt another, it would have made me doubt. He'd been right.

I stirred the knife through the blood and flung blood on the waiting zombies with the blade. Only a few drops fell on them, but every time the blood touched one, I could feel it, a shock of power, a jolt. I ended in the center of the once walled room, surrounded by the zombies. When the blood touched the last one, a shock ran through me that tore a gasp from my throat. I felt the blood close round the dead. It was similar to closing a circle of power, but it was like the closure was inside me, rather than outside.

'Back,' I said, 'back into your graves, all of you. Back into the ground.'

The dead shuffled around me, positioning themselves like sleep-walkers in a game of musical chairs. As each one reached its place, it lay down, and the raw earth poured over them all like water. The earth swallowed them back and smoothed over them as if a giant hand had come to neaten everything up.

I was alone in the room with the earth still twitching like a horse thick with flies. When the last ripple had died away, I looked out of the blasted wall at the others.

Jean-Claude and Richard stood at the opening of the wall. The three werewolves clustered around them. Even Cassandra had knelt on the ground beside the wolf that was Jason. Dominic stood behind them, watching. He was grinning at me like a proud papa.

I walked towards them, my legs a touch rubbery, and I stumbled, splashing blood down the side of the bowl. Crimson drops fell onto the swept earth.

The wolf was suddenly there, licking the ground clean. I ignored it and kept walking. Vampires next. Everyone moved to let me pass as if they were afraid to touch me. Except for Dominic. He crowded almost too close.

I felt his own power crackle between us, shivering over my skin, down the ropes of power that bound me to Richard and Jean-Claude.

I swallowed and said, 'Back up.'

'My apologies.' He moved back until I couldn't feel him quite so tightly. 'Good enough?'

I nodded.

The three vampires waited with hungry eyes. I sprinkled them with the cooling blood. They twitched when the blood touched them, but there was no rush of power. Nothing. Shit.

Dominic frowned. 'The blood is still warm. It should work.'

Jean-Claude moved closer. I could feel it without turning around. I could feel him coming down the line of power between us like a fish being reeled in. 'But it is not working,' he said.

'No,' I said.

'They are lost then.'

I shook my head. Willie was staring at the bowl of blood. The look was feral, pure hunger. I'd thought that the worst thing that could happen would be for Willie to simply lie down in his coffin and be truly dead. I was wrong. Having Willie crawl out of his coffin craving nothing but blood, knowing nothing but hunger, would be worse. I would not loose him, not yet.

'Any bright ideas?' I asked.

'Feed them the blood in the bowl,' Dominic said, 'but hurry before it grows colder.'

I didn't argue; there was no time. I wiped the knife on my jeans and sheathed it. I'd have to clean it and the sheath later, but I needed my hands free. I dipped my fingertips into the blood. It was still warm, but barely. The eyes were still brown as they followed my hand, but it wasn't Willie looking out of them. It just wasn't.

I lifted the gold bowl to Willie's mouth and said, 'Willie, drink.' His throat moved, swallowing furiously, and I felt that click. He was mine again. 'Stop, Willie.'

He stopped, and I took the bowl away from him. He didn't grab for it. He didn't move at all. His eyes were blank and empty above his bloody mouth. 'Go back to your coffin, Willie. Rest until nightfall. Back to your coffin to rest.'

He turned and walked back down the hallway. I'd have to trust he was going back to the coffin. I'd check later. One down, two to go. Liv left like a good little puppet. The blood was getting pretty low by the time I raised it to Damian's lips.

He drank at it, his pale throat swallowing. The blood passed down his throat and something brushed me. Something that wasn't my magic. Something else. Damian's chest rose in a great breath like a man struggling back from drowning. And that something thrust me backwards, cast out my power, turned it back on me. It was like a door slammed, but it was more than that. A force thrust at me, hit me, and the world swirled around. My vision was eaten away in greyness and white spots. I heard my own heartbeat impossibly loud. The thudding chased me down into the darkness, then even that was lost.

33

I woke, staring up at the white drapes above Jean-Claude's bed. There was a damp washcloth folded over my forehead and voices arguing. I lay there for a few seconds, just blinking. I couldn't remember how I'd gotten here. I remembered the sensation of being cast out of Damian. I'd been cast out like an intruder, something to be protected against. The force that touched me hadn't been evil. I'd felt evil before, and that wasn't it. But it certainly hadn't been a beneficent force, either. More neutral, maybe.

The voices were Jean-Claude and Richard. The argument was about me. Big surprise.

'How can you let her die when you could save her?' Richard asked.

'I do not believe she is dying, but even if she was, without her permission, I will never again invade her mind.'

'Even if she was dying?'

'Yes,' Jean-Claude said.

'I don't understand that.'

'You don't have to understand it, Richard. Anita would agree with me.'

I brushed the rag from my head. I wanted to sit up, but it seemed too much effort.

Richard sat down on the bed, taking my hand. I wasn't sure I wanted him to, but I was still too weak to stop him.

Jean-Claude stood behind him, watching me. His face was blank and perfect, a mask.

'How do you feel?' Richard asked.

I had to swallow before I could speak. 'Not sure.'

Dominic walked into view. He had, wisely, stayed out of the argument. Besides, he was already a vampire's human servant. What was he going to say? That the mark was evil, or that it was no big deal. Lies either way.

'I am very glad to see you awake.'

'It thrust me out,' I said.

He nodded. 'Indeed.'

'What thrust her out?' Richard asked.

Dominic looked at me.

I shrugged.

'When the power that animates the vampire returned and found Anita still inside the body, the power cast her out.'

Richard frowned. 'Why?'

'I shouldn't have been there.'

'Did the soul return as you touched it?' Jean-Claude asked.

'I've felt the brush of a soul before, that wasn't it.'

Jean-Claude looked at me.

I looked back.

He was the one who looked away first.

Richard touched my hair where it had gotten wet from the rag. 'I don't care if it was a soul or the bogeyman. I thought I'd lost you.'

'I always seem to survive, Richard, no matter who else dies.'

He frowned at that.

I let him. 'Is Damian all right?' I asked.

'He seems to be,' Jean-Claude said.

'What were you two arguing about?'

'Dominic, could you leave us now?' Jean-Claude asked.

Dominic smiled. 'Gladly. I am eager to speak with Sabin. Tomorrow, you and Richard can raise him, and you, Anita –' he touched my face lightly – 'can heal him.'

I didn't like him touching me, but there was almost a reverence in his face. It made it hard to yell at him.

'I'll do my best,' I said.

'In all things, I think.' With that, he bid us a good day and left.

When the door closed behind him, I repeated my question. 'What were you two arguing about?'

Richard glanced behind at Jean-Claude, then back to me. 'You stopped breathing for a few seconds. No heartbeat, either. I thought you were dying.'

I looked at Jean-Claude. 'Tell me.'

'Richard wanted me to give you the first mark again. I refused.'

'Smart vampire,' I said.

He shrugged. 'You have made yourself very clear, *ma petite*. I will not be accused of forcing myself upon you again. Not in any sense.'

'Did someone do CPR?'

'You started breathing on your own,' Richard said. He squeezed my hand. 'You scared me.'

I drew my hand out of his. 'So you offered me to him as his human servant.'

'I thought we'd agreed to be a triad of power. Maybe I don't understand what that means.'

I wanted to sit up but still wasn't sure I could do it, so I had to be content with frowning up at him. 'I'll share power with you both, but I won't let Jean-Claude mark me. If he ever forces himself on me again, I'll kill him.'

Jean-Claude nodded. 'You will try, *ma petite*. It is a dance I do not wish to begin.'

'I'm going to let him mark me before I leave for the pack tonight,' Richard said.

I stared up at him. 'What are you talking about?'

'Jean-Claude can't come tonight. He isn't a member of the pack. If we're joined, I can still call the power.'

I struggled to sit up, and if Richard hadn't caught me, I'd have fallen. I lay cradled in his arms, digging fingers into his arms, trying to make him listen to me. 'You don't want to be his servant for all eternity, Richard.'

'The joining of master and animal is not the same as between master and servant, *ma petite*. It is not quite as intimate.'

I couldn't see the vampire over Richard's broad shoulders. I tried to push myself up, and Richard had to help me. 'Explain,' I said.

'I will not be able to taste food through Richard, as I could through you. It is a minor side effect, but in truth one I miss. I enjoyed tasting solid food again.'

'What else?'

'Richard is an alpha werewolf. He is an equivalent power to mine in some ways. He will have more control over my entering his dreams, his thoughts. He would be able to keep me out, as it were.'

'And I couldn't,' I said.

He looked down at me. 'Even then, before you had explored your powers of necromancy, you were harder to control than you should have been. Now,' he shrugged, 'now I am not sure who would be master and who would be servant.'

I sat up on my own. I was feeling just a tad better. 'That's why you didn't mark me while you had the chance and Richard to take the blame. After what I did today, you're afraid that I'd be the master and you'd be my servant. That's it, isn't it?'

He smiled softly. 'Perhaps.' He sat on the bed on the other side of Richard. 'I have not worked for over two hundred years to be Master of my own lands to give up my freedom to anyone, even you, *ma petite*. You would not be a cruel master, but you would be an exacting one.'

'It's not pure master and servant. I know that from Alejandro. He couldn't control me, but I couldn't control him, either.'

'Did you try?' Jean-Claude asked.

That stopped me. I had to think about it. 'No.'

'You simply killed him,' Jean-Claude said.

He had a point. 'Would I really be able to order you around?'

'I have never heard of another vampire choosing a necromancer of your power as human servant.'

'What about Dominic and Sabin?' I asked.

'Dominic is no match for you, *ma petite*.'

'If I agreed to the first mark, would you do it or not?' I asked.

Richard tried to hug me to his chest, but I moved away. I had to put both arms down to prop myself up, but I was sitting on my own.

Jean-Claude sighed, looking down at the floor. 'If we truly joined, no one could stand against us. That much power is very tempting.' He looked up suddenly, letting me see his eyes. Emotions rolled across his face. Excitement, fear, lust, and finally, just weariness. 'We could be bound together for all eternity. Bound together in a three-way struggle for power. It is not a pleasant thought.'

'Jean-Claude told me that he would not be my master,' Richard said. 'We would be partners.'

'And you believed him?' I said.

Richard nodded, looking terribly earnest.

I sighed. 'Jesus, Richard, I can't leave you alone for a minute.'

'It is not a lie, *ma petite*.'

'Yeah, right.'

'If it's a lie,' Richard said, 'I'll kill him.'

I stared at him. 'You don't mean that.'

'Yes, I do.' Something moved through his brown eyes, something low and dark and inhuman.

'Once you decide to kill someone, it becomes easier to kill others, doesn't it?' I said.

Richard didn't flinch or look away. 'Yes, it does, but that's not it. I won't be anyone's servant. Not Jean-Claude's, not yours, not Marcus's, not Raina's.'

'Do you understand that once you're bound to him, that hurting him can hurt you? Killing him can kill you?'

'I'd rather be dead than trapped.'

I watched the absolute certainty in his eyes. He meant it. 'You'll kill Marcus tonight,' I said.

Richard looked at me, and an expression passed over his face that I'd never seen before, a fierceness that filled his eyes and sent his power shivering through the room. 'If he doesn't back down, I'll kill him.'

For the first time, I believed him.

34

There was a knock on the door. Richard and Jean-Claude spoke at the same time. 'Enter.' 'Come in.' They stared at each other as the door opened.

Edward walked in. His cool blue eyes took in the three of us at a glance. 'What happened to you?'

'Long story,' I said. 'It wasn't the assassin if that's what you're worried about.'

'I wasn't. Your wolves are guarding my backup. They wouldn't let me bring him in without somebody's approval.' He looked at Jean-Claude and Richard. 'They weren't absolutely clear on whose permission I was supposed to get.' He didn't smile while he said it, but I knew him well enough to see the shadow of humor on his face.

'This is my home,' Jean-Claude said. 'It is my permission that is needed.'

I slid to the edge of the bed and found I could sit up. The movement put me between the two men. Richard hovered close to help me if I fell onto my face. Jean-Claude just sat there, not touching me, not offering to. In many ways, he understood me better than Richard did, but then he'd known me longer. I was sort of an acquired taste.

Jean-Claude stood up. 'I will go escort your guest in.'

'I better go with you,' Edward said. 'Harley doesn't know you, but he'll know what you are.'

'What's that supposed to mean?' I asked.

'If a strange vampire walked up to you in this place and said follow me, would you do it?'

I thought about that. 'Probably not.'

Edward smiled. 'Neither would Harley.'

Edward and Jean-Claude left to fetch Edward's friend. I tried standing while they were gone, just to see if I could do it. I always like to meet new people, especially new hired muscle, on my feet.

Richard tried to help me, and I pulled away. I had to grab for the wall to keep from falling.

'I was trying to help,' he said.

'Don't try so hard.'

'What is the matter with you?'

'I don't like being helpless, Richard.'

'You aren't superwoman.'

I glared at him. 'I fainted, for God's sake. I never faint.'

'You didn't faint,' he said. 'Whatever it was threw you out of Damian. I was still tied to you when it happened, Anita. I felt it brush me.' He shook his head, hugging his arms to his chest. 'You didn't faint.'

I leaned my back against the wall. 'It scared me, too.'

'Did it?' He came to stand in front of me. 'You don't seem scared.'

'Are *you* scared about joining with Jean-Claude?'

'That bothers you more than me killing for the first time tonight, doesn't it?'

'Yeah.'

The door opened before we could continue the conversation. It was just as well. We'd found something else we disagreed on. Letting someone tie themselves to my mind, my soul, frightened me a lot more than killing someone.

The man that followed Edward didn't look that impressive. He was slender, only a couple of inches taller than Edward. He had curly brownish red hair receding in a soft circle to nearly the middle of his head. He slouched even when he walked, and I couldn't tell if it was habit or some sort of spinal problem. Brown

T-shirt over black corduroy pants, and sneakers. Everything looked like it had come from the Salvation Army. He wore a patched leather aviator's jacket that might have been original World War II issue. Under the jacket, I got a glimpse of guns.

He was wearing a double shoulder holster so that he had a 9 millimeter under both arms. I'd seen holsters like it, but never knew anyone who actually wore one. I thought they were mostly for show. Very few people are equally good with both hands. There was a crisscross of straps beneath the T-shirt that I didn't understand, but I knew it was for carrying something lethal. He had a duffel bag in one hand, crammed full and big enough to carry a body in. He wasn't even straining. Stronger than he looked.

I met his eyes last. They were pale and greyish green with lashes so gingery red they were almost invisible. The look in the eyes was the emptiest I'd ever seen in another human being. It was as if when he looked at me, he wasn't seeing me at all. It wasn't like he was blind. He saw something, but I wasn't sure what he saw. Not me. Not a woman. Something else. That one look was enough. I knew that this man walked in a circle of his own creation. Saw a version of reality that would send the rest of us screaming. But he functioned, and he didn't scream.

'This is Harley,' Edward said. He introduced us all, as if it was an ordinary meeting.

I stared at Harley's pale eyes and realized that he scared me. It had been a long time since another human being frightened me just by entering a room.

Richard offered his hand, and Harley simply looked at it. I wanted to explain to Richard why he shouldn't have made the gesture, but I wasn't sure I could.

I did not offer to shake hands.

'I found out the name of the money man behind the attempts on your life,' Edward said. He said it without preamble.

Three of us stared at him. Harley, disquietly, kept staring at me. 'What did you say?' I asked.

'I know who we have to kill.'

'Who?' I asked.

'Marcus Fletcher. The head of our local werewolf pack.' He smiled, pleased with himself, on the effect the news was having on Richard.

'You're sure?' Richard said. 'Absolutely sure?'

Edward nodded, studying Richard's face. 'Does he hate you enough to kill Anita?'

'I didn't think so.' Richard turned to me, the look on his face stricken, horrified. 'My God, I never dreamt he'd do something like this. Why?'

'How well would you have fought tonight with *ma petite* dead?' Jean-Claude asked.

Richard stared at him so obviously overwhelmed by the dastardliness of what Marcus had done that I wanted to pat his head and tell him it was all right. I nearly get killed twice and I wanted to comfort him. Love is just plain stupid sometimes.

'It's all so convenient,' Edward said, with a happy lilt to his voice.

'What do you mean?' Richard asked.

'He means you are supposed to kill him tonight, Richard, so we don't have to,' I said.

'I just can't believe that Marcus would do something so . . .'

'Evil,' I suggested.

He nodded.

'It would seem more Raina's sort of idea than Marcus's,' Jean-Claude said.

'It's twisted enough for her,' I said.

'Marcus could have said no,' Richard said. He ran his hands through his hair, combing it back from his face. His handsome face was set in very stubborn lines. 'This has got to stop. He'll do anything she asks, anything, and she's crazy.'

My eyes flicked to Harley. I couldn't help it. He caught my look and smiled. I didn't know exactly what he was thinking, but it wasn't pleasant and it wasn't pretty. Having Harley as backup made me wonder if I was on the right side.

'Edward, can I talk to you a minute in private?' I didn't want to be this obvious, but Harley was bothering me that much.

I walked away from the others and Edward trailed behind. It was kind of nice to walk across the room, lower my voice, and know the person I was whispering about wouldn't hear me. Both Jean-Claude and Richard would.

Edward looked at me, and there was that same touch of amusement to him, as if he knew what I was going to say and thought it was a hoot.

'Why does he keep looking at me?'

'You mean Harley?'

'You know damn well who I mean,' I said.

'He's only looking, Anita. No harm.'

'But why me?'

'You're a girl maybe?'

'Stop it, Edward. Whatever he's thinking, it isn't sex, and if it is, I don't want to know the details.'

Edward stared at me. 'Ask him.'

'What?'

'Ask him why he's staring at you.'

'Just like that?'

He nodded. 'Harley will probably get a kick out of it.'

'Do I want to know?' I asked.

'I don't know. Do you?'

I took a deep breath and let it out slowly. 'You're stringing me along here, Edward. What's the deal?'

'If something happens to me during the fighting, Harley needs at least one other person that he'll mind.'

'Mind?'

'He's absolutely reliable, Anita. He'll stay at my back, never flinch, and kill anyone I tell him to, but he's not good without specific orders. And he doesn't take orders from just everybody.'

'So you designated me?'

Edward shook his head. 'I told him to pick someone in the room.'

'Why me?'

'Ask him.'

'Fine.' I walked back towards the others, and Edward followed me. Harley watched us like he was seeing other things. It was too damned unnerving.

'Why are you staring at me?' I asked.

His voice was quiet, as if he never yelled. 'You're the scariest motherfucker in the room.'

'Now I know you can't see.'

'I see what's there,' he said.

'What the hell is wrong with you?'

'Nothing.'

I tried to think of a better question and finally asked, 'What do you see when you look at everybody in the room?'

'The same thing you see: monsters.'

'Why do I think the monsters I see in the room aren't the same ones you see?'

He smiled, a bare upturning of lips. 'They may look different, but they're still monsters. They're all monsters.'

He was a card-carrying, rubber-room-renting psychotic. By the time most people got to the point where they weren't seeing reality, they were so far gone that there was no going back. Sometimes drug therapy helped, but without it, the world was a frightening, overwhelming place. Harley didn't look frightened or overwhelmed. He looked calm.

'When you look at Edward, he always looks the same to you. I mean you recognize him?'

Harley nodded.

'You'd recognize me,' I said.

'If I make an effort to memorize you, yes.'

'That's why you were staring.'

'Yes,' he said.

'What happens if Edward and I both go down?'

Harley smiled, but his eyes shifted to one side as if something low to the ground and rather small had run across the room. The movement was so natural that I looked. Nothing.

'Harley,' I said.

He looked back at me, but his eyes were just a little higher up than my face should have been. 'Yes,' he said, his voice so quiet.

'What happens if Edward and I are both killed?'

Harley stared at me. His eyes shifted to my face for just a second, as if the fog had cleared. 'That would be bad.'

35

There would be no backing down for Marcus tonight. He had to die, one way or another. Richard wasn't arguing anymore. But there was still the chance that Raina would lead a revolt of the other lukoi. Their loyalty was divided enough for a war, even with Marcus dead. Jean-Claude came up with a solution. We'd put on a better show. A better show than Raina and Marcus? He had to be kidding. Richard agreed to let Jean-Claude costume him up for the night. As his lupa, that meant I had to get dressed up, too.

Jean-Claude took Richard off to dress him. He sent Cassandra with a white cardboard clothes box to me. She was supposed to help me change, she said.

I opened the box and all that was in it was a pile of black leather straps. I kid you not. I drew it out of the box and it didn't improve. 'I don't know how to get into this, even if I was willing to.'

'I'll get Stephen,' Cassandra said.

'I don't want to undress in front of Stephen.'

'He's a stripper,' she said. 'He dressed me last night at Danse Macabre, remember.' She patted my hand. 'He'll be a perfect gentleman.'

I sat down on the bed and scowled at the door. I was not wearing this crap.

An hour later, Stephen and Cassandra were turning me in front of the bathroom mirrors so I could see myself. It had been embarrassing at first having a man help squeeze me into the thing, but

Cassandra was right. Stephen was not only a perfect gentleman, he simply didn't seem to be moved at all by the fact that I was mostly naked. It was like having two girlfriends help me. One just happened not to be a girl.

The top was mostly a leather bra with lining for comfort. It was one of those that lifted and showed your cleavage to absolute best advantage. But it was tight and held in place. Nothing was falling out. My cross was visible, though. I taped it. I'd peel the tape when I left the Circus. Werewolves on the menu tonight, not vamps.

The bottom was sort of leather shorts, except that where the shorts stopped, straps took over. I wouldn't be caught dead or alive in something like this, not even to make a good show of things for Richard, except that there were extras.

Two leather sheaths covered my upper arms, complete with a knife apiece. The knives were high quality, high silver content. If the hilts were a little elaborate for my taste, the balance was good, and that's what counted. Two more sheaths covered my lower arms with two more knives, smaller, balanced more for throwing, though they both had hilts and weren't true throwing knives. The bulge under Harley's T-shirt had been throwing knives, the real McCoy, slender and innocent looking until you saw them used.

There was a leather belt around the top of the shorts that my Browning's shoulder holster fit on nicely. Edward had bought me a new Browning. It wasn't my very own gun, but it was still nice to have. Harley had fished a clip-on holster for the Firestar out of his duffel. The small clip-on rode to one side of my waist for a cross draw.

The straps down my legs had small silver loops, sheaths, two more knives, one on each thigh. No knife sheaths below the knees because boots came with the outfit. Jean-Claude had finally gotten me out of my Nikes. The boots were soft black suede with heels only a touch higher than I would have liked. A tiny stoppered vial fit in small loops just below the top of each boot. I held one up to the light, and knew what it was. Holy water. A nice gift from my vampire boyfriend, heh?

I stared at myself in the mirror. 'How long has Jean-Claude been planning this outfit?'

'A little while,' Stephen said. He was kneeling by me, tugging the straps into place. 'We all had a running bet that he'd never get you to wear it.'

'Who's we?'

'His flunkies.' Stephen stood up, stepped back, and nodded. 'You look amazing.'

'I look like a biker slut from hell meets soldier of fortune pinup.'

'That, too,' Stephen said.

I turned to Cassandra. 'Be honest.'

'You look dangerous, Anita. Like somebody's weapon.'

I stared in the mirror, shaking my head. 'Somebody's sex toy, you mean.'

'A dominatrix maybe, but nobody's toy,' Cassandra said.

Why didn't that make me feel better?

Cassandra had insisted on helping me with my makeup. She was a great deal more skilled at it than I. Years of practice, she'd said. My hair was tight and curling, falling just below my shoulders now. It needed a cut. But for tonight, the hair was perfect. The face was still pretty. Makeup is a wonderful thing. But the outfit stripped away the pretense. I looked like what I was: something that would kill you before it would kiss you.

We walked out of the bathroom and found Edward and Harley waiting for us. They had brought two straight-backed chairs to sit on the white carpet, facing the bathroom door. I froze as Edward stared at me. He didn't say a word, just sat there with a sort of half-smile on his face.

'Well, say something, dammit.'

'I would say it isn't you, but in a way, it is.'

I took a deep breath. 'Yeah.'

Harley stared at me with vacant eyes. He was smiling, but not at the outfit. Smiling at some internal music or vision that only he could perceive.

There was a long leather coat on the bed. 'One of the vampires dropped it off,' Edward said. 'Thought you might want something to cover up with until the big unveiling.'

'You're enjoying this, aren't you?'

'I'd feel better if I could guard your back.'

'You're going to do that with a rifle from the closest hill, remember.'

'Night vision and scope, fine, but I can't kill them all from a distance.'

'You couldn't kill them all if you were johnny on the spot, either,' I said.

'No, but I'd feel better.'

'Worried about me?'

He shrugged. 'I'm your bodyguard. If you die under my protection, the other bodyguards will make fun of me.'

It took me a second to realize he was making a joke. Harley looked back at him with an almost surprised look. I don't think either of us heard humor from Edward much.

I walked towards Edward. The leather made that little creaking sound it makes. I stopped in front of him, legs a little apart, staring down at him.

He widened his eyes a little. 'Yes.'

'I can't imagine anyone making fun of you, Edward.'

He touched one of the leather straps. 'If I went around dressed like this, they might.'

I had to smile. 'You probably would be dressed like this if you were going to be down in the clearing with us tonight.'

He turned pale blue eyes to me. 'I've worn worse than this, Anita. I'm a fine actor when I have to be.' The humor drained away from his face, leaving something feral and determined behind.

Edward would still do things that I wouldn't, still had fewer rules than I did, but in some ways, Edward was a mirror for me. A warning of what I was becoming, or maybe a preview.

Richard would have said it was a warning. I hadn't made up my mind yet.

There was a knock on the door. Richard came in without waiting for an invitation. He was scowling, but the grumpy look faded when he got a good look at me. His eyes widened. 'I was going to come in and complain about my outfit.' He shook his head. 'If I complain, will you just shoot me?' A smile spread across his face.

'No laughing,' I said.

The smile got wider. His voice was a little choked, but he managed, 'Wonderful. You look wonderful.'

There are only two things you can do when you're dressed like *Barbie Does Bondage*; you can be embarrassed or you can be aggressive. Guess what my choice was.

I stalked towards him, putting a little extra sway into my walk. The boots made it easier, somehow, giving just the right roll. I put into my eyes, my face, what the outfit promised: sex, violence, heat.

The humor faded from Richard's face, replaced by an answering heat and a hesitation, like he wasn't exactly sure we should be doing this in public.

He was wearing black leather pants with soft suede boots that were almost a match to my own. His hair had been slicked back, tied off with a black ribbon. His shirt was silk and a vibrant blue, somewhere between turquoise and royal. It looked splendid against his tanned skin.

I stopped just in front of him, legs apart. I stared up at him, defying him to think it was funny. I put a finger to his lips, trailing my fingertip down his cheek, his neck, caressing the edge of his collarbone, tracing the skin until it vanished down the buttoned front of his shirt.

I stalked to the bed, fetching the leather coat. I threw it over one shoulder so that it trailed down like a limp body, not hiding much of the outfit. I opened the door and stood for just a moment framed in it. 'Coming?' I said. I walked away without waiting for an answer. The look on his face was enough. He looked like I'd hit him between the eyes with a sledgehammer.

Great. Now all I had to do was try the outfit out on Jean-Claude, and we could go.

36

The May woods were a warm, close darkness. Richard and I stood outside the barn where Raina shot dirty pictures. The pack meeting place was among the trees around the farmhouse. There were so many cars that they were parked on every bit of spare ground, some so close to the woods that they touched the trees.

There may have been a full moon up there somewhere, but the clouds were so thick, the darkness so complete, that it was like standing inside a cave. Except this cave had movement. A small oozing wind trailed through the thick, night-darkened leaves. It was like some invisible giant trailed fingertips through the trees, bending them, rattling the leaves, giving movement to the night that made my shoulders tight. It was like the night itself was alive in a way that I'd never seen before.

Richard's hand was warm and slightly moist. He'd dampened that creeping energy so that it wasn't uncomfortable to touch him. I appreciated the effort. His leather cloak whispered as he moved closer. It was tied across his chest, covering only one shoulder. The cloak, combined with the full sleeves of the brilliant blue shirt, made the whole outfit seem antique.

Richard pulled on my hand, bringing me against his body, into the circle of his arms, the brush of the leather cloak. The clouds slid apart and suddenly we were bathed in a thick, silver glow. Richard was staring outward. He seemed to be listening to something that I couldn't hear. His hands convulsed around my hands, an almost painful squeeze. He stared down at me as if just remembering I was there.

He smiled. 'Can you feel it?'

'What?'

'The night?'

I started to answer, no, then stopped. I looked around at the hurrying woods, the feeling of movement. 'The woods seem more alive tonight.'

His smile widened, a brief flash of teeth, almost a snarl. 'Yes.'

I tried to pull away, but his hands tightened. 'You're doing it,' I said. My heart was suddenly thudding in my throat. I'd thought to be afraid of a lot of things tonight, but not of Richard.

'We're supposed to share power. That's what I'm doing. But it has to be my power, Anita. The pack won't be impressed with zombies.'

I swallowed past my beating heart and forced myself to stand very still. Made myself return the grip of his hands. I hadn't thought what it would mean. I wasn't going to be in charge. Not my power but his. I was going to be fuel for his fire, not the other way around.

'It's Jean-Claude's mark,' I said. 'That's what's doing it.'

'We hoped it would work this way,' Richard said.

And I knew that the *we* he was referring to didn't include me. 'How does it work?'

'Like this.' That trembling energy broke over his skin like a rush of warmth. It plunged through his hands into my hand. It rode like a wave over my body, and everywhere it touched, the hair and skin of my body raised and shivered.

'Are you all right?'

'Sure,' but my voice was a breathless whisper.

He took me at my word. Some barrier went down, and Richard's energy crashed into me like a fist. I remembered falling, and the feel of Richard's arms around my waist, catching me, then it was like I was elsewhere. I was everywhere. I was over there in the trees, staring at us with eyes that tried to turn and see me, but I wasn't there. It was like the wind that opened inside me when I walked a cemetery, except it wasn't power that was spreading outward. It *was* me. I flashed through a dozen eyes, brushed bodies, some furred, some still skinned. I hurried outward, outward, and touched Raina. I knew it was her. Her power lashed out like a shield, casting me away from her, but not before I felt her fear.

Richard called me back, though call implies a voice. I slipped back inside myself in a rush of curling golden energy. I could see the color behind my eyes, though there was actually nothing to see. I opened my eyes, though I wasn't a hundred percent sure that they'd been closed. That golden energy was still there, swirling inside, along my skin. I curled my hands over Richard's shoulders and felt an answering energy in him.

I didn't have to ask what I had just experienced. I knew. It was what it meant, at least for someone as powerful as Richard, to be alpha. He could fling his essence outward and touch his pack. It was how he kept the werewolf from changing form two days ago. It was how he could share blood. Marcus couldn't do it, but Raina could.

Jean-Claude's power, even my own power, never felt so alive. It was like I was drawing energy from the trees, the wind, like being plugged into a vast battery, as if there was enough magic to go on forever. I had never felt anything like it.

'Can you run?' Richard asked.

The question meant more than just the words, and I knew that. 'Oh, yeah.'

He smiled, and it was joyous. He took my hand and flung us into the trees. Even if he'd been human, I couldn't have kept up with Richard in a dead run. Tonight, he didn't run so much as flowed into the woods. It was like he had sonar telling him where every branch, every tree root, every fallen trunk would be. It was like the trees moved away from him like water, or maybe moved into him like something else that I had no words for. He pulled me with him. Not just with his hand, but with his energy. It was like he'd entered me and tied us together somehow. It should have been intrusive and frightening, but it wasn't.

We spilled into the great clearing and Richard's power filled it, flowed over the lycanthropes like a fire springing from one dry branch to another. It filled them and made them turn to him. Only Marcus, Raina, Jamil, Sebastian, and Cassandra were untouched. Only they kept him out by force of will. He swept everyone else before him, and I knew that part of what let him do that was me. Distant as a dream or a half-remembered nightmare, was Jean-Claude, down that twisting power that was almost buried under Richard's shining light.

I felt every movement. It was like the world was suddenly crystalline, almost like the effect from an adrenaline rush, or shock, where everything seems carved and hard-edged and terribly, frightfully clear. It was like being dipped in reality, as if anything else would forever be a dream. It was almost painful.

Marcus sat in a chair that had been carved from rock so long ago the edges were rounded with weather and hands and bodies. I knew that this clearing had been the meeting place for the lukoi for a very long time.

Marcus wore a brown satin-lapeled tux. The shirt was of gold cloth, not gold lamé, but the real deal, as if they'd melted down jewelry and beaten him out a shirt. Raina curled on the edge of the stone chair. Her long auburn hair was done in an elaborate swirl of soft curls on top of her head, down along her face. A gold chain cut across her forehead with a diamond the size of my thumb in it. More diamonds burned like white fire at her throat. She was absolutely naked except for a sprinkling of gold body glitter, done thick enough on her nipples to make them seem metallic. A diamond anklet glittered on her right ankle. Three gold chains rode low on her hips, and that was it.

And I'd complained about my outfit.

'Welcome, Richard, Anita,' Marcus said. 'Welcome to our happy family.' His voice was deep and thick. It flowed with its own edge of power, but it wasn't enough. It would never be enough. Richard could have worn his jeans and T-shirt, and still he would have won them over. There are things beyond clothing that make a king.

'Marcus, Raina.' Richard released my hand slowly, and as he pulled away, the tie remained. It was a shadow of the way I'd bound Richard and Jean-Claude's auras to me, but more. He took a few steps away to stand a little in front of me. I could feel him like a large, shimmering *thing*. His energy was amazing. The closest thing I'd ever felt was the power of a Daoine Sidhe, a fairie of the highest court.

'You naughty boy,' Raina said. 'You've made her one of us.'

'No,' Richard said, 'she is what she always has been: herself.'

'Then how can you ride her power? How can she ride yours?' Raina pushed away from the chair, stalking along the ground in front of it, pacing like a caged animal.

'What have you done, Richard?' Marcus asked.

'She is my mate.'

'Raina, test it,' Marcus said.

Raina smiled, most unpleasant, and stalked over the open ground. She swayed, transforming walking into a seductive dance. I felt her power tonight. Her sex rode the air like the threat of lightning, prickling along the skin, drying out the mouth. I felt every male watch her, even Richard. I didn't resent it. Hell, I watched her. She was magnificent in her sheer, naked lust. It was like sex for Raina was power, literally.

I slipped off the long, black coat and let it fall to the ground. There was a collective gasp from the human throats. I traced my hands over the bare skin of my waist, trailing down my leather-clad thighs. I laughed. A loud, joyous bark of noise. It was Raina. I was riding her power, dancing along the edge of her energy.

I stalked towards her, not waiting, but meeting her in the middle of the circle. We moved around each other, and I could match her dance. I pulled her aura of sex and violence into me, pulled it like a hand reaching inward and stealing bits of her. Fear widened her eyes, brought her breath faster.

She knew how to protect herself against another werewolf, but my brand of power was just different enough that she didn't know what to do with me. I'd never done anything like this before, didn't understand exactly what I was doing, until Raina backed off. She didn't run back to Marcus, but the shine was gone. She slunk back with her tail between her legs, and I could taste her inside my mind like I'd licked her skin.

I turned back to Richard and stalked towards him in the high-heeled boots. I felt every man watching. I knew it. I wrapped it around me and threw it all back into Richard. He stood almost frozen, his dark eyes filled with a heat that was part sex, part energy, part something else. And for the first time, I understood that something else. I heard that music, felt it dance inside my body.

I grabbed the leather cloak and pulled him down to me. We kissed and it burned, as if more than flesh was mingling. I released him abruptly, and my eyes didn't go to his face but fell lower. Without touching him, I knew he was hard and ready. I could still feel the pack, distant, but touchable. Jason's great wolf head brushed my thigh. I dug my fingers into that thick fur and knew that if Richard and I made love, the pack would know it. Here tonight, they'd be along for the ride. It wouldn't just be sex. It would be magic. And it didn't seem shameful or pagan or wrong.

'You can't let them do this,' Raina said.

Marcus pushed himself to his feet. He seemed tired. 'No, I don't suppose I can.' He looked at Raina, naked, beautiful, fearful. 'But it is not your blood that will be spilled tonight, is it, my love?' The irony was thick enough to walk on, and for the first time, I realized that Marcus knew what Raina was, maybe had always known.

Raina went to her knees in front of him, hands clutching at his legs. She rubbed her cheek along his thigh, one hand smoothing perilously close to his groin. Even now, it was what she knew best. Sex and pain.

He touched her hair gently. He stared down at her, and the naked tenderness on his face made me want to look away. It was a terribly intimate look, more intimate than sex, more powerful. The fool loved her.

If he hadn't been paying to kill me, I'd have felt sorry for him.

Marcus stepped away from Raina. He began walking across the clearing. His power opened like a door, flowing like electric water across the wolves, across me. He undid his tie, opened the first few buttons of his shirt. 'No more preliminaries, Richard. Let us do this.'

'I know you tried to have Anita killed,' Richard said.

Marcus stopped in midmotion. His small, sure fingers hesitated. Surprise chased across his face, then changed into a smile. 'You have surprised me twice tonight, Richard. Let's see if you can make it three.'

'I will kill you tonight, Marcus; you know that.'

Marcus shrugged out of his jacket. 'You can try.'

Richard nodded. 'I'd planned on giving you the chance to just leave.'

'I tried to have your mate killed. You can't leave me alive now.' He undid the cuffs of his shirt.

'No, I can't.' Richard undid the cloak's tie, letting it fall to the floor. He pulled his shirt out of his pants and slid it over his head in one quick movement. The moonlight made shadows on the muscles of his arms and chest. I suddenly didn't want him to do it. I could shoot Marcus, and it would all be done. Richard would never forgive me, but he'd be alive. They wouldn't kill each other with power. They'd use claws and teeth for the killing. All Richard's trembling, eager power wouldn't keep him from getting his throat ripped out.

37

Richard turned to me, wearing only the leather pants and the boots. Marcus had asked that they not strip down, said something about saving an old man's dignity. Bullshit. There was something in the air that I didn't like, as if Marcus had known what was coming and he was ready.

'As acknowledged Ulfric, Marcus gets to choose the form we fight in,' Richard said.

'What form did he choose?'

Richard raised his hand in front of my face. 'Touch my hand.'

He made it sound so serious for such a small request. I touched the back of his hand lightly.

'Grip my palm, Anita.'

I wrapped my fingers around the lower part of his hand. Before I could look to his face or ask a question, I felt it. Energy welled up his hand like oil up the wick of a lamp. His skin flowed under my hand. I felt the bones lengthening. I felt his body give as if the boundaries that confined him to skin and bone and flesh had dissolved. It felt almost like he would scatter himself outward like I'd done earlier, but it wasn't his essence that was reaching outward. It was his body.

He held up his other hand, and I took it. I locked my fingers in his and felt his bones grow across my skin, watched claws form as his flesh flowed like clay. Distant as a scream, I knew I should have been scared or sickened. The power flowed down his shifting hands to my hands, flowing between us like cool fire.

He stopped when his hands were human claws with talons that

could have ripped me apart. The power didn't stop abruptly; it wasn't like turning off a switch. It was like turning off a faucet, slowing the flow down to a trickle, a drop, then nothing.

I was on my knees and hadn't remembered getting there. Richard knelt in front of me, hands still clasped in mine. It took me two tries to be able to talk. 'How can you stop like that?'

He drew his newly formed hands carefully out of my hands. I shivered as the tips of his claws trailed over my skin.

'Controlling the change is what separates the sheep from the wolves,' he said.

It took me a second to realize he'd made a joke. He leaned into me and whispered, 'If I lose control in the fight, or if I'm losing, I'll shift completely. I want you to come touch me, if I ask you.'

'Why?'

His breath was warm against my cheek. He wrapped his arms around me, held me in the circle of his body, claws playing along the leather straps of the outfit. 'I want you to feel the rush of power. I want you to know what it can be like between us.' His arms tightened. 'If I'm losing, you can ride the power and use it to get my wolves out of here. The others will kill anyone they think is disloyal.'

I pushed away enough to see his face. 'How can I use the power to do that?'

'You'll know.' He kissed my forehead ever so gently. 'Save them, Anita. Promise me.'

'I promise.'

He stood, my hands slipping over his body as he got to his feet. I caught one of his hands. My hand slid down the long, curved claw. It was as hard and solid and unreal as it looked. I'd felt his body shift, and yet, staring up at Richard's handsome face and those monstrous hands, it was jarring. Still, I held on. I didn't want to let him go.

'Careful of the claws, Anita. I'm not in human form anymore.'

He meant that a scratch might make me furry, might not. Hard to tell. But it was enough to make me let go. No matter how good Richard felt, I wasn't ready to throw humanity completely behind me.

Richard stared down at me, and there was a world in his eyes of things unsaid, things undone. I opened my mouth, closed it. 'Do you have this much control over every body part?'

He smiled. 'Yes.'

I was so scared I couldn't speak. I'd made my last joke. The only thing left was truth. I raised up, putting my hands on his legs for support and kissed the back of his hand. The skin was still as soft, still smelled and tasted like Richard, the bones underneath felt like someone else.

'Don't get killed.'

He smiled. There was a sadness in his eyes that was bottomless. Even if he won this fight, it would cost him dearly. Murder, that's how he would see it. No matter how justified. Moral high ground is dandy, but it'll get you killed.

Raina kissed Marcus goodbye, pressing her body so tightly against him, it was like she was trying to walk through him, part him like a curtain and slip inside.

She pushed him away with a rich, throaty laugh. It was the kind of laughter that made you turn your head in bars. A joyous, slightly wicked sound. Raina stared across the clearing at me, the laughter still sparkling in her eyes, on her face. One look was enough. She was going to kill me if she could.

Since I was pretty much thinking the same thing about her, I gave her a little nod and a salute. We'd see who was dead come morning. It might be me, but somewhere on the lists of the dead would be Raina. That I could almost promise.

Marcus raised his clawed hands over his head. He turned in a slow circle. 'Two alphas fight for you here tonight. One of us will leave this circle alive. One of us will feed you tonight. Drink of our blood, eat of our flesh. We are pack. We are lukoi. We are one.'

Jason threw his head back and howled, so close to me that I jumped. Furred throats echoed him, human throats joining the chorus. I stood alone among the pack and did not join in. When the last echo faded off in the rolling, wooded hills, Marcus said, 'Death between us then, Richard.'

'I offered you life, Marcus. You chose death.'

Marcus smiled. 'I suppose I did.'

Marcus jumped straight at him, no feinting, no practice, just a blur of speed. Richard rolled to the ground, up and away, coming to his feet. Three thin lines bled across his belly. Marcus didn't give him a chance to recover. He covered the distance between them like a bad dream. I couldn't even keep track of it with my eyes. I'd seen lycanthropes move before, and I'd thought they were fast, but Marcus was breathtaking.

He slashed Richard, forcing him back towards the edge of the clearing where Raina stood. Richard wasn't being hurt, but the flurry of attacks forced him backwards, kept him from attacking. I needed to ask a question. I looked down at Jason. He turned pale wolf eyes to me.

'If anyone else helps Marcus, it's cheating, right?' It felt vaguely stupid talking to something that looked like an animal, but the look in those eyes wasn't animal. I wasn't sure it was human, but it wasn't animal.

The wolf nodded its head. Awkwardly.

Richard's back was almost within Raina's reach. Jamil, the black werewolf from two nights ago, had joined her. Sebastian was already at her side. Shit.

'If they cheat, can I shoot them?'

'Yes,' Cassandra joined us, walking up through the pack like a warm, prickling wind. I got the first real brush of her power and knew she could have been lupa if she wanted to be.

I pulled the Browning out, and it felt odd in my hands, as if I didn't need it. I was channeling more of the pack than I knew if I didn't want my gun. A dangerous amount more. I wrapped my fingers around the butt of the Browning, digging my hand around it, remembering the feel of it. The sensory memory brought it back to me, pushed some of the glow of power away.

I didn't see a weapon, but Richard's back was to Raina and Sebastian. I raised the Browning, not aiming, not yet. I yelled, 'Behind you.'

I saw Richard's back spasm. He collapsed to his knees. Everything slowed down, carved in crystal. Sebastian's hand moved with a flash of silver blade. I was already aiming at him. Marcus's claw drew back for a downward swipe at Richard's unprotected throat. I pulled the trigger and turned the gun towards Marcus, but it would be too slow, too late.

The top of Sebastian's head exploded. I had a fraction of a second to wonder what ammunition Edward had put in the gun. The body started to fall backwards. Marcus's claw came sweeping down, and Richard drove his hand under the arm, into Marcus's upper stomach. Marcus stopped, froze for a second, as the claws dug into his stomach, up under his ribs. Richard's hand went into Marcus's body past the wrist.

I kept the Browning pointed at Raina in case she got any ideas about picking up the knife.

Marcus drove his claws into Richard's back. Richard tucked his face and neck against the other man's body, protecting himself from the claws. Marcus shuddered. Richard broke away from him, bringing his bloody hand out of Marcus's chest. He tore the still-beating heart out of his chest and flung it to the wolves. They fell on the morsel with small yips and growling.

Richard collapsed to his knees beside Marcus's body. Blood poured down his lower back where the knife had gone in. I walked to him, the gun still pointed at Raina. I knelt, still keeping a bead on her. 'Richard, are you all right?' It was a stupid thing to ask, but what else was I supposed to say?

'Put up the gun, Anita. It's over.'

'She tried to kill you,' I said.

'It's over.' He turned his face to me, and his eyes were already gone. His voice fell towards a growl. 'Put it away.'

I stared up at Raina and knew if I didn't kill her now, I'd have to kill her later. 'She'll see us dead, Richard.'

Richard's hand was suddenly there, faster than I could see. He hit my hand, and the gun went spinning. My hand was numb. I tried to back away, but he grabbed me, wrapping his clawed hands around my upper arms. 'No more killing . . . tonight.' He threw back his head and howled. His mouth was full of fangs.

I screamed.

'Ride the power, Anita. Ride it or run.' His hands convulsed around my arms. I backpedaled, dug my heels in, and tried to get loose. He collapsed on top of me, too hurt for the struggle, too far gone to fight the change. His power roared over me, into me. I couldn't see anything but the glow of power behind my eyes. If I could have breathed, I'd have screamed again, but there was nothing but the force of his power, and it spread outward from him like a rock in water. The waves touched the pack, and where it touched, fur flowed. Richard shifted and took everyone with him. Everyone. I felt Raina struggle next to us. I felt her fight it. Heard her shriek, but in the end she fell to the ground and changed.

I held onto Richard's arms, and fur flowed under my hands like water. Muscle formed and shifted, bones broke and reknit. My lower body was trapped underneath him. Clear liquid gushed from his body, pouring over me in a near scalding wave. I screamed and struggled to get out from underneath him. And the power rode me down, filled me up, until I thought my skin wouldn't hold, couldn't hold it.

Finally, he rose off me, not a wolf, but man-wolf, covered in fur the color of cinnamon and gold. His genitalia hung large and full underneath him. He stared at me with amber eyes and offered me a clawed hand as he rose on two slightly bent legs.

I ignored the hand and scooted backwards. I got to my feet, a little unsteady, and stared. The wolf form was actually taller than his human shape, about seven feet, muscled, and monstrous. There was nothing left of Richard. But I knew how good it had felt to let loose the beast. I had felt it rise out of him like a second mind, soul, rising upward, outward, filling him, spilling out of his skin.

My body was still tingling with the brush of his beast. I could feel the thick softness of his fur under my fingertips like a sensory memory that would haunt me.

Marcus's very human-looking body lay on the ground at Richard's feet. The scent of fresh blood ran through him, ran through them all. I felt it thrill through my body. I stared down at the dead man and wanted to go down to my knees and feed. I had a strong visual image of tearing flesh, warm viscera. It was a memory. It jerked me back a step.

I stared at the man-wolf. I stared at Richard and shook my head. 'I can't feed. I won't.'

He spoke, but it was twisted and guttural. 'You're not invited. We will feast, then hunt. You can watch. You can join the hunt, or you can go.'

I backed away slowly. 'I'm going.'

The pack was creeping closer, gigantic wolves mostly, but here and there were man-wolves, watching me with alien eyes. I couldn't see the Browning that Richard had knocked from my hand. I drew the Firestar and started to back away.

'No one will hurt you, Anita. You are lupa. Mate.'

I stared into the cool eyes of the nearest wolf. 'Right now, I'm just food, Richard.'

'You refused the power,' he said.

He was right. In the end, I'd panicked and hadn't gotten the full dose. 'Whatever.' I eased through the wolves, but they didn't move. I walked out, brushing through fur like wading through a fur coat factory. Every brush of breathing, living animal scared me. Panic climbed at my throat, and I still had enough glow left to know that my fear excited them. The more scared I got, the more I smelled like food.

I kept the gun ready, but I knew if they went for me, I was dead. There were too many of them. They watched me walk. They stubbornly refused to move, forcing me to brush their furred bodies. I realized they were using me for a sort of appetizer, my fear to spice their food, the brush of my human body to flavor their chase.

When I passed the last furred body, the sound of tearing flesh brought my head around. I couldn't stop myself in time. Richard's muzzle was raised skyward, slick with blood, throwing down a piece of meat that I tried not to recognize.

I ran. The woods that I'd glided through with Richard's help suddenly became an obstacle course. I ran, and tripped, and fell, and ran some more. I finally got back to the parking lot. I had driven because nobody but me was going home tonight. They'd stay here and have a moonlight jamboree.

Edward and Harley had watched all of it from a nearby hill with night scopes. I wondered what they thought of the show.

38

Edward made me promise to go back to the Circus for one more night. Marcus was dead, so there was no more money, but if someone else had taken the contract, they might not know that yet. It would be a shame to get killed after all the effort we'd put in to save me. I walked all the way down the damn stairs to the iron-bound door before I realized I didn't have a key, and nobody was expecting me.

The clear liquid that had gushed out of Richard's body had dried to a sticky, viscous substance somewhere between blood and glue. I needed a bath. I needed clean clothes. I needed to stop seeing Richard's mouth while he ate pieces of Marcus. The harder I tried not to flash on it, the clearer the image got.

I banged on the door until my hands stung, then I kicked it. No one came. 'Shit!' I screamed at no one and everyone. 'Shit!'

The feel of his body on top of mine. His bones and muscle sliding on top of me like a bag of snakes. The warm rush of power, and that moment when I had wanted to drop to my knees and feed. What if I had swallowed the power whole? What if I hadn't backed off? Would I have fed on Marcus? Would I have done that and enjoyed it?

I screamed wordlessly, smacking my hands into the door, kicking it, beating on it. I collapsed to my knees, stinging palms pressed against the wood. I leaned my head against the door and cried.

'*Ma petite*, what has happened?' Jean-Claude stood behind me on the stairs. 'Richard is not dead. I would feel it.'

I turned and pressed my back against the door. I wiped at the tears on my face. 'He's not dead, not even close.'

'Then what is wrong?' He came down the steps like he was dancing, too graceful for words, even after an evening spent with shapeshifters. His shirt was a deep, rich blue, not quite dark enough to be navy, the sleeves were full, with wide cuffs, the collar high but soft, almost as if it were a scarf. I'd never seen him in blue of any shade. It made his midnight blue eyes seem bluer, darker. His jeans were black and tight enough to be skin, the boots were knee-high, with a trailing edge of black leather that flopped as he moved.

He knelt beside me, not touching me, almost like he was afraid to. '*Ma petite*, your cross.'

I stared down at it. It wasn't glowing, not yet. I wrapped my hand around the cross and jerked, snapping the chain. I flung it away. It fell against the wall, glinting silver in the faint light. 'Happy?'

Jean-Claude looked at me. 'Richard lives. Marcus is dead. Correct?'

I nodded.

'Then why the tears, *ma petite*? I do not think I have ever seen you cry.'

'I am not crying.'

He touched my cheek with one fingertip and came away with a single tear trembling on the end of his finger. He raised it to his lips, the tip of his tongue licked it off his skin. 'You taste like your heart has broken, *ma petite*.'

My throat choked tight. I couldn't breathe past the tears. The harder I tried not to cry, the faster the tears flowed. I hugged myself, and my hands touched the sticky gunk that covered me. I held my hands away from my body like I'd touched something unclean. I stared at Jean-Claude with my hands held out in front of me.

'*Mon Dieu*, what has happened?' He tried to hug me, but I pushed him away.

'You'll get it all over you.'

He stared at the thick, clear gunk on his hand. 'How did you get this close to a shapeshifting werewolf?' An idea flowed across his face. 'It's Richard. You saw him change.'

I nodded. 'He changed on top of me. It was . . . Oh, God, oh, God, oh, God.'

Jean-Claude pulled me into his arms. I pushed at him. 'You'll ruin your clothes.'

'*Ma petite, ma petite*, it's all right. It is all right.'

'No, it's not.' I sagged against him. I let him wrap me in his arms. I clutched at him, hands digging into the silk of his shirt. I buried my face against his chest and whispered, 'He ate Marcus. He ate him.'

'He's a werewolf, *ma petite*. That's what they do.'

It was such an odd thing to say, and so terribly true, that I laughed – an abrupt, almost angry sound. The laughter died in choking, and the choking became sobs.

I held onto Jean-Claude like he was the last sane thing in the world. I buried myself against him and wept. It was like something deep inside me had broken, and I was crying out bits of myself onto his body.

His voice came to me dimly, as if he had been speaking for a long time, but I hadn't heard. He was speaking French, softly, whispering it into my hair, stroking my back, rocking me gently.

I lay in his arms, quiet. I had no more tears left. I felt empty and light, numb.

Jean-Claude smoothed my hair back from my forehead. He brushed his lips across my skin, like Richard had done earlier tonight. Even that thought couldn't make me cry again. It was too soon.

'Can you stand, *ma petite*?'

'I think so.' My voice sounded distant, strange. I stood, still in the circle of his arms, leaning against him. I pushed away from him gently. I stood on my own, a little shaky, but better than nothing.

His dark blue shirt was plastered to his chest, covered with were-wolf goop and tears. 'Now we both need a bath,' I said.

'That can be arranged.'

'Please, Jean-Claude, no sexual innuendo until after I'm clean.'

'Of course, *ma petite*. It was crude of me tonight. My apologies.'

I stared at him. He was being far too nice. Jean-Claude was a lot of things, but nice wasn't one of them.

'If you're up to something, I don't want to know about it. I can't handle any deep, dark plots tonight, okay?'

He smiled and gave a low, sweeping bow, never taking his eyes off me. The way you bow on the judo mat when you're afraid the person may pound you if you look away.

I shook my head. He *was* up to something. Nice to know that not everyone had suddenly become something else. One thing I could always depend on was Jean-Claude. Pain in the ass that he was, he always seemed to be there. Dependable in his own twisted way. Jean-Claude dependable? I must have been more tired than I thought.

39

Jean-Claude opened the bedroom door and stepped inside, ushering me through with a sweep of graceful hands. The bed stopped me. There'd been a change of bedding. Red sheets covered the bed. Crimson drapes formed a half canopy over the nearly black wood. There were still a dozen pillows on the bed and they were all screaming, brilliant red. Even after the night I'd had, it was eye-catching.

'I like the new decor, I guess.'

'The linens needed to be changed. You are always complaining that I should use more color.'

I stared at the bed. 'I'll stop complaining.'

'I will run your bath.' He went into the bathroom without a single joke or risqué comment. It was almost unnerving.

Whoever had changed the sheets had also removed the chairs that Edward and Harley had used. I didn't want to sit on the clean sheets still covered in whatever the hell I was covered in. I sat down on the white carpet and tried not to think. Not thinking is a lot harder than it sounds. My thoughts kept chasing each other, like a werewolf chasing its tail. The image tore a laugh from my throat, and on the end of it a sound like a sob or a moan. I put the back of my hand against my mouth. I didn't like that sound coming out of me. It sounded hopeless, beaten.

I was not beaten, dammit, but I was hurt. If what I felt had been an actual wound, I'd have been bleeding to death.

The bathroom door opened at long last. A puff of warm, moist air flowed around Jean-Claude. He had taken off his shirt, and the cross-shaped burn scar marred the perfection of his chest. He held his boots in one hand, a towel as scarlet as the sheets in the other.

'I washed up in the sink while the tub filled.' He walked barefoot across the white carpeting. 'I'm afraid I used the last clean towel. I will fetch you more.'

I took my hand away from my mouth and nodded. I finally managed to say, 'Fine.'

I stood before he could offer to help me up. I didn't need any help.

Jean-Claude moved to one side. His black hair lay in nearly tight curls across his pale shoulders, curled from the humidity of the bathroom. I ignored him as much as it was humanly possible and walked inside.

The room was warm and misty, the black marble tub full of bubbles. He offered me a black lacquer tray from the vanity top. Shampoos, soap, bath crystals, and what looked like oils were grouped on the tray.

'Get out so I can undress.'

'It took two people to dress you tonight, *ma petite*. Won't you need help getting undressed?' His voice was utterly bland. His face so still, his eyes so innocent, it made me smile.

I sighed. 'If you get the two straps in back, I think I can manage the rest. But no monkey business.' I held my hands over the bra because one strap would loosen it. The other strap, as far as I could tell, was the pivot point for the rest of the outfit.

His fingers moved to the top strap. I watched him in the fogged mirror. The strap came unbuckled, and the leather gave with a small sigh. He moved to the second strap without so much as an extra caress. He undid it and took a step back. 'No monkey business, *ma petite*.' He backed out of the room, and I watched him go like a phantom in the mist-covered mirrors. When the door was shut, I started on the rest of the straps. It was like peeling myself to get the goo-soaked leather off.

I put the tray of bath accessories on the tub edge and slipped into the water. The water was hot, just this side of too hot. I sank into it up to my chin, but I couldn't relax. The gunk clung to my body in patches. I had to get it off me. I sat up in the tub and started scrubbing. The soap smelled like gardenia. The shampoos smelled like herbs. Trust Jean-Claude not to buy a name brand from the grocery store.

I washed my hair twice, sinking under the water and coming up for air. I was scrubbed and virtuous, or at least clean. The mirrors had cleared and I had only myself to stare at. I'd washed off all the careful makeup. I smoothed my thick, black hair back from my face. My eyes were enormous and nearly black. My skin so pale, it was almost white. I looked shocked, ethereal, unreal.

There was a soft knock on the door. '*Ma petite*, may I come in?'

I glanced down at myself. The bubbles were still holding. I drew a pile of them a little closer to my chest and said, 'Come in.' It took a lot of effort not to hunch down in the water. I sat up straight, trusting in the bubbles. Besides, I would not huddle. So I was naked in a tub of bubble bath. So what. No one can embarrass you unless you let them.

Jean-Claude came in with two thick, red towels. He closed the door behind him with a small smile. 'We wouldn't want to let the hot air out.'

I narrowed my eyes but said, 'I guess not.'

'Where do you want the towels? Here?' He started to lay them on the vanity.

'I can't reach them there,' I said.

'Here?' He laid them on top of the stool. He stood there, staring down at me, still wearing nothing but the black jeans. His feet were startlingly pale against the black carpet.

'Still too far away.'

He sat down on the edge of the tub, placing the towels on the floor. He stared down at me as if he could will the bubbles away. 'Is this close enough?'

'Maybe a little too close,' I said.

He trailed fingertips over the bubbles at the edge of the tub. 'Do you feel better now, *ma petite*?'

'I said no sexual innuendo, remember.'

'As I remember, you said no sexual innuendo until after you were clean.' He smiled at me. 'You're clean.'

I sighed. 'Trust you to be literal.'

He trailed his fingers in the water. He turned his shoulder enough that I could see the whip scars on his back. They were slick and white, and I suddenly had an urge to trace them with my fingers.

He turned back to face me. He wiped his wet fingers across his chest, trailing shining lines of moisture across the flat slickness of the burn scar, down along his belly. His fingers played with the line of dark hair that vanished into his pants.

I closed my eyes and let out a sigh.

'What is the matter, *ma petite*?' I felt him leaning over me. 'Are you faint?'

I opened my eyes. He had leaned his entire upper body across the tub, right arm on the far rim, the left near my shoulder. His hip was so far over the water that if I'd touched his chest, he'd have fallen in.

'I don't faint,' I said.

His face leaned down over mine. 'So glad to hear it.' He kissed me lightly, a brush of lips, but even that small movement made my stomach jerk.

I gasped and pushed him away. He fell into the tub, going completely under, only his feet sticking out. He landed on my naked body, and I screamed.

He came up for air, his long, black hair streaming around his face, across his shoulders. He looked as surprised as I'd ever seen him. He crawled off me, mainly because I was shoving at him. He struggled to his feet. Water streamed down his body. He stared down at me. I was huddled against the side, staring up at him, pissed.

He shook his head and laughed. The sound filled the room, played along my skin like a hand. 'I have been a ladies' man for nearly three hundred years, Anita. Why is it only with you that I am awkward?'

'Maybe it's a hint,' I said.

'Perhaps.'

I stared up at him. He stood there, knee deep in bubble bath. He was soaking wet and should have been ridiculous, but he wasn't. He was beautiful.

'How can you be so damn beautiful when I know what you are?'

He knelt in the water. The bubbles covered his waist, so he looked naked. Water trailed down his chest in fine beads. I wanted to run my hands over him. I wanted to lick the water off his skin. I drew my legs to my chest and locked my arms around them, not trusting myself.

He moved towards me. The water sloshed and curled around my naked body. He stayed kneeling, so close that his jeans brushed my huddled legs. The feel of him in the water, that close, made me hide my face against my knees. The pounding of my heart gave me away. I knew he could taste my need on the air.

'Tell me to go, *ma petite*, and I will go.' I felt him lean over me, his face just above my wet hair.

Slowly, I raised my face.

He placed a hand on the tub edge, one arm on either side of me, bringing his chest dangerously close to my face. I watched the water bead on his skin, the way that he sometimes watched blood on mine: a need almost too overwhelming to deny, an urge so complete that I didn't want to say no.

I unclenched my arms from my knees and leaned forward. I whispered, 'Don't go.' I touched hands to his waist, tentative, as if it should burn, but his skin was cool under the slickness of water. Cool and smooth to the touch. I glanced up at his face and knew that there was something close to fear on my own face.

His face was lovely, and uncertain, as if he didn't know what to do next. It was a look I never thought to see on Jean-Claude's face when I was naked in his arms.

I kept my eyes on his face as I moved my mouth towards his stomach. I ran my tongue over his skin, a quick, tentative movement.

He sighed, eyes fluttering shut, body almost sagging. I pressed my mouth against his skin, drinking the water off of him. I couldn't reach his chest. I moved to my knees, hands steadying me against his slender waist.

The air was cool against my naked breasts. Kneeling had bared them. I froze, suddenly unsure. I wanted desperately to see his face and was afraid to look up.

His fingertips brushed my shoulders, sliding down the wet skin. I shivered and glanced up. The look on his face caught my breath in my throat. Tenderness, need, amazement.

'You are so beautiful, *ma petite*.' He put his fingertips to my lips before I could protest. 'You are beautiful. On this I do not lie.'

His fingers moved across my lips, down my chin. He slid his hands to my shoulders, down my back, in slow, teasing lines. His hands stopped on either side of my waist, mirroring my hands on his own waist.

'Now what?' My voice was a little breathless.

'Whatever you like, *ma petite*.'

I massaged my hands against his waist, feeling the flesh underneath, feeling him under my hands. I spread my hands wide, splaying my fingers tense against his skin, dragging my hands up his ribs.

He kneaded his fingers into my waist, pressing his hands against my ribs. He inched his hands upward along my sides. Strong fingers pressed into my skin just enough to make me sigh. He stopped with his thumbs below my breasts. His touch was feather light, almost not touching at all. But that one small brush of his skin against my breasts made my body react, tightening, nipples hardening. My body wanted him. Wanted him so badly that my skin felt large and aching with the thought of it.

My own hands were pressed against his chest. I realized that he was still mirroring me, waiting for me to move.

I stared up into his face. I searched that beauty, those dark eyes. There was no pull to them, no power, except the thick black line of his lashes, and the rich color like the sky just before darkness swallows the world when you think all is black, but there in the west is a shade of blue, dark and rich as ink. Beauty had its own power.

I slid my hands up his chest, fingers brushing across his nipples. I stared at his face while I did it, heart pounding in my throat, breath coming too fast.

His hands slid upward, cupping my breasts. The touch of his hands made me gasp. He scooted lower in the water, still touching me. He bent over my breasts and laid a gentle kiss on them. He licked the water off my skin, lips working gently.

I shuddered and had to steady myself on his bare shoulders. All I could see was his long, dark hair bent over me. I caught sight of us in the mirrors. I watched his mouth close over my breast, felt him take me into his mouth as far as he could. Fangs pressed against my breast. For a second I thought they would sink into my flesh, draw blood in a fine hot line, but he drew back. He dropped to all fours in the water, which made me taller, allowed me to look down into his face.

There was no uncertainty in his face now. His eyes were still lovely, still human, but there was a knowledge in them now, a growing darkness. Sex, for want of a better word, but that look in a man's eyes is too primitive for vocabulary. It's the darkness we all have inside of us, peeking out. That part of us that we trap in our dreams and deny in daylight hours. He stayed crouched in the water with that feral light in his eyes, and I went to him.

I kissed him, light, a brush of lips. I flicked my tongue along his lips and he opened his mouth for me. I cupped his face between my hands and kissed him, tasted him, explored him.

He came up out of the water with a sound between a moan and a cry. His arms locked behind my back and he rolled us in the water like a shark. We came up gasping. He pushed away from me to lean against the far edge of the tub. I was breathing so hard I was trembling. My pulse thudded at the back of my throat. I could taste it on my tongue, almost roll the beating pulse in my mouth like candy. I realized it wasn't just my heart I was hearing. It was Jean-Claude's.

I could see the pulse in his neck like something alive and separate, but it wasn't only my eyes that could see it. I could feel it like it was my own. I had never been so aware of the blood coursing through my body. The pulsing warmth of my own skin. The thick pumping of my heart. My life thundering inside me. Jean-Claude's body pulsed in time to mine. It was like he was riding my pulse, my blood. I felt his need, and it wasn't just sex, but for the first time, I understood it wasn't just the blood, either. It was all of me. He wanted to warm himself in my body, like holding hands to a flame, gathering my warmth, my life, to him. I felt his stillness, a depth of quiet that nothing living could touch, like a still pool of water hidden away in the dark. In one crystalline moment, I realized that, for me, this was part of the attraction: I wanted to plunge my hands into his stillness, into that quiet place of death. I wanted to embrace it, confront it, conquer it. I wanted to fill him up with a burning wash of life, and I knew in that moment that I could do it, but only at the price of drinking in some of that still, dark water.

'My deepest apologies, *ma petite*, you have almost undone me.'

He sank into the water, leaning against the edge of the tub. 'I did not come here to feed, *ma petite*. I am sorry.'

I felt his heartbeat going away from me, pulling away from me. My pulse slowed. The only heart thudding in my ears was my own.

He stood, water dripping down his body. 'I will go, *ma petite*.' He sighed. 'You rob me of my hard-won control. Only you can do that to me, only you.'

I crawled through the water towards him and let the darkness fill my eyes. 'Don't go,' I said.

He watched me with a look that was part amazement, part amusement, part fear, as if he didn't trust me – or didn't trust himself.

I knelt at his feet, running my hands up the soaked cloth of his jeans. I dug my nails lightly into the cloth over his thighs and stared up at him. My face was dangerously close to places I had never touched before, not even with my hands. This close, I couldn't help noticing that he was stretched hard and firm under the tight, heavy cloth. I had a terrible urge to lay my cheek over his groin. I ran my hand lightly over him, barely touching. That small touch brought a soft groan from him.

He stared down at me like a drowning man.

I met his eyes. 'No teeth, no blood.'

He nodded slowly. He tried twice before he found his voice. 'As my lady wishes.'

I laid my cheek across him, feeling him firm and large against my skin. I felt his whole body tense. I rubbed my face against him like a cat. A small sound escaped him. I looked up. His eyes were closed, his head thrown back.

I grabbed the waistband of his jeans and used it to pull myself to my feet. Water ran down my body, suds clung to my skin.

His hands encircled my waist, but his eyes went lower. He met my gaze and smiled. It was the smile he always had. That smile that said he was thinking wicked little thoughts, things you'd only do in the dark on a dare. For the first time, I wanted everything that smile promised.

I tugged at his jeans. 'Off.'

He unsnapped the jeans carefully. He peeled the wet cloth away from his body. If there'd been underwear, I never saw it. The jeans ended up on the carpet. He was somehow suddenly nude.

He was like carved alabaster, every muscle, every curve of his body pale and perfect. Telling him he was beautiful was redundant. Saying golly gee whiz seemed too uncool. Giggling was out. My voice came small and strangled, hoarse with all the words I couldn't find. 'You're not circumcised.'

'No, *ma petite*. Is that a problem?'

I did what I'd wanted to do since I first saw him. I wrapped my fingers around him, squeezing gently. He closed his eyes, shuddering, steadying his hands on my shoulders. 'Not a problem,' I said.

He pulled me against him suddenly, pressing our naked bodies together. The feel of him hard and firm against my stomach was almost overwhelming. I dug fingers into his back to keep my suddenly weak knees from giving out.

I kissed his chest. I rose on tiptoe and kissed his shoulders, his neck. I ran my tongue along his skin and tasted him, rolling the scent of him, the feel of him in my mouth. We kissed, a nearly innocent brush of lips. I locked my hands behind his neck, arching my body against him. He made a small sound low in his throat.

He slid down my body, arms locked behind my back, holding me against him as he left my arms and left me standing, staring down at him.

He licked my stomach with quick, wet flicks of his tongue. His hands played along my buttocks, teasing. He licked back and forth where stomach ended and lower things began. His fingers slid between my legs.

I gasped. 'What are you doing?'

He rolled his eyes upward, mouth still pressed low on my stomach. He raised his face just enough to speak. 'You may have three guesses, *ma petite*,' he whispered. He put a hand on each of my thighs and spread my legs wider. His hand slid over me, exploring me.

My mouth was suddenly dry. I licked my lips and said, 'I don't think my legs will hold.'

He ran his tongue down my hip. 'When the time comes, *ma petite*, I will hold you.' He kissed his way down my thigh. His finger slid inside of me. My breath fell outward in a sigh.

He kissed the inside of my thighs, running his tongue, his lips along my skin. The feel of his fingers between my legs tightened my body, and I could feel the beginnings of something large and overwhelming.

He stood, hand still between my legs. He bent and kissed me, long and slow. The movement of his hand matched his mouth. Slow and lingering, teasing along my body. When his fingers plunged inside me, I cried out, shuddering against him.

He left me standing in the water, alone and shivering, but not from cold. I couldn't even think enough to ask where'd he gone. He appeared in front of me with a condom in his hand like he'd plucked it from the air. He traced the foil down my body.

I touched him while he unwrapped it. I held him in my hands and felt the velvet smoothness of him. The skin was unbelievably soft. He drew himself gently out of my hands with a shaking laugh.

When he was ready, he picked me up, hands on the backs of my thighs. He pressed himself against me without entering, rubbing himself where his hand had touched. I whispered, 'Please.' He spread my legs and eased inside of me. Slowly, so slowly as if he were afraid he'd hurt me, but it didn't hurt.

When he was sheathed inside me, he looked at me. The look on his face was haunting. Emotions flowed over his face. Tenderness, triumph, need. 'I have wanted this for so long, *ma petite*, so very long.' He eased in and out, slowly, almost tentatively. I watched his face until the play of emotions was too much, too honest. There was something like pain in his eyes, something that I didn't even come close to understanding.

The movements of his hips were still slow, careful. It was amazing, but I wanted more. I brought my mouth up to his and said, 'I won't break.' I pressed my mouth to his hard enough to feel the press of fangs.

He went to his knees in the water, pressing me against the side of the tub. His mouth fed at mine, and there was a small, sharp pain. Sweet copper blood filled my mouth, filled his mouth, and he plunged inside of me, hard and fast. I watched him in the mirrors. Watched his body coming in and out of mine. I gathered him in my arms, in my legs. I held him to me, feeling his body plunging inside of mine. Felt his need.

Someone was making a high moaning sound, and it was me. I wrapped my legs around his waist. The muscles in my lower abdomen spasmed, tightened.

I pressed my body against Jean-Claude as if I would climb through him, into him. I grabbed a handful of his long hair and watched his face from inches away. Watched his face while his body pumped into mine. The emotions were gone. His face was almost slack with need. Blood spilled down the corner of my mouth, and he licked it away, his body tightening against me.

He slowed the rhythm of his body. I felt the effort strain through his arms and back. He slowed. Every time he thrust into me, it was like I could feel it into the middle of my chest. As if he'd grown impossibly large within me. My body spasmed around him, tightened like a hand. He cried out, and his body lost its rhythm. He plunged inside me faster, harder, as if he would meld our bodies together, weld us into one flesh, one body. A wave of pleasure burst over me in a skin-tingling, body-sweeping rush. It burst over me like a rush of cool flame, and still he was not done. Every thrust of his body reached inside of me and caressed things that should never have been able to be touched. It was as if his body could reach the places his voice could touch, as if it were more than his body that plunged inside of me. The world became for a moment a shining whiteness, a melting thing. I dug fingers into Jean-Claude's back. Noises fell from my mouth that were too primitive for screams. When I realized I was drawing blood on his back, I scratched my own arms. I hadn't asked what he thought about pain.

I cuddled around him, letting him hold the full weight of my body. He climbed up the edge of the tub, lifting me out of the water. He crawled on all fours to the raised area around the tub with me hanging onto him. He lowered his body and I moved away from him. He slid out of me and was still as hard and ready as when he had started.

I looked at him. 'You didn't come.'

'I have not waited this long to end it so quickly.' He lowered himself in a sort of push-up and ran his tongue down one of the scratches on my arm. He rolled his tongue around his lips. 'If you did this for my benefit, I appreciate it. If you did it to keep from damaging me, it was not necessary. I do not mind a little pain.'

'Me, either.'

He slid his body across mine. 'I noticed that.' He kissed me slowly. He lay beside me, then scooted until he was lying on his back and I was almost back in the tub. 'I want to watch you move, *ma petite*. I want you above me.'

I straddled his waist and slid slowly over him. It was deeper from this angle, sharper somehow. His hands moved up my body, over my breasts. He lay back underneath me. His long, curling, black hair was almost completely dry. It fanned out around his face in a thick, soft wave. This was what I wanted. Seeing him like this. Feeling him inside me.

'Move for me, Anita.'

I moved for him. I rode his body. He tightened inside me, and I gasped. I watched us in the mirrors. Watched my hips swaying above him.

'*Ma petite*,' he whispered, 'look into my eyes. Let it be between us as it always could have been.'

I stared into his dark blue eyes. They were lovely, but they were just eyes. I shook my head. 'I can't.'

'You must let me inside your mind, as you let me inside your body.' He spasmed inside of me, and it was hard to think.

'I don't know how,' I said.

'Love me, Anita, love me.'

I stared down at him and did. 'I do love you.'

'Then let me in, *ma petite*. Let me love you.'

I felt it like a drape being pulled away. I felt his eyes, and they were suddenly drowning deep, an endless midnight blue ocean that somehow managed to burn. I was aware of my body. I could feel Jean-Claude inside my body. I could feel him like a brush of silk inside my mind.

The orgasm hit me unexpectedly, opened my mind to him more than I'd planned. Flung me wide open and falling into his eyes. He cried out underneath me, and I realized I could still feel my body, feel my hands on his chest, feel my pelvis riding him. I opened my eyes and for a dizzying second I saw his face go slack, that moment of total abandon.

I collapsed on top of him, trailing my hands down his arms, feeling his heart pound against my chest. We lay quietly for a few moments, resting, holding each other, then I slid off him, curling beside him.

'You can't hold me with your eyes anymore. Even if I let you, I can still break the hold at any time.'

'Yes, *ma petite*.'

'Does that bother you?'

He lifted a lock of my hair, running it between his fingers.

'Let us say it does not bother me as much as it might have a few hours ago.'

I raised up on one elbow so I could see his face. 'Meaning what? That now that I've had sex with you, I'm not dangerous?'

He stared up at me. I couldn't read his eyes. 'You will always be dangerous, *ma petite*.' He raised upward, bending at the waist, bringing his lips against mine in a gentle kiss. He moved back from me just enough to speak, propping himself on one arm. 'There was a time when you would have taken my heart with stake or gun.' He took my hand in his and raised it towards his mouth. 'Now you have taken it with these delicate hands and the scent of your body.' He kissed the back of my hand ever so gently. He lay back, drawing me with him. 'Come, *ma petite*, enjoy your conquest.'

I held my face back, avoiding a kiss. 'You aren't conquered,' I said.

'Nor, *ma petite*, are you.' He ran his hands up my back. 'I am beginning to realize that you will never be conquered, and that is the greatest aphrodisiac of all.'

'A challenge forever,' I said.

'For all eternity,' he whispered. I let him draw me down into a kiss, and part of me was still not sure if I'd done a good thing or a bad thing. But just for tonight, I didn't care.

40

I woke surrounded by bloodred sheets, naked, and alone. Jean-Claude had kissed me goodbye and gone to his coffin. I didn't argue. If I'd awakened to him cold and dead beside me . . . Let's just say I'd had all the shock I could handle from my boyfriends for awhile.

Boyfriend. That was a word for someone who walked you to your class. It didn't seem the right word after last night. I lay there, clutching the raw silk sheets to my chest. I could smell Jean-Claude's cologne on the sheets, on my skin, but more than that, I could smell him. I cuddled that scent to me, rolled in it. He said he loved me and for a time last night, I believed him. In the light of day, I wasn't so sure. How stupid was it to half-believe the vampire loved me? Not nearly as stupid as half-loving him. But I still loved Richard. One night of great sex didn't change that. I think I had hoped it would. Lust may die that easily, but love doesn't. True love is a much harder beast to kill.

There was a soft knock on the door. I had to reach under two red pillows before I came out with the Firestar. I held it at my side and said, 'Come in.'

A man entered the room. He was tall, muscular, with hair shaved on either side, the back left in a long ponytail.

I pointed the gun at him and clutched the sheets to my chest. 'I don't know you.'

His eyes went wide; his voice shook, 'I'm Ernie, I'm supposed to ask if you want breakfast.'

'No,' I said. 'Now, get out.'

He nodded, eyes on the gun. He hesitated in the doorway, even staring down the barrel of a gun. I made a guess.

'What did Jean-Claude tell you to do?' It was amazing how many people were more afraid of Jean-Claude than of me. I pointed the gun at the ceiling.

'He said I was to be at your disposal, anything you want. He said I was to make that very clear to you.'

'It's clear. Now, get out.'

He still hesitated.

I'd had enough. 'Ernie, I am sitting here naked in a bed, and I don't know you. Get out or I'm going shoot you on principle.' I aimed the gun at him for dramatic emphasis.

Ernie ran for it, leaving the door open. Great. Now I had the choice of walking to the door naked and closing it, or draping a king-size sheet around me and stumbling to the door and closing it. Sheet. I was sitting on the edge of the bed, with the sheet in front of me and most of my backside not covered, gun still clutched in one hand, when Richard appeared in the doorway.

He was dressed in jeans, white T-shirt, jeans jacket, and white tennis shoes. His hair foamed around his face in a mass of golden brown waves. A claw had caught him across the face, leaving angry red welts that chased across the entire left side of his face. The injury looked days old. It had to have happened after I left last night.

He had my leather coat in one hand and the Browning in the other. He just stood there in the doorway.

I sat on the bed. Neither of us said anything. I wasn't slick and sophisticated enough for this. What do you say to boyfriend A when he finds you naked in the bed of boyfriend B? Especially if boyfriend A turned into a monster the night before and ate someone. I bet Miss Manners didn't cover this at all.

'You slept with him, didn't you?' His voice was low, almost soft, as if he was trying very hard not to yell.

My gut tightened. I was not ready for this fight. I was armed, but I was naked. I would have traded the gun for clothes in a hot second.

'I would say it's not what it looks like, but it is.' My attempt at humor did not work.

He strode into the room like an approaching storm, his anger riding before him in a crackling wave. The power poured over me and I wanted to scream.

'Stop leaking all over me.'

It stopped him, almost literally in midmotion. 'What are you talking about?'

'Your power, aura, it's raining all over me. Stop it.'

'Why? Does it feel good? Until you panicked last night, it felt good, didn't it?'

I shoved the Firestar under the pillow and stood, clutching the sheet to me. 'Yeah, it felt good until you shapeshifted on top of me. I was covered in that clear gunk, thick with it.' The memory was new enough that I shuddered and looked away from him.

'So you fucked Jean-Claude. Oh, that makes perfect sense.'

I looked at him and felt an answering anger. If he wanted to fight, he'd come to the right place. I held up my right hand. It was covered in a wonderful multicolored bruise. 'You did this when you knocked my gun away.'

'There'd been enough killing, Anita. No one else had to die.'

'Do you really think that Raina is just going to let you take over? No way. She'll see you dead first.'

He shook his head, his face set in stubborn lines. 'I am Ulfric now. I'm in control. She'll do what I say.'

'Nobody bosses Raina; not for long. Has she offered to fuck you yet?'

'Yes,' he said.

The way he said it stopped me, brought my breath up short. 'Did you, after I left?'

'It would serve you right if I had.'

I couldn't meet his eyes on that one. 'If you make her lupa, she'll let it go. She just doesn't want to lose her power base.' I forced myself to look up, to meet his eyes.

'I don't want Raina.' Something passed over his face so raw, that it brought tears to my eyes. 'I want you.'

'You can't want me now, not after last night.'

'Is that why you slept with Jean-Claude? Did you think it would keep you safe from me?'

'I wasn't thinking that clearly,' I said.

He laid the coat and the gun on the bed. He gripped the end of the bed. The wood groaned under the strength of his hands. He jerked back from it as if he hadn't meant to do it. 'You slept with him in this bed. Right here.' He put his hand over his eyes as if he was trying to erase an image inside his head.

He screamed wordlessly.

I took a step towards him, hand out, and stopped. How could I comfort him? What could I say to make this better? Not a damn thing.

He jerked at the bottom sheet, tugging it until it came loose. He grabbed the top mattress and pulled it off the bed. He grabbed the bottom of the bed and lifted.

I screamed, 'Richard!'

The bed was antique solid oak, and he tossed it on its side like it was a toy. He pulled the bottom sheet off. The silk tore with a sound like skin peeling back. He was on his knees with the butchered silk in his hands. He held his hands out to me and the sheets fell away like blood.

Richard got to his feet, a little unsteady. He caught himself against the bed and took a step towards me. The Firestar and the Browning were somewhere on the floor in the welter of red silk and tossed mattress.

I backed away until I hit the corner, and I had nowhere else to go. I was still clutching the sheet around me like it was some kind of protection.

I held out a hand towards Richard, as if that would help. 'What do you want from me, Richard? What do you want me to say? I'm sorry. I am sorry that I hurt you. I'm sorry that I can't handle what I saw last night. I'm sorry.'

He stalked towards me, not saying anything, hands balled into fists. I realized that I was afraid of Richard. That I wasn't sure what he'd do when he reached me, and I wasn't armed. Part of me felt like I deserved to be hit at least once, that I owed that to him. But after seeing what he'd done to the bed, I wasn't sure I'd survive it.

Richard grabbed the front of the sheet, balling it in his fist, jerking me against him. He used the sheet to raise me to tiptoe. He kissed me. For a second I froze. Hitting, yelling, that I'd expected, but not this.

His mouth bruised against my lips, forcing my mouth open. The moment I felt his tongue, I jerked my head back.

Richard put a hand on the back of my head like he'd force me to kiss him. The rage in his face was frightening.

'Not good enough to kiss now?'

'I saw you eat Marcus last night.'

He let me go so suddenly I fell to the floor, stumbling over the sheet. I tried to get to my knees, but my legs had tangled. The sheet slipped over one breast. I struggled to cover myself. Embarrassed at last.

'Two nights ago, you let me touch them, suck them. Now I can't even see them.'

'Don't do this, Richard.'

He went to all fours in front of me, so we'd be on eye level. 'Don't do what? Don't be mad that you let the vampire fuck you?' He crawled forward until our faces were almost touching. 'You fucked a corpse last night, Anita. Did it feel good?'

I stared at him from inches away, not embarrassed anymore. Instead, I was getting pissed. 'Yeah, it did.'

He jerked back from me like I'd hit him. His face crumpled, and his eyes searched the room frantically. 'I love you.' He looked up suddenly, eyes wide and pain-filled. 'I love you.'

I kept my eyes very wide so the tears in them wouldn't fall out and run down my cheeks. 'I know, and I'm sorry.'

He turned away from me, still kneeling. He slapped his hands against the floor. He pounded his hands into the floor over and over until blood smeared on the white carpet.

I got to my feet. I hovered over him, afraid to touch him. 'Richard, Richard, don't, please don't.' The tears fell and I couldn't stop them.

I knelt beside him. 'You're hurting yourself. Stop it!' I grabbed his wrists, held his bleeding hands in mine. He stared at me, and the look on his face was raw, human.

I touched his face, gently tracing the claw marks. He leaned into me, tears spilling down his cheeks. The look in his eyes held me immobile. His lips brushed mine, soft. I didn't flinch, but I didn't kiss him back, either.

He moved back from me, just enough to see my face clearly. 'Goodbye, Anita.' He got to his feet.

I wanted to say so much, but none of it would help. Nothing would make it better. Nothing would erase what I'd seen last night or how it had made me feel. 'Richard . . . I . . . I'm sorry.'

'So am I.' He walked to the door. He hesitated with his hand on the doorknob. 'I'll always love you.'

I opened my mouth, but no sound came. There was nothing left to say but, 'I love you, Richard, and I am sorrier than I know how to say.'

He opened the door and stepped through it without looking back. When the door closed behind him, I sat on the floor, huddled in the silk sheet. I could smell Jean-Claude's cologne on the silk, but I could smell Richard now, too. His aftershave clung to the sheets, to my mouth.

How could I let him go like this? How could I call him back? I sat on the floor and did nothing, because I didn't know what to do.

41

I called Edward's answering service and left a message. I couldn't stay where I was. I couldn't stay here staring at the wrecked bedroom and remembering Richard's wounded eyes. I had to get out. I had to call Dominic and tell him I wasn't coming. The triad of power didn't work without at least two of us on the spot. Jean-Claude was in his coffin and Richard was out of the picture. I wasn't sure what would happen with our little triumvirate now. I didn't see Richard standing around watching me grope Jean-Claude, if I wasn't groping him, too. I couldn't blame him on that.

Strangely, the thought of him sleeping with Raina still made me see green. I had no right to be jealous of him now, but I was. Go figure.

I dressed in black jeans, a black, short-sleeved blouse, and a black blazer. I had to work tonight, and Bert would kick a fit about me wearing black. He thought it gave the wrong image. Screw him. Tonight, black fit my mood.

The Browning in its shoulder holster, Firestar in the Uncle Mike's sidekick holster, a knife on each arm, and a knife down my spine. I was ready for work.

I was going to give Edward ten more minutes, and then I was out of there. If there was still an assassin lurking around, I'd almost have welcomed him or her.

There was a knock on the door. I sighed. 'Who is it?'

'Cassandra.'

'Come in.'

She opened the door, caught one sight of the wrecked bed, and grinned. 'I've heard of rough sex, but this is ridiculous.' She was wearing a long, white dress that fell nearly to her ankles. White hose and white canvas flats completed the outfit. She looked light and summery with her long hair trailing down her back.

I shook my head. 'Richard did it.'

The smile left her face. 'He found out you slept with Jean-Claude?'

'Does everyone know?' I asked.

'Not everyone.' She walked into the room, shutting the door behind her. She shook her head. 'Did he hurt you?'

'He didn't hit me, if that's what you mean, but I feel pretty shitty.'

Cassandra walked to the bed, staring up at it. She grabbed the edge of the frame. She pulled with one hand and steadied with the other. She pulled several hundred pounds of wood and metal around like it was nothing. She settled the bed gently to the carpet.

I raised an eyebrow. 'That was impressive.'

She smiled, almost shyly. 'One of the fringe benefits of being a lycanthrope is that you can pretty much lift anything you want.'

'I see the appeal of that.'

'I knew you would,' she said. She started picking up the pillows and ripped sheets. I joined her. 'We should probably put the mattress back first,' she said.

'Okay. You need help?'

She laughed. 'I can lift it, but it's awkward.'

'Sure.' I grabbed the other side of the mattress.

Cassandra came up beside me, lifting the mattress with her left hand. A look passed over her face. 'I am sorry.'

'I meant what I said about you and Richard earlier. I want him to be happy,' I said.

'That's very flattering. I like you, Anita. I like you a lot. I wish I didn't.'

I had time to frown at her, then her delicate fist came out of nowhere, a blur of speed that smashed into my face. I felt myself fall backwards. I smashed into the floor and couldn't save my head from that extra smack against the carpet. It didn't hurt. I didn't feel a damn thing when blackness closed over me.

42

I rose out of the darkness slowly, dragging upwards like being awakened from deep sleep. I wasn't sure what woke me. I couldn't remember going to sleep. I tried to roll over and couldn't. I was suddenly very awake, eyes wide, body straining. I'd been tied up before; it was one of my least favorite things. I had a few moments of pure panic. I bucked against the ropes that tied me at the wrists and ankles. I fought, pulling until I realized that the knots were getting tighter as I struggled.

I forced myself to lie very still. My heart pounded in my ears so loudly that I couldn't hear anything else. My wrists were tied over my head at an angle sharp enough to squeeze my shoulder blades and put strain all the way down to my wrists. Even raising my head the little bit I needed to see my ankles was painful. My ankles were tied together to the foot of an unfamiliar bed. I rolled my head back and saw the rope that tied my wrists to the head of the bed. The rope was black and soft, and if I had to guess, I'd say it was woven silk. It looked like something Jean-Claude might have lying around in a closet somewhere. I considered it for only a split second, then reality stepped into the room, and my heart stopped for just a second.

Gabriel came to the foot of the bed. He was wearing black leather pants so tight they looked poured on, and high black boots that rode his thighs all the way up, with straps at the top to hold the soft leather in place. He was naked from the waist up, a silver ring through his left nipple and another through the edge of his belly button. More silver marched up his ears to the curve, glittering as he walked around the bed. His long, thick black hair fell across his face, framing his pale, storm grey eyes. He walked around behind the headboard, out of sight, then slowly back into frame.

My heart had started beating again. It was beating so hard I was going to choke on it. They'd taken the Browning and Firestar, holsters and all. The wrist sheaths were gone. I tensed my back and could still feel the back sheath. When I put my head back, I didn't feel the knife's handle. I guess I was grateful they hadn't stripped me to get the sheath. The way Gabriel was circling the bed, I was betting we'd get to that.

I tried to talk, couldn't, swallowed, and tried again. 'What's going on?' My voice sounded amazingly calm. Even to me.

A woman's laugh, high and rich, filled the room. But of course, it wasn't a room. We were at the farm where they made dirty movies. The room I was tied in had only three walls. The lights hung above me were dead, not on yet.

Raina stalked into sight on high, spiked heels the color of blood. She was wearing what looked like a red leather teddy that left most of her long legs and hips bare. 'Hello, Anita, you're looking well.'

I took a deep breath in through my nose and let it out slowly. My heart slowed a bit. Good. 'You should talk to Richard before you do anything drastic. The position of lupa just opened up today.'

She cocked her head to one side, puzzled. 'What are you talking about?'

'She slept with Jean-Claude.' Cassandra came to stand on the edge of the fake room, back to the wall. She looked like she'd always looked. If she felt uncomfortable having betrayed me to Raina, it didn't show. I hated her a lot for that.

'Aren't you going to sleep with both of them?' Raina asked.

'Hadn't planned on it,' I said. Every time I opened my mouth and nobody touched me, I got a little calmer. If Raina had done this to get me out of the way, then she didn't need to go any further. If it was revenge for Marcus, I was in deep shit.

Raina sat down on the end of the bed near my feet. I tensed when she did it; I couldn't help myself. She noticed and laughed. 'Oh, you are going to be a lot of fun.'

'You can be alpha female. I don't want the job,' I said.

Raina sighed, running her hand along my leg, massaging the muscle in my upper thigh, almost absently like you'd pet a dog. 'Richard doesn't want me, Anita. He thinks I'm corrupt. He wants you.' She squeezed my thigh until I thought she was going to grow claws and tear out the muscle. She forced a small sound out of my throat before she stopped.

'What do you want?'

'Your pain.' She smiled when she said it.

I turned my head to Cassandra. There had to be someone sane in this room. 'Why are you helping them?'

'I am Sabin's wolf.'

My eyes narrowed. 'What are you talking about?'

Raina crawled up on the bed, lying beside me, insinuating her body against mine, one finger tracing over my stomach. It was an idle gesture, as if she wasn't really concentrating. I didn't want to be here when she started concentrating.

'Cassandra was a plant from the very beginning, weren't you dear?'

Cassandra nodded, coming to stand beside the bed. Her hazel eyes were calm, too calm. Whatever she was feeling was there behind that pretty face, carefully controlled. The trick was, was there anything behind that face that could help me?

'Dominic, Sabin, and I are a triumvirate. We are what you and Richard and Jean-Claude could have been.'

I didn't like her using the past tense. 'You're the woman he gave up fresh blood for?'

'I believe in the sanctity of life. I thought I valued that above all. Watching Sabin's golden beauty rot away has convinced me otherwise. I will do anything, *anything* to help him recover.' Something like pain crossed her eyes and she looked away. When she looked back, her face was forcibly blank, the effort trembling down her hands. She noticed and hugged her hands to her arms. She smiled, but it wasn't a happy smile. 'I have to make it up to him, Anita. I am sorry that you and yours have become entangled in our problems.'

'How am I caught up in it?'

Raina slid her arm over my stomach, putting her face very near mine. 'Dominic has a spell to cure Sabin of the rotting disease. A transfer of magical essence, you might say. All he needed was exactly the right donor.' She leaned in so close that only my turning my head kept our lips from touching. She whispered against my skin, breath warm, 'A perfect donor. A vampire who shares Sabin's powers exactly, a perfect match, and a servant, either alpha were-wolf, or necromancer, bound to that same vampire.'

I turned and looked at her. I couldn't help it. She kissed me, pressing her mouth against mine, trying to force her tongue inside. I bit her lip hard enough that I tasted blood.

She jerked back with a startled scream. She put her hand to her mouth and stared down at me. 'That is going to cost you dearly.'

I spit her blood at her. It spattered along my chin. It was a stupid thing to have done. Making her angrier was not helpful, but watching the blood drip down her lovely face had almost been worth it.

'Gabriel, entertain Ms Blake.'

That got my attention. Gabriel slid onto the bed, folding himself against me as Raina had done on the other side. He was taller, six feet, so he didn't fit quite as well, but what he lacked in matching size he made up for in technique. He straddled my body and leaned over me in a sort of push-up, bringing his mouth close and closer. He licked my bloody chin, one quick flick of his tongue. I jerked my head away.

He grabbed my chin with one hand, forcing me to look at him. He held my chin like a vise, fingers digging in when I struggled. The strength in his fingers was enough to crush my jaw if he squeezed. He licked the blood off my chin and lips in slow, lingering licks.

I screamed, then mentally cursed myself. This was what they wanted. Panic would not help. Panic would not help. I kept repeating it over and over until I stopped pulling at the ropes. I would not lose it, not yet, not yet.

Cassandra crawled up on the bed. I could only see her white dress out of the corner of my eye. Gabriel still held me immobile.

'Let go of her face so she can look at me.'

Gabriel glanced at her and hissed.

A low, rolling growl trickled out from behind her lips. 'I'm in the mood for a fight tonight, kitty, don't make it easy for me.'

'Aren't you expected at the ceremony?' Raina said. 'Doesn't Dominic need you there for it to work?'

Cassandra reared back, and the voice that came was low and fell from her human lips with effort. 'I will speak with Anita before I go, or I will not go.'

Raina came to stand on the other side of the bed. 'You'll never find another master vampire who matches your master as perfectly as Jean-Claude. Never. You'd jeopardize his one chance at a cure?'

'I will do as I wish on this one thing, Raina, for I am alpha. When Richard is gone, I will lead the pack. Do not forget that.'

'That wasn't our bargain.'

'Our bargain was that you would kill the Executioner before we arrived in town. You failed.'

'Marcus hired the best. Who knew she would be so hard to kill?'

'I did, the first time I met her. You are always underestimating other women, Raina; it is one of your weaknesses.' Cassandra leaned towards Raina. 'You tried to kill Richard before Dominic could use him in the spell.'

'He was going to kill Marcus.'

Cassandra shook her head. 'You panicked, Raina. You and Marcus. Now Marcus is dead, and you can't hold the pack. Too many of them hate you. And many of them love Richard, or at least admire him.'

I wanted to ask where Jean-Claude and Richard were, but I was afraid I knew. A ceremony, sacrifice, but they needed Cassandra to make it work. I didn't want her to rush off.

'You were Dominic's alibi,' I said. 'Not that I'm complaining, but why am I still alive?'

Cassandra looked down at me. 'Gabriel and Raina want you on film. If you would give me your word that you would seek no revenge against any of us for the deaths of your two men, then I would fight to see you go free.'

I started to open my mouth and promise.

She waved a finger in front of my mouth. 'No lies, Anita, not between us.'

'Too late for that,' I said.

Cassandra nodded. 'True, and that grieves me. Under other circumstances, we might have been friends.'

'Yeah.' Of course, that made it hurt all the more. Nothing rubs salt in the wounds like betrayal. Richard could probably compare notes with me right now.

'Where are Richard and Jean-Claude?'

She stared down at me. 'Even now you think you can save them, don't you?'

I would have shrugged, but I couldn't. 'It was a thought.'

'You were a lure and a hostage for the two men,' Cassandra said.

Gabriel had settled on top of me, body pressing along the length of my body. He was heavy. You never noticed how heavy a man was when you were enjoying yourself. He had sunk down, so that his feet trailed off the bed, and he could fold his arms across my chest. His chin rested on his arms, and he stared at me like that, like he knew he had all day, all night, all the time in the world.

'I am very surprised that you broke up with Richard today, Anita,' Raina said. 'We sent him a lock of your hair with a note saying we'd send a hand next. He came alone and told no one, as we had said to do. He really is a fool.'

It sounded like something Richard would do, but it surprised me, anyway. 'You didn't get Jean-Claude to hand himself over for a lock of my hair.'

Raina moved where I could see her better and smiled down. Her lip was already beginning to heal. 'Very true; we didn't even try. Jean-Claude would have known we meant to kill you, regardless. He'd have come with all his vampires, all the wolves that are loyal to him. It would have been a bloodbath.'

'How did you get him then?'

'Cassandra betrayed him. Didn't you, Cassandra?'

Cassandra just looked at us. 'If Richard hadn't broken with you, you might have been able to cure Sabin. Seeking your aid was originally only an excuse to enter Jean-Claude's territory, but you were more powerful than Dominic first thought. You surprised us by bearing none of the vampire's marks. You were supposed to be part of the sacrifice, but without at least the first mark, it will not work.'

Hurrah for me. 'You saw me heal Damian's cut and the zombie. I can heal Sabin. You know I can, Cassandra. You saw it.'

She shook her head. 'The sickness has moved inside Sabin. His brain is going. If you had cured him today, it would be moot. But he must be sane for the spell to work. Even one more day might be too late.'

'If you kill Richard and Jean-Claude, I won't have the power to heal Sabin. If Dominic came here planning to sacrifice all three of us, then the spell must need all three of us to work.'

Something flickered across her face. I was right. 'Dominic's not sure it will work without a human servant in the loop, is he?'

Cassandra shook her head. 'It has to be tonight.'

'If you kill them both and it doesn't cure Sabin, you've destroyed the only real chance he has. Our triumvirate can cure him. You know it can.'

'I know no such thing. You would promise me the moon itself if you thought it would save you all.'

'That's true, but I still think we can cure him. If you kill Richard and Jean-Claude, the chance is gone. Let us at least try. If it doesn't work, you can sacrifice them tomorrow. I'll let Jean-Claude give me the first mark. We'll either cure Sabin tomorrow or we'll be the perfect sacrifice for Dominic's spell.' I willed her to listen to me. To believe me.

'Will Sabin be able to read his part of the spell tomorrow night?' Raina asked. She moved in very close to Cassandra. 'Once his brain is rotted away, there will be nothing left to do but lock him in a box with crosses on it. Hide him away.'

Cassandra's hands balled into fists. A fine trembling ran through her body. Raw fear showed on her face.

Raina turned to me almost conversationally. 'Sabin won't die, you understand. He'll melt down into a little puddle of slime, but he won't die. Will he, Cassandra?'

'No,' Cassandra almost shouted. 'No, he won't die. He'll just go insane. He'll still have all the powers of the triumvirate, but he'll be mad. We'll have to lock him away and pray that Dominic's spells can hold his power in check. If we can't hold his powers prisoner, the council will force us to burn him alive. Only that would be sure death.'

'But if you do that,' Raina said, 'you and Dominic will die, as well. All those vampire marks dragging you down to hell with him.'

'Yes,' Cassandra said, 'yes.' She stared at me, anger and helplessness in her face.

'Am I supposed to feel sorry for you?' I asked.

'No, Anita, you're just supposed to die,' she said.

I swallowed hard and tried to think of something useful. It was hard to do with Gabriel lying on top of me, but if I didn't think of something, we were all dead.

Cassandra startled as if someone had touched her. A prickle of energy swept over my body from her, raising goose bumps where it touched. Gabriel ran his fingertips over the skin of my arms, making the gooseflesh stay just a little longer.

'I must go,' Cassandra said. 'Before the night is over, you may wish you were being sacrificed.' She looked from Gabriel to Raina. 'A slit throat would be quicker.'

I agreed with her, but I wasn't sure what to say. We were discussing different ways to kill me. None of them seemed particularly good choices.

Cassandra stared down at me. 'I am sorry.'

'If you're really sorry,' I said, 'untie me and give me a weapon.'

She smiled wistfully. 'Sabin has ordered me not to.'

'You always do what you're told?' I asked.

'On this one thing, yes. If you'd watched Jean-Claude's beauty rot before you, you'd do anything to help him.'

'Who're you trying to convince, me or you?'

She swayed slightly, and I felt the roll of power out of her body and along mine. Gabriel licked my arm.

'I must go. The circle will be closed soon.' She stared down at me, at Gabriel running his tongue up my arm. 'I am truly sorry, Anita.'

'If you're looking for forgiveness, pray. God may forgive you; I won't.'

Cassandra stared down at me for another heartbeat. 'So be it. Goodbye, Anita.' She ran in a blur of white, like a fast-forward ghost.

'Good,' Raina said, 'now we can set up the lights and make some test shots.' The lights sprang into a dazzling brightness.

I closed my eyes against the glare.

Gabriel moved up my body, and I opened my eyes. 'We were going to strip you naked and tie you spread-eagled, but Cassandra wouldn't let us. But now she's too busy with the spell.' He put a hand on either side of my head, pinning some of my hair. 'We did makeup on your face while you were out. We can make the body makeup part of the show. What do you think?'

I tried to think of anything useful. Anything at all. Nothing came to mind. He leaned over me, bringing his face close and closer. He opened his mouth enough to show fangs. Not vampire fangs but small leopard fangs. Richard had told me once that Gabriel spent too much time in animal form so he didn't come completely back anymore. Great.

Gabriel kissed me, lightly, then harder, forcing his tongue in my mouth. He drew back from me. 'Bite me.' He kissed me, then raised his lips back just enough to whisper, 'Bite me.'

Pain excited Gabriel. I didn't want him more excited, but with his tongue halfway down my throat, it was hard not to give him what he wanted. He ran his hand over my breasts, squeezing hard enough to make me gasp. 'Bite me, and I'll stop.'

I bit his lip. I bit him until he pulled back, the flesh straining between us. Blood poured from his mouth to mine. I let go and spit blood into his face. He was close enough that it splattered in a red rain.

He laughed, wiping his fingers on the bloody lip, putting them in his mouth, sucking the blood off of them.

'Do you know how I became a wereleopard?' he asked. I looked at him.

He slapped me lightly, casually. Starbursts exploded across my vision. 'Answer me, Anita.'

When I could focus, I asked, 'What was the question?'

'Do you know how I became a wereleopard?'

I didn't want to play this game. I didn't want to participate in Gabriel's idea of pillow talk, but I didn't want to be hit again, either. It wouldn't take much for him to knock me unconscious. If I ever woke up again, I would be in worse shape than I was now. Hard to believe, but true.

'No,' I said.

'I've always liked pain, even when I was human. I met Elizabeth. She was a wereleopard. We fucked, but I wanted her to change while we did it. She said she was afraid she'd kill me.' He leaned over me. Blood dripped from his lip in slow, heavy drops.

I blinked, turning my face, trying to keep the blood out of my eyes.

'I almost died.'

I had turned my head completely to the side, while his blood dropped on the side of my face. 'Was the sex worth it?'

He leaned down and began to lick the blood off my face. 'Best sex I ever had.'

A scream started in my throat. I swallowed it, and it hurt going down. There had to be a way out of this. There had to be.

A man's voice said, 'Lie on top of her like you're going to do for the shot, and let's get some light readings.'

I realized that there was a crew here. A director, a cameraman, a dozen people scurrying around, not helping me.

Gabriel drew a knife out of his high, black boot. The hilt was black, but the blade had a high silver sheen. I watched that knife, couldn't help myself. I'd been scared before, but not like this. The fear burned at the back of my throat, threatened to spill out in screams. It wasn't the sight of the blade that frightened me. A moment ago I'd have done anything to have him cut the ropes. Now I would have given anything for him not to cut the ropes.

Gabriel put his hand on my stomach and slid one knee between my tied legs. There wasn't a lot of give. I was grateful. He twisted his upper body and reached downward with the knife. I knew what he was going to do before I felt the ropes give at my ankles. He cut my feet loose and collapsed his lower body against me at almost the same time. No time to struggle, no time to take advantage. He'd done this before.

He wiggled his hips against me, spreading my legs wide enough that I could feel him against me through the jeans. I didn't scream, I whimpered and hated it. My face was pressed into his naked chest just above his pierced nipple. His chest hair was coarse, scratchy against my cheek. His body covered me almost completely. They couldn't have seen much more than my hands and my legs from the camera.

I had a very strange idea. 'You're too tall,' I said.

Gabriel had to raise up a little to look down at my face. 'What?'

'The camera will never see anything but your backside. You're too tall.'

He crawled backwards, raising himself in a little push-up position. He looked thoughtful. He turned around without getting off of me. 'Frank, can you see her at all?'

'Nope.'

'Shit,' Gabriel said. He stared down at me, then smiled. 'Don't go anywhere. I'll be right back.' He slid off me.

With my feet free, I could sit up. My hands were still above my head, but I could huddle against the headboard. It was an immense improvement.

Gabriel, Raina, and two men in scruffy clothes were talking in a huddled group. I caught snatches of the conversation. 'Maybe if we hang her from the ceiling?' 'We'll have to change the room setup for that.'

I had bought some time, but time for what? There was a long table near the room. My weapons were on it, laid in neat lines like props. Everything I needed was right there, but how could I get to it? Raina wasn't going to hand me a knife so I could cut myself loose. No, Raina wouldn't, but maybe Gabriel would.

He walked towards the bed, moving as if he had more muscles, more something, than a human did. He moved like a cat, if a cat could walk on two legs.

He knelt on the bed and started untying the rope from the head-board, but leaving my wrists bound.

'Why not cut the rope?' I asked.

'Frank got pissed that I cut the first one. This is real silk. It's expensive.'

'Nice to know that Frank's fiscally responsible.'

Gabriel grabbed my face, forcing me to meet his eyes. 'We're going to change the room and tie you standing up. I'm going to fuck you until you go with me inside you, then I'm going to change and I'll rip you apart. You may even survive like I survived.'

I swallowed and spoke very carefully. 'Is that really your fantasy, Gabriel?'

'Yes.'

'Not your best fantasy,' I said.

'What?'

'Raping me while I'm helpless isn't your idea of hot sex.'

He grinned, flashing fangs. 'Oh, yes it is.'

Don't panic. Don't panic. Don't panic. I leaned into him, and he released my face so I could do it, but he jerked the rope up tight, making sure my hands stayed in sight. He had definitely done this before.

I forced myself to lean into his naked chest, my tied hands pressed against his skin. I leaned my face towards him and whispered, 'Don't you want a blade inside you while you do it?' I touched the silver ring in his nipple, pulled on it until the flesh bowed outward and he gave a little gasp.

'Don't you want the feel of silver burning up inside you while you're shoving yourself inside of me?' I went up on my knees so our faces would be closer together. 'Don't you want to know I'm trying to kill you while you fuck me? Your blood pouring over my body while you fuck me, isn't that your fantasy?' I whispered the last against his lips.

Gabriel had gone very, very still. I could see the pulse in his throat thudding against the skin. His heart beat fast and hard against my hands. I jerked the ring out of his nipple and he let out a low moan. Blood trickled down his chest. I raised the ring, and he let the rope go so I could move my hands. I raised the bloody ring between our lips, almost as if we'd both kiss it.

'You'll only have one chance to fuck me, Gabriel. One way or another, Raina will see me dead tonight. You'll never get another chance at me.'

The tip of his tongue curled out and caught the ring, licking it from my fingers. He rolled it in his mouth and brought it back out, clean and free of blood. He held it out to me on the tip of his tongue. I picked the ring off and wrapped my fingers around it.

'You just want me to give you a knife,' he said.

'I want to shove a silver blade so deep inside you that the hilt bruises your flesh.'

He shuddered, breath escaping in a long sigh.

'You'll never find anyone else like me, Gabriel. Play with me, Gabriel, and I'll be the best sex you ever had.'

'You'll try and kill me,' he said.

I slid my fingers along the top of his leather pants. 'Oh, yeah, but have you ever really been in danger of dying since that first time with Elizabeth? Since she shape-shifted underneath you, have you ever feared for your life during sex? Did you ever ride that thin, shining line between pleasure and death again?'

He turned away from me, not meeting my eyes. I touched his face with my bound hands, turned him back to me. 'Raina hasn't let you, has she? Just like she won't let you tonight. You're alpha, Gabriel, I can feel it. Don't let her steal this from you. Don't let her steal *me* from you.'

Gabriel stared at me, our bodies touching, faces close enough to kiss. 'You'll kill me.'

'Maybe, or you'll kill me.'

'You might survive,' he said, 'I did.'

'Are you still fucking Elizabeth, now that you survived?' I kissed him softly, running my teeth along his skin.

'Elizabeth bores me.'

'Would you bore me, Gabriel? If I survive, would you be boring?'

'No,' he whispered. I knew I had him, just like that. I either had the beginnings of a brilliant plan, or I'd bought myself some time, some options. It was an improvement. The real question was how much time did Jean-Claude and Richard have? How long until Dominic cut them open? If I couldn't get there in time, I didn't want to get there at all. If they both died, I almost wanted Gabriel to finish me. Almost.

43

They kept me tied to the bed, but Gabriel slipped the knives back in the wrist sheaths. He held the big knife that went down along my spine up to the light. I thought he wouldn't give it back, but in the end, he swept my hair to one side and slipped it into the sheath.

'Don't cut the ropes until I'm in the shot. I want the camera to know why you're scared. Promise not to spoil it.'

'Give me a gun and I'll wait until you're on top of me to pull the trigger.'

He smiled and waved a finger in my face like you'd scold a child. 'Uh, uh, uh. No rough stuff.'

I took a deep breath and let it out. 'Can't blame a girl for trying.'

Gabriel laughed, high and nervous. 'No, can't blame you for trying.'

We had lights, camera, all we needed was action. Gabriel had wiped the blood off his chest and put the silver ring back into his flesh. We were starting over for the camera. They'd even cleaned the blood off my mouth and freshened the makeup. It was the young woman, Heidi, the lycanthrope that did the makeup. Her eyes were too wide. Her hands shook when she touched me.

She whispered as she dabbed at my face. 'Be careful when he kisses you. He ate a girl's tongue out once.'

'Can you get me a gun?'

She shivered, eyes rolling white and panicked. She shook her head. 'Raina'd kill me.'

'Not if she's dead.'

Heidi shook her head over and over and backed off the bed.

Most of the rest of the crew walked out. When the director realized they were going to lose too many people to run things, he offered bonuses. Big bonuses, and a few people stayed. The rest left. They didn't do snuff films. They wouldn't watch Gabriel kill me, but they wouldn't stop it, either. Maybe one of them would call the police. It was a nice thought, but I didn't pin any hopes on it.

Power rushed over me in a skin-prickling wave. It tugged at something low and deep in my body. The sensation was gone almost as soon as it came, but a smell lingered over my skin like I'd walked through somebody's ghost. I smelled Richard's aftershave. Richard was trying to tell me something, either on purpose or because he was being driven by fear. Either way, time was running out. I had to save them. I had to. There was no other choice. Saving them meant bringing Gabriel in close enough to kill him. Close to me. A mixed blessing at best.

'Get on with it,' I said.

'You are terribly eager for someone who's about to die a truly horrible death,' Raina said.

I smiled. I made the smile everything Gabriel wanted it to be, confident, dangerous, sexual. 'I don't plan to die.'

Gabriel's breath sighed outward. 'Let's do it.'

Raina shook her head and stepped back out of the shot. 'Fuck her, Gabriel, make her cry out your name before you kill her.'

'My pleasure,' he whispered. He stalked onto the floor of the fake bedroom.

I unsheathed a wrist knife and cut the rope that held me to the headboard. My wrists were still bound. I watched him while I turned the blade to cut between my hands. He could have jumped me then, but he didn't. He glided around the bed while I cut my hands loose.

He ended on his knees beside the bed, staring at me. I backed away from him, knife in my right hand. I was going to get off the damn bed.

Gabriel crawled up on the bed as I crawled off it. He mimicked my movements but made them graceful and painfully slow. He shimmered with contained energy. He wasn't doing a damn thing but crawling across a bed, but the promise of violence and sex rode the air like lightning.

He was faster than me. His reach was almost twice mine. He was certainly stronger than I was. The only thing I really had going for me was the fact that I planned on killing him as quickly as possible, and he planned on raping me first. It meant I was willing to do things he wasn't. At least at first. If it wasn't over quickly, I was sunk.

I dropped to one knee and braced myself, with a blade in each hand. He wanted to come in close. He even wanted to be hurt, so no feinting, no trying each other's skill. I'd make him come to me, and I'd cut him up.

Power curled inside my stomach. It burst over me in a wave of sensations. The smell of the summer woods was so strong it was choking. For a second, I couldn't see the room. I had a glimpse of somewhere else, chaotic bits and pieces like a jig-saw puzzle thrown across the ground. I came away with three thoughts; fear, helplessness, and need.

My vision cleared to Gabriel frowning down at me. 'What is wrong with you, Anita? Did Cassandra hit you a little too hard?'

I shook my head and took a shaky breath. 'Are you all talk and no bite, Gabriel?'

He smiled, a slow, lazy grin that showed his fangs. He was suddenly there. I slashed out without thinking, pure reaction, no thought. He leaped away, and blood seeped down his stomach in a thin, crimson line.

He rubbed his fingers in the blood slowly, sensuously, then licked them with long, slow tongue movements. Playing for the camera. He crawled onto the bed and wrapped the white sheets around his body, rolling in them until he was tangled. He leaned over backwards, exposing his neck. Almost within reach of me. 'Come play, Anita.'

It was tempting, and it was meant to be, but I knew better. I'd seen Richard rip sheets earlier like they were paper. 'I'm staying here, Gabriel. You're going to have to come to me.'

He rolled onto his stomach. 'I thought I'd get to chase you. This isn't any fun.'

I smiled. 'Come closer, and it'll be a lot of fun.'

He rose onto his knees. The sheets were smeared with blood as he crawled out of them. Gabriel was just suddenly there, too fast for me to see it. He was by me and past me before I could react.

I fell back on my butt, trying desperately to keep him in sight. But he stood there, just out of reach. A second later, a sharp pain ran through my right arm. I glanced, and found bleeding claw marks on my upper arm.

He raised one hand in front of his face, and claws sprang out from under his fingernails. 'Meow,' he said.

I tried to swallow my beating heart and couldn't. This meant that even if he didn't kill me, a month from now I might be sprouting fur.

It wasn't a scream that you could hear with your ears. It wasn't a sound. I had no words for it, but I felt Richard scream inside me. His power poured over me, and down that long line I felt Jean-Claude. Something tight and painful held him down. I tried to get to my feet and stumbled.

'What's wrong, Anita? I didn't hurt you that badly.'

I shook my head, and got to my feet. He wasn't going to come to me. Richard was growing desperate. I reached outward with that flare of power and I could feel Dominic's spell. He'd been shielding it somehow, but he couldn't hide from me. The spell was growing. The time of sacrifice was coming. I didn't have time for Gabriel to play with me. 'Stop playacting, Gabriel, or don't you want me?'

His eyes narrowed. 'You're up to something.'

'You bet. Now, fuck me, Gabriel, if you've got the balls for it.'

I put my back to the wall and hoped it would be enough, and knew it wouldn't be. I threw a thread of power back to Richard, hoping he'd get the hint and not interrupt for the next few minutes. If he distracted me at the wrong time, it would be all over.

Gabriel stalked in front of me, daring me to come out from the wall and get him. I did what he thought I would do. I tried for him and he just wasn't there. It was like trying to cut air.

He slashed out with one hand and sliced the back of my left hand open. I slashed at him with my right hand, trying to hold onto the left-hand knife. He hit the hand again, not with claws but backhanded. My hand spasmed, and the knife went spinning.

His body hit mine full out, slamming me to the floor. I shoved the right-hand knife into his stomach before my back hit the ground. But shoving the knife in meant I took the full force of the fall. It stunned me for a heartbeat. A heartbeat was all he needed.

He ran his hands under my arms, not trying to pin them, but forcing them up away from the knife in his stomach. He pinned me to the floor with his body. I expected him to draw out the blade, but he didn't. He pressed the hilt against my body and pushed. He shoved the blade into him up to the hilt and kept pressing. The hilt bruised against my stomach and he ground it into both of us.

He shuddered over me. He raised his upper body off me, pinning me with his lower body, snuggling it between my legs so I could feel him, hard and firm. He pulled the blade out in a burst of crimson and plunged it downward so fast my arms were only halfway up to protect my face when the blade bit into the carpet. He drove the blade hilt deep into the plywood floor, so close to my head that it pinned my hair on one side.

He undid the button on my jeans. He wasn't even trying to control my hands, but I only had one knife left. If I lost it, I couldn't kill him. We were about to find out just how good my nerves were.

Richard's power flowed over me again, but it wasn't the same. It was less frantic, more as if he was trying to whisper something to me, offer me something. Then I realized what it was. The first mark. Jean-Claude and Richard, for it was they, couldn't do it now without my permission. I was too powerful to be forced, at least psychically.

Gabriel kept my legs pinned with his hips and grabbed the front of my jeans, fingers pointing outward, away from my body. His claws sprang out through the cloth, and he ripped upward, slicing the cloth nearly to my pubic bone.

I screamed and let Richard do me. Better the monster you know than the monster about to go down your pants. A line of warmth ran through my body. It had been even simpler when Jean-Claude did it on his own, once upon a time. Even knowing what it was, it didn't feel like much.

But I felt better instantly; clearer-headed, more . . . something. Gabriel hesitated on top of me. 'What the hell was that?' The skin of his bare arms was prickled with gooseflesh. He'd gotten a taste of the power.

'Didn't feel a thing,' I said. I tugged on the knife in the floor, pulling at it. Gabriel ripped my jeans in both hands, and they split down the middle, leaving nothing between him and me but my panties and his leather pants. I was at a bad angle for the knife and it was only halfway out when he slid his hand down my panties.

I screamed. I screamed, 'Richard!'

The power flowed over me. With Jean-Claude, I had watched his burning blue eyes enter me. With Richard as focus, there was nothing to see, but smells, the forest, his skin, Jean-Claude's perfume. I could taste them both in my mouth like drinking two strong wines one mouthful after another.

Gabriel's hand froze down the front of my body. He was

staring down at me. 'What did you just do?' His voice was a whisper.

'Did you think raping me would be easy?' I laughed, and it unnerved him. I saw something close to fear in his storm grey eyes. He'd moved his hand. Not having him down my underwear was too big an improvement for words. I never wanted him to touch me like that again. Never.

I had two choices. I could bluff and hope I could run, or I could reinitiate sex and kill him. The second mark didn't give me that much more power. In fact, it gave the boys more pull on my power than the other way around. So, sex it was.

'What's wrong?' Raina asked out of camera range. 'Gabriel's getting cold feet,' I said. I raised up on my elbows. The knife he'd shoved in the floor held my hair pinned, and I kept raising up, tearing a hunk of my hair out. It was a small pain, but I knew it would appeal to Gabriel. It did.

I was sitting up with my legs on either side of his thighs. He picked me up, hands sliding over my undies, cupping my buttocks. He leaned back on his knees, supporting my weight. He watched me, and I saw something slide through his eyes, felt it tremble through his hands. For the first time, he thought I really might kill him, and it turned him on. Fear was the rush.

He kissed the side of my face gently. 'Go for the last knife, Anita. Go for it.' He leaned into me while he said it, biting gently down my face. I felt the pressure of his fangs down my jawline, onto my neck. He set his teeth into the side of my neck, bearing down, hard and harder, a slow, building pressure. His tongue licked across the skin.

I didn't go for the knife. I ran my hands through his thick hair, pulled it back from his face. His teeth continued to press into my skin. His hands slid inside my underwear, cupping my bare buttocks. I stiffened, then forced myself to relax. This would work. It had to work.

I traced my fingers along his face. His teeth bit in enough to draw the first faint blood. I gasped, and his claws dug into me. I ran my fingers along either side of his face, tracing his cheeks, his eyebrows. He came up for air, eyes wide and unfocused, lips half-parted. I caressed his face and pulled him in for a kiss. I traced his thick eyebrows. As he kissed me, he closed his eyes, and I put my thumbs over his eyelids. His eyelashes fluttered against my skin. I shoved my thumbs into both eyes, digging, trying to shove my thumbs into his brain and out the other side.

Gabriel reared back, shrieking. His claws ripped up my back. I gasped but didn't have time for screaming. I drew the big knife from the back sheath.

Raina screamed instead.

I shoved the blade under Gabriel's ribs. I shoved it into his heart. He tried to fall backwards, but my weight pinned his knees, so his back bowed backwards, but he didn't fall. I shoved the blade through him. I felt the tip of it burst out the other side.

Raina was suddenly there, grabbing me by the hair, flinging me off him. I flew through the air, smashed into the fake wall, and kept going. The wall splintered. I lay on my stomach, relearning how to breathe. My pulse was so loud in my head, I was deaf for a few seconds. My body stopped being numb in stages, and let me know it was scraped and bruised, but nothing was broken. It should have been. Two marks and I was suddenly Anita the human battering ram. When it happened the first time, I hadn't appreciated it. Now I did. I wasn't hurt badly, hurrah, but I still had to get past Raina. Everybody else would fold and run for cover if she were dead. Question was, how to get her there?

I looked up and realized I was right next to the prop table with my guns on it. Were they loaded? If I went for them and they weren't, Raina was going to kill me. Of course, if I just lay here and bled, she'd kill me anyway.

I heard her high heels coming my way. I pushed to my knees,

my feet, and went for the table. She still couldn't see me through
the partial wall, but she could hear me. She rushed up her side of
the wall in those ridiculous high heels.

I grabbed for the Firestar and rolled over the table as I moved.
I ended on my back, staring up as she leapt over the table. I hit
the safety with my thumb and pulled the trigger. The gun exploded
in my hand and took her in the upper stomach. The bullet seemed
to slow her in midmotion, and I had time for another shot, higher
up in the chest.

Raina collapsed to her knees, honey brown eyes wide with shock.
She reached out one hand, and I scooted backwards, still on my
butt and lower back. I watched her eyes go, that light sliding away.
She slumped over on her side, her long hair spilling like auburn
water across the floor.

The crew had hightailed it. Only Heidi was crouched by the
wall, crying, covering her ears as if afraid to leave or stay.

I got to my feet, using the prop table for support. I could see
Gabriel's body now. Blood and clear fluid flowed down his face from
his eyes. His body still hadn't fallen. It knelt in a strange parody of
life, as if he would open his eyes and it would all be pretend.

Edward came in through the covered door. He had a shotgun
at his shoulder. Harley followed at his side with a machine gun.
He surveyed the room and finally came back to me. 'Is Anita in
this room?'

'Yes,' Edward said.

'I can't recognize her,' Harley said.

'Hold your fire. I'll go find her for you.' He walked towards
me, eyes taking it all in.

'How much of this blood is yours?' he asked.

I shook my head. 'How'd you find me?'

'I tried to return your message. Nobody knew where you'd
gone. Then nobody knew where Richard had gone, or Jean-Claude,
or Raina.'

I felt Richard scream through me and I didn't fight it this time, I let the scream come out my mouth. If Edward hadn't caught me, I would have fallen. 'We've got to get to Jean-Claude and Richard. Right now!'

'You can't even walk,' he said.

I grabbed his shoulders. 'Help me, and I'll run.'

Edward didn't argue; he simply nodded and slid one arm around my waist.

Harley handed my knives and the Browning to Edward. I was inches away, but he didn't try to touch me. He looked past me as if I wasn't there. Maybe, for him, I wasn't. I cut the legs of my jeans off, which left me in nothing but underwear and Nikes from the waist down, but I could run now, and we needed to run. I could feel it. I could feel the power growing on the summer night. Dominic was preparing the blade. I could taste it. I prayed as we ran. Prayed that we'd be in time.

44

We ran. I ran until I thought my heart would burst, jumping trees and dodging things in the dark only half-felt and not seen at all. Branches and weeds raked my legs in thin scratches. A branch caught my cheek and sent me stumbling. Edward caught me. Harley said, 'What is that?'

There was a bright, white glow through the trees. It wasn't fire. 'Crosses,' I said.

'What?' Harley asked.

'They've hung Jean-Claude with crosses.' As the words left my mouth, I knew they were the truth. I ran towards the glow. Edward and Harley followed.

I spilled out to the edge of the clearing with them at my back. I raised the Browning without thinking about it. I had a second to take it all in. Richard and Jean-Claude were bound so thick with chains that they could barely move, let alone escape. A cross had been thrown around Jean-Claude's neck. It glowed like a captive star, resting on the folds of chain. Someone had blindfolded him as if afraid the glow would hurt his eyes. Which was odd, since they meant to kill him. Considerate murderers.

Richard was gagged. He'd managed to work one hand free, and he and Jean-Claude were touching fingertips, straining to retain that touch.

Dominic stood over them in a white ceremonial robe. The hood was thrown back, his arms wide, holding a short sword half the length of my body. He held something dark in his other hand.

Something that pulsed and seemed to live. It was a heart. Robert the vampire's heart.

Sabin sat in Marcus's stone chair, dressed as I'd seen him last, hood up, hiding in the shadows. Cassandra was a shining whiteness on the other side of the circle of power, forming the last point of a triangle with her two men. My two men lay bound on the ground.

I pointed the Browning at Dominic and fired. The bullet left the gun. I heard it, I saw it, but it didn't go near Dominic. It didn't seem to go anywhere. I blew my breath out and tried again.

Dominic stared at me. His dark-bearded face was calm, totally unafraid. 'You are of the dead, Anita Blake, neither you, nor anything of yours may pass this circle. You have come only to watch them die.'

'You've lost, Dominic, why kill them at all, now?'

'We will never find what we need again,' the necromancer said.

Sabin spoke, his voice thick, awkward, as if talking was hard. 'It must be tonight.' He pushed to his feet and shoved the hood back. His flesh was almost completely gone, only straggles of hair and raw, putrefying tissue were left. Dark liquid oozed from his mouth. Maybe he didn't have one more night of sanity. But that wasn't my problem.

'The vampire council has forbidden any of you to fight each other until Brewster's Law is either passed or voted down. They'll kill you for disobeying them.' I was half guessing on this, but I'd been around enough masters of the city to know how very seriously they took disobedience. The council was, in fact, the biggest, baddest, master of the city around. They would be less forgiving, not more.

'I will take that chance,' Sabin said, every word careful, showing the effort it took to speak.

'Did Cassandra tell you about my offer? If we can't cure you tomorrow, I'll let Jean-Claude mark me. Tonight you only have part of what you need for the spell. You need me, Sabin, one way or another, you need me.' I didn't tell them I was already marked. They obviously hadn't felt it. If they knew I was already marked, all I could offer was to die tonight with the boys.

Dominic shook his head. 'I have searched Sabin's body, Anita. Tomorrow will be too late. There will be nothing to save.' He dropped to his knees beside Richard.

'You don't know that for sure,' I said.

He laid the still-beating heart on top of Richard's bare chest. 'Dominic, please!'

It was too late for lies. 'I'm marked, Dominic. We're the perfect sacrifice. Open the circle, and I'll come inside.'

He looked at me. 'If this is true, then you are all far too dangerous to trust. The three of you together without the circle would overwhelm us. You see, Anita, I have been part of a true triumvirate for centuries. You have no dreams of the power you can touch. You and Richard are more powerful than Cassandra and I. You would have been a force to be reckoned with. The council itself might have feared you.' He laughed. 'They may forgive us for that alone.'

He spoke words that curled power over me.

I walked to the edge of the circle and touched it. It was like my skin tried to crawl off my bones. I fell forward and slid down something that couldn't be there. Jean-Claude shrieked. It hurt too much for me to scream. I lay curled by the circle, and even when I breathed, I could taste death, old, rotting death in my mouth.

Edward knelt by me. 'What is it?'

'Without your other parts, you do not have the power to force this circle, Anita.' Dominic got to his feet, raising the sword two-handed for a downward blow.

Dolph had passed the circle earlier in the room where they had taken Robert's heart. I grabbed Edward's shirt. 'You pass the circle. Now. And kill that son of a bitch.'

'If you can't, how can I?'

'You're not magic, that's how.'

It was one of those rare moments when you understand how great trust can be. Edward knew nothing about the ceremony, yet he didn't argue. He accepted what I said, and simply did it. I wasn't a hundred percent sure it would work, myself, but it had to.

Dominic brought the sword down. I screamed. Edward crossed the circle like it wasn't there. The sword bit into Richard's chest, pinning the beating heart to his body. The pain of the blade drove me to my knees. I felt it enter Richard's body. Then I felt nothing, like a switch had been turned off. Edward's shotgun blast took Dominic in the chest.

Dominic didn't fall. He stared at the hole in his chest and then at Edward. He pulled the sword out of Richard's chest and slid the still-beating heart off it. He faced Edward with the sword in one hand and the heart in the other. Edward fired again, and Cassandra leapt on his back.

Harley crossed the circle then. He grabbed Cassandra around the waist and pulled her off of Edward. They fell, rolling to the ground. A gun sounded, and Cassandra's body jerked, but her dainty fist came up and smashed downward.

Edward fired the shotgun until Dominic's face vanished in a spray of blood and bones, and he fell slowly to his knees. His outstretched hand spilled the heart onto the ground beside Richard's terribly still body.

Sabin levitated upward. 'I will have your soul for that, mortal.'

I ran my fingers over the circle and it was still there. Edward started to turn the shotgun towards the vampire. The naked heart pulsed and shimmered in the cross's glare.

'The heart, shoot the heart!'

Edward didn't hesitate. He turned and shot the heart, exploding it into so much meat. Sabin hit him a second later and he went flying. He ended up very still on the ground with Sabin on top of him.

I pushed my hand forward. It met empty air. I fired two-handed at Sabin as I walked towards him. I put three shots into his chest, forcing him to his feet, back from Edward.

Sabin raised a hand in front of his skeletal face, almost a pleading gesture. I stared down the barrel of the gun into his one good eye and pulled the trigger. The bullet took him just above the crumbling remains of his nose. It made a nice big exit wound like it was supposed to, spattering blood and brains on the grass. Sabin collapsed backwards onto the grass. I fired two more shots into his skull until it looked like I'd decapitated him.

'Edward?' It was Harley. He was standing over Cassandra's very still, very dead body. His eyes searched wildly for the one person he recognized.

'Harley, it's me, it's Anita.'

He shook his head, as if I was a buzzing fly. 'Edward, I still see monsters. Edward!' He raised the machine gun at me, and I knew I couldn't let him fire. No, it was more than that, or less. I raised the Browning and fired before I'd had time to think. The first shot sent him to his knees. 'Edward!' He squeezed off a round of fire that went inches above the men's heads. I fired another into his chest, and put one through his head before he fell.

I approached him, gun at the ready. If he'd twitched, I'd have shot him again. He didn't twitch. I knew nothing about Harley except he was genuinely crazy and very good with weapons. Now I'd never know because Edward didn't volunteer information. I kicked the machine gun out of Harley's dead hand and went for the others.

Edward was sitting up, rubbing the back of his head. He watched me walk away from Harley's body. 'Did you do it?'

I faced him. 'Yes.'

'I've killed people for less.'

'So have I,' I said, 'but if we're going to fight, can we unchain the boys first? I don't feel Richard anymore.' I couldn't say the word *dead* out loud, not yet.

Edward got to his feet, a little shaky, but standing. 'We'll fight later.'

'Later,' I said.

Edward went to sit by his friend. I went to sit by my lover and my other boyfriend.

I holstered the Browning, slipped the cross off Jean-Claude's neck, and threw it spinning into the woods. The darkness was suddenly velvet and intense. I bent to undo his chains and one of the links went spinning by my head.

'Shit,' I said.

Jean-Claude sat up, sweeping the chains down his body like a sheet. He slipped off the blindfold last. I was already crawling to Richard. I'd seen the sword pierce his heart. He had to be dead, but I searched for the big pulse in his neck, and I found it. It beat against my hand like a weak thought, and I slumped forward with relief. He was alive. Thank you, God.

Jean-Claude knelt on the other side of Richard's body. 'I thought you could not bear his touch, that is what he told me before they gagged him. They were afraid he would call his pack to aid him. I have already called Jason and my vampires. They will be here soon.'

'Why can't I feel him in my head?'

'I am blocking it. It is a fearful wound, and I am better practiced at dealing with such things.'

I pulled the gag from Richard's mouth. I touched his lips gently. The thought of how I'd refused to kiss him earlier that day bit at me. 'He's dying, isn't he?'

Jean-Claude broke Richard's chains, more carefully than his own. I helped him clear them from Richard's limp body. Richard lay on the ground in the bloodstained white T-shirt I'd last seen him in. He was just suddenly Richard again. I couldn't imagine the beast I'd seen. I suddenly didn't care. 'I can't lose him, not like this.'

'Richard is dying, *ma petite*. I feel his life slipping away.'

I stared up at him. 'You're still keeping me from feeling it, aren't you?'

'I am protecting you.' There was a look on his face that I didn't like.

I touched his arm. His skin was cool to the touch. 'Why?'

He turned away.

I jerked him hard, forced him to look at me. 'Why?'

'Even with only two marks, Richard can try and drain us both to stay alive. I am preventing that.'

'You're protecting us both?' I asked.

'When he dies, I can protect one of us, *ma petite*, but not both.'

I stared at him. 'You're saying that when he dies, you're both going to die?'

'I fear so.'

I shook my head. 'No. Not both of you. Not all at once. Dammit, you're not supposed to be able to die.'

'I am sorry, *ma petite*.'

'No, we can share power just like we did to raise the zombies, the vampires, like we did tonight.'

Jean-Claude slumped suddenly downward, one hand on Richard's body. 'I will not drag you to the grave with me, *ma petite*. I would rather think of you alive and well.'

I dug my fingers into Jean-Claude's arm. I touched Richard's chest. A shuddering breath ran up my arm from him. 'I'll be alive, but I won't be well. I'd rather die than lose you both.'

He stared at me for a long second. 'You do not know what you are asking.'

'We are a triumvirate now. We can do this, Jean-Claude. We can do this, but you have to show me how.'

'We are powerful beyond my wildest dreams, *ma petite*, but even we cannot cheat death.'

'He owes me one.'

Jean-Claude flinched as if in pain. 'Who owes you?'

'Death.'

'*Ma petite* . . .'

'Do it, Jean-Claude, do it. Whatever it is, whatever it takes. Do it, please!'

He slumped on top of Richard, head barely raised. 'The third mark. It will either bind us forever, or kill us all.'

I offered him my wrist. 'No, *ma petite*, if it is to be our only time, come to me.' He lay half on Richard's body, arms open for me. I lay in the circle of his arms, and realized when I touched his chest there was no heartbeat. I turned and stared into his face from inches away. 'Don't leave me.'

His midnight blue eyes filled with fire. He swept my hair to one side and said, 'Open for me, *ma petite*, open for us both.'

I did, sweeping my mind open, dropping every guard I'd ever had. I fell forward, impossibly forward, down a long, black tunnel towards a burning blue fire. Pain cut the darkness like a white knife, and I heard myself gasp. I felt Jean-Claude's fangs sink into me, his mouth sealing over my flesh, sucking me, drinking me.

A wind swept through the falling darkness, catching me like a net before I touched that blue fire. The wind smelled of growing earth and the musty scent of fur. I felt something else: sorrow. Richard's sorrow. His mourning. Not of his death, but of my loss. Dead or alive, he'd lost me, and among his many faults was a loyalty that went beyond reason. Once in love, he was a man to stay there, regardless of what the woman did. A knight errant in every sense of the word. He was a fool, and I loved him for it. Jean-Claude I loved in spite of himself. Richard I loved because of who he was.

I wouldn't lose him. I wrapped his essence like winding myself in a sheet, except that I had no body. I held him in my mind, my body, and let him feel the love, my sorrow, regret. Jean-Claude was there, too. I half-expected him to protest, to sabotage it, but he didn't. That blue fire spilled upward through the tunnel to meet us, and the world exploded into shapes and images that were too confusing. Bits and pieces of memory, sensations, thoughts, like three separate jigsaw puzzles shaken and tossed into the air, and every piece that touched formed a picture.

I padded through the forest on four feet. The smells alone were intoxicating. I sank fangs into a dainty wrist, and it wasn't mine. I watched the pulse underneath a woman's neck and thought of blood, warm flesh, and far-off and distant sex. The memories came fast, then faster, flowing like some sort of carnival ride. Blackness gained on the images, like ink filling water. When the darkness ate everything, I floated for an impossible second, then went out like a candle flame. Nothing.

I didn't even have time to be scared.

45

I woke in a pastel pink hospital room. A nurse in a matching pink smock smiled down at me. Fear pumped like fine champagne. Where was Richard? Where was Jean-Claude? What I finally managed to ask, was, 'How did I get here?'

'Your friend brought you.' She motioned with her head.

Edward sat in a chair by the far wall, leafing through a magazine. He looked up and our eyes met. His face gave away nothing.

'Edward?'

'My friends call me Ted, Anita, you know that.' He had that good ol' boy smile that could only mean he was pretending to be Ted Forrester. It was his only legal identity that I'd ever met. Even the cops thought he was this Ted person. 'Nurse, can we have a few minutes alone?'

The nurse smiled, looked curiously from one to the other of us, and left, still smiling.

I tried to grab Edward's hand and found my left hand was taped to a board and stuck with an IV. I grabbed at him with my right hand, and he held it. 'Are they alive?'

He smiled, a mere twitch of lips. 'Yes.'

A relief like I'd never known flowed through my body. I collapsed back against the bed, weak. 'What happened?'

'You came in suffering from lycanthrope scratches and a very nasty vampire bite. He almost drained you dry, Anita.'

'Maybe that's what it took to save us.'

'Maybe,' Edward said. He sat on the edge of the bed. His jacket gaped enough to flash his shoulder holster and gun. He caught me looking. 'The police agree that the monsters might hold a grudge. There's even a cop outside your door.'

We weren't holding hands now. He stared down at me and something very cold passed over his face. 'Did you have to kill Harley?'

I started to say yes, but I stopped myself. I replayed it in my mind. Finally, I looked up at him. 'I don't know, Edward. When you were knocked out, he couldn't see you anymore. I tried to talk to him, but he couldn't hear me. He started to raise the machine gun.' I met Edward's empty blue eyes. 'I shot him. You saw the body. I even put one through his head. A coup de grâce.'

'I know.' His face, his voice gave nothing away. It was like watching a mannequin talk, except that this mannequin was armed and I wasn't.

'It never occurred to me not to shoot, Edward. I didn't even hesitate.'

Edward took a deep breath through his nose and let it out through his mouth. 'I knew that's what had happened. If you'd lied to me, I'd have killed you.' He walked away to stand at the foot of the bed.

'While I'm unarmed?' I tried to make light of it, but it didn't work.

'Check your pillow.'

I slid my hand under and came up with the Firestar. I held it in my lap, laying it on my sheet-covered legs. 'What now?'

'You owe me a life.'

I looked up at that. 'I saved your life last night.'

'Our lives don't count, we'd back each other up, no matter what.'

'I don't know what you're talking about then.'

'Occasionally I'll need help, like Harley. Next time I need help, I'll call you.'

I wanted to argue because I wasn't entirely sure what mess

Edward would drag me into, but I didn't. Looking into his empty eyes, holding the gun he'd put under my pillow, I knew he'd do it. If I refused his bargain, his trade as it were, he'd pull down on me, and we'd find out once and for all who was better.

I stared down at the gun in my hands. 'I've already got the gun out; all I have to do is point.'

'You're injured. You need the edge.' His hand hovered near the butt of his gun.

I laid the gun on the sheets beside me, and looked at him. I lay back on the pillows. 'I don't want to do this, Edward.'

'Then, when I call, you'll come?'

I thought about it for another brief second, then said, 'Yeah, I'll come.'

He smiled, his Ted (good ol' boy) Forrester smile. 'I'll never find out how good you really are until you draw down on me.'

'We can live with that,' I said. 'By the way, why the invitation to come monster hunting now? And don't tell me it's about Harley.'

'You killed him, Anita. You killed him without thinking about it. Even now, there's no regret in you, no doubt.'

He was right. I didn't feel bad about it. Scary, but true. 'So you invited me to come play because I'm now as much of a sociopath as you are.'

'Oh, I'm a much better sociopath,' he said. 'I'd never let a vampire sink his fangs into my neck. And I wouldn't date the terminally furry.'

'Do you date anyone, ever?'

He just smiled that irritating smile that meant he wasn't going to answer. But he did. 'Even Death has needs.'

Edward dating? That was something I had to see.

46

I got out of the hospital with no permanent scars. That was a switch. Richard had touched the wounds Gabriel gave me, his face very serious. No one had to say it out loud. In a month, we'd know. The doctors offered to put me in one of the shapeshifter halfway houses (read prisons) for the first-time furry. It has to be voluntary, but once you sign yourself in, it's almost impossible to sign yourself out. I told them I'd take care of it myself. They scolded me, and I told them to go to hell.

I spent the night of my first full moon with Richard and the pack, waiting to see if I was going to join the killing dance. I didn't. Either I'd gotten incredibly lucky or just as a vampire can't catch lycanthropy, neither could I. Richard wouldn't have much to do with me after that. I can't blame him.

I still love him. I think he still loves me. I love Jean-Claude, too. But it's not the same kind of love. I can't explain it, but I miss Richard. For brief moments in Jean-Claude's arms, I forget. But I miss Richard.

The fact that we are both bound to Jean-Claude doesn't help. Richard has accidentally invaded my dreams twice. Having him that close to me is too painful for words. Richard fought it, but he finally agreed to let Jean-Claude teach him enough control so that he doesn't leak all over both of us. He talks to Jean-Claude more than he talks to me.

The triumvirate is useless. Richard is too angry at me. Too full of self-loathing. I don't know how he's doing with the pack. He's forbidden anyone to speak of pack business with me, but he hasn't chosen a new alpha female.

Willie McCoy and the rest of the vampires I accidentally raised seem fine. Big relief there. Monica's baby is due in August. Her amnio came back clean. No Vlad syndrome. She seems to think I'm her friend now. I'm not, but I help out sometimes. Jean-Claude is playing the good master and taking care of her and the baby. Monica keeps talking about me babysitting. I hope she's kidding. Auntie Anita, she calls me. Gag me with a spoon. Funnier still, is Uncle Jean-Claude.

My dad saw me on television in Jean-Claude's arms. He called and left a very worried message on my answering machine. My family are devout Catholics. There is no such thing as a good vampire to them.

Maybe they're right. I don't know. Can I still be the scourge of vampire kind when I'm sleeping with the head bloodsucker?

You bet.

It's time to satisfy your bloodlust . . .

Turn the page for a preview of the next sensational novel featuring Anita Blake.

LAURELL K. HAMILTON

Burnt Offerings

An Anita Blake,
Vampire Hunter, Novel

headline

I

Most people don't stare at the scars. They'll look, of course, then do the eye slide. You know, the quick look, then drop the gaze, then just have to have that second look. But they make it quick. The wounds aren't like freak show bad, but they are interesting. Captain Pete McKinnon, firefighter and arson investigator, sat across from me, big hands wrapped around a glass of iced tea that our secretary, Mary, had brought in for him. He was staring at my arms. Not the place most men look. But it wasn't sexual. He was staring at the scars and didn't seem a bit embarrassed about it.

My right arm had been sliced open twice by a knife. One scar was white and old. The second was still pink and new. My left arm was worse. A mound of white scar tissue sat at the bend of my arm. I'd have to lift weights for the rest of my life or the scars would stiffen and I'd lose mobility in the arm, or so my physical therapist had said. There was a cross-shaped burn mark, a little crooked now because of the ragged claw marks that a shapeshifted witch had given me. There were one or two other scars hidden under my blouse, but the arm really is the worst.

Bert, my boss, had requested that I wear my suit jacket or long-sleeved blouses in the office. He said that some clients had expressed reservations about my ah . . . occupationally acquired wounds. I hadn't worn a long-sleeved blouse since he made the request. He'd turned the air conditioner up a little colder every day. It was so cold today I had goose bumps. Everyone else was bringing sweaters to work. I was shopping for midriff tops to show off my back scars.

McKinnon had been recommended to me by Sergeant Rudolph Storr, cop and friend. They'd played football in college together, and been friends ever since. Dolph didn't use the word 'friend' lightly, so I knew they were close.

'What happened to your arm?' McKinnon asked finally.

'I'm a legal vampire executioner. Sometimes they get pesky.' I took a sip of coffee.

'Pesky,' he said and smiled.

He sat his glass on the desk and slipped off his suit jacket. He was nearly as wide through the shoulders as I was tall. He was a few inches short of Dolph's six foot eight, but he didn't miss it by much. He was only in his forties, but his hair was completely grey with a little white starting at the temples. It didn't make him look distinguished. It made him look tired.

He had me beat on scars. Burn scars crawled up his arms from his hands to disappear under the short sleeves of his white dress shirt. The skin was mottled pinkish, white, and a strange shade of tan like the skin of some animal that should shed regularly.

'That must have hurt,' I said.

'It did.' He sat there meeting my eyes with a long steady look. 'You saw the inside of a hospital on some of that.'

'Yeah.' I pushed the sleeve up on my left arm and showed the shiny place where a bullet had grazed me. His eyes widened just a bit. 'Now that we've proven we're big tough he-men, can you just cut to the chase? Why are you here, Captain McKinnon?'

He smiled and draped his jacket over the back of his chair. He took the tea off my desk and sipped it. 'Dolph said you wouldn't like being sized up.'

'I don't like passing inspections.'

'How do you know you passed?'

It was my turn to smile. 'Women's intuition. Now, what do you want?'

'Do you know what the term firebug means?'

'An arsonist,' I said.

He looked expectantly at me.

'A pyrokinetic, someone who can call fire psychically.'

He nodded. 'You ever seen a real pyro?'

'I saw films of Ophelia Ryan,' I said.

'The old black-and-white ones?' he asked.

'Yeah.'

'She's dead now, you know.'

'No, I didn't know.'

'Burned to death in her bed, spontaneous combustion. A lot of the firebugs go up that way, as if when they're old they lose control of it. You ever see one of them in person?'

'Nope.'

'Where'd you see the films?'

'Two semesters of Psychic Studies. We had a lot of psychics come in and talk to us, demonstrate their abilities, but pyrokinetics is such a rare ability, I don't think the prof could find one.'

He nodded and drained the rest of his tea in one long swallow. 'I met Ophelia Ryan once before she died. Nice lady.' He started to turn the ice-filled glass round and round in his large hands. He stared at the glass and not at me while he talked. 'I met one other firebug. He was young, in his twenties. He'd started by setting empty houses on fire, like a lot of pyromaniacs. Then he did buildings with people in them, but everybody got out. Then he did a tenement, a real firetrap. He set every exit on fire. Killed over sixty people, mostly women and children.'

McKinnon stared up at me. The look in his eyes was haunted. 'It's still the largest body count I've ever seen at a fire. He did an office building the same way, but missed a couple of exits. Twenty-three dead.'

'How'd you catch him?'

'He started writing to the papers and the television. He wanted credit for the deaths. He set fire to a couple of cops before we got him. We were wearing those big silver suits that they wear to oil rig fires. He couldn't get them to burn. We took him down to the police station, and that was the mistake. He set it on fire.'

'Where else could you have taken him?' I asked.

He shrugged massive shoulders. 'I don't know, somewhere else. I was still in the suit, and I held onto him. Told him we'd burn up together if he didn't stop it. He laughed and set himself on fire.' McKinnon sat his glass very carefully on the edge of the desk.

'The flames were this soft blue color almost like a gas fire, but paler. Didn't burn him, but somehow it set my suit on fire.

The damn thing is rated for something like 6,000 degrees, and it started to melt. Human skin burns at 120 degrees, but somehow I didn't melt into a puddle, just the suit. I had to strip it off while he laughed. He walked out the door and he didn't think anyone would be stupid enough to grab him.'

I didn't say the obvious. I let him talk.

'I tackled him in the hallway and slammed him into a wall a couple of times. Funny thing, where my skin touched him, it didn't burn. It was like the fire crawled over a space and started on my arms, so my hands are fine.'

I nodded. 'There's a theory that a pyro's aura keeps them from burning. When you touched his skin, you were too close to his own aura, his own protection, to burn.'

He stared at me. 'Maybe that is what happened, because I threw him hard up against the wall over and over. He was screaming, 'I'll burn you. I'll burn you alive.' Then the fire changed color to yellow, normal, and he started to burn. I let him go and went for the fire extinguisher. We couldn't put the fire on his body out. The extinguishers worked on the walls, everything else, but it wouldn't work on him. It was as if the fire was crawling out of his body from deep inside. We'd dampen some of the flames, but there was just more of it until he was made of fire.'

McKinnon's eyes were distant and horror-filled as if he was still seeing it. 'He didn't die, Ms Blake, not like he should have. He screamed for so long and we couldn't help him. Couldn't help him.' His voice trailed off. He just sat there staring at nothing.

I waited and finally said, gently, 'Why are you here, Captain?'

He blinked and sort of shook himself. 'I think we've got another firebug on our hands, Ms Blake. Dolph said that if anyone could help us cut the loss of life, it was you.'

'Psychic ability isn't technically preternatural. It's just talent like throwing a great curve ball.'

He shook his head. 'What I saw die on the floor of the station that day wasn't human. It couldn't have been human. Dolph says you're the monster expert. Help me catch this monster before he kills.'

'He or she hasn't killed yet? It's just property damage?' I asked.

He nodded. 'I could lose my job for coming to you. I should have bucked this up the line and gotten permission from the chain of command, but we've only lost a couple of buildings. I want to keep it that way.'

I took in a slow breath and let it out. 'I'll be happy to help, Captain, but I honestly don't know what I can do for you.'

He pulled out a thick file folder. 'Here's everything we've got. Look it over and call me tonight.'

I took the folder from him and sat it in the middle of my desk blotter.

'My number's in the file. Call me. Maybe it's not a firebug. Maybe it's something else. But whatever it is, Ms Blake, it can bathe in flames and not burn. It can walk through a building and shed fire like sprinkling water. No accelerant, Ms Blake, but the houses have gone up as if they've been soaked in something. When we get the wood in the lab, it's clean. It's like whatever is doing this can force the fire to do things it shouldn't do.'

He glanced at his watch. 'I'm running late. I am working on getting you on this officially, but I'm afraid they'll wait until people are dead. I don't want to wait.'

'I'll call you tonight, but it may be late. How late is too late to call?'

'Any time, Ms Blake, any time.'

I nodded and stood. I offered my hand. He shook it. His grip was firm, solid, but not too tight. A lot of male clients that wanted to know about the scars squeezed my hand like they wanted me to cry 'uncle.' But McKinnon was secure. He had his own scars.

I'd barely sat back down when the phone rang. 'What is it, Mary?'

'It's me,' Larry said. 'Mary didn't think you'd mind her putting me straight through.' Larry Kirkland, vampire executioner trainee, was supposed to be over at the morgue staking vampires.

'Nope. What's up?'

'I need a ride home.' There was just the slightest hesitation to his voice.

'What's wrong?'

He laughed. 'I should know better than to be coy with you. I'm all stitched up. The doc says I'll be fine.'

'What happened?' I asked.

'Come pick me up and I'll tell all.' Then the little son of a gun hung up on me.

There was only one reason for him to not want to talk to me. He'd done something stupid and gotten hurt. Two bodies to stake. Two bodies that wouldn't have risen for at least another night. What could have gone wrong? As the old saying goes, only one way to find out.

Mary rescheduled my appointments. I got my shoulder holster complete with Browning Hi-Power out of the top desk drawer and slipped it on. Since I'd stopped wearing my suit jacket in the office, I'd put the gun in the drawer, but outside the office and always after dark I wore a gun. Most of the creatures that had scarred me up were dead. The majority I'd done personally. Silver-plated bullets are a wonderful thing.

Guilty Pleasures

An Anita Blake, Vampire Hunter, Novel

Laurell K. Hamilton

'I don't date vampires. I kill them.'

My name is Anita Blake. Vampires call me the Executioner.
What I call them isn't repeatable.

Ever since the Supreme Court granted the undead equal rights,
most people think vampires are just ordinary folks with fangs.
I know better. I've seen their victims. I carry the scars . . .

But now a serial killer is murdering vampires – and the most
powerful bloodsucker in town wants me to find the killer.

978 0 7553 5529 7

headline

Skin Trade

An Anita Blake, Vampire Hunter, Novel

Laurell K. Hamilton

'I'd worked my share of serial killer cases, but none of the killers had ever mailed me a human head. That was new.'

My name is Anita Blake and my reputation has taken some hits. Not on the work front, where I have the highest kill count of all the legal vampire executioners in the country, but on the personal front. No one seems to trust a woman who sleeps with the monsters. Still, when a vampire serial killer sends me a head from Las Vegas, I know I have to warn Sin City's local authorities what they're dealing with.

Only it's worse than I thought: several officers and an executioner have been slain paranormal style. When I get to Las Vegas, I'm joined by three other federal marshals. Which is a good thing because I need all the back up I can get when hunting a killer this powerful and dangerous.

978 0 7553 5255 5

headline

Now you can buy any of these bestselling
books by **Laurell K. Hamilton** from your bookshop
or *direct from her publisher*.

FREE P&P AND UK DELIVERY
(Overseas and Ireland £3.50 per book)

Guilty Pleasures	£7.99
The Laughing Corpse	£7.99
Circus of the Damned	£7.99
The Lunatic Cafe	£7.99
Bloody Bones	£7.99
The Killing Dance	£7.99
Skin Trade	£7.99

TO ORDER SIMPLY CALL THIS NUMBER

01235 400 414

or visit our website: www.headline.co.uk
Prices and availability subject to change without notice.

J. M. W. Turner

Watercolours from the R. W. Lloyd Bequest
to the British Museum

J. M. W. Turner

Watercolours from the R. W. Lloyd Bequest to the British Museum

Kim Sloan

Published for the Trustees of the British Museum by
British Museum Press

© 1998 The Trustees of the British Museum
Published by British Museum Press
A division of The British Museum Company Ltd
46 Bloomsbury Street, London WC1B 3QQ

First published 1998

British Library Cataloguing in Publication Data
A catalogue record for this book is available from the British Library

ISBN 0-7141-2613-6

Designed and typeset in Janson by Ronald Clark

Printed and bound in Italy
by Grafiche Milani

Half-title page: Bookplate of R. W. Lloyd.

Frontispiece: John Scarlett Davis (1804–44), *The Library at Tottenham, the seat of B. G. Windus, Esq*. Watercolour with gum arabic, 1835. The watercolour is in its original frame, which was designed to match those of the Turners hanging in the room, nearly all of which are from the *England and Wales* series (see p. 89).

Contents

Preface

Forty years ago, R. W. Lloyd bequeathed fifty of Turner's finest watercolours to the British Museum, where they joined the bequests of Turners made by George Salting and the Reverend Charles Sale forty years earlier. Together, these gifts to the Department of Prints and Drawings, the British national collection of works on paper, make it the repository of one of the finest collections of the artist's work in the world. At times – because the conditions of Lloyd's will forbid the loan of the watercolours from his bequest outside the Museum, and because they are only a small fraction of holdings of well over 20,000 works by British artists – the British Museum's Turners may have seemed to be one of the best-kept secrets of British art. The fortieth anniversary of Lloyd's generous bequest provides an appropriate occasion for a very public reminder and celebration in the form of an exhibition and catalogue.

Lloyd's gift also included ten pencil and wash drawings by Turner and the Monro school, as well as a watercolour of a *Dead blackcock* by the artist (they could not all be illustrated here, but are listed in Appendix 1). But the works by Turner often overshadow the fact that Lloyd's bequest to the Museum included three further demonstrations of his widely varied collecting activities: a collection of 76 additional British watercolours; 51 examples of Chinese lacquerware; and 202 Japanese swords. Few examples from the last two groups are on public display, but the British watercolours, listed in Appendix 1, are always available for study in the Students' Room of the Department of Prints and Drawings.

Lloyd religiously protected his watercolours from exposure to light, and the terms of his will specified that they could only be exhibited during the first two weeks in February when the winter sun in the top-lit gallery of the Department (see fig. 9) was at its weakest. This condition was adhered to until controlled lighting conditions were installed in 1971. In 1975 several of the Turners were included in the exhibition *Turner in the British Museum*, and in 1985 a selection from the entire R. W. Lloyd Bequest was included in the exhibition *British Landscape Watercolours 1600–1860*, but the Museum still housed the Turner Bequest at that time and this has led to a great deal of confusion. The Turner Bequest has been back at the Tate Gallery since 1987 – the British Museum's own Turners are listed here in Appendix 2.

The present exhibition includes for the first time all the Turner watercolours from Lloyd's 1958 bequest. Although he bequeathed them in their ornate gold Agnew's frames, with their distinctive wash-line mounts and gold slips, and roller blinds to protect them from the light, Lloyd's executors were aware of the danger of acid present in the mounts and agreed to their removal for the protection of the watercolours. The frames were too deep for display in the Museum's glass cases and were largely forgotten, but nine have been retrieved and the watercolours carefully restored to them for this exhibition, enabling the public to view them in the manner in which Lloyd and his contemporaries preferred for the first time since they came to the Museum.

Much of my information about the activities of R. W. Lloyd in the 1950s has been gleaned from conversations with Reginald Williams, formerly of the Department of Prints and Drawings, and with Evelyn Joll and Dick Kingzett of Agnew's. I would like to record here my enormous thanks to them for so patiently giving their time to answering my many queries. Angus Lloyd kindly solved several last-minute problems, and Noël Annesley of Christie's and Giles Pemberton of Lee and Pemberton's, Lloyd's solicitors, generously provided photocopies of sales and lists of items from his collections. When I began this project, my former colleague Paul Goldman passed to me all his research and the results of many interviews he conducted in preparation for his own article on Lloyd. I could not have written the introductory essay without their contributions.

The catalogue entries include prices and provide the most complete provenances and exhibition history ever given for these works. For this I am grateful again to Evelyn Joll for his guidance through Agnew's records and to Christopher Kingzett and the staff of Agnew's for putting up with my frequent presence in their library and for permission to quote from their records. Full references to literature on Turner's works in the British Museum would have left little room for catalogue text, so I have tried to ensure that references are made to the most important sources of information on these watercolours in the footnotes to each entry.

Many people were involved in my quest to solve various problems arising from Lloyd's frames: their superb restoration was carried out by Charles Collinson of this Department. The mounts were recreated by Dylan Owen and Christina Angelo of the Department of Conservation. But I also owe a great deal to the useful advice and quick responses of the following: Jacob Simon, Jenny Bescoby, Stephen Wildman, James Deardon, Richard Hallas, Elizabeth Oliver, Lynn Roberts, Michael Gregory, Pippa Mason, Maggi Simms and Claire Stuart. Queries about Lloyd's various collecting activities led me into new areas for which I was grateful to have the guidance of colleagues in the British Museum, especially Christopher Date, Stephen Coppel, Victor Harris and Jane Portal, as well as scholars in other institutions, especially George Bankes of the Manchester Museum, Margaret Ecclestone of the Alpine Club and Jacqueline Ruffle of the Royal Entomological Society. I hope I have acknowledged the kind assistance of others in the appropriate places in the notes.

I have no claims to be a Turner scholar and was therefore extremely grateful to Ian Warrell of the Tate Gallery for agreeing to read through the catalogue entries, on very short notice and with a Turner exhibition of his own about to open. He saved me from several obvious mistakes but I hasten to add that those that remain are my own. In my preparations for the exhibition, I have benefited from the earlier work of several of my predecessors in the Department of Prints and Drawings, Andrew Wilton, Ann Forsdyke and Lindsay Stainton, as well as from the support of the present Keeper, Antony Griffiths. I am thankful to the Head of British Museum Press, Emma Way, for her request for a catalogue, and to Teresa Francis, who has once again been the most patient and encouraging of editors. Julie Young has guided the production of the photographs taken by Bill Lewis through to the most beautiful printed results.

I am very much aware that a great deal of the burden of writing a catalogue like this is borne by those at home, so I would like to record here my thanks and my apologies to my husband, Paul Chaffe, and our daughter, Morwenna, for all the lost weekends. Finally, I should like to express my heartfelt gratitude to three people who taught me to appreciate and enjoy the myriad wonders of Turner's watercolours long before I came to live in England: my friend the late Pat Holmes; my university professor, Lee Johnson; and especially my father, Bill Sloan.

Fig. 1. R. W. Lloyd (centre) with his two Alpine guides, Joseph and Adolph Pollinger. Reproduced, with permission, from *Alpine Journal* 39 (1927).

The Collector as Creator: Robert Wylie Lloyd (1868–1958)

'A famous man in business circles'

One of the most distinguished of [Christie's] directors is its Chairman, Mr. R. W. Lloyd. Mr Lloyd is a famous man in business circles in London and Manchester. He is Fellow and Vice-President of the Royal Entomological Society of London, Member and a past Vice-President of the Alpine Club – he was Hon. Treasurer of the last Expedition that set out to conquer Mount Everest – and a Fellow of the Royal Geographical Society. And, not least of his qualifications to occupy his important post at Christie's, he possesses one of the finest collections of Turner's drawings in England, a unique collection of Swiss prints, some splendid Old Masters and Chinese lacquer. He is kindly, considerate, and genial, and is held in affection and respect by all who come in contact with him.[1]

Thus Percy Colson described Robert Wylie Lloyd (fig. 1) in his history of Christie's, published in 1950. In fact this list of 'qualifications' provides only a hint of Lloyd's myriad involvements in the financial, artistic, cultural and scientific life of England this century. Yet he was born in 1868, and it would be difficult to think of another twentieth-century businessman and collector who so little characterised our own modern era and remained so firmly entrenched in the Victorian age into which he was born. This sense of a northern-born Victorian businessman constantly driven by a passion for working, collecting and involvement in worthy societies is not based on the evidence of any diaries or correspondence, as an exhaustive search has revealed almost none,[2] but comes instead from piecing together evidence from the widely varied businesses, societies and dealers with whom Lloyd was involved.

This research into Lloyd's activities was begun in an attempt to understand why and how he came to put together one of the finest collections of Turner watercolours and the reasons why he left it to the British Museum. As this essay will indicate, the search has only been partially successful in answering these particular questions, but has incidentally been very revealing on a number of other issues relevant to collecting in the twentieth century.

Where no documentation exists, rumours, gossip and reputation are often contradictory. Colson was writing in 1950, when Lloyd was in his eighties, but 'kindly, considerate and genial' were not the only characteristics for which he was remembered. Instead, many who met him were struck by 'a dour strain and vein of ruthlessness in his character': he did not tolerate second-class work or lack of effort, and he 'liked his money's worth' and was known to drive a hard bargain.[3] His reputation for parsimony was remarkably reminiscent of George Salting, another great benefactor of Turner watercolours to the British Museum. Salting was said to buy a shilling cake on Sunday for guests, who knew better than to accept a slice as he could return it whole to the baker the next day for ninepence: first-time visitors who accepted a piece were never asked back.[4] However, in Lloyd's case, such characteristics were tempered by the knowledge that he had lost a leg from thrombosis in 1937 and by the 1950s was constantly in great pain, walking only with the aid of two sticks, so barely mobile that Christie's board meetings had to be held in his rooms at Albany. The authors of his many obituaries, while acknowledging his hardness and reticence, noted his generosity to deserving young people and were universal in their admiration of his phenomenal perseverance and self-reliance.

Other contradictions arise from comparing Colson's printed account with Lloyd's reputation as it survives among those who knew and worked for him. Apart from its invaluable collection of sale catalogues, all Christie's records were destroyed by a bomb that demolished the building on King Street in 1941. With the blitz went any proof for what is not written in any accounts of Christie's but is nevertheless understood – that Lloyd's collections of Turners, old masters and other works were not his chief qualifications for his chairmanship of Christie's. It was because of his sound and proven business acumen that, when war broke out in 1939 and all the partners joined the forces, leaving one behind to run a firm nearly broken by the effects of the depression, that partner, Alec Martin, invited Lloyd to join Christie's as an advisory director. Shortly afterwards, probably on Lloyd's advice, Christie's became a private limited company with himself as its chairman.

During temporary accommodation in Derby House and then Spencer House, Lloyd ran the finances while Alec Martin took care of the day-to-day business until the rest of the partners returned as directors after the war. An uncompromising businessman, Lloyd was insistent that Christie's should be run in as professional a manner as possible, and was concerned that the staff should receive business training.[5] He remained a director of the company until his death, and had continued to attend the monthly meetings even when they had to come to him.

Throughout this period Lloyd was also a constant buyer at Christie's sales, but, unlike Salting,[6] Henry Tate,[7] Lord Beaverbrook[8] and many others, it was not during the last decades of his life that he formed the collections he was to leave to the nation. Those had been been begun and nearly all completed long before he had any connection with Christie's, and it is to these early days of collecting that we must turn if we are to understand the reasons for the formation and ultimate destination of the collection of Turners and almost 100 other watercolours and drawings that he bequeathed to the British Museum in 1958.

Robert Wylie Lloyd was born on 17 March 1868 at Oswaldtwistle, Lancashire, the second son of John Lloyd, a bleacher, and grandson of Nathaniel Lloyd of Foxhill Bank Hall, Church, Lancashire, a calico printer and bleacher. Lloyd's mother was a Wylie of Glasgow. His parents separated when he was young, and his mother took him and his elder brother Nathaniel (1867–1933) to live in Clapham, London. As a child Robert's health was poor, so he had little formal education: his first job was as a junior clerk in a Mincing Lane warehouse.[9] He once revealed to a friend that, as a boy, it had shocked him to see his mother having to economise and it was this that gave him the determination to succeed. However, she died shortly after he had managed to set himself up satisfactorily in his early twenties: 'the blow was one he never forgot. From then on, . . . he simply concentrated on extending his business activities and it was from this concentration that there arose that dour strain and vein of ruthlessness in his character that struck many that encountered him.'[10] His acumen as a businessman seems to have been due to his ability to apply himself thoroughly to the job in hand and also to a sound judgement of men and affairs.[11]

Exactly what form Robert's first business took is unclear: according to *Who was Who*, his brother Nathaniel was educated in Manchester and founded the firm of Nathaniel Lloyd & Co., Lithographic Printers, in 1893, retiring from the business in 1909.[12] Alec Martin later wrote that he met Robert Wylie Lloyd before the First World War when he used to come into Christie's on Saturday mornings on his way to Nathaniel Lloyd and Co., poster printers in Blackfriars, 'founded by his brother and himself'.[13] Robert Lloyd seems to have stayed on to run the company when his brother left for an architectural career with Sir Edwin Lutyens: the brothers had also been joint managing directors of the Star Bleaching Co. Ltd until it was sold to the Bleaching Association in 1912. Clearly they found it profitable to continue the type of businesses their father and grandfather had run. Robert Lloyd's other business interests were all associated with cloth and printing: he was chairman of Druce and Co. Ltd, a large department store and estate agents on Baker Street; of Chadwicks, Manchester, Ltd, cotton piece goods finishers;[14] and he was a director of the *Morning Post* when it was sold to the *Daily Telegraph* in 1937 while he was in hospital. It was said that he greatly regretted that a newspaper that accorded so well with his own political views should cease to exist, and, had he known he was to survive, he would have purchased the *Morning Post* and kept it running himself.[15]

Lloyd's first documented purchase, a watercolour of *Crowland Abbey* by Peter de Wint (fig. 4), was no. 5 in Thomas Agnew and Sons' Annual Watercolour exhibition in Bond Street and Lloyd paid £475 for it on 22 February 1912.[16] Certainly this confirms the date when Alec Martin recalled that Lloyd began to collect, just before the First World War, but Martin also stated that Lloyd had been given a Turner watercolour, 'which had whetted his appetite', and implied that this gift had been the impetus to the formation of Lloyd's collection of Turners. However, all the Turner watercolours that Lloyd gave to the British Museum can be accounted for with notes of their purchase, and this 'gift' thus becomes an apocryphal one; we must search elsewhere for the reasons why he became such an assiduous collector, not only of Turners but of other English watercolours as well.

Beetle 'captures'

In 1885, when he was only 17, Lloyd was elected a Fellow of the Royal Entomological Society. He served on its Council and was four times Vice-President; the Society's annual reports also record his many generous contributions, including the panelling and furnishing of the Society's new meeting room when it moved to 41 Queen's Gate, the presentation of two important manuscripts, and financial assistance with the publication of *Nomenclator Zooliogicus* in order to keep its subscription price low. In addition he presented original drawings by Jacob Hubner to the British Museum (Natural History) so that they could be studied alongside the collections, and he assumed the ownership and editorial management of the *Entomologists' Monthly Magazine* in 1904, frequently subsidising colour illustrations: his firm took over the actual printing in 1924.[17]

Lloyd began collecting insects on Wimbledon and Clapham Commons as a young boy, and the quality of his collection was shown by his early election to a distinguished society, by his accounts of his 'captures' in their publications, and by the additions he made to his collection through the selective purchase of others. His assiduity in collecting in the field was not lessened by the amputation of his leg in 1937; he merely shifted his attention from butterflies to beetles, remarking that 'beetles are no more active than I am now'.[18] His chauffeur would drive him to promising spots and bring material to him to examine on a folding table; this he would later mount and set in his study at home. Friends were invited to his country houses, Treago Castle in Herefordshire and

11

later Bampton Grange, Oxfordshire, to join him in his collecting. On business trips to Manchester he would visit the University Museum to 'talk beetles' and was always full of enthusiasm for the subject. He enabled the museum to purchase the fine Spaeth collection of Cassidinae and bequeathed it his entomological collection and library: his own collection of British Coleoptera has been described as one of the treasures of the Manchester Museum.[19]

The President of the Royal Entomological Society described Lloyd as one of its last links with the Victorian era,[20] and indeed one of his main concerns was that the Society should continue to cater for the amateur collector like himself who had not taken any special training.[21] His perceived connection with the Victorian age must have been due to his emphasis on 'captures' and their correct labelling and display, indicative of his amateur, as opposed to professional, status in the Society. It also provides the first clue to the link between this particular collecting passion and his others: his insect 'captures' might be regarded as parallel activities to his successful Alpine 'ascents' and to the Turners that he 'went after' and 'acquired'.[22]

Lloyd seems to have shared his fear of the professionalisation of the natural sciences with John Ruskin, the Victorian critic and collector of Turners *par excellence*, who spoke out loudly against the new science from his Chair of Fine Arts at Oxford.[23] A fellow Alpinist, Ruskin was also a botanist and mineralogist who, in his pioneering Saint George's Museum at Sheffield, created a museum where working men could study the interrelationships between the natural sciences and the fine arts. Before it moved in 1890, the first small gallery received extensive notice in the papers as a 'treasure-box' in which 'rare stones, fine engravings, choice pictures [Verrochios, Mantegna drawings, and watercolours by Turner, the Pre-

Raphaelites and Ruskin himself], valuable books and manuscripts', as well as sculptures and casts were arranged on the walls and in cases and cabinets designed by Ruskin himself. The curator was directed to have catalogues ready to hand and drawers were to be kept open for students to inspect specimens.[24]

Alpine ascents

We shall recall Saint George's Museum when we come to examine the display of Lloyd's various collections in Albany. First, however, mention should be made of another 'collecting' society of which Lloyd was a keen member – the Alpine Club. In this he displayed a rigorous physical self-discipline, another characteristic he shared with Victorian naturalists: 'brought up to feel guilt at idleness and an utter abhorrence of sloth, recreation for them could never mean relaxation . . . every single moment needed to be filled with some useful activity and that productive power which so impresses us today owed much to the meticulous way in which the Victorians learned to plan their time.'[25] It was when Lloyd joined an entomological friend in Austria in 1896, on one of his summer holidays spent on collecting trips on the Continent, that he was introduced to the Alps and developed his great passion for climbing.[26] Ruskin, too, had begun to visit the Alps on field trips; but whereas for him they were the 'beginning and end of all natural scenery', seemingly 'built for the human race, as at once their schools and cathedrals',[27] for Lloyd the Alps quickly became two further collecting challenges: the first, a collection of 'ascents', 'variations' and 'traverses' to be claimed, described and labelled in the form of articles and illustrations in the *Alpine Journal*; and the second, a collection of eighteenth-century Swiss prints, each one carefully mounted or inserted in folders, labelled, catalogued and

stored in solander boxes in specially made cabinets (fig. 2).[28]

Elected in December 1901, Lloyd served the Alpine Club well in advice and finance, acting variously as Auditor, com-

Fig. 2. One of four mahogany cabinets in which Lloyd kept his collection of Swiss prints, which came to the British Museum with the rest of his bequest.

mittee member, Vice-President and, from 1949 to 1956, as Honorary Treasurer, when he was active raising funds for the expeditions to Everest. He funded a climber's hut on Ynys Ettwys in Wales, and subsidised illustrations, sometimes in colour, for the Club's official publication. The Valais and Mont Blanc range were the areas of his principal climbs, which he made in what is now described as an old-fashioned, recognisably Victorian manner, with a guide, usually Joseph Pollinger (fig. 1), and a preference for snow routes. All his climbs are listed in the *Alpine Journal*, the most important ones delivered as illustrated talks to the Club and then published in detailed articles written by Lloyd himself.[29] Lloyd's climbing 'firsts' were mainly achieved after the First World War when he was over 50; they displayed great stamina, courage and curiosity and show that he and his guide steered clear of any irresponsible attraction to obvious danger. After his last great ascent, that of the north face of the Aiguille de Bionnassay in 1926 (when he was 58), he and Pollinger tended to climb in the Dolomites. When Lloyd's operation in 1937 put an end to all serious climbing, they toured the Alps by car.[30]

Lloyd used two eighteenth-century Swiss prints from his collection to illustrate in colour the area described in his account of his climb of the Aiguille de Bionnassay, and he permitted a large selection to be used as the illustrations to T. Graham Brown and Sir Gavin de Beer's account of the *First Ascent of Mont Blanc* in 1957. There had been an exhibition of Alpine prints at the Club in 1909[31] and in 1924 Lloyd organised another, borrowing from the collections of other members, including that of Madame Paravicini, the wife of the Swiss ambassador, as well as from his own. He wrote the three-page introduction to the catalogue, demonstrating his intimate knowledge of the artists, engravers and aquatint techniques, evidently gained not only from his own collecting

VOYAGE DE M^r DE SAUSSURE A LA CIME DU MONT-BLANC, AU MOIS D'AOUT MDCCLXXXVII. II^{de} Planche

Ce célèbre Physicien Genevois defend le Mont-Blanc avec l'intrépide Jaques Balmat, dit *le Mont-Blanc*, et les autres Guides, après avoir fait le 3e Aout, sur la Cime elevée de cette fameuse Montagne diverses observations et experiences interessantes, qui se trouvent detaillées dans le 8e Volume de ses Voyages

Publié par Chr: de Mechel l'an 1790, et se vend chez lui à Basle.

Fig. 3. One of Lloyd's rarest Swiss prints, showing Horace de Saussure (1740–99) on the descent from Mont Blanc, 1787. Etching probably by Marquard Wocher (1758–1830) after his own design, published by Christian von Mechel, 1790. The middle-aged and portly de Saussure, who made one of the earliest ascents of the mountain, is shown seated, about to be pulled across a crevasse. The plate was suppressed and reissued showing him as a young man about to step across without any assistance.

activities, in which he was assisted by the famous Geneva dealer Kundig, but also from studying with the curator of prints at the Technical School in Zurich.[32] Most of an Alpine climber's time is spent waiting for the right weather and conditions, and it is clear that Lloyd typically put this time to constructive use. His impressive collection of nearly 5,000 prints, the finest private collection in the world (see fig. 3), was left to the British Museum, along with the cabinets in which they were housed and almost 200 very fine, often rare, books with plates of Swiss costumes and views, with Lloyd's distinctive bookplate inserted inside the cover of each (half-title page).[33] Lloyd's Alpine library, which contained many unique early accounts, was left to the National Library of Scotland.

From the distribution of his collections already mentioned, it is apparent that Lloyd was intent on disposing of them in places where they would be most accessible to any member of the public with an informed interest and where they would form an appropriate complement to an existing collection. When he invited members of the various societies with which he was involved to visit his rooms at Albany, they invariably recalled not only his great pride and enjoyment in showing his collections, but his enthusiasm for teaching others about them: 'the evening was to look, learn and appreciate'.[34]

This essay may seem to have become – as Peter Bicknell, another climber and book- and print-collector, once described his own visit to Lloyd's rooms – 'somewhat of an ordeal, because we had to be shown the collections of beetles, butterflies, Japanese sword-blades, etc. before getting to the *bonne-bouche* of the Turner drawings'.[35] However, without this examination of the other apparently unrelated activities of R. W. Lloyd's life it would be impossible to understand his motivation and method in putting together 'perhaps the most splendid collection of Turner watercolours assembled by any individual since Ruskin'.[36]

Watercolour acquisitions

As mentioned above, Lloyd's first documented purchase of an English watercolour was not a work by Turner but a view of *Crowland Abbey* by de Wint (fig. 4), for which he paid the substantial sum of £475 at Agnew's exhibition in February 1912. This period before the First World War was a time when the market in English watercolours was booming and prices were high; but this was one of the highest priced items in Agnew's exhibition that year and to put it in perspective it might be noted that Sir Hickman Bacon purchased his version of Thomas Girtin's *White House at Chelsea* at the same exhibition for £215, while comparable works by Samuel Prout and Copley Fielding were priced at around £150.[37] Agnew's sold the de Wint to Lloyd with the proviso that they would 'exchange it, provided it is kept in good condition; at any time for other Drawings in our possession, or take back within 12 months, at 10% less than the amount charged'.

Fig. 4. Peter de Wint (1784–1849), *Crowland Abbey*. Watercolour, R. W. Lloyd Bequest, 1958-7-12-343.

Why Lloyd began to collect watercolours in February 1912 can only be surmised. Evidently he was prepared to spend large amounts, and it may be significant that his brother had retired from Nathaniel Lloyd & Co. in 1909 and the Star Bleaching Company which they directed jointly was sold in 1912. R. W. Lloyd had moved into chambers at I.5 Albany a few years previously;[38] perhaps he made his acquisitions in this fresh field, at the age of 44, because he found he had extra funds available or needed to decorate the walls of a new residence. Nevertheless, already with this first purchase in a different collecting area, characteristics of Lloyd the collector with which we are familiar can be perceived: he made a large financial commitment for a 'first', but, as when he used a guide in a new Alpine 'ascent', he placed himself in the hands of an expert and at the same time did not take any unnecessary risks. Agnew's were well established in Manchester and London as the premier dealers in watercolours, having held annual watercolour exhibitions in those cities as well as in Liverpool almost from the date of their first opening. They were renowned particularly for the role they had played in forming the collection of watercolours at the Whitworth Art Gallery in Manchester, the Lees collection in Oldham, and George Salting's vast collections which had recently and famously been bequeathed to the nation, including eighteen Turner watercolours to the British Museum. In fact, Turner watercolours were their speciality, and they had handled most of the important ones to pass through the market in the past half-century.[39]

Morland Agnew was himself a serious collector of the watercolours of John Robert Cozens and Turner, having begun with works left in stock after the Charles Sackville Bale sale in May 1881 and eventually buying late Swiss watercolours by Turner for record prices. During the period before the war, he ran the Bond Street rooms with Lockett Agnew (with whom George Salting mainly dealt) while his son Gerald looked after the Manchester sale rooms, before coming to London when his father retired in 1913.[40] It has been claimed that Gerald Agnew bought for Lloyd at the J. E. Taylor sale in 1912 and was the guiding hand behind Lloyd's collection of Turners.[41] However, an examination of Agnew's records of Lloyd's first purchases indicates that, on the contrary, they did not buy for him at the Taylor sale and it was Lloyd himself, with the possible assistance of a previously unremarked salesman at Agnew's, E. G. Cundall, who formed his collection of English watercolours.

It is worth emphasising here that although the sixty works by Turner certainly formed the heart of Lloyd's 1958 bequest to the British Museum, his will in fact stated specifically that the bequest included all the drawings and watercolours dating from before 1885; it numbered a total of 154 works, not all by English artists but a handful by Dutch, French and Swiss artists as well (see Appendix 1). By far the majority, nearly 100, were purchased at Agnew's between 1912 and 1929; there was also a large group of watercolours by John 'Warwick' Smith which Lloyd bought privately in 1927, while most of the remainder were either connected with his collection of Swiss prints or were later purchased for him by or on the advice of Alec Martin from the late 1930s onwards. These included two of the Turner watercolours: *Criccieth* (no. 37) and *A Storm (Shipwreck)* (no. 25).

Edward George Cundall was a salesman at Agnews from 1888 to 1925. His initials appear in the Day Books of Agnew's London branch recording Lloyd's purchases, from the first one in 1912 until 1918, when the initials of an office clerk and then those of 'CGA' (C. Gerald Agnew) begin to replace them on occasion, the latter taking over completely after

Cundall's retirement early in 1925. Apart from his initials and the dates he worked at Agnew's, there is nothing about Cundall at all in the published history of the company.[42] He himself wrote one book, *Fonthill Abbey. A Descriptive Account of five watercolour drawings by J M W Turner, R.A.*, printed privately in London in 1915 (thirty-five copies) for Ralph Brocklebank, Esq. of Haughton Hall, Tarporley, the owner of a number of these watercolours and another sometime client of Agnew's. This small book served as a catalogue of all Turner's views of Fonthill and provided a history of the Abbey, with transcriptions of contemporary reports of the building and a bibliography.

With his insider's access to and knowledge of Agnew's archives, Cundall was ideally placed to catalogue Lloyd's collection, or at least to provide him with information about the provenance and exhibition history of his acquisitions. Lloyd's typescript catalogue of his watercolours fortunately survives, passed to the British Museum with the drawings in 1958, along with a handful of letters from Gerald Agnew, W.G. Rawlinson, A.J. Finberg, Alec Martin and one from Cundall himself. Just as the box of index cards which accompanied the 5,000 Swiss prints provided their 'find spots' and 'labels' detailing their 'species', so the carefully compiled catalogue provides the same type of information for the watercolours.

Cundall had just retired to Whitstable when he wrote to Lloyd on 27 March 1925 to thank him for lunch at the Gresham Club three weeks previously. He sent further information about a view of *Lake Nemi* by J. R. Cozens that he had researched for Lloyd's catalogue, and went to the trouble of typing out the relevant extract from the article, 'as you may like to correct the error in your MSS of the Catalogue'.[43] He went on to offer Lloyd his copy of a catalogue the latter had been searching for, the illustrated version of the Stephen

Holland sale (1908), which included a number of important Turners, including one purchased by Lloyd in 1917, *Messieurs les Voyageurs . . .* (no. 39).

As this letter is the only actual evidence of anyone advising Lloyd on his collection, it is worth quoting from it at length:

Have you been again to see the 'Water Colour' Exhibition at Agnew's? – I made a note of some of the drawings, that I thought worth your attention, when I was there. – There is a very good Gainsborough 'The Corner of the Wood' (No. 76) on the First Screen – of course it is sketchy, but I have never seen a finished drawing by Gainsborough, as far as I remember, & he is not represented amongst your *drawings*; it would be difficult to get a better example – A beautiful little upright drawing by 'Harpignies' hangs on the other side of the same screen (No. 104?); this I much admired: – of course he is a foreign artist, but you have one or two French pictures. – Also at the opposite end of the same screen, there is a very good example of George Chambers – 'Off Deal' – (No. 87) – which you might like for your portfolios. – A drawing that I covet is 'The Huguenot' by Sir J. E. Millais (No. 99), but it may not appeal to you, and it is not for sale.

Lloyd took none of this advice and in fact his collecting at Agnew's was nearly at an end by this date: he was only to buy eight more watercolours by Turner, plus a group of his early drawings, almost all purchased at sales, on commission.

The last transaction Cundall himself recorded at Agnew's was the sale to Lloyd on 5 March 1925 of six copies of *The Water Colours of Turner, Cox and de Wint* at £2 2s. each, less a special discount of 25 per cent. This was a lavish publication introduced by A. P. Oppé and illustrated with colour plates which served as a souvenir of the Spring watercolour exhibition held by Agnew's the previous year. Lloyd lent eight watercolours to the exhibition, several of which were discussed by Oppé in his introduction, and two of his Turners were reproduced.[44] Interestingly, Oppé noted that 'for good or ill, the trio continue to represent English landscape painting' and complained that there was no proper history of the eighteenth-century watercolour school providing a background for these artists of the nineteenth century to spring from, rather than appearing already miraculously fully-fledged.[45]

To what extent did Lloyd have a similar purpose in mind while forming his own collection of English watercolours, and how far was he in fact advised by Cundall or any other member of staff at Agnew's in his purchases? Without further letters it is impossible to state categorically, but the evidence of the catalogue compiled for him by Cundall[46] and Agnew's own records provide revealing patterns in his purchasing and a context for his Turner watercolours.

Altogether Lloyd bought 110 watercolours, drawings and oil paintings from Agnew's between 1912 and 1936. He purchased his second watercolour from Agnew's less than a week after the first. It was Turner's view of *Marxburg* (no. 21) and, surprisingly, it had not been in the annual Spring exhibition where he had purchased the de Wint. Charles Fairfax Murray had bought this important work, painted by Turner for Sir John Swinburne, at Agnew's in 1910 for £1,600 and Agnew's sold it for him to Lloyd, adding a commission, on 1 April 1912, for £985.[47]

The next two purchases were made at Agnew's annual exhibition in Manchester later the same year, Turner's *Winchelsea* (no. 28), which had once belonged to Ruskin, and a lovely *Mont St Michel* by John Sell Cotman. Both works had been bought for stock earlier that year, for about half what Lloyd was to pay for them, although the profits had to absorb

the £5 10s. that it cost Agnew's to frame each. Returning to London, another Turner that had formerly belonged to Ruskin was offered to Lloyd, *Caernarvon Castle* (no. 33), which he bought in January 1913 for the more substantial sum of £1,750 (this time Agnew's mark-up was £250).

After this purchase, a pattern begins to emerge. Each spring Agnew's held an exhibition of English watercolours in London, with proceeds from the catalogue going to the Artists' General Benevolent Institution, which Turner had chaired in 1823. Every year they would include a number of items that they had sold during the previous year, borrowed back for the exhibition from the purchasers. Each year, Lloyd would lend a number of works he had purchased the year before and buy one or two of the new works for sale.

In 1913 the annual exhibition was very small; Agnew's had decided to focus instead in April and May on an exhibition of the works of Turner, because in the previous July they had acquired large numbers of his works from three very important collections: those of Frederick Fawkes, who owned what remained of the famous collection formed by Walter Fawkes of Farnley Hall, H. E. Heyman, who owned a number of works from the Swinburne collection, and J. E. Taylor, proprietor of the *Manchester Guardian* and, with William Agnew, largely responsible for forming the Whitworth's collection, having given the gallery a substantial number of works in 1892.[48] All these collectors had bought from Turner himself or formed their collections very soon after his death.

R. W. Lloyd lent the three Turners he had bought so far to the 1913 exhibition and also took advantage of the abundance of fine Turners to create a foundation for his growing collection, although the fact that he negotiated a deferred payment for some of them suggests that he did not yet have to hand the funds to finance such collecting. He bought three works at the exhibition almost on the day it opened, including two more fine examples from the Swinburne collection (*Tancarville* (no. 43) and *Biebrich* (no. 20), the companion to *Marxburg*), but the prices had risen since he had bought the last and he paid £6,000 for these two alone (Agnew's profit on the pair was £2,000). When the exhibition closed, a number of the smaller but lovely Rhine drawings from the Fawkes collection were still with Agnew's and Lloyd managed to buy a group of five in August for £3,350, 'payable half cash – half in six months'.[49] Agnew's made a note when they originally bought each work of what it had cost them for 'F+G' (framing and glazing), usually around £4 10s. on the Rhine drawings. But on all the ones Lloyd purchased there was an additional note, 'blind', with the added cost of £2 15s. A note on his invoice explained that the cost was 'including spring roller blinds'.

Mounting and display

A number of Agnew's frames survive that incorporate a roller blind mechanism inserted into the upper portion of the frame from the back, with a silk or polished cotton blind which can be pulled down along slots set into the sides just above the glass; the blind has one or two small brass tags that can be hooked onto a pin set into the lower edge (see fig. 5). Most of the few that survive, however, are in private collections; large bequests of watercolours in elaborate gilt frames present museums with problems of space – both on display and in store they require much more room than the eighteenth-century method of storing watercolours on wash-line mounts in portfolios. But the main reason why museums do not leave framed watercolours on display is that they fade. Thus museums have tended to remove them from frames, preferring to have them securely and safely mounted on stiff acid-free

Fig. 5. J. M. W. Turner, *Hirzenach* (no. 16), in an Agnew's frame with its blind partly lowered.

boards which provide wide margins for handling and enable them to be stored in solander boxes, away from harmful air, dust and light.

There were extensive debates in the second half of the nineteenth century about the safest way to store and display watercolours. A long and public argument ran in the columns of *The Times* in the 1880s, between Ruskin, quoted as the greatest authority, who said it was safe to hang them in subdued light or covered; the artist and critic John Charles Robinson, who claimed there had been great damage to the collection at South Kensington (Victoria and Albert Museum) and it was only safe to show them in artificial light at night; and Sir James D. Linton, President of the Royal Institute of Painters in Water Colours, who had his own obvious agenda on behalf of his members. He not only claimed that watercolours did not fade, but even went so far as to say that some works that had been on display for thirty years in the South Kensington Museum were richer and deeper in tone than when they were first painted. After protracted arguments about whether they faded at all, then long experiments to see which pigments were stable and which were not, it was finally agreed that watercolours must be protected most of all from air, dirt and dampness, and from direct sunlight.[50] It was concluded that the environment provided by frames, with well-fitting glass and well taped at the back, was as good as boxes for protecting watercolours from dirty air, but something must block the sunlight, and this could be achieved by placing curtains over them or by storing the frames themselves in cabinets. Ruskin and Henry Vaughan had special cabinets made for storing the collections they gave to various public institutions.[51] Because the frames had to fit into slots in cabinets and were constantly being put in and taken out, they had to be sturdy and fairly plain. Such cabinets were intended for study and display in institutions and were in effect just much larger versions of a solander box.

From the time around the beginning of the nineteenth century when watercolours began to be exhibited alongside oil paintings and to compete with them on walls in houses, they began to be elaborately framed. Brief histories of how they were framed and displayed have begun to be written,[52] and it is clear that Turner himself close-framed his large exhibition watercolours with elaborately carved gilt frames.[53] There are specific instances of his advising purchasers how to frame in this way, and on one occasion he complained that the margins were too wide and advised the insertion of a 'small flat of matted gold'.[54] The most graphic illustration of the way he and his contemporaries preferred to see his larger finished watercolours framed and displayed is provided by John Scarlett Davis's watercolour of Benjamin Godfrey Windus's collection of watercolours from Turner's *England and Wales* series as they were hung in the Library of his house at Tottenham (frontispiece). Windus commissioned this work in 1835 to hang with the watercolours themselves, and it was framed in the same style as the Turners, which were closely hung in groups, with little wall space visible between the gold frames. Smaller works were kept in cabinets and tables, cases and portfolios, visible in this watercolour and described by Windus's daughter in her notes about his collection.[55]

Around 1850, when admiration for 'pure' watercolour landscapes, with their thinner, broader washes and more delicate colours began to compete with more heavily finished watercolours, often with a thick overlay of bodycolour, some artists and collectors considered that the large fancy gilt frames and gold slips overwhelmed the more delicate works, and they began to mount watercolours with broad cream borders and plainer frames. These were the forerunners of those used by Ruskin and Vaughan for their cabinets, and there are many views of interiors, including Arthur Severn's well-known picture of Ruskin's bedroom, showing watercolours framed in this way and hung with more space around each work.[56]

Throughout the second half of the nineteenth century and the first decades of the twentieth, controversy raged in watercolour exhibiting societies and in museums over white or cream mounts versus elaborate gold frames with gold slips. One authority in 1857 complained of the large white mount on *A Storm (Shipwreck)* (no. 25), then on exhibition in Manchester – 'in contact with its present abominable white margin, it looks vulgarly "painty", and positively disagreeable' – and went on to say there was even less excuse for white mounts around vignettes.[57] As late as 1935 the controversy still raged, but Martin Hardie at the Victoria and Albert Museum was finally claiming 'victory', as he himself had made a gradual attempt 'to get rid of all the gold mounts and to change what a recent writer has described as "serried ranks of plummy Victorian pieces in heavy frames and broad gold mounts" into a more orderly arrangement of watercolours shown in historical sequence, in simple frames with mounts of white or cream with bordering lines and washes.' But even he conceded that 'the large water-colour, especially if broadly painted in a high key of rich colour, demands the close frame'.[58]

Turner himself gave his early smaller watercolours wash-line mounts similar to those onto which eighteenth-century artists affixed their watercolours so that they might be stored in portfolios. These were framed less elaborately, with the wash-line borders showing.[59] Sometime around the beginning of the twentieth century Agnew's seems to have devised a compromise for the watercolours they displayed in their annual exhibitions. They left the wash-line borders on cream mounts around the medium and smaller size watercolours, in a shade which was intended to complement those in the watercolour, but prevented objections to large areas of cream mounts by giving them gold slips which framed the wash borders and provided a transition to the fairly elaborate composite gold frames in which their clients who wished to hang their watercolours wanted to display them in their dining and reception rooms.

It seems that Morland Agnew, protective of his own fine collection of Cozens and Turner watercolours, may have been responsible for Agnew's own framers creating for him the ingenious roller blind.[60] Although there are earlier frames with curtains on pulleys or on rods or simply attached at the top of the verso, no examples of these roller blinds can be dated before around 1905.[61]

Glancing through Agnew's accounts of all the Turner watercolours they sold in the 1910s, when Lloyd was building his collection, it is significant that few other collectors requested this additional expensive yet vital protection for their purchases. Lloyd paid for blinds for nearly every Turner watercolour he owned.[62] Stephen Courtauld had them on some, but not all, of the Turner and other watercolours he bought during this time,[63] and the Towneley Art Gallery in Burnley bought a large Girtin of *Lincoln* with a blind which cost Agnew's £4 5s. of their profit.[64] It should perhaps be pointed out that the roller blinds required that the frame be of substantial depth to accommodate them and they could not be inserted into plain frames of the type recommended by Ruskin or Martin Hardie.[65]

Patterns of acquisition – 'driving a hard bargain'
When Agnew's annual exhibition opened in February 1914 Lloyd was still somewhat short of funds, and, having decided he must have a de Wint watercolour and one by Cox, he made a very complicated deal including part payment in cash, one month's delayed payment and the part-exchange of an oil of a *View in Wales* by B. W. Leader.[66] The de Wint *View of Lincoln*[67] was one of the artist's greatest works and came from one of his descendants: Lloyd paid £800 for it and requested blinds for both it and the Cox watercolour of *The Terrace, Haddon Hall*. However, the Cox was bought back by Agnew's one month later for what it had cost Lloyd, since he preferred two other works in the exhibition which would leave him with £25 credit – Girtin's *Road through a village with pond on left* (now identified as 'The Old Cottage' at Widmore, Bromley, the oldest house in the borough) and the lovely W. H. Hunt of *A Girl plucking a fowl* from the Nettlefold collection.[68] The price included a 'new swept frame and sprung roller blind' for

the Girtin, but the Hunt did not have one and Lloyd did not order one to be put in.[69]

After this, Lloyd began to commission Agnew's to bid for him at sales. He was not limiting himself completely to earlier English watercolours and drawings: he had purchased a drawing by Charles Sims, ARA and was to buy several more by this artist he obviously admired; he also bought an oil painting of *The Prodigal* by E. Luminais at Christie's through Agnew's in 1915. It must have been around this year that he started to tour the auction rooms on his Saturday rounds and to become more aware of other important collections of English watercolours. The Reverend Charles Sale had acquired a number of notable Turners from the Munro of Novar collection in the 1880s, and in March 1915 six of the finest were left to the British Museum on the death of his widow (see Appendix 2).[70] One or two works left in her collection were sold anonymously at Christie's in July, and Lloyd commissioned Agnew's to buy *Lowestoffe* (no. 35). Even with the 5 per cent commission, Lloyd must have realised that the £504 he paid for this watercolour was much less than if he had waited for it to appear in the following year's exhibition with Agnew's usual mark-up of a few hundred pounds. In fact they had paid £777 for the same work at the Munro of Novar sale in 1878.

Similarly, when further Turner watercolours from the Swinburne collection appeared in 1916 Lloyd again managed to obtain them at the sale through Agnew's for the 5 per cent commission charged to customers for bidding on their behalf. Understandably this became Lloyd's preferred method for adding to his collection, but occasionally Agnew's, with their privileged access to certain clients, would make private purchases from them; they obviously informed Lloyd of these, and invariably his purchase of the work from Agnew's would be recorded in their books less than a week after they acquired it. This was the case for the *Richmond Bridge, Surrey* (no. 29), which the ledger (and presumably the invoice) proudly noted was 'Ruskin's first Turner drawing, given to him by his father'.[71] Agnew's had paid £1,000 privately for two Turners and sold this one alone to Lloyd for £1,400, and this type of 'cat and mouse' game of commissions and attempts to claw back profits through private sale characterised their dealings with Lloyd. Occasionally, he seems to have been aware that they were desperate to sell something that had been on their books too long and to have bought works from them for the same price or even less than they had paid. There were attempts to keep him sweet, however: two months after Lloyd purchased *Richmond Bridge*, Agnew's presented him with an India paper proof-before-letters of the engraving.[72] They charged Stephen Courtauld £27 for a similar proof in 1917.[73]

The purchases proceeded in this manner through the next ten years or so, with Lloyd still buying works by other English watercolourists and building up a collection of one or two excellent examples by most of the important artists, but concentrating mainly on what was becoming a very significant collection of Turners from a careful selection of important original collections – those of Ruskin, Munro of Novar, Fawkes, Swinburne and Windus. He watched carefully for the sales of 'second-generation' Turner collectors, whose collections were well known through the popular press and written up in the newspapers before and after the sales, recording prices paid and the previous history of the most important works. One of these was Sir Joseph Beecham's sale in May 1917, when Agnew's successfully purchased five extremely important Turner watercolours for Lloyd for nearly £8,000: *Florence* (no. 40), *Hastings* (no. 22), *Saltash* (no. 26), *Venice* (no. 45) and *Messieurs les Voyageurs . . .* (no. 39). Lloyd, ever the astute businessman, still seems to have been looking for advantageous methods of settling his account: Agnew's ledger recorded 'Invoice sent May 5th, payable by June 1st'.[74]

Sir Joseph Beecham's sale was very significant for several reasons. It included works he had purchased from the Stephen Holland sale in 1908, which at the time the *Daily Telegraph* had written up as incomparable, stating that, like Joseph Gillot, Holland 'was of the breed of collectors . . . who used to say "The Best of everything is good enough for me" ' and mentioning the Turner watercolours of *Saltash* and *Messieurs les voyageurs* specifically. Lloyd was still looking for an illustrated copy of this catalogue in 1925 when Cundall offered him his. The *Daily Telegraph* made a similar fuss of Beecham's sale, which broke individual records for prices for Turner, Constable, de Wint and others, as well as for the total fetched.

W. H. Smith's 'soothing six' and Agnew's 'record price' Turner of *Zurich*

In their report on the Beecham sale, the *Telegraph* related in detail Lockett Agnew's description of the formation of an earlier collection by the Rt Hon. W. H. Smith (1825–91), which Beecham had also absorbed into his own:

> Years ago this eminent 'business man' . . . seeking a sure distraction, asked Mr Woods of Christie's to pick for him half a dozen of Turner's best drawings. There was no better judge to do it and it was done. Mr Smith kept the soothing six in a portfolio, and would contemplate them in quietude. At his death they were found in his house in Grosvenor Place, still in their portfolio, and Mr Agnew bought them, eventually letting Sir Joseph Beecham have them.[75]

They went on to report that at the sale Agnew's had purchased three of them back, listing them and reporting how much was paid; but the newspaper was not aware that two of these had been purchased by them for Lloyd – *Florence* (no. 40) and *Venice, the Grand Canal* (no. 45). Members of Sir Joseph Beecham's family bought the other three, but Lloyd was not defeated: when they were sold on the following year he managed to acquire two of them, *Worcester* (no. 34) and *Saumur* (no. 41), reuniting in his own collection four of W. H. Smith's original 'soothing six'. However, at the 1916 sale he paid around £1,500 for most of the Turners he purchased, while in 1917 he had to pay twice that much and more.

Lloyd managed to add Beecham's watercolour of *Windsor* (no. 30) to his collection at the same time, but for a few years afterwards he mainly limited himself to relatively inexpensive but fine works by other English watercolourists. The exceptions were *Lucerne by moonlight* (no. 47), which Agnew's acquired privately just before their annual exhibition in 1920 and Lloyd bought for nearly £5,000 as soon as the exhibition went up, and two less expensive works with Ruskin and Fawkes provenances, *Keswick Lake* (no. 36) and *The Johannisberg* (no. 19). Lord Northwick's sale in 1921 provided the opportunity to fill gaps of Turner's earlier work not yet represented in his collection, and it was on this and the more topographical type of watercolour and drawing that Lloyd concentrated for the rest of the decade. The Brocklebank sale in 1927 offered the chance to buy a few more items with Munro and Fawkes provenances at reasonable prices. But one further purchase made from Agnew's was perhaps his greatest coup, and cost Agnew's, specifically Morland Agnew, dearly.

In 1919 Agnew's paid the record price of £6,510 for Turner's *Zurich* (no. 46) at the Drummond sale. They had purchased it for Morland Agnew, who had retired from the firm in 1913, and their records indicate that he paid them £7,000 for it two weeks after the sale. In May 1924 Agnew's bought it back from him for £4,500 specifically to sell to Lloyd, who paid £5,000, noting in the ledger, 'Payable: £1000 on delivery, £2000 in three months, and £2000 in six months.'[76] Thus Lloyd managed to acquire the 'record price' Turner, without actually paying the record price himself. His catalogue proudly described it as 'No. 10 of the ten [Swiss] drawings of 1842' and quoted Ruskin's story of their creation which had been published in the 1878 Fine Art Society exhibition of his collection.[77] It was thus one of the artist's most famous works. In a note appended to his catalogue, Lloyd wrote: 'In event of my ever selling this picture separately I have promised to let Mr Gerald Agnew have the first offer of it. R. W. Lloyd. 22/6/24.'

Collecting in the 1920s and 1930s

This was one of Lloyd's last major purchases of Turner watercolours and almost the last of his dealings with Agnew's. E. G. Cundall retired shortly afterwards. Through the twenties, Lloyd continued to buy other English watercolours and the occasional oil painting. These included a small oil on panel by Turner of *Tummel Bridge, Perthshire* (1802), purchased from stock for £250 in 1927 and now in the Yale Center for British Art,[78] and two oils by Richard Wilson, *On the River Tiber* and *Villa Adriana*, purchased for Lloyd on commission at the Richard Ford sale in June 1929.[79] It is curious that alone among the pre-1885 works he purchased at Agnew's, these three oil paintings, all lovely works with impeccable provenances, were not destined to grace a national collection. However, two other oil paintings were thought by Lloyd to be important enough to be left to the National Gallery: a portrait, once in the collection of the Marquis of

Exeter, of a woman whom Lloyd believed to be Anna Maria van Schurman, painted by Cornelius Johnson (signed and dated 1655; NG 6280) and a painting by Gainsborough of a *Woody Landscape with Sheep* (NG 6281). Both of these were bought by Lloyd in 1917 from the Samuel Joseph collection, which he was assured by Cundall had been formed in the late nineteenth century under the supervision of Sir Walter Armstrong, Director of the National Gallery of Ireland.[80] Although the paintings were accepted in 1958, the Johnson is only occasionally on view and the Gainsborough, which Ellis Waterhouse accepted and catalogued but the staff at the National Gallery were convinced was a nineteenth-century fake, was transferred to the Tate six months later and has never been displayed.[81] Agnew's had paid £1,400 for the two; Lloyd paid them nearly £2,000 more.[82]

Lloyd bought very little in the 1930s, but managed to acquire *Criccieth* (no. 37) for a small sum at a Christie's auction. Significantly, Alec Martin at Christie's arranged a private sale for him in 1936 with the Trustees of the estate of F. E. Loyd for the 'Wreckers', now known as *A Storm (Shipwreck)*, enclosing in his letter a transcription from a contemporary account of its exhibition in 1823 written in A. J. Finberg's hand (see no. 25). It is around this time that Alec Martin seems to have begun to play a greater role in forming Lloyd's collection. Lloyd had made the occasional purchase of an oil painting or a drawing by a foreign artist that interested him, but he added little to the collection of British watercolours he had already formed through Agnew's. Instead the character of what he purchased changed completely: modern oil paintings and drawings by artists exhibiting at the Royal Academy, drawings by Corot, Dutch and Italian old masters, genre paintings by Landseer, including one of his most famous, *The Cat's Paw*, and portraits by Romney, Lawrence and Reynolds as well as some marble and bronze sculpture.[83] This later collection was the one Alec Martin was referring to when he wrote in Lloyd's obituary: 'In recent years, knowing my intense love of oil paintings he got me to buy for him, giving me a free hand, a small collection of works by artists of the Flemish, Dutch and Italian Schools of the fifteenth to the seventeenth centuries and by English artists of the eighteenth and nineteenth centuries.'[84] Martin oversaw the paintings department at Christie's and these works were probably purchased mainly to fill the walls of the four chambers Lloyd then occupied at Albany (I.5, I.6, I.3 and I.4), as well as those of Bampton Grange in Oxfordshire, which Lloyd had bought in the 1940s, and the offices of Druce and Co. at 1 Baker Street.[85] Some of this collection was retained by Lloyd's family, but most of it was sold by Christie's on 29 May 1959. The most valuable painting in the sale, however, was one that we know Lloyd himself chose to purchase while he was Chairman of Christie's, Henry Thompson's *Crossing the Brook*.[86]

It seems clear that Lloyd's collection of British watercolours was already nearly complete by the end of the 1920s, perceived as a complete entity and possibly already destined for the national collection to complement the group of Turners given to the British Museum by Salting and Sale.[87] In spite of the proviso guaranteed by Agnew's on his first purchase, and the one occasion when he sold an oil painting and a Cox watercolour, Lloyd did not, like Salting or many other collectors, 'weed' or sell off works from his collection in order to 'trade up' or acquire better ones.[88] He certainly did not collect as an investment, unless it was an investment in the cultural and artistic heritage of the country.

Exhibitions, Lloyd's library, and membership of art societies

Extremely proud of his collection, Lloyd was a generous lender to Agnew's annual watercolour exhibitions. Occasionally they would focus on Turner's work and he would lend a large number, as in the 1924 Cox, de Wint and Turner exhibition and late in 1928, when he lent several items to their showrooms in Manchester. He carefully retained newspaper reviews of the Agnew's exhibitions that mentioned his works, although the lender's names were never given in the catalogues.

In his typescript catalogue of his collection Lloyd carefully noted the exhibition history of each watercolour he purchased, and the care he took to buy works which were not only in excellent condition but from collections which had been formed by Turner's own clients meant that they had been included in some very important exhibitions indeed. These included the 1878 exhibition of his own collection that Ruskin organised and catalogued for the Fine Art Society,[89] as well as the four important winter exhibitions of British art at the Royal Academy in 1886, 1887, 1889 and 1891 and several of the 'international' exhibitions that followed in the wake of Crystal Palace, held in Manchester, Leeds and Glasgow. These exhibitions were carefully recorded on new or transferred labels on the back of the frames when they were reframed for Lloyd by Agnew's, along with the work's previous owners. Lloyd himself was equally generous in loans to other institutions besides Agnew's. He lent regularly to exhibitions held at the Burlington Fine Arts Club and in 1934 he was on the Honorary General Committee of the Royal Academy's important *Exhibition of British Art c.1000–1860*, held under the patronage of the King and Queen to celebrate the nation's greatest achievements in painting, sculpture and objets d'art, during a time when the country needed a boost to morale.

In 1951, the centenary of Turner's death, Lloyd lent a number of works to the exhibition at the Royal Academy and to the complementary exhibition held by Agnew's of 100 of Turner's best watercolours in private hands. The catalogue introduction by Hugh Agnew indicated that he only met with one refusal to lend (because the drawing could not be found), but did not record that he was forced to hold the exhibition in February and March because those were the only months during which Lloyd, who lent twenty-one works, would allow his to go on display. But not only did the 83-year-old chairman of Christie's dictate when Agnew's should hold their exhibition, he also seems to have dictated which of his works they should borrow. Geoffrey Agnew's interesting annotations on their copy of the catalogue includes, next to no. 23, *The Colosseum*, 'not very exciting & definitely out of drawing. RWL rather forced this on us.'[90]

Just as Lloyd was not a passive lender, so he was not a passive collector. Although Cundall wrote to let Lloyd know which sales were coming up, it is clear that Lloyd himself toured the sale rooms and dealers and made his own informed choices about which works he added to his collection. As mentioned, their provenance and condition was paramount. As with his other collections, he took great pains to make himself as informed as possible. His library contained a complete run of Christie's catalogues from 1874, Walter Armstrong's various monographs on British artists, Collins Baker on Crome, Binyon on Girtin, Oppé on Cotman, the complete works of Ruskin in their original editions (seventy-one volumes altogether), and the published, bound versions of prints by J. C. Nattes, Cotman and others, and especially Turner – *England and Wales, Liber Studiorum, Sussex, South Coast, Richmondshire, Harbours and Rivers* and his illustrations to Scott, as well as everything Rawlinson and Finberg had written on the artist.[91] Shortly after making his first purchases, Lloyd became a member of, and thus subscriber to, the publications of the Walpole Society (1920–54) and the Old Watercolour Society's Club from its foundation in 1923 until his death, serving on the Consultative Committee from the beginning.

The Alpine Club was in Savile Row, near the premises of one of the oldest and most established fine arts associations in London, the Burlington Fine Arts Club. Formed in the second half of the nineteeth century to hold *conversazioni* where collectors and amateurs could display, compare and discuss their acquisitions, it occupied a building which boasted a Member's Writing Room, Library, Reading Room, Smoking Room and of course a Gallery, where the *conversazioni* soon developed into exhibitions. Dealers were excluded from membership, which from 1910 to 1920 hovered around 300–400, while visitors to the exhibitions numbered 2,000–3,000. Members received copies of the exhibition catalogues. Lloyd was proposed for membership by Thomas Girtin on 24 February 1918 and seconded by Geoffrey Blackwell, shortly before Arnold Bennett, Bernard Berenson and Osbert Sitwell joined. Manufacturers were strongly represented among the membership, and Lloyd himself proposed Henry Allen, a professional bleacher, in 1918.[92] The spur for Lloyd to join may have been the exhibition of the collection of English drawings formed by Herbert Horne, held in the winter of 1916–17. The guiding lights of the club at this time were A. P. Oppé, Thomas Girtin, C. F. Bell, Robert Witt, W. Rawlinson and Tancred Borenius, whose names also appear regularly in the Visitors Books to the Department of Prints and Drawings of the British Museum. Lloyd was not a regular visitor himself, but seems to have made at least one visit, in 1915.[93]

Fig. 6. A Japanese 'Tachi' mounted sword in a gold lacquered scabbard of the type that would have been carried in the annual procession of feudal lords to their formal mansions in the capital Edo (Tokyo). The blade is signed by Sukesada of Bizan Province, active in the early sixteenth century. L. 99 cm. British Museum, Department of Japanese Antiquities, R. W. Lloyd Bequest.

Fig. 7 (below). Pair of vases of carved red lacquer (Chinese, Qing Dynasty, late eighteenth century) and a box and cover of carved red, black and yellow lacquer and gilt bronze (Qing Dynasty, Qianlong mark and period, 1736–95). Ht of vases 28.5 cm. British Museum, Department of Oriental Antiquities, R. W. Lloyd Bequest.

Several members of the Burlington Fine Arts Club were from the British Museum's staff, including Laurence Binyon, Sidney Colvin, A. M. Hind and Campbell Dodgson. With this type of constituency, it is not surprising that many of their exhibitions focused on British art, but there was a growing interest among many of these men in oriental art as well. They organised important exhibitions of Chinese art in 1915 and Japanese art in 1933, which may have been instrumental in leading Lloyd to begin collecting in this field. No research has yet been done on where or when he began to collect Chinese red lacquerware (fig. 7) or Japanese antiquities, particularly swords and their fittings (fig. 6), but both collections came to the British Museum in 1958.

Display

It seems as if once one collection was complete, Lloyd went on to form another; or, as Alec Martin described this new direction, 'when increasing wealth enabled him to pursue

more expensive quarry he was at first, like many other successful young industrialists, less selective than accumulative, though he did seek advice from the well-known oriental experts, H. L. Joli, K. Tomita and others, on the vast array of Chinese and Japanese lacquer, Japanese ivories and swordblades.' In fact he was not as well served by his experts in this area as he had been by Agnew's and his own eye in collecting Turners. He believed his collection of fifty pieces of Chinese red lacquer was a representative collection from the Ch'ing dynasty, mainly eighteenth century, including several imperial pieces and possibly two from the sixteenth century. The Museum collection was weak in this field, which was little studied at the time, and now most of the collection is recognised to be from the Qing dynasty of the nineteenth century.[94] The British Museum was well provided with *inro*, *netsuke*, ironwork, etc., and was happy to see Lloyd's examples go to the Manchester Museum (fig. 8),[95] but it was very pleased to retain the 200 swords which formed one of the two best private collections in the country, richer in fine blades than the collection at the Victoria and Albert Museum.[96]

Alec Martin recalled that all these antiquities were crowded into a few glass cases in Albany, more suggestive of a store than of artistic display, and all the framed drawings hung over the glass cabinets, two or three deep, close to the ceiling, and covered with blinds to protect them from the sun and artificial light.[97] Another visitor described the sitting room as typically Edwardian, green in tone and luxuriously comfortable, full of *objets de vertu* and watercolours on the walls, uncovered

Fig. 8. Three pieces of Japanese ironwork from Lloyd's collection: from top, a snake (articulated) and crow, signed Munesuke (1688–1735), and a dragon (articulated). Such pieces were usually made to show that armourers could make things other than suits of armour. L. of dragon 37.8 cm. The Manchester Museum, University of Manchester.

because the light had gone.[98] The list of contents of Lloyd's chambers in Albany drawn up for probate indicates that the Turner watercolours were mainly hung in the sitting and dining rooms, but there were also framed drawings and watercolours not hanging, as well as numerous portfolios, albums and boxes of engravings. With the addition of four large cabinets of Swiss prints, in folders that only the valet was allowed to handle, and the drawers of speared butterflies and beetles, as well as photos of the Alps, Lloyd's chambers must have resembled nothing so much as Ruskin's 'treasure-box', the Saint George's Museum at Sheffield.

Conditions of bequest to the British Museum

Lloyd did everything in his power to ensure that the care with which he himself housed, preserved, labelled and displayed his collections would also be taken by those to whom he bequeathed them. His will, dated 5 February 1954, included a number of conditions attached to the bequest of the Turner watercolours, including:

> . . . that it be accepted as a whole, 3. that the said drawings shall be kept in a mahogany cabinet or cabinets so as not be be accessible to light and shall only be shown by special request and then so far as practicable for not more than half an hour at a time but so that any drawings comprised in this present bequest may be exhibited during the first fourteen days of February in each year, 4. than none of the said drawings comprised in this bequest are any time to be taken away from the said Museum at Bloomsbury whether for loan or for any other purpose save in case of a national emergency AND I express my wish that subject to the discretion of the Museum Trustees the present frames of the said drawings shall be retained but shall be protected so as

to prevent damage by handling AND that the drawings comprised in this and the next following bequest to the museum Trustees shall be known as 'the R.W. Lloyd Bequest of Drawings'. [99]

Lloyd clearly visualised them in cabinets in the Print Room and, in February, on display in the great top-lit gallery next to that room in the King Edward VII Wing of the Museum (fig. 9).

However, before accepting the bequest, the then Keeper had checked with Alec Martin, one of Lloyd's executors, to ensure there would be no objection to removing them from their frames and acid backing boards for their own protection, and promised to retain the wash-line mounts. Forty years later, the frames have unfortunately suffered, though not irredeemably, from the terrible pressure on space in the Museum; but the watercolours have not. Modern lighting conditions enable them to be shown during months other than February, but, true to the terms of the will, they are never lent. Several frames have now been restored and the wash-line mounts have been recreated[100] so that the public has for the first time an opportunity to see them as Lloyd himself displayed them and to judge for itself the merits of gold versus white mounts.

Collector as creator

Robert Wylie Lloyd was a mountain climber, but he did not collect Turner watercolours for their depictions of the Alps; rather he acquired each one because it was a fine specimen in perfect condition, with the best provenance he could find. His collection mainly consisted of finished works, not executed on the spot but carefully painted afterwards for a particular patron, for engraving or for exhibition. Modern collectors of Turner's works have tended to covet his late views of Venice, loose sketches and colour beginnings, now familiar to them from decades of exhibitions from the Turner Bequest: their taste has been formed by exposure to the work of the Impressionists and modern artists who have taught many to admire the unfinished sketch over meticulous detail or craftsmanship, or by such arbiters of taste in watercolours as Martin Hardie, whose definition of the finest watercolour was one which consisted of pure broad washes. Lloyd, on the other hand, shared the taste of Turner's own Victorian patrons and collectors, prizing the artist's consummate skill and his genius in interpreting landscape which remained recognisable but was imbued with drama and sentiment.

As the century has progressed, there has been an increasing amount of research on individual collectors of British watercolours, most recently A. P. Oppé (1878–1957) who died the year before Lloyd,[101] and it has become clear that these collectors fall into two main types. Only ten years older than Oppé

Fig. 9. The King Edward VII Wing Prints and Drawings exhibition gallery, British Museum, 1934. Watercolours from the Turner Bequest are shown on the front screen, which incorporated curtains that could be drawn to protect them from the light.

and beginning to collect ten years after him, Lloyd was clearly a 'Victorian' collector who paid large sums for 'guaranteed' quality and provenance by well-known names which would illustrate the history of English watercolours, while Oppé, Iolo Williams, L. G. Duke and others looked for unattributed works that they could use to document the written history. Lloyd and others like him – Stephen Courtauld, Herbert Powell and Agnes and Norman Lupton – were the descendants of collectors like Salting and Sale who collected in many areas and intended their collections of watercolours to grace public institutions where they could be viewed and studied.

In 1931, introducing the catalogue of Herbert Powell's bequest to the nation, another contemporary, Sir Robert Witt, whose collection was destined for the Courtauld Institute, described the method and motives of men like Lloyd:

> . . . the collector makes his selection – good, better, or best, as his taste and growing experience dictate. So the first timid, tentative purchases become the nucleus of something more – a gathering of works of art carefully chosen, . . . that may hope to express the artist that lies in almost everyone. He will go on to try his strength with other collectors in some exhibition. The critics publicly appraise his collection and, in so doing, his taste. He is encouraged to do still better. Others ask his advice, what to buy, what to discard. Has he anything good enough to be welcomed by his local gallery, even, dare he hope, the National Gallery at Millbank, or the Victoria and Albert Museum? What a privilege to lend, what an honour to present, a permanent memorial of his taste and courage! So the collector becomes one with the creator, the layman with the artist, each complementing the other in the fulfilment of their high purpose.[102]

NOTES

1. Colson, p. 160.

2. Enquiries were made of Lloyd's descendants, of his solicitors, Lee and Pembertons, the companies of which he was chairman, including Christie's, the various societies of which he was a member or fellow, and the present owners of Nathaniel Lloyd and Co. An enquiry at the National Register of Archives revealed a small amount of mountaineering correspondence between Lloyd and fellow Alpinists in the National Library of Scotland (Acc. 11022).

3. Blakeney, p. 233. Rumours circulating after his death included tales of charging staff at Christie's for portions of the Christmas venison he was sent every year by the Duke of Devonshire and of sending his staff out to deliver letters by hand rather than spending the pennies on stamps. He could be economical about the electric light, while offering his guests almost priceless wines although he drank little himself (Brown, p. 238). His friend Alec Martin said he appeared reticent and hard to the outside world, but 'kindness itself' to his friends, to whom he was known as 'Robin' (Martin, *The Times*).

4. Frank Davis, *Victorian Patrons of the Arts: 12 Collections and their Owners* (Country Life, 1963), p. 80; see also Coppel 1996a, p. 193.

5. Goldman, p. 67. Dick Kingzett, employed for a time at Christie's, also provided much useful information about Lloyd's chairmanship.

6. Salting collected objets d'art from the 1860s but did not begin to collect watercolours by Turner until the last decade of his life: see Coppel 1996a, pp.190–91, and 1996b, pp. 9–11.

7. See R. Hamlyn, *Henry Tate's Gift: A Centenary Celebration*, exh. cat., Tate Gallery, London, 1997 (n.p.).

8. K. Sloan, *Victorian Painting in the Beaverbrook Art Gallery*, exh. cat., Fredericton, New Brunswick, 1989, especially 'Lord Beaverbrook as a Victorian collector: "An eye for beauty and a hard-nosed sense of value"', pp. 3–8.

9. Martin, *The Times*.

10. Blakeney, p. 233.

11. Champion, p. 97.

12. *Who Was Who 1929–1940*, p. 817: Nathaniel Lloyd (1867–1933), OBE 1918, FSA, FRIBA, was an architect, author and lecturer on architectural subjects.

13. Martin, *The Times*. Nathaniel Lloyd & Co. were lithographers who printed advertis-

ing posters, labels and leaflets, and in the 1940s were responsible for the first tear strips on cellophane and the silver strips in paper currency.

14. 'Works of art for British Museum: Mr R. W. Lloyd's will', *The Times*, Friday [13?] July 1958 (photocopy in Paul Goldman's dossier on Lloyd in P&D).

15. Martin, *The Times*.

16. Agnew's, London Day Book 27: 155.

17. Champion, pp. 97–9, and 'The President's remarks', *Proceedings of the Entomological Society* 23 (1959), pp. 71-2.

18. Champion, p. 98.

19. 'H., W.D.', p. 59. Lloyd's entomological collections are all now in the Museum of Manchester, still in his own cabinets.

20. 'The President's remarks' (n. 17 above), p. 72.

21. Champion, p. 97.

22. The words in quotations were used in his various obituaries, including Alec Martin's, to describe his activities.

23. Allen, pp. 164-5.

24. Casteras, pp. 187-92.

25. Allen, p. 70.

26. Champion, p. 97.

27. Quoted from *Modern Painters*, vol. 4, 'Of mountain beauty', 1856, in Abbot Hall, Kendal, exh. cat., pp. 21, 23.

28. BM P&D register nos 1958-7-12-473 to 2974. When they came to the BM, some folders contained more than one print, with good and bad impressions, mounted and unmounted, all mixed together. This may have been done for probate, in order to list them more easily. A box of index cards and a typescript catalogue which came with the prints describes each print and gives its provenance and value. Lloyd began to collect prints first in the 1900s, then from the bookseller Kundig in Geneva, who purchased for him at sales, and also from Sotheby's and English booksellers. Most were purchased in the 1920s, but Lloyd continued to collect into the 1950s. The solanders were made by H.J. Wood, who also made them for the BM, and the cabinets, two of which stand in the Students' Room in Prints and Drawings and two on the mezzanine level, were made for him by an unknown cabinet-maker.

29. Blakeney, pp. 234–5, lists each of Lloyd's articles in the *Alpine Journal*. Pollinger's son, Adolph, joined them on several of their later climbs, and Lloyd was the author of the elder guide's obituary in the *Alpine Journal* 54, no. 268 (1944), pp. 301–3.

30. Ibid.

31. *The Alpine Club Exhibition: A Loan Collection of Alpine Prints, Engravings and Black and White Drawings*, exh. cat., Alpine Club, 23 Savile Row, 9–29 December 1909. Lloyd lent twenty-eight items including costume prints by G. Lory and Reinhardt and several prints of de Saussure on Mt Blanc. I am grateful to Margaret Ecclestone, Librarian of the Alpine Club, for providing a photocopy of this catalogue and much other relevant material from the *Alpine Journal*.

32. *Exhibition of Swiss Coloured Prints lent by the Members of the Alpine Club and their Friends*, exh. cat., Alpine Club, 1–30 December 1924; lenders' names were not given.

33. Register nos 1958-7-12-2975 to 3149. In his obituary of Lloyd, Professor T. Graham Brown, p. 237, noted that Lloyd had begun his collection of both Alpine books and prints with the purchase of the collection made by Godfrey Ellis, who had lent many works to the 1909 exhibition.

34. The Hon. Patrick Lindsay in coversation with Paul Goldman (dossier in BM).

35. Quoted in a letter from Charles Warren to Paul Goldman, 18 March 1984, in dossier.

36. Agnew, p. 46.

37. Agnew's records indicate that they had purchased the de Wint from Abel Buckley, a well-known Victorian collector, in 1904 for £300 and sold it to J. R. Smith for £472 in 1906, from whom they bought it back in Manchester for the same amount nearly six years later (see Appendix 1).

38. Lloyd became a tenant at I.5 Albany around 1906 and purchased the property at a later date. By the time of his death he resided in I.5, I.6 (on one landing) and also owned I.3 and I.4 (on the landing below). It is not known when he began to rent his country residence, Treago Castle, Herefordshire; he appears to have purchased The Grange, Bampton, Oxfordshire, sometime in the 1940s.

39. Whitworth 1996, p. 17.

40. Agnew, pp. 43–6; a copy of Gerald Agnew's 1932 typescript catalogue of Morland Agnew's (d. 1931) collection of works by Turner and J. R. Cozens is in the P&D library.

41. Agnew, p. 46.

42. Agnew, p. 89, where retirement date given incorrectly as 1924. It is not known what

his relationship was to Herbert Minton Cundall, who wrote widely on English water-colours in the 1920s and worked at the Victoria and Albert Museum from 1865 to 1910, when he retired as Keeper of Paintings.

43. He had discovered that Thomas Ashby in a recent article in the *Burlington Magazine* had confirmed that the view was indeed of Nemi and not Albano. The identification of the lake was evidently a sore point with Cundall, as there was a similar work called 'Lake Albano' in the British Museum: 'I was rather snubbed by Mr Lawrence Binyon – for suggesting that the title should be altered to "Lake Nemi" –, as he said that their drawing came from the – "Cashrode (?) [Cracherode] Collection" – & the title must be correct –; so I was rather glad to have Mr. Ashby's confirmation of my views.'

44. The watercolours borrowed from Lloyd and other private collectors were catalogued, with details of earlier provenance, by Hugh Agnew. Lloyd's watercolours which were reproduced were pl. VII, *Windsor Castle*, and pl. XIV, *Venice: the Grand Canal*.

45. Oppé, pp. 1–2.

46. The typescript catalogue is uniform in typing and format up to *c*.1924, and was afterwards typed by various hands as each group was purchased.

47. Agnew's Drawings stock 7692. Fairfax Murray was a consultant to Agnew's and in 1910 sold his collection of old master drawings to J. Pierpont Morgan.

48. He had died in 1905, but left the rest of his collection to his widow, at whose sale at Christie's in July 1912 Agnew's and a number of other collectors purchased heavily. For Taylor see Craig Hartley, 'John Edward Taylor's collection of Turner watercolours', *Antique Dealer and Collector's Guide*, April 1984, pp. 42–5, and M. Croal's essay, 'Collectors of Turner watercolours in nineteenth century Manchester', in Whitworth 1996, pp. 15–20.

49. Agnew's, London Day Book 28: 70.

50. 'M.I.H.' in a letter in *The Builder* first commented extensively on the fading of indigo in Turner's works in 1857. The same year, Ruskin had written a letter (reprinted in his *Arrows of the Chase*) about the exposure to damp and dirt of four Turners lent to the Manchester exhibition. His own explanation of this letter and a complete reprint of all the correspondence in *The Times* was published as part of *A Catalogue of the Exhibition of Water Colour Drawings by Deceased Masters of the British School*, Royal Institute of Painters in Water Colours, July 1886, with a preface by Linton. Several other articles followed in 1886 and 1887 (listed by S. Wilcox in Rosenthal, p. 325, n. 31). See also Burlington Fine Arts Club, *Reports I. and II. of a Sub-Committee appointed to test certain methods devised for the Preservation of Drawings in Water Colour*, 1895, a private response

to the failure of a promised successor to the *Report to the Science and Art Department of the Committee of Council on Education, on the Action of Light on Water Colours*, 1888.

51. Ruskin had the cabinets made for the Turner drawings in the National Gallery (see Warrell 1995, pp. 24–7, figs 12–13) and for his collections given to Oxford and Cambridge (see Hewison, pp. 126–34, with illus. of Ruskin's cabinets for these institutions). Ruskin's own frames were similar to those used in these cabinets and were specially made for him by Foord & Dickinson, Wardour Street (see ibid., p. 129) and were too shallow to hold roller blinds. For Vaughan's cabinets in the National Gallery of Ireland, see Dawson, pp. 39–40, illus. p. 41. For his own collection Ruskin wrote that he had noted no change since he was ten in the condition of his father's watercolours by Prout and Lewis, which were in 'quiet light', and the Turners at their house in Denmark Hill, 'like the rest of our Turner collection, were protected by covers when no one was looking at them, & were always uncovered at breakfast time, and often, when we had visitors, during the day' (Ruskin, Royal Institute exh. cat. (see n. 50 above), pp. 27, 30).

52. See P. Mason, 'The framing and display of watercolours', in Leeds 1995, pp. 28–38; Jane Bayard, *Works of Splendor and Imagination: The Exhibition Watercolour, 1770–1870*, exh. cat., Yale Center for British Art, New Haven, 1981; Giles Waterfield, *Palaces of Art: Art Galleries in Britain 1790–1990*, exh. cat., Dulwich Picture Gallery, London, 1991–2, *passim*; N. Walker, 'Feature it or file it: mounting and framing at the Whitworth Art Gallery', in N. Bell (ed.), *Historic Framing and Presentation of Watercolours, Drawings and Prints*, Institute of Paper Conservation, 1996, pp. 43–50.

53. One of these survives on *St Huges in the valley of d'Aoust*, 1803 (W 364) in the Soane Museum.

54. Gage 1980, p. 79, with sketch in letter to Robert Stevenson re *Bell Rock lighthouse* frame; see also 'H., M.I.', pp. 25–6, for Turner's own advice on mounts, framing and display.

55. Whittingham 1993, p. 83.

56. Severn's watercolour of *Ruskin's Bedroom at Brantwood* is illustrated in Whitworth 1989, p. 40.

57. 'H., M.I.', p. 26.

58. M. Hardie, 'The framing of water-colours', *Museums Journal* 35 (Sept. 1935), pp. 223–6, first published in *The Times* 10 June 1935. Hardie wrote that the gold mount and frames were pushed by picture dealers and were 'calculated to make the recipient feel that he had obtained good value for his money as well as a suitable accompaniment to the plush and gilt furniture of his Victorian drawing room'.

59. For an illustration, see engraved frontispiece by Henry Moses to Fawkes's 1819 Grosvenor Place exh. cat. (copy in V&A library). According to Thornbury, Turner saved

Fawkes the expense of having the Rhine series mounted: he 'stuck them rudely on cardboard with wafers, to the infinite detriment of the drawings, as it was found when they came to be re-mounted' (II, p. 86). For an example of one of Turner's own early wash-line mounts, see BM 1975 (1).

60. According to D. Kingzett, Morland Agnew had a house built around 1905, which had very bright sunny rooms.

61. Some Turner watercolours which are in these frames with roller blinds are known to have belonged to Ruskin, who was concerned to cover his own watercolours. On occasion it has been thought these were Ruskin's own original frames, but in each case the watercolours went through Agnew's between c.1905 and 1935, when they were reframed and given the blinds.

62. The Monro school watercolours, the early pencil drawings, and *Bonneville*, which had a narrow flat-reed type frame, and the small *Loch Katrine*, which was in a thin elaborate pierced frame, neither of which could take a blind, were without them. Several of Lloyd's other English watercolours had blinds.

63. For example on *Heaped Thundercloud over sea and land - tide coming in* (Agnew's stock 8385, bt 9 December 1915).

64. Agnew's stock 8404, 7 April 1914. Blackburn Art Gallery has Agnew's frames with blinds on three of their Turners: *Terni* (W 701), *Mayence* (W 1110) and *Ramah* (W 1245). Although two had belonged to Ruskin and J. E. Taylor, they had all been through Agnew's in the twentieth century, when they were given the frames with blinds.

65. The lighter frames were recommended by Hardie especially for pure wash watercolours: 'the best watercolour is of such a scale that the painter . . . can get from side to side with one stroke of the brush' (p. 226). In his article Hardie did not mention exposure to light or acid-free boards and since such watercolours are the most susceptible to fading, it is not surprising that most examples by the type of watercolourists he admired, such as Charles Knight, are now sadly very faded and often badly stained.

66. Agnew's Day Book 28: 266. The Leader was bought from Lloyd by Agnew's jointly with Vicars Brothers; it was to be credited towards payment of the account and one-half of any profit over £100 was to go to Lloyd (Picture Stock Book J.1704). A further complication was that interest on a Stanfield painting of *The Shipwreck* was also to go to Lloyd (J.1711).

67. Illustrated in BM 1985 (146).

68. See Appendix 1. The Hunt is illustrated in BM 1985 (152).

69. Agnew's Day Book 28: 321.

70. For the collection of the Rev. Charles Sale (1817–96) of Holt Rectory, Worcestershire, see Estelle Gittins, 'The Sale bequest of nineteenth-century watercolours in the British Museum and Worcester City Art Gallery', BA report for Warwick University, 1995 (copy in P&D library).

71. Agnew's Day Book 29: 168.

72. Ibid., 29: 180.

73. Ibid., 29: 497.

74. Ibid., 29: 324.

75. *Daily Telegraph*, 5 May 1917 (newspaper clipping in Agnew's copy of the Beecham sale catalogue). The Rt Hon. William Henry Smith the younger (1825–91) had built up his father's newsagent business by obtaining the concession to set up stalls on all the important railway stations in England. A philanthropist and later MP, on his death his son, the Hon. William Frederick Danvers Smith (1868-1928; from 1913 Viscount Hambledon), inherited the business and his estate.

76. Agnew's Day Book 32: 378; invoice sent 6 May, but stock book (item 477) indicates it was sold to Lloyd on 5 May but bought by Agnew's from Morland Agnew on 8 May.

77. In 1920 when he bought the *Lucerne*, Agnew's had sent a transcript (now with Lloyd typescript catalogue in P&D). For the most recent and thorough account of these watercolours, see Warrell 1995, Appendix II.

78. B&J 41; Agnew's stock 6623.

79. Agnew's Painting Stock J.7037, 7040; purchased at Christie's sale 18 June 1929 (17, 22). See W. G. Constable, *Richard Wilson*, London 1953, pp. 221 (pl. 113a) and 205 (pl. 85a).

80. Letter from Cundall to Lloyd, National Gallery archives (copy courtesy of Judy Egerton). Armstrong was the author of a number of monographs on British artists, including Turner in 1902.

81. Accepted by the National Gallery Board at a meeting of 12 June 1958 (information kindly communicated by Judy Egerton, letter 30 June 1997). See M. Davies, *National Gallery Catalogues: The British School*, 2nd edn, London, 1959. When Lloyd purchased the Gainsborough it was titled 'An Open Glade in a Forest'.

82. Agnew's Painting Stock 4795 (Gainsborough) and 4804 (Johnson).

83. The collection can be reconstructed from the Valuation for Probate drawn up by Christie's in August 1958 (a copy of which was kindly lent to me by Giles Pemberton of Lee and Pembertons, Lloyd's solicitors) and from the Christie's sale of 'Paintings by Old

Masters and Water-Colour Drawings from the Collection of The Late R. W. Lloyd, Esq.', Friday 29 May 1959. The provenances given for works at this sale indicate they were purchased mainly in the 1940s and 1950s.

84. Martin, *Alpine Journal*, p. 236.

85. His residences at the time of his death are given in the probate list (see n. 83).

86. D. Kingzett remembers Lloyd commissioning a bid for this work. In Lloyd's sale it was lot 108, 6,000 gns to Davidge.

87. Indeed Lloyd's collection of Turners was similar in type and quality to those in their bequests, rather than complementary to Turner's Bequest to the Nation, mainly sketches and colour beginnings and at that time housed in cabinets in the Tate. The Turner Bequest was deposited in the British Museum in 1931 (it has been back at the Tate since 1987).

88. Salting's process of endlessly purifying his collections earned him the nickname 'Prince of Weeders'; see Coppel 1996b, p. 6.

89. The exhibition was repeated at the Fine Art Society, revised and with new catalogue numbers, to reflect alterations to the collection, shortly after Ruskin's death in 1900. Many were sold shortly after the exhibition by the Severns, who had inherited them.

90. See List of Exhibitions, Agnew's 1951. Agnew's copy is annotated with comments by Geoffrey Agnew. Both Evelyn Joll and Dick Kingzett recall that Lloyd would only lend to the exhibition if it was held in February and March when the winter light was weakest.

91. Sale Christie's 29 June 1959: Lloyd's collection was in lots 1–105 (photocopy of catalogue kindly provided by Noël Annesley).

92. Burlington Fine Arts Club Candidates' Book, vol. VIII, no. 1428 (23 November 1918, seconded by Thomas Girtin); Lloyd's membership number was 1414. The Club's papers, including the General Committee and General Meeting Minutes Books, are in the National Art Library (Victoria and Albert Museum).

93. BM P&D Visitors Books. With 6,000 visitors per year (a similar number to the present), it has only been possible to make a cursory check of those covering 1913–22 and 1950. Alec Martin and E. G. Cundall were also regular visitors.

94. Jane Portal, my colleague in the Department of Oriental Antiquities, informs me that although one hat stand from Lloyd's bequest is on display in the Hotung Gallery, most of his lacquerware is now in store because there is not enough room to display it in the gallery. The bequest is nearly all Qing dynasty; some of the better pieces are from the eighteenth century but the majority is nineteenth century. Little research has been done on Chinese lacquer in recent years and Lloyd's bequest was rather overshadowed by the 1974 Garner bequest of predominantly Ming lacquer.

95. Dr George Bankes, Keeper of Ethnography at the Manchester Museum, has kindly informed me that Lloyd's collection included Japanese lacquer, ivories, wood carvings, metalwork (including insects, such as a horned beetle) and weapons. Much of this collection is on permanent display: see booklet on Lloyd's bequest, *A Picture Book of Japanese Art*, intro. J. Forde-Johnston, Manchester Museum, 1965.

96. Basil Gray's report to the Director, June 1958 (BM Central Archives). The BM had only half a dozen of any quality and was permitted to retain the racks on which Lloyd kept them in his chambers (now in storage). Victor Harris, Keeper of Japanese Antiquities, has indicated that, although Lloyd was collecting when the study of Japanese swords was in its infancy and the finest examples were going to American collections, his collection did contain a comparatively high percentage of very fine blades, as well as a number of highly decorative items which were produced by the Japanese in the nineteenth and twentieth centuries for the 'tourist trade'.

97. Martin, *Alpine Journal*, p. 236.

98. Described by Lady Chorley, who visited in the 1940s (quoted in Goldman, pp. 67–8).

99. An extract of the relevant portion of Lloyd's will is in the Central Archives, BM (sent by Lee and Pembertons for the Executors 29 April 1958).

100. Restored by Charles Collinson after a week's course kindly arranged by Richard Hallas at the National Portrait Gallery. The BM's mounters were able to reproduce the wash-line mounts based on examples sent by Claire Stewart of the Towneley Art Gallery, Burnley, and Maggi Simms of Blackburn Museum and Art Gallery.

101. R. Hamlyn and A. Lyles, *British Watercolours from the Oppé Collection*, exh. cat., Tate Gallery, London, 1997, pp. 9–18.

102. Sir Robert Witt, in his preface to C. E. Hughes, *Catalogue of the Herbert Powell Collection of Water-Colours and Drawings of the Early British School*, 1931 (n.p.); Powell's bequest was made to the nation through the National Art Collections Fund, which arranged a touring exhibition of the collection throughout Great Britain, then the Dominions and Colonies, after which, in 1967, the Tate Gallery was offered first choice from the collection.

CATALOGUE OF WORKS BY J.M.W. TURNER IN THE R.W. LLOYD BEQUEST

1(a) Malvern Priory, gatehouse 1793

Pencil, 205 × 263 mm

INSCRIBED: *Malvern Abbey Gate*

PROVENANCE: Charles Stokes; by descent to his niece, Hannah Cooper, 1853; Thomas Hughes; by descent to his niece, Mrs F. Hughes; her sale Sotheby's 28 November 1922 (128), bt Agnew's for Lloyd, £21 plus 5% commission £1 1s. (stock 230)

R.W. Lloyd Bequest 1958-7-12-391

1(b) St Mary's Church, Dover 1793

Pencil, 271 × 211 mm

INSCRIBED: *S Mary. Dover*

PROVENANCE: Charles Stokes; by descent to his niece, Hannah Cooper, 1853; Thomas Hughes; by descent to his niece, Mrs F. Hughes; her sale Sotheby's 28 November 1922 (124), bt Dunthorne, £20 10s.; A.A. Allen, his sale Sotheby's 4 April 1935 (119), bt Agnew's for Lloyd, £25 plus 5% commission £1 5s. (stock 1731)

R.W. Lloyd Bequest 1958-7-12-401

Turner's first signed and dated drawings, made in 1787, are of architectural subjects, and two years later he was working with Thomas Malton junior (1748–1804), a specialist in watercolours and prints of architectural views. By 1792 Turner had begun making summer tours to sketch landscape as well as the buildings within it, and had already developed his own distinctive drawing style, clearly evident in the drawings reproduced here.

In 1921 A.J. Finberg, who had catalogued the Turner Bequest for the National Gallery, where it was then housed, published a booklet about a group of early pencil drawings not in Turner's bequest to the nation. Some of the drawings made by the 18-year-old artist on his important summer tour of 1793 to Hereford, Great Malvern, Tewkesbury and Tintern (see no. 3) were still in the Turner Bequest (TB XII and XIII), but most of them had belonged to Charles Stokes, an early collector of Turner's works, who became his stockbroker from the 1830s and later one of his executors. He died in 1853 and left his collections to his niece, who over the years kept some and sold or exchanged others.[1] When Finberg published four, then in a private collection, the importance of the large group of early draw-

ings which came from the Stokes collection became known to all serious Turner scholars and collectors.

R.W. Lloyd managed to acquire all four drawings that Finberg published as well as five others (see Appendix 1), including the two shown here. Turner had made several drawings of Great Malvern Priory, Worcestershire, especially of the porch, tower, and gatehouse – all that remains of the original monastery – and exhibited a finished watercolour of the porch at the Royal Academy the following spring. The present whereabouts of these pencil drawings, and thus their relationship to the finished watercolours, has not been known to recent cataloguers,[2] but it is now clear that the finished versions were not taken directly from these pencil sketches.

Turner visited Kent and Sussex in the autumn of 1793, and it was then that he made the drawing of St Mary's in Dover. Other drawings made in Canterbury on the same trip were the basis for another watercolour he exhibited at the Royal Academy the following year.

1. See Warrell 1997, pp. 199–200.
2. See Whitworth 1984, p. 11, and 1996, no. 5.

a

b

2(a)   Mont Blanc from the banks of the Arve, near Sallenches in Savoy

Blue and grey wash over pencil, 231 × 376 mm

PROVENANCE: W. G. Rawlinson; ? his sale (Different Properties), Christie's 28 June 1912 (87), bt Agnew's, £21; Agnew's 1913 (85); bt Lloyd 8 April 1913, £35 (stock 7746)

EXHIBITIONS: BFAC 1922–3 (75)

R. W. Lloyd Bequest 1958-7-12-387

2(b)   Posillipo

Blue and grey wash over pencil, 203 × 323 mm

PROVENANCE: Dr Thomas Monro, his sale Christie's 26-28 June, 1, 2 July 1833 (?), ? bt John Rushout, 2nd B. Northwick (d. 1859); by descent, Lord Northwick's sale Sotheby's 6 July 1921 (177), bt Agnew's for Lloyd, £3 10s. plus 5% commission 3s. 6d. (stock 45)

EXHIBITIONS: BFAC 1922–3 (77)

R. W. Lloyd Bequest 1958-7-12-392

Dr Thomas Monro (1759–1833) was a specialist in mental illness and, as a dedicated amateur artist, had known John Robert Cozens long before he was consigned to his care in 1792. Monro moved in a circle of collectors, amateurs and patrons of British art, and when he took up residence in one of the great new houses in the Adelphi in the Strand he invited these friends and young artists, including Turner, Thomas Girtin, Thomas Hearne and Edward Dayes, to gather there to study and copy his collection. His friends also lent works from their collections, among them many watercolours, drawings and sketchbooks by Cozens. Monro's purpose in running this 'academy' was partly to offer the artists the opportunity to study and improve their own work, but he also paid them a small amount for their copies, which he kept.

In November 1798 Turner and Girtin told the diarist Joseph Farington that they 'had been employed by Dr. Monro 3 years to draw at his house in the evenings. They went at 6 and staid till Ten. Girtin drew in outlines and Turner washed in the effects. They were chiefly employed in copying the outlines or unfinished drawings of Cozens &c &c of which Copies they made finished drawings'.[1] At Dr Monro's sale these drawings were described variously as by Turner or Girtin, but many were the combined efforts of both artists. The work of determining the different hands has barely begun; Lloyd purchased his watercolours as examples by Turner alone, and indeed they do not bear any of the hallmarks of Girtin's distinctive pencil style found on many of the Monro school drawings.

Lloyd acquired the view of Mont Blanc early in his collecting career, when he was visiting Agnew's annual exhibitions and buying works without a particular collecting policy in mind. This clearly caught his eye as a view of a mountain that was the focus of his own Alpine climbing expeditions. The composition is based on a watercolour which once belonged to Richard Payne Knight, with whom Cozens made his first visit to the Alps in 1776.[2] The view of Posillipo is based on sketches made by Cozens on his second trip to Italy, in the company of William Beckford in 1782, but, like no. 2(a), it is not an exact copy of Cozens's original.[3] It is from a group Lloyd purchased at Lord Northwick's sale in 1921, when he was concerned to fill gaps in his collection of Turner's work.

1. Quoted in Wilton 1984, p. 9.

2. BM 1900-4-11-13; Bell and Girtin (5).

3. See Bell and Girtin (282, 294).

a

b

3 Tintern Abbey, the transept *c.* 1795

Watercolour, 345 × 254 mm

PROVENANCE: J. E. Taylor by 1887; Mrs Taylor's sale Christie's 5 July 1912 (59), bt Agnew's, £399, for J. F. Haworth (stock 7766); his sale Christie's 25 June 1926 (151), bt Agnew's for Lloyd, £273 plus 5% commission £13 13s. (stock 902)

EXHIBITIONS: RA 1887 (26); Agnew's 1913 (81); Agnew's 1951 (8); RA 1951–2 (513); BM 1959, 1960; BM 1966, 1969 (1)

R. W. Lloyd Bequest 1958-7-12-400 (W 59)

In 1788, at the age of 13, Turner was copying plates from William Gilpin's guidebook to the 'picturesque', *Observations on a tour in the mountains and lakes of Cumberland and Westmoreland* (1782).[1] He made his first visit to the Wye valley, which had been the subject of another of Gilpin's famous 'picturesque' tours, in 1792 and returned there during his summer tour the following year. He exhibited his first watercolour of Tintern Abbey (a view of the choir) at the Royal Academy in 1794 (W 57, Victoria and Albert Museum) and another, *The Transept of Tintern Abbey, Monmouthshire*, in 1795. Gilpin's *Tour of the Wye* had already made the site extremely popular with the growing number of tourists in search of picturesque ruins that nature had made her own, where time had 'worn off all traces of the rule . . . blunted the sharp edges of the chisel; and broken the regularity of opposing parts . . . adding its own ornament'.[2] Turner's training enabled him to make the most of the architectural framework of this ruin, but that may not have been the only reason why his most successful views of it were taken from the inside – Gilpin had also pointed out that its outward appearance was spoilt by the shabby houses surrounding it, inhabited by beggars.

Lloyd believed his version to be the one shown at the Royal Academy in 1795, as it had been identified as such when it was lent to the Royal Academy Winter Exhibition in 1887 by the great Turner collector John Edward Taylor (1830–1905). Confusion about the two versions of this subject had been compounded by Finberg, who in 1909 stated that the version owned by Taylor was a view of the choir and 'probably not by Turner'.[3] In 1917 C. F. Bell identified the work shown at the Royal Academy in 1795 as the version now in the Ashmolean Museum (W 58).[4] When Lloyd purchased this drawing, Gerald Agnew wrote to him explaining that Finberg had recently informed him that when he saw the drawing again at Taylor's sale in 1912 he had changed his mind and decided the drawing was by Turner. But Finberg never published his reattribution and many writers still doubted the authenticity of Lloyd's version. In 1975, however, Andrew Wilton suggested that, 'if anything', the Ashmolean version, 'with its hard summary detail and possibly false signature, is the imitation'.[5]

Certainly Lloyd's version bears all the hallmarks of Turner's best work of the period; however, this watercolour may have been the combined effort of Turner and another artist – the three main figures are more beautifully and elegantly drawn than those Turner usually produced, the area of watercolour immediately surrounding them shows signs of having been filled in later, and the figure of the gardener is clearly surrounded by a pencil sketch of a much larger, clumsier figure.

1. Wilton 1987, p. 45.

2. Gilpin 1782, pp. 31–7.

3. Finberg 1909, I, p. 37, under TB XXIII A.

4. *Walpole Society* V (1915–17), p. 77.

5. BM 1975 (5).

4 St Erasmus in Bishop Islip's Chapel, Westminster Abbey 1796

Watercolour over pencil, 546 × 398 mm

INSCRIBED: *WILLIAM TURNER NATUS 1775*

PROVENANCE: Purchased by Edward Lascelles, jun. (d.1814) 17 May 1797, 3 gns; by descent to Lord Harewood; his sale Christie's 1 May 1858 (36), bt Colnaghi, £109; John Dillon, his sale Christie's 17 April 1869 (47), bt Agnew's, £178 10s.; bt John Heugh of Gaunt's House, Dorset, 19 April 1869; his sale Christie's 17 March 1877 (35), bt Vokins, £231; John Morris by 1884; D. S. Thompson, 1912; sale Christie's 1917, bt Boswell; Agnew's, purchased from Boswell and Sons 22 November 1917, £250, bt Lloyd 4 December 1917, £400 (stock 8701)

EXHIBITIONS: RA 1796 (395); BFAC 1871 (89); BFAC 1884 (166); ? Guildhall 1899 (83: 'Westminster'); BFAC 1919 (38); Agnew's 1920 (13); RA 1951–2 (505); BM 1959, 1960; BM 1966, 1969 (2); BM 1975 (9); BM 1985 (85)

R.W. Lloyd Bequest 1958-7-12-402 (W 138)

If Lloyd had any doubts that his version of *Tintern Abbey* was the one exhibited at the Royal Academy by Turner in 1795, he could have entertained no such doubts that this view of the interior of Westminster Abbey was the one shown the following year. This was also the year the 21-year-old artist exhibited his first oil painting at the Royal Academy, and he seems to point to his own prodigious genius in a self-conscious, if not modest manner in the quasi-memorial inscription on the tomb in the foreground. Several writers on Turner have since endorsed his own opinion of his abilities by using this work to illustrate not only his early mature mastery of architectural draughtsmanship and the watercolour medium, but also the strength of his unique vision, even genius, which has achieved such a monumental effect in a relatively small-scale work on paper.[1]

The artist's 'own' monument serves to mark the viewpoint as from the eye level of a visitor standing in the north ambulatory of the abbey, a shaft of light falling on Bishop Islip's double-tiered, screened chapel. The doorway further to the right leads to a vestibule containing the Chapel of St Erasmus, which Bishop Islip had moved twice: first when he laid the foundation of Henry VII's Chapel where the saint's once stood, and, secondly, when his own chapel was built over the spot to which he had transferred it.[2] This explains the very precise wording of the title Turner gave this watercolour, which has caused much confusion in the past.

St Erasmus is the patron saint of sailors, and the subject was a fortuitous choice for a young artist who was not only exhibiting his first marine painting but was to make the sea such a significant aspect of his future work. The spectator's eye is drawn to the visitor in black and others beyond, and to the realisation that they are dwarfed by towering pillars and arches, shafts of light falling blue and clear from the upper windows in the crossing and the clerestory, out of our sight. The natural gloom of the abbey on a dull day is transformed into glowing golden stone. All the lessons Turner learnt from his early study of perspective, the prints of G. B. Piranesi and the watercolours of Louis Ducros have been put to use: pentimenti around the steps to the left show that he reduced their horizontal intrusion into the composition, and he has manipulated light and shade to minimise and strip the surfaces of the distracting accretions of hundreds of years, leaving the pure lines of the architecture to emphasise the upward thrust and glorious soaring space.

1. See Hill 1984, p. 26; Wilton 1987, p. 8; Gage 1987, pp. 101–2; Egerton 1995, p. 48.
2. Macmichael, pp. 55–9.

42

5 St Edmund's Church, Salisbury

Watercolour, 384 × 270 mm

SIGNED: *W Turner*

PROVENANCE: Sir Richard Colt Hoare; by descent to Sir Henry Hoare, his sale Christie's 30 July and 4 and 7 August 1883 (in a volume), bt Rev. J. H. Ellis; H. Arthur Steward, his sale Christie's 28 July 1927 (9), bt Agnew's for Lloyd, £141 15s. plus 5% commission £7 1s. 9d.

EXHIBITIONS: Agnew's 1928 (18); BM 1959, 1960; BM 1966, 1969 (3); BM 1975 (23)

R. W. Lloyd Bequest 1958-7-12-403 (W 205)

Sir Richard Colt Hoare, 2nd Bt (1758–1838), an antiquarian and talented amateur, inherited Stourhead in Wiltshire from his grandfather the banker Henry Hoare in 1785. The latter had created the magnificent gardens and begun the picture collection, but Sir Richard added the Picture Gallery and Library and proceeded to fill them not only with old master paintings picked up on his many tours of the Continent, but also with the works of contemporary artists and a unique collection of books on British history and topography. His own great study, *The Ancient History of Wiltshire* (1810–21), was one of the earliest objective field studies in British archaeology.[1]

Colt Hoare was an accomplished landscape painter in watercolours, having taken lessons from John 'Warwick' Smith. In Italy he had commissioned several large, highly finished watercolours from the Swiss artist Louis Ducros, which he hung in his Library, not far from several watercolours by John Robert Cozens in the Ante-Room. He also admired the work of Philip James de Loutherbourg, whose *Avalanche* he had copied for his own collection. It is not surprising, then, to learn that Hoare was an early patron of Turner, who probably first visited Stourhead in 1795. We know that while there he carefully examined Hoare's collection of prints by Piranesi, whose influence along with that of Ducros was immediately evident in the the architectural interiors he exhibited at the Royal Academy the following year (see no. 4).

Turner's first works for Hoare were views of the garden at Stourhead, followed by a series of views of Salisbury, including the Cathedral, which had recently undergone restoration by James Wyatt (1787–92). A list made in about 1798 recording twenty subjects to be drawn is among Turner's papers (TB CCCLXVIII A). The ten of the Cathedral were to be larger in size; they were begun around 1797 but only eight were completed (by 1805); by 1822 they were hanging together in the Column Room at Stourhead. A group of ten smaller watercolours, all views in and around the city, were also planned but probably never completed, work on them ceasing with the large group in 1805. They included no. 3, 'Ancient Arch in Mr Wyndham's Garden', one of the first to be finished, *c.* 1797 (see no. 6), and no. 9, 'St Edmund's Church', the present drawing.[2]

This small parish church was probably included in this group because its main body was once the chancel and chancel chapels of the large collegiate church of St Edmund which once stood on this site. This lovely Perpendicular-style church, set in a spacious turfed churchyard next to the Council House in Bedwin Street, was declared redundant in 1973.[3]

1. See K. Woodbridge, *Stourhead*, National Trust 1975, p. 9.

2. Gage 1974, pp. 65–8; Whittingham 1976, pp. 45 (n. 92), 54–5.

3. Pevsner 1975, p. 435.

6   The ancient arch in Mr Wyndham's garden, Salisbury   *c.* 1797

Watercolour over pencil, 379 × 293 mm

SIGNED: *W Turner*

PROVENANCE: Sir Richard Colt Hoare; by descent to Sir Henry Hoare, his sale Christie's 30 July and 4 and 7 August 1883 (in a volume), bt Rev. J. H. Ellis; H. Arthur Steward, his sale Christie's 28 July 1927 (7), bt Agnew's for Lloyd, £68 5s. plus 5% commission £3 8s. 3d.

EXHIBITIONS: Agnew's 1928 (14); BM 1959, 1960; BM 1966, 1969 (4); BM 1975 (22)

R. W. Lloyd Bequest 1958-7-12-404 (W 206)

Of the nine completed smaller views of Salisbury drawn for Sir Richard Colt Hoare between 1797 and 1805, three are now in the British Museum: the present watercolour, *St Edmund's Church, Salisbury* (no. 5), and *St Martin's Church* (1948-10-9-8). The fact that this series of views was kept in a volume while at Stourhead, and probably for some time afterwards, meant that unlike the larger series, which hung in the Column Room at Stourhead from 1822 until the 1883 sale, these smaller ones still retained their wonderful fresh condition and bright colours when they were sold in 1927. The debt we owe R.W. Lloyd for preserving his own collection of Turner watercolours from exposure to light is clear when we compare those he purchased in 1927 with *St Martin's Church* and another purchased at the same sale, *Gateway to the Close*, both now sadly faded.[1]

It is thus due to Lloyd's insistence on blinds that we can still appreciate the hollyhocks lining the curving pink garden path in *The ancient arch in Mr Wyndham's garden*. This was the title given in Hoare's list of the series but it has also traditionally been titled *A gothic porch*, a more accurate description of the structure, which was in fact the porch of a door in the north transept of Salisbury Cathedral. James Wyatt's renovations in the early 1790s had concentrated on emphasising the lightness, elegance and harmony of style of an outstandingly simple and monumental Gothic structure by removing screens and other objects and partitioning walls which cluttered the interior. He also removed anything which he felt was not part of the 'original' pure Gothic building, including this porch which

> was not intended for the use that was made of it . . . and was probably brought from Old Sarum: this porch, with the consent of the Dean and Chapter, is removed to a garden belonging to Henry Penruddocke Wyndham, Esq., near Salisbury, [a friend of Colt Hoare] who has added a spire and other Gothic ornaments to it, which it is supposed originally to have had.[2]

Wyatt's renovations were controversial even in his own day: Colt Hoare had not appreciated his alterations to Durham, but did approve of the 'neo-classical' effect on the light and shade in Salisbury Cathedral, which he must have hoped that Turner's watercolours would record. That Turner was indeed sympathetic to these effects cannot be surprising in view of his own interest in the work of Piranesi and Ducros. However, the Society of Antiquaries and the *Gentleman's Magazine* expressed strong opposition in a series of articles to Wyatt's 'improvements' and dubbed him Wyatt 'the Destroyer'.[3]

1. Munro, p. 66.

2. W. Dodsworth, *A Guide to the Cathedral Church of Salisbury . . . with an account of Wyatt's improvements . . .* , pp. 30–31, quoted in Gage 1974, p. 71.

3. Colvin, p. 1109.

7 St Agatha's Abbey, Easby   *c.* 1797–8

Watercolour, 270 × 371 mm

SIGNED: *W Turner*

PROVENANCE: John Ruskin after 1878; bequeathed to Arthur Severn; Fine Art Society, bt Agnew's 10 May 1900, £630 (stock 3069); bt Walter F. Morice 16 February 1901, £600; his sale Christie's 12 May 1922 (60), bt Agnew's for Lloyd, £441 plus 5% commission £22 1s. (stock 154)

EXHIBITIONS: Fine Art Society 1900 (6); Agnew's 1951 (3)

R. W. Lloyd Bequest 1958-7-12-406 (W 274)

The Hon. Edward Lascelles (d. 1814) was, like Colt Hoare, the Capel family (Earls of Essex) and Dr Monro, an important early patron of Turner. He probably met Dr Monro, Turner and Thomas Girtin through the Capels, who had a house near the doctor at Bushey, Hertfordshire. Lascelles' father had inherited Harewood in 1795; he immediately began to fill it with paintings and new furnishings, and the following year his son also began to use his own new allowance to collect. Paul Sandby, William Payne and, not surprisingly, Girtin were among the artists whose work he purchased, and in May 1797 he bought his first picture by Turner, of Westminster Abbey (see no. 4), exhibited at the Royal Academy the previous year. He invited Turner to visit Harewood, and in June 1797 the artist set out, filling two large sketchbooks with views of Yorkshire, Durham, Northumberland and the Lake District, which he toured *en route* before settling in to draw Harewood itself and its more immediate surroundings.[1] The sketches were to provide rich material for Turner over the next thirty years.

St Agatha's Abbey is only a mile downstream from Richmond in Yorkshire, on the Swale river, in almost as sequestered a setting as when it was founded in 1155.[2] Turner made two sketches of it in his *North of England* sketchbook: one a detailed study of its north range, the other the view from downstream (TB XXXIV 24, 25). The present watercolour shows the abbey from near the mill in the opposite direction, and is on a sheet of the same size and paper as the other sketchbook he used on this tour, *Tweed and Lakes* (TB XXXV): as David Hill has pointed out, it seems to be a detached sheet from it.[3] He used the other views for several finished watercolours, one of the most successful of which is now also in the British Museum (1915-3-13-48; W 561) and dates from *c.* 1818 when Turner was working on illustrations for *Whitaker's History of Yorkshire*.[4] In the present view, the buildings in the distance distract the eye from the ruin. The other views show the abbey, with its cracking, leaning solarium, silhouetted on the banks of a river plain, the setting more romantic than the 'picturesque' one shown here, which owes a great deal in composition, colouring and even mannerisms to Turner's fellow pupil at Dr Monro's, Thomas Girtin. The records at Agnew's have established that it was this version that was acquired by Ruskin after 1878 and exhibited with his other Turner watercolours at the Fine Art Society in 1900. It was an acquisition which enabled him to represent in his own collection the vital early mutual influence of Turner and Girtin on each other's work.

1. See Hill 1984, pp. 24–6, 33.

2. Hill 1996, p. 42.

3. Ibid, pp. 42 (n. 58), 193.

4. Hill 1980, nos 7, 129.

48

W Turner

8 Mountain study: a view in North Wales? *c.* 1798–1800

Watercolour over pencil, 247 × 418 mm

PROVENANCE: John Edward Taylor, his sale Christie's 8 July 1912 (133), bt Agnew's 40 gns (stock 7811); Agnew's 1913 (111), bt Ralph Brocklebank 23 May 1913, £70; his sale (late of Haughton Hall, Cheshire) Christie's 7 July 1922 (39), bt ? 50 gns; G. T. Veitch; his sale Sotheby's 7 December 1927 (118), bt Agnew's for Lloyd, £40 plus commission £2 (stock 1068)

EXHIBITIONS: BM 1985 (86)

R. W. Lloyd Bequest 1958-7-12-405 (W 258)

John Edward Taylor purchased a watercolour of Llyn Cwellyn, North Wales, in 1863 and presented it to the Whitworth Art Gallery nearly thirty years later.[1] It was based on a sketch Turner made on his first visit to the mountains of North Wales in 1798 and showed the large cliff that was the most popular starting point for the ascent of Snowdon. The sketch was inscribed 'Hon Mr Lacelles', indicating that the finished work may have been intended for Harewood (see no. 4). Mr Taylor's watercolour was badly faded in comparison with the sketch, and it is not surprising to find that the present watercolour, which also came from Taylor's collection, also shows signs of having faded, particularly in the blue edge visible along the top. Thus the slate-like greys and blues that at first seem to confirm that it depicts a Welsh view are deceptive.

The present watercolour is clearly a working out rather than a finished piece, and bore the rather vague title 'Mountain study' at J. E. Taylor's sale. While it was at Agnew's in 1913 'Langdale Pikes' was inscribed on their copy of the catalogue. Certainly this view resembles some of the wilder passes north of Grasmere in Cumbria, but on the whole it shares the same brooding, romantic, misty approach to the landscape that characterises Turner's views in North Wales, not all of which, especially those around Snowdon, have been clearly identified.[2] Andrew Wilton noted that the size of the sheet fits the *Smaller Fonthill* sketchbook (TB XLVIII) associated with views in a similar technique made on a tour in the north-west in 1801; but

he also felt that the watercolour probably related to a Welsh tour, resembling the large colour studies of scenes in Snowdonia (TB LX (a), see entry under W 258). The limited range of colours in the present work, its reliance on rough pencil notes to indicate the path and rocks in the foreground, the broadness with which the washes were applied, as well as the finger-scumbling in the stream on the left, all point to this watercolour being drawn on the spot. When compared, for example, with his view of *St Agatha's Abbey* of the previous year (no. 7), another work possibly begun in the open air but worked up later, it is abundantly clear that Turner's approach not only to mountainous landscape, but also to the watercolour medium, was profoundly affected by his tours of North Wales in 1798 and 1799. It was this experience that prepared him for his brief encounter with the Alps in 1802 and, perhaps more importantly, for his response to the Rhine in 1817.

Thomas Girtin also made a tour of North Wales in 1798, reacting to the Welsh scenery in a way new to his work; but his response was usually grounded in reality, with the insertion of recognisable detail in the foreground – a village, bridge or stepping stones – the overall effect remaining lyrical rather than reflecting the brooding monumentality and drama of Turner's response.

1. Whitworth 1996, no. 16.
2. See Lyles 1989, p. 37.

50

9 Bonneville 1802

Watercolour with pen and brown ink over pencil, touched with white, on white paper prepared with a grey wash on recto and verso, 308 × 473 mm

PROVENANCE: Rev. Stopford A. Brooke of 1 Manchester Square by 1899; Mrs L. Jacks, sale Christie's 17 December 1920 (51), bt in, then bt Agnew's 110 gns for Lloyd 29 December 1920, £115 10s. (stock 9865)

EXHIBITIONS: Guildhall 1899 (96); Birmingham 1899 (36); BM 1959, 1969; BM 1966, 1969 (5)

R. W. Lloyd Bequest 1958-7-12-407 (W 354)

Nine separate watercolours by Turner are on sheets that were originally pages in his *St Gothard and Mont Blanc* sketchbook (TB LXXV; W 354-62), which he used on his first tour of the Alps in 1802. Most are on this type of paper (Whatman 1801, although no watermark is visible on this sheet), prepared with grey wash just like that he was to use in several of the Rhine sketches (see no. 14). Several of them were used as the basis for finished commissions for patrons such as W. B. Cooke and the Swinburne family (see no. 10). Turner produced a small group of finished works in oil and watercolour of this particular view in Savoy, interpreting them through the influence of the pictorial structure he had found in a group of paintings by Poussin which had been brought to England by Sir Peter Bourgeois and Noel Desenfans.[1] This work, however, was the basis for an oil (B&J 148) painted for Walter Fawkes.

John Ruskin particularly admired the group of sketches of Bonneville, Chamonix and the Valley of the Cluses, all in this part of Savoy, and may have been responsible for their removal from the sketchbook. He himself at one time owned most of them, although his earlier ownership of this particular view has not been established. Some he felt were coloured on the spot and others worked up later, and he found them not 'delightful and exhilarating', as did his contemporaries, but 'an unbroken influence of gloomy majesty, making him [Turner] henceforth of entirely solemn heart in all his work'.[2]

The grey washed paper and muted tones of this view add to the impression that it is an unfinished work or a sketching out for a later, larger composition, but the white bodycolour in the distant mountains has flaked slightly and, although there is no clear evidence, the overall tones appear slightly faded. Almost alone among Lloyd's purchases of Turner watercolours, this one was not given a new frame with a roller blind when he bought it through Agnew's after it was bought in at the Jacks sale in 1920. The frame was a gilt flat reed type with no gold slip and bore the framer/dealer's label of Samuel Jenkins, established 1824, of Duke Street, Manchester; it was too narrow to support the insertion of a roller blind.

1. Wilton 1987, pp. 6–9.
2. Quoted in Whitworth 1989, p. 46.

10 Lake of Brienz 1809

Watercolour, 388 × 556 mm

INSCRIBED: *J M W Turner RA PP 1809*

PROVENANCE: Sir John Swinburne of Capheaton, Northumberland; by descent to Miss Julia Swinburne; the late Miss Isabel Swinburne, sale Christie's 26 May 1916 (118: as 'Lake Thun'), bt Agnew's for Lloyd, £630 plus 5% commission £31 10s. (stock 8410)

EXHIBITIONS: RA 1887 (47); Agnew's 1919 (34); BM 1959, 1960; BM 1966, 1969 (6); BM 1975 (38); BM 1985 (88)

R. W. Lloyd Bequest 1958-7-12-409 (W 386)

In February 1802 Turner was elected to the Royal Academy, and later that year, like many of his fellow Academicians, he took the opportunity provided by the Treaty of Amiens to make his first visit to the Continent. Unlike most of the others, however, Turner headed immediately for the Alps. Many of the places he visited he had first seen in the watercolours by Cozens that he had copied at Dr Monro's (see no. 2). The drawings he himself made in these places were slight pencil sketches which he had worked up with black chalk and white washes by the time he reached Paris. Bonneville (see no. 9), the source of the Arveron, and the St Gothard Pass were among the first Alpine scenes to appear in both watercolours and oils.

In the 1790s Turner gave drawing lessons to Julia Bennett, later Lady Gordon, who became a faithful patron. Her sister was married to Sir John Swinburne, 6th Bt (1762–1860), of Capheaton, Northumberland. Sir John himself was to play a formative role as a patron of British art[1] and purchased his first oil painting from Turner in 1813 (see no. 43). His brother Edward (1765–1847) was an accomplished amateur, and the name 'Mr. Edward Swinburne' appeared in one of Turner's sketchbooks as early as 1799; ten years later 'Ed. Swinburne Esq.' paid 40 guineas for a watercolour of Grenoble (now lost). Family tradition stated that it was Sir John who commissioned this view and its companion, as well as the two views on the Rhine painted in 1820, *Biebrich* and *Marxburg* (nos 20 and 21). The Swin-

burne family's patronage of Turner continued until at least 1840, when he painted the magnificent view of *Tancarville on the Seine* (no. 43) for one of them, but the details have been complicated by the fact that Sir John's son was also called Edward (1788–1855).[2] In fact Sir John and his brother Edward, who spent much of his life at Capheaton and died without issue,[3] were both very active patrons in Northumberland, closely involved with Newcastle institutions and often lending to their exhibitions.[4]

The Swinburnes' friend Walter Fawkes selected a number of sketches from Turner's 1802 Swiss sketchbooks to be worked up into finished watercolours; the Swinburnes were among the few other patrons to do the same. This watercolour is based on a sheet in the *Grenoble* sketchbook which Finberg correctly identified as 'On the Lake of Brienz'.[5] The Falhorn range is clearly identifiable in the distance. However, it was always called 'Lake Thun' by the Swinburne family and was exhibited under this incorrect title until 1976.[6]

1. Heleniak, pp. 162, 258 (n. 11).

2. See Lyles 1988, pp. 28 and 46 (nn. 61, 74).

3. See Hill 1981/2, p. 2.

4. Usherwood 1984, pp. 29, 81 and 97.

5. TB LXXIV 43: see Wilton 1982 (12).

6. Russell and Wilton, p. 56.

11   Castle of Chillon   *c.* 1809

Watercolour, 281 × 395 mm

INSCRIBED: *I M W Turner RA*

PROVENANCE: Sir John Swinburne of Capheaton, Northumberland; by descent to Miss Julia Swinburne; the late Miss Isabel Swinburne, sale Christie's 26 May 1916 (119), bt Agnew's for Lloyd, £682 10s., plus 5% commission £34 2s. 6d. (stock 8411)

EXHIBITIONS: RA 1887 (46); Agnew's 1919 (18); BM 1959, 1960; BM 1966, 1969 (7)

R. W. Lloyd Bequest 1958-7-12-410 (W 390)

In 1810 Turner exhibited in his own gallery in Harley Street an oil painting of the *Lake of Geneva* from a high point above Montreux, showing the Castle of Chillon and the mouth of the Rhône in the valley at the end of the lake beyond (B&J 103). The mood of the oil painting was Italianate, with stone pines dominating the composition and a group of dancing women in the foreground reminiscent of nymphs in a painting by Claude. It was purchased by Walter Fawkes, a friend of Sir John Swinburne who commissioned the present watercolour and the view of the *Lake of Brienz* while Turner was working on the oil. All were based on sketches made on his first visit to the Alps in 1802. The larger watercolour (no. 10) has often been described, like the large oil painting, as Italianate in mood; but the smaller view of the *Castle of Chillon*, although it could be taken from a detail of the composition in oil, could never be described as anything but Swiss. The costumes of the women in the foreground and the activity they are engaged in are specific to the location: their pointed hats and the gloves for bleaching worn by the figure on the left have all been carefully studied and recorded by the artist, as have the fishermen in the boat to the right.

The fresh breeze coming from the lake stirs up the ripples and waves on the shore and billows out the sheet held by the standing figure in white, whose gesture points to the castle in the shadow of the steep mountainside. Lights glimmer from its windows and shine from the tips of its turrets, but the shade in which it stands heightens the cold white snow on the Dents du Midi beyond. A mood of sunny calm would be totally inappropriate for a view of a fortress famous for its dungeons, which held the 'Prisoner of Chillon' - a prior of Geneva who was chained to one of its pillars for four years in the sixteenth century for attempting to introduce the Reformation to Catholic Savoy. A few years after Turner painted this watercolour, the location became even more renowned as the setting of Byron's celebrated poem *The Prisoner of Chillon* (1816). The poet had been inspired by the romantic site of the castle and its tale during his notorious visit to Switzerland in 1816 when he met Percy Bysshe Shelley and his young wife, Mary. She too had been greatly moved by her experience of Chillon, and the future authoress of *Frankenstein* pronounced the dungeons to be an enduring symbol of 'that cold and inhuman tyranny, which it has been the delight of man to exercise over man'.[1]

1. Quoted in Wilton 1982 (13).

12 Rosehill, Sussex 1816

Watercolour, 379 × 556 mm

PROVENANCE: John Fuller of Rosehill Park; by descent to Sir Charles then Sir Alexander Acland-Hood, Bt (d. 1908); his sale Christie's 4 April 1908 (97), bt Colnaghi, 340 gns; Rev. J. W. R. Brocklebank; by descent to Lieut. Brocklebank, RN, his sale Christie's 25 November 1927 (92), bt Agnew's for Lloyd, £294 plus 5% commission £14 14s. (stock 1053)

EXHIBITIONS: London, 1862 (1898); Agnew's 1928 (26), Manchester (43); BM 1959, 1960; BM 1966, 1969 (8); BM 1975 (47)

R. W. Lloyd Bequest 1958-7-12-411 (W 438)

John ('Mad Jack') Fuller, the Tory MP for Sussex 1801–12, was one of Turner's most eccentric patrons. His vast fortune was based on West Indian sugar plantations and he was, not surprisingly, a strong advocate of slavery. He insulted the Speaker of the House during a debate on the issue in 1810, upsetting his local constituency.[1] He seems to have been at pains to appease it, however, since shortly afterwards, in April 1810, Farington recorded that Fuller had engaged Turner to make three or four watercolour views of the area around his 6,000-acre estate in Sussex, which were intended to be engraved. An oil painting of Rosehill Park (B&J 211), showing the alterations to the vast estate on the Downs, possibly carried out by Humphry Repton around 1806, was also probably painted that year.[2] Rosehill Park, now Brightling Park, is about four miles from Battle and about ten from Hastings. The vales of Pevensey and Ashburnham can be seen from its grounds, and Turner executed four large watercolours of these beautiful rolling valleys with their views of Rosehill and neighbouring estates and the distant coastline, as well as one of Battle Abbey. They were engraved between 1816 and 1818 by Joseph Stadler in coloured aquatint (R 822-5) and printed privately for Fuller to circulate amongst his friends.

Fuller eventually owned thirteen watercolours of Rosehill and its neighbourhood. Apart from the four that were aquatinted, several others were engraved by W. B. Cooke for *Views in Sussex* (1817–18). They were large watercolours: two of the loveliest, even larger than the present work, of the vales of Ashburnham and Heathfield, came to the British Museum with the Salting Bequest (W 425, 427). The present more intimate view (based on a pencil study in the second Hastings sketchbook, TB CXXXIX 32v-34) was never engraved and shows some signs of having been hung for a long period. It seems to have been intended as a more personal family record of Rosehill itself, emphasising the 'natural' gardens recently created for Fuller by Repton and carefully detailing the alterations carried out to the house in 1810–12 by the 'truly Tory' architect Robert Smirke. When Turner painted this watercolour view, Smirke was engaged on alterations and additions to Montagu House (the British Museum), including the temporary room for the Elgin marbles.[3]

During this period, while Smirke was carrying out alterations to Fuller's house and adding buildings to his garden, he was also commissioned by Fuller to build a pyramidal mausoleum in Brightling churchyard. Fuller's reputation as an eccentric was literally 'sealed' upon his death when he was interred inside it, seated upright, fully clothed, wearing a top hat and holding a glass, surrounded by bottles of his favourite claret.[4]

1. See Kriz, pp. 98–9.
2. For Repton's plans see Colvin, p. 802, and Stroud, p. 172.
3. Colvin, pp. 875–9.
4. Shanes 1981, p. 5.

Lurlei-berg and St Goarshausen.

J. M. W. Turner R.A.

Cat. no. 15

Turner's series of views on the Rhine, from the Fawkes collection at Farnley Hall (nos 13–19)

In August 1817 Turner spent ten days exploring the middle Rhine between Cologne and Mainz, travelling southwards mainly on foot and returning downstream more swiftly by boat. Although it is generally agreed that the pencil sketches in his Rhine sketchbooks (TB CLX and CLXI) were done on the spot, there is some disagreement as to when and where Turner executed the fifty-one watercolours on grey prepared paper that he produced on his arrival at Farnley in autumn 1817, 'in a slovenly roll, from his breast-pocket'. According to Walter Thornbury, Turner's early biographer and the source of this anecdote, the bundle was promptly purchased by Walter Fawkes for £500.

Thornbury stated that the watercolours were executed on the spot at the rate of three a day, but others have suggested that they were begun from nature and then worked up each night back at the inn, or that the series was produced from the pencil sketches after Turner's return to England, either at Raby Castle, where he stayed before going on to Farnley, or possibly even at Farnley itself as a special commission from Fawkes. Certainly some of the watercolours, especially the view of an *Abbey near Coblenz* (no. 13), have the spontaneity and hastily applied effects we have come to associate with works done from the motif, *en plein air*; but the application of bodycolour and the occasional rearrangement of the elements of the composition, to conform with an artistic rather than a topographically correct viewpoint, indicate that they are comparable with the series of Swiss scenes Turner was to produce after his tours of the early 1840s and which were to be used to gain commissions for more detailed finished works (see nos 46–7). It seems most likely that the Rhine views were produced by Turner shortly after his tour with the same purpose: a little more worked-up than sketches, they were intended to give an idea of the appearance of a finished work on which future patrons could decide to commission a larger, more highly wrought watercolour for their walls. Such a comparatively sketchy style as that found in the fifty-one views along the Rhine would not have been to the taste of most purchasers at that time, and Turner must have been greatly surprised to find a buyer for the entire group so quickly. It is interesting that they were not included in the exhibition of watercolours from his collection that Walter Fawkes held in his London house at 45 Grosvenor Place in 1819.

In keeping with their 'sketchy' quality, Fawkes did not frame his Rhine views. According to Thornbury, Turner himself mounted them crudely on cardboard, clearly intending them to be stored in a portfolio. Indeed, in 1850, when Fawkes's son sent a list of them to Turner so that he could check the titles, it was headed 'Sketches on the Rhine in a Case', and we can be grateful that their colours and freshness were thus retained. In 1889, they were all lent to the Royal Academy Exhibition, but the following year the family sold thirty-five through Christie's, retaining the best sixteen for themselves. In 1902 these were shown at Lawrie & Co. for the benefit of King's Hospital, and around 1912 Alex Finberg catalogued and reproduced them in a lavish publication, after which they were sold to Agnew's.

The finest works retained by the Fawkes family thus came onto the market shortly after R. W. Lloyd began to collect, and he was fortunate to acquire seven of them (nos 13–19). Thornbury, who saw them all together at Farnley in the 1850s, found them 'most exquisite for sad tenderness, for purity, twilight poetry, truth, and perfection of harmony. They are to the eye, what the finest verses of Tennyson are to the ear. They do what so few things on earth do: *completely satisfy* the mind.'

LITERATURE: Thornbury, II, pp. 84–7; Finberg 1912, *passim*; Hill 1980, pp. 64–71; Stader, pp. 17–27; Wilton 1982, nos 14-25; Hill 1988, p. 22 (where they were incorrectly said to have been exhibited in 1819); Morrell, *passim* (who argues they were done on tour); Powell 1991, pp. 11–36, 97–105, and 1995, pp. 9–29, 89–105.

13　Abbey near Coblenz　1817

Watercolour, with bodycolour, on white paper [J. Whatman 1816] prepared with grey wash on recto and verso, 195 × 313 mm

PROVENANCE: Walter Fawkes of Farnley, 1817; by descent to Rev. Ayscough Fawkes then Frederick H. Fawkes, bt Agnew's 22 July 1912 (with 20 others), £500 (stock 7867); Agnew's Manchester 1912 (6), 700 gns; Agnew's 1913 (3); bt Lloyd 20 August 1913 (with four others for £3,350)

EXHIBITIONS: RA 1889 (57); Lawrie & Co. 1902 (20); RA 1934 (900) (766, where incorrect provenance given); Agnew's 1951 (58); BM 1959, 1960; BM 1966, 1969 (9); BM 1975 (50); BM 1985 (89a)

R. W. Lloyd Bequest 1958-7-12-412 (W 672)

As with many of Turner's watercolours of the Rhine, the traditional title of this work has caused confusion concerning the exact spot depicted. Coming to the Rhine from Holland, Turner walked southward, or upstream, mainly staying on the west bank; however, most guidebooks to the Rhine describe the river from a boat travelling downstream (i.e. northwards), from Mainz towards Cologne. The pencil study for this view in Turner's *Waterloo and Rhine* sketchbook (TB CLX 56v) was once thought to be inscribed *Abernath*, which was interpreted as Andernach, a town some distance north of Coblenz. However, Cecilia Powell convincingly reread the inscription as *Oberwerth* and was thus able to identify the view as taken looking up the Rhine from the village of Pfaffendorf.[1] While staying in Coblenz, Turner crossed the river to study the great fortress of Ehrenbreitstein on its enormous rock overlooking the city at the confluence with the Moselle. The fort's monumental shape was to occupy many of Turner's compositions later in his career. Pfaffendorf was only a short walk away and had been particularly recommended by the Reverend John Gardnor, whose 1792 guide to the Rhine Turner had studied carefully.[2] Indeed, a later guidebook noted that 'near Pfaffendorf is a stone bench, shaded by three poplars, whence there is a fine view of Coblenz and Ehrenbreitstein'.[3]

When he sketched this view, however, Turner had already spent two days in Coblenz and, having finished his studies of the dark looming citadel on his right, he turned to look southwards towards the next stage of his journey. Rays of sunlight filtered through the trees onto the path and beyond it men towed a barge in the shallow waters of the river as it flowed past the island of Oberwoerth. The island's nunnery had been suppressed thirty years previously and its ruined arches can be glimpsed in Turner's watercolour through the lattice of poplar trees lining the bank. Upstream on the left, the river meanders around the edge of the island and the town of Oberlahnstein, its church spires clearly visible on the far bank of the Lahn river where it flows into the Rhine. Schloss Stolzenfels stands guard on its mountainous perch on the opposite bank, and the castle of Marxburg rises on a blue hill just visible in the far distance beyond the trunk of the poplar on the far left.

The misty tones and dappled sunlight in this view are much fresher than the deeper, darker tones found in most of the other Rhine views, and it is this *plein-air* effect which has suggested to many writers on this series that they were painted by Turner on the spot or the same evening once he was back at his hotel.

1. Powell 1991, p. 197.
2. Ibid., p. 56 (n. 25).
3. Schreiber, p. 223.

14 Oberlahnstein 1817

Watercolour, touched with bodycolour, on white paper prepared with a grey wash on recto and verso, 198 × 316 mm

PROVENANCE: Walter Fawkes of Farnley; by descent to Rev. Ayscough Fawkes, his sale Christie's 27 June 1890 (20), bt Agnew's, £147 (stock 9866); Agnew's 1891 (263), 250 gns; 1892 (155), 200 gns; Agnew's Liverpool 1893 (199), 200 gns; Agnew's 1894 (293), 180 gns; bt Walter F. Morice 20 February 1897, £150; his sale Christie's 12 May 1922 (61), bt Agnew's for Lloyd, £252 plus 5% commission £12 12s. (stock 155)

EXHIBITIONS: RA 1889 (55); BM 1959, 1960; BM 1966, 1969 (10)

R. W. Lloyd Bequest 1958-7-12-413 (W 654)

Schloss Stolzenfels, on its perch opposite the mouth of the River Lahn, featured in the distance of no. 13 but is here seen dominating the view from the well of Oberlahnstein. This town, on the southern bank of the Lahn at its confluence with the Rhine, was a substantial one, which Turner's guidebook by Charles Campbell informed him was mentioned by Ausonius in his poem on the Moselle. The book also noted the town's 'fine gardens' with 'beautiful prospects from its windows and terraces', and continued: 'The Rhine here is very broad, and on the left bank we have a prospect of some rural dwellings, called Krippe; and not far from the village, of Kapellen, is the dismantled castel of Stolzenfels, built upon a mountain.'[1] Krippe is just visible on the far shore in Turner's view; and although his guidebook did not inform him of it, the castle had in fact been dismantled by the French in 1689 and was not rebuilt until after Turner's visit, by Friedrich Wilhelm IV between 1836 and 1842. Campbell did not pay much attention to the architecture of these buildings, merely pointing out particularly picturesque ones and noting any references to classical authors or more recent poets such as Byron. He did not, for example, describe the substantial Martinsburg which dominates Turner's view of the town; but a later guidebook explained that it was the old castle, belonging to Nassau, and had become the residence of the bailiff.[2] Its terrace and windows commanded a fine view and there was a mineral spring in the vicinity. It is the well of this spring that forms the focus of Turner's watercolour.

Turner started to inscribe 'Children playing at a Well w[. . .]' on his sketch for this view.[3] In his final version, however, he concentrated on the mineral properties of the well, focusing on a group of women filling stone bottles with its water, which they will carry away in a type of panier-wheelbarrow. It is a warm sunny day; a figure approaches along the shaded roadway on the right, while the sun lights on the women's dresses, the well, and the walls of the castle behind, and falls on the arm of the cross in the left foreground. Turner created these highlights by scraping away the preparatory grey wash to reveal the white paper underneath, or sometimes by wetting and rubbing the paper to lighten the grey. The patch of sky above the Schloss Stolzenfels has been left to show the grey wash with which the paper was prepared and clearly indicates the medium tone the artist was working up with brighter washes of blue and green and highlighting with bodycolours of gold, amber, red, brown and blue. A close examination reveals all the tricks Turner used to work his magic on a plain sheet of washed grey paper, and his thumbprint is clearly visible working light and shade into the trees on the right.

1. C. Campbell, p. 192.

2. Schreiber, p. 222.

3. *Waterloo and Rhine* sketchbook, TB CLX 93, now inserted between 57 and 58; see Powell 1991, p. 197.

15   Lurleiberg and St Goarshausen   1817

Watercolour, with bodycolour, on white paper [Whatman 1816] prepared with grey wash, recto and verso, 197 × 309 mm. Verso: slight pencil sketch of same subject

PROVENANCE: Walter Fawkes of Farnley; by descent to Rev. Ayscough Fawkes then Frederick H. Fawkes, bt Agnew's 22 July 1912 (with 20 others), £400 (stock 7871); Agnew's, Manchester 1912 (109), 600 gns; Agnew's 1913 (4), bt Lloyd 20 August 1913 (with four others for £3,350)

EXHIBITIONS: RA, 1889 (41); Lawrie & Co. 1902 (50); BM 1959, 1960; BM 1966, 1969 (11); BM 1975 (48)

R. W. Lloyd Bequest 1958-7-12-416 (W 684)

While preparing for his tour, Turner made a note in his sketchbook of a place a small distance below Oberwesel, where there was 'a dangerous whirlpool a mile below where banks are very close'.[1] When he arrived at St Goar and began his walk towards Oberwesel, Turner would have found, as his guidebook described, that at this point the river was of 'extraordinary depth, and the majestic mountains are crowned with forests which leave little more than a rod between their feet and the water'. Travelling from the south, as Turner was to do on his journey home, the guidebook noted that

> here the river, after winding to the right, brings us within sight of an immense rock upon the right bank, called Lurleyberg; here an echo is said to repeat the voices of the people in the boats, etc. three or four times . . . The spot called *Bank*, in this part of the Rhine, is more dangerous than the *Trou* of Bingen, especially at low water. Immediately under this shelf, or *banc*, is a whirlpool called the Labryinth, and which, as the wrecks of vessels lost here have been found in the Trou of Bingen, is supposed to communicate with it.[2]

The romantic legend of the siren who lured boatmen to their death upon the rock was not yet part of popular folklore when Turner visited the Lorelei, but its origins were clear in the deep waters, echoing cliffs and dangerous whirlpools with their communicating wrecks; the ruined castles on crags above would have intensified the attraction of the area for an artist like Turner, attuned to and searching for the sublime.

This particular view appears to have been taken from midstream, perhaps from a boat on Turner's return journey; indeed, a quick series of sketches he made of this area, squeezed onto an opening out of sequence in the front of his *Waterloo and Rhine* sketchbook, includes the first sketch for this composition, which shows Burg Katz on its crag above the town of St Goarshausen in the distance.[3] In the finished watercolour the dark rock with its falls of water dwarfs the fisherman in the shadows below, and the scratched highlights and salmon boat moored to stakes midstream hint at the whirlpool and dangers at the foot of the cliff beyond. Once the dangers have been negotiated, a safe haven is promised in the distant town lit by the setting sun falling through breaking clouds. This now famous rock of the Lorelei seems to have haunted Turner after his Rhine tour in 1817, as the group of fifty-one watercolours at Farnley Hall included seven in which the 427-foot (130 m) precipice dominated the composition, and many of his late watercolours included other mountains and cliffs whose shapes echoed its massive form.

1. TB CLIX 24; Powell 1991, p. 191.

2. C. Campbell, pp. 189–90.

3. TB CLX 1v (1); Powell 1991, pp. 59 (n. 59), 195.

16   Hirzenach below St Goar   1817

Watercolour, with bodycolour, on white paper [Whatman 1814] prepared with grey wash, 210 × 325 mm

PROVENANCE: Walter Fawkes of Farnley; by descent to Rev. Ayscough Fawkes then Frederick H. Fawkes, bt Agnew's 22 July 1912 (with 20 others), £800 (stock 7870); Agnew's, Manchester 1912 (90), 1,100 gns; Agnew's 1913 (7); bt Lloyd 20 August 1913 (with four others for £3,350)

EXHIBITIONS: RA 1889 (50); Lawrie & Co. 1902 (48); Agnew's 1951 (54)

R. W. Lloyd Bequest 1958-7-12-415 (W 681)

Widely acclaimed as the finest road in Europe, the *route Napoléon* ran along the west bank of the Rhine from Cologne to Mainz. As Turner's tour along the river in 1817 was made mainly on foot, frequently walking as many as thirty-five miles a day, he had reason to be grateful to the French engineers who during their occupation of the Rhineland had blasted through the basaltic rocks and levelled the surface of the old mountain road. Where swollen torrents had once swept over it, taking much of the surface of the road with them, the French had built arched sewers for the torrents to pass beneath it; one of these is clearly visible on the left of this view, which was based on a sketch showing the bend of the river at Hirzenach, looking downstream from the west bank.[1]

In fact the road might be described as the main subject of this watercolour, which otherwise depicts what at first appears to be one of the less remarkable stretches of the river, featuring no castles or other notable sites. Hirzenach itself was situated close to an ancient priory and was apparently picturesquely surrounded by the huts of vine-dressers. Apart from a hint of vines climbing the slopes on the left, none of this was visible from the spot Turner chose for his picture, which seems to focus instead on the achievements of engineers. However, closer inspection indicates that this feat of engineering was not allowed to dominate the view completely. The guidebooks pointed out that Hirzenach was located on a part of the Rhine where the river formed a beautiful bay. Turner inserted his usual reference to the local 'commerce and manufactures' in the form of the fishermen on the river and upon the bank, some of their silvery-blue catch spilling out of the basket in the foreground, and he emphasised the calm expanse of the river here by placing other fishermen in a boat to draw our eyes to the far right and the sunlit bend in the distance. The grey that he used as a mid-tone preparation on this side of the sheet only, and the overall lightness which was the result of leaving the lower edge and right corner blank, lend a poetic peacefulness to the watercolour. The guidebooks also noted that the river here was surrounded by heights rich in silver, copper, marble, slate, lime and lead. Touches of bodycolour in pinks, yellows, ochres and deep reds and browns remind us of the wealth of the minerals underground and in the rich fertile earth.

1. TB CLX 60 (1); see Powell 1991, pp. 19, 197.

17   Burg Sooneck with Bacharach in the distance   1817

Watercolour, with bodycolour, on white paper prepared with grey wash, 220 × 360 mm

PROVENANCE: Walter Fawkes of Farnley; by descent to Rev. Ayscough Fawkes then Frederick N. Fawkes, bt Agnew's 22 July 1912 (with 20 others), £800 (stock 7873); Agnew's, Manchester 1912 (96) 1,150 gns; Agnew's 1913 (39); bt Lloyd 20 August 1913 (with four others for £3,350)

EXHIBITIONS: RA 1889 (33); Lawrie & Co. 1902 (17); Agnew's 1951 (61); BM 1959, 1960; BM 1966, 1969 (12)

R. W. Lloyd Bequest 1958-7-12-417 (W 671)

The grey wash Turner used to prepare most of the fifty-one views along the Rhine that once belonged to Fawkes lends a poetic and calm uniformity to the series. Some, like the present work and the view of *Hirzenach* (no. 16), were prepared with the grey washes on one side only; others are washed on both recto and verso, and occasionally have a rough graphite sketch on the back. The same restricted group of green, brown and grey watercolours are highlighted and deepened with yellow, blue, red, ochre and occasionally bright green bodycolours, used throughout the series, each one scraped, rubbed and thumbprinted into a work of beauty, or given detailed form with lines created by the finest point of a brush.

This view, like *Hirzenach*, emphasises the peaceful expanse of one of the wider parts of the river, its beauty captured so successfully that Turner chose it as the basis for one of the larger finished watercolours he created around 1820 for the Swinburne family (see no. 20). The larger work was more detailed and Turner even went so far as to make a colour study in preparation;[1] but the present smaller watercolour is faithful to the original sketch in the *Waterloo and Rhine* sketchbook.[2] Taken from vineyards being harvested part-way up a slope, the view downstream shows a succession of castles, themselves strung on alternating high and low peaks as if on a vine. On the left, or west, bank the sunlit ruins of Burg Sooneck are followed by two smaller castles, with the sunlit town of Bacharach nestled below Burg Stahleck on a distant bend. On the opposite bank, the large town of Lorch lies in a shadow, protected by Burg Nollig high above it.

When in the autumn of 1912 Agnew's exhibited in their Manchester rooms the large group of twenty Rhine watercolours they had purchased from F. N. Fawkes that summer, they attached higher values to the present watercolour and to the views of *Hirzenach* and the *Johannisberg*, priced at 1,100, 1,150 and 1,350 guineas respectively. Contemporary taste clearly favoured the brighter, more peaceful and serene landscapes over the darkly romantic works more highly valued in our own day, such as the *Lurleiberg*, which was then priced at 600 guineas, or the more overtly topographical ones like *Oberlahnstein*, which they had difficulty selling in the 1890s at 180 guineas and which Lloyd managed to acquire in 1922 for only £252.

1. TB CCLXIII 120; see Wilton 1982 (20) and Powell 1991 (16, 17).
2. TB CLX 62.

18   Bingen from the Nahe   1817

Watercolour, with bodycolour, on white paper [Whatman 1816] prepared with grey wash, 195 × 316 mm. Verso: pencil sketch of the Lorelei on paper prepared with grey wash, inscribed *Laureligh*

PROVENANCE: Walter Fawkes of Farnley; by descent to Rev. Ayscough Fawkes then Frederick H. Fawkes, bt Agnew's 22 July 1912 (with 20 others), £450 (stock 7874); Agnew's, Manchester 1912 (70), 700 gns; Agnew's 1913 (8); bt Lloyd 20 August 1913 (with four others for £3,350)

EXHIBITIONS: RA 1889 (29); ? Lawrie & Co. 1902 (47?)

R. W. Lloyd Bequest 1958-7-12-414 (W 682)

This watercolour has always previously been titled 'Bingen from the Lorch' or 'Lake' or 'Loch', a conflation of three locations: the towns of Bingen and Lorch and a place where the Nahe river enters the Rhine and 'foams and murmurs like the sea in passing through the famous lock, called the Bingerloch'.[1] It is not surprising that Turner's lack of German and general British unfamiliarity with the intricacies of the place-names along the Rhine have resulted in such strange titles, which were retained because they were the ones with which the works were christened when they were in Walter Fawkes' collection.[2] The presence and location of the bridge and the lack of an island in the middle of the river made nonsense of the traditional titles for this work. Fortunately, Cecilia Powell has convincingly corrected all the Rhine titles, explained the exact viewpoints and locations depicted, and matched them with the corresponding drawings in Turner's sketchbooks.[3] She has identified the present view as the Drusus Bridge over the Nahe river, looking eastwards down the Nahe to the town of Bingen at the river's confluence with the Rhine. Burg Ehrenfels, 'on a high cliff, broken, craggy, and impending',[4] is on the far bank of the Rhine, and Burg Klopp, largely destroyed in 1711, sprawls on the hill behind Bingen on the right.

The drawing on the prepared grey verso of this watercolour is more detailed than most and appears to be almost the same composition found in two finished views of the *Lorelei* (W 646, Whitworth

Art Gallery, and W 686, Thaw Collection). Turner scratched particularly deeply in places on this sheet to create the white highlights of the figures on the bridge, the washing on the wall and the ripples in the river; but he knew exactly what his paper could withstand and never went right through. There are indications that the finished drawing was not able to sustain all the rough treatment it received, both in the distant and the more recent past. There was much old damage to the left edge of the drawing, even loss of pigment where it was particularly bent, and the lower right corner was lost altogether. When the drawing originally came to the British Museum it was placed in a mount with a perspex verso so that the drawing on the back could be seen. However, a type of tape was used to fix the perspex which eventually seeped into the drawing itself, causing an oily mark to appear along the right and upper edges.[5] Most of this oily residue has now been painstakingly removed.

1. C. Campbell, p. 184.
2. See Finberg 1912, pp. 23–4.
3. Powell 1991, pp. 59 (n. 59), 195ff.
4. C. Campbell, p. 183.
5. See the reproduction in Wilton 1982, pl. 21.

19 The Johannisberg 1817

Watercolour with bodycolour on white paper [Whatman 1814] prepared with grey wash, 214 × 338 mm

PROVENANCE: Walter Fawkes of Farnley; by descent to Rev. Ayscough Fawkes then Frederick H. Fawkes, bt Agnew's 22 July 1912 (with 20 others), £800 (stock 7868); Agnew's, Manchester 1912 (41), 1,350 gns; bt H. E. Walters 7 February 1913, £1,450; sold to Agnew's 27 March 1918, £1,300 (one of a group of watercolours purchased by them from Walters; stock 8774); group sold by Agnew's 6 May 1918 to A. E. Lawley for £10,000; his sale Christie's 25 February 1921 (127), bt Agnew's for Lloyd, £126 plus 5% commission £6 6s. (stock 9924)

EXHIBITIONS: RA 1889 (27); Lawrie & Co. 1902 (15); Agnew's, 1913 (12); Agnew's 1951 (59); BM 1959,1960; BM 1966, 1969 (13); BM 1975 (49); BM 1985 (89b)

R. W. Lloyd Bequest 1958-7-12-418 (W 673)

On his journey up the Rhine, Turner covered the thirty-five miles from St Goar to Mainz in one day, 25 August. He walked the first half on the west bank, making quick sketches as he passed the Lorelei, Hirzenach, Sooneck, Lorch and all the villages and castles dotted between them, and then, pausing in Bingen long enough to make sketches of the town, he caught a boat for the remainder of that day's journey. In this, the final section of the Rhine he was to visit, the river assumes a completely different character from the winding bends and cliffs of the Middle Rhine with its picturesque villages, sharply sloping vineyards and omnipresent castles and ruins. Known as the Rheingau, this stretch is tranquil and peaceful, its calm expansive width dotted with islands and bordered by spreading villages and more gentle hills, their slopes covered with undulating vineyards.

Turner probably boarded the regular passage boat, which was drawn by horses, and as a result of this and the completely different landscape before him, his sketches for this stage are understandably more panoramic, recording long stretches of the river's banks, its villages dotted with spires and low hills capped with palaces and monasteries, including the famous priory of St John on the hill in the distance here. Even at horse-pace, impressions followed one another in quick succession, as witnessed by Turner's notes on his sketch for this view: 'Edrich; Johannisberg; Vines; Elfeldt; Clouds'.[1] This watercolour and the view of *Biebrich Palace* (no. 20) demonstrate Turner's ability to respond instantly to a completely different atmosphere as well as a different landscape. The broad expanse of the river enabled him to display a wide variety of the river craft he had been studying so carefully as he progressed along it, and gave him ample opportunity to work his magic in the sparkling reflections on its calm surface and the scattered clouds dragging a misty shower across the sky.

1. TB CLX 70v-71; Powell 1991, p. 198, and 1995, pp. 25–6.

20 Biebrich Palace on the Rhine 1820

Watercolour with touches of bodycolour, 293 × 453 mm

PROVENANCE: Painted for a member of the Swinburne family; by descent to Julia Swinburne by 1887; H. E. Heyman; bt Agnew's 31 July 1912 (with *Tancarville*, £4,000 plus 10% commission £400); bt Lloyd 8 April 1913, £2,500 (stock 7879)

EXHIBITIONS: Newcastle 1828 (74); RA 1887 (61); Agnew's, 1913 (24); Agnew's, Manchester 1913 (107); Agnew's, 1924 (23); RA 1934 (896) (770); BFAC 1936-7 (103); Agnew's, 1951 (56); BM 1959, 1960; BM 1975 (79)

R. W. Lloyd Bequest 1958-7-12-420 (W 691)

Although the 'sketchy' character of the watercolours in the Rhine series purchased by Walter Fawkes would not have been to the taste of most patrons of the time, there were a few who envied Fawkes his possession of them and requested their own copies of some of the compositions. The publisher and engraver W. B. Cooke was one of these, and in 1819 he contracted Turner to produce thirty-six views of the Rhine to be engraved by J. C. Allen and published by Cooke and John Murray. Turner had already produced several of these when the project was abandoned the following year owing to the appearance of a rival publication, and Cooke himself purchased three of the finished watercolours. They were slightly smaller than the originals, but far more elaborate in detail, as one would expect of a series to be engraved for the armchair traveller.

The Swinburne family of Capheaton, Northumberland (see no. 10), were friends of Walter Fawkes (both had London residences in Grosvenor Place) and were among the small group of patrons who owned (possibly commissioned) copies of the series at Farnley Hall. The original watercolour of *Biebrich* owned by Fawkes was sold in 1890 and bequeathed by its purchaser to the National Gallery of Wales, Cardiff, eight years later (W 638). It measures 229 × 343 mm, smaller than the present watercolour, and contains fewer details; it is as if all the components of the landscape and objects in the fore- and middle-grounds of the first version have been brought forward and

into greater focus in this larger version produced for the Swinburne family. The palace was renowned as the most princely on the banks of the Rhine, with vast and beautiful gardens extending behind it.[1] It was built at the beginning of the eighteenth century by Prince George Augustus, with a central dining room in the form of a rotunda (clearly visible in Turner's view). Campbell pointed out that it was once tenanted for one night by King George II and his brother the Duke of Cumberland.[2]

Turner exaggerated the length of the wings of the palace in this larger work and increased the number of men working on the long wooden jetty reaching into the river, using the addition of a small skiff at its end to draw our attention across the image to the bustle of activity in the reeds on the left. In spite of all this busyness, half the composition is given to one of Turner's most stunning skies, and the emphasis on the horizontal creates a work of serene beauty, providing a fitting complement to its companion from the Swinburne collection, *Marxburg* (no. 21), with its hills, trees and castles reaching upwards in a symphony of forms and colours.

1. See Wilton 1982 (23).
2. C. Campbell, p. 180.

21 Marxburg 1820

Watercolour with touches of bodycolour, 291 × 458 mm

INSCRIBED: *IMW Turner 1820* and *MARXBOURG and BRUGBERG* [Braubach] *on the RHINE*; piece of old mount preserved
in backboard of frame, inscribed: *Marxbourg on the Rhine / JMW Turner* and *1823*

PROVENANCE: Painted for a member of the Swinburne family; by descent to Miss Julia Swinburne by 1887; her sale,
Christie's 17 March 1900 (78) ('property of a lady'); bt Vokins, £840; Agnew's, 1910 (186), 1,600 gns; bt Charles Fairfax Murray;
sold by him through Agnew's, 1 April 1912, £886 10s. plus £60 10s. (commission) to Lloyd, April 1912 (stock 7692), £985

EXHIBITIONS: Newcastle 1828 (71); RA 1887 (59); Agnew's 1913 (61); RA 1934 (890) (769); BM 1959, 1960; BM 1966, 1969 (16);
BM 1975 (80); BM 1985 (89c)

R. W. Lloyd Bequest 1958-7-12-422 (W 692)

Turner's first glimpse of the Marxburg had been from Pfaffendorf just south of Coblenz (no. 13), where its distinctive shape appeared in the furthest distance on the left. The castle took its name from St Mark the Evangelist, and was famous for being the only castle on the Rhine never to have been captured or wrecked. Its good condition is manifest in this large finished watercolour, where it rises in the centre of the composition, the crowning glory of a rich and prosperous scene. The original watercolour on which this was based, painted for Walter Fawkes (W 653, Indianapolis Museum of Art), captured Turner's first proper view of the castle as recorded in his sketchbook (TB CLX 52), looking up at the impregnable fortress from the path below. This viewpoint was highly extolled and even illustrated in Gardnor's 1792 guidebook, which Turner had studied carefully before setting out on his tour.[1]

In contrast to the companion view of *Biebrich* (no. 20), where he brought everything forward in the finished work, here Turner added more foreground to the finished version and pushed the fluid central group of entwining trees further back, to frame and enhance the strong upward thrust of the crag on which the castle stood. Not only was this version larger and more detailed than the one in the original series, but like *Biebrich* it was painted on white paper which had not been prepared with grey wash, and the result was a brilliant luminosity of a type quite different from the sombre beauty of the earlier group. Detailed still-life vignettes of flowers and a panier-wheelbarrow laden with refreshments were added to the foreground to give the entire work the substance and content needed to compete with oil paintings on the walls where these works were intended to hang. Although at first sight there is little sign of the Rhine itself, we are not allowed to forget the presence of the river whose existence brings the wealthy harvest manifest on its banks; the streams which are its source flow down the slopes to the left of the castle, and the standing woman in the foreground points to a blue strip of the Rhine itself, a light mist rising to envelop the town of Braubach beside it.

1. Powell 1991, p. 29 (fig. 19).

22 Hastings from the sea 1818

Watercolour, 398 × 591 mm

SIGNED AND DATED: *I M W Turner RA 1818*

ENGRAVED: By R. Wallis for E. Gambart in 1851 (R 665)

PROVENANCE: W.B. Cooke; Benjamin Windus of Tottenham by 1835; ? Ernest Gambart (by 1851; but second state of print published with dedication to C.S. Bale); Charles Sackville Bale by 1871; his sale Christie's 13 May 1881 (197), bt Vokins, £1,102 10s.; Stephen G. Holland; his sale Christie's 26 June 1908 (258), bt Agnew's for Sir Joseph Beecham £1,680 (stock 6738); his sale, Christie's 3 May 1917 (150), bt Agnew's for Lloyd, £1,260 plus 5% commission £63 (stock 8572)

EXHIBITIONS: W. B. Cooke 1822 (9); BFAC 1871 (127); RA 1891 (94); Agnew's 1909 (31); BM 1959, 1960; BM 1966, 1969 (14); BM 1975 (54); BM 1985 (90)

R. W. Lloyd Bequest 1958-7-12-419 (W 504)

The fishing town of Hastings on the East Sussex coast had by the end of the eighteenth century become a health resort to rival Brighton, and in the following years its growth was stimulated by its role as a garrison town during the Napoleonic wars.[1] According to the evidence of his sketchbooks, Turner's first encounters with Hastings took place around 1805, but he probably spent more time there when he was working for John Fuller in the area around Rosehill Park in 1810 and again in 1815–16 (see no. 12).

The publisher W. B. Cooke was able to use some of Turner's watercolours of the Downs for his *Views in Sussex*, published in 1818–20, and he hoped to follow these with a series of *Views at Hastings and its vicinity*, but Turner was slow meeting deadlines and the project was abandoned. The present large watercolour was titled 'Hastings from the Sea' in Cooke's exhibition of 1822, and it was singled out for praise in Ackermann's *Repository of Arts* as displaying 'great power and truth'.[2] Benjamin Godfrey Windus seems to have seen it there and made it the first of over 200 watercolours by Turner that he was to own:[3] it is shown clearly over the fireplace on the left of Scarlett Davis's 1835 watercolour of his house at Tottenham (frontispiece). When Windus's collection was partly catalogued by William Robinson in 1840, this painting was called 'Hastings, from

the sea'.[4] It has often been confused with the smaller watercolour lent by Henry Vaughan to the Art Treasures exhibition in Manchester in 1857, under the same title. Vaughan's watercolour, painted around 1826–7, is now known as *Shipwreck off Hastings* (W 511).[5]

Further confusion has been caused by the fact that Lloyd's watercolour has been known as 'Hastings: deep sea fishing' since at least 1871, but as Eric Shanes has pointed out, the title was misleading because there is no deep-sea fishing in the area at all.[6] The boats in the foreground may in fact be engaged in line-fishing, which Turner was to depict in a later oil painting (Victoria and Albert Museum; B&J 368) which seems to be loosely based on this watercolour. Whatever its title, however, there can be no doubt that this is a *tour de force* of marine painting in watercolour and deserved its pride of place in Windus's collection.

1. Hastings, pp. 3–8.

2. Quoted in BM 1985 (90).

3. Gage 1987, p. 173.

4. Shanes 1984a, p. 56.

5. See Dawson, pp. 80–81, and Warrell 1997, p. 196.

6. Shanes 1981 (13).

23 The Colosseum, Rome 1820

Watercolour, 277 × 293 mm

INSCRIBED: *Colliseum Rome W Turner 1820*

PROVENANCE: W. Fawkes; by descent to Frederick H. Fawkes; bt Agnew's 22 July 1912, £450 (stock 7859); Agnew's Manchester 1912 (80), 600 gns; Agnew's 1913 (73), 750 gns; Agnew's 1914 (161), 600 gns; bt Rev. J.W.R. Brocklebank, 28 March 1914, £500 (stock 7859); by descent to Lieut. Brocklebank, RN, his sale Christie's 25 November 1927 (91), bt Agnew's for Lloyd, £441 plus 5% commission £22 1s.

EXHIBITIONS: Leeds 1839 (70); Lawrie & Co. 1902 (64); Grafton Galleries, 1911 (211); Agnew's 1928 London (27), Manchester (46); Agnew's 1951 (23); BM 1975 (74)

R. W. Lloyd Bequest 1958-7-12-421 (W 723)

In August 1819 Turner finally set out from Calais to satisfy his long-cherished desire to see Italy. Arriving in Rome near the end of October, he filled over a dozen sketchbooks in that city alone, working up water- and bodycolour studies on grey-washed grounds in his lodgings in the evenings. Having thus filled his sketchbooks with reference material and armed himself with compositional studies suggestive of colour, atmosphere and mood, on his return Turner was able to begin to execute commissions arising from this journey, which had been of vital significance for his development as an artist. A series of watercolours were intended for Charles Heath's *Picturesque Views in Italy*; another group were to appear much later as vignettes in Samuel Rogers's *Italy*, and eight carefully chosen subjects were to be worked up into watercolours for his favourite patron, Walter Fawkes of Farnley Hall.

The paintings for Fawkes included four views of Rome, two city views and two studies of single buildings to represent the great achievements of Rome in modern and ancient times – *St Peter's* and the *Colosseum*. Turner may have delivered the latter, which is dated 1820, on his Christmas visit to Farnley in 1821. He had a great deal of reference material to draw on for this watercolour: in 1818, before he had even visited the city himself, he had worked up watercolours

of Rome from James Hakewill's drawings made with the camera obscura[1] and during his own visit he drew the Colosseum from every possible angle in his sketchbook (TB CLXXXIX). For this particular watercolour, he eventually settled on a careful drawing he had made in pencil on paper prepared with grey wash, in which he had rubbed out the highlights.[2] Turning lounging cattle into sprightly goats, angling the building and bringing it slightly forward to eliminate the distracting view into the distance on the right, Turner relied on his recollection of the blue sky and golden-pink tinge of the stones to make a perfect exterior companion to his view of the nave and aisles of the interior of *St Peter's* (W 724): row upon row of arches radiate out from the centre of the Colosseum to complement perfectly the rows of arches moving into the heart of the basilica.

When he saw this watercolour at Farnley Hall in 1902, Armstrong noted that it was slightly faded;[3] Finberg recorded its condition in his catalogue of the Fawkes collection in 1912 (pl. XIV), and it may have faded further before Lloyd acquired it fifteen years later.

1. Powell 1982, pp. 408–25.

2. f. 23; see Powell 1987, pp. 106–9.

3. p. 274.

24 Val d'Aosta *c.* 1820–22

Watercolour, 408 × 302 mm

SIGNED: *J M W Turner*

PROVENANCE: Commissioned from the artist by James Rivington Wheeler; by descent to his nephew, Henry James Wheeler, his sale Foster's, 1 June 1864 (49), bt in (Parnell) for Capt. H. R. Ray; Gertrude Emma Hunt, her sale Foster's, 22 April 1874 (158), bt Agnew's, £1,178 2s.; bt Abel Buckley 14 May 1874, £1,178 2s. (stock 2467); bt Agnew's 4 February 1904, £3,000 (stock 4495); Agnew's 1904 (215), 2,200 gns; bt George J. Gould, of New York, 23 August 1904, 1,650 gns, less duty and excise, £1,493 9s. 4d; his widow's sale Christie's 26 November 1926 (25), bt Agnew's, £861; bt Lloyd 27 November 1926, £950

EXHIBITIONS: RA 1887 (62); Glasgow 1901 (806); Agnew's 1951 (65); BM 1959, 1960; BM 1966, 1969 (19); BM 1975 (96)

R. W. Lloyd Bequest 1958-7-12-425 (W 403)

Less than half a metre high, this watercolour has an inherent monumentality that lends it the presence of a painting in oil. This is in large part due to the deep tones which still retain so much of their freshness, but also to the composition, constructed on planes in the manner of a painting by Poussin. In fact, unusually for Turner at this date, the elements of the composition have been taken from several sources: the bridge is a real one he sketched over the Doire at Villeneuve (TB LXXIV 5), where the Tour Colin is indeed visible on a hill in the distance, but Turner has rebuilt the Château d'Argent from the ruin that exists in reality and brought it down to dominate the hill on the right. The height of the bridge is greatly exaggerated and the mountains beyond are brought forward and made steeper and more dramatic than the hills that actually surround the Doire.[1] Villeneuve stands at the point in the Val d'Aosta where one leaves behind the better-known, more spectacular Alpine scenery and begins to head towards Italy and the landscape of antiquity; it is not surprising therefore that this watercolour has also been described as 'Narni' (famous for its ruined Roman bridge) or a 'fantasy on the theme of the Bridge at Villeneuve'.[2] It is loosely based on a colour sketch of 1813 which once belonged to Ruskin (W 397), who was equally unsure of its exact location.

This lovely watercolour with its strong classical overtones was executed at a time when Turner was creating second, larger versions of watercolours in Fawkes's collection for other patrons, such as the Swinburnes, and he was beginning to play with the elements of these landscapes, heightening atmosphere, altering the physical reality and creating works with a much stronger presence. James Wheeler (1758–1834), a wealthy lawyer and a significant collector of watercolours, already owned a view of Cologne (W 689a) adapted from one of Fawkes's Rhine series. Shortly after it was delivered, around 1818–19, Wheeler commissioned two upright pendant compositions: the present watercolour and another Rhine scene, *Rafts on the Rhine* (Bolton Art Gallery).[3] As in *Val d'Aosta*, in the latter Turner has taken artistic liberties with nature and exaggerated the height of the cliffs, not only to accommodate the vertical format, but also to create an 'ideal', generic depiction of the Rhine.

1. See Boase 1956, pl. 59, p. 286; also Hill 1982, pp. 78–82.

2. BM 1975 (96) and Boase, pl. 59d.

3. See Yardley, pp. 54–5.

25 A Storm (Shipwreck) 1823

Watercolour, 434 × 632 mm

SIGNED: *J M W TURNER RA*

PROVENANCE: Commissioned by W. B. Cooke; B. G. Windus of Tottenham until at least 1840; Lewis Loyd by 1857; by descent through his son, Lord Overbury, to F. E. Loyd; bt from his estate by Christie's for Lloyd, December 1936, 2,000 gns

EXHIBITIONS: W. B. Cooke 1823 (no number, companion to *A Calm (Sunrise)*, W 507); Manchester 1857 (330); BM 1959, 1960; BM 1966, 1969 (18); BM 1975 (87)

R. W. Lloyd Bequest 1958-7-12-424 (W 508)

There are at least three colour beginnings for this watercolour,[1] which does not seem to be based on an actual shipwreck and was painted for a series of *Marine Views*, another of W. B. Cooke's publishing projects that was never completed. It has been variously called 'A Storm', the title used in Cooke's exhibition and while in Windus's collection,[2] or 'Shipwreck', as it was described by a contemporary reviewer. It was known as 'Wreckers' during the entire time it was with the family of the banker Lewis Loyd, who lent it under this title to the 1857 Art Treasures exhibition in Manchester.

When R. W. Lloyd purchased the painting from Loyd's descendants in 1936, Sir Alec Martin sent him transcriptions of the advertisements and reviews this virtuoso perfomance in watercolour had attracted in 1823, including the following extract from an article in the *Literary Gazette* (24 May 1823):

> Exhibition of Drawings by British Artists Soho Square. An addition has been made by Mr Cooke to this varied and attractive Exhibition, of two very spendid Drawings, by J. M. W. Turner RA in which the artist has depicted, with his usual ability, the powerful and sublime effect of a Shipwreck, contrasted with the quiet serenity of a Calm. . . . The chaotic & destructive character of the former is, we think, hurt by the interferance [*sic*] of vivid colour. How far a sudden burst of sunshine might light up a scene like this, and, as if in mockery to misery, tinge it with the gaudy hues of a fairy vision, we are not prepared to say . . .

Certainly, everywhere one looks in the composition figures are being drawn towards disaster: the small boat in the foreground is about to be swamped by the weight of those clinging to its stern, but it is in any case ultimately doomed as it heads for the huge rock before it. Sunlight may fall on the cliffs in the centre, but only to illuminate the waves that crash over them, and there is no sign of beach, ship or shore to offer hope in the bright chalk cliffs in the distance on the left. We should recall, however, that shipwrecks were much more a part of life at this time, a symbol of the inevitable triumph of the power of nature. Seldom was hope an element in the background of scenes of shipwrecks, as it had been in Géricault's *Raft of the Medusa* shown in London in 1820, where man rather than nature was the main subject.[3] Perhaps the reviewer still had this painting in mind when writing of Turner's 'mockery to misery', but in Turner's many paintings of shipwrecks nature was nearly always the main protagonist and hope was absent, except perhaps in redemption after death.

1. TB CCLXIII 371, 377, 379; see Warrell 1991, p. 29.

2. Shanes 1981 (68) and 1984a, p. 56.

3. See Boase 1959, p. 340.

LOWESTOFT
J. M. W. TURNER, R.A.

Cat. no. 35

Picturesque Views in England and Wales, from drawings by J. M. W. Turner, 1827–38 (nos 26–37)

The R. W. Lloyd Bequest included twelve of the series of ninety-six magnificent watercolours produced by Turner for *Picturesque Views in England and Wales*, which has been described by Andrew Wilton as 'the central document of his art'. The idea for the series of engravings was that of the publisher Charles Heath, who, noting the success of W. B. Cooke's *Picturesque Views on the Southern Coast of England*, commissioned Turner to paint him '120 Drawings of England and Wales'. On 19 February 1825 he wrote that he had just taken delivery of the first four watercolours, 'the finest things I ever saw'. Heath was thrilled: he had paid 30 guineas each for them and already had offers of 50 guineas each from various collectors, while the publishers Hurst and Robinson were prepared to put up all the capital on condition they received half the work. Engraving began, but Hurst and Robinson went bankrupt the following year and no prints were actually published until Heath found his feet again with the first publication of his lucrative annual *The Keepsake* in 1827.

Combining forces with a series of printsellers and publishers, Heath eventually managed to produce twenty-four parts of the series (instead of the thirty planned initially), each consisting of four plates. He promoted the series while it was in production by exhibiting Turner's finished watercolours to the public. Forty-one were put on display in the Egyptian Hall in Piccadilly in June 1829 and five were sent up to the Society of Artists exhibition in Birmingham in the autumn of that year. In 1833, in an attempt to obtain more subscribers so that he could complete the series, Heath and his new publishers, Moon, Boys and Graves, mounted an exhibition at their gallery in Pall Mall, showing ten newly finished watercolours still with Heath. They also borrowed nearly seventy watercolours back from their purchasers, including Turner's dealer Thomas Griffith and B. G. Windus of Tottenham (see frontispiece). The last eight drawings were delivered by Turner in July 1836, and the final engravings were issued in 1838.

The ninety-six copper plates became the property of Longman, the publishers, and in 1839 Turner purchased them, along with the print stock, for £3,000, in order to prevent further printing from them. He kept them in his house until his death, and they were finally destroyed in 1874 to retain the market value of the prints. But this most ambitious of all Turner's publishing ventures, undertaken for profit as well as to disseminate his work, was a financial disaster, and it has been argued that the prints, in spite of their delicacy and the impressive range of landscapes they reproduced, never really did justice to the originals. However, the eighty-seven watercolours that survive 'unsurpassed in their range and power' stand as a testimony to Turner's consummate skill and as the legacy of his unique vision of the life and landscape of England and Wales in the early nineteenth century.

The British Museum is fortunate to possess not only the twelve that Lloyd preserved for posterity by protecting them in frames with drawn blinds, but also three other examples, in equally fine condition, which were part of George Salting's bequest in 1910: *Richmond Castle, Yorkshire* (1910-2-12-276, W 791), *Lancaster Sands* (1910-2-12-279, W 803), and *Louth, Lincolnshire* (1910-2-12-278, W 809). These three works had been published by W. G. Rawlinson in his recent catalogue of Turner's engravings, and their bequest to the British Museum was immediately celebrated in an exhibition that attracted a great deal of media attention, including a statement in *The Times* that, thanks to this noble benefaction, 'the greatest of our landscape painters will be adequately represented in the British Museum' (quoted in Coppel 1996b, p. 17). No doubt Salting's generosity was in Lloyd's mind when he decided in his will, made in 1954, to add to this representation.

LITERATURE: W, pp. 173–92; BM 1975, pp. 20–26; Shanes 1979 and 1984b; Herrmann pp. 112–40.

26 Saltash, Cornwall 1825

Watercolour with touches of bodycolour, 273 × 408 mm

SIGNED AND DATED: *J M W Turner RA 25*

ENGRAVED: For *England and Wales* by W.R. Smith in 1827 (R 218)

PROVENANCE: Benjamin Godfrey Windus of Tottenham by 1833; John Hornby Maw; R. R. Davies by 1857; anon. sale Christie's 3 March 1862 (52), bt in; J. Knowles, sale Christie's 7 April 1865 (122), bt Vokins, 210 gns; F.R. Leyland, sale Christie's 9 March 1872 (36), bt White, £472 10s.; anon. sale Christie's 10 March 1876 (130), bt S. Addington, £420; his sale Christie's 22 May 1886 (57), bt Vokins, £204 5s.; S. G. Holland, sale Christie's 26 June 1908 (261), bt Agnew's for Sir Joseph Beecham, £1,102 10s. plus 10% commission £110 5s.; his sale Christie's 4 May 1917 (152), bt Agnew's for Lloyd, £1,470 plus 5% commission £73 10s. (stock 8573)

EXHIBITIONS: Egyptian Hall, Piccadilly, 1829 (17); Moon, Boys and Graves Gallery 1833 (48); Manchester 1857 (337); Agnew's 1909 (157); Agnew's 1919 (30); Agnew's 1927 (18); BM 1959, 1960; BM 1966, 1969 (21); BM 1975 (90); BM 1985 (92)

R. W. Lloyd Bequest 1958-7-12-427 (W 794)

As *Saltash* is the only dated watercolour in the entire series Turner made for *Picturesque Views in England and Wales*, it was probably among the first group that the artist delivered to Charles Heath in February 1825. At that time, Heath mentioned that a number of gentlemen had already offered him 50 guineas each for these watercolours, and although engraving began immediately, the first plates did not appear until March 1827. In fact, Heath held an exhibition of forty-one of Turner's works, many for the *England and Wales* series, at the Egyptian Hall in Piccadilly in June and July 1829.[1] Benjamin Godfrey Windus and Thomas Griffith were amongst the earliest owners of the original watercolours, and they lent the greatest numbers to Heath's later exhibition at the Moon, Boys and Graves gallery in 1833 (Griffith lent thirty and Windus sixteen).[2] This watercolour can be seen at the end of the lower right row in John Scarlett Davis's watercolour of Windus's gallery (frontispiece).

Although it was amongst the first of the series Turner delivered to Heath, *Saltash* was not amongst the first group to be engraved. This may have been because, with its large groups of figures and naval vessels dominating the fore- and middle-grounds, it may not have represented the type of 'picturesque' landscape view with which Heath would have wished to launch and advertise the forthcoming series. The first plate issued was a much more typically 'Turneresque' and 'picturesque' view of the ruins of Rievaulx Abbey nestled in its river valley in the Yorkshire moors. With *Saltash*, however, Turner was signalling his own intentions for this series: he planned to explore the life and people of the towns and harbours of England and Wales, not just the physical attractions of the landscape itself. In fact Andrew Wilton has described the series as 'modern "history pictures" in which the common man is the hero': here the lives of the families of the marines are played out in great detail before us; women, children, sailors, officers and their ships are all lovingly depicted, and even their reflections in the still waters are given far more prominence than the pale town hovering on its hill in the distance.

1. Gage 1980, pp. 237–8.
2. See Shanes 1979, p. 157.

27 Prudhoe Castle, Northumberland *c.* 1825

Watercolour, 292 × 408 mm

INSCRIBED: *JMW* [monogram] *Turner*

ENGRAVED: For *England and Wales* by E. Goodall, 1828 (R 222)

PROVENANCE: Rev. William Kingsley of South Kilvington, Thirsk; bequeathed to his niece Miss L.L.A. Taylor; her sale Christie's 22 February 1918 (24), bt Agnew's for Lloyd, £1,627 10s. plus 5% commission £81 7s. 6d. (stock 8748)

EXHIBITIONS: RA 1889 (3); Agnew's 1919 (22); Agnew's 1951 (76); BM 1959, 1960; BM 1966, 1969 (22); BM 1975 (106)

1958-7-12-428 (W 798)

Although everything about the series of views of *England and Wales* – published for the armchair traveller or as 'souvenirs' of favourite places – might seem to indicate that topography should have governed Turner's brush, as always when called upon to create a watercolour he painted his 'conception' or 'sense' of the place rather than a strictly accurate rendering of reality. This is true to a greater or lesser degree of all the watercolours in this series, but perhaps most clearly here, where even the figures have lost their usual identifying traits of local costume or commerce. Prudhoe Castle and its hill are reduced to a silhouette resembling a castle on a crag on the Rhine, which in turn seems to have been transposed to the warmth of a Claudian summer in the south of France or Italy. All references to the town or to the burgeoning industry along the Tyne have been erased.[1]

Rawlinson relates two somewhat apocryphal stories about the work, reported to him by its first owner, Ruskin's friend the Reverend William Kingsley. However, like the watercolour, both probably have some basis in reality. Evidence of some extra scraping and sponging around the sun and its reflections makes it quite plausible that, as Kingsley reported, when the drawing was damaged in the centre of the sun's reflection, 'Turner moistened his finger with saliva, rubbed the colour off and touched it in again'. He also took the opportunity to scratch his name into the lower left corner of the previously unsigned drawing. Less likely is the story that the watercolour was made by Turner from memory, 'having been struck by the view as he was being driven past, whilst on a visit to the Swinburne family in August 1825'. Apart from the fact that Turner was in London that month, the composition bears too close a resemblance to sketches made of the area on a visit in 1817 (TB CLVII 77, 78) to have been made completely from memory;[2] but what Turner may indeed have recalled, and employed to effect, was the fleeting impression of a surprisingly classical landscape produced by a late summer sun on a northern English river.

1. See Shanes 1979 (11).
2. BM 1975 (106).

92

28 Winchelsea, Sussex *c.* 1828

Watercolour and bodycolour over a pencil sketch, 293 × 425 mm

ENGRAVED: For *England and Wales* by J. Henshall, 1830 (R 245)

PROVENANCE: Thomas Griffith by 1833; bt John James Ruskin, who gave it to John Ruskin, Oxford, 1840; bequeathed to Arthur Severn 1900; Fine Art Society 1900; bt Brown & Phillips from whom bt Agnew's February 1912 for £475 (stock 7655); Agnew's, Manchester 1912 (73), 1,450 gns, bt Lloyd November 1912, £892 10s.

EXHIBITIONS: Moon, Boys and Graves Gallery 1833 (26); Fine Art Society 1878 (34), 1900 (32); Agnew's 1913 (59); BM 1959, 1960; BM 1966, 1969 (23); BM 1985 (93)

R. W. Lloyd Bequest 1958-7-12-429 (W 821)

When Ruskin lent his collection of Turner watercolours and memorabilia to the Fine Art Society in 1878, he wrote notes on them for the catalogue. This scene of tired soldiers approaching their barracks refers back to Turner's memories of his first visit to Winchelsea, during the Napoleonic Wars. It was one of the earliest Ruskin had owned: 'My father gave me the drawing for a birthday present, in 1840, and it used to hang in my rooms at Oxford; no mortal would believe, and now I can scarcely understand myself, the quantity of pleasure it gave me. At that time, I loved storm, and dark weather, and soldiers. *Now*, I want blue sky, pure air, and peace.'

This explanation enables us to begin to understand how much influence Ruskin's own feelings about a subject affected his interpretation of Turner's art. However, we can now stand back from Ruskin's very personal injections and even rejection of the artist's motives and see them for what they often were – a reflection of events in Ruskin's own life and his own personal prejudices. This is seldom more clear than in his 1878 notes:

Turner was always greatly interested, I never could make out why, in the low hill and humble antiquities of Winchelsea. The tower and East gate, though little more, either of them, than heaps of old stone, are yet made each a separate subject in the 'Liber Studiorum' . . . Here, the piece of thundrous light and wild hailstorm among the houses on the hill to the left is entirely grand, and so also the mingling of the shaken trees (all the grace of their foliage torn out of them by the wind) with the wild rain as they melt back into it. But he has missed his mark in the vermilions of the foreground, which fail in distinction of hues between sunlight and shade . . . He is, throughout, ill at ease, both in himself, and about the men and the camp-followers; partly laughing the strange, half-cruel, half-sorrowful laugh that we wonder at, also, so often in Bewick: thinking of the trouble the poor fellows are getting into, drenched utterly, just as they stagger up the hill to their quarters, half dead with heat and thirst, and white with dust.

The engraving of this watercolour included a lightning flash over the troops, never there but easily imagined in the original, and modern writers have interpreted the image as a metaphor for war. The fainting camp-followers and use of vermilion tones in the foreground may have alienated Ruskin's sympathies, but the power of the storm about to engulf the exhausted troops and their own compassion for the small group of women convince us of the sincerity of Turner's never-flagging fascination with, and feeling for, his fellow man.

29 Richmond Hill and Bridge, Surrey *c.* 1828–9

Watercolour, with bodycolour and white highlights, 291 × 435 mm

ENGRAVED: For *England and Wales* by W.R. Smith, 1832 (R 257)

PROVENANCE: T. Griffith by 1833; John Ruskin 1839; bequeathed to Arthur Severn 1900; Fine Art Society, bt Agnew's 7 May 1900, £900 (stock 3058); bt G.P. Dewhurst, 18 June 1900, £1,450; Capt. Dewhurst; bt Agnew's 2 August 1916 (£1,000 with Turner's *Absolom's Tomb*); bt Lloyd 11 August 1916, £1,400 as 'Richmond Bridge, Surrey: Play' (stock 8437)

EXHIBITIONS: Egyptian Hall, Piccadilly, 1829 (27: 'Richmond Hill and Bridge with a Pic-nic Party'); Moon, Boys and Graves Gallery 1833 (18); FAS 1878 (33), 1900 (29: 'Play: Richmond Bridge, Surrey'); Agnew's 1919 (20); Agnew's 1951 (78); BM 1959, 1960; BM 1966, 1969 (29); BM 1975 (174)

R. W. Lloyd Bequest 1958-7-12-435 (W 833)

In the 1830s Ruskin's father, John James Ruskin, began a modest collection of watercolours by British artists such as David Cox, Copley Fielding and Samuel Prout, an artist his son particularly admired. His first expensive purchase was a view of Venice by James Holland, for which he paid 25 guineas in 1836. He also shared his son's growing admiration for the work of Turner and in 1839 bought this watercolour of Richmond, Surrey, for him for 55 guineas.[1] Reminiscing many years later, the younger Ruskin explained that his father had bought it for him 'thinking I should not ask for another, – we both then agreeing that it had nearly everything *characteristic* of Turner in it, and more especially the gay figures!'[2] It was, however, only the beginning of a growing passion, John James spending over £1,200 on fifteen more watercolours by Turner in the next five years and at the same time building up an increasing acquaintance with the artist himself.

The younger Ruskin, meanwhile, became a significant collector and certainly the most important interpreter of the artist's work, his words informing nearly every commentary up to the present day. When he agreed to lend his collection of Turner watercolours to the Fine Art Society for exhibition in 1878, his accompanying *Notes* shared all the vagaries of his own changing taste for different periods

of the artist's work. Explaining that the present work had been the foundation of his collection, he also stated, 'A more wonderful or instructive piece of composition I could not have had by me; nor was I ever weary of trying to analyze it. After thirty years' endeavour I finally surrender that hope.' When this watercolour was first shown by Charles Heath in 1829, its title was 'Richmond Hill and Bridge, with a Pic-nic Party'. In his 1878 exhibition, Ruskin hung it to contrast with a dark watercolour of a heavily industrialised *Dudley* (W 858) which he subtitled 'Work'; the accompanying subtitle 'Play' was appended to the the Richmond view for the next hundred years.

1. Deardon, p. 15.
2. FAS 1900, pp. 34–5.

30 **Windsor Castle** *c.* 1828–9

Watercolour, 288 × 437 mm

ENGRAVED: For *England and Wales* by W. Miller, 1831 (R 253)

PROVENANCE: Thomas Tomkinson by 1833; Benjamin Godfrey Windus by 1839; John Smith, sale Christie's 4 May 1870 (59), bt Agnew's, £714; bt William Moir; Mrs Moir by 1887, bt from her by Agnew's 1899; George Agnew; R. E. Tatham; his sale Christie's 7 March 1908 (84), bt Agnew's for Sir Joseph Beecham, £1,785 plus 5% commission; his sale Christie's 4 May 1917 (148), bt Freeman for Sir Thomas Beecham, £3,360; his sale Christie's 10 May 1918 (85), bt Agnew's for Lloyd, £3,150 plus 5% commission £157 10s. (stock 8912)

EXHIBITIONS: Egyptian Hall, Piccadilly, 1829 (26); Moon, Boys and Graves Gallery 1833 (43); RA 1887 (68); Guildhall 1899 (141); Agnew's 1909 (34); Agnew's 1913 (58); Agnew's 1919 (24); Agnew's 1924 (37); RA 1934 (881) (772); Agnew's 1951 (70); BM 1959, 1960; BM 1966, 1969 (26); BM 1975 (148)

R. W. Lloyd Bequest 1958-7-12-432 (W 829)

Turner would have been familiar with the work of Paul Sandby (1730–1809), who has often been described as 'the father of English watercolour painting', as most of his early patrons and teachers, especially Dr Monro and Edward Dayes, owned and admired his work. The Duke of Cumberland, Ranger of Windsor Great Park, was an important early patron of Paul Sandby and his brother Thomas, who lived in the Duke's household at Windsor for many years. Their most successful and best-known watercolours were of Windsor and Eton – the town, the Castle, the Great Park, and the people who inhabited them. These were painted mainly for the tourist market, but Sir Joseph Banks purchased around sixty before 1773, most of which later came into the Royal Collection.[1] R. W. Lloyd was able to purchase one which had once belonged to Banks when it came onto the market two years after he bought this view of *Windsor Castle* by Turner.

The Castle was a 'must' in any series of picturesque views in England and Wales: situated on a long, flat hill over the Thames, with its medieval towers and ancient and modern accretions, including alterations carried out in the early nineteenth century by the Prince Regent, it provided an image which had naturally appealed to

artists for centuries. Turner drew and painted it many times: here, in his final depiction of the Castle, he repeated a barge (on the right) that he had included in one of his earliest drawings, engraved in 1795 in the *Pocket Magazine*.[2] The Claudian glow of the sunset suffuses the substantial and busy town below, tinting all the horses and figures in the foreground yellow and thereby causing the organisers of the 1886 exhibition at the Royal Academy to assign it to a late period of Turner's work. However, it is based on drawings made in the area around 1827 (TB CCXXV 2, 2v) and was one of the works exhibited by Heath at the Egyptian Hall in 1829. It had been purchased by Thomas Tomkinson by the time of Heath's 1833 exhibition, and it must have passed into Windus's collection between then and 1839 – presumably after 1835, as it does not seem to appear in John Scarlett Davis's watercolour (frontispiece).

1. See Roberts, *passim.*
2. Shanes 1979 (40).

31 Coventry, Warwickshire *c.* 1832

Watercolour, 288 × 437 mm

ENGRAVED: For *England and Wales* by S. Fisher, 1833 (R 273)

PROVENANCE: Charles Heath 1833; H. A. J. Munro of Novar, his sale Christie's 2 June 1877 (49), bt Wallis, £1,081; bt Agnew's 16 April 1878 (stock 4600); Agnew's Liverpool 1878 (172), 1,030 gns; bt C. Wheeley Lea 26 May 1879, 1,030 gns plus 10%; Mrs Wheeley Lea of Parkside, near Worcester, her sale Christie's 11 May 1917 (33), bt Agnew's for Lloyd, £1,155 plus 5% commission £57 15s. (stock 8581)

EXHIBITIONS: Moon, Boys and Graves Gallery 1833 (62); Agnew's 1919 (33); BM 1959, 1960; BM 1966, 1969 (28); BM 1975 (197)

R. W. Lloyd Bequest 1958-7-12-434 (W 849)

Messrs Moon, Boys and Graves were in partnership with Charles Heath in the publication of various parts of *England and Wales* from 1831 onwards. In June 1833 they exhibited sixty-six of the finished watercolours in their gallery in Pall Mall, borrowing fifty-six back from the relatively small number of original purchasers. The exhibition also included ten watercolours belonging to Heath, which were presumably newly finished or still in the process of being engraved, including the present work. It was later sold to one of Turner's most faithful patrons, Munro of Novar, and it was while it was in his collection that Ruskin saw it and wrote enthusiastically about it in his paean to Turner, volume I of *Modern Painters*:[1]

> Impetuous clouds, twisted rain, flickering sunshine, fleeting shadow, gushing water and oppressed cattle, all speak the same story of tumult, fitfulness, power, and velocity. Only one thing is wanted, a passage of repose to contrast with it all; and it is given. High and far above the dark volumes of the swift rain-cloud, are seen on the left, through their opening, the quiet, horizontal, silent flakes of the highest cirrus, resting in the repose of the deep sky.

The preparatory drawings and colour sketches for this watercolour in the *Birmingham and Coventry* sketchbook (TB CCXL 15v, 25v-27) were drawn on a tour in 1830 which included visits to Worcester and Dudley in the heart of England's Black Country. Writing after several decades of growing industrialisation and his own increasing antipathy towards it, Ruskin's words do not convey the excitement and wonderment that these scenes of the 'modernisation' of their country must have generated in the minds of Turner and many of his contemporaries. This view of Coventry is just one in the series of views of *England and Wales* that he filled with turnpikes and coaches and metal processing in the midst of country fields, and cities spreading into the surrounding countryside and connecting outwards along their main roads to other cities;[2] here a young boy catches the toll from a passing coach on the turnpike road to Birmingham, while Coventry rises as a kind of 'celestial city' beyond.

1. p. 250.
2. See Berg, pp. 124–8

32 Penmaen-Mawr, Caernarvonshire *c.*1832–3

Watercolour, 312 × 440 mm

INSCRIBED: (on verso) *Pass of Penmanmawr, North Wales*

ENGRAVED: For *England and Wales* by J. T. Willmore, 1834 (R 276)

PROVENANCE: Charles Heath, 1833; ?Benjamin Godfrey Windus of Tottenham; John Leigh Clare of Toxteth Old Hall, Liverpool, sale Christie's 28 March 1868 (98), bt Maclean, £493 10s.; Murrieta, sale Christie's 30 April 1892 (51), bt Agnew's, 330 gns; bt Securities Insurance Co., 4 May 1892, £346 10s. (stock 517); Leopold Salomon, Norbury Park; his sale, Knight, Frank & Rutley, 11 September 1916 (127), bt Agnew's for Lloyd, £451 10s. plus 5% commission £22 11s. 6d. (stock 8442)

EXHIBITIONS: Moon, Boys and Graves Gallery 1833 (57); Agnew's 1894 (300)

R. W. Lloyd Bequest 1958-7-12-437 (W 852)

This unfortunate wreck of a watercolour must once have been breathtaking. It was exhibited in 1833 while it was still in Charles Heath's hands for engraving and was probably sold on shortly afterwards, as the engraving was published the following year. It is not known when John Leigh Clare purchased it; Benjamin Windus is known to have owned forty watercolours from this series by 1839, although not all have been identified, and Eric Shanes has suggested that it may be the watercolour depicted on the lower register just behind the door on the right in the Davis watercolour (frontispiece).[1] Most of the watercolours once owned by Windus are in good condition, so it seems likely that this work suffered at the hands of a later owner. Its condition by 1916 is reflected in the price Lloyd paid for it. A hint of the blues and greys it once contained, most of which have turned a reddy brown, can be seen in the line across the top and a slightly narrower one along the right edge. Either Turner used far more of this particular blue, indigo, which is more light-sensitive than most pigments, or it was hung in fairly direct sunlight at some time in the nineteenth century.[2]

Nevertheless, this is one of the most powerful and dynamic images in the entire series, as if Turner has transferred all the power of one of his alpine snowstorms or spectacular shipwrecks to a road on the Welsh coast. In the diary of his trip to North Wales in 1792 another, unknown traveller wrote of 'that tremendous Mountain – running by the Sea Side with the Puffin or Preston's Island & the Isle of Anglesea on the opposite shore'.[3] The roadway was an extremely dangerous one, even after the sea-wall was built in 1792, constantly threatened not only by landslides washed down by storms, rendering the road impassable, but also by the sea washing over it, as it does in the foreground here, the horses rushing to pass before the next gathering wave crashes over them.[4]

1. Shanes 1984a, p. 57.
2. See 'H., M.I.', p. 25.
3. Gage 1980, p. 16, where diary incorrectly ascribed to Turner.
4. See Shanes 1979 (61); also Wilcox, pp. 45–6, for an account of the road *c.*1777.

33 Caernarvon Castle *c.*1832–3

Watercolour over traces of pencil, 278 × 418 mm

ENGRAVED: For *England and Wales* by W. Radclyffe, 1835 (R 281)

PROVENANCE: H. A. J. Munro of Novar, sale Christie's 2 June 1877 (46), bt Severn, £798, for John Ruskin; bequeathed to Arthur Severn 1900; Fine Art Society, bt Agnew's 7 May 1900, £900 (stock 3061); bt R. E. Tatham, 15 May 1900, £1,525; his sale, Christie's 7 March 1908 (85), bt Agnew's, £1,023 15s. plus 10% for Walter Jones (stock 6423); bt Agnew's 26 November 1912, £1,500 (stock 7893); bt Lloyd 27 January 1913, £1,750

EXHIBITIONS: Fine Art Society 1878 (40), 1900 (34); Agnew's 1910 (30); Agnew's 1913 (65); BM 1959, 1960; BM 1966, 1969 (31); BM 1975 (199); BM 1985 (94)

R. W. Lloyd Bequest 1958-7-12-439 (W 857)

This view of Caernarvon is quite different in mood from the artist's romantic and often 'sublime' interpretations of the landscape of North Wales which he produced after his first visits there in the late 1790s. In 1800, however, he exhibited at the Royal Academy a very Claudian vision of Caernarvon, with the castle a focal point in the distance. Returning to the subject for this later series of watercolours, he attempted in one of his colour beginnings[1] to work out a composition in which the castle was brought forward to create a backdrop to a twilight scene, where the shape of the castle and its reflection, and a darker bulk indicating a bank on the right, were bathed in a diffuse, floating mass of light. He managed to transfer this successfully to the final watercolour, using the palest yellows and touches of vermilion and purple to convey the overwhelming hazy heat at the end of a summer's day. Desperate to find relief, horses bathe in the river by the still moored boats, their sails useless without a breeze, while a group of young women have sought refuge by bathing in the harbour. Two already in the water are depicted as classical nude nymphs, but nineteenth-century modesty has halted one of the others, her cheeks blushing in the realisation that there is an audience on the bank. If the castle's outline did not make the Welsh location immediately evident, the costumes of the children on the right and the coracle beside them left no room for doubt.

Ruskin was obviously fond of this watercolour, hanging it with his favourites in his bedroom and retaining it until his death.[2] In his notes for the Fine Art Society exhibitions in 1878 and 1900 he described it as

> Quite one of the most exquisite pieces of Turner's twilight mist. Its primrose-coloured sky has been often objected to . . . But any one with real eyes for colour, who will look well into the drawing of the rosy towers, and purple mountains and clouds beyond the Menai, will be thankful for them in their perfectness, and very glad that Turner did not what a common painter would, darken them all down to throw out his twilight.[3]

1. TB CCLXIII 9; BM 1975 (198); Shanes 1997 (12).

2. See Whitworth 1989 (34), which reproduces in colour A. Severn's watercolour of *Ruskin's bedroom, Brantwood*, 1900.

3. FAS 1900, pp. 40–41.

34 **Worcester** *c.* 1834

Watercolour with bodycolour, 292 × 439 mm

ENGRAVED: For *England and Wales* by T. Jeavons, 1835 (R 286)

PROVENANCE: Hon. William Henry Smith, MP (d. 1891); his son, Hon. William Frederick D. Smith, MP; bt Agnew's 6 April 1908, 100 gns (with five others) (stock 6492); bt Sir Joseph Beecham 26 June 1908; his sale, Christie's 3 May 1917 (151), bt Freeman, £3,150, for Sir Thomas Beecham; his sale Christie's 10 May 1918 (86), bt Agnew's, £3,150 (stock 8193); bt Lloyd 23 November 1918, £3,400

EXHIBITIONS: Guildhall 1896 (10, where the catalogue mistakenly said it had been engraved by J. Basire in 1804); Agnew's 1909 (30); Agnew's 1919 (25); Agnew's 1951 (77); BM 1959, 1960; BM 1966, 1969 (30); BM 1975 (200)

R. W. Lloyd Bequest 1958-7-12-438 (W 862)

In 1833, when Charles Heath exhibited the sixty-six watercolours Turner had so far completed for the *England and Wales* series, two of the views showing the exciting new economic growth in the Black Country, *Coventry* (no. 31) and *Dudley* (W 858), were included. This watercolour of *Worcester* was not, but the sketches on which it was based (TB CCXXXIX 80v, 81) were made on the same Midland tour, and it must have been completed during the following year, as it was engraved in 1835.

The cathedral city and county town of Worcester was an active and growing centre. The Severn river and its canals were its busy roadways, linking it with the south-west and the new industrial Midlands to the north-east. As in his watercolour of *Coventry*, with its donkeys, sheep and cattle in a meadow sharing the foreground with the turnpike road rushing to connect it with other expanding centres, in this view Turner contrasts traditional rural means of livelihood – the women with their eel traps in the middle of the river - with the boats on the right heavily laden with their bundles of wool for the carpet manufactories or clay for the porcelain works, while other river craft and boats line the banks of the canal as it winds its way through the city. This watercolour shares with *Coventry* the motif of a passing storm and its lovely pinks, blues and greys, and it

may have been conceived as a pendant to Turner's vision of the latter as a new 'celestial city' in his own pilgrim's progress through 'modern' Britain. There are no dark chimneys here with ominously rising smoke, but the sun's rays slant diagonally from a passing storm-cloud to reveal another cathedral city where the old religion with its shining spires is making room for a new one with square mills and warehouses rising at its feet.

35 Lowestoffe, Suffolk *c*. 1835–6

Watercolour, 275 × 427 mm

ENGRAVED: For *England and Wales* by W. R. Smith, 1837 (R 293)

PROVENANCE: Benjamin Godfrey Windus of Tottenham by 1844; H. A. J. Munro of Novar; his sale Christie's 6 April 1878 (92), bt Agnew's, £777; bt Rev. Charles John Sale of Holt Rectory 13 April 1878 (stock 4581); Mrs Sale; her sale, Christie's 9 July 1915 (85), bt Agnew's for Lloyd, £504 plus 5% commission £25 4s. (stock 8370)

EXHIBITIONS: Worcestershire 1882 (552); RA 1891 (86); Agnew's 1919 (31); BM 1959, 1960; BM 1966, 1969 (33); BM 1975 (208); BM 1985 (95)

R. W. Lloyd Bequest 1958-7-12-441 (W 869)

At first, there may seem to be little in this desolate scene of men struggling against the sea to entitle it to be a part of a series of 'picturesque views': it contains almost no topographical references to identify a particular town or harbour. However, those familiar with the location of the first established lifeboat service in 1807, and the notorious occasion in 1821 when it was turned away by local 'wreckers' to enable salvage at the cost of four lives, would recognise the cliffs, the town and the apparently ineffective lighthouse at Lowestoft, Suffolk.[1]

Lloyd's typescript catalogue of his collection transcribed several passages from Ruskin's *Modern Painters* praising this work in particular: 'The Land's End, and Lowestoft, and Snowstorm . . . are nothing more than passages of the most hopeless, desolate, uncontrasted greys, and yet are three of the very finest pieces of colour that have come from his hand'.[2] In 1844 Windus, who then owned *Lowestoffe* (as it has always been known), offered to exchange it for Ruskin's father's *Land's End*; but even though he preferred Windus's watercolour, Ruskin refused because at that date he was really only interested in acquiring the late Swiss watercolours.[3]

Several writers have commented on the desolate moods found within so many of the watercolours in this series and have identified the source in Turner's loss during the previous decade of both his greatest friend and patron, Walter Fawkes, who died in 1825, and his own father, in 1829. Certainly a number of these works show the awesome, even dark power of nature over man, but this was a force Turner had recognised and admired from the time he became an artist, and they indicate less a mournful disposition than a truthful reflection of the life and 'modern history' of England and Wales that he wished to document in this series. By this date he was already friendly with a new and promising patron, the Scottish landowner Hugh Andrew Johnstone Munro of Novar. Freedom from family commitments meant Turner could travel abroad more easily, and in 1836 he accompanied Munro, a keen amateur draughtsman, to Switzerland. Munro was an avid collector of Dutch seventeenth-century marine paintings and, as this view of Lowestoft was painted around this time and Windus seems to have been willing to part with it around 1844, it is not surprising that it became one of several in the *England and Wales* series to be purchased by Munro (see also nos 38, 40–42, 46–7), who eventually owned 130 watercolours by the artist.[4]

1. Shanes 1979 (76).

2. Vol. I, 2nd edn 1898, p. 373.

3. Whittingham 1993, p. 103.

4. Gage 1987, p. 169.

36 Keswick Lake, Cumberland (Derwentwater) *c.*1835

Watercolour, 275 × 435 mm

ENGRAVED: For *England and Wales* by W. Radclyffe, 1837 (R 295)

PROVENANCE: John Ruskin by *c.*1860 [Thornbury, II, p. 395]; J. E. Taylor by 1871; his sale Christie's 5 July 1912 (43), bt Agnew's, 2,200 gns; bt Baroness Goldschmidt Rothschild; returned to Agnew's March 1914; bt H. E. Walters; sold to Agnew's 27 March 1918, £2,500 (stock 8773); bt A.E. Lawley 6 May 1918 (one of a group for £10,000); his sale Christie's 25 February 1921 (123), bt Agnew's for Lloyd, £2,415 plus 5% commission £120 15s. (stock 9928)

EXHIBITIONS: Leeds 1868 (2244); BFAC 1871 (120); RA 1886 (2); Guildhall 1899 (135); ? Agnew's Liverpool 1908 (6); Agnew's 1914 (157); Agnew's 1924 (35); RA 1934 (901) (775); Agnew's 1951 (74); BM 1959, 1960; BM 1966, 1969 (34); 1975 (203)

R. W. Lloyd Bequest 1958-7-12-442 (W 871)

In 1769 the poet Thomas Gray had described this view as 'the vale of Elysium in all its verdure; the sun then playing on the lake; and lighting up all the mountains with its lustre'.[1] On his 1797 tour of the north of England, Turner made Keswick his base for the first few days of his exploration of the Lake District. The area had become increasingly popular with artists and writers over the past few decades, especially since the publication of William Gilpin's *Tour of the Lakes* in 1782 and of Turner's friend Joseph Farington's *Views in the Lakes* of 1789.

Turner's viewpoint for this watercolour of the lake, now better known as Derwentwater, was from Calfclose Bay, with Lodore Falls tumbling over the grey-blue hills in the centre of the composition and the valley of Borrowdale disappearing at the end of a rainbow in the misty sunlit distance to the right. The lake was first drawn by Turner in a series of pencil and then watercolour studies in the sketchbook used on this first visit (TB XXXV 26, 82); it was the subject of a more finished watercolour he later presented to Farington (TB XXXVI H), and in 1801 it again caught his imagination for further studies and finished works. In the 1820s Turner used his sketches of Derwentwater to illustrate Samuel Rogers's poems, and in 1831 he revisited Keswick to collect material for his illustrations to Walter Scott.

The present watercolour was the culmination of these compositions – a virtuoso performance of technique and vision, set off by the human incident in the foreground which elucidates the weather effects and gives imagination free rein to unravel the story being told. In fact, David Hill has recently suggested that the figure of a distinctive dark-haired man being helped from the boat whose occupants have been caught by the rain on the lake was Turner's personal tribute to the 'Lake Poet' Robert Southey, who apparently did not much care to be out of doors and exposed to the weather.[2] Turner had paid him a visit in 1831, two years after the poet's 'Stanzas Addressed to J M W Turner Esq RA on his view of the Lago Maggiore from the Town of Arona' were published in the *Keepsake* of 1829.

1. Quoted in Hill 1996, p. 104.

2. Ibid., p. 108.

37 Criccieth Castle, North Wales *c.* 1836

Watercolour, with touches of bodycolour, 290 × 425 mm

SIGNED: *IMW*

ENGRAVED: For *England and Wales* by S. Fisher, 1837 (R 300)

PROVENANCE: H. A. J. Munro of Novar; his sale Christie's 2 June 1877 (40), bt Agnew's (stock 4281); bt W. Dunlop 28 June 1877;
Col. H. J. Holdsworth, his sale Christie's 4 May 1889 (78), bt Gooden; William Newall by 1899; his sale Christie's 30 June 1922 (74),
bt King, 850 gns; Lt.-Col. James B. Gaskell of Roseleigh, Liverpool, his sale Christie's 30 April 1926 (77), bt W. W. Sampson,
1,550 gns; Gilbert Lees Hardcastle, sale Christie's 4 May 1933 (34), bt in at 380 gns; bt Lloyd (price and date unrecorded)

EXHIBITIONS: Guildhall 1899 (131, where incorrect Fawkes provenance given); Agnew's 1913 (34); BM 1959, 1960;
BM 1966, 1969 (32); BM 1975 (206)

R. W. Lloyd Bequest 1958-7-12-440 (W 876)

As in *Lowestoffe* (no. 35), the subject of this watercolour is not just man's relationship with the sea, but also his attempt to take advantage of its power; here customs officers inspect salvage collected from a wreck by the local inhabitants on this rugged part of the Welsh coast, the storm which caused the wreck still lashing the cliffs and churning the waves. This watercolour also dates from around 1836 and belonged to the same owner, the Scottish collector and admirer of marine paintings H. A. J. Munro of Novar.

Two or three colour beginnings in the TB CCLXIII series may be associated with this composition,[1] but the only drawings Turner made of this part of the Welsh coast date from his tour of 1798.[2] Prince Llewellyn's thirteenth-century castle, which stands on a rocky hill at the base of the Lleyn peninsula, was later enlarged by the English. They were driven out, however, by the Welsh in 1404, and the castle was sacked and burnt, its ruins standing as a reminder of Wales' ancient struggle for independence. Turner was presumably aware of the site's history when deciding to include it in the series of *Picturesque Views in England and Wales*, but, as usual, he treats it only

as the background to a scene from 'modern life'. Also, as was his habit, he has taken some degree of licence with the height of the cliffs and the extent of the beach, and this has led to some discussion concerning his exact viewpoint. Even with the tide well out, it would be difficult for the water to be deepest at the base of the cliff rather than where the artist has most of the action taking place; but he needed a platform for his drama and an explanation for the event, as well as a backdrop in the form of a raging sea. Playing 'god' with the elements himself, Turner simply reversed the direction of the tides.[3]

1. Shanes 1997, pp. 45–6.
2. BM 1975 (206).
3. See *On the Trail of Turner in North and South Wales*, Welsh Historic Monuments, Cardiff, 1995, pp. 30–31, and letter from the Rev. A. D. Hall, 1996, in BM dossier.

38 Loch Katrine *c.* 1832

Watercolour, 96 × 149 mm

ENGRAVED: For *The Poetical Works of Walter Scott* by W. Miller, 1833, as frontispiece to vol. VIII (R 507)

PROVENANCE: Robert Cadell; H. A. J. Munro of Novar, his sale Christie's 6 April 1878 (73), bt Agnew's, £336 (stock 4566); bt Mansell Lewis of Stradey, Llanelly, Carmarthenshire, £336 plus 10%; bt Agnew's 31 May 1879 (stock 5116); bt C. Wheeley Lea 7 June 1879, £369 12s.; Mrs Wheeley Lea of Parkside, near Worcester, her sale Christie's 11 May 1917 (39), bt Agnew's for Lloyd, £325 plus 5% commission £16 5s. 6d. (stock 8585)

EXHIBITIONS: Agnew's 1924 (85); RA 1934 (863) (773); BM 1975 (178)

R. W. Lloyd 1958-7-12-436 (W 1084)

Turner made his first long visit to Scotland in 1801 as the logical conclusion of his series of tours around Britain. He travelled there again late in 1818, commissioned by Sir Walter Scott to prepare designs for his *Provincial Antiquities of Scotland* (1818–26). Ten water-colours and two vignettes were eventually used in the book and retained by Scott; eight hung in one frame in the breakfast room at Abbotsford. In 1831 Turner was persuaded by the Edinburgh pub-lisher Robert Cadell to tour Scotland again in order to prepare illus-trations for a complete edition of Scott's works. Turner had met Sir Walter in 1818 and the two men had not taken to each other, but in April 1831 Scott invited Turner to stay with him at Abbotsford. The artist, the author and the publisher spent several days in August exploring the nearby sites in the Vale of the Tweed which Scott hoped would illustrate specific poems, before Turner set off to sketch in the Borders and around Stirling and the Trossachs, going on to a blustery west coast as far north as Staffa.[1] After Turner left Abbotsford, Scott wrote to his son: 'I think he will make a superb book of it if he is not as Burn[s] sa[y]s, "killd by highland bodies/And eaten like a weather haggis".'[2]

The drawing used for this watercolour of *Loch Katrine* appears in the *Stirling and the West* sketchbook (TB CCLXX 47), one of several Turner used on this tour. When the artist, publisher and author had originally discussed which subjects would be most appropriate for which work, they had changed their minds several times about those for volume VIII, which was to be introduced by *The Lady of the Lake*. In the end they settled on *Loch Katrine* for the frontispiece and *Loch Achray* (W 1085) for the vignette.[3]

Cadell's twelve-volume edition of Sir Walter Scott's *Poetical Works* appeared in 1834 with twenty-four illustrations by Turner (a title-page vignette and frontispiece in each); the *Prose Works* appeared between 1834 and 1836 with forty illustrations by him. He was paid 25 guineas for each of the first group, and most of them, including the present work, were purchased from Cadell by Munro of Novar. Like all the final watercolours made in preparation for this publication, Turner painted it in the size at which it was to be engraved. Undisturbed by distracting figures, the result is a jewel-like vision filled with the royal blues of the lake and hills and the pinks and purples of the heather overlain by a smoky mist; magically repaying ever closer inspection, it is a visual poem no engraver could ever hope to recreate.

1. See Finley, pp. 103–42.
2. Quoted ibid., p. 123.
3. Ibid., p. 242.

39 *Messieurs les voyageurs* on their return from Italy (*par la diligence*) in a snow drift upon Mount Tarrar – 22nd of January 1829   1829

Watercolour and bodycolour, 545 × 747 mm

PROVENANCE: Thomas Griffith by 1854 (where seen by Ruskin 8 February – information from Ian Warrell); William Moir; Mrs Moir; bt Agnew's 1899; S. G. Holland, sale Christie's 26 June 1908 (259), bt Agnew's, £546 plus £54 12s. for Sir Joseph Beecham; his sale Christie's 4 May 1917 (157), bt Agnew's for Lloyd, £714 plus 5% commission £35 14s. (stock 8576)

EXHIBITIONS: RA 1829 (520); Agnew's 1909 (37); Agnew's 1927 (19); Agnew's 1951 (82); RA 1951-2 (509); BM 1959, 1960; BM 1966, 1969 (25); BM 1975 (147); BM 1985 (92)

R. W. Lloyd Bequest 1958-7-12-431 (W 405)

In 1828 Turner made his third visit to Italy. This was during a period of increased exploration of the use of vibrant colour in his work and, unlike on his previous visits, when he made meticulous sketches of the monuments and atmospheric colour-washed sketches, he concentrated instead on producing a series of oils, which he exhibited in his rooms in Rome. Anxious to return to commitments in London, he left Italy in January and experienced a crossing of the Alps so disastrous that he swore he would never leave so late in winter again. He had already survived one terrifying crossing of Mt Cenis, returning from Italy a decade earlier, which he vividly recorded in a much smaller watercolour for Walter Fawkes showing his carriage careering along a mountain road, cut off from its baggage wagon by a fall of rocks and snow, the vortex of a great storm swirling beyond (W 402).

Fawkes's small watercolour record of the earlier experience bore echoes of Turner's fascination with Hannibal's legendary crossing of the Alps, but his 1829 passage over Mt Tarrar was less life-threatening and of a more personal, wet and miserable nature. Nevertheless, he recorded it on such a scale - the size of a large oil painting – as to monumentalise the experience for posterity, an experience he recounted in February in a letter to Charles Eastlake:

. . . the snow began to fall at Foligno, tho' more of ice than snow, that the coach from its weight slide about in all directions, that walking was much preferable, but my innumerable tails would not do that service so I soon got wet through and through, till at Sarre-valli the diligence zizd into a ditch and required 6 oxen, sent three miles back for, to drag it out . . . consequently half starved and frozen we at last got to Bologna . . . . But there our troubles began instead of diminishing . . . all bad til Firenzola being even the worst for the down diligence people had devoured everything eatable (Beds none) . . . crossed Mont Cenis on a sledge – bivouaced in the snow with fires lighted for 3 Hours on Mont Tarate while the diligence was righted and dug out, for a Bank of Snow saved it from upsetting – and in the same night we were again turned out to walk up to our knees in new fallen drift to get assistance to dig a channel thro' it for the coach, so that from Foligno to within 20 miles of Paris I never saw the road but snow![1]

1. Gage 1980, pp. 125–6.

116

40 Florence from San Miniato *c.*1828

Watercolour and bodycolour, 286 × 418 mm

PROVENANCE: H. A. J. Munro of Novar; Sir John Pender, his sale Christies 29 May 1897 (16), bt Agnew's 340 gns (stock 2042); bt Sir Donald Currie 31 May 1897, £357 plus 5% commission £17 17s.; Hon. William Henry Smith, MP; by descent to his son, Hon. William Frederick D. Smith, MP; bt Agnew's 4 April 1908 (with five others), £700; bt Sir Joseph Beecham 26 June 1908 (£5,500 for six watercolours); his sale Christie's 3 May 1917 (149), bt Agnew's for Lloyd, £2,362 10s. plus 5% commission £118 2s. 6d. (stock 8571)

EXHIBITIONS: Guildhall 1899 (148); Birmingham 1899 (47); Glasgow 1901 (800); Agnew's 1909 (166); Agnew's 1919 (29); Agnew's 1927 (20); Agnew's 1951 (83); BM 1959, 1960; BM 1966, 1969 (20); BM 1975 (145)

R. W. Lloyd Bequest 1958-7-12-426 (W 728)

Turner first made studies of this view, from a spot actually half a mile north of San Miniato, during his momentous tour of Italy in 1819, when he spent Christmas in Florence before setting out for home again in January.[1] He did not return to Florence until 1828, but the composition of this view is so close to three others of *c.*1826–8 that it must have been produced before his second visit to the city. These watercolours were part of another of Charles Heath's many publishing schemes, *Picturesque Views in Italy*, which never reached fruition. One of the other versions of this watercolour did actually appear as a small engraving in 1827 in yet another of Heath's publishing ventures, but this time a very successful one with which Turner was to be involved for the next ten years.

Small 'pocket-books' or 'annuals', a cross between a diary and a literary selection, had been published for the Christmas market since the eighteenth century. With the invention of steel engraving in the 1820s, enabling much larger runs to be taken from plates without loss of detail or quality, the annuals began to include more illustrations, and from this time the demand for them increased dramatically. Charles Heath launched his new annual, *The Keepsake*, in 1827, including engravings after watercolours by Turner; priced at a guinea each, he sold 15,000 copies.[2] Rather than specially producing small watercolours for these octavo volumes, Heath seems to have used larger finished works Turner had to hand, and this may be one of the reasons why this publication project was so successful – the anguish of meeting publishers' deadlines had caused many of Turner's publishing projects to flounder.

John Ruskin was familiar with the original watercolour of Florence that was engraved for the *Keepsake* (W 727), which was very similar to the present work. Although he considered it 'a glorious drawing, as far as regards the passage with the bridge and sunlight on the Arno', he complained that 'the vines and melons of the foreground are disorderly, and its cypresses conventional; in fact, I recollect no instance of Turner's drawing a cypress except in general terms'.[3] Nevertheless, the figures are so reminiscent of a *fête champêtre* and the character of the city is captured so faithfully that two of Turner's most assiduous patrons, including Munro of Novar who owned the present work, were to commission copies.[4]

1. Powell 1987, pp. 93–4.

2. Herrmann, pp. 164–5.

3. *Modern Painters*, I, p. 130.

4. See Warrell 1991, pp. 66–7.

41 Saumur *c.* 1829–30

Watercolour with touches of bodycolour, 283 × 421 mm

ENGRAVED: For *The Keepsake* (of 1831) by R. Wallis, 1830 (R 324)

PROVENANCE: Benjamin Godfrey Windus until at least 1840; H. A. J. Munro of Novar, sale Foster's 1855, bt John Dillon; his sale Foster's 7 June 1856 (144), bt ?, £204 15s.; J. H. Maw, 1857; Hon. William Henry Smith, MP, by descent to his son, Hon. William Frederick D. Smith, MP; bt Agnew's 4 April 1908, £3,600 (with five others); bt Sir Joseph Beecham 26 June 1908 (£5,500 for six watercolours); his sale Christie's 3 May 1917 (153), bt Freeman 2,800 gns for Sir Thomas Beecham; his sale Christie's 10 May 1918 (87), bt Agnew's for Lloyd, £3,150 plus 5% commission £157 10s. (stock 8194)

EXHIBITIONS: Guildhall 1899 (147, as 'Namur, on the Meuse'); Birmingham 1899 (46, where Ruskin is incorrectly added to the provenance); Agnew's 1909 (27); Agnew's 1919 (23); Agnew's 1951 (66); BM 1959, 1960; BM 1966, 1969 (24); BM 1975 (168)

R. W. Lloyd Bequest 1958-7-12-430 (W 1046)

In 1819 Turner and W. B. Cooke began work on a planned series of engravings to be based on the 1817 Rhine views, but the publication was abandoned when a rival illustrated tour appeared first. Through the 1820s, however, the two men successfully produced the mezzotints for the *Rivers of England*, and by the middle of the decade Turner had begun to gather material for *Turner's Annual Tour*, which he planned in collaboration with another publisher, Charles Heath. Rather than appearing as individual prints, however, these views were published in the same format as the hugely popular series *The Landscape Annual* (1829–38), in volumes with complete texts of tours. Turner held enough cachet that his series bore his own name, and the first volume, with its alternative title of *Wanderings by the Loire*, appeared in December 1832.[1] But long before this ambitious series even got into production, Turner and Heath had already devised another, more expeditiously lucrative use for the magnificent series of watercolours of the rivers of France the artist was producing – the *Keepsake* annuals (see no. 40). This view of *Saumur* appeared in the volume for 1831.

Turner had made drawings of the area in a sketchbook of 1826 and studies on blue paper by 1829.[2] The freshness of style and colour in this work is remarkably close to the views of *Florence* (no. 40) and

Marly-sur-Seine (no. 42) in Lloyd's collection, which also appeared in the *Keepsake* and which share with it an interest in costume and a sparkling detail and quality of light achieved with the finest lines and hatching touches of a brush loaded with pure colour. These qualities lend the watercolours a distinctly European feel not found in the similar-sized finished watercolours for *Picturesque Views of England and Wales* which Turner and Heath were producing at the same time.

Because this drawing was incorrectly titled 'Namur on the Meuse' when it was exhibited at the Guildhall in 1899, it was thought to have once belonged to Ruskin, but he gave his watercolour of this title to the Fitzwilliam Museum in 1861 (W 1025). We can be certain, however, that this view of *Saumur* and its companion, *Nantes*, engraved in the same *Keepsake*, were both once owned by Benjamin Godfrey Windus, although they do not appear in Davis's watercolour of the collection at Tottenham (frontispiece).[3]

1. See Warrell 1997, pp. 185–95.
2. Wilton 1982, nos 49–50.
3. See Whittingham 1987, p. 33.

120

42 Marly-sur-Seine *c.* 1832

Watercolour and bodycolour, 286 × 425 mm

Engraved: For *The Keepsake*, by William Miller, 1832 (R 327)

PROVENANCE: H. A. J. Munro of Novar; his sale Christie's 2 June 1877 (37), bt White, £420; John Heugh; his sale Christie's 10 May 1878 (157), bt C. Harrison, £409 10s.; property of a lady, sale Christie's 19 July 1918 (16), bt Agnew's, £1,050; bt Rev. J. W. R. Brocklebank, 2 October 1918, £1,260 (stock 8984); by descent to Lieut. Brocklebank, RN, his sale Christie's 25 November 1927 (88), bt Agnew's for Lloyd, £1,627 10s. plus 5% commission £81 7s. 6d.

EXHIBITIONS: Agnew's 1920 (17); Agnew's 1928 (23); Agnew's 1951 (84); BM 1959, 1960; BM 1966, 1969 (27); BM 1975 (175); 1985 (96)

R. W. Lloyd Bequest 1958-7-12-433 (W 1047)

Like *Saumur* (no. 41), *Marly-sur-Seine* was based on studies made in France late in the previous decade in preparation for *Rivers of France* (TB CCLX 58, CCLXIII 30), but used instead to make this watercolour, which appeared in Charles Heath's annual *The Keepsake*. Also like the previous work (and *Florence from San Miniato* (no. 40)), it was once owned by Hugh Munro of Novar. Both French river views are much larger than the engravings related to them and were probably created specifically for the *Keepsake*, then exhibited for sale to publicise each new volume.[1]

This view of Marly was painted as a pair to another view of this part of the Seine, *St Germain-en-Laye* (W 1045), also of 1832. In the latter, the river is on the left, its bank filled with working figures wearing the costume of the time of Henri IV rather than the contemporary dress of Louis-Philippe worn by the women in the present work. In *St Germain*, the aqueduct of the Machine de Marly is visible running across the horizon in the distance, while in Lloyd's watercolour it rises like a ruin in a vignette on the far left, from which the sun casts diagonal shafts of light over the gate and through the trees as if through stained-glass windows in a Gothic nave.

Turner used a thick white wove paper with a cream finish for these works, leaving the finish to lend a creamy tone to the work in many parts of the sky while scraping it away in other places for white highlights. In *Saumur* he used very little bodycolour – only a few touches of red, and some ochre for the boats and straw in the foreground – but in *Marly* he employed more than in most of his works of this period. The bright green was a new emerald green pigment developed about this date, and the jewel-like blue, the ochres and reds, even blacks, were used to unite the group of figures and other more far-flung elements of the composition; but most unusual of all in this work is the use of white pigment on top of areas of scratched-out highlights, such as on the dogs, the parapet and the women's dresses. This may have been an experiment with media in response to Turner's study of Venetian painting: Ruskin noted that the group of trees on the left could be found in Tintoretto's *Death of Abel* in the Accademia[2] and in 1833 Turner exhibited two oils with Venetian subjects at the Royal Academy. The type of costumes worn by the women has been the subject of much discussion,[3] but previous writers have failed to notice that the men poling the pleasure boats on the river are dressed as gondoliers – a further reference to Turner's current fascination with all things Venetian.

1. See Warrell 1997, pp. 184–5 and p. 212 (n. 5).

2. *Modern Painters*, I, 1898 edn, p. 84, n. 1.

3. See, for example, Alfrey, p. 55.

43 Tancarville on the Seine 1839

Watercolour and bodycolour, 344 × 477 mm

PROVENANCE: 'Painted for a member of the Swinburne Family in 1839' [according to label post-1887 on back of frame]; by descent to Julia Swinburne by 1887; H. E. Heyman; bt Agnew's 31 July 1912 (with *Biebrich*, £4,000 plus commission £400; stock 7879); bt Lloyd 8 April 1913, £3,500

EXHIBITIONS: RA 1887 (71); Agnew's 1913 (23); Agnew's Manchester 1913 (106); Agnew's Manchester 1928 (49); Agnew's 1932 (96); BM 1959, 1960; BM 1966, 1969 (17); BM 1975 (264)

R. W. Lloyd Bequest 1958-7-12-423 (W 1379)

In 1811 Turner exhibited an oil painting of *Mercury and Herse* at the Royal Academy. At the annual banquet that year, the Prince Regent spoke of 'landscapes which Claude would have admired' and it was generally thought that he was referring to Turner's painting and that he would be its purchaser. The reviews were enthusiastic and two other patrons who wished to buy it were turned down by Turner in anticipation of the Prince's offer, which never actually came. 'The victim of etiquette and delicacy',[1] Turner exhibited it again in his own gallery in 1812 and Sir John Swinburne bought it early the following year, one of several works he and his family were to purchase and commission from the artist (see nos 10–11, 20–21).

Nearly twenty-five years later, after Turner had returned to producing large oil paintings Claudian in atmosphere and composition, plans were afoot to engrave Sir John's painting as a companion plate to one after the painting *Mercury and Argus*, which Turner had exhibited at the Royal Academy in 1836.[2] The project proceeded slowly and the plates were finally published in 1841 and 1842.[3] In the meantime, however, it appears that the renewed contact with the Swinburnes, who had not purchased a work from Turner since 1820, prompted a new commission for a similarly 'Claudian' watercolour, this view of *Tancarville on the Seine*.

Like *Marly-sur-Seine* and *Saumur*, Turner made his original drawings for this composition when he was working on ideas for the planned *Annual Tours* of French rivers. Although the preparatory works for this watercolour therefore date from *c*.1828-30,[4] Wilton argued for a date of *c*.1840 for the finished work on stylistic grounds.[5] In light of the family tradition regarding its commission recorded on the label on the verso, there are strong reasons for believing that it can be firmly dated to 1839, the date it was given when it was exhibited at the Royal Academy in 1887, while it was still in the hands of the Swinburne family. The subject is French in title, and the format is horizontal rather than vertical like the two paintings depicting Mercury, but it shares with them certain elements of the composition and particularly the golden, Italianate, Claudian light which permeates the ruins, lifting them to float on a distant landscape turned into a misty sea of reflections. Whereas in the oils the glowing light is achieved by multiple layers of paint, in watercolour Turner laid only the palest, thinnest washes around the sun and rubbed out, blotted and scraped layers away to create its rays and reflections.

1. See B&J 114.

2. Ibid., 367.

3. Herrmann, pp. 225–6.

4. TB CCLIX 169, CCLXIII 17, 77. Shanes 1997, p. 97.

5. Wilton 1982, p. 54.

44 Lake Nemi *c.* 1840

Watercolour, 347 × 515 mm

INSCRIBED: *JM*[*WT*?] very faintly, centre foreground

ENGRAVED: For Finden's *Royal Gallery of British Art* by R. Wallis, 1842 (R 659)

PROVENANCE: Benjamin G. Windus; J. E. Fordham; John Fowler, Esq. by 1871, his sale (Sir John Fowler), Christie's 6 May 1899 (29), bt Vokins, £3,150; William Cooke, his sale Christie's 8 June 1917 (66), bt Agnew's for Lloyd, £2,152 10s. plus 5% commission £107 12s. 6d. (stock 8598)

EXHIBITIONS: BFAC 1871 (116); RA 1889 (21); Agnew's 1919 (26); Agnew's Manchester 1928 (45); Agnew's 1951 (113); BM 1959, 1960; BM 1966, 1969 (36); BM 1975 (263); BM 1985 (97)

R.W. Lloyd Bequest 1958-7-12-444 (W 1381)

In several of the watercolours in the R. W. Lloyd Bequest Turner attempted to capture in this difficult medium the warmth and atmosphere found in paintings by the greatest painters of 'classical' landscape, artists such as Claude, Poussin and Dughet. Lake Nemi, 'the mirror of Diana', like the neighbouring volcanic crater of Lake Albano, had been a site of pilgrimage for every visitor to Rome, patron or artist, since the seventeenth century. In the work of John Robert Cozens, in particular, it was a motif that was repeated time after time, with a little variation in the viewpoint, types of trees, or figures, and Turner and Girtin must have copied several examples while working from Dr Monro's collection in the 1790s (see Appendix 2, p. 145). Turner himself had painted the lake in watercolour in 1818 before he had even been to Italy, basing his work on a drawing by James Hakewill, for engravings to illustrate the latter's *Picturesque Tour in Italy* (1819). This earlier watercolour belonged to Ruskin and has often been confused with Lloyd's later view.[1]

Employing similar techniques to those he used for his Italianate view of *Tancarville* (no. 43), Turner created this atmospheric watercolour of the most 'classical' of all Italian subjects, not by using layers of paint to achieve texture and depth, but by laying on washes in the thinnest of colours and then sponging them and scraping away highlights, finally conveying a sense of form with the tiniest hatches of coloured brush. The iridescent patches where light seems to sparkle over the hazy landscape, catching the mist in the trees, on the hills and over the lake's surface, are reminiscent of the flecks of white brushwork that flickered over the surface of Constable's painted canvases, attempting to achieve the same effect but by a completely different means.

In 1847 Thomas Tudor, himself a collector of Turner watercolours, made four visits to see Windus's collection at Tottenham. He described this view of Lake Nemi as 'the first work in the collection & no description of it can convey its merits'.[2] Unfortunately it was painted after Scarlett Davis's watercolour of the Windus collection of 1835 (frontispiece), so is not recorded there. When it was exhibited at the Burlington Fine Arts Club in 1871 the catalogue noted that the watercolour was inscribed 'JWT'. All impressions of the first state of the engraving bear the monogram and date 'JMWT 1840' inside the plate-line (R 659).

1. FAS 1900 (18).

2. Whittingham 1987, pp. 30–31.

126

45 Venice: the Grand Canal, looking towards the Dogana *c.* 1840

Watercolour, 221 × 320 mm

PROVENANCE: Hon. William Henry Smith, MP, by descent to his son, Hon. William Frederick D. Smith, MP; bt Agnew's 4 April 1908
(with five others); bt Sir Joseph Beecham 26 June 1908 (£5,500 for six watercolours); his sale Christie's 4 May 1917 (156),
bt Agnew's for Lloyd, £1,732 plus 5% commission £86 12s. 6d. (stock 8575)

EXHIBITIONS: Agnew's 1909 (168); Agnew's 1924 (94); RA 1934 (897) (778); BM 1959, 1960; BM 1966, 1969 (35); BM 1975 (259); BM 1985 (98)

R. W. Lloyd Bequest 1958-7-12-443 (W 1359)

Venice held a special fascination for Turner, as for so many other artists, and his watercolours and oils of the city have a magical quality which has received more universal acclaim than perhaps any other aspect of his work. He made his third and last visit to Venice in 1840, staying for fourteen days at the end of August and basing himself at the Hotel Europa. Even on this third visit he was still so completely engrossed in capturing the nuances of the city's atmosphere and light that the artist William Callow recorded being made to feel guilty by the older man's unflagging labours: 'One evening whilst I was enjoying a cigar in a gondola I saw in another one Turner sketching San Giorgio, brilliantly lit up by the setting sun. I felt quite ashamed of myself idling away the time whilst he was hard at work so late.'[1]

Most of Turner's watercolours of Venice remained in his studio, and are now to be found in his sketchbooks and colour beginnings in the Turner Bequest at the Tate Gallery. He may have hoped that the the result of his 1840 tour would be commissions for large finished works like his late Swiss watercolours of *Zurich* and *Lucerne* (see nos 46–7) but, apart from one possible commission from the Ruskins,[2] these were not forthcoming. Instead, over two dozen sheets were removed from the sketchbooks and sold to Turner's patrons, probably by his dealer at the time, Thomas Griffith. At least six (from TB CCCXV) were purchased by John Ruskin. One characteristic common to nearly all his late Venetian watercolours is the use of red tones to make objects stand out and blues to make them recede, creating a sense of depth with the minimum of detail. Some previous writers have suggested that the red lines which sketch the architecture in this work and others were drawn by the artist with pen and ink; a close examination, however, shows that some may have been drawn with pen dipped in watercolour,[3] while others could have been made with the finest of brushes, as one would expect from an artist who from a fairly early stage seldom relied upon pencil or pen to indicate architectural details.

Turner's viewpoint was probably from the steps of S. Maria della Salute, but the misty campanile of S. Marco and the even paler ghosts of gondolas floating across the foreground make it seem unlikely that it was completely finished on the spot.

1. *Autobiography*, quoted in BM 1985 (98).

2. See Warrell 1995, pp. 96–7.

3. See ibid., p. 45.

46 Zurich 1842

Watercolour with touches of bodycolour, 300 × 456 mm

PROVENANCE: Painted for H. A. J. Munro of Novar, sale Christie's 6 April 1878 (87), bt Agnew's, £1,260 (stock 4575); bt J. Irvine Smith 8 April 1878; bt Agnew's 10 January 1907 (stock 6114); bt Sir George Drummond 29 January 1907; his sale Christie's 27 June 1919 (129), bt Agnew's, £6,510; bt C. Morland Agnew 10 July 1919, £7,000 (stock 9317); bt Agnew's 8 [sic] May 1924, £4,500 (stock 477); bt Lloyd 5 May 1924, £5,000

EXHIBITIONS: Agnew's 1907 (39); Agnew's 1920 (19); RA 1934 (884: incorrectly said to have been exh. FAS 1878); Agnew's 1951 (116); BM 1959, 1969; BM 1966, 1969 (38); BM 1975 (286); BM 1985 (100)

1958-7-12-445 (W 1533)

Turner's 1836 tour to the Val d'Aosta with his friend and patron Munro of Novar reawakened his interest in Switzerland, and from 1840 until 1845 he went there every year. He not only returned to favourite sites, seeking to reinterpret them, but also sought out new alpine scenes. The small group of finished watercolours from these tours, produced when Turner was at the height of his technical and creative powers, must have been the most desirable from Lloyd's point of view, but those available were finite in number and he only managed to secure two – although undoubtedly two of the finest.

Turner returned from his travels in 1841 bearing the usual results of such a tour – hastily made pencil sketches in small notebooks and 'composed' views broadly sketched in watercolour in larger soft-bound notebooks that he carried with him, rolled in his pocket. The following spring he decided to produce a group of twenty finished watercolours based on the large colour sketches, but he was unwilling to undertake such a substantial group without commissions for at least some of them. In order to attract such commissions, he thought of showing potential clients his colour sketches, but because they were not of uniform size or style, he produced another set all of the same size, carefully ensuring that he reproduced the character of 'the original sketch in the primitive state'.[1] In the end he only managed to produce fifteen of these 'samples' and four finished works derived from them, which he gave his dealer Griffith to try to organise buyers at 80 guineas each. Turner's earlier patron Benjamin Windus thought them too dramatic a departure from his earlier work, but Munro of Novar bought three of the finished watercolours and commissioned one more from the samples – this view of *Zurich*.[2] One of the finished works purchased by Munro was *The Pass of the Splügen* (W 1523), the one most coveted by John Ruskin, who described this group from 1842 as 'the most finished and faultless works of his last period'.[3] In this watercolour, which has been described as 'ecstatic', suggesting 'perhaps, the apotheosis of city life',[4] Turner seems to have finally realised the union he had been striving to achieve through subject matter and medium for decades – that of man, history and landscape.

1. Warrell 1995, p.12, also Appendix II for the most thorough discussion of all the late Swiss watercolours, 1841–51.
2. Based on sample study TB CCCLXIV 291, inscribed on verso 'J.A. Munro Esqr/4' and in red chalk '10'; see Warrell 1995 (22), illus.
3. FAS 1900, p. 65.
4. Wilton 1982 (99).

47 Lucerne by moonlight 1843

Watercolour, with touches of bodycolour and some black chalk, on white paper [J WHATMAN 1816], 290 × 476 mm. Verso: slight pencil sketches of gondolas and small boats with sails

PROVENANCE: H. A. J. Munro of Novar; his sale Christie's 2 June 1877 (34), bt Agnew's, 850 gns (stock 4280); bt J. Irvine Smith 28 June 1877; bt Agnew's 10 August 1903 for 3,500 gns with a group of other Turners; Agnew's 1904 (209); bt R. E. Tatham, 2,400 gns (stock 4408); bequeathed by Tatham to W. G. Gibbs, his partner; bt Agnew's 25 February 1920, £4,000; bt Lloyd 28 February 1920, £4,750 (stock 9517)

EXHIBITIONS: Manchester 1857 (378); Agnew's 1920 (18); Agnew's 1924 (52); BFAC 1936-7 (102); Agnew's 1951 (115); BM 1959, 1960; BM 1966, 1969 (38); BM 1975 (292)

R. W. Lloyd Bequest 1958-7-12-446 (W 1536)

In 1843 Turner again returned from his travels to Switzerland with the aim of producing a further set of watercolours. Only six were completed, of which four were commissioned by H. A. J. Munro, including this view of *Lucerne by moonlight*. Based on TB CCLXIV 324,[1] the finished watercolour may not have actually come into Munro's possession until 1844. Ruskin included this finely wrought work in his list of the three best paintings from the entire series of Swiss watercolours, and seems to have missed the opportunity of acquiring it with the others because 'I wanted to make Turner do more – which he never did'.[2] In 1878 Ruskin described the two watercolours he owned from this 1843 group as 'Done passionately; and somewhat hastily, as drawing near the end. Nevertheless, I would not take all the rest of the collection put together for them.'[3]

Recently removed from its mount, this watercolour was found to have slight sketches of an unrelated subject on the verso; but more interesting is that it is on the same paper Turner had used over twenty years previously when working up larger versions of his views on the Rhine. This paper is whiter and thinner and is sized to give a smoother, shinier finish than the rather creamy, thick, matt paper he used for the *England and Wales* series, suggesting that the final effect he was trying to achieve in these late Swiss works was quite different

in tone and texture from the picturesque views of Britain. The final results were, as was appropriate for Switzerland, somehow crisper and cooler in atmosphere and effect, but the play of light on buildings, people, water, distant landscape, or even in darkness, as here, was the motif he was most concerned to capture.

The only moonlit view of the finished late Swiss series, this watercolour has been described by Andrew Wilton as a 'symphony in black and silver worthy of Whistler'. The focal point is the dramatic silhouette of the picturesque wooden bridge, constructed in the fourteenth century to serve not only as a bridge but also as a rampart against Austrian incursion. From the seventeenth century its rafters had been hung with paintings depicting scenes from Swiss history and the lives of the patron saints of Lucerne, and the bridge was thus not only a symbol of Lucerne's independence but also a focal point for Swiss national pride.[4]

1. Illus. Warrell 1995, p. 150.

2. Ibid., p. 152.

3. FAS 1900, p. 64.

4. J. Russell, *Switzerland*, 1950, quoted in Wilton 1982 (110); sadly, the bridge was recently almost destroyed by fire.

Abbreviations and Primary Sources

Agnew's – Thomas Agnew and Sons
Archives consulted include:
CLIENTS BOOK: lists of purchases made by important clients in order purchased
LONDON DAY BOOKS: records of invoices out (referred to by volume: followed by folio)
DRAWINGS STOCK BOOKS: records of stock, with details of purchase of drawings by Agnew's and their later sale (referred to by stock number)
PAINTINGS STOCK BOOKS: records of stock, with details of purchase of paintings by Agnew's and their later sale (referred to by stock number)
TURNER CARD INDEX: consisting of catalogue entry from Sir Walter Armstrong's *Turner*, 1902 (pp. 238–86, unnumbered) cut out and pasted to card, with MS annotations of additional provenance and exhibition history by Agnew's staff

BFAC – Burlington Fine Arts Club, London

B&J – Butlin, M., and Joll, E., *The Paintings of J. M. W. Turner*, rev. edn, 2 vols, New Haven and London, 1984

BM – British Museum

FAS – Fine Art Society, London

P&D – Department of Prints and Drawings, British Museum
Archives/collections consulted include:
LLOYD'S TYPESCRIPT CATALOGUE: of his collection (compiled for him by E. Cundall?)
FRAMES: information taken from labels and marks on the frames in which the Lloyd collection was acquired, and from which the Museum removed the watercolours for storage and conservation purposes shortly after they were bequeathed in 1958

R – Rawlinson, W. G., *The Engraved Work of J. M. W. Turner R.A.*, London, 1908–13

TB – Turner Bequest, originally housed in the National Gallery, then National Gallery of British Art (Tate Gallery) until 1931 when deposited in the British Museum, and from 1987 housed in the Clore Gallery of the Tate Gallery, London (for catalogue of collection see Finberg 1909)

TS – *Turner Studies*, a bi-annual journal published in association with the Tate Gallery, 1981–92 (11 vols)

W – Wilton, A., *The Life and Work of J. M. W. Turner*, London, 1979 (includes catalogue raisonné of watercolours)

Exhibitions in which works from the Lloyd Bequest have been included

NB Thomas Agnew and Sons (Agnew's) held annual watercolour 'exhibitions', which included works lent and works for sale, in Liverpool, Manchester and London. In the present catalogue they are listed under PROVENANCE if they were for sale at that time, with the price, and under EXHIBITIONS if they were lent. 'Agnew's' refers to London unless otherwise stated. Only special Turner exhibitions at Agnew's are listed below.

1822, 9 Soho Square, London, W. B. Cooke's *Exhibition of Drawings by Modern and English Masters and Old Masters*

1823, 9 Soho Square, London, Feb.–May, W. B. Cooke's *Exhibition of Drawings by British Artists*

1828, Newcastle, Northern Academy of Arts

1829, Egyptian Hall, Piccadilly, London, June/July, Charles Heath (watercolours for *England and Wales*)

1833, Moon, Boys and Graves Gallery, 6 Pall Mall, London (watercolours for *England and Wales*)

1839, Leeds, Music Hall, *Leeds Public Exhibition in Aid of the Mechanics Institute*

1857, Manchester, *Catalogue of the Art Treasures of the United Kingdom collected at Manchester in 1857*

1862, London, *Handbook to the Fine Art Collections in the International Exhibition of 1862*

1868, Leeds, *Official Catalogue of the National Exhibition of Works of Art, at Leeds, 1868*

1871, Burlington Fine Arts Club, *Exhibition of Drawings in Water Colours by Artists Born Anterior to 1800 and now Deceased, Illustrative of the Progress and Development of that Branch of the Fine Arts in Britain*

1878, Fine Art Society's Galleries, 148 New Bond St., London, *Notes by Mr Ruskin on his Drawings by the late J. M. W. Turner, R.A.* (see also 1900)

1882, Worcestershire, *Official Catalogue of the Worcestershire Exhibition, Fine Arts Section* (held for the benefit of the Worcester Public Library)

1884, Burlington Fine Arts Club, *Exhibition of Architectural Subjects by Deceased British Artists*

1886, Royal Academy, Burlington House Winter Exhibition, *Exhibition of Works by the Old Masters, and Deceased Masters of the British School, including a Selection from the Works of Joseph Wright (of Derby) and a Collection of Water-Colour Drawings by Joseph M. W. Turner, R.A.*

1887, Royal Academy, Burlington House Winter Exhibition, *Exhibition of Works by the Old Masters . . . including a Collection of Water-Colour Drawings by Joseph M. W. Turner, R.A.*

1889, Royal Academy, Burlington House Winter Exhibition, *Exhibition of Works by the Old Masters . . . and a Collection of Water-Colour Drawings by Joseph M. W. Turner, R.A.*

1891, Royal Academy, Burlington House, *Exhibition of Works by the Old Masters . . . including a Collection of Drawings illustrating the Progress of the Art of Water Colour in England*

1896, Corporation of London Art Gallery, Guildhall, *Catalogue of the Loan Collection of Water Colour Drawings*

1899, Corporation of London, Guildhall,

Catalogue of the Loan Collection of Pictures and Drawings by J. M. W. Turner, R.A., and a selection of Pictures by some of his Contemporaries

1899, Birmingham, Corporation of City of Birmingham Museum and Art Gallery, *Catalogue of the Loan Collection of Pictures and Drawings by Joseph Mallord William Turner R.A.*

1900, Fine Art Society's Galleries, 148 New Bond St., London, *Notes by John Ruskin on His Water-Colours by J. M. W. Turner, R.A.*, new edition of the 1878 exhibition and catalogue, with several new numbers

1901, Glasgow Exhibition, *Fine Arts Section . . . Official Catalogue of Art Objects*

1902, Messrs. Lawrie & Co Galleries, 159 Bond Street, London, *Catalogue of the Farnley Hall Collection of Pictures and Drawings by J. M. W. Turner, R.A.* (taken from mimeograph version in Agnew's library, dated '1902' in pencil on title page; proceeds to King's Hospital)

1911, Grafton Galleries, London, 4 Oct.–28 Dec., *Loan Exhibition of Old Masters, including an Historical Collection of British Water Colours lent by members of the Walpole Society, in aid of the National Art Collections Fund*, selected and catalogued by A. J. Finberg

1913, Agnew's, Apr.–May, *Exhibition of Water Colour Drawings by J. M. W. Turner RA*

1919, Burlington Fine Arts Club, *Catalogue of a Collection of Early Drawings and Pictures of London*

1922–3, Burlington Fine Arts Club, *Catalogue of a Collection of Drawings by John Robert Cozens*

1924, Agnew's, *Exhibition of Watercolour Drawings by Turner, Cox and De Wint* (see Oppé 1925)

1934, Royal Academy of Arts, 6 Jan.–17 Mar.,

Exhibition of British Art, c.1000–1860, cat. published in 1934; rev. edn 1935 with different cat. nos, as *Commemorative Catalogue of the Exhibition of British Art, Royal Academy of Arts, London Jan.–Mar. 1934*

1936–7, Burlington Fine Arts Club, *Catalogue of an Exhibition of Pictures, Drawings, Furniture and other Objects of Art*

1951, Agnew's, Feb.–Mar., *Centenary Loan Exhibition of Watercolour Drawings by J. M. W. Turner, R.A.*

1951–2, Royal Academy of Arts, Winter Exhibition, Dec. 1951–Mar. 1952, *The First Hundred Years of the Royal Academy. 1769–1868*

1953, Agnew's, *Loan Exhibition of Water-Colour Drawings by Thomas Girtin*

1959, BM, 4–15 Feb., *The R. W. Lloyd Bequest*, mimeograph Introduction, no numbered checklist, but list of works exhibited in BM P&D Mounters' Book, 30 Dec. 1958

1960, BM, repeat of above exhibition

1966, BM, P&D, 1–14 Feb., *Turner Water-Colours from the R. W. Lloyd Bequest*, mimeograph Introduction and checklist (38 items)

1969, BM, P&D, 9–23 Feb., repeat of above exhibition

1975, BM, P&D, 9 May 1975–18 Jan. 1976, *Turner in the British Museum: Drawings and Watercolours* (cat. by Andrew Wilton)

1985, BM, P&D, *British Landscape Watercolours 1600–1860* (cat. by Lindsay Stainton)

Bibliography

Abbot Hall Art Gallery, Kendal, *Sublime Inspiration: The Art of Mountains from Turner to Hillary*, exh. cat. (ed. Edward King), Kendal, 1997

Agnew, Geoffrey, *Agnew's 1817–1967*, London, 1967

Alfrey, Nicholas, Review of A. Wilton, *Turner Abroad*, in *TS* 3/1 (1983), p. 55

Allen, David Elliston, *The Naturalist in Britain: A Social History*, London, 1976 (2nd edn Princeton, 1994)

Armstrong, Walter, *Turner*, London and New York, 1902

Bell, C. F., and Girtin, Thomas, 'The drawings and sketches of John Robert Cozens: a catalogue with an historical introduction', *Walpole Society* XXIII, Oxford, 1934–5

Berg, Maxine, 'Representations of early industrial towns: Turner and his contemporaries', in Rosenthal *et al.*, pp. 115–30

Blakeney, T. S., 'In Memoriam: R. W. Lloyd', *Alpine Journal* 63, no. 297 (1958), pp. 232–6

Boase, T. S. R., 'English artists and the Val d'Aosta', *Journal of the Warburg and Courtauld Institutes* XIX, London, 1956, pp. 283–93

Boase, T. S. R., 'Shipwrecks in English Romantic painting', *Journal of the Warburg and Courtauld Institutes* XXII, London, 1959, pp. 332–46

Bower, Peter, *Turner's Papers: A Study of the Manufacture, Selection and Use of his Drawing Papers 1787–1820*, exh. cat., Tate Gallery, London, 1990

Brown, T. Graham, 'In Memoriam: R. W. Lloyd', *Alpine Journal* 68, no. 297 (1958), pp. 237–8

Campbell, Charles, *The Traveller's Complete Guide through Belgium and Holland . . . with a Sketch of a Tour in Germany*, 2nd edn 1817

Campbell, Mungo, *A Complete Catalogue of Works by Turner in the National Gallery of Scotland*, Edinburgh, 1993

Casteras, Susan P., ' " The germ of a museum" . . . the curating of the Saint George's Museum', in *John Ruskin and the Victorian Eye*, exh. cat., Phoenix Art Museum (with essays by Casteras, R. Hewison, *et al.*), New York, 1993, pp. 184–210

Champion, H. G., 'In Memoriam: Robert Wylie Lloyd, F.R.E.S.', *Entomologists' Monthly Magazine* 94 (1958), pp. 96–9

Colson, Percy, *A Story of Christie's*, London, 1950

Colvin, Howard, *A Biographical Dictionary of British Architects 1600–1840*, 3rd edn, New Haven and London, 1995

Coombs, Trevor, *Watercolours: The Charles Lees Collection at Oldham Art Gallery*, exh. cat., Oldham, 1993

Coppel, Stephen, 'George Salting (1835–1909)', in A. Griffiths (ed.), *Landmarks in Print Collecting: Connoisseurs and Donors at the British Museum since 1753*, London, 1996, pp 189–203 (=1996a)

Coppel, Stephen, 'The Australian collector George Salting 1835–1909: Prince of Weeders', typescript of paper given at symposium 'Turner in Australia', Canberra, 1996, 19 pp. (=1996b)

Davis, Maurice, *Turner as Professor: The Artist and Linear Perspective*, exh. cat., Tate Gallery, London, 1992

Dawson, Barbara, *Turner in the National Gallery of Ireland*, Dublin, 1988

Deardon, James, *John Ruskin: An Illustrated Life, 1819–1900*, Coniston, 1973; rev. edn 1981

Egerton, Judy, *Making and Meaning. Turner: the Fighting Temeraire*, exh. cat., National Gallery, London, 1995

Fawkes, Walter, *A Collection of Water Colour Drawings in the Possession of Walter Fawkes, 45 Grosvenor Place*, London, 1819 (National Art Library, Victoria and Albert Museum, Box I 38 ZZ)

Finberg, Alex J., *A Complete Inventory of the Drawings of the Turner Bequest*, 2 vols, National Gallery, London, 1909

Finberg, Alex J. *Turner's Water-Colours at Farnley Hall*, London, 1912

Finberg, Alex J., *Notes on Four Pencil Drawings of J M W Turner*, published privately, London, 1921

Finley, Gerald, *Landscapes of Memory: Turner as Illustrator to Scott*, London, 1980

Gage, John, 'Turner and Stourhead: the making of a classicist?', *Art Quarterly* XXXVII (1974), pp. 59–87

Gage, John (ed.), *Collected Correspondence of J. M. W. Turner*, Oxford, 1980

Gage, John, *J. M. W. Turner: 'A Wonderful Range of Mind'*, New Haven and London, 1987

Gardnor, Rev. John, *Views taken on and near the River Rhine*, London, 1788–91; 2nd edn 1792

Goldman, Paul, 'The perfectionist collector: R. W. Lloyd', *The Antique Collector* 9 (1985), pp. 66–71

'H., M.I.', 'The use of indigo. Turner's drawings'

(reprinted from *The Builder*, 24 Oct. 1857, p. 609), *TS* 5/1 (1985), pp. 25–6

'H., W.D.', 'Robert Wylie Lloyd 1868–1958', *Journal of the Society of British Entomologists* 6 (May 1959), p. 59

Hartley, Craig, 'John Edward Taylor's collection of Turner watercolours', *Antique Dealer and Collector's Guide*, Apr. 1984, pp. 42–5

Hastings Museum and Art Gallery, *Turner to Burra: Painters of Hastings 1780–1950*, exh. cat., 1991

Heleniak, K. M., *William Mulready*, New Haven and London, 1980.

Herrmann, Luke, *Turner Prints: The Engraved Work of J. M. W. Turner*, Oxford, 1990

Hewison, Robert, *Ruskin and Oxford: The Art of Education*, exh. cat., Ashmolean Museum, Oxford, 1996

Hill, David, *Turner in Yorkshire*, exh. cat., York City Art Gallery, 1980

Hill, David, 'A newly discovered letter by Turner', *Turner Society News*, no. 23 (1981/2), pp. 2–3

Hill, David, *Turner in the Alps. The Journey through France and Switzerland in 1802*, London, 1982

Hill, David, *In Turner's Footsteps – Through the Dales and Hills of Northern England*, London, 1984

Hill, David, *Turner's Birds: Bird Studies from Farnley Hall*, exh. cat., Leeds City Art Gallery, Oxford, 1988

Hill, David, *Turner in the North*, New Haven and London, 1996

Kriz, K. Dian, *The Idea of the English Landscape Painter: Genius as an Alibi in the Early Nineteenth Century*, New Haven and London, 1997

Leeds City Art Gallery, *Watercolours from Leeds City Art Gallery*, exh. cat. with essays by C. Miller, P. Mason, *et al.*, Leeds, 1995

Lyles, Anne, *Turner and Natural History: The Farnley Project*, exh. cat., Tate Gallery, London, 1988

Lyles, Anne, *Young Turner: Early Works to 1800*, exh. cat., Tate Gallery, London 1989

Lyles, Anne, *Turner: The Fifth Decade Watercolours 1830–1840*, exh. cat., Tate Gallery, London, 1992

Macmichael, N. H. (ed.), *Westminster Abbey Official Guide*, new edn 1977

Martin, Alec, 'Industrialist and collector' (obituary of R.W. Lloyd), *The Times*, 30 April 1958

Martin, Alec, 'In Memoriam: R. W. Lloyd', *Alpine Journal* 63, no. 297 (1958), pp. 236–7

Miller, Frank, *J. M. W. Turner Paintings in Merseyside Collections*, National Museums and Galleries on Merseyside, Liverpool, 1990

Morrell, Mary Tussey, 'J. M. W. Turner's working methods in his 1817 series of 51 Rhenish Drawings', Ph.D. thesis, Stanford, 1993, printed U.M.I., Ann Arbor, 1994

Munro, Jane, *British Landscape Watercolours 1750–1850 (in the Fitzwilliam Museum)*, London and Cambridge, 1994

Oppé, A. P., *The Water Colours of Turner, Cox and De Wint* (cat. of an exhibition held at Agnews Apr. and May 1924), London and New York, 1925

Pevsner, N. P., *Wiltshire* (1963), rev. B. Cherry, Harmondsworth, 1975

Pocklington, G. R., *The Story of W. H. Smith and Son*, London, 1921

Powell, C., 'Topography, imagination and travel: Turner's relationship with James Hakewill', *Art History* 5/4 (1982), pp. 408–25

Powell, C., *Turner in the South: Rome, Florence, Naples*, New Haven and London, 1987

Powell, C., *Rivers of Europe: Turner's Rhine, Meuse and Mosel*, exh. cat., Tate Gallery, London, 1991

Powell, C., *Turner in Germany*, exh. cat., Tate Gallery, London, 1995

Roberts, Jane, *Views of Windsor: Watercolours by Thomas and Paul Sandby from the Collection of Her Majesty Queen Elizabeth II*, London, 1995

Rosenthal, M., Payne, C., and Wilcox, S. (eds), *Prospects for the Nation: Recent Essays in British Landscape 1750–1880*, New Haven and London, 1997

Royal Academy, *Turner 1775–1851*, exh. organised jointly with Tate Gallery (cat. by M. Butlin and A. Wilton), London, 1974

Ruskin, John, *Notes by John Ruskin on his Water-Colours by J M W Turner* (exh. at FAS 1878 and 1900), London, 1900

Ruskin, John, *Modern Painters*, 2nd edn, London, 1898

Russell, John, and Wilton, Andrew, *Turner in Switzerland*, Zurich, 1976

Schreiber, A., *The Traveller's Guide to the Rhine*, 4th edn, London, 1836

Shanes, Eric, *Turner's Picturesque Views in England and Wales 1825–1838*, London and New York, 1979

Shanes, Eric, *Turner's Rivers, Harbours and Coasts*, London, 1981

Shanes, Eric, 'Picture notes: John Scarlett Davis, *The Library at Tottenham . . .*', *TS* 3/2 (1984), pp. 55–8 (= 1984a)

Shanes, Eric, 'New light on the "England and Wales" series', *TS* 4/1 (1984), pp. 52–4 (= 1984b)

Shanes, Eric, *Turner's Watercolour Explorations 1810–1842*, exh. cat., Tate Gallery, London, 1997

Stader, Karl H., *William Turner und der Rhein*, Bonn, 1981

Stainton, Lindsay, *Turner's Venice*, London, 1985

Stroud, Dorothy, *Humphry Repton*, London, 1962

Tate Gallery 1974: see Royal Academy

Thornbury, Walter, *The Life of J. M. W. Turner, R.A.*, 2 vols, London, 1862

Upstone, Robert, *Turner: The Final Years, Watercolours 1840–1851*, exh. cat., Tate Gallery, London 1992

Usherwood, Paul, *Art for Newcastle: Thomas Miles Richardson and the Newcastle Exhibitions 1822–1843*, exh. cat., Laing Art Gallery, Newcastle upon Tyne, 1984

Warrell, Ian, *Turner: The Fourth Decade, Watercolours 1820–1830*, exh. cat., Tate Gallery, London, 1991

Warrell, Ian, *Through Switzerland with Turner: Ruskin's First Selection from the Turner Bequest*, exh. cat., Tate Gallery, London, 1995

Warrell, Ian, *Turner on the Loire*, exh. cat., Tate Gallery, London, 1997

Whitley, W. T., *Artists and their Friends in England 1800–1820*, 2 vols, London, 1928

Whittingham, Selby, *Constable and Turner at Salisbury*, Salisbury, 1972, rev. edn 1976

Whittingham, Selby, 'The Turner collector: Benjamin Godfrey Windus 1790–1867', *TS* 7/2 (1987), pp. 29–35

Whittingham, Selby, 'Windus, Turner and Ruskin: new documents', *J. M. W. Turner, R.A.*, no. 2 (Dec. 1993), pp. 69–116

Whitworth Art Gallery, *Turner Watercolours in the Whitworth Art Gallery*, exh. cat. (text by C. Hartley), Manchester, 1984

Whitworth Art Gallery, *Ruskin and the English Watercolour from Turner to the Pre-Raphaelites*, exh. cat. (text by A. Sumner), Manchester, 1989

Whitworth Art Gallery, *Turner Watercolours from Manchester*, exh. cat., The Trust for Museum Exhibitions, touring USA and ending at Whitworth Art Gallery in 1998 (text by Charles Nugent and Melva Croal), Manchester and Washington, D.C., 1996

Wilcox, Timothy, *Francis Towne*, exh. cat., Tate Gallery, London, 1997

Wilton, Andrew, see W under Abbreviations

Wilton, Andrew, *Turner Abroad*, London, 1982

Wilton, Andrew, 'The "Monro school" question: some answers', *TS* 4/2 (1984), pp. 8–23

Wilton, Andrew, *Turner in his Time*, London and New York, 1987

Yardley, Edward, 'The Turner collector: "that munificent gentleman" – James Rivington Wheeler', *TS* 6/2 (1986), pp. 51–60

Appendix 1

British Drawings and Watercolours in the R. W. Lloyd Bequest to the Department of Prints and Drawings, British Museum, 1958

The following appendix includes a few works by Turner from Lloyd's Bequest that it was not possible to include in the catalogue entries. It lists all the works by British artists in the bequest, but does not include 18 additional works, mostly anonymous, of the Dutch, Italian, French and Swiss schools.

ANONYMOUS (formerly attributed to Paul Sandby)
Rocky waterfall at Bettwys-y-Coed; falls centre left, with figures
Watercolour, with bodycolour and pink bodycolour border, 452 × 577 mm
INSCRIBED: *P. Sandby*
PROVENANCE: purchased by Lloyd from W. T. Spencer, Isle of Wight, 1920s
1958-7-12-318

ANONYMOUS (formerly attributed to Paul Sandby)
Rocky waterfall at Bettwys-y-Coed; falls centre foreground, with figures above
Watercolour, with bodycolour and pink bodycolour border, 524 × 650 mm
INSCRIBED: *P. Sandby*
PROVENANCE: as above
1958-7-12-319

ANONYMOUS (formerly attributed to Paul Sandby)
Rocky waterfall at Bettwys-y-Coed; falls in background, with figures in distance
Watercolour, with bodycolour and pink bodycolour border, 451 × 576 mm

INSCRIBED: *P. Sandby*
PROVENANCE: as above
1958-7-12-320

ANONYMOUS
Village on the Cornish coast; view of quarry by bay, village in foreground
Watercolour, with bodycolour and pink bodycolour border, 449 × 573 mm
PROVENANCE: as above
1958-7-12-321

GEORGE BARRET the younger (1767–1842)
Returning from labour: sunset; woody landscape on a hill with figures and dog on a road, towns on plain in distance
Watercolour with gum arabic, 326 × 488 mm
PROVENANCE: Murray sale, Christie's 2 February 1920 (10), bt Agnew's for Lloyd, £54 12s. plus £2 14s. 6d. (stock 9469)
1958-7-12-322

J. S. BARTH (*fl.* 1797–1810)
Mer de Glace, Chamonix, 1810; figures in foreground on ice, glacier stretching length of valley beyond, goats to left
Watercolour and grey wash, with bodycolour, 515 × 710 mm
SIGNED and dated; INSCRIBED on verso: *The Sea of Ice, otherways known by the name of Glacier du Montagn Vert. Chammonni. Savoy*
PROVENANCE: N. D. Newall, Northumberland, bt Lloyd 4 November 1937, £20
1958-7-12-323

J. S. BARTH (*fl.* 1797–1810)
Waterfall (at Dawlish, Devon?), 1810; picnic in foreground, at base of waterfall in three tiers from steep cliffs
Watercolour, with bodycolour, 571 × 447 mm
INSCRIBED on verso: *J. S. Barth. N 288. High Holborn London/ Dawlish in Devon Ag¹ 1810.*

PROVENANCE: N. D. Newall, Northumberland, bt Lloyd 4 November 1937, £10
1958-7-12-324

HERCULES BRABAZON BRABAZON (1821–1906), after Turner
The Castle of Chillon, after Turner
Watercolour and bodycolour over pencil, on grey paper, 229 × 356 mm
VERSO: Head of a woman, to right. Pencil on grey paper
INSCRIBED: *HBB* and *Chillon*
PROVENANCE: Mrs Brabazon Combe, sale Christie's 18 March 1926 (45), bt Agnew's £28 7s.; bt Lloyd 19 March 1926, £35 (stock 770)
1958-7-12-325

HERCULES BRABAZON BRABAZON (1821–1906) after Turner
Venice, after Turner
Watercolour, 219 × 296 mm
INSCRIBED: *HBB*
PROVENANCE: Mrs Brabazon Combe, sale Christie's 18 March 1926 (93), bt Agnew's for Lloyd £157 10s. plus 5% commission £7 17s. 6d. (stock 773)
1958-7-12-326

WILLIAM CALLOW (1812–1908)
View at Falmouth; from the water, town in distance
Watercolour, with touches of bodycolour, over pencil sketch, 240 × 321 mm
INSCRIBED: *W. Callow*
PROVENANCE: Lewis H. Samuel, S. Kensington; his sale, Christie's 16 July 1915 (105), bt Agnew's for Lloyd, £12 12s., plus 5% commission 12s. 6d. (stock 8371)
1958-7-12-327

JOHN CONEY (1786–1833)
St Mary Overy, Southwark; warehouse with

draymen and cart to right
Watercolour over pencil sketch, 197 × 298 mm
PROVENANCE: A. A. Allen, Esq., sale Sotheby's
4 April 1935 (25), bt Agnew's for Lloyd, £7 plus
5% commission 7s. (stock 1730)
1958-7-12-328

JOHN SELL COTMAN (1782–1842)
Gormire, Yorkshire (probably a view of Cader Idris
from Barmouth ?), *c.* 1803–4; two figures in
foreground with cattle on shore of lake,
mountains in distance
Watercolour, 372 × 546 mm
PROVENANCE: RA 1804 (928 or 375?); W.
Richardson, bt Agnew's 24 January 1919, £150
(for this and another); Agnew's 1919 (74), bt
Lloyd 3 March 1919, £240 (stock 9113); BM
1959, 1960, 1985 (116)
1958-7-12-329

JOHN SELL COTMAN (1782–1842)
Mont St Michel, Normandy; seen from the water at
low tide, group of horses and figures on left
Watercolour over pencil, 307 × 530 mm
PROVENANCE: BFAC 1888 (77), lent by John
Gunn, Norwich; his widow's sale, Christie's 26
April 1912, bt Agnew's, £105; Agnew's
Manchester 1912 (5), bt Lloyd 15 November,
£231 (stock 7704); BM 1959, 1960
1958-7-12-330

attr. to JOHN SELL COTMAN (1782–1842)
Mount and Fort of St Marion, Bay of la Hogue; fort
seen from the water
Watercolour over pencil, 233 × 398 mm
PROVENANCE: Sir Hickman Bacon, bt Agnew's
January 1913; Agnew's 1913 (4); bt W. B.
Patterson; exh. Patterson's, 5 Old Bond St.,
London, June and July 1913 (19), bt Lloyd 2
December 1913; BM 1959, 1960
1958-7-12-331

DAVID COX (1783–1859)
Boys fishing; fields divided by river, horse on left
Watercolour, with touches of bodycolour, over
black chalk sketch, 272 × 371 mm
PROVENANCE: John Graham; H. E. Walters;
sold to Agnew's 27 March 1918, £240 (one of a
group: stock 8783); group bt A. E. Lawley 6 May
1918, £10,000; his sale Christie's 25 February
1921 (79), bt Agnew's for Lloyd, £493 10s. plus
5% commission £24 13s. 6d. (stock 9917);
Agnew's 1924 (14)
1958-7-12-335

attr. to DAVID COX (1783–1859)
Town on a river
Watercolour, 178 × 311 mm
PROVENANCE: H. E. Walters; sold to Agnew's
27 March 1918, £30 (one of a group: stock 8787);
group bt A. E. Lawley 6 May 1918, £10,000; his
sale Christie's 25 February 1921 (86), bt Agnew's
for Lloyd £35 14s. plus 5% commission £1 15s.
(stock 9918)
1958-7-12-336

DAVID COX (1783–1859)
The crossroads, 1849; two men on horseback
passing each other on muddy track
Pen and brown ink and brown wash, with
watercolour, touched with bodycolour,
607 × 873 mm
INSCRIBED: *David Cox 1849*
PROVENANCE: Bullock sale 1870, £388 10s.;
T. H. Ismay sale 1908, £262 10s., bt Agnew's for
James Ismay; his sale Sotheby's August 1930, bt
Vicars Brothers for Lloyd, £300
1958-7-12-337

JOHN ROBERT COZENS (1752–97)
Lake Nemi; lake in crater to right, town on ridge
on far side
Watercolour over pencil, 360 × 522 mm
PROVENANCE: John Rushout, 2nd Baron

Northwick; by descent to Lord Northwick, his
sale, Sotheby's 3 November 1920 (348), bt
Agnew's for Lloyd, £205 plus 5% commission
£10 5s. (stock 9824); BFAC 1922-3 (61); Bell and
Girtin 145(i); BM 1959, 1960, 1985 (59)
1958-7-12-332

JOHN ROBERT COZENS (1752–97)
Lake Nemi; lake in crater to left, town on ridge to
right
Watercolour over pencil, 366 × 530
PROVENANCE: John Rushout, 2nd Baron
Northwick; by descent to Lord Northwick, his
sale Sotheby's 6 July 1921 (125), bt Agnew's for
Lloyd, £155 plus 5% commission £7 15s. (stock
36); BFAC 1922-3 (46); Bell and Girtin 141(III);
BM 1959, 1960
1958-7-12-333

attr. to JOHN ROBERT COZENS (1752–97)
A hilly landscape with a winding road; lined with
trees, hills and cliffs
Brush drawing in grey wash over pencil sketch,
480 × 617 mm
PROVENANCE: unknown before bequeathed to
BM
1958-7-12-334

attr. to JOHN CROME (1768–1821)
On the Wensum, near Norwich
Brush drawing in brown ink over pencil,
259 × 362 mm
PROVENANCE: Kirkman Hodgson, MP; Major
Swann, bt Agnew's November 1926, exh.
Agnew's 1926 (31), price £475; bt Lloyd 19
November 1926, £420 (stock 6621)
1958-7-12-338

EDWARD DAYES (1763–1804)
Conway Castle
Blue and grey wash over pencil, 245 × 378 mm
PROVENANCE: John Rushout, 2nd Baron

Northwick; by descent to Lord Northwick, his sale, Sotheby's 4 November 1920 (475, as Turner, after Hearne ?), bt Agnew's for Lloyd, £40 plus 5% commission £2
1958-7-12-339

EDWARD DAYES (1763–1804)
Conway Castle
Blue and grey wash over pencil, 240 × 375 mm
PROVENANCE: John Rushout, 2nd Baron North-wick; by descent to Lord Northwick, his sale Sotheby's 6 July 1921 (180, as Turner), bt Agnew's for Lloyd, £25 plus 5% commission £1 15s. (stock 48; bt with a number of Monro school works)
1958-7-12-340

PETER DE WINT (1784–1849)
Lincoln from the river
Watercolour, 670 × 1113 mm
PROVENANCE: purchased by Vicars Brothers from a descendant of the artist; bt Agnew's 9 February 1914, £500 (+ glazing £1 12s. 10d., + frame £7 10s.) (stock J.8222); Agnew's 1914 (34), bt Lloyd, £800 (including blind for frame); BM 1985 (146)
1958-7-12-341

PETER DE WINT (1784–1849)
A view of Lancaster; stone quarry in right foreground with road leading to town on hill in middle distance
Watercolour, 765 × 1320 mm (sight)
PROVENANCE: Society of Painters in Water Colours exh. 1826 (238); Earl of Lonsdale; Frances Summer, Earl of Glossop; Col. Joseph Ruston, his sale Christie's 17 December 1920 (38), bt Agnew's £756; bt Lloyd 18 December 1920, £945
1958-7-12-342

PETER DE WINT (1784–1849)
Crowland Abbey; River Welland with fishermen in

foreground, abbey and windmill beyond
Watercolour, 394 × 742 mm
PROVENANCE: Abel Buckley; bt Agnew's, February 1904, £300; bt J. R. Smith, Manchester, 2 January 1906, £472 (stock 4514); bt Agnew's, 31 May 1911, £472 (stock 7547); Agnew's 1912 (5), bt Lloyd, 22 February 1912, £475
1958-7-12-343 (see p. 15, fig. 4)

PETER DE WINT (1784–1849)
St Alban's Abbey; seen from river meadows
Watercolour, 257 × 367 mm
PROVENANCE: R. Forbes Carpenter; his sale Christie's 23 May 1910 (31), £99 15s.; Agnew's 1912 (52); bt H. E. Walters 5 March 1912; bt Agnew's 27 March 1918, £185 (one of a group: stock 8779); bt A. E. Lawley 6 May 1918, £10,000 for group; his sale Christie's 25 February 1921 (131), bt Agnew's for Lloyd, £241 10s. plus 5% commission £12 1s. 6d. (stock 9926)
1958-7-12-344

THOMAS GAINSBOROUGH (1727–88)
Italianate landscape with figure on horseback crossing a bridge; wooded landscape, bridge at left, waterfall below
Black chalk and stump, touched with white chalk, 277 × 370 mm
PROVENANCE: Agnew's; BM exh. *Gainsborough and Reynolds in the British Museum*, 1978 (69); J. Hayes, *Gainsborough's Drawings*, supplement (959)
1958-7-12-345

THOMAS GIRTIN (1775–1802)
Old cottage at Widmore, near Bromley, c.1798–9; Elizabethan manor house behind wall at right, horse and rider at pool by road in foreground
Watercolour over pencil sketch, 308 × 512 mm
SIGNED: *Girtin*
PROVENANCE: William Gratwick?; Rev. Thomas Baugh; his widow Mrs Baugh; A. Pearse; bt

Agnew's 27 March 1914, £100 as 'Landscape with cottage'; bt Lloyd, 7 April 1914, £150 ('including new swept frame and sprung roller blind': stock 8272); *The Studio*, Special No. 1922, pl. xi; Agnew's 1931 (105); Agnew's Girtin exh. 1953 (103); T. Girtin and D. Loshak, *Girtin*, (276); BM 1959, 1960, 1985 (75)
1958-7-12-346

JAMES DUFFIELD HARDING (1797–1863)
Dunstanborough Castle, Northumberland; castle on cliff, seen from rough sea, and boat near rocks
Watercolour, touched with white bodycolour, over pencil sketch, 220 × 323 mm
PROVENANCE: unknown before bequeathed to BM; BM 1985 (159)
1958-7-12-347

WILLIAM HENRY HARRIOTT (d. 1839), after Turner
Copy of 'A Storm' by J. M. W. Turner (see no. 25)
Watercolour and bodycolour, 457 × 645 mm
PROVENANCE: unknown before bequeathed to BM
1958-7-12-348

THOMAS HEARNE (1744–1817)
View on the Wye, c.1788; river bank with cows in foreground and high banks in distance
Watercolour, over pencil, on contemporary wash-line mount, 188 × 266 mm
INSCRIBED: *Hearne*; and on verso of mount: *A scene from a window of Moccas Court, Herefordshire. Sir George Cornwall's Bart.*
PROVENANCE: unknown before bequeathed to BM
1958-7-12-349

ALFRED WILLIAM HUNT (1830–96)
Dolwydellan Castle, early spring, 1856; castle in mid-distance

Watercolour, 274 × 384 mm
SIGNED: *A. W. Hunt April 1856*
PROVENANCE: Sir George A Drummond, of
Montreal; his sale Christie's 27 June 1919 (119),
bt Agnew's for Lloyd, £42 plus 5% commission
£2 2s. (stock 9316); BM 1985 (192)
1958-7-12-350

WILLIAM HENRY HUNT (1790–1864)
Merry Hill, Bushey (formerly called 'The cottage
porch'), *c.* 1820–25; Dr Monro's summer house,
probably with his wife on balcony and daughter
Sally in porch (see R. Witt, *Hunt*, no. 29)
Watercolour with pen and grey ink over pencil,
336 × 269
INSCRIBED: *W. HUNT*
PROVENANCE: unknown before bequeathed to
BM; BM 1959, 1960
1958-7-12-351

WILLIAM HENRY HUNT (1790–1864)
A village in a valley (Hemel Hempstead, Herts.?),
c. 1820; seen from meadow (Witt, no. 26)
Watercolour over pencil sketch, 267 × 375 mm
SIGNED: *W. HUNT*
PROVENANCE: C. D. Rudd sale, Christie's 2 May
1919 (30), bt Agnew's for Lloyd, £13 13s. plus 5%
commission 13s. 9d. (stock 9248); BM 1985 (151)
1958-7-12-352

WILLIAM HENRY HUNT (1790–1864)
Plucking the fowl, 1832; girl seated in barn,
plucking fowl over a pot, wicker baskets to left,
and straw in foreground
Watercolour with bodycolour, 346 × 362 mm
SIGNED: *HUNT*
PROVENANCE: Nettlefold sale, Christie's 5 June
1913 (28), bt Agnew's, £57 15s. (+ frame £2 14s.);
Agnew's 1914 (74), bt Lloyd, £75 (stock 8045);
BM 1959, 1960, 1985 (152)
1958-7-12-353

WILLIAM HENRY HUNT (1790–1864)
Bushey churchyard; edge of church to right,
tombstones in foreground, trees and village
beyond
Watercolour over pencil, 320 × 418 mm
PROVENANCE: Dr Monro; John Rushout, 2nd
Baron Northwick; by descent to Lord
Northwick, his sale Sotheby's 6 July 1921 (136)
(one of group of views of Bushey (134–44), all bt
at Monro's sale), bt Agnew's for Lloyd, £28 plus
5% commission £1 8s.; BM 1959, 1960
1958-7-12-354

WILLIAM LEIGHTON LEITCH
(1804–83)
Swiss valley scene; chalets on either side of river
cascading through centre
Watercolour and bodycolour on blue paper,
197 × 146 mm
PROVENANCE: (studio stamp) artist's sale
Christie's 13–17 March and 17 April 1884;
otherwise unknown before bequeathed to BM
1958-7-12-355

HENRI L'EVEQUE (1769–1832)
Death of General Sir John Moore at Corunna; battle
scene, soldiers charging on horseback and on
foot, Moore being tended centre foreground
Brush drawing in grey wash, with watercolour,
and pen and grey ink over pencil, with drawn
washed border, 322 × 507 mm (image),
373 × 560 mm (sheet)
INSCRIBED: *H L'Eveque*
PROVENANCE: Earl of Abingdon, his sale
Sotheby's 21 May 1935 (3), bt Lloyd £7
(purchased because same artist responsible for
some of the illustrations for Saussure's *Ascent of
Mt Blanc*)
1958-7-12-356

THOMAS MALTON (1748–1804)
The Old Palace Yard, Westminster; Abingdon
Street with houses and east end of Westminster
Abbey
Pen and grey ink with watercolour, 329 × 481 mm
PROVENANCE: anon. sale Christie's 26 May 1919
(35), bt Agnew's £50 10s. (+ frame £5 10s.);
Agnew's 1920 (35); bt Lloyd 28 February 1920,
£120 (stock 9276); BM 1959, 1960
1958-7-12-357

THOMAS MALTON (1748–1804)
The Provost's House and Trinity College, Dublin
Pen and grey ink and wash, with watercolour, on
original wash-line mount, 276 × 390 mm
INSCRIBED on verso of mount: *College Green
Dublin*
PROVENANCE: B. T. Batsford; bt Agnew's
£15 2s. 6d.; bt Charles R. Williams 5 January
1919, £20 (stock 8475); bt Agnew's 3 June 1921,
£20; bt Lloyd 27 November 1923, £25 (stock
9965: bt with an aquatint printed in colour of the
above, £3; watercolour bt as Malton, with figures
by Francis Wheatley)
1958-7-12-358

formerly attr. to J. MAURER (*fl.* 1713–61)
Blackfriars Bridge under construction, *c.* 1765;
looking east from Temple gardens with London
Bridge in distance
Watercolour with pen and black ink,
337 × 482 mm
PROVENANCE: anon. sale Christie's 7 April 1919
(8), bt Agnew's £39 18s.; bt Lloyd 8 April 1919,
£50 (stock 9207); BM 1959, 1960
1958-7-12-359

SAMUEL PALMER (1805–81)
A pastoral landscape, *c.* 1878; moonlit river scene,
with figures on bank, birds rising from hill
beyond castle to right (R. Lister, *Palmer*, no. 678)
Watercolour with bodycolour, pen and grey ink
and gum arabic over black chalk, on card,
229 × 353 mm

INSCRIBED: *S Palmer*
PROVENANCE: ? Old Water Colour Society exh.
1878 (238: 'River Banks at Even'); Rev. E.
Gurney, lent to FAS 1881 (41)?; R.H. Shillito; his
sale Christie's 18 March 1935, bt Lloyd £27 6s.;
BM 1985 (176); BM 1959, 1960
1958-7-12-360

WILLIAM PAYNE (1760–1830)
Rocky waterfall; bridge and cottage in distance,
waterfall flanked by overhanging mossy boulders
to left
Brush drawing in brown and grey wash and
watercolour, 398 × 602 mm
PROVENANCE: purchased privately at Christie's
by Lloyd (according to Lloyd's typescript
catalogue)
1958-7-12-362

WILLIAM PAYNE (1760–1830)
River or lake landscape with ruined abbey; mountain
in distance
Brush drawing in brown and grey wash and
watercolour over pencil, 371 × 498 mm
PROVENANCE: as above
1958-7-12-363

SAMUEL PROUT (1783–1852)
Fishing boats on the Thames estuary; boats with
figures in foreground, further vessels in distance
Watercolour with bodycolour, 259 × 397 mm
INSCRIBED: *S. Prout*; on verso: *on the Thames*
PROVENANCE: unknown before bequeathed to
BM; BM 1959, 1960
1958-7-12-361

JAMES BAKER PYNE (1800–70)
Langdale valley, 1840; seen from height, figures
and dogs on left
Watercolour touched with white, over pencil
sketch, 321 × 476 mm
SIGNED AND DATED: *J B.Pyne.1840.*

PROVENANCE: James Gresham; his sale
Christie's 9 May 1919 (126) bt Agnew's for
Lloyd, £44 2s. plus 5% commission £2 4s. (stock
9263)
1958-7-12-364

JAMES BAKER PYNE (1800–70)
Shipyard on an estuary (formerly called 'A view in
Italy, Evening'), 1857
Watercolour and bodycolour, 277 × 435 mm
INSCRIBED: *PYNE 57*
PROVENANCE: exh. Blackburn, lent by James
Gresham; his sale Christie's 9 May 1919 (127), bt
Agnew's for Lloyd, £75 12s. plus 5% commission
£3 15s. (stock 9264); BM 1985 (163)
1958-7-12-365

DAVID ROBERTS (1796–1864)
A view of Cairo
Pen and brown and grey ink and watercolour,
over pencil with some bodycolour, 323 × 483 mm
PROVENANCE: the late Thomas Wallis, his sale
Christie's 26 May 1916 (26: as 'Constantinople'),
bt Agnew's for Lloyd, £13 13s., plus 5%
commission 13s. 6d.
1958-7-12-366

PAUL SANDBY (1730–1809)
*Windsor Castle and the King's engine house, from the
river*
Pen and grey ink wash with watercolour, over
pencil, with black ink and grey wash border,
323 × 521 mm
PROVENANCE: Sir Joseph Banks?; anon. sale
Christie's 22 December 1920 (8), bt Agnew's £19
19s.; bt Lloyd 23 December 1920, £25 (stock
9864); BM 1959, 1960
1958-7-12-367

JOHN 'WARWICK' SMITH (1749–1831)
Glacier of Montanvert, Chamonix, 1802; river flows

from glacier in centre, figures in foreground
Watercolour, touched with bodycolour,
535 × 823 mm
INSCRIBED on verso with subject, artist's name
and date 1802 (according to Lloyd's typescript
catalogue)
PROVENANCE: anon. sale Sotheby's 14 April
1937 (16), bt Howell 2 gns; bt Lloyd £2
1958-7-12-368

JOHN 'WARWICK' SMITH (1749–1831)
*The course of the Rhône in the Pays de Valais,
Switzerland*, 1802; rocks in foreground, looking
down onto valley plain with river and town
Pen and brown wash with watercolour,
528 × 823 mm
INSCRIBED: as above
PROVENANCE: as above, lot 17, bt Howell, £4
10s.; bt Lloyd £2
1958-7-12-369

JOHN 'WARWICK' SMITH (1749–1831)
*View of the Abbey of the Vale of Crucis, near
Llangollen*, 1790; abbey in field surrounded by
trees, ruins on hill beyond
Watercolour with pen and brown ink,
133 × 211 mm
INSCRIBED with full details of title, location and
date on labels on mount
PROVENANCE: Lady Gunning; bt Lloyd 30
January 1927, £50 for group of eight
1958-7-12-370

JOHN 'WARWICK' SMITH (1749–1831)
Llewenny bleachery, near Denbigh, North Wales; low
hills and buildings at left of open space
Watercolour with pen and brown ink,
130 × 208 mm
INSCRIBED: as above
PROVENANCE: as above
1958-7-12-371

JOHN 'WARWICK' SMITH (1749–1831)
Course of the River Dee between Llangollen and Corwen, 1795; seen from road on hillside, woman mounted on horse passing a woman knitting beside road
Watercolour with pen and brown ink, 144 × 216 mm
INSCRIBED: as above
PROVENANCE: as above
1958-7-12-372

JOHN 'WARWICK' SMITH (1749–1831)
River Dee seen from the road through the valleys above Llantysilio, 1795
Watercolour with pen and brown ink, 143 × 218 mm
INSCRIBED: as above
PROVENANCE: as above
1958-7-12-373

JOHN 'WARWICK' SMITH (1749–1831)
Ruins of Oystermouth Castle, overlooking bay of Swansea, 1795; seen on mound beyond small bay, figures and boat in foreground
Brush drawing in grey wash, with watercolour, over pencil, 136 × 220 mm
INSCRIBED: as above
PROVENANCE: as above
1958-7-12-374

JOHN 'WARWICK' SMITH (1749–1831)
St Donat's Castle, 1787; seen on a hill from the side, sea in distance to right
Watercolour over pencil, 129 × 208 mm
INSCRIBED: as above
PROVENANCE: as above
1958-7-12-375

JOHN 'WARWICK' SMITH (1749–1831)
Cave on sea coast, called 'Reynard's Church', near St Donat's Castle, 1787; cliff with two entrances to cave
Watercolour over pencil, 129 × 208 mm

INSCRIBED: as above
PROVENANCE: as above
1958-7-12-376

JOHN 'WARWICK' SMITH (1749–1831)
On the ascent to Snowdon, from Llyn Cywelyn, 1790; figures on horseback and on foot climb slope in foreground, mountain range beyond
Watercolour over pencil, 138 × 208 mm
INSCRIBED: as above
PROVENANCE: as above
1958-7-12-377

JOHN 'WARWICK' SMITH (1749–1831)
View of Worcester; cathedral to right, Malvern hills beyond
Watercolour, 130 × 206 mm
PROVENANCE: unknown before bequeathed to BM
1958-7-12-378

JOHN 'WARWICK' SMITH (1749–1831)
Ruins of Oxwich Church; on cliff-top, castle to right, bay in distance to left
Watercolour over pencil, 132 × 220 mm
PROVENANCE: unknown before bequeathed to BM
1958-7-12-379

JOHN 'WARWICK' SMITH (1749–1831)
Ruins of Penrice Castle; view from top of hill, castle to left, sea in distance
Watercolour over pencil, 131 × 224 mm
PROVENANCE: unknown before bequeathed to BM
1958-7-12-380

JOHN 'WARWICK' SMITH (1749–1831)
View of Llangollen and bridge; bridge in mid-distance, town beyond
Watercolour, over pencil, 131 × 208 mm

PROVENANCE: unknown before bequeathed to BM
1958-7-12-381

JOHN 'WARWICK' SMITH (1749–1831)
Llangollen from near the cottage of Lady Eleanor Butler and Miss Ponsonby; town viewed from height, large white house on hill at left, mountains beyond
Watercolour 135 × 213 mm
PROVENANCE: unknown before bequeathed to BM
1958-7-12-382

JOHN 'WARWICK' SMITH (1749–1831)
Vale of Crucis; valley from a height, edge of house on left, coach on road in distance
Watercolour with pen and brown ink, 130 × 209 mm
PROVENANCE: unknown before bequeathed to BM
1958-7-12-383

JOHN 'WARWICK' SMITH (1749–1831)
View of Goodrich Castle; in mid-distance on small hill, other hills beyond, river in foreground
Watercolour, with pen and brown ink, over pencil, 130 × 209 mm
PROVENANCE: unknown before bequeathed to BM
1958-7-12-384

JOHN 'WARWICK' SMITH (1749–1831)
Malvern Abbey; seen from height, hills to left
Watercolour over pencil, 137 × 230 mm
PROVENANCE: unknown before bequeathed to BM
1958-7-12-385

FRANCIS TOWNE (1740–1816)
Rydal Water looking towards Grasmere, Westmoreland, 1786; seen from height, trees to right, mountains in distance

Pen and grey and brown ink and watercolour on four joined sheets, 298 × 568, on artist's wash-line mount, 395 × 680 mm
INSCRIBED: *F.Towne delt 1786*; extensive inscription with title, date and description of view on verso of mount
PROVENANCE: unknown before bequeathed to BM; BM 1959, 1960
1958-7-12-386

J. M. W. TURNER (1775–1851)
*Tewkesbury Abbey from the north east, c.*1793
Pencil, 208 × 271 mm
INSCRIBED: *Tewkesbury Abbey*
PROVENANCE: Charles Stokes; Thomas Hughes; by descent to his niece, Mrs F. Hughes; her sale Sotheby's 28 November 1922 (129), bt Agnew's for Lloyd £15 10s. plus 5% commission 15s. 6d.
1958-7-12-388

J. M. W. TURNER (1775–1851)
*Tewkesbury Abbey, church gate, c.*1793
Pencil, 281 × 406 mm
INSCRIBED: *Tewkesbury Abbey*
PROVENANCE: Charles Stokes; N.W. Underdown, his sale Sotheby's 10 December 1925 (92), bt Agnew's for Lloyd, £28 plus 5% commission £1 8s. (illus. in Finberg 1921)
1958-7-12-389

J. M. W. TURNER (1775–1851)
*Malvern Priory, tower, c.*1793; seen beyond house with tiled roof
Pencil, 205 × 263 mm
INSCRIBED: *Malvern Abbey*
PROVENANCE: Charles Stokes; Thomas Hughes; by descent to his niece, Mrs F. Hughes; her sale Sotheby's 28 November 1922 (127), bt Agnew's for Lloyd, £15 plus 5% commission 15s.
1958-7-12-390

J. M. W. TURNER (1775–1851)
*Hereford, a small priory church, c.*1793–4
Pencil, 206 × 272 mm
PROVENANCE: Charles Stokes; N.W. Underdown, his sale Sotheby's 10 December 1925 (94), bt Agnew's for Lloyd, £24 plus 5% commission £1 4s. (illus. in Finberg 1921; has also been called 'St John's Church, Chester')
1958-7-12-396

J. M. W. TURNER (1775–1851)
Old ruins (at Evesham?), *c.*1793; with cart in ruins of undercroft
Pencil, 267 × 216 mm
PROVENANCE: Charles Stokes; N. W. Underdown, his sale Sotheby's 10 December 1925 (91), bt Agnew's for Lloyd, £10 plus 5% commission 10s. (illus. in Finberg 1921)
1958-7-12-397

J. M. W. TURNER (1775–1851)
*Evesham, All Saints Church, c.*1793
Pencil, 267 × 209 mm
INSCRIBED: *Evesham*
PROVENANCE: Charles Stokes; N.W. Underdown, his sale Sotheby's 10 December 1925 (93), bt Agnew's for Lloyd, £24 plus 5% commission £1 4s. (illus. in Finberg 1921)
1958-7-12-398

J. M. W. TURNER (1775–1851)
*Unidentified Perpendicular church, c.*1793–4; possibly a view of Peterborough or Lincoln, with an arched passage on lower ground level and a kiln amongst houses and buildings in distance
Pencil, 212 × 269 mm
PROVENANCE: Charles Stokes; Thomas Hughes; by descent to his niece, Mrs F. Hughes; her sale Sotheby's 28 November 1922 (133), bt Agnew's for Lloyd £11 10s. plus 5% commission 11s. 6d.
1958-7-12-399

J. M. W. TURNER (1775–1851)
Solfatara, near Naples (Monro school, after John Robert Cozens), *c.*1795–7; interior of crater filled with water
Blue and grey wash, over pencil, 201 × 345 mm
PROVENANCE: John Rushout, 2nd Baron Northwick; by descent to Lord Northwick, his sale, Sotheby's 6 June 1921 (178), bt Agnew's for Lloyd, £10 plus 5% commission 10s. (stock 46: with a number of other Monro school drawings at this sale); ? BFAC 1922–3 (71)
1958-7-12-393

J. M. W. TURNER (1775–1851)
Lake Albano (Monro school, after John Robert Cozens), *c.*1795–7
Blue and grey wash, over pencil, 318 × 452 mm
PROVENANCE: John Rushout, 2nd Baron Northwick; by descent to Lord Northwick, his sale, Sotheby's 6 June 1921 (179), bt Agnew's for Lloyd, £28 plus 5% commission £1 18s. (stock 47: with a number of other Monro school drawings at this sale); ? BFAC 1922–3 (86)
1958-7-12-394

J. M. W. TURNER (1775–1851)
View over Baia to Ischia, from the road leading to the Scuola di Virgilio (Monro school, after John Robert Cozens), *c.*1795–7
Blue and grey wash, over pencil, 306 × 532 mm
PROVENANCE: John Rushout, 2nd Baron Northwick; by descent to Lord Northwick, his sale, Sotheby's 4 November 1920 (478), bt Agnew's for Lloyd, £40 plus 5% commission £2 (stock 47: with a number of other Monro school drawings at this sale); BFAC 1922–3 (85); see Bell and Girtin 286 (II)
1958-7-12-395

J. M. W. TURNER (1775–1851)
*A dead blackcock, c.*1815–20; hanging suspended by its feet

Watercolour and bodycolour, over pencil, on paper with pink-grey wash, 258 × 231 mm
INSCRIBED: *I M W Turner RA*
PROVENANCE: Amelia Hawksworth (Mrs Hotham), ? to whom given by the artist; J. E. Taylor, exh. Guildhall 1899; his sale Christie's 8 July 1912 (122), bt Brown & Phillips, £31 10s.; Capt. J. Audley Harvey; his sale Christie's 30 March 1928 (63), bt Agnew's for Lloyd, £17 17s. plus 5% commission 18s. (stock 1076); BFAC 1936-7 (101) (colour illus. Gage 1987, fig. 240; see also Lyles 1988, no. 59)
1958-7-12-408

formerly attr. to J. M. W. TURNER
Portrait of a young man (once thought to be a portrait of Turner); head and shoulders, facing left
Black, red and white chalk with charcoal, heightened with white, on buff paper, 387 × 338 mm
INSCRIBED: *J. M. W. Turner*
PROVENANCE: unknown before bequeathed to BM
1958-7-12-447

JOHN VARLEY (1778–1842)
Hackney church, 1830; church tower at end of path through cemetery in foreground
Watercolour, 275 × 382 mm
SIGNED AND DATED: *J Varley. 1830* and inscribed by the artist on a separate piece of paper with light pencil sketches of figures, attached to the mount: *Hackney Church, a Study from Nature. J. Varley, July 22d, 1830*
PROVENANCE: ? Old Water Colour Society exh. 1831 as 'Sketch of the Old Tower at Hackney' (either this or another version, sold Sotheby's 8 June 1982 (18) and Sotheby's 11 July 1990 (97)); R. Norton; his sale Christie's 26 May 1919 (142), bt Agnew's for Lloyd, £39 18s. plus 5%

commission £2 (stock 9291); BM 1959, 1960, 1985 (110)
1958-7-12-448

JOHN VARLEY (1778–1842)
Landscape with stream and castle; track leading uphill through rocky landscape
Watercolour, touched with gum, over pencil sketch, 244 × 405 mm
PROVENANCE: Thomas Smelt; Whitworth Institute Water Colour exh. Manchester 1912 (166); anon. sale, Christie's 29 November 1918 (32), bt Agnew's for Lloyd, £23 2s. plus 5% commission £1 3s. (stock 9059)
1958-7-12-449

ELIJAH WALTON (1833–80)
East side of Monte Rosa, Switzerland; snow-capped mountain and densely wooded hill before it
Watercolour, touched with white and blue bodycolour, over pencil, 248 × 349 mm
INSCRIBED on separate label on verso with previous owner's name and exh. label
PROVENANCE: C. E. Mathews, Four Oaks nr Birmingham; R.W. Lloyd, exh. Alpine Club (n.d.)
1958-7-12-450

ELIJAH WALTON (1833–80)
A glacier; seen from height, across meadows to glacier in mid-distance
Watercolour, touched with white bodycolour, 350 × 247 mm
PROVENANCE: unknown before bequeathed to BM
1958-7-12-451

ELIJAH WALTON (1833–80)
Moonlit mountain landscape; starlight, tops of snow-capped mountains
Watercolour, touched with white bodycolour, 138 × 224 mm

PROVENANCE: unknown before bequeathed to BM
1958-7-12-452

GEORGE YATES (*fl.* 1824–37)
Southwark Bridge, 1830; view from Thames looking east
Pen and grey and black ink and watercolour, with artist's yellow wash-line border, 327 × 570 mm
INSCRIBED: *G. Yates. 1830*
PROVENANCE: sale Christie's 12 June 1924, bt Lloyd, £36
1958-7-12-453

THOMAS YATES (1765–96)
View on the Thames looking towards St Paul's; in hazy light
Watercolour over pencil, 374 × 563 mm
PROVENANCE: sale Christie's 12 June 1924, bt Lloyd, £36
1958-7-12-454

Appendix 2

Other Drawings and Watercolours by J. M. W. Turner in the Department of Prints and Drawings, British Museum

Works are listed roughly in chronological order. Descriptions are given only for those not illustrated in W (Wilton, see Abbreviations). References in brackets after the register number of each work have been confined to: LB (Laurence Binyon, *Catalogue of the Drawings by British Artists in the Department of Prints and Drawings in the British Museum*, vol. IV, 1907); W; and BM 1975 and 1985 (see Exhibitions). Those works by Turner in the Lloyd Bequest which are not included in the foregoing catalogue entries are listed in Appendix 1.

NB: The Department of Prints and Drawings has an almost complete collection of Turner's prints – over 900 compositions – kept in Rawlinson catalogue order, as well as 49 cancelled plates from the *Liber Studiorum* and 2 from the so-called 'Little Liber'. All drawings and watercolours referred to with the prefix TB (Turner Bequest) are now in the Clore Gallery at the Tate Gallery.

*Officer of the Third Regiment of Foot Guards, c.*1792 (etching by T. Kirk, after Edward Dayes, coloured by Turner); full length
Watercolour over etching, 277 × 168 mm
PROVENANCE: According to inscription on verso, given by Mr Colnaghi, for whom it was coloured, to J. T. Smith; purchased from W. Ward, exh. RA 1974 (B13)(another similar work acquired at the same time (LB 15) may have been coloured by Girtin and is kept with English prints by T. Kirk)
1890-8-6-2 (LB 14)

*Malvern hills, c.*1793
Pencil, 210 × 265 mm
INSCRIBED: *Malvern Hills*
Bequeathed by E. H. W. Meyerstein
1953-4-11-35

*View near Bunkers Bridge, Dover, c.*1793; after TB XVI J
Watercolour over pencil, 257 × 177 mm
Presented by Miss M. Ball
1980-10-11-43

Old houses with castle ruins beyond; road in foreground, woman in doorway, figures dismounting and ruins in distance
Watercolour and pencil, 209 × 303 mm
PROVENANCE: John Henderson sen.; by descent to John Henderson jun., by whom bequeathed to BM
1878-12-28-50 (LB 1)

*Magdalen College, Oxford, c.*1794
Watercolour over pencil, 357 × 263 mm
INSCRIBED: *W Turner*
PROVENANCE: J. Palser; Agnew's; bt George Salting, 1902, by whom bequeathed to BM
1910-2-12-286 (W 68)

*Magdalen Tower and Bridge, Oxford, c.*1794
Watercolour and pencil, 285 × 224 mm
PROVENANCE: John Henderson, sen.; by descent to John Henderson jun., by whom bequeathed to BM
1878-12-28-39 (LB 2; W 70)

*Tintern Abbey, west front, c.*1794; after TB XII D
Watercolour over pencil, 419 × 316 mm
INSCRIBED: *Turner*
PROVENANCE: as above
1878-12-28-41 (LB 16; W 60)

*Christ Church, Oxford, c.*1794
Watercolour over pencil sketch, 319 × 425 mm

INSCRIBED: *Turner*
PROVENANCE: as above
1878-12-28-42 (LB 18; W 71; BM 1975:6)

*Worcester Cathedral, west front, c.*1794–5
Watercolour over pencil, 419 × 318 mm
INSCRIBED: *W Turner 1794* [or *5 ?*] and *Turner*
PROVENANCE: as above
1878-12-28-43 (LB 17; W 67)

Lincoln Cathedral and Exchequer Gate from Bailsgate, 1795
Watercolour over pencil, 446 × 348 mm
INSCRIBED: *W Turner 1795*
PROVENANCE: as above
1878-12-28-48 (LB 19; W 124; BM 1975: 7)

Edinburgh Castle (after Thomas Hearne)
Watercolour and pencil, 178 × 248 mm
PROVENANCE: as above
1878-12-28-49 (LB 6; W 74)

Dover, pier and castle (after John Henderson sen.); pier in foreground, cliffs to right, castle on hill beyond
Watercolour over pencil, 177 × 260 mm
PROVENANCE: as above
1878-12-28-45 (LB 10)

Dover, inner harbour and town (after John Henderson sen.); vessel anchored in harbour to right, town beneath cliffs beyond
Watercolour over pencil, 199 × 263 mm
PROVENANCE: as above
1878-12-28-46 (LB 9)

Dover, inner harbour (after John Henderson sen.); wharf and warehouses to left, boats moored alongside, houses beyond
Watercolour over pencil, 198 × 261 mm
PROVENANCE: as above
1878-12-28-47 (LB 8)

Dover harbour (after John Henderson sen.); ships

at pier, harbour buildings on right
Watercolour over pencil, 208 × 259 mm
PROVENANCE: as above
1878-12-28-44 (LB 7)

Paris, from the Pont Neuf; Louvre beyond
Watercolour over pencil, 191 × 158 mm
PROVENANCE: as above
1878-12-28-38 (LB 12)

Paris – Ile de la Cité from the Seine; Notre-Dame
to left
Watercolour and pencil, 190 × 357 mm
PROVENANCE: as above
1878-12-28-40 (LB 11)

Dover harbour (attr. to Turner); view of the quay,
town beyond
Blue and grey washes over pencil, 199 × 145 mm
Presented by Miss M. H. Turner
1944-10-14-184

Emblematic subject for frontispiece (attr. to Turner);
broken frieze in pile with ruins beyond
Pen and blue ink with blue wash, 121 × 188 mm
Presented by Miss M. H. Turner
1944-10-14-185

Lake of Wallenstadt (Monro school, probably after
John Robert Cozens)
Brush drawing in grey wash, over pencil,
241 × 371 mm
INSCRIBED on verso with title and name of artist
PROVENANCE: C. S. Bale, sale Christie's 14 May
1881 (179); bt Rev. C. J. Sale; bequeathed by his
widow, Mrs Mary Sale
1915-3-13-82

Tell's Chapel, Lake of Lucerne (Monro school,
probably after John Robert Cozens)
Brush drawing in grey wash, over pencil,
246 × 355 mm
PROVENANCE: C. S. Bale, sale Christie's 14 May

1881 (174); bt Rev. C. J. Sale; bequeathed by his
widow, Mrs Mary Sale
1915-3-13-83

Lake Como (Monro school, after John Robert
Cozens (Bell and Girtin 50))
Brush drawing in grey wash and pencil,
242 × 377 mm
PROVENANCE: C. S. Bale, sale Christie's 14 May
1881 (169); bt Rev. C. J. Sale; bequeathed by his
widow, Mrs Mary Sale
1915-3-13-84

Newport Castle, *c.* 1796
Watercolour over pencil sketch, 230 × 302 mm
INSCRIBED: *W Turner*
Engraved by W. B. Cooke
PROVENANCE: Sir Joseph Heron; Mrs Kershaw;
George Salting, by whom bequeathed to BM
1910-2-12-289 (W 167)

A watermill, *c.* 1796
Watercolour over pencil sketch, 342 × 495
Bequeathed by P. C. Manuk and Miss G. M.
Coles through the National Art Collections Fund
1948-10-9-9 (W 169)

Wakefield Bridge, *c.* 1798
Watercolour with touches of pen and brown ink,
260 × 434 mm
Engraved by W. B. Cooke
PROVENANCE: Gooden and Fox; bt Agnew's
1903; Agnew's 1904 (42); bt George Salting, by
whom bequeathed to BM
1910-2-12-283 (W 241)

Stream cascading over rocks; leaf from the *Smaller
Fonthill* sketchbook (TB XLVIII)
VERSO: rocky landscape
Pencil, 416 × 265 mm
PROVENANCE: John Ruskin (?); Alexander J.
Finberg; Mrs Hilda Finberg, by whom presented
to BM
1946-11-9-1

Stream passing around a rock; leaf from the *Smaller
Fonthill* sketchbook (TB XLVIII)
Pencil and grey wash, 410 × 263 mm
PROVENANCE: as above
1946-11-9-2

View on a river, with barges; leaf from the *Smaller
Fonthill* sketchbook (TB XLVIII)
Pencil, 264 × 413 mm
INSCRIBED on verso by Finberg, suggesting it is
a view on the Tyne
PROVENANCE: as above
1946-11-9-3

Scene on a quay?, harbour beyond; leaf from the
Smaller Fonthill sketchbook (TB XLVIII)
Pencil, 264 × 414 mm
INSCRIBED on verso by Finberg, suggesting it is
a view on the Tyne
PROVENANCE: as above
1946-11-9-4

St Martin's Church, Salisbury, *c.* 1800
Watercolour with pen and ink over pencil sketch,
318 × 432 mm
INSCRIBED: *J M W Turner*
PROVENANCE: Sir Richard Colt Hoare, by
descent to Henry Hoare; Rev. J. H. Ellis; H. A.
Steward; Permain; P. C. Manuk and Miss G. M.
Coles, by whom bequeathed to BM through
National Art Collections Fund
1948-10-9-8 (W 207)

East Street, Chichester
VERSO: design for a Gothic frame for nine
drawings of Salisbury Cathedral commissioned
by Sir Richard Colt Hoare
Pencil, 472 × 626 mm
INSCRIBED on verso: *Sarum Cathedral*, with
Hoare's key to display of drawings
Purchased from E. Kersely
1949-6-27-1

View on the Thames, c. 1806
Watercolour, 251 × 353 mm
Engraved by W. B. Cooke
PROVENANCE: Joseph Gillot; Sir John Fowler;
Agnew's; George Salting, by whom bequeathed
to BM
1910-2-12-285 (W 415; BM 1985:87)

Bonneville, Savoy, 1808–9
Watercolour, 277 × 394 mm
INSCRIBED: *J M W Turner RA 08* [or *09* ?]
Engraved by W. B. Cooke
PROVENANCE: Abel Buckley; Agnew's; George
Salting, by whom bequeathed to BM
1910-2-12-284 (W 385; BM 1975:37)

Bolton Abbey, Yorkshire, 1809
Watercolour with bodycolour, 278 × 395 mm
INSCRIBED: *I M W Turner RA PP 1809*
Engraved by W. B. Cooke; also etched by
E. Finden in 1826 for the *Literary Souvenir*
PROVENANCE: Walter Fawkes?; Agnew's;
George Salting, by whom bequeathed to BM
1910-2-12-282 (W 532; BM 1975:39)

Malham Cove, Yorkshire, c. 1810
Watercolour, 279 × 533 mm
INSCRIBED: *I M W Turner RA*
Engraved by W. B. Cooke
PROVENANCE: Christie's 10 May 1907 (47), bt
Agnew's; Agnew's 1908 (5), bt George Salting, by
whom bequeathed to BM
1910-2-12-277 (W 533)

Sketch of ship, 1815; a three-masted sailing vessel,
possibly a sketch for W. B. Cooke's engraving of
the *Mew Stone, Plymouth* for the *South Coast* series
Pencil, 183 × 223 mm
INSCRIBED: *Sketch by Turner RA. – in reference to
the Mew Stone for Coast. 1815*
PROVENANCE: Purchased from F. Smith 1849
1849-2-10-504 (LB 13)

Loch Fyne, 1815
Watercolour, 278 × 388 mm
INSCRIBED: *J M W Turner RA 1815*
Engraved by W. B. Cooke
PROVENANCE: Walter Fawkes, sale Christie's
1890; Sir Donald Currie; bt Agnew's 1908, exh.
(169), bt George Salting, by whom bequeathed
to BM
1910-2-12-275 (W 351)

Vale of Ashburnham, 1816
Watercolour, 380 × 564 mm
INSCRIBED: *J M W Turner RA 1816*
Engraved by W. B. Cooke
PROVENANCE: John Fuller, by descent to Sir
Alexander Acland-Hood; London International
Exhibition 1862; Acland Hood sale Christie's
4 April 1908 (91), bt Agnew's; bt George Salting,
by whom bequeathed to BM
1910-2-12-272 (W 425; BM 1975:45)

Vale of Heathfield, 1816
Watercolour, 380 × 563 mm
Engraved by W. B. Cooke
PROVENANCE: as above
1910-2-12-273 (W 427; BM 1975:46)

Landscape studies; castles and hills, on the Rhine?
VERSO: sketches of landscape studies
Pencil, 160 × 236 mm
Presented by Mrs Cecil Eldred Hughes
1946-10-30-1

Heysham and Cumberland mountains, 1818
Watercolour, 290 × 424 mm
INSCRIBED: *J M W Turner RA 1818*
Engraved by W. B. Cooke; also by W. R. Smith
for Whitaker's *History of Richmondshire*, 1822
PROVENANCE: John Ruskin; FAS 1878; RA
1886; Guildhall 1899; W. Sopper 1902, bt
Agnew's; bt George Salting, by whom
bequeathed to BM
1910-2-12-274 (W 579)

On the Washburn, under Folly Hall, c. 1815
Watercolour, 277 × 393 mm
INSCRIBED: *I M W Turner RA*
PROVENANCE: Sir H. Pilkington; John Dillon;
R. Leake; F. Stevenson; James Orrock; Agnew's
1904; bt George Salting, by whom bequeathed
to BM
1910-2-12-287 (W 538; BM 1975:56)

Weathercote Cave, c. 1818
Watercolour, with gilding around the edge of the
sheet, 299 × 421 mm
PROVENANCE: Abel Buckley; bt Agnew's 1904;
bt George Salting, by whom bequeathed to BM
1910-2-12-281 (W 580; BM 1975:55; BM
1985:91)

Simmer Lake, near Askrigg, c. 1820
Watercolour, 287 × 412 mm
INSCRIBED: *I M W Turner RA*
Engraved by W. B. Cooke; also by H. Le Keux in
1822 for Whitaker's *History of Richmondshire*
PROVENANCE: Cosmo Orme; Agnew's 1905
(190); George Salting, by whom bequeathed to BM
1910-2-12-280 (W 571)

St Agatha's Abbey, near Richmond, Yorkshire,
c. 1821
Watercolour over pencil, on buff-toned paper,
288 × 415 mm
Engraved by J. Le Keux, 1822 for Whitaker's
History of Richmondshire, 1819–23
PROVENANCE: Sir Thomas Lawrence; Rev.
Charles Sale; Mrs Mary Sale, by whom
bequeathed to BM
1915-3-13-48 (W 561)

Sion House, Isleworth, c. 1822; seen in distance
from across park; possibly intended for but not
used in the *Liber Studiorum*
Pen and brown ink with brown wash,
219 × 280 mm

PROVENANCE: John Heywood Hawkins; purchased from Colnaghi, Scott & Co. 1861-8-10-29 (LB 4)

Pan and Syrinx, *c.* 1822; in wooded landscape with pool to right, etched for *Liber Studiorum* but never completed or published
Pen and brown ink with brown wash, 211 × 276 mm
PROVENANCE: as above
1861-8-10-30 (LB 3)

Huntsmen in a wood, *c.* 1824; sportsman with gun and dogs on footbridge over stream, intended for *Liber Studiorum*, but not engraved
Pen and brown ink with brown and grey wash, 194 × 263 mm
VERSO: pencil sketches
PROVENANCE: as above
1861-8-10-31 (LB 5)

Richmond, Yorkshire, *c.* 1826
Watercolour, 275 × 397 mm
Engraved by W. B. Cooke and W. R. Smith for *England and Wales*
PROVENANCE: Benjamin Godfrey Windus; John Leigh Clare, his sale Christie's 28 March 1868 (98); bt Isaac; John Farnworth, his sale Christie's 18 May 1874 (49); Andrew G. Jurtz, his sale Christie's 9–11 May 1891 (200); bt Tooth; George Salting, by whom bequeathed to BM
1910-2-12-276 (W 791)

Lancaster Sands, *c.* 1826
Watercolour with bodycolour, 278 × 404 mm
Engraved by W. B. Cooke; also by R. Brandard in 1828 for *England and Wales*
PROVENANCE: Tomkinson; H. A. J. Munro of Novar; J. Irvine Smith; F. Stevenson; R. C. Tatham; bt Agnew's 1903; bt George Salting, by whom bequeathed to BM
1910-2-12-279 (W 803)

The horse fair, Louth, Lincolnshire, *c.* 1827
Watercolour with bodycolour and pen and brown ink, 285 × 420 mm
Engraved by W. Radclyffe for *England and Wales*
PROVENANCE: Thomas Griffith; H. A. J. Munro of Novar; John Ruskin; T. H. Ward; bt Agnew's 1904; bt George Salting, by whom bequeathed to BM
1910-2-12-278 (W 809)

Glacier des Bossons, 1836
Watercolour, 231 × 331 mm
PROVENANCE: Thomas Greenwood; Albert Levy; sale Christie's 1 April 1876 (277), bt 'Seele' (Sale ?); Rev. Charles Sale; Mrs Mary Sale, by whom bequeathed to BM
1915-3-13-49 (W 1440)

Venice, a storm
Watercolour, 219 × 318 mm
PROVENANCE: William Quilter; Agnew's; Rev. Charles Sale; Mrs Mary Sale, by whom bequeathed to BM
1915-3-13-50 (W 1354; BM 1975:260)

Bellinzona, *c.* 1843
Watercolour and pencil, 228 × 287 mm
On verso of mount, copy of letter from Ruskin who once owned a version of this drawing
PROVENANCE: FAS 1904; bt Agnew's; bt 1905 George Salting, by whom bequeathed to BM
1910-2-12-288 (W 1490; BM 1985:99)

Essays in colour to try his palette
Watercolour, 480 × 345 mm
Inscribed on a separate sheet with a list of drawings and descriptive note
Presented by Mrs A. J. Finberg
1939-12-9-1 (BM 1985:101)

Sketchbook, *c.* 1845; seventy leaves all blank except for sketches of coastal scenes on the last ten, and on f.1 the draft of a letter referring to the

Fighting Temeraire as 'my Darling'
Pencil, 70 × 114 mm
Presented by Mrs Edward Croft Murray in memory of her husband
1981-12-12-15 (1...70)

Formerly attributed to Turner
Sunset at sea
Watercolour, 237 × 356 mm
Several labels from verso of mount now in dossier
Bequeathed by E. H. W. Meyerstein
1953-4-11-34

Index

This index is selective and does not cover the appendices, but all the main names in the provenances have been included except dealers and auctioneers. Numbers in *italics* refer to figure numbers and those in **bold** (under Turner only) to catalogue numbers. For places depicted in Turner's watercolours, see under Turner.